PAL... POWERS

Rulke of the Charon: Is he truly the Great Betrayer—or the last victim of a crime so terrible that its horror has tainted all of human history?

Karan of Gothryme: Can she forge a bridge between worlds—or will the attempt be the path to her own destruction?

Llian the Chronicler: His ambition to find the lost Great Tale cost him his honor—will his resolve to find the truth cost Llian his life?

Maigraith: Is she merely a pawn to be used by the mighty—or the bearer of an unimaginable power?

Mendark: He's used murder, magic, and immortality to maintain his reputation—but is his wizardry great enough to save Santhenar?

Faelamor of the Faellem: Did she commit genocide to save her race—and will she destroy whole worlds to lead her people home?

"A great find! Irvine writes beautifully . . . refreshing, complicated, and compelling."

—Kate Elliott, author of *King's Dragon*

Books by Ian Irvine

A Shadow on the Glass
The Tower on the Rift
Dark is the Moon

IAN IRVINE

THE WAY BETWEEN THE WORLDS

An AOL Time Warner Company

WARNER BOOKS EDITION

Cover illustration by Mark Sofilas

This edition is published by arrangement with Penguin Books Australia, Ltd.

Warner Books, Inc.
1271 Avenue of the Americas
New York, NY 10020

Visit our Web site at www.twbookmark.com.

An AOL Time Warner Company

Printed in the United States of America

First Warner Books Printing: October 2002

10 9 8 7 6 5 4 3 2 1

I would like to thank Angus and Simon Irvine
for the brilliant cover concept artwork

Contents

MAPS

PART ONE

PART TWO

PART THREE

"What though the field be lost?
All is not lost; the unconquerable Will,
And study of revenge, immortal hate,
And courage never to submit or yield . . ."

MILTON, *PARADISE LOST*

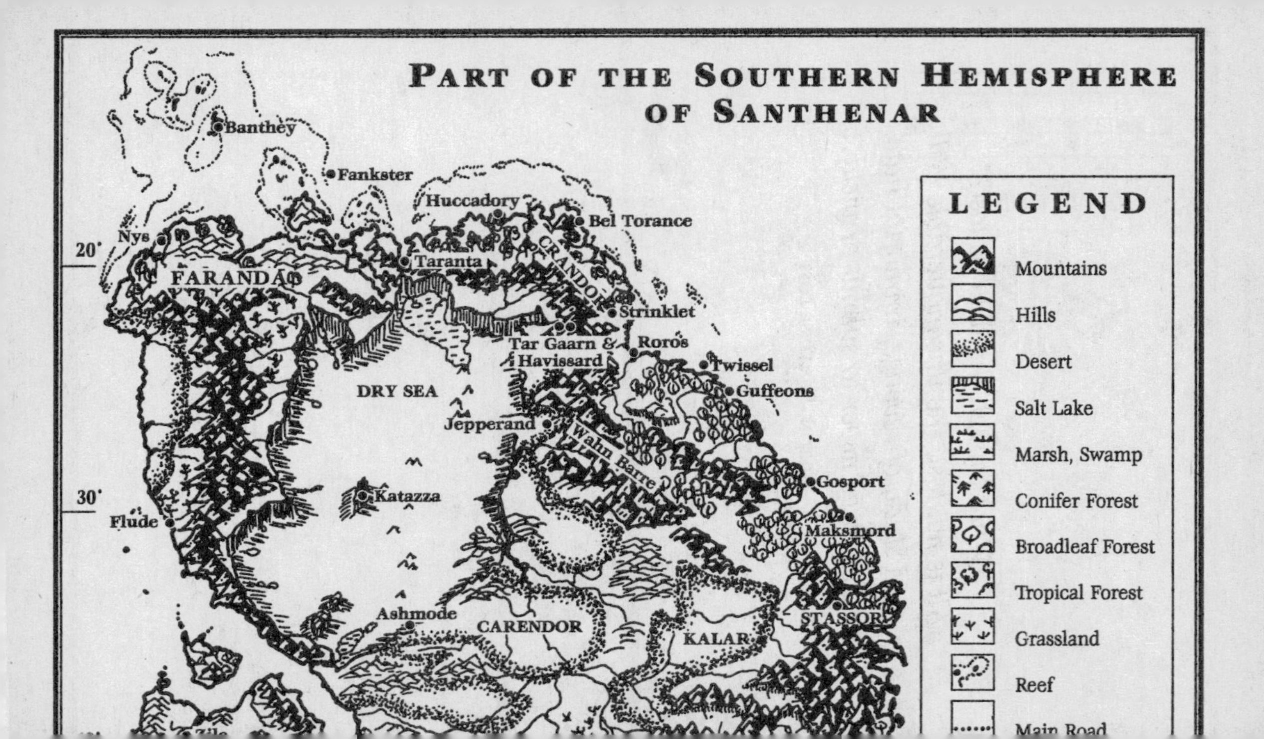
PART OF THE SOUTHERN HEMISPHERE OF SANTHENAR
LEGEND
Mountains
Hills
Desert
Salt Lake
Marsh, Swamp
Conifer Forest
Broadleaf Forest
Tropical Forest
Grassland
Reef
Main Road
Banthey
Fankster
Huccadory
Bel Torance
Nys
20˚
Taranta
CRANDOR
FARANDA
Strinklet
Tar Gaarn &
Havissard
Roros
Twissel
Guffeons
DRY SEA
Jepperand
Wahn Barre
Gosport
30˚
Katazza
Flude
Maksmord
Ashmode
CARENDOR
KALAR
STASSOR

Great Mountains
Tirthrax
Tiksi
Burning Mountain
Fiz Gorgo
LAURALIN
MIRRILLADELL
50˚
KARAMA MALAMA
(Sea of Mists)
OOLO
HA-DROW
LUUMA NARTA
SHAZABBA
Steppe
60˚
70˚
N
W
E
S
SCALE
KILOMETERS
0 100 200 300 400 500 600 700 800 900 1000
0 40 80 120 160 200
LEAGUES
Maps by the author

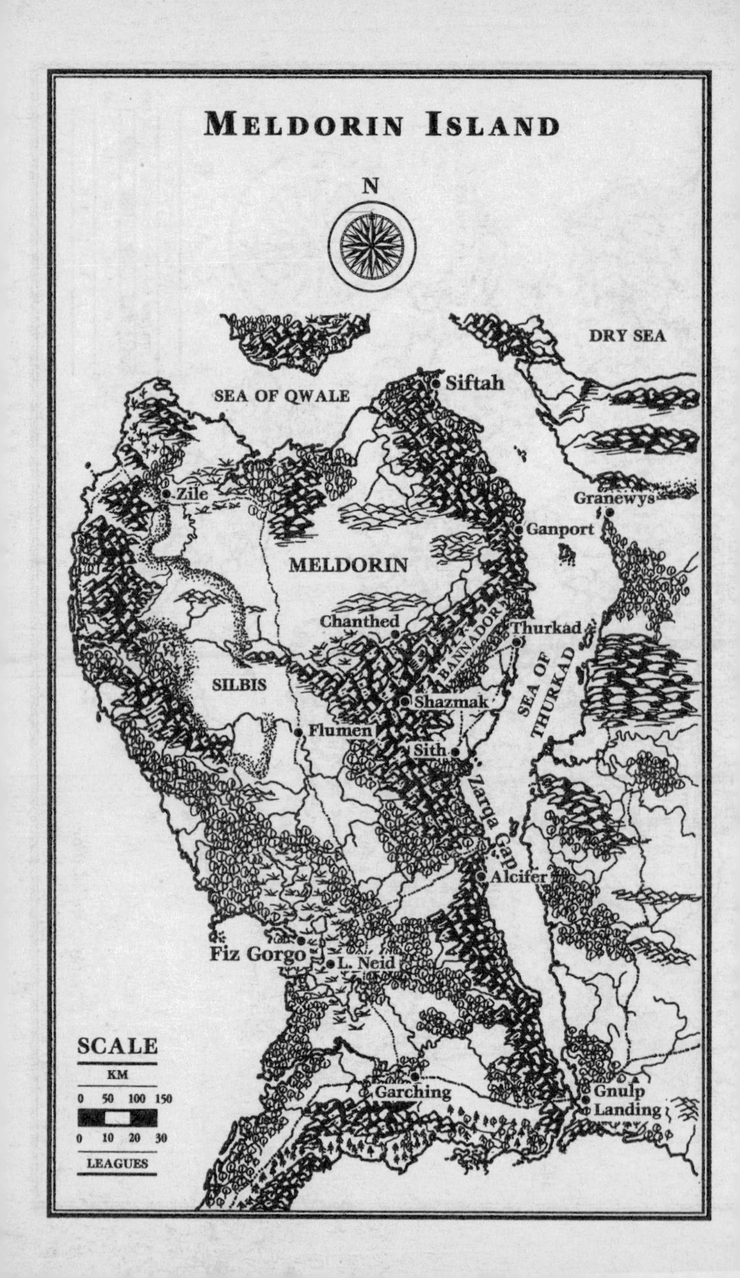
MELDORIN ISLAND
N
DRY SEA
SEA OF QWALE
Siftah
Zile
Granewys
Ganport
MELDORIN
Chanthed
BANNADOR
Thurkad
SEA OF THURKAD
SILBIS
Shazmak
Flumen
Sith
Zarqa Gap
Alcifer
Fiz Gorgo
L. Neid
SCALE
KM
0 50 100 150
0 10 20 30
LEAGUES
Garching
Gnulp Landing

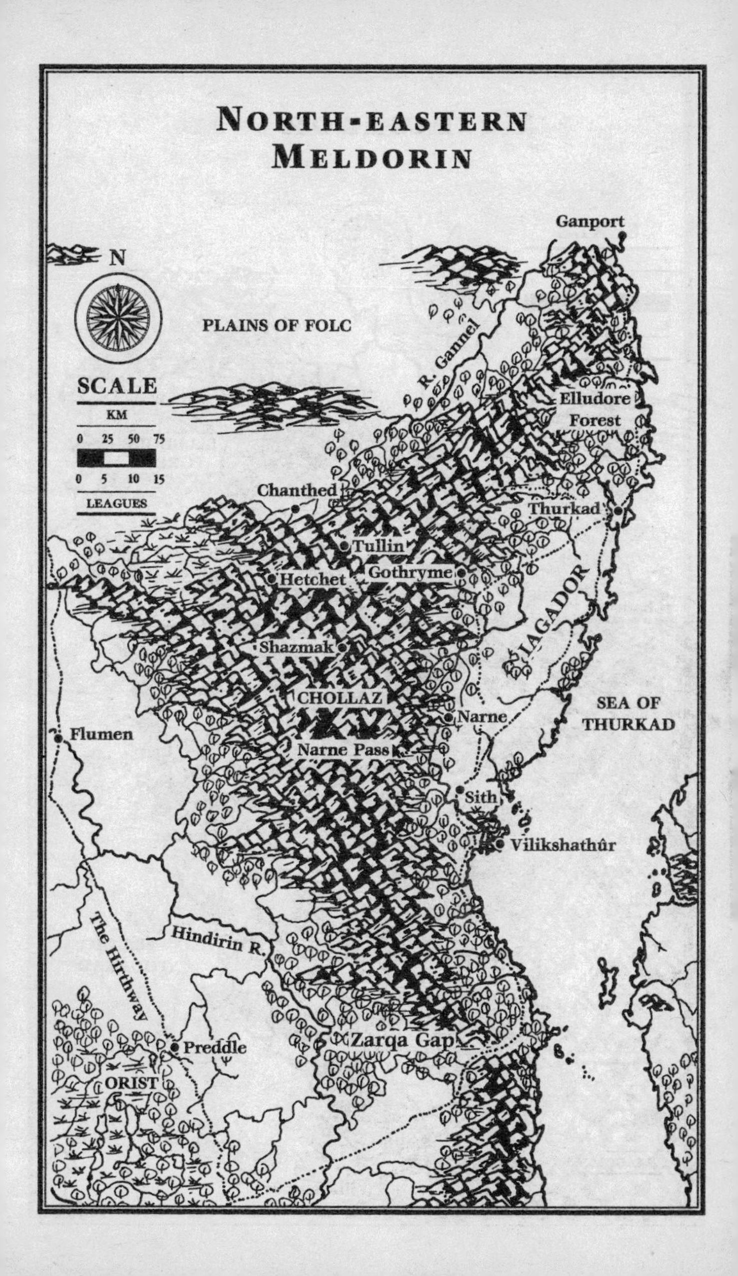
NORTH-EASTERN MELDORIN
N
PLAINS OF FOLC
SCALE
KM
0 25 50 75
0 5 10 15
LEAGUES
Ganport
R. Gannel
Elludore
Forest
Chanthed
Thurkad
Tullin
Hetchet
Gothryme
IAGADOR
Shazmak
CHOLLAZ
Narne
SEA OF
THURKAD
Flumen
Narne Pass
Sith
Vilikshathûr
The Hirthway
Hindirin R.
Zarqa Gap
Preddle
ORIST

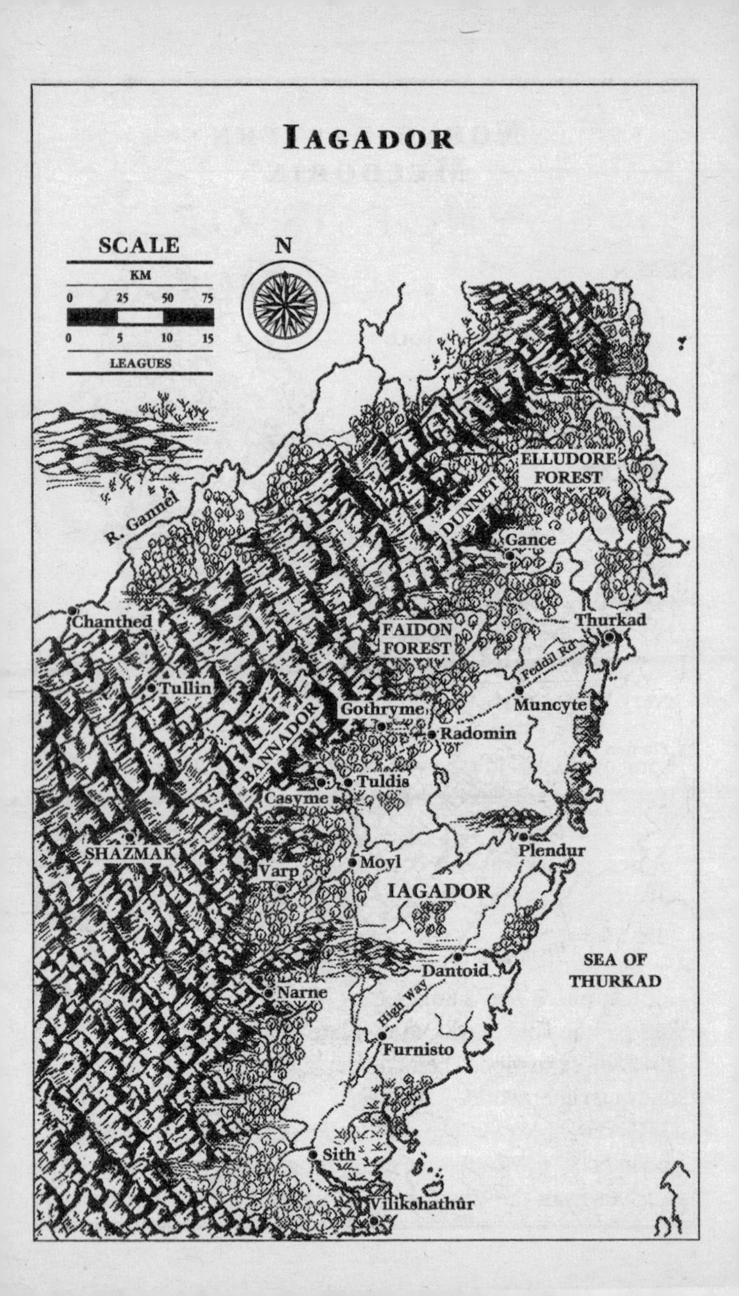
IAGADOR
SCALE
KM
0 25 50 75
0 5 10 15
LEAGUES
N
R. Gannel
ELLUDORE FOREST
DUNNET
Gance
Chanthed
Thurkad
FAIDON FOREST
Feddil Rd
Tullin
Muncyte
Gothryme
Radomin
BANNADOR
Tuldis
Casyme
SHAZMAK
Plendur
Moyl
Varp
IAGADOR
Dantoid
SEA OF THURKAD
Narne
High Way
Furnisto
Sith
Vilikshathûr

SYNOPSIS OF

THE VIEW FROM THE MIRROR

The View from the Mirror is a tale of the Three Worlds, *Aachan, Tallallame* and *Santhenar*, and of the four human species that inhabit them: *Aachim, Charon, Faellem* and *old human*. The setting is Santhenar, a world where wizardry—the *Secret Art*—is difficult, and doesn't always work, and every using comes at a price—*aftersickness*.

Long ago a whole race was betrayed and cast into the void between the worlds, a Darwinian place where life is more desperate, more brutal, more fleeting than anywhere. In the void none but the fittest survive, and only by remaking themselves constantly. A million of that race died in the first few weeks.

The terrible centuries ground on. The exiles were transformed into a new human species, but still they could not survive the void. Reduced to a handful, they hung over the abyss of extinction. Then one day a chance came, an opening to another world—Aachan!

Giving themselves a new name, Charon, after a frigid moonlet at the furthest extremity of the void, they took Aachan from the Aachim. The Hundred, as the remaining

Charon became known, dared allow nothing to stand before the survival of their species.

But they did not flourish on Aachan, so one of the Hundred, *Rulke*, commissioned the golden flute, an instrument that could open the Way between the Worlds. Before it could be used, *Shuthdar*, the old human who made it, stole the flute and fled with it to Santhenar. Unfortunately for Rulke, Shuthdar blundered. He opened all the paths between the worlds, and the four species scrambled to get the flute for themselves. Rather than be taken Shuthdar destroyed it, bringing down the *Forbidding* that sealed Santhenar off completely. Now the fate of the Three Worlds is bound up with those marooned on Santhenar. They have never ceased to search for a way home, but none has ever been found.

Volume 1
A SHADOW ON THE GLASS

•

Llian, a brilliant young chronicler at the College of the Histories, presents a new version of an ancient Great Tale, the *Tale of the Forbidding*, at his graduation *telling*, to unprecedented acclaim. But *Wistan*, the master of the College, realizes that Llian has uncovered a deadly mystery—evidence that a crippled girl was murdered at the time the golden flute was destroyed. The crime must have occurred to conceal a greater one, and even now such knowledge could be deadly, both for him and for the College.

Llian is also *Zain*, an outcast race despised for collaborating with the Charon in olden times. Wistan persecutes Llian to make him retract the tale, but Llian secretly keeps on with his research. He knows that it could be the key to a brilliant story—the first new Great Tale for hundreds of years—and if he were the one to write it, he would stand shoulder to shoulder with the greatest chroniclers of all time.

Karan, a young woman who is a *sensitive*, was at the graduation telling when Llian told his famous tale. She loves the Histories and is captivated by the tale and the teller. Karan returns to Gothryme, her drought-stricken and impoverished home, but soon afterwards *Maigraith* appears. Karan owes an obligation to Maigraith, the powerful but troubled lieutenant of *Faelamor*, and Maigraith insists that she repay it by helping to steal an ancient relic for her liege. Faelamor is the age-old leader of the Faellem, exiled on Santhenar by the Forbidding. Desperate to take her people back to her own world, she believes that the relic may hold the key.

Yggur the sorcerer now holds the relic in Fiz Gorgo. Karan and Maigraith steal into his fortress, but Karan is shocked to learn that the relic is the *Mirror of Aachan*, stolen from the Aachim a thousand years ago. Being part-Aachim herself, she knows that the Aachim have never stopped searching for it. She must betray her father's people or refuse her debt to Maigraith—dishonor either way. And Karan has a dangerous heritage: part Aachim, part old human, she is a *blending*. Blendings, though prone to madness, can have unusual talents, as she has. They are also at risk: sometimes hunted to enslave the talent, as often to destroy it.

Maigraith, fascinated by something she sees on the Mirror, is surprised by Yggur. Finally she is overcome but Karan flees with the Mirror into the flooded labyrinth below the fortress, pursued by Yggur's dreadful *Whelm* guards. Karan eventually escapes but is hunted for weeks through swamp and forest and mountains, the Whelm tracking her through her nightmares. In a twist of fate, Karan saves the life of one of them, *Idlis the healer*. She heads toward

Chanthed, a place of haunting memories because of Llian's wonderful tale. Pursued by the Whelm and their dogs, she reaches out to him in her dreams.

Mendark, a mancer and Yggur's bitter enemy, hears that the Mirror has been stolen and sends his lieutenants to find it. Learning from *Tallia* that Karan is heading for Chanthed he asks Wistan to find her. Wistan, who would do anything to get rid of Llian, orders him to find Karan and take her to Mendark's city, Thurkad.

At the village of Tullin, Llian dreams that Karan is calling for help and wakes to find two Whelm at his throat, trying to trace her *sending*. He is rescued by *Shand*, an old man who works at the inn but is more than he seems. Llian heads out into the snow to find Karan. Eventually he does, after many perils. Full of mixed feelings about Llian, Karan flees with him into the high mountains. After a number of narrow escapes they lose their pursuers, but Llian gets mountain sickness and Karan has no choice but to head for Shazmak, a secret city of the Aachim, where she grew up.

After they arrive Karan learns that *Tensor* is on his way to Shazmak. She knows she can never keep the Mirror secret from him. Unknown to her, Tensor already knows she has it. Soon Karan is brought to trial, for the Mirror cannot be found. It is impossible to lie to the *Syndics*, but Karan, in a desperate expedient, plants a false dream in Llian's mind, and through a *link* with him, reads it back to the Syndics at her trial. Because Llian believes it to be truth, it is truth, and despite Tensor's protests she is freed. Karan and Llian escape from Shazmak, hotly pursued by the Aachim. Stealing a boat, they flee down a wild river.

In Yggur's stronghold, Maigraith is tormented by the Whelm, who have an instinctive hatred of her. Later, under Yggur's relentless interrogation, she gives away Karan's destination, the city of Sith. Yggur needs the Mirror desperately, for his coming war. However as the weeks pass a bond grows between them, Maigraith finding in the tormented Yggur the complement to her own troubled self.

Faelamor uses her mastery of illusion to snatch Maigraith out of Fiz Gorgo but is furious when she learns that Karan, whom she hates, has escaped with the Mirror. Inwardly Faelamor despairs because the Mirror, which she has sought for so long, has eluded her again. Once before she almost had it, but *Yalkara* the Charon, her greatest enemy, defeated her. Yalkara used the Mirror to find a warp in the Forbidding, the only person ever to escape from Santhenar. Now Faelamor's own world, Tallallame, cries out for aid and she is desperate to return.

Faelamor and Maigraith set off to find Karan. Maigraith falls back under Faelamor's domination. Yggur, finding Maigraith gone, marches to war on the east.

Karan and Llian flee through mountains and caverns, hotly pursued by Tensor and his Aachim. At a forest camp she has a terrible nightmare and wakes to find that the Whelm have tracked her down again. This time she is helpless for they have learned how to control her. Desperate, Karan makes a link to Maigraith, now not far away. Unfortunately the link is captured by a terrifying presence, who uses it to speak directly to the Whelm, reminding them that they are really Ghâshâd, ancient enemies of the Aachim. Llian escapes but Karan is captured.

Not long after, Faelamor is taken by Tensor and sent to Shazmak, where to her horror she learns about Karan's Aachim heritage. Faelamor already suspects that Karan has Faellem ancestry as well. If so, she is *triune*: one with the blood of three worlds. A terrifying prospect—no one can tell what unpredictable talents a triune might have. Faelamor decides that the risk to her plans is too great—Karan must die. Faelamor escapes but the Ghâshâd find a way into Shazmak.

Clumsy Llian somehow rescues Karan, hires a boat and *Pender* takes them down the river to Sith. There they find Yggur's armies just across the river. The city cannot stand against him. Nor is Faelamor there to take the Mirror. Karan collapses, unable to drive herself any further. There is nowhere to go but to Mendark. Karan is afraid of him too.

They reach Thurkad not far ahead of the war to find that Mendark has been overthrown by *Thyllan*. A street urchin, *Lilis*, guides Llian to Mendark's refuge. Mendark and Tallia offer to take Karan in but, angered by Mendark's imperious manner, she refuses him. Shortly, Thyllan captures Karan and the Mirror.

As all the powers gather in Thurkad, Mendark realizes that the only way to recover the Mirror is to call a Great Conclave, which Thyllan must obey. As the Conclave ends, news comes that the army is defeated and Yggur at the gates of the city. Faelamor shatters Tensor by revealing that the Whelm are actually his ancient enemies, Ghâshâd, one-time servants of Rulke, who have taken Shazmak and slaughtered the Aachim there. She lies, blaming Karan for this treachery.

Karan is sentenced to death, while the Mirror is given to Thyllan to use in the defense of Thurkad. Seizing the moment, Faelamor calls forth Maigraith, and Tensor knows by her eyes that she is descended from the hated Charon. He breaks and uses a forbidden *potency*, or mind-blasting spell, that lays the whole Conclave low. Only Llian the Zain is unaffected. Thinking Karan dead, in grief and fury he attacks Tensor but is easily captured. Tensor sees a use for someone who is immune to the potency. He flees with Llian and the Mirror.

Volume 2
THE TOWER ON THE RIFT

•

Mendark and Tallia wake in the ruins of the Conclave. Tensor and Llian have disappeared, and Karan too. Mendark takes over the hopeless defense of the city but Thurkad soon falls. He flees with his little company, a few guards, Tallia and Lilis, then finds that his boat has been captured. They are forced to take refuge with the *Hlune*, a strange subculture that has made the vast, ancient wharf city of Thurkad their own. Tallia eventually hires Pender's boat and after a series of pursuits, escapes and mishaps they reach Zile, an old, declining city famous for its Great Library. The librarian, *Nadiril*, is a capricious old man who has the knowledge of the world at his fingertips. Nadiril takes Lilis as his apprentice but cannot suggest where Tensor may have taken refuge.

Tensor drags Llian through bloody war to a hideout where a small band of the Aachim wait for him, including *Malien*, his one-time consort. Tensor tells the terrible news about the destruction of Shazmak and the climax of the Conclave, but when he admits that he violated the Conclave with a forbidden potency the Aachim are outraged at his dishonor.

In the uproar Llian tries to get away but is speared in the side. The Aachim flee, taking Llian with them. They are hunted for weeks by Yggur's Whelm. They flee north, escaping many traps, and some among them would kill Llian, the treacherous Zain as they see him, but Tensor has a purpose for him. Llian, grieving for the loss of Karan and plagued by dreams of death and doom, is slow to recover. He often talks to Malien, who is disturbed by his dreams. Finally they are joined by other Aachim, refugees from ruined Shazmak. Their tales drive Tensor into a frenzy of hate and bitterness.

Maigraith and Faelamor are also laid low by Tensor's potency. Maigraith recovers, but Faelamor has lost her powers and sinks into despair. Thurkad is now controlled by Yggur and there is no way of escape. Maigraith has only one recourse—she goes to Yggur. Their meeting is tense, for neither has been able to forget the other and each is afraid of rejection. However, in time they become lovers.

Karan wakes from pain, nightmares and madness to find herself in a dingy room with a stranger. At first she barely knows who she is, and can remember only fragments of the past weeks. The stranger turns out to be Shand, who rescued her from the Conclave. She does not know why.

Karan is devastated to find that Llian has disappeared. As Thurkad capitulates, Shand leaves her in the wharf city, a place that she has a horror of, while he goes to find help. She is put to work at a disgusting and painful job—cleaning jellyfish and packing them in barrels. Finally Shand returns and they go across the sea.

Shand reveals that he knew Karan's father long ago, which is why he rescued her. They travel on, having adventures alternately comical, palpitating and gruesome, and eventually come to a cliff as tall as a mountain, below which is a vast emptiness, the Dry Sea, that was once the magnificent Sea of Perion.

Karan senses that Llian is out there somewhere. Throughout the salt plains there are tall mountains, once islands in the sea, and the largest of them, Katazza, was the seat of the fabulous empire of *Kandor*, one of the three Charon who came to Santhenar for the flute. The empire was destroyed when the sea dried up, but the fortress of Katazza remains.

Karan senses that Llian has been taken there. Shand

agrees to accompany her, but it is not a journey to be taken lightly. They set out across the salt, a terrible journey, pursued by bounty hunters and attacked by venomous desert creatures. There is never enough water and at the end, deadly volcanic country to cross before they get to Katazza. There they are stuck, too weak to tackle the great cliffs.

Much earlier, the Aachim also go down onto the Dry Sea. They cross quickly and climb the cliffs and mountains of Katazza to reach Kandor's fortress. Tensor begins his great project, to find within the Mirror the way of making gates from one place to another. He plans to open the *Nightland*, Rulke's prison of a thousand years, and have his revenge.

For a long time Tensor makes no progress, the memories of the Mirror being locked, then one day finds a way in. Only when he begins to make his gate do the Aachim realize what his real plan is. They try to stop him but Tensor seizes Llian, locks the Aachim out of the tower and continues with his work. Soon the gate is ready for its first test.

Back in Zile, Tallia has worked out what Tensor's destination must be. Mendark, his guard *Osseion*, and Tallia set off. After crossing the Dry Sea, to their astonishment they come across recent tracks at the base of Katazza. After a scuffle in the dark they realize that they have found Karan and Shand. Together they climb the cliffs and at the top are met by a deputation of the Aachim.

Mendark agrees to help them against Tensor. Karan is interested in only one thing, that Llian is here, and races off to find him. Unfortunately they can only communicate through a slit in the wall.

Tensor tests his gate but it goes astray, for he has used the Mirror to see the destination. It was often called the Twisted Mirror—a deceitful, treacherous thing. Karan, afraid for

Llian, climbs the tower, a terrifying ordeal that she barely survives. Soon after that, Tensor seizes Llian, who is immune to the potency, as a defense against Rulke. Then he opens the gate.

In Thurkad, Faelamor recovers her powers and warns Yggur that Tensor has made a gate, risking their ruin. Yggur manages to draw the gate away from the Nightland to Thurkad, though when it opens he dares not enter. Faelamor curses him for a coward and a fool and leaps into the gate. Later Yggur follows her, leaving Maigraith behind.

In Katazza, Tensor expects Rulke to come through the gate but Faelamor appears instead. She confuses him with illusion, snatches the Mirror and hides. Yggur appears. Shortly after, the gate begins working of its own accord. Tensor seizes Llian, preparing to blast his enemy, Rulke. Karan knows Llian won't survive the confrontation. She hurls a block of rubble in Tensor's face and Llian gets away. Then Rulke leaps out of the gate, terrible in his power and majesty, and the potency fizzles into nothing.

Rulke attacks his enemies one by one. First Yggur, then Tensor, whom he cripples. Faelamor, having found what she wanted in the Mirror, flees back through the gate. The Aachim are broken; Mendark is afraid to act by himself. Finally Rulke turns to Karan and realizes that she is the one whose link he used to wake the Ghâshâd. He needs her for his own project. He advances on Karan. With no other resort, she flings herself through the gate, dragging Llian after her.

Mendark now sees an opportunity, reaches into Yggur's mind and frees him from Rulke's possession of long ago. The tide begins to turn; the allies realize that together they can defeat Rulke, if they have the courage. They attack. Rulke flees to the top of the tower. There they corner him and hurl him out, but he curses them with a foretelling—that when the dark side of the moon is full in *hythe* (mid-winter's day) he will return and Santh will be his.

Shand replies with a riddle, "Fear the thrice born, but beware the thrice betrayed," then Rulke vanishes. Finally Shand takes the Mirror, "in memory of the one whose birthright it was', though no one knows what he means.

Volume 3
DARK IS THE MOON

•

In Thurkad, there comes a tremendous storm and Maigraith finds the Whelm waiting on the roof of Yggur's fortress. In a flash of lightning Rulke appears, exulting in his freedom. He commands the Whelm, or Ghâshâd as he calls them, to make a show of his strength. Seeing Maigraith, he orders the Ghâshâd to guard and protect her with their lives. Maigraith is equally captivated by him, though she has no idea why.

The Ghâshâd spread terror throughout the land, turning the armies of Yggur on one another. Maigraith escapes and is saved by *Vanhe*, one of Yggur's few surviving officers. In a hopeless gamble Vanhe uses Maigraith as a figurehead against Thyllan, who is besieging Thurkad with an overwhelming army. Surprising even herself, she humiliates Thyllan in a one-on-one struggle. The soldiers rally around her.

In Katazza, Yggur is desperate, now that his great enemy, Rulke, is at large. Mendark convinces the company to try to seal the gate into the Nightland, even knowing that this must trap Karan and Llian there. They draw power from the rift but at the last minute Yggur's nerve breaks. The attempt ends disastrously, bringing down the Great Tower. The survivors set out across the Dry Sea on foot.

Karan and Llian are hurled apart in the gate. Llian lands in an alien palace, bitterly reproaching himself for helping Tensor. He comes face to face with a colossal *construct*, a complex device of unknown but deadly purpose. Later Karan finds him, Rulke returns and they feel an attack on the gate, the company trying to seal it. To defend the gate Rulke has to draw on the energy holding the Nightland together. It begins to collapse around them. Eventually Rulke wins and tempts Llian with the offer of secret knowledge.

Karan, finding Rulke and Llian together, is troubled. She manages to escape through the gate to Katazza. Rulke catches Llian, interrogates him about the Histories, puts a hidden compulsion on him, to bring Karan when he calls, then allows Llian to escape to Katazza too.

Karan is suspicious about his escape, at first. They catch up to the company, who also mistrust Llian now. The Dry Sea is unbearably hot, and their progress hindered by salt-storms that last for days. Yggur, who lost most of his sight at the rift, is bitter and harries Llian constantly.

In order to counter Rulke's construct, Shand proposes that they remake the golden flute, banish Rulke and seal Santhenar from the other worlds forever. It is an exciting, impossible proposal, but they will need four things: the right kind of gold; the way to make the flute; the way to use it; the one to use it. Perhaps the Mirror has some of this information. Mendark demands it but Shand refuses, pointing out that it cannot be used *save by one who knows the use of it, and that way lies only within the Mirror.* Llian is consumed by this paradox, but Shand will say no more.

The others agree to remake the flute. But first they must have gold for its forging, and only red gold of Aachan will suffice.

Tensor confesses to Karan that, when she was a child, he recognized a great danger in her: that she was *triune*. He wanted to send her away to die, to rid the Aachim of the menace. However the Aachim took her in, so he blocked the development of her triune talents. He begs her forgiveness. Karan is shocked. It explains why she has been hunted all her life. She cannot forgive him.

The company finally return to Faranda. Yggur hurries back to Thurkad, desperate to find Maigraith. Mendark and Tallia go east on Pender's boat. There, Mendark sets out alone to Yalkara's abandoned fortress, Havissard.

Mendark finds Havissard to be a very strange place. Eventually he gets inside but the Aachan gold he came for has recently been stolen. Soon after, he is attacked without warning. He manages to escape Havissard but has to renew his failing body to save his life. The renewal turns him into a hideous travesty of his former self.

Maigraith leads an army to Bannador to liberate Bannador from the Ghâshâd. The expedition is nearly a disaster, for the Ghâshâd are able to link their minds into a communal will to control the other army. In a desperate struggle, Maigraith just succeeds in breaking their control.

That night Faelamor returns and lies, saying that Yggur is dead. Suddenly all that has driven Maigraith seems pointless. Faelamor wakes an old compulsion and soon Maigraith falls under her liege's thrall again.

They go to the rugged forests of Elludore. Faelamor is sure that there *is* a way to break the Forbidding. She calls the

Faellem, who are far away. It is now a race against Rulke and Mendark. Faelamor makes a gate to Havissard, a continent away. While she searches for something there, Maigraith wanders, curious to see what Yalkara was like. She finds a writing tablet. The last thing Yalkara wrote was a name—Aeolior. For some reason she can't explain, Maigraith keeps the page.

Faelamor finds what she is looking for—the Aachan gold. But in the library, one of Yalkara's journals disturbs her greatly. The writing is in a script that is terrifyingly familiar. She has no time to consider it further, for Mendark appears, and in striking him down she loses the journal.

Karan is haunted by what Tensor told her about herself. Karan and Llian travel to Chanthed, where Llian is now received with honor. However, in the library he discovers that drawings he was looking for, from the time of the Forbidding, have been stolen by Faelamor.

In Tullin Karan's nightmares begin again, and Rulke is always in them. Karan thinks that Llian is spying for Rulke. She tries by a link to snatch control. Rulke attempts to *compel* them both but Karan knocks Llian out and the compulsion fails. Shand arrives home and, thinking Llian possessed by Rulke, forces Karan to reject him. They take a now despairing Llian to Gothryme. The country is devastated by war.

One day they learn that the Ghâshâd have occupied Carcharon, an old stronghold built by a mad ancestor of Karan's, high in the mountains. Shortly they are summoned to a meet in Thurkad. Mendark is returning by ship from the east. Llian, knowing he is mistrusted, is in despair.

The company meet. So far their efforts have been fruitless. No Aachan gold has been found. Yggur, who is even more suspicious of Llian now, sends him to the execution yard. Karan manages to free him and they escape back to Gothryme.

* * *

In Gothryme, Rulke begins calling Llian again, demanding that he bring Karan to Carcharon. Mendark appears unexpectedly and, discovering this, interrogates Llian, resorting to powerful charms to get at the truth. Between the two of them, Llian is in agony.

Finally Karan wakes to what is going on. Drawing the truth from Llian, she is mortified to discover that all along he had been protecting her from Rulke. They are reconciled. Karan knows there is only one way to end Llian's torment. She must go to Carcharon. Llian refuses to let her go alone. He is convinced that the time of the foretelling is at hand, for hythe is only a few days away now.

Llian challenges Rulke to a telling. If he wins, Karan and he are to go free. If he loses, they will do what Rulke wants. To Llian's surprise Rulke accepts the challenge. Three Ghâshâd will adjudicate, including Idlis the healer.

Rulke's tale is a barbaric splendor, the story of how a hundred Charon conquered a world, Aachan. But Llian sees that the tale jars against the codes of the Ghâshâd. Rulke put his own glory before the security of his people. Llian makes a new tale to take advantage.

Llian's reply is a tale of a servant race who served not wisely but too well. This tale strikes a chord in the Ghâshâd, wakening their deepest fears, as Llian intends. Rulke is enraged, accusing Llian of cheating, but Idlis's casting vote gives Llian the victory.

Rulke sends Llian through a gate but it goes wrong, dropping him into the snow below Carcharon. There he is found by Tallia and Mendark. Llian's reappearance, alone, confirms Mendark's suspicions.

Karan is the triune Rulke needs to seek out the Way between the Worlds. He tries to coerce her but she delays, sensing that time is important. Rulke forces her to choose between aiding him and seeing Llian tormented. She makes a bargain—Llian to be freed of the compulsion first. Rulke has no more time, and he agrees. Karan, believing that Llian is safe, agrees to do what Rulke wants.

The dark full moon rises, and it is hythe—mid-winter's day. The weight of the prophecy crushes the company. Rulke's victory cannot be averted, Shand tells them. The one who was to be the Restorer is dead.

PART ONE

1

THE ARROW

The construct, a menace that warped even the light around it, slowly revolved above the decapitated tower of Carcharon. Rulke stood tall on top, holding his levers in one negligent hand. The other was thrust out at the rising moon, whose dark face, mottled red and purple-black, had just heaved its swollen mass over the horizon. That was a hideous omen. The moon had not been full on hythe, mid-winter's day, for 1,830 years. Rulke's foretelling was already coming to pass.

When the dark moon is full on mid-winter's day, I will be back. I will crack the Forbidding and open the Way between the Worlds. No one has the power to stay me. The Three Worlds will be Charon evermore.

Karan, chest-high beside Rulke, was a stark white, staring shadow surrounded by a corona of flaming hair. Llian wept for her, but even if he could step the air between them there was no way to wrest her free. No one would help him now. He was a pariah, accused of betraying Karan to Rulke, accused of being Rulke's spy. Nothing would convince the company otherwise. Wherever he looked he received dark looks in return, especially from Basitor the Aachim, who blamed him for the destruction of Shazmak. Basitor would kill him given the least opportunity.

Llian had only one friend left, little Lilis, but what could she do? The most powerful people of Santhenar were here but not one of them—not Mendark, not Yggur or the crippled Tensor, not Tallia or Shand or Malien—had the courage to strike at Rulke.

The construct rumbled. The tower wobbled. Wavering discharges rose up from the spiny protrusions embedded in the walls. The Ghâshâd guards, stick-men and stick-women, resumed their posts, pacing with stiff-limbed gait. The red glare from inside faded and flared, faded and flared.

Llian eyed the construct. It was an impossible thing, made of metal so black that it stood out against the night sky. There was nothing on Santhenar to compare it with. It required no beast to pull it; it had no wheels; and yet it slipped through the sky like silk. It hung in the air like a balloon, though Llian knew it was heavier than a boulder. Its sides bulged in complex shapes that were alien, then curved away into corrugations underneath. The long front soared up to a flaring binnacle crammed with knobs and wheels, behind which was a thicket of levers, a place to stand and a high seat of carven serpentine.

Llian knew that the inside was just as strange, equally packed with controls and glowing plates, for he had seen it in the Nightland. Evidently Rulke preferred to ride on top where he could display, and dominate.

"Karan!" Llian sang out in anguish. His voice echoed back across the amphitheater to mock him.

Karan must have seen him standing there on the rim, for she went quite rigid. At the same instant the construct lurched beneath her. Her arms thrashed. Llian thought she was going to go over, but Rulke jerked her back. She looked up at him, looming head and shoulders above her, and spoke. Her words were not even a sigh on the wind.

Yggur adjusted glasses as thick as bottle ends. When Rulke first appeared Yggur had resolved to face his fears and die, rather than be overcome by them yet again. Already that resolve was weakening. "Look at them together," he said, grinding his teeth. "He has possessed her mind. I can feel it, the way he possessed me for so long."

"I hope so," replied Mendark in an even more chilly voice. "Otherwise Karan has betrayed us and must suffer for it." He looked more haggard, wasted and bitter than ever.

The way they talked was horrible. Llian was stabbed all over by pain pricks, as if his blood had crystallized to needles. He sucked at the air but could not fill his lungs. Everything wavered; he felt faint.

Yggur's cheek began to twitch, then locked rigid in a spasm that twisted up one side of his face. Remembering that Yggur had once been mad, Llian wondered if he was cracking again.

Yggur clutched at Malien's arm. "Who is your best archer?" he gasped.

"Basitor has the strongest pull by far. But I should say Xarah is the most accurate at this distance. Xarah!"

Xarah came forward. She was small for an Aachim, not much bigger than Karan, with limp hair the color of mustard and a scatter of freckles on her cheeks. She looked much younger than the others.

"You are the best among you?" Yggur asked, his fists clenched, his knuckles white.

Xarah looked down at the snow, fingering a bracelet on her wrist. She knew what was going to be asked of her. Then she gazed up at the construct, gauging the distance. Only Karan's head could be seen now.

"The best that is able," she said. "I can hit any target in Carcharon from here."

"And on the construct?"

"An uphill shot, but I can do it."

Yggur followed her gaze. He spasmed again, tried to take control but failed. "Then put an arrow in Karan's eye, for pity's sake! For her and for us."

She did not move. "Do it this minute!" he shouted, and there were flecks of foam at the corners of his mouth. He looked as if he had just fought a monumental battle with himself, and lost. He would do anything to avoid Rulke possessing him again.

Xarah shivered. She looked up at Malien, her midnight-dark eyes expressionless in the red light.

Malien put out her hand. "Stay, Xarah!"

Mendark looked thoughtful. "Rulke has made an error of judgment. If we were to neutralize her, it might cripple him."

Llian staggered between them, the ice-crusted manacles tearing his legs until the blood flowed. He took no heed of that pain; it was nothing beside what he was feeling inside.

"No!" he screamed, crashing into Mendark, who pushed him away.

"Don't interfere, chronicler!"

"But Karan—" Llian wept.

"It's a choice between her life and our world, Llian!" But still Mendark stared at the construct and did not give the order.

Nadiril the librarian was bent right over on his walking staff, looking frailer than ever. Shand, a head shorter beside him, held his arm. Lilis stood by Nadiril, hopping from one foot to another, crying, "Stop them, Nadiril!"

"This deed will come back to haunt you, Yggur," said Nadiril. "She—"

"Just do it!" Yggur screamed.

"No more will I do evil," said Malien softly, "even if the greatest good comes out of it. Xarah, put down your bow."

Tensor slid his legs over the side of the litter and with a convulsive wrench forced himself to his feet. He was as gaunt as a skeleton now, the once huge frame nothing but bone and sinew that was all twisted from Rulke's blow in Katazza last summer. Llian tried to claw his way over the snow but Basitor's huge foot slammed into the middle of his back, pinning him down.

"A chance," Tensor rasped. "A chance sent for my torment! What evil did my forefathers do that I should suffer so? Do you give the order, Malien?"

"No!" she whispered, and a tear froze to crystal from each eye.

"You have always been true," he said, clinging to her for a moment.

Tensor took a lurching step toward Xarah, and another. He wavered toward her like the grim reaper, an animated skeleton covered in skin. She watched him come, the long bow hanging from one hand, the red-feathered arrow in the other. At the last moment she tried to put them behind her, but the look in his eyes paralyzed her.

Tensor plucked the bow from one hand, the arrow from the other. The arrow went to the bowstring. The string was drawn back. Llian's arms and legs thrashed as if swimming in the snow, but Basitor's boot held him in place.

"I'm sorry, Karan," said Tensor ever so gently.

"Shoot, damn you!" cried Yggur, shaking so hard that his head nodded like a child's toy.

Karan's red hair looked to be on fire in the boiling glare

from the tower. Her face was a white blotch, but Llian had no doubt that Tensor could hit her eye from here. Before he even released the arrow, Llian could see it flying straight and true toward her lovely face, to spear straight through her skull with a shock that would carry her backward off the construct and down, down dead onto the rocks at the bottom of the gorge.

"*No!*" Llian shrieked with every fiber and atom of himself, broadcasting his love and terror across ridge and valley and mountain, trying to speak back across the link Karan had closed down only a few days ago.

The company stopped their ears against the curdled shriek. Twisting around, Llian sank his teeth into Basitor's calf. Basitor yelped and sprang backward. Tensor did not even shiver. He stood up straight, sighted along the arrow and let it fly. It disappeared into the night.

At the same time the construct lurched sideways like a puppet whose strings had broken. It shuddered in the air and fell like a rock. Rulke was suspended above it for a moment then stood up straight and tall, his hands dancing. The machine slammed into solid air, bounced, drifted around in a circle and veered back toward Carcharon, listing like a sinking yacht. Karan was nowhere to be seen.

Rulke almost had it under control, but it shuddered again, the front tilted and it began to glide downward, accelerating and plunging straight toward the rocky ridge side. Llian held his breath. Rulke struggled desperately, mastered it a moment before impact and began to inch it back up again.

"We've done it!" Yggur shouted. "He's weak! Do you dare use power against him *now*?" he challenged Mendark.

Mendark hesitated, then, "Yes, *yes! Together!*" They shot out their arms. Red and blue fire flared out, writhing like colored cables across the night. The Aachim fired as one. A dozen arrows arched in formation toward their target, but immediately an opaline spheroid sprang into life around the construct. The fiery blasts reflected dangerously back at them, melting the snow into glassy patches as they ducked for shelter. The arrows sighed harmlessly into a dough-like barrier, then one by one fell free, quite spent.

"That showed him!" Tensor crowed. "He won't be so bold next time."

Mendark's wit was quicker. "You're a fool, Tensor," he said in a dead voice. "He uses our power against us. The construct is proof against any force we can direct at it, and I was a bigger fool to think any different."

The construct regained its even keel, lifted smoothly and hung on the ruined brass lip of the tower. Rulke reached down with one hand, hauled up Karan and shook her at his enemies. *She was still alive!* He roared defiance, then the machine slipped back into the tower like a black egg into its nest. As it went down, the walls bulged outward around it like a snake swallowing a chicken. The eerie red glow reappeared.

"What was that all about?" asked Tallia.

"Intimidation," said Yggur. "Maybe he's not ready."

"He's ready!" said Shand.

The moon rose higher, its blotched face illuminating the scene raggedly. They stood together on a bowl-shaped rim of the ridge top. In front of them the living rock had been carved away to form a small amphitheater that looked back to Carcharon. Its shallow lower lip dropped in a series of steep steps that narrowed downward to a winding track running along the knife-edged crest of the ridge. The track was barely wide enough for two abreast, and deadly on account of ice and gale. On either side the rock fell steep, sometimes sheer, into a mighty chasm. The track wound down and then back up, broadening at the other end before a long, steep and upward-flaring stair which terminated at a landing outside the brass gates and iron-plated doors of Carcharon itself.

Carcharon had once been an ugly tower of nine uneven sides, squatting on the sheerest part of the ridge. A high wall ran from the back of the tower, steeply up one side of the ridge and down the other, enclosing a large yard. The tower was built of glassy-smooth gabbro, violet-gray in color. Its walls were covered in clusters of rods, hooks, vitreous spheres and opaline spines like those of a sea urchin. The roof had been a spiky helmet of brass and green slate, but the slate was scattered and the brass remnants now hung down like metal petals. The place had never had harmony or proportion, but with the roof torn open and the walls deformed as if they had begun to melt, it was hideous.

Behind the company the high back of the amphitheater descended by a steeper stair onto a winding, soaring ridge-top track, down and down and down for hours, eventually to reach a strip of plateau cut by ravines, encircled on the lower side by granite cliffs and covered in Karan's magnificent but inaccessible Forest of Gothryme. Below the cliffs lay Gothryme, her impoverished estate in the valley of the Ryme, and further on, Tolryme town and the road to Thurkad.

The red light sank to an uncanny glare. A freezing wind sprang up, so they moved into the shelter of the arena. Llian lay on the snow. If his rage had been a weapon, Yggur and Tensor would now lie dead among the rocks. His legs hurt, a torment that gave him no rest, but at least Karan was alive. He had to get her out. He knew she would do the same for him.

"Lilis!" he whispered.

Lilis came scuttling across. Her thin face was pinched. Her cold nose touched his even colder cheek. She was shivering.

"What you warn't?" she said, reverting for a moment to her street-brat argot.

"I've got to get inside. Will you help me?"

Lilis visibly took herself in hand. A street brat no longer, she was an apprentice librarian now and the great Nadiril was her tutor. She schooled her voice to calmness. "What do you want me to do?"

"See if you can get these shackles off."

Lilis bent down, her hair caressing his boots. "Oh," she said. "Your leg is all bloody. And your other leg too."

Llian couldn't have cared less. "The ice scratches the skin. It's not serious."

Her fingers worked at the irons. "They're locked," she said. "Do you know who has the key?"

"Mendark! I don't suppose—No, it's too much to ask."

She moaned under her breath and stood up. "Poor Llian," she said, looking into his eyes. In the light from Carcharon hers were the size of apricots. "Of course I'll go. For you I will even rob Mendark himself; though I'm very frightened."

"I'm ashamed to ask you, dear Lilis." He hugged her thin frame. "But I've got to get in."

She crept across the snow and ice. Llian was more ashamed than Lilis realized, for she was just a diversion. She would be discovered as soon as she tried to rob Mendark, but it might just give him time enough. He did not wait to see what happened.

Everyone else was huddled at the back of the amphitheater out of the worst of the wind. No one seemed to be watching him. Llian slipped down between the snow-covered stone benches. He was just above the steps and the path to Carcharon.

There came an outcry from the other side of the platform. Lilis must have been caught! Llian slid over the edge and crashed down the steps feet first, bumping hard on his bottom. Landing right at the edge of the ravine, he staggered as fast as his hobbles would allow him along the treacherous path.

"What are you doing, you little thief?" he heard Mendark roar. Lilis's frightened squeak of an answer was inaudible. A minute later Mendark roared again, "He's gone! After him!"

Llian redoubled his efforts, his terror of being caught before he found Karan more powerful than his fear of Rulke, or the hideous pain in his legs.

He reached the bottom of the steps that led in an upcurving arch to the front gate. He dragged himself up fifty or sixty steps, but near the top had to rest, no matter what. Llian slumped over the stone rail. At least there was one here, though each of the balusters was covered with gargoyle faces of profound hideousness, all grinning and jeering at him. In his fevered mind the railing seemed to move beneath his hand, as if they reached out for him. Llian snatched his hand away and looked up to be confronted by a sight even more palpitating.

At the top of the stairs was a landing, on the far side of which the stairs curved away from the gate to meet the side of Carcharon tower. In the open space between the left-hand rail and the wall loomed a vast menace out of legend, a creature half-human and half-beast, with short though massive legs and a barrel chest, long hanging arms and overarching bat-wings that cast the crested head and fanged mouth into shadow. Its hands were the size of Llian's head, with retractable claws. The joints of its wings and the bony crest of its head were tipped with spikes. In one hand it clutched a flail, each lash being tipped with a spiked ball like a tiny morning-star, while the other hand gripped a rod like a wizard's baton.

Llian fell back against the railing before realizing that the beast was just a statue, though a brilliantly lifelike one. It was made of brass, impervious to time and the elements. On the other side of the landing crouched another of the creatures, equipped with a spear in one hand and a set of pincers in the other. This one had wings that soared out on either side and the chest armor was curved to accommodate a pair of breasts as large as melons.

Between the statues was a great gate of wrought-iron, clustered with heads and faces and squatting gargoyle figures. The gate was ajar but beyond was a solid door set with decorated metal plates. Even knowing that the statues were mere metal, Llian could not move, they so embodied the mythical terrors his childhood had been steeped in. Then, looking back, he saw his pursuers emerge out of shadow below the arena. They were only a minute away. Basitor was well ahead, his impossibly long legs flashing.

Squawking in terror, Llian clawed his way up the remaining steps like a lame crab. One, two, three, four, five. Five to go! He could see the fury on Basitor's face; the snarl; the bared teeth. No mercy there! Basitor would bash out his brains against the steps, or throw him over the side without a thought.

Llian hurled himself up the last high step, stuck for a moment as his hobbles caught on the broken stone, then with a tremendous heave freed himself, skidded across the landing, flung the gate open and crashed head first into one of the decorated plates on the door. It clanked; something inside gave forth a hollow boom that echoed on and on. He bashed at the door until his knuckles bled. It was too late. Basitor was already at the bottom of the steps. He leapt up, four steps at each stride.

"Got you, you treacherous swine," he gasped, striking

Llian a blow in the belly that doubled him over helpless. "I should have done this a year ago."

He picked Llian up by the collar and the seat of the pants, shaking him until his brains felt like jelly. Llian tried to kick him but Basitor was too big and strong. The rest of the company was still too far away to do anything, even supposing that they cared to.

"You're dead!" raged Basitor, holding Llian out over the precipice and punctuating every phrase with another shake. "Do you remember Hintis? Dead because of you! Do you remember Selial, Shalah, Thel, Trule?" He went on with a litany of names, most unknown to Llian, as if he blamed him for every death in Shazmak and since, and planned to list each one too. "Do you remember the kindness my brethren in Shazmak showed you, treacherous Zain? Do you remember Rael? All dead because of you. Because of you beloved Shazmak lies in ruins! This is the *least* I can do for them."

Llian looked down. The gorge was bathed in the baleful glare from the dark moon. The beckoning rocks were as clear as daylight. Basitor shook him until it all became a blur again, then drew back his arm.

As he did, Llian's hand struck one of the many metal projections that stuck out from the walls of the tower. He gripped it like a drowning man, heaved and his knee struck Basitor in the eye. Basitor fell against the wall, relaxing his grip for a second. Llian kicked free and went hand over hand up the wall, using the rods and hooks like a ladder. His fear of heights was nothing to his terror of Basitor. One of his hobbles snagged on a hook and he almost fell. He freed himself, his upstretched hand caught the lip of an embrasure and without looking he threw himself in head first.

Eventually his brain stopped whirling, his eyes uncrossed. He was in the upper chamber where the great telling had been held a week ago. There was a mound of wreckage on the floor—beams, tiles and metal, the remains of the roof—but the space around the construct was swept clear as if the rubble had been repelled from it. Snowflakes drifted down through the broken roof and covered every surface, though the construct was as black and clean as ever.

Llian lay on the floor, literally unable to get up. His body had suffered too many injuries, too many insults in the past two weeks. He lifted his head. Rulke was sitting on the high seat of the construct concentrating hard on something. As his eyes adjusted, Llian saw that the room was hung with a ghostly web of light, like a barely visible fishing net curving from one wall to another. The fibers of the net began to glow more brightly, the light spreading and smearing out until the net became a shimmering wall, a barrier across which iridescent lights danced. Ripples passed gently across its surface.

It was the Wall of the Forbidding made visible, curving through the ten dimensions of space and time. It touched all parts of Santhenar, the Three Worlds and even the Nightland equally, while separating these inhabited spaces from the Darwinian nightmare of the void. Rulke's tale of a week ago had told Llian all that he cared to know about the violent creatures that dwelt in the void, and what they would do to Santh if they ever got out.

Where was Karan? He picked her out across the other side, sitting cross-legged on a window ledge with a brazier glowing in front of her. Her eyes were closed but she looked alert, concentrating intensely on something.

"Karan!" he screamed.

Her eyes sprang open. The net of light vanished. "Llian!" she whispered, anguished and ashamed. "What are you doing here? Go back!"

"Not without you." He tried to get to his feet but only managed his knees.

Rulke snapped back to reality with a shock that almost tumbled him off his seat. For a moment he looked dazed, as if the switch from one dimension to the other was like trying to think in a foreign tongue.

"Take what you want and pay the price!" she said. "I am paying for my choices."

"The price is too high," Llian said, hungering for her. He was helpless. His shredded legs were too painful to move. "Come with me." He felt ashamed that Karan had bought his freedom with her own.

"It's too late," she said softly. "It's gone too far now and can't be undone. Please go, or all I've done will be in vain."

"She's right, chronicler," said Rulke, recovering rapidly. "I don't know what fool let you in, but it's no use. If she refuses me I'll take you back."

"I won't go! Karan, don't do this."

"I have no choice," she said in her own agony. "Go away, Llian!"

Llian was desperate to take her in his arms, and knew that despite her words she felt the same. She was weakening.

Rulke shook his fist at the watching guards. "How can I work?" he roared. *"Get rid of him!"*

Two came forward—Idlis, he of the scarred face, who had hunted Karan for so long, and the woman Yetchah. They had been banished to the lowest duties, in disgrace at having voted for Llian's tale instead of Rulke's a week ago. Taking Llian under the arms, they dragged him down the coiled stairway, past statues every bit as alarming as those outside the gates. Before he reached the bottom of the stairs, the room was lit up by the Wall of the Forbidding again.

The front door of Carcharon was flung open. The wind

whistled in. Idlis put his foot in Llian's back and sent him flying through. He skidded halfway across the landing.

Llian wished he was dead. He wiped the snow out of his eyes, turned over and looked up into the grim faces of the company. No one said a word. Basitor gripped him by the collar then marched down the steps, dragging him behind. The others followed in his wake.

2

THE WAY

The previous night, Karan had lain squirming in her sleeping pouch, desperate for sleep. Tomorrow would be hythe, mid-winter's day—the day she would betray her people and her world. To save Llian she had agreed to find the Way between the Worlds for Rulke. But what would the consequences be? Would she survive it? Would any of them? What was the word of Rulke, the Great Betrayer, worth anyway?

A week had gone by since the great telling, after which he had used the construct to cast Llian out of Carcharon. Since then Rulke had worked Karan impossibly hard, day and night, in exercises her brain could scarcely comprehend. She practiced as though her life depended on mastering his lessons. She knew it did. The void was a brutal place and hers a deadly job, and the knowledge that he would torment Llian if she refused was all the goad she needed.

Karan found it hard to concentrate. She made a lot of mistakes but Rulke never criticized her. A good teacher, he patiently instructed her over and again, yet she felt sure he found her stupid and incapable.

She wriggled in her pouch but could not get warm. And being a sensitive, she could feel the age-old emotions stirring in this place. The stones were saturated with the death agonies of the hundreds of workers who had died building Carcharon, with the mad cunning of her ancestor, Basunez, and with strange, older passions that she could not disentangle from the rocky matrix.

Karan hated Carcharon. Her beloved father had been killed here too, seventeen years ago, a senseless crime. After all this time she still missed him. Just to think of Galliad was to bring back her childhood longings. She could not sense him here, but how she wanted to.

Exhausted, she kicked off her pouch, drew on socks and crept across to where Rulke slept beside the construct. Evidently he was impervious to cold for he lay on the floor wrapped in only a single blanket, and his mighty chest was bare. His shoulders were each the size of her head. Karan eyed them in uncomfortable awe.

"There is something I need to know," she said.

He woke instantly. "What is it?"

"A question of the most surpassing interest to me."

"Then ask it," he said, sitting up. His muscles rippled. She pulled her eyes away.

"My father was killed here. Do you know why?"

"I don't know anything about your father, except that he was a blending of human and Aachim. What happened to him?"

"He was the rock of my childhood," she said in melancholy tones. "He was coming back from Shazmak but never arrived. Finally he was found here, beaten to death for the few coins in his pocket. No one could understand why."

"Why would he come here, so far off the path to Shazmak?"

"He was fascinated by this place, and by Basunez."

"Mad Basunez!" said Rulke. "He can't have been quite as mad as he was made out."

"Why do you say that?"

"The bronze statues are too perfect. He found something here, and he had to have looked into the void for it. That was what first attracted me to this place."

"Last summer?"

He smiled at her naivety. "Little Karan! You still think all this came about by accident, by some chance of fate."

"What do you mean?" Suddenly she felt panicky, all shivery afraid and choked up. "*What wasn't an accident?*"

"Even from the Nightland I could sense Basunez working here. His corrupt experiments had thinned the wall between Santhenar and my prison, and the void too. Had he succeeded your old human species would probably no longer exist. Fortunately he failed, but I've been watching this place ever since. For six hundred years I kept vigil! I even noticed *you*."

Karan writhed, imagining that he might have looked down on her most private moments. "What do you mean, *noticed* me?"

"I mean that I sensed you. This place is one of the most potent sites on all Santhenar for working the Secret Art, which is why Basunez built Carcharon here. What he did here allowed me to detect him, and you too."

She turned away abruptly.

"Don't worry, I couldn't actually *see* anything from the Nightland. I felt that he was carrying out dangerous experiments which were of great interest to me, but I couldn't find out what they were. Then, not so long ago, I sensed something here again, where there had been nothing for centuries. Someone strange and rare. It turned out to be you!"

Karan trembled. "Does this mean that other people can tell that I am . . . triune?" Her heritage had caused her enough trouble already.

"I wouldn't think so! Not even I can sense you from Santhenar. The Nightland is different; a higher plane."

"When did you sense me?" But she knew all too well.

"Time has funny habits in the Nightland. It might have been ten years ago, or thirty."

"I came here with my father when I was eight, not long before he died. And to think you were spying on us!" Her voice rose in outrage.

"Not spying. I had no idea if you were young or old, man or girl. All I knew was that there was a unique talent in Carcharon. It made me sweat. This place might have been full of dangerous secrets, for all I knew."

"But I have no powers at all," said Karan. "Tensor made sure of that when I was a child. I cannot wield the Secret Art. All I have are a few minor talents like *sensing* and *sending* and *linking*, abilities that often fail me."

"The right lever can move the world. Anyway, as soon as you left Carcharon I lost you, and no matter what I did I could not find you again. Not until you picked up the Mirror in Fiz Gorgo did I detect you once more, for the Mirror was tied to Yggur, and he tenuously to me, because I had possessed him long ago."

Even as a child, a watch was being kept out for her. It made Karan feel that her destiny had never been in her control.

"The Mirror started it all," he went on. "I still didn't know who you were, but I could sometimes get into your dreams and give you a nudge. And now I'm here," he said with great satisfaction. "Without you I would still be in the

Nightland with no chance of ever getting out. I owe you a great debt, Karan."

"You can repay it by letting me go!"

He roared with laughter.

Karan stared into nothingness, trying to concentrate on what he had said. Without her, none of this would have happened. She had always known that, in a way, but she'd had no idea that it went back to her distant ancestors. *Nothing comes out of nothing*. It better explained Maigraith's interest in her, and Faelamor's unease, and Tensor's attitude too. How she had been exploited!

"And did you learn anything about Basunez's work?" she asked.

"Not much," said Rulke. "I tried to compel his shade, but whatever he found is lost forever."

Karan looked out the window, wondering if he spoke the truth. "I couldn't care less what Basunez found," she murmured. "But I would dearly love to know who killed my father, and why. It must be connected with this place."

Rulke rubbed his jaw. "Well, there's all day to wait until moonrise. If I can put your mind at ease it will help later on. Come with me."

It was still dark as they went out into the yard, but the flagstones were lit by a ray of light from an upstairs window. Rulke lifted a trapdoor and shone his lantern down a metal ladder. "Go down!" He followed her, extinguished his lamp and by means that were invisible to her in the dark conjured up the shade of Basunez.

At first it was no more than a black and white outline on the wall. Shortly, two specks began to gleam at the top, as if she was being watched by someone who was bitterly angry.

"Come out, shade!" said Rulke sternly. "Focus your misery on the particles of air and make them speak."

The outline took on a more human shape, then the ghost

emerged part-way from the wall, hawk-nose first. Its thin lips moved but the squeaky wail of its voice seemed to come from the middle air.

"Why do you call me back again?" it piped in querulous tones. "Let me go to my rest."

"You shall have no rest while your sins remain unpunished! Here is your granddaughter more than twenty generations on, Karan Elienor Melluselde Fyrn." Rulke pushed her forward.

Karan resisted. She was afraid.

Coming halfway out of the wall, the shade of Basunez spat at the floor near her feet. The phosphorescent stuff evaporated to nothing in the air. "Hideous little mite," he fluted.

"She demands to know what happened to her father, Galliad, who died here."

Basunez flapped his hands in agitation. "Never heard of him," he muttered, vainly trying to pass back through the stone.

"Liar!" she shouted. "He often came here. He used to tell me stories about the ghosts of Carcharon, at bedtime." The tales of Basunez had always frightened her.

Basunez came right out of the wall, fluttering through the air at them. His lean bearded face was furious, his nostrils flaring. He had an arching nose and black eyes, no resemblance to her at all. He shouted in her face and flapped his cloak at her. Karan jumped, falling backward against the ladder.

"Stop that!" Rulke roared. By the time she recovered Basunez was back in the wall, only his eyes and hook-nose showing.

"I wonder . . ." said Rulke.

"What?"

"You say Galliad was beaten to death for a few coins.

What robber would lie in wait here, so far from anywhere? I wonder if he might not have pestered Basunez's ghost too much."

"My father was not afraid of ghosts."

"Out with it, shade," said Rulke, and did something in the dark that made the ghost glow like a red-hot poker. "What did you do to her father?"

"Unpleasant, inadequate man," wailed Basunez, wrenching himself out of the wall again. "Always prying and trying to learn my secrets. Hah! I burned everything to ashes before I died. No one will get the benefit of my labor, not even you, Rulke! Anyway, the struggle is the answer! But he took the easy way—he ripped my bones out of their crypt and dared to raise me from the dead. And don't think I was the first either!" he sneered at Karan. "He was well practiced in the unwholesome art of necromancy." The ghost blurred back into the wall, fading almost to nothing.

"Don't go," said Rulke in a velvet voice. "Why did he die?"

"He was not as cunning as I was!" Basunez's eyes gleamed, rat-like. "I led him on a playful dance, a merry climb right to the very tower top. Still he pestered me, and I grew angry and flew at him. He fell to his death."

"You killed him!" Karan screamed. "*You* murdered my father." She tried to strike the shade with her fists but all she got for it was bloody knuckles.

"A death for a life," said the ghost of Basunez with grim irony. "He reanimated my dead bones, a greater crime by far than easing his miserable life out of him."

"Murderer!" she shrieked, thrashing about wildly. Rulke held her arms.

"*Life-giver!*" Basunez spat. "I am dead six hundred years and still I cannot lie in my grave. Send me back!"

"Enough!" said Rulke. His lantern flared brightly and

Basunez faded to nothing, though his cries could still be heard, "Send me back, send me back!" as Karan hurried up the ladder and Rulke closed the trapdoor of the cellar.

Back in the upper tower he sat Karan down and put a cup to her lips. She was trembling. She held the vessel in two hands and sipped from it, staring at the floor for a long time. Finally she gave a great shudder and looked up at him. The light made her malachite-green eyes glow. She took a deep breath.

"He wasn't murdered at all, was he? It was just a stupid accident that means nothing."

"No more than a malicious accident," he said. "Ghosts can't do murder. Do you feel better for knowing?"

"That my beloved father practiced the black art, necromancy? No! But only the child of eight thought he was perfect. *I had to know the truth.*"

Nonetheless she paced back and forth, as agitated as she had been down below. Behind her back, Rulke did something with his fingers and suddenly her head nodded. "Oh, I'm so tired."

"Sleep," he murmured, drawing his fingers down over her face. "It's nearly dawn and there'll be no rest for either of us tonight." Her eyes fell closed, she subsided on the floor and he drew the sleeping pouch up around her.

"Well," Rulke said just before moonrise that evening. "Are you ready?"

"Almost!" She was still wondering what her father had been up to. "But before we begin I must know what has happened to Llian."

"Another condition! He's out there with the rest of the company." He gestured to the embrasure that faced east toward the amphitheater.

"I must know that he's safe."

Rulke restrained his impatience. "Very well. Come up!"

"What?"

"Come up and I'll show you. I had thought to make a demonstration anyway."

She walked over to the construct, rather anxiously. One of the Ghâshâd, a man with gray warts all over his face, flung her up. Rulke caught her, setting her down beside him.

"Hold tight to this rail," he said, manipulating levers, knobs and wheels with practiced ease.

The construct radiated light that wove a spherical shield around them, their surroundings grew dim and with a shriek the machine lifted abruptly. The sensation was sickening—her stomach felt left behind. Then it caught up, they rose faster and faster and the shield burst through the brass and slate roof of Carcharon, flaring like a miniature sun. Debris rained down at them. Karan flinched but the shield hurled it all to the sides. Then it faded and they floated in the air above the tower, Rulke roaring his delight at his enemies.

Looking down, Karan saw the company, like a family of helpless ants on the far side of the amphitheater. She saw Llian too, staring desperately at her, and felt his pain. She was ashamed of what she was going to do, and afraid of his contempt, but there was no alternative.

Rulke flung out his arm, pointing over their heads. The moon was rising, huge and dark and full. The dark moon was in hythe, signaling that the foretelling would come to pass. Karan clutched her stomach. The bimonthly waxing of the dark face always gave her a pang, ill-omen that it was, but this was unimaginably bad.

Rulke played with the construct, sending it soaring and swooping above the chasm, displaying it and taunting the company with it while Karan stood statue-like beside him. This might be the end of her world. Then, as clearly as looking through Rulke's paired glasses, she saw Tensor lurch to his feet, take the bow and the red-feathered arrow from Xarah and draw the arrow back.

She knew that it was aimed at her; knew that Tensor could hit her too, but she was paralyzed. Maybe this was meant to be. She watched him sight along the arrow, unable to save herself. Rulke had not noticed; he was looking elsewhere. Then she felt an explosion of love and terror, as Llian shrieked, "*No!*" That sparked an equally wild broadcast of her own agonies.

She threw herself down between the bulkheads. The arrow slammed into the cowl where her head had been, smashing into splinters. Rulke threw up his arms as her crazed sending tore through his mind. The construct plunged at the rocks while he worked furiously to control it. At the last minute he forced it to answer his levers again and wrested it back up.

"I've had enough!" he said roughly as they regained the top of the tower. Rulke looked quite shaken. Soberly he brought the construct back down inside. Settling it down, he took her by the shoulders. His eyes flamed like lighthouse beacons.

"There, Llian is safe, and he knows you are safe, and they have seen my power. *Now will you honor your promise?*"

She bowed her head.

"Are you ready?"

"Almost," she said, shaking.

"Then steady yourself. Be calm."

"Why did you pick me?" Anything to put it off a bit longer. "There are other sensitives."

"No triunes though! Have *you* ever sensed another?"

"No. Once or twice I sensed other sensitives, but I never found them."

"You must feel quite lonely," he observed shrewdly, "having none of your own kind."

Karan would have none of this subtle manipulation. "Don't tell me what my kind is!" she said. "I am content with my life."

Rulke said no more about it. "What matters that? You are here; I have no other. And perhaps if I had the choice of many I might still choose you. I knew the Way to Aachan once, but everything is changed so much that I no longer have the ability to find it. Let's begin."

She tensed.

"Don't look so worried. This is what we're going to do. First I'll focus the construct on making a hole through the Forbidding. It must be a tiny opening that no creature can get through, because the void is violent beyond your imagining. Then you must make a . . . kind of sending through the hole, and seek out the Way between the Worlds, as I've taught you already. Together we will look for the way to Aachan. That will take all my strength and wit." What Rulke planned to do on Aachan he did not say. "But first I must tune the construct. It's not answering my will as it ought. It's difficult to control."

Karan struggled with her conscience. Terrible things had flowed from her previous actions—the wakening of the Ghâshâd, the fall of Shazmak, the liberation of Rulke—and she had vowed to take no further part in the affairs of the world because of it.

Yet now she collaborated in a worse crime for her own selfish reasons. For Llian, to make up for the wrong she had done him before, and because she loved him. But still, a crime. Would the next hundred generations, groaning in slave chains, curse her name? Would even Llian come to hate her?

And, she could not deny it, curiosity about her triune nature drove her too. That temptation was impossible to resist.

And curiosity about Carcharon. What *had* her father and old Basunez been searching for?

But then again, perhaps this was fated to be; perhaps Rulke was the one who could finally liberate Santhenar from all its petty squabbles. How could she tell? How could she choose? She could not, and so she kept her faith with Llian and her word to Rulke.

3

The Void

Rulke sat on the high seat of the construct (and how he gloried in his wonderful machine) but Karan found that the very presence of the device took away her mind's ability to *see* and to seek. They tried several times but the metallic bulk of it oppressed her inner eye, warped her *seeing*. She had to be as far away from it as possible.

She went around the corner to a small alcove where the room and the stairs were shielded by a wall. It was the place where Llian had emerged through the concealed stone panel a week earlier, before the great telling, and where she had been captured after Llian's reply to Rulke's telling. On the other side was an embrasure, taller than she was and as wide, glazed with plain glass in small panels. The glass was so old that it had a purple tinge.

It was frigid against the window. Karan nested herself down on a pile of rugs and wrapped a blanket around her. She stared out through the bubbly glass. The window faced west of north, and the moon would come through it later on, before setting behind the mountains that were tall and jagged in the west.

"I'm ready," Rulke called down to her.

"I am too."

She sat still, watching and waiting for him to begin. The lights faded, the room grew dark, ghostly webs formed and extended to become nets of light. She closed her eyes.

Before she could begin, a ragged bundle flopped in through an embrasure. "Karan!" Llian screamed.

His wracked face stabbed her like a moth on a pin. Karan wanted to die of shame, that he should see her doing this. How it hurt to send him away, and when it was done she wept uncontrollably.

Rulke had remade the nets of light that were the Forbidding, but now he sighed and let them fade away again. "This is not working," he said aloud. "Maybe she's not up to it. That's the problem with sensitives. Still, better to find out now than later."

Waving the Ghâshâd out of the room, he leapt off the construct and sat beside Karan. "Talk to me."

Karan felt like bawling her eyes out. "Did you see him?" she wailed. "How contemptuous he looked. How I must disgust him!"

He put his arm around her. "I saw that he was in pain; that he was terribly afraid for you."

"I hate myself," said Karan. "I want to go home."

"Don't be a child," he said. "Hate me, if you must hate. I know how you feel for each other. I spied on you and him together, remember?"

"I *do* hate you!" she shouted, pushing him away. "You are the wickedest and most evil man in all the Three Worlds. Everything you say is just to get me to do what you want."

"Indeed it is," he said, and laughed. "Now here is an

offer. Go! I absolve you of your debt to me. Walk free from Carcharon, right now."

The offer was so absurd that she was not even tempted. "Why do you taunt me?" she said coldly. "I know you will never let me go."

"Unless you are willing, we will fail. Unless we can trust each other we will never find the Way. I would be better off looking for a new sensitive, even if it took me a hundred years to find one."

Karan stood up. "You are the Great Betrayer, the bane of two worlds. I can never trust *you*."

"Of course not. But do you?"

She sat down again. "It's impossible, but I do believe you."

"Then go. Your debt is absolved."

She did not move. "You can't absolve it! I gave you my promise in exchange for Llian's freedom. Even if I *could* go back on my word, I must expect you to do the same."

Rulke smiled, but she sensed relief as well.

"You knew that all along, didn't you!" she snapped, feeling that she had been cleverly manipulated.

"I know your character. But, on the other hand, you have free will. I didn't know what you would do. Shall we begin?"

"Let's get it over with."

"Link with me."

She allowed him to touch that small, cut-off portion of her mind that had not been used since Narne, more than a year ago. Then she shied away instinctively, like an unbroken filly, expecting to feel some horror or loathing. There was nothing like that. The touch of his mind was quite gentle, even a little tentative.

It surprised her. He was too clever for her, this Great Betrayer. She allowed him to continue, and through the contact she sensed many things. An overwhelming purpose; an urge to dominate and possess; to crush his enemies; never to yield. The Charon were rulers of Aachan but prisoners there, unable to increase, surrounded by the legions of the Aachim, the threat of extinction hanging over them. But what she most feared—the depravity and corruption of Emmant, a mind so diseased that the touch of it had been like that rodent she had pulled out of the water barrel in the wharf city of Thurkad, rotted into jelly and matted fur—there was not the least trace of *that* here.

I might be committing a terrible, wicked crime, she thought, one that no one can ever forgive me for. But at least I'm working with a man who is not totally evil. Not for anything could she have collaborated with Emmant.

"Are you all right?"

"Yes," she murmured.

Rulke got busy with the construct. Karan felt a sick dizziness, then encouragement poured across the link, steadying her.

"Now comes the most delicate stage of all—finding the right way to penetrate the Forbidding. It must be done delicately, so as not to alert the creatures that dwell in the void."

"Are you going to take the construct to Aachan?"

"If only I could!" he sighed. "But everything's different now. The best I can do is find the Way there, with your help, and using your senses linked to me, try to speak to my people."

Karan wriggled under her blanket. She was cold. She stretched, rubbed her chilly fingers together, waited. Nothing happened for some time and her mind drifted away onto familiar paths, familiar longings that were stronger than ever, now that it seemed they would never be fulfilled.

She longed to be back in Gothryme, her shabby little manor that had been damaged in the war. It would probably never be repaired, for war and drought had cost her everything she had, and Yggur's tax collector was due in the spring, only months away. And when she could not pay him, surely Gothryme would be stripped from her. That would not have happened in the old days, but Bannador was a free nation no longer. It lay under the yoke of Yggur, and she knew how ruthless he could be.

She longed for her own people, especially faithful old Rachis, her steward for nearly twenty years, the mainstay of Gothryme. He had always been steadfast. He should be enjoying his rocking chair by the hearth now, not working day and night to keep Gothryme from falling apart.

She longed for her gardens that she had just begun to lay out, and for the feel of the poor soil of Gothryme in her fingers. But most of all she ached for Llian, for the comfort of his arms around her, for his jokes and tales, and his lovemaking too. Not much of that lately. Rulke had come between them on the way back from Katazza, and dear mistaken Shand had poisoned her mind against Llian, raising the worm of treachery that had made the past few months such a misery for them both.

And that woke another yearning that was still a little thing but growing—an heir for Gothryme. She did not feel ready for that, but the women of her family were not fertile for long, and Karan knew her time was running out. If she did not produce an heir, one day her beloved home would fall into the hands of a stranger, some distant cousin who might care nothing for its Histories or its people.

Suddenly the nets of light sprang into place again and the networks smeared out to make the Wall of the Forbidding. All at once her world—the tower walls, the window—faded, and she saw that she was outside (or perhaps inside) a translucent surface that seemed to curve away in many dimensions, further than she could sense it. It was a little akin to the stuff of which the Nightland had been made, faintly shimmering on its folds, curves and convolutions. The Wall was in constant motion, sometimes billowing, sometimes shivering but never in the same place twice. Sometimes it went in many directions at once, a thing that her mind could not accommodate. Carcharon was a very strange place, and here the Secret Art behaved in unpredictable ways.

She closed her eyes to try to escape from the dizziness, but that made no difference. At times a wave would pass across the Wall from one direction or another, or it would ripple like a stone thrown into a pond. At other times it rang silently, like a gigantic gong, or shook violently as if rattled from the other side.

Mostly the Wall was milkily translucent, but there were occasions when rainbows shimmered across it in muted, pastel colors, and other times when parts of it would darken to opacity or burst with brief bright radiance. Nothing was visible on the other side, if there could be said to be another side to something like an ultra-dimensional Möbius plane.

She was growing used to it now. Though it was endlessly variable, endlessly fascinating, she had work to do. The sound of the construct moved up to a higher pitch. Waves of color pulsed across the translucency like a frightened cuttle-fish. The nature of reality changed again; the walls of Car-charon began to warp around and away from the construct. Karan could not see this, but she could feel it. The floor felt as if it had sagged down. She had to brace herself to avoid sliding toward the construct.

The sound rose to a whine and the Wall became solid with moving color. Now it was like lying beneath the sur-face of a pool, watching drops fall from above. The drops were invisible, but each made a nipple sticking out at her, and a series of concentric ripples spread out from it like a corrugated breast. The drops began to fall faster and harder, the ripples chasing each other continuously. Now they rebounded and reformed, and sometimes a tiny globe would break off and drift away, or fall back and be slowly resorbed. Once one of these came drifting toward her nose and she half-expected it to burst the way a soap bubble might, but it just rebounded with no sensation at all.

Sometimes bubbles seemed to be forming on the other side too. Perhaps that was what Rulke was trying to achieve. "It thins!" he sang out. "Can you feel it?"

The whine rose in pitch. The whole Forbidding reverberated like a gong. The colors and motions made her feel bilious, then suddenly a corona of bubbles soared past and right in front of her was a tiny perforation in the Wall.

Rulke was quietly triumphant. "There it is! Now it's your turn, Karan. Find the Way between the Worlds."

She hesitated, wondering what would happen if the hole snapped shut while her *sensing* was beyond. He must have known what she was thinking, for he said quietly, "Courage! I won't fail you. But you must do it quickly. This takes a toll of my strength."

Great Betrayer! But, strangely, she felt safe. At least, as safe as he was. "I'm ready."

"I'll put you in a trance, else your eyes and ears will distract you."

She submitted, and he did that. Her body sat motionless in Carcharon but now her eyes saw nothing. Karan sought out through the Wall as he had instructed her, her mind totally blank, only her senses live. All around her stretched the void. She had thought it to be just emptiness, but in this state she saw that it was a maze of spaces, ever changing, like the Forbidding itself only extending in many dimensions. The structure of the void was impossible to comprehend, but there was a Way through it; perhaps many Ways.

She floated past a murky clot that suddenly sprang

against the layer between her and it. It clung there like a black spider, bristly limbs rasping against the barrier, trying to get at her. Karan was shocked out of her drifting complacency. The void swarmed with violent life; she could sense it all around. She knew that it sensed her too. Her disembodied spirit might not be in danger, but those creatures would soon realize that there was a break in the Forbidding. Freedom! A way out of the void! They would find it easily enough, for the Ways between the Worlds were their garden paths. And her body lay helpless before the portal in Carcharon, an invitation to a feast.

For a moment she lost concentration, but Rulke was there, steadying her across the link. *I am very afraid*, she sent to him.

And you should be. There are things here that will rend us in an instant, if I fail. But I'm protecting you.

The pressure of their violent urges hurt her, almost physically. How easy it would be to go mad in this task. Rulke helped her to get control of herself again. She kept on and at last found a track and knew that it was the Way to Aachan. *I've found it!* she sang out across the link.

Back in Carcharon Rulke shouted with delight. He took his seat upon the construct, his will locked totally to the task, trusting her as he must. The Way, tenuous and ever-changing, skidded from her questing senses. The very act of seeking and finding it, the *seeing* of it in her mind seemed to change it, so that she must not only see what it is *now*, and how it will be *then,* but must also know the unknowable—in what way it would shy away from her mind—and put all these together into a path that Rulke could follow.

She slid her triune senses, that she barely knew how to use, along the Way, preparing it as he had taught her to. The strain of holding it was terrible. She could feel his struggle too.

It hurts! he cried.

Again Karan sensed an alien presence scratching at the boundaries of the Way, sniffing it out even as she did. Then another! They began to move past, first a trickle, then a flood of them, but though she cringed they passed by without sensing her life force.

This Way was almost mapped now. Ahead Karan sensed the cold dark globe that was Aachan. Behind her, through the link with Rulke, she felt the creatures clustered about the pore through the Wall. How they clawed at it, trying to get into Carcharon.

Karan felt a shock behind her as the first void-creature came up against Rulke's will. Across the link she sensed his unguarded thoughts.

It's strong. Far stronger than I expected! We've been out of the void too long. I'd forgotten how desperate they are. Unknowingly, his guard over the pore through the Wall began to slip.

She continued mapping the Way, though now she could sense his whole body shuddering with the strain, his knuckles white on the levers of the construct, his eyes staring but seeing nothing. *I can't keep it up!* She felt the burning pain in his limbs as if he was being torn between two straining horses. *Aaaaah!* he screamed aloud, and did not realize it. *I can't! I can't do it!* Then nothing.

Karan stopped at once, shocked at how quickly he had been overcome. What was she to do? She hesitated, then the link was back. Rulke was back.

She felt the ache as he took control again. *It's not far now. Once I get there, they can't touch me. She's done a better job than I dared hope. Karan, where are you?*

Here I am. Karan remained where she was, afraid to map the Way any further, afraid of the creatures in the void, afraid that Rulke would fail again.

Aachan! he exulted. *I know the way from here!*

Rulke put his body into a trance and sent his senses through the pore, tracking her link, following the Way she had mapped. Consumed by his triumph he raced past Karan, leaving her to follow as she might. But who was guarding their bodies now? This thought distracted Karan so badly that she lost touch with her own job. She forgot the Way.

Karan could hear Rulke calling the Charon with all his might, trying to reach those to whom he had not spoken in thousands of years. *Yalkara! Vance! Grendor! We have a chance now, to survive on another world.*

Lost somewhere in his turbulent wake, Karan sensed that they answered cautiously. But so quickly had he disappeared, leaving such chaos behind him, disrupting her *seeing*, that she could not follow. It was like being lost in a gate, unable to remember the destination. Then the voices were abruptly cut off. She had lost Rulke, lost the link, everything. Her physical body in Carcharon was unprotected.

The little intangible part of her that had sensed out the Way now drifted in the limitless void, lonely and terrified. She was so alone, while around her everything was black, menacing and alien.

In the distance a fast-moving spark lit up the void, a comet that left a luminous trail. A few lines of verse popped into Karan's mind as she floated there.

A restless zephyr ruffles my soul,
Sculpting chunks of darkness into form,
While from the emptiness around,
Twin vortices of piercing sound,
Whisper to each other.

Where had that come from? Her father? The scribblings of mad old Basunez? Wherever, it summed up the void at this moment.

Just then the invisible cord that led back to her helpless body twanged as if something had plucked it. Karan couldn't sense what it was. Rulke had gone where she could not follow. Her increasingly panicked sendings raised no response. He had abandoned her—he didn't need her any more.

There came an unpleasant sucking sound. Her disembodied senses sought around in the void. The cord vibrated again and she realized what it was. Something had begun to haul itself toward the hole in the Wall. Her senses struggled desperately to find the way home, but whatever the thing was, it blocked her path. She sang out across the Way, imagining her body about to be devoured. Would she even know, or would she just fade out to nothing? Using one of her triune talents that Rulke had developed, by supreme efforts Karan roused her flesh and bones from the trance, just enough so that she could see what was happening in Carcharon.

The Wall had grown transparent around the hole, so that she could just make out something approaching. It settled over the pore with a splatting sound. It had the shape of a blob of stuff with tentacles, though its form was in flux. It glistened wetly like a slug.

Rulke had said she was safe, that nothing could get past his protection through the Wall. Clearly the slug-thing did not know that, for it extruded a shiny pseudopod like a needle and slid it right through the pore. It lengthened until it extended halfway across the room, while the body on the other side grew smaller and smaller, and eventually the last of it popped through. The creature resumed its former blobby shape.

Karan tried to mobilize her limbs, jerking this way and that like a beetle trapped in a spider's web, but could not come any further out of her trance. She could not get away from the creature either, for it was attached like a limpet to her life-cord. Now the void-leech, or whatever it was, glided up to her, its mucus-covered foot squelching across the floor.

Karan screamed as it put out a slug foot at her face, slug tentacles questing this way and that. She tossed her head but another pseudopod thrust at her from the other side. It slurped across her cheek. Karan felt a pain in one ear as it tried to drill into her head. She was almost insane with disgust and horror.

4

FROZEN FOOD

Karan felt horribly betrayed. Rulke's promises of protection had come to nothing. He had abandoned her. And if those promises were lies, so was everything else.

The void-leech extended its pulpy pseudopods around her head, trying to envelop her face with its grainy matter so as to drill through her ears and eyes and suck out her brain. But Karan was a prisoner of the trance. She could barely move a finger.

The pain grew in her ear. She lost sight as the blob settled on her face. A rude probe began to insinuate its way up her nose, questing for a way into her skull. Another pressed against the jelly of her eyeball, a disgusting sensation. Initially soft, it began to harden so as to spear right through.

Karan directed a furious sending of rage, hate and rapacious hunger at the void-leech, trying to make herself seem like a rat or a hyena, something that might prey on such creatures. It shot away a span or two, its transparent mantle fluttering in what could have been agitation. Taking the opportunity, she screamed, broadcasting her horror and betrayal right across the void. Instantly Carcharon and her body vanished. She was a disconnected consciousness in the void again. Now Rulke's path shimmered in front of her. She flashed across the Way, following his trail to Aachan and into the Council chamber of the Charon.

Who summons the Summoner? she heard someone roar in a voice of thunder.

It is I—

Karan spat her fury at them, broadcasting the horrible image of the void-leech into all their minds. *Betrayer!* she screamed. *Look how he keeps his promises. He will betray you too!*

She sensed the Charon shrink back as if they had embraced a viper.

Who are you? they cried. *What do you want of us?*

Unable to see her or Rulke, they must have feared that it was the first skirmish of a war. Karan hurled the image of the void-leech, now pulsating as it began to settle on her head again, right into their minds. Back in Carcharon she was screeching out her terror. She flung that at them too.

Karan! Rulke exclaimed. She sensed his mortification, that he had failed to protect her, though that was swiftly overlaid by regret at having to abandon Aachan.

You deserted me! she sent to him, then blocked out the link and fled into the folds and corrugations of the void.

You fool! he shouted. *Let me help you. I can't find the Way back by myself. We'll both die!*

In that schizophrenic nightmare, her body in Carcharon, her conscious self lost in the void, Karan felt the disgusting probe in her nose again. Whatever Rulke had in mind could be no worse than that. She allowed him to find her and all at once the Way back to Santhenar was clear. They hurtled back through the mazes and corridors, and every passage they took, every wrong turn, she was aware of the current of creatures surging toward the hole—their way out of the void.

There was still some way to go when Karan felt a shocking pain in her ear. Her head was completely covered by the void-leech. She arched her back and drummed her heels on the floor. Her blind hands tore the mantle of the creature to shreds but it just re-formed. In her trance-like state she could do no more; she could not get it off.

They rushed down the last shimmering tunnel of the Way, leapt the last barrier. The Wall appeared in front of them. They shot through the Wall; their senses flashed back into their bodies. Her eardrum felt as if it had been torn open. Karan let out a despairing wail, a sending that once more disturbed the void-leech, temporary reprieve for her assaulted eyeball. The creature flopped back down onto her face. *Rulke!* Her mind screamed at him. *Rulke, help me!*

Rulke lay motionless, unable to find the way out of the trance. It was up to her. She fired up every painful, shocking and horrible emotion she had ever felt, mixed them up with her disgust and terror of the amorphous thing now flapping at her face, and bounced them back and forth between the mirrors of her mind, amplifying them at every turn, until they burst out in all directions, emotions so strong and raw that no one could resist them.

Rulke jerked as if he had taken hold of an electric eel and fell off the construct, hitting his head so hard that she was sure he had fractured his skull. However he turned over and came to hands and knees. "Karan?" he said dazedly.

Help! she screamed over the link, since her mouth was full of leech.

He crawled toward her, ever so slowly. With bare hands he ripped the void-leech off her face and flung it at the Wall. It splattered into jelly that slid down, already collecting itself together for another assault. Hauling himself back onto the construct, he spun an aiming wheel then fell against a purple knob. Light roared out of the front and boiled the creature into a sickly sweet-smelling vapor.

It burned a crater right through the Wall. A bulge appeared in the fabric of the Forbidding, then another. An arm thrust through the hole and out leapt the most frightening thing Karan had ever seen. She felt the shock in Rulke's mind, the memory of long ago: *thranx!* It leapt at them and its great shoulder struck the construct, rattling that massive machine like a child's toy.

Karan was slow to move. Her brain seemed to have lost the ability to control her body. Experimenting with crawling, she lifted an arm and a leg at the same time and toppled on her side like a baby. Her belly ached; her head spun. She rolled sideways and tried to look like a piece of rubble, and knew that she didn't.

The thranx went after Rulke, who was still clinging to his seat. A crack of leather wings propelled it up on top of the construct, where it lunged at him. He ducked, the construct rolled and he fell off again. The thranx leapt after him, landed with a thud that shook the tower and slashed at Rulke with long yellow claws. He scuttled backward, darting and ducking around the other side, and sprang from the floor up into his seat. Yellow light came out of a rod at the front, searing the thranx's thigh and melting part of a low wall behind it.

The thranx reared up, its wings soaring so high that they touched the mess of tangled roof beams suspended above them. Though it made no sound, it screwed up its face and clenched its fists. For an instant Karan sensed its agony, its desperation to get out of the void and find a safe place to nest. Its emotions flashed and faded like misty breath on a window. Karan was confounded. Its fears and longings were similar to her own.

The light touched the winged creature's thigh again, tracing a fiery line toward its groin. The thranx made a sound like a scalded cat, sprang at an embrasure which was too small and went out the side of Carcharon in an explosion of broken stone. Part of the wall collapsed behind it. The wind howled in through the new opening. Karan crawled into the rubble pile as other creatures strained against the gossamer walls of the Forbidding. She was too exhausted to blink.

The dark moon shone straight down through the broken roof of the tower—it was midnight. Momentarily Rulke wrestled with some hideous, many-clawed and fanged beast that appeared out of nowhere. It got away from him and leapt toward Karan, who scurried up onto the rubble, desperate to get out of its reach. "Karan, here!" Rulke shouted, tossing her the knife he had taken a week ago.

She caught it and ran up a slender beam, but the creature jumped on the other end, flicking her hard against the wall. The knife fell into the rubble, out of reach. She lay winded as the creature crept toward her.

The commotion had brought a squad of Ghâshâd racing up the stairs. "To me!" Rulke roared, and they ran to his aid with swords and spears. Together they forced Karan's assailant back through the Wall.

Karan picked herself up, wondering if her ribs were broken. Now only Rulke's strength held back the things that clawed at the Wall. If he were overcome, they would pour in until they choked all Santhenar. And she had helped to make this disaster.

Out of the vent surged other beasts, smaller than the thranx but seeming equally cunning. They appeared more or less human, though immensely hairy. They separated, one feinting and slashing at Rulke with unnaturally long arms, while another sprang up on the construct. A third bailed up the Ghâshâd on the other side of the room.

"Lorrsk!" said Rulke. "And I'm already spent."

These were not dumb beasts either. The one on top slammed into the seat and gripped the levers of the construct in a very knowing way, with feet that were like huge clawed hands. Its bucket-sized mouth grinned at Rulke, flashing many yellow teeth.

Rulke swung a jagged length of wood at the first lorrsk, clouting it over the side of the head and sending it sprawling into the rubble. It staggered out, blood pouring from a gash in its thigh to pool on the floor, then abruptly flung itself on Rulke and wrestled him to the ground. They rolled over and over, grunting and groaning. Karan found another billet of wood and whacked the lorrsk over the head, but it hardly noticed.

The other beast banged the levers forward. The construct groaned, lurched backward and sideways, then began to sink down until the lower side was below the level of the floor. The stone appeared to have softened beneath it. The lorrsk chittered, flinging the levers opposing ways. The construct bucked and blurred, seemingly trying to rearrange its component atoms. Molten yellow gushed out of an aperture at the front, splashing golden on the floor.

Karan had not appreciated how the Forbidding protected them. Fragments of tales burst in her mind—myths and fairy stories from the distant past. This was all too horrible! She danced around the wrestling pair like a dervish and, seeing an opportunity, stabbed the lorrsk in the ear with the jagged end of her billet. It yelped.

It was the chance Rulke needed. Gaining the upper hand in his wrestling match, he slammed the lorrsk down on its back. He manipulated something with his fingers, whereupon the construct bucked. The second lorrsk described an arc in the air, still holding onto one lever. The construct flung itself upward. The lorrsk soared through the air to land on its hairy backside right in the molten puddle. It screamed so harsh and shrill that Karan had to stop her ears. An awful smell of burnt hair and charred flesh filled the room. The lorrsk moved away, its buttocks sweating blood like meat on a hotplate, and fell through the embrasure.

The other lorrsk flung Rulke on his back, slammed its knee into his belly then lunged, trying to bite his throat. Karan yelled and pronged it in the ear again, snapping its head sideways so hard that its teeth jarred. With a superhuman effort Rulke hurled it off him into the rubble. He staggered to his feet, wrenched a long jagged beam hanging down from the roof and tried to spear the creature with it. It yelped, rolled flat head over pointy heels, ended up near an embrasure and tumbled out head first.

Karan slid to the floor, panting, wrung dry. The broken roof groaned where Rulke had pulled the beam out. Two of the Ghâshâd and the third lorrsk lay dead. Three Ghâshâd heaved the body out the window while the others tried to hold the roof from collapsing completely. Rulke flopped on his face, so exhausted that he could not even stand. I'm free, she thought, if I can hold off the aftersickness.

Rulke's vacant stare touched her. "Too . . . hard," he gasped, scarcely able to frame the words. "I was not strong enough."

"You overreached yourself and betrayed my trust," she shouted.

"Not intentionally . . ."

Karan realized that she could hardly hear on her left side. She put her hand to her ear. It came back all bloody. "I've finished with you!" she screamed. "I've paid my debt."

"Not until I say so." Rulke raised his hand weakly, but

could not hold it up. "Aftersickness is like a fire in my brain," he mumbled and collapsed.

The broken roof rumbled and slid further down, to halt just over Rulke's head. The Ghâshâd struggled frantically to maneuver a prop under it. The Wall faded almost to nothing. Out of the corner of her eye Karan saw something ease apart the ragged hole.

"You'd better seal that up, quick!" she shouted. Scooping up pack and cloak—she'd not survive outside without them—Karan hurtled down the stairs.

Near the bottom she saw that one wall of the tower had collapsed below as well as above, though the stairs and most of the floor still hung there. There was a hole in the wall three arm-spans wide. Lights shone out onto the snow. Below was a huge gouge where the thranx had landed, and a white mound thrown up against the outer wall.

Karan was just about to take a flying leap down when she realized that the mound was made of rubble, and a broken ankle was the most likely result. The freezing wind roared in, pressing her against the wall. She wrestled the cloak around her and continued down. On the ground floor she raced toward the front door, then stopped dead. A thranx stood by the doorway. Further down an odd-shaped hall, other creatures clustered together. With a squawk of terror she turned the other way, saw more in front of her, then realized that they were just bronze statues.

As she edged by, half-expecting them to come to life, the first spasm of aftersickness doubled her over. Not now! she thought, tearing at the brass bolt. Her skin stuck to the frigid metal. Karan peeled her fingers off, hastily put on gloves and slammed back the bolt.

The wind flung the door open and a blast of snow blinded her. She ran out, peering all around from the wide landing, hoping to see the company. There was no one in sight.

They'd fled. She would never catch them. In her condition she might not even reach the amphitheater. Where could she go?

Something screamed upstairs, and she knew that it was some *thing*, a creature out of the void. No human throat could have formed that wailing screech, no human mouth shaped it into such an ululating cry. They must still be coming through the Wall!

The night was punctuated by a series of thuds that shook the building and made the metal gate rattle. It could have been one monstrous creature battering another against the walls. The scream sounded again.

"To me!" came a feeble shout from above. That was Rulke, crying for his remaining Ghâshâd.

Karan began to go down the steps, then stopped, smelling blood. There was a body beside her, all broken, mangled and partly eaten. *Llian?* No, it was a tall soldier. "Llian," she shouted, "where are you?" Just to think of him out here hurt her. She could not sense him at all. Karan tried to renew the link but instantly felt Rulke's presence on the edge of her mind.

As she began to creep down, across in the amphitheater a flare illuminated a flying, thranx-like shadow. Her courage failed her. Karan turned back up the steps, and the bloody moon touched a pair of the creatures between her and the doors of Carcharon.

She stood there for a full minute before realizing, from their unnatural stillness, that they were also statues. An awful scream echoed across the ravine. Perhaps it was the injured lorrsk. Karan ran in through the doors and bolted them behind her.

Where could she go? The cold outside was terrible, as bad as the night she and Llian had almost frozen to death on the way to Shazmak last winter. Karan knew how to survive in the mountains, but she must be prepared. She had to disappear. Where? There was nowhere to hide on the ridge path. She heard footsteps on the stairs. Racing down the back, she ducked into a dark room next to the galley. It smelled like a larder. There was only one way to go now—up the mountain!

Karan felt around, finding something long and bony that reeked of smoked fish or eel. The smell was unpleasant but it was better than nothing. She scooped up several lengths, along with a cheese shaped like a breadstick, a string of onions, another that seemed to be giant radishes, and some dried fruit, hurled the lot into her pack and turned to run.

There was another cry from upstairs, then a bellow of rage and shouting in a language she did not know. It sounded as if Rulke was recovering. Boots scraped on the stone. The door out into the yard banged. She pressed back against the pantry wall as several Ghâshâd ran past. They too headed up the stairs.

Karan ran out into the yard, pulling on her overgloves. It was so cold! The wind was a blast, a gale of roaring snow that made it impossible to see. Where could she go? She tried to recall the layout of the yard. She'd looked down on it many times in the past week, but what she'd seen fitted poorly with the blizzard-struck geography she was confronted by now.

There were several places where she might get onto the wall. One was up the back of the yard, a steep stair beside lean-to sheds. She felt her way across, conscious that there was a cistern here somewhere and if she fell in she would go straight through the ice and be dead in a minute.

In the dark her progress was painfully slow. Behind her came a *Boom!* The wind crushed it into insignificance, but immediately a column of light lit up the tower, the embrasures flaring yellow. Karan jumped and cracked her knee against stone. She put out her hands to steady herself. It was the cistern; she could feel the smooth convexity of the rim. The stairs must be to her right.

They could not have seen her. Not even *that* light could have picked her out in the snowfall, but she was frightened, ill and becoming flustered. Hobbling around the edge of the cistern, Karan tripped over something in the dark. The fall jarred the wrist she had broken last year and the food spilled out of her pack—she'd forgotten to tie the flaps. She felt around in the snow, stuffing what she could find back in, but it might have been stones for all she could tell. There came a cry from behind her, an answering cry to one side. They were searching the yard.

Forget the food! Even in this weather she couldn't hide here. Rulke would be able to sense her, so close had their minds been. Lights moved toward the cistern. She groped along the wall, the pain in her knee and wrist forgotten.

Karan found the steps with her shin, then heard, even above the shriek of the wind, the sound of heavy feet running along the top of the wall. The cries came from several places now but the feet stopped directly above. She cursed; they were cutting off the exits from the yard. She fumbled around on the ground for a stone, crept halfway up the stairs and heaved it to her right. It clattered against one of the sheds. Almost immediately a flare erupted over that way. She heard the Ghâshâd calling but could not tell where they were.

Karan went up the stairs as fast as snow, ice and darkness would allow, but at the top heard Rulke's voice, an angry shout, and the footsteps came running back. She felt the force of his will too, exhausting and confusing her. She crouched at the top of the wall. The footsteps were close—another flare and they would have her. She rolled over and the guard caught a foot on her hip and went sprawling.

Metal clattered on stone. A woman's voice swore in pain. Karan kept rolling and suddenly there was nothing beneath her. She fell silently into darkness.

It was a long way down, eight or ten spans. She landed *whoomph* in the powdery snow of the deep drift below the wall. The snow fell back on her head. Her first impression was that it was much warmer than she had expected. The next, that she could easily suffocate. Karan packed the loose snow away from her nose and mouth and pushed her arm up to make an air hole. Then she lay back for a few minutes' rest, lest illness overcome her completely.

Muffled shouting came from above, and the dull flash of flares, but they moved away. In darkness it was too far down to see the slight impression, almost closed over, that she had made in the snow. The search moved back inside the yard, though Karan knew this fortunate state of affairs could not last.

Climbing out was exhausting, and walking through the drifts almost impossible. Karan, who had hiked in these mountains since the time she could walk, understood that very well. She was above the steepest slope of the deep valley between Carcharon and the adjoining ridge, the ridge up which wound the eastern way leading eventually to Shazmak, the path her father had come down just before he died. She could still remember the day they brought his body back.

Enough of that! She had to get well away before looking for a place to hide. The only sensible way out of this wilderness was down, but that risked sheer falls of hundreds of spans into the rocky bottom of the gorge. They would expect her to head east down the ridge, toward the hard snow, the path and Gothryme Forest.

Perhaps they were already hunting down there. Certainly they would be in the morning, and they would find her easily enough once the blizzard let up. Karan turned in the other direction, up the ridge.

There was no protection from the wind on this side. It was wild and gusty, occasionally dropping to nothing so that the flakes settled, then rising again to a shrieking blast that plastered hard pellets of snow to the side of her hood. The snow was piled against the wall of Carcharon in drifts higher than her head, though on the very edge of the precipice the ledge had been scoured bare. Karan picked her way carefully along the rim. She recalled that the wall ran west up the ridge for a few hundred paces before looping back down the other side. Beyond, the ridge went up and up, to become a spur of the mountains.

Up there she would have plenty of warning of their coming. Karan followed the bare rock on hands and knees, feeling every step of the way ahead, afraid that the ledge would run out and leave her nowhere to go.

Then an image of the country flashed into her head as she had seen it from a window a few days ago. She knew exactly where she was. Ahead was a rocky gully, not much more than a ditch, and beyond that a broken cliff ran behind the western wall of Carcharon. On this side it swung sharply to the west, blending into the precipitous rim of the ravine a little to her left. She would have to be careful there.

On she crawled. Her hands were stiff, unfeeling blobs and her knee hurt. So did her ear. By the time Karan reached the top it was beginning to get light, a slow seeping grayness, the air so thick with driven snow that she could see only a few steps ahead. But that was enough. Any more and her enemies could see her, for she was still so close to Carcharon that she could have hurled a pebble over the western wall.

On the steep slope above her the loose snow had been scoured away by the wind. What remained was a rough crust that was quite hard. By mid-morning she was high above Carcharon. Further up, the ridge was dotted with boulders and outcrops. Karan planned to make a snow shelter in the lee of one of these, where there were snow drifts.

After much searching she found a long outcrop that was eroded underneath. Snow had piled against the uphill side, higher than her head. She made a shelter the way she had seen her father do long ago, the snow hollowed out and packed tightly to secure the walls and roof, leaving a tiny cave against the rock. The door was a ball of snow that she could roll back or forward. The space was just large enough for her to sit, or lie curled up on her cloak to sleep. The only way she could be found was if someone walked right up to the rock, and it was one among thousands.

Now her cares came back redoubled. Was her collaboration with Rulke the most terrible crime of all? When the thranx had shaken the construct with one blow of its shoulder, when it had gone through the wall as if it were made of a child's blocks, she had felt truly afraid. The price of Llian's life might be the death of everyone she cared about. And Llian too! And below, Gothryme lay in its path.

It began to snow heavily, which pleased her. Karan emptied her pack on the tiny patch of floor in front of her, sorting out her supplies. There were two slabs of smoked eel, now frozen so hard that she risked breaking teeth on them, the long stick of cheese, a string of purple onions, very strong, some with bad spots, an orange-like *marrim*, a few pieces of dried fruit and half a loaf of dark bread she had brought from Gothryme. The rest had been lost in the snow. It wasn't much, but she could survive on it for a few days. Worst of all, she had no knife. She missed her little knife, her companion on the road.

She put the fish inside her coat where it would warm and gnawed on the end of the loaf. Stale even before they left

Gothryme, now it was like eating sawdust. She peeled away the skin of the onion with her teeth, nibbling at the shoot end, which had thawed a little in her hand. It was crisp and hot. Hunger improved the taste immeasurably.

The dried fruit was unfamiliar, rust-colored on the outside but crimson within. Karan recalled seeing the Ghâshâd eating it once or twice. She tasted a small piece, rather tentatively. It was leathery, like a dried apricot. The first impression was a tangy flavor like ginger and just as hot, though the aftertaste was strange, slightly off.

Her lips began to tingle. A warm glow ran all the way down to the pit of her stomach. Little beads of perspiration sprang out on her forehead. Her heart began to race and suddenly Karan felt hot all over. Even her fingers and toes started to tingle. Her mouth tasted odd though. She put the rest of the piece back.

The snow must have stopped, for the light was brighter now. Karan rolled the ball of snow away and put her eye to the tunnel. She could see right across the ridge. She wriggled out, trying not to disturb the opening.

It was still snowing, though not so as to impede her vision. The walls and tower of Carcharon were clearly visible half a league below. Quite a lot of snow had fallen since she had made her cave, enough to cover her tracks. Occasionally the sun peeped through low, rushing clouds.

Karan scanned the slope—up, down, across. Nothing but snow, ice and rocks. There was no sign of activity at Carcharon either. She backed into the shelter, which now gave off a warm fishy reek that grew stronger every time she moved. The eel had begun to thaw inside her coat.

Her lunch was a piece of fatty smoked eel, dry bread, hard cheese and the rest of the onion. The eel had a river-bottom muddy flavor that was unpleasant, and it was full of tiny wire-like bones that caught in her teeth and throat. The onion fumes made her nose drip.

Karan curled up in the sleeping pouch and was soon asleep, but had troubling, hallucinatory dreams that she was being hunted by a blood-drenched lorrsk and woke sweating, almost unbearably hot. Surely the weather can't have changed that much, she thought, taking her coat off. She stuck her head out of the entrance to find that it was late afternoon and the blast as wintry as ever.

Karan felt ravenous. Her supplies now looked even less appetizing than before. Wanting something sweet, she felt in her pack, found the piece of dried fruit and popped it in her mouth. Instantly she felt the most delicious thrill course through her veins. Her blood pumped like hot metal. Nothing was beyond her—she could challenge Rulke himself for the construct.

"Yes!" she cried, leapt up and her head brought down half the roof of the cave. It seared her roaring red cheeks and a clot of snow went down the back of her neck. Another huge lump landed on her head, flattening her to the floor. She felt suffocated in cold, all the more shocking because she had been so hot. Choking, she coughed the piece of fruit out into the snow.

By the time Karan dug herself out and repaired the hole in the roof the feelings of euphoria were quite gone. She now felt desperately cold. Even wrapped in cloak, coat and sleeping pouch, she could not get warm. Her head was throbbing in the beginnings of a migraine. Eventually she drifted back into her alarming dreams.

When she woke it was long after dark, and still snowing. Once she made out the lights of Carcharon, then a snow squall swept past and blotted it out. The snow she had so painstakingly packed into her water bottle had melted, generating less than a cup of icy water. She drank it, repacked the flask and pulled her sleeping pouch up again.

She dozed off at once but did not sleep for long—one unpleasant dream followed another, and all on the same topic: the hunting of her younger self a year ago. Always running, always powerless. *Not any more!* She was wakeful and cold, and the pressure of her rage built up until she felt a sudden violent urge to strike; to make a link and transmit a killing impulse across it at Rulke.

For a moment Karan reveled in this violent thought, this thrill of power, but reality intervened. If she dared to make a link this close, after their minds had been linked, he would have her instantly. Who was she to think of such things anyway?

No, she would sit quietly, attempt nothing. They could not know where she was. In a day or two she could go free. She dozed again.

"*Skelaaarr!*"

The guttural cry shocked Karan awake, for it came from not far away. Ghâshâd! She crawled to the entrance, put her head out and recoiled in horror. A weak sun shone on the snow, illuminating the dark figures of five Ghâshâd climbing up the slope toward her. She watched them for a moment, just long enough to be sure. They were heading directly toward her as if following a line drawn on the snow.

Though she was faster and more agile, it would not help her here, for they were spread out across the whole top of the ridge. She was trapped!

For a few moments Karan sat paralyzed like a rabbit in a burrow; then she stuffed her goods in her pack and darted hopelessly up the slope.

5

The Thranx

They waited in the arena for hours, staring at Carcharon. There was nothing else they could do. Someone kindled a fire with sticks that the Aachim had brought with them. The blaze was a meager thing about the size of a plate, always in danger of being blown out. It did little to warm or cheer them.

Llian's eyes darted back and forth over the company. It included a squad of about a dozen of Yggur's guard, battle-hardened veterans who never relaxed. Behind them the cold stick-figure of Vartila the Whelm stalked back and forth, shaking with passion. Most of the Whelm had abandoned Yggur a year ago, reverting to their old name—Ghâshâd—and serving their master of old, Rulke. But a few, unable to recognize him, had remained loyal to Yggur. *I am blind to my master!* Vartila had wept when Rulke first appeared. From the look on her hatchet face, Vartila's loyalty was now being severely tested.

Yggur was talking to Vanhe by the fire. A squat, bullet-headed man, Marshal Vahne had once led the First Army, but after the battle with the Second Army in Bannador, and Maigraith's disappearance, Yggur had broken Vanhe to a common soldier.

Yggur's adjutant, Dolodha, a nervous young woman perennially dressed in ill-fitting robes, scuttled back and forth. Her promotion from servant-girl had been equally abrupt and she lived in fear of offending Yggur, who was notoriously unstable. No one could be a more generous master when things were going well. However in adversity he became dangerously capricious, changing in an instant to unforgiving brutality and sometimes to a kind of madness, the echo of that insanity he had suffered when Rulke was exiled in the Nightland. No one knew how to predict his mood.

Mendark, who looked more like a bird of prey every day, was perched on a log staring into the fire. His guards, Osseion and Torgsted, were playing a game of dice on a slab of rock. As Llian watched, Torgsted threw back his head and roared with laughter. The firelight caught his broad, handsome face and the mop of dark curls. Osseion, who was almost twice his friend's size, clapped Torgsted on the shoulder and threw his dice on the slab.

On the other side of the fire sat Nadiril of the Great Library, with Lilis, her father Jevi, and Tallia. Shand had also been with them but was nowhere to be seen. Probably spying on Carcharon, Llian thought moodily. The Aachim made a third group, equally spaced about the fire. There were a dozen of them, including red-haired Malien, a silent Tensor and Old Darlish, an ancient Aachim whom Llian had not previously met. He was thin in the limbs but round in the belly, a rare thing in an Aachim. His hairy ears hung down to the level of his voice-box and his chin was as pointed as a trowel.

"What are we waiting for?" asked Lilis.

"The end of the world," said Tensor direfully.

"What mischief is he hatching now?" asked Old Darlish in a gravelly eastern accent.

"Who can predict it?" said Nadiril.

They stood ankle-deep in soft snow, and there was ice beneath that. Once or twice there were flurries of snowflakes, but even they seemed dispirited and did not last. The potential of the construct overpowered them. *It is fated to be*, the dark moon told them. Almost as one they drew away from Llian. His culpability was self-evident.

Tallia strode across to where he huddled in the snow, to check his bonds. She wore a short sword on her right hip. Llian had not seen her bear arms before.

"Tallia . . ." he began, then went silent. What was the use? The sullen moon washed the color out of even her chocolate skin. Though her long face was quite expressionless, she looked very beautiful. Her hair was blacker than the night. Llian noticed, not for the first time, just what a striking woman she was. But she could have been made of granite as far as he was concerned. His thoughts were back in the tower.

He realized that she was speaking to him.

"I said, is that too tight?"

"What does it matter?"

"I know not whether you're guilty or innocent. That will be a matter for trial, if we survive. But I would not have you lose your hands, and that's an easy thing on a night like this."

Llian tested the bonds absently. Tight, but not too tight. She began to move away. Something burst inside him—he made a groaning, choking sob.

Tallia peered into his face. The moonlight touched one cheek, leaving shadows with tinged edges.

"So now you're feeling sorry for yourself! Or is it remorse?"

"I'm terrified for Karan."

The tone of his voice seemed to unsettle her. She peered at him again, turning him by the shoulder so that the light was full on him, as if trying to read his face.

"That surprises you? You all think that I betrayed her."

"There's good evidence for it," she said. "What have you to say for yourself?"

"Nothing!" Llian raged. "Words mean nothing!"

He no longer cared what she thought of him. What was Rulke going to do with Karan? That was the only question with any meaning. She was a sensitive with rare abilities and Rulke would never give her up.

Llian examined the bowed backs and defeated faces around him. No help there. Tallia opened her mouth but whatever she had been about to say was cut off as Mendark approached.

The fulfilment of the prophecy had come as a shattering blow to Mendark. He was greatly diminished, and whenever he saw other people engaged in quiet conversation his face would darken, as though he suspected that they were libelling him, or laughing at him. Mendark's reputation meant everything to him and he would do anything to protect his place in the Histories. He could not bear for his long, long reign as Magister to end in such a failure.

The veil which had been hanging across the moon parted and it shone out, red, purple and black, brighter than before. The light caught Mendark on the snow and for a moment he hesitated. He was so changed from the man Llian had known that he scarcely seemed to be the same person. The experience in Havissard a few months ago had almost killed him, and trapped in the brambles there he'd had no option but to renew his failing body one time too many.

Mendark now looked like a withered raptor—his formerly broad nose was shrunken into a beak, hands to claws, narrow shoulders hunched forward. His hair was lank and his beard scanty. Huge creases ran from the corner of his mouth across half the length of his face and the skin hung loosely as if the flesh beneath had all dried up. The once full lips were just hard slashes across his face.

Hopping across the snow like a condor circling a corpse, Mendark also checked Llian's bonds. "What do you say now, chronicler?"

"Only that I'm innocent."

Mendark bent to check the other leg, but so slowly and with such a shudder of pain that Llian, even now, felt a flash of empathy for him. Mendark straightened, even more painfully.

"Maybe you are, Llian, but your actions speak otherwise."

"If I had died in Yggur's dungeon in Thurkad, you'd still be standing here, waiting on Rulke's whim!"

"Hmn," Mendark said. He made his awkward way back to the fire.

The night grew colder. Carcharon was silent. The Aachim went down the ridge to their wood stockpile, to return hours later bearing huge bundles on their backs. They built another fire in the most sheltered part of the amphitheater and everyone huddled between the two.

Later still, to Llian's amazement, Yggur brought him a mug of soup. Perhaps he felt remorse for his earlier fit of madness. Llian wanted to hurl it in his face but that would not help Karan. He took off his gloves to warm his hands on the mug. His feet were turning to blocks of icy jelly. The soup was scalding. He looked up and Yggur was watching him.

"You wanted me dead without trial, a month ago," said Llian. "Do you judge me differently now, or do you want something from me?"

"Rulke has made no effort to possess me," Yggur replied. "I may have been wrong about you."

"Why don't you go after him then? You were brave enough with your armies at your back, destroying half of Meldorin." In his time as a tale-spinner Llian had developed his teller's *voice* to a fine art, until he could move people to almost any emotion he desired. His talents had not been much used lately. Could he drive these cowards into some action that would help Karan? "You're *supposed* to be a great mage. Why don't you do something?"

Yggur smiled. "You can't manipulate *me* so easily, chronicler, despite that I am not what I was. It is a wondrous thing to have been great, and then to be laid low; and then to try and rise again. Things that were once important now seem trivial. Things that once had been of no account . . . But that is bye the bye. About Rulke I can do nothing—I'm too afraid. I admit it. The thought of being possessed by him again turns my bowels liquid—"

At that moment a white light shot up from the cratered tower top of Carcharon. Yggur ran to the lower edge of the amphitheater, shielding his eyes from the glare as he stared at the tower. He cursed and ran down the steps, and the rest of the party followed.

Llian felt a momentary attack of vertigo. *It was beginning!* Karan was up there because of him, and he was powerless to help her. He hobbled after the group as fast as his irons would allow. They were hard with ice now. In a minute his shins were a bloody ruin. Soon he was alone in the darkness.

He bumped down the steps, along the winding path and back up the steep track. The rest of the company were already on the stairs below the gate, but the light that had attracted them was fading. Now it disappeared, leaving them in a blacker darkness, for the moon was hidden again. Llian hung back where he could not be seen. He felt a vague physical discomfort in his guts, a certain disorientation in his head, a veritable shivering of the spaces around him. When he closed his eyes strange scenes, like the paintings of that alien world of Aachan that he had seen in Shazmak, and yet unlike—a little more twisted, a little more unreal—played inside his head.

He knew what it was; he had felt it only a week ago. It was the construct. Rulke wasn't just flying it now, he was beginning to *operate* it. This quivering of every inner cell was something that he had felt when Rulke flung him out of Katazza. But this was different from the other time—much stronger. This was *the time*!

High winds tore the clouds to shreds. It became a wild night, a gale howling from the south, carrying frost crystals that tore the exposed skin. A night when all the lower air was filled with ice, but the stars above were brittle and cold. Blue-white auroras flickered across the sky.

The company waited on the gargoyle-haunted steps of Carcharon. Above them the winged statues seemed to flex their wings as if preparing to ride the gale. For a long time nothing happened, except that it grew ever colder, an empty cold that drew every speck of warmth out of them. For a minute it was completely calm, then the night fell apart.

A wind came thundering down the mountain, before which all previous winds were nothing. They saw it coming, a formless shadow sweeping toward them, touched with billows and eddies like the luminous air of the Nightland. It blasted round the corners of the tower, so strong that they had to cling to each other lest they be blown right off the stairs. Driven ice crystals eroded the snow off the rail. Ice shards tore at their cheeks. The gale ripped away a section of the ruined roof, hurling it over their heads to crash on the path below the stairs right in Llian's face. He flattened himself, expecting it to sweep him off like a jagged metal broom. It rocked there for a moment, then was flung over the precipice. The blast whirled everyone around and was gone, racing down the slopes and pulling up trees at the edge of the forest.

The moon sprang out of the stillness like a highwayman. It was soon blotted from the sky by a harsh red light that leapt up from Carcharon; a light so intense that the stronghold seemed transparent except for its bones—black shadows against the red. A bright light that did not waver, and all in silence.

A blast of hot air gushed out of the tower. The sky filmed over and rain fell, a downpour lasting for a few minutes. Rain in the mountains in winter? But it made no pools or cascades, for the water turned instantly to ice on the ground, and the stair rails and the gate were hung with a curtain of icicles, and the rocks were glazed with it.

Now the music began. An arrhythmic whistling and clicking and rattling like a plague of cicadas all trying to sing in harmony was mixed in with a subterranean boom as of a metal drum the size of a house, and a graveyard keening that took only three notes and repeated them over and over. Now the noise was so loud that the eardrums hurt, now so soft and terrible that the hairs stood up all over Llian's body. The light began to pulse in sequence with the wailing sound, and when that broke off, the light throbbed in sympathy with those unearthly booms, which was even more horrible. Then the glow faded and the sound was muted, though both kept on.

The moon was almost overhead now. It began to snow,

huge flakes falling out of a clear sky, heavier and heavier until all that could be seen was a dim red light and a dim dark moon, and the shadow of the tower against the snow.

A bright flare lit the tower from inside. Thuds shook the walls, dislodging the last few slates to smash on the landing above them. They heard cries and the sound of falling masonry. With a vicious shriek, something came through the wall of Carcharon like a thunderbolt, in an avalanche of broken stone. It landed on the narrow ledge that encircled the tower, sending up a great spray of snow and ice. The creature hurtled toward them. They could hardly see what it was, only that against the light it was larger than human. Was that a flash of wings?

"*Thranx!*" screamed Shand. "He's opened the way into the void. Run for your lives!"

The Aachim were furthest up the stairs. Two of them took up Tensor's litter and ran. They went only a few steps before the thranx flapped over the rail and landed among them. The litter revolved in the air and Tensor fell face-down underneath it. That saved him, but the nearest Aachim was broken in a moment. Llian was exposed on the path. He clawed his way toward the stairs, icy hobbles tearing the fresh scabs off his legs. In his terror he scarcely felt it. What had happened to Karan? If this monster had fled, what was it like inside? Gaining a shaded drift, he rolled into it. The company rushed down the stairs without noticing him, and along the path toward the amphitheater.

The thranx stood up, a vast winged outline, gave one last retching gobble and bounded into the air. It soared over Llian's head and down onto the path, tearing apart one of Yggur's guards, smashing down another. It was a monstrous, uncertain thing in the gloom; rapacious and desperate. Someone screamed: it was a woman's cry, horrible in her pain.

"*Light!*" roared Tallia, then a blue light flared blindingly from Yggur's upraised staff. The creature propped, and in its still menace Llian saw the statue outside the gate. There was a momentary silence, through which the snow fell softly. Behind Llian someone wailed. It sounded like Lilis.

Llian didn't know what to do. His hands were still bound. He could not see Lilis; he could not get to Karan. He forced his face down into the snow. The thranx raced down the path, half-bounding, half-flying. One of Tensor's guard put a spear in it, though it might as well have been a bee sting. He found no protection from the semi-dark, as his dismal cry testified.

In the flare from Yggur's staff, Llian saw that the company were almost to the amphitheater, fleeing for their lives. The thranx hurtled after them, arching wings lifting it into the air at every bound.

A red light flashed some distance from Yggur's blue. The creature soared into the air on pinions impossibly large. It glided down, taloned feet extended like a hunting eagle, then the red light turned night into day. For an instant the creature was a black shadow in the air, a claw-perfect cut-out. It gave a hideous screech, beat the air, climbed above Mendark's head and disappeared over the precipice in the darkness.

"Fall back!" Llian heard Yggur cry as another shape leapt through the broken wall. This was smaller, more human-looking, but still menacing. The company took up their wounded and scuttled into the uncertain safety of the arena.

Llian pressed down into the snow. The creature took the steps in a series of bounds, not seeing him. When he finally dared raise his head, he was alone. In Carcharon the light was almost gone, the ghostly sounds faded to nothing, but through the snow he could just make out the jagged outline where the thranx had come through the wall. The other creature had disappeared too. There was a lumpy shape on the steps not far above him, the remains of one of the thranx's victims.

He crawled past it, his heart pounding. "Karan!" he cried weakly. "Karan!" His movements became slower and slower. He cracked his forehead on the next step and lay down in the snow. Rulke had opened the way into the void.

The void! Even the chroniclers knew little about it, except that it was a dark, desperate place that fostered only two urges: to survive; to escape. The thranx! Equally unknown, but stronger, more cunning, more deadly than any other creature that dwelt there.

How his legs hurt. Llian climbed painfully to his feet and promptly collapsed again. Karan was within a stone's throw but he was too weak to crawl up the steps to her. Whatever had happened to her, there was absolutely nothing he could do about it.

For the first time he thought of his own safety, of being rent apart by some unspeakable horror. There were *Tales of the Void*, his fevered mind reminded him, though he had read few of them. His interests had lain in other directions, and they were not tales at all as far as he was concerned, for they seemed to have little basis in truth. So, for Llian and most of the chroniclers and tellers they formed part of the Apocrypha, the pre-Histories; the unproven or unprovable, not worthy of study.

He struggled to recall. By the time he became a master chronicler he could remember perfectly anything that he had read twice. That was his training. But the *Tales of the Void* had been learned much earlier, when he was a mere journeyman, long before his training was perfected.

Shand had recognized the thranx. He could still hear the panic in his voice, see the way he had flung up his hands, the red light from Carcharon on his face. How would Shand know such a thing?

The snow began to fall heavily—a blizzard that blotted everything out. Blood was freezing to slush in his boots. Llian's shivers turned to a convulsive shuddering. Even the pain in his ankles was gone now. He could feel nothing from the shins down. He forced himself to his knees but as soon as he tried to move fell over again. Llian had just wit enough to realize that he no longer had to worry about the thranx. He would be dead within the hour.

6

THE LORRSK

Lilis was standing halfway up the steps of Carcharon with Nadiril and Jevi when the thranx came through the wall. Jevi, a small wiry man with long platinum hair like Lilis's, knocked Nadiril down on the step and flung himself on top of Lilis.

"Stay still," he hissed in her ear. "Don't move; don't scream."

"I wasn't going to," she muttered, her mouth full of snow. Though she loved Jevi as much as anyone could, she had been looking after herself for so long that she sometimes found his care smothering.

They lay motionless while the thranx gobbled its prey, bounded into the air and attacked further down the track. Light flared from an upraised staff, then it disappeared in the night.

"Quickly now," said Jevi. "Be careful on the path, Lilis."

Nadiril did not move. Lilis bent over him, crying, "Are you all right?"

"I'll live, child. I banged my head. Help me up!" But when they lifted him to his feet the old man tottered. "Leave me," he said. "Get down to the forest. There might be more of them."

"We're not leaving you. Jevi, please do something," begged Lilis, in great distress.

Jevi heaved Nadiril over his shoulder like a lanky bag of bones and set off, Lilis close at his heels. In the dark they went past Llian without seeing him.

"Such indignity," said Nadiril in a chuckling wheeze.

At the dip in the path Jevi had to stop for a breather. It was slightly wider here.

"Put me down," said Nadiril. "I feel better now."

Jevi looked toward the steps that led over a lip into the amphitheater, gauging the distance. "I think I can carry you that far."

"What's *that*?" Lilis hissed.

A flare from inside the tower outlined something racing down the stairs of Carcharon, a man-sized creature like a wingless thranx. "It's a *lorrsk* out of the void, child," said Nadiril, staggering against Jevi's shoulder. "More than our equal, even were we armed."

Jevi whipped out a short knife. "Get behind me, up the steps," he said urgently.

Neither Lilis nor Nadiril was armed. "Where are our friends?" the girl cried in dismay. "Tallia! Help! Help!" Her little voice was whipped away by the wind.

Tallia was not far off, helping the injured up the high back of the amphitheater, when she caught the whisper of Lilis's cry. "I'm going back!" she shouted to Shand.

Shand did not look up. He and Malien were attempting emergency work on Xarah, who had been clawed down one side from shoulder to hip. Several sausage coils of intestine pressed out of the wound. They bound her up again. Any meaningful surgery was impossible here.

"Tallia, quick," screamed Lilis, as Tallia appeared at the top of the steps.

Jevi was defending the narrowest part of the path, wielding the knife expertly, but the short weapon was no match for the lorrsk's reach and its clawed fingers. With one furious slash it sent the knife flying. Jevi retreated, step by step, ducking and dancing, but Tallia knew he must fall.

Tallia felt an unaccustomed pang in her heart. She hurled herself down the icy steps, a barely controlled fall that landed her between Nadiril and Lilis. Bounding to her feet she stabbed at the creature with her short sword. The lorrsk tried to bat the blade away, cutting the heel of its hand. It ducked back. Tallia pressed forward beside Jevi on the narrow track.

Lilis, squatting in shadows on the lowest step, began to pack snowballs and hurl them at the lorrsk, to no effect.

"Try this one," Nadiril said.

She threw it and it struck the lorrsk right in the eye. "Take that!" she yelled fiercely. "I hope it hurt."

It must have, for the lorrsk held its eye with one hand while slashing feebly with the other. "Was that a magic snowball?" Lilis asked breathlessly. "Make me another!"

"It had a not-so-magic rock in the middle of it," said Nadiril with a grim chuckle. "Here you are."

The lorrsk gave forth a wild shriek, leapt right over Jevi's head and lunged at Lilis. She tried to hurl her weapon and fell off the edge of the steps, to disappear without a sound.

The lorrsk reached out to gut Nadiril. He said calmly, "*Thuggah ghoe maddarha! Vunc!*"

The creature stopped dead, squinting into the darkness. "*Maddarhan?*" it said, then Tallia stuck it in the ribs. It leapt high in the air and went over the side.

"I didn't know you knew words of power," she said. "What did you say?"

"Words *are* power. I said, in one of the languages of the void, *Stop! I am your father!* An excusable deceit under the circumstances. I can't even remember where I read it."

"Where's Lilis?" cried Jevi, running around frantically.

Nadiril looked around. "She was standing just there."

They peered down, but this slope was in the moon shadow and nothing could be seen. "I'm going down," said Jevi.

"Could she possibly be alive?" asked Tallia.

"She could," said Nadiril. "It's a fair way down to the cliff just here. It wouldn't take much to stop her."

"We need light," Tallia muttered. "Jevi, run up and get a brand from the fire." He raced off.

"Why did you send him away?" asked Nadiril.

She whipped out her lightglass. Its glow revealed a steep slope blotched with round outcrops and veneered with snow. "He saved me from a chacalot. And afterwards he was so gentle and kind, and expected nothing of me in return. I can't let him go down there. Lilis adores him—"

"And so do you," observed Nadiril.

"She might be alive," she said hurriedly. "And there's a hungry lorrsk down there. I think I can see a way."

She eased herself over the edge, feeling with her boot, knowing that what she was doing was foolish in the extreme. She would never have attempted it in daylight. Tallia found a foothold, another, tested it then moved down. Stones slid underfoot and she skidded half a span before catching herself. She went even more gently the next time, but the same thing happened and she slid another span or two before coming to rest against an ice-glazed outcrop. Her heart was pounding like a piston. "Lilis!" she shouted.

A flare soared high in the air over Carcharon. "What's happening?" she shouted.

"I can't see," Nadiril yelled back. "The snow is too thick. But Carcharon is all lit up now. Something's going on! Are you all right?"

"No!" She had done a crazy, stupid thing. "I'll have to come back up." She pressed gently against her foothold, her boot skidded and she shot down again. The lightglass was jolted out of her hands to disappear down the slope, still shining until the whirling snow obscured it.

"Tallia?"

Now she couldn't see Nadiril either. "I can't get back up." Why had she done this foolish thing? "Lilis!" she roared. There was no response. "Lilis!" Nothing could be heard above the howling of the wind. Tallia clung to the slippery slope, not daring to move. Exposed to the full blast, it was perishingly cold. She kept calling but Lilis did not answer. She must have gone over the cliff.

Some time later a light appeared above her, a blazing brand. "Tallia, where are you?" Jevi's voice had never been so welcome.

"Straight below you. Don't come down, it's too slippery."

"Have you found her?" She could hear the agony in his voice.

"No!"

"Are you stuck?"

"Yes," she shouted.

"Don't move!"

Tallia felt a sudden spasm of fear. She did not want him risking his life for her. She braced one foot and the slope slipped under her, hurtling her down half a dozen spans before she thumped back and head into a clot of ice, a frozen seep. She lay utterly still, hurting all over. The sheer plunge could not be far below her. She prepared herself for death.

"Tallia, Lilis! Tallia, Lilis!"

Jevi's torch moved back and forth, a long way above. It must be snowing less now. "Go back," she said weakly. The cold attacked her bruises and lacerations. She couldn't get out of the accursed wind. Her clothes were shredded. The snow stopped for a minute and through rags of cloud she saw stars shining brightly. It would have been peaceful, save for the wind. Pebbles rattled past once or twice. She called Lilis until she was hoarse, but there was no answer. A pain at the base of her skull grew sharper. The stars began to wobble across the sky, making her dizzy. She closed her eyes, which made it worse.

All at once the torch was spluttering in her face and Jevi had his hand under her chin. "Tallia! Are you hurt?"

"Nothing broken," she said softly.

"Have you heard Lilis?"

"No. How did you get down?"

"I'm a sailor, remember?" Taking off his gloves, he felt her head. She flinched as his callused fingers roved over the bruise. "I've climbed many an icy mast on a stormy night, and I don't go anywhere without a length of rope."

"Oh!" she said in a daze. "Where *is* it?"

"It didn't reach this far. Hold my hand."

She clung to his fingers, her lifeline. His courage made her heart ache. Jevi held up his torch, pointing out where to put her hands and feet. Going up was easier, for she could test her footholds before putting weight on them. After much slipping and sliding they found the dangling end of the rope.

"Can you climb it?"

Her head was spinning. "No!"

He tied the rope through their belts and went up behind her, heaving her up with his hand on her backside. Eventually they saw Nadiril's face looking over the edge. He extended his hand to her.

"Look after her," Jevi said, "she's banged her head." He moved the rope over to the bottom of the steps and went down again.

Tallia watched in a daze where every second seemed to take an hour. The light drifted back and forth across the slope like a firefly. She sweated blood for Jevi, knowing that he was far beyond his rope. He was a small, wiry, unhandsome man that she could have held up in one hand. Her bottom remembered the imprint of his fingers. I care for him, she realized, in a way that I care for no one else. I have ever since I met him. That reminded her of her tropical homeland, beloved Crandor, of helping Jevi to escape from the corsair's island, and how he had saved her from the jaws of a chacalot.

Poor Jevi. He loves Lilis more than his own life. He'll never find her. Now the light was moving up again, very slowly and wearily. After an eternity he came in sight, alone.

Nadiril helped him over the edge. Jevi had tears frozen on his face. "Where was Lilis standing?" he asked hoarsely.

"Just there!" Nadiril pointed to the edge of the steps. Jevi hobbled to the spot. "Exactly here?"

"A little bit to the left. You must give her up, Jevi," Nadiril said gently. "She can't have survived."

"I won't!" he shouted. "Not for anything! What happened after she stood here?"

"I didn't see! She just disappeared."

Jevi dashed the frozen tears away. Tallia knew he was going to do something foolish. "Don't go down again!" she begged.

"I have to," said Jevi, and quite deliberately stepped backward over the edge.

Tallia let out a wail of anguish. Nadiril cursed dismally.

"I'll go for help. I expect the Aachim have some rope. Stay here. Don't go down."

She laughed hysterically. "I won't." She felt as if she was frozen to the stone. The two people she cared about most in the world were down there, probably dead.

Tallia sat on the edge, and with the pain in her head and her heart she quite lost track of time. Yellow lights flashed and flared inside Carcharon. Nadiril reappeared with several Aachim, including Basitor, and Yggur. Everything happened in a kind of waking nightmare.

Basitor knotted another length to Jevi's rope and tied one end into a harness around his own chest. The other Aachim braced themselves and lowered him slowly, right where Lilis and Jevi had fallen. The rope moved across and back, many times. Basitor signaled with tugs, they added a third length and the search continued.

Tallia heard an urgent whisper behind her. She looked around.

"There's someone at the gates!" hissed Nadiril. "What are we going to do now?"

Tallia's headache felt worse than ever. "We'll have to defend the path." She pushed herself up with the point of her sword, sure they were all going to die.

"Signal to Basitor," said Yggur. "He's got to come up *now*!"

Tallia, Yggur and Old Darlish went down to the lowest point of the path. There they drew their weapons and waited in the shadows. A light grew in the doorway but disappeared again. A shadow ghosted down the steps. As it reached the dip in the path, Yggur stepped into view. "Go no further, Ghâshâd!" he said.

The guard stopped still, inspecting them. It peered past Tallia at the scene up by the steps. She wondered how well it could see in the dark.

Better than she could, evidently, for it gave a grim chuckle. "You'd better be gone before we come back," it rasped, then headed back to Carcharon.

They returned to the steps. "Come on!" snapped Yggur. "What's the matter?"

"He's found something," said the Aachim holding the rope.

"Well, signal him to hurry or we'll leave him behind."

The man gave three jerks on the rope, three jerks came back and they began to haul it up.

"Faster!" snapped Yggur, watching the tower. "I think someone's coming."

Basitor appeared. A body was bound over his shoulders. It was Jevi, his long hair hanging down. Tallia felt speared through the heart. Taking hold of the rope she hauled them up. Basitor wearily unfastened the bundle and lay Jevi on the path.

"Jevi!" she sang out, and threw herself at him. He was battered blue and black, and very cold.

"Careful," panted Basitor. "He's alive, but he's broken some bones."

"What about Lilis?" she asked in a frozen voice.

The rest of the rope still hung over the edge. Basitor began to pull it in. Suddenly the rope went slack as the load came off it. Tallia cried out.

"They were close together," said Basitor.

"Tallia," came a scream from below, and the miracle had occurred. Lilis was on the end, scrambling up the last little distance.

"Well done, Basitor!" said Nadiril.

Lilis's face was scraped raw down one side and the knee of her trousers was bloody, but she was alive! Tallia pulled her up and folded Lilis in her long arms.

"They were an awful long way down," said Basitor. "In

a little gully full of snow, just before the precipice. I thought they'd gone over. I would never have found her but Jevi had landed close by, and I heard her squeaking." He ruffled Lilis's hair.

"I heard you calling, Tallia," Lilis said hoarsely. "I shouted until I had no voice left. But I knew you would find me," she said with childlike certainty.

Tallia bent over Jevi, who groaned and opened his eyes. He smiled up at her and Lilis.

"That was the stupidest thing I've ever seen," Tallia said.

"I found her though, didn't I?"

She embraced him and he groaned. His right arm was broken, and three fingers, and a good number of ribs.

"What if she'd gone over the cliff?" Tallia said.

"I'd still want to be with her," Jevi replied, and that was the end of the matter.

7

Operating Theater

"Where's Llian?" Lilis said sharply, after they rejoined the others above the amphitheater.

"He was below me when the thranx attacked," said Tensor.

"Poor Llian!" exclaimed Lilis. "I forgot all about him."

"There's been no sign of him," said Nadiril. "I'd say he's . . . not made it."

"He must be still up there!" cried Lilis.

"We can't go back," Mendark said roughly.

Lilis glared at him. "Llian is my friend! I'll go by myself, *if none of you are game*!"

"I'll have a look," Shand sighed. "Come on then, Lilis."

There were still lights showing in Carcharon, and the stick-figures of the guards occasionally flashed in front of them. The group crept along the path, more than a little afraid, and up the broad steps to the front door. There was no sign of Llian. Lilis searched, very gingerly, behind the statues. As she did so, something banged inside the tower, so loud that the door shook. Letting out a little moan, she leapt out of the way.

"Come on," said Shand, catching her hand. "He's gone. We can't do any more."

They hurried down the steps. In the darkness near the bottom Lilis trod on something yielding. She cleared the snow away to uncover a body. Llian lay quite motionless.

"He's dead," sobbed Lilis, touching his cold cheek.

"No, but near it," Shand muttered. "And I'm to blame."

He hefted Llian and staggered down the perilous track. Halfway along Tallia appeared. "I thought I saw something move down the side of the ridge," she said.

"The lorrsk," said Shand, rolling his r's.

"Feet hurt," Llian mumbled. He looked ghastly.

Shand pulled up the bottom of Llian's trousers and gasped. His calves were raw, the flesh rasped off by the hobbles. A gum of blood, ice and grated meat had frozen in a ring around each ankle.

Llian shuddered. "How did you know its name?" He was delirious.

"Never mind! If we don't get him to shelter he'll die," Shand said to Tallia. "He might lose his feet anyway. How could I have been so stupid?"

He turned away, swearing at the night, and himself, then carried Llian to the fires in the amphitheater and banked them with the remaining wood. "Keep watch, Tallia! Run up for help, Lilis!"

Cutting off Llian's boots, he wrapped his half-frozen feet in blankets and put him in a sleeping pouch with warm stones at the bottom. He was dribbling a mug of soup down his throat when Basitor came running back.

"There's someone at the gates again!" Tallia shouted "We've got to go, Shand."

"Can I trust you to bear Llian down, Basitor?" asked Shand. "I'm spent."

Basitor's eyes glittered dangerously. "I'll carry him," he said harshly.

"And not drop him over?"

"No!" whispered Lilis. A bond had grown between her and Basitor after the rescue, yet she knew how he hated Llian. "You carry him, Shand."

Basitor bent down and thrust his fierce face at Lilis's. She did not flinch. "Your loyalty is a fine and noble gift, child. My word means as much to me. I won't harm your friend, *though I want to*!"

They departed hastily. By the time they reached the rest of the company Llian was thrashing in a fever wherein the void and the thranx, and Karan and Rulke, roiled in a blood-red, pain-driven subconscious.

Malien and Asper inspected the injuries. "We've got to have fire and hot water or we won't save him, or Xarah either," said Malien.

They hurried down, terrified that the thranx would suddenly reappear, or the Ghâshâd come hunting. Dawn broke before they reached the forest, a bleak winter's morn, and it began snowing again, tiny flakes that fluttered in the wind. They took refuge in the stone pavilion at the edge of Black Lake, which was frozen over now. The Aachim rigged up windbreaks from tents while Yggur's guards built three huge fires in the pavilion. The healers set up a surgery in the center to work on Xarah and Llian, and Jevi's broken bones. Guards patrolled in pairs out in the forest.

Lilis was too tired to sleep. She went down to the lake where Osseion, the captain of Mendark's guard, was hacking a hole through the ice with his axe. She stood beside him, marvelling at his deft strokes.

"Ow!" she said, rubbing her nose where a chip of ice had just stung her.

"Stand back," said Osseion, turning so that she was shielded by his massive body. He struck the last blows and levered out a rectangular plug of ice. Lilis began to fill leather buckets with a dipper.

"This takes me back to our first adventure together, fetching the water," said Osseion.

"You were kind to me." Lilis smiled at the memory. "Even after I helped to chop your finger off."

Osseion held up his hand. There was a gap where the gangrenous middle finger had been. "Had to be done," he said, "though I didn't care for it at the time." He hefted a bucket in each hand and they headed back to the fires, chatting about past journeys.

The company was subdued. The thranx had cast a shadow over them. "A hundred such creatures could overrun the whole of Meldorin," said Shand, honing his knife.

"And a thousand, perhaps all Santhenar," Mendark agreed gloomily. "My life's work is coming undone."

"How is he?" Tallia asked, when they had cut the bloody rags of Llian's trousers off to reveal his eroded calves. The bone was exposed on both shins. Lilis looked quite ill at the sight.

"Sick and sore, but I expect he'll live."

Malien went on with the delicate operation, picking dirt out of the collar of abraded flesh around Llian's calves and shins while Shand and Asper sewed up Xarah's wounds with a large needle. Xarah watched her surgeons with never a complaint.

"She's a tough one!" said Shand admiringly, as they completed the stitches across her belly.

Llian woke when Malien was nearly done. He moaned. His legs and feet were a mess of pain.

"He's coming round," he heard Shand say. "Hold him down."

Llian opened his eyes. Malien wiped sweat from his brow. "I seem to have spent half my life patching you up, chronicler," she said with a pretense at cheerfulness.

"Is it bad?" Llian asked, gritting his teeth as he tried to sit up.

"I think we can save your feet."

He fell back. The self-destructive fever that had possessed him last night was gone, frozen out of him. His helplessness had been proven all too vividly. What could he do without feet?

"You'll hurt for a bit, but then I know what a philosophical attitude you have." She chuckled. The Aachim had a high tolerance for pain and thought Llian to be rather feeble.

"But I will be able to walk?"

"It's a long time since I heard such heart-rending moans. I expect so, chronicler, though you'll be limping for months."

"I'm freezing!" His teeth chattered.

"Soup's nearly ready," said Lilis, stirring a cauldron on the smoky fire. Her eyes were red raw.

They fed Llian soup and wrapped him up again. He lapsed back into a semi-comatose state, hearing snatches of talk. Once or twice, tormented by helplessness and failure, he groaned Karan's name.

"We can't stay here," he heard Yggur say. "The Ghâshâd are out on the mountain."

"What about the thranx?" croaked Tensor.

"No sign of it, nor the other creature."

"We've got to help Karan," Llian mumbled, tossing on his stretcher.

"There's nothing we can do," said Malien. "Try to sleep now."

One of the patrols hurried in to report a band of Ghâshâd gathered on the slope above the forest.

"We'd better get down," said Yggur. "I don't like this place—we're too vulnerable."

"It'll be dark in a few hours. Call the guards in closer."

They spent a miserable night in the pavilion, prey to all kinds of fears, though the Ghâshâd seemed content to guard the track up to Carcharon. At the first glimmer of dawn the bearers took up their stretchers and they all retreated through the forest to the granite cliff.

Shand had equipped himself with a stave made of a hard wood almost as black as charcoal. One end was knobbly and fitted neatly into his hand. The making of this staff, or perhaps the possession of it, seemed to give him particular pleasure. "This reminds me of my wandering days. I feel that I could defend myself against anything, with it." He stroked his beard with his free hand.

"You delude yourself," said Mendark coldly.

"It's a very comforting delusion," Shand grinned. He liked to provoke Mendark.

They reached the edge of the plateau. Here the path came out of forest to snake across a strip of wind-twisted scrub, no more than head-high, then between massive outcrops of pink granite, crusted with lichens and capped with snow, that marked the edge of the escarpment.

"We're too exposed," Shand muttered.

Tensor lifted his head from the stretcher to sniff the air. He shivered.

"Let's move!" said Mendark. His voice cracked.

They skidded their way between the boulders with their stretchers and onto the narrow path at the top of the cliff. It was icy, and an updraught sent flurries of snow whirling and tumbling in their faces. They turned down the track, treading carefully.

"Gothryme will seem like paradise after this," said Tallia to Shand. They were at the rear.

"And Tullin, heaven. I wish I'd never left," said Shand.

Tallia and Jevi were immediately behind Llian, not speaking, but walking so close together that their arms touched. Jevi's broken arm was in a sling and the three fingers had been strapped together. At that moment the leader, Basitor, recognizable among the tall Aachim by his bandaged head, stopped so abruptly that Yggur bumped into him.

"Watch—" Yggur broke off.

Standing before them on the path, looking like a devil from the deepest pits of the void, with its wings forming a hood high above it, was the thranx. Its skin was a threatening blood-purple color, like a bruise, its belly swollen from feeding. Massive thigh muscles rippled. Claws as long as knives tightened on the path, crushing the ice and rotten rock beneath its feet. One thigh bore a red wound, like a burn.

Yggur stood paralyzed, as he had when Rulke's construct had appeared. One hand groped for his sword hilt but did not recognize it. His mouth hung open.

Basitor whipped out his long sword and held it out before him. "Stay behind me, blind man!" he said contemptuously. He swung the weapon in the air. It made a humming sound.

The thranx bared its teeth. Its mouth seemed to contain a hundred of them and they were shiny brown. It could have bitten his arm off at the shoulder. "*Skunngg!*" it said, purring.

"I think that means 'breakfast!' " Nadiril coughed.

To Llian, sitting up on his stretcher, the events seemed unreal: the thranx smiling, Basitor waving his sword in circles as if winding himself up. "He's going berserker," Llian said softly, "just like he did in Katazza." Lilis gripped his hand.

Basitor humped his great shoulders, roared mad defiance and leapt at the thranx. It continued to grin at him, then at the last possible moment its left arm flashed. It held a flail tipped with little spiked balls, like the statue outside the gate of Carcharon.

The lashes whipped around Basitor's chest, the balls embedding themselves in his flesh with thuds like a butcher's meat mallet. Basitor screamed. The sword fell from his hand. With a backhanded flick of the flail, he was lifted off his feet and sent whirling through the air like a spinning top, to disappear over the edge of the cliff in the falling snow.

The thranx, still grinning, snapped the bloody flail at Yggur. Llian, who was directly behind him, saw Yggur's weak knee wobble. His fingers clutched at the sword hilt but Yggur did not seem to have the strength to draw it. Surely this time he was going mad, and they were all going to die.

8

A TRANSFORMATION

Behind Llian someone was screaming. It took a long time to work out that it was Lilis.

"You *can* do it, Yggur!" said Nadiril.

"Move aside!" said Yggur to the thranx, struggling to control his fear but failing miserably. He wrenched out his sword. His knee wobbled again and he sagged on that side. "Fall back!" he gasped over his shoulder.

The thranx swung its flail at Yggur's head. He did not move, though the whizzing balls went so close that they ruffled his hair. The thranx took another step forward, and only then did Llian realize how huge it was. Yggur was a tall man but it was shoulders and head above him and the arch of its spiked wings as high again. It raised the flail. Yggur did not move. How can he just stand there? Llian thought. It'll turn him into mince. He must be paralyzed with terror.

Yggur squinted at the flail hand through his thick glasses. It twitched, and at the same instant the thranx shot out its other hand, which held a gray rod tipped with black. From the end of the rod, black light sprang out at Yggur's eyes.

Yggur slashed down his left hand. The cable of light writhed across the path like paste squeezed from a tube. It struck the rock face, which crumbled. A wall of shattered granite collapsed onto the path, burying the thranx to the knees. A twitch of the cheek was its only acknowledgment of the pain.

The thranx lashed the flail at Yggur. He tipped up his long sword and four of the five thongs whipped themselves around the blade, then fell to the path. The fifth ball curled past the blade, embedding itself in his shoulder. The thranx grinned and tore it free in a spray of blood. Yggur staggered, went to one knee and dropped the sword. The creature thrust the flail in its belt, half-freed a leg from the rubble and extended the claws of its empty hand.

Yggur's shoulder gushed blood. *He's finished!* Llian thought. *And we're next!* Judging from the cries behind him, the rest of the company must have felt the same.

Yggur came up with a knife in his hand and shot forward. The thranx's blow carved the air behind him. While it tried to free its legs, he stabbed upward with his good arm at the creature's unprotected groin. The thranx screeched, lashed out blindly and its armored knee caught Yggur in the belly, flinging him against the cliff. It took two limping hops, staggered and fell sideways off the path, trailing purple blood from between its legs. It spiraled downward, the wings began to beat and it disappeared.

Tallia and Shand forced past Llian, sending his stretcher swaying dangerously near the edge of the cliff. They feared the worst but Yggur sat up. There was a bruise the size of a peach on the side of his head and his shoulder was gruesomely lacerated.

"Bravely done, sir," said Shand. "The tellers will tell *this* tale for a thousand years."

"An incredible feat," echoed Mendark, who had been at the rear. "Though you are my enemy, I praise you ungrudgingly. I hope I can show the same courage when I'm put to the test."

"There was no time to think," said Yggur, his chest heaving. "Sometimes we surprise ourselves. But it's not finished yet. Let's get down before you have to carry me too."

Lilis was sobbing her heart out. "Poor Basitor! What will happen to him?"

Shand put an arm about her shoulders. "The fall would have killed him instantly, child. His suffering is over."

Asper bandaged Yggur's shoulder, then they hurried on. They stopped briefly halfway down, on a platform just wide enough for all of them to stand together. From here the way was very steep, making it hazardous to maneuver the stretchers. Tensor went on foot for a while but his gait was so awkward that he was always in danger of going over. Snow began to fall more heavily, reducing visibility to a few paces and making the ground underfoot even more slippery.

Llian and the injured Aachim had to be carried, while Nadiril was looking more like a stretcher case every minute. Llian found it terrifying, for his Aachim bearers swayed around hairpin corners as if the track was a garden path. He wished Karan were there to hold his hand, as she had on the way up. But that thought led only to unpleasant conjectures.

At Gothryme there were explanations to be made yet again. Llian was given more dark looks by Rachis and the whole household. Karan's sitting room was turned into a hospital. Nadiril went to bed with pneumonia. Xarah's terrible wound had become infected and she tossed in a fever. The healers gathered round her bed, fearing that she would not live the night. A messenger was sent across the range to Casyme, where Yggur had a small garrison. Other messengers went down the valley of the Ryme to warn the neighboring counties of their peril. The manor's paltry defenses were readied.

In the morning two of the Aachim went back to search for Basitor's body, but returned without it.

"We found where he fell," said Old Darlish somberly, "but there was nothing left except a bloody splash on the snow. The thranx had been there before us—we saw its prints."

"What a terrible day," said Malien. "It hurts us bitterly when we cannot lay our dead to rest."

Llian knew that the Aachim ever looked backward, and every death made them weep for lost Aachan that none of them would ever return to. They still thought of it as home, though almost all had been born on Santhenar. The Aachim could not bear to lay their dead in alien soil.

"What's to be done about Llian?" said Mendark that evening. "I'm anxious to get back to Thurkad."

"He'll have to go there too. He needs medicines that we don't have here," said Nadiril from his bed. He was recovering but still weak. A coughing fit cut him off.

"Agreed," said Shand quickly, before Mendark could say more. "Then let's get on to the other matter—what to do about Rulke, and Karan."

"A while ago we talked about finding enough gold to make the golden flute anew—a weapon against Rulke," said Mendark. "A way of making our own gates."

"We don't have the gold," said Yggur. "I plan to go my own way now. This partnership has failed."

"I see!" Mendark said coldly. "You were happy to ally with us when you were weak. Now we don't matter any more!"

"We never pretended to be friends," Yggur replied. He looked ennobled by his great victory. "I don't see any merit in your plan. I've always argued against it, if you recall."

Mendark leapt up from his chair. "You want the construct for yourself!"

"*I* don't want it at all. My life has been transformed. I'm not afraid of Rulke now, and I'm not going to help you with your scheming."

"Gentlemen, please," Nadiril croaked. "We're doing Rulke's work for him. Remember Katazza! United we can face him, but divided we're nothing. Let the alliance stand, at least until we return to Thurkad.

"Well, Yggur?" he snapped after neither had made any move. "What about you, Mendark?"

They agreed grudgingly.

"I'd say the thranx shocked Rulke as much as it did us," said Malien. "We've got to find out what happened up there."

"Who would dare return to Carcharon now?" said Yggur.

"Where did the thranx come from?" asked Lilis. She was sitting on the floor by the fire, brushing her long hair. Jevi sat back in the corner watching her, and Tallia beside him with her long legs stretched out, enclosing Lilis.

"What anyone knows about the void is just rumor, Lilis," said Nadiril. "It is a dark place between the worlds, from which, even before the time of the flute, when some chance alignment allowed them, things sometimes crept into Santhenar."

"What kind of things?" asked Lilis.

"Sometimes wild beasts or monsters. Other times, cunning and clever creatures that were almost human, like that lorrsk back there, though merciless in their violence. In the void only survival matters. But all that ended with the Forbidding, for afterwards nothing could get through. All we remember is a rumor of terror and a name or two—*thranx* is one such. Llian might tell you some of those tales, when he's better."

Lilis's curiosity was far from exhausted. "How can the thranx even fly? It's nothing like a bird or a bat. How can its wings hold up such a big body?"

"Well, child," said Nadiril, "it doesn't fly that well—it mostly soars and glides. But even that must require a prodigious expenditure of the Secret Art, for its wings weren't designed for a world as heavy as ours. I reckon it will need a lot of rest after the last few days."

"That gives me hope for our coming struggle," said Yggur.

"And as you say, someone has to go back," Tallia said. "I'll go—"

"I need you in Thurkad," said Mendark.

"I've served my ten years and more," she said angrily, a rare rebellion. "My indenture is finished."

"But you're still my lieutenant, until you resign!" Mendark's eyes challenged her. Then he changed his mind. "Yes, good idea. Go in the morning. Find out everything you can about his plans; *and his construct*!"

"I'll come with you, Tallia," said Shand. "I prefer the company up there."

The following night the whole house was sleeping but for Llian, who lay by himself in the old keep near the front door. Gothryme was crowded with refugees and he was at the bottom of the list for the best bed. Llian's legs throbbed constantly, though he hardly noticed. What had Karan and Rulke done? And what happened inside Carcharon, after the thranx came?

He lay staring up at the invisible ceiling, drifting into dreams and immediately back to wakefulness. After some hours, a sudden movement caught his eye. A shadow had flitted through the door leading from the west wing into the keep.

Llian watched without curiosity as someone glided into the room, moving so smoothly that their feet must have scarcely touched the floor. The manor was full of people, and it was not surprising that one of them, unable to sleep, should go for a midnight walk.

But whoever it was, they quested about as if searching for something. Or as if the layout was unfamiliar. Llian closed his eyes as the figure came close, conjured ghost light from its fingertips and inspected his face. The light disappeared. After an interval he opened his eyes to see the shadow moving noiselessly up the steps toward Karan's bedroom. He didn't dare follow, cripple as he was. It was not long before the intruder reappeared, a shadow surrounded by a faint nimbus of light. It shook him by the shoulder and light again flared from its fingertip, dazzling him so that he could see nothing but a golden-skinned, blue-veined hand.

"Where is she, chronicler?" The voice was a disguised hiss. He could not tell if it belonged to man or woman.

"I don't—"

Nails dug into his shoulder, piercing the skin. "Where is Karan?"

Surely it wasn't Rulke then, unless Karan had somehow escaped from Carcharon. That didn't seem likely.

"At Carcharon!" he gasped. "Rulke has her. Unless he has taken her to Shazmak, *or between the worlds*."

The hiss was a shriek in his ear. The nails wrenched painfully then the light went out. By the time Llian's night vision recovered, the intruder was gone.

Still he tossed on his straw mattress, worried senseless about Karan. It must be after midnight now. Suddenly something struck the door near his head. It was not a hard blow, but enough to shake the door and startle him. Another blow followed, and Llian heard a thin cry, though he could not make out the words. Maybe Tallia and Shand had returned unexpectedly.

Something scratched at the door, then that cry came again. It sounded like a child. Llian lit his candle and crawled across the freezing floor, which was easier than trying to walk. The door handle was out of reach. Three times he tried to force himself up, urged on by those pitiful cries, and as many times fell back groaning.

"Help! Oh please help!" came the cry again.

Llian scrabbled at the timbers, caught the handle and forced back the bolt. The door swung open and someone fell through. It was a boy about twelve years old, clad in stained rags. What was he doing out on a night like this? Then Llian saw that the stains were blood, and the rags, good winter clothes that had been torn apart.

Putting down the candle he helped the boy up. Gouges down his chest ebbed blood. One arm hung limp. He opened his eyes, wide and terrified.

"It came out of the sky," the boy wailed.

9

CONFINEMENT

Llian's shout roused the household. Someone knew the boy, who came from a farmhouse halfway between the manor and the village.

Yggur stared down at the stricken child, his jaw muscles spasming. "If we don't see to the thranx right now, this scene will be repeated a thousand times across Santhenar."

"And if others get through," said Mendark gloomily, "if it breeds . . ."

"Let's get a hunting party together, quickly!" Yggur gave orders to his guards.

In a few minutes they were gone, Mendark and Yggur, Yggur's guard and Vartila the Whelm, Osseion and Torgsted. All the able-bodied Aachim went too, except Malien and Asper, who remained behind to tend the injured.

Sometime later, Llian was woken by a smashing, wrenching noise, as if the whole roof had been torn open. There was a scream of timbers above his head, then something came crashing down the stone stairs, careened across the room and thudded into the wall between Llian and the door. Llian felt a sharp pain in his earlobe. The whole keep shook with the impact, then the candle went out.

Before he managed to light it, Malien had come running with a lantern. "What was that?" she screamed above the groaning of roof timbers.

A boulder half a span across lay on the floor. "It must be part of the upper wall."

"I don't think so," said Malien. "It's still got yellow earth on one side. It's been wrenched out of the ground and dropped, to crack us open."

Llian felt weak all over. "Better see if it has," he whispered.

She put one foot on the rubble-littered step, then stopped. Further up, the stairs were partly blocked by a tangle of beams. "This reminds me of the way the Charon took our world from us. They came out of the void too."

Llian was just as afraid. He felt his way around the wall to her, and every step was agony to his ruined calves. But he couldn't bear to lie here, waiting for it. He went up the steps on hands and knees. Malien was beside him, tread for tread. They negotiated a gap between the broken timbers and the wall. Llian stopped. Cold sweat was pouring off him. "Give me your arm!" he panted.

They reached the third floor, where a long landing was littered with shards of slate. To the right was Karan's bedroom. Above was an attic whose floor was smashed open. Llian and Malien looked up though it. The wind howled. There was a hole in the roof that a horse and cart could have bolted through.

Silhouetted against the stars was the unmistakable arching shape of a wing. The thranx stood straddling the broken roof. Darting its head through, it gave a hiss of pleasure.

Llian could feel Malien's tension through her shoulder. "Of all places in the valley," he said, "why did it have to pick us?"

"Maybe it watched the others going out."

"Or maybe it likes the smell of us. What are we going to do?" He clung onto her shoulder.

"Have you got a knife?"

"Do you think they'd let me keep one?" he said with a trace of bitterness.

"Quick, have a look in Karan's room. See what you can find." She threw up her arms, crying out to the thranx in the Aachim tongue.

Llian slid behind her in through Karan's door. The only time he'd been in here had been after Mendark's attack on him a couple of weeks ago. Then he'd been too sick and sore to notice his surroundings. The room was dimly lit by Malien's lantern. The center was occupied by a huge square box bed. He saw linen chests and cupboards, a lantern on a lampstand, but nothing that could conceivably be used as a weapon.

Turning to go, he was reminded of that distant night when he'd rescued Karan from the old house in Narne. He had smashed a lantern in the hall in front of Vartila, sending a curtain of flame roaring up to the ceiling. Llian swirled the lantern. It was half full. Clicking the striker until the wick lit, he lurched back out to Malien.

She stood in that same frozen attitude, her hands upraised. The thranx watched Malien with its hooded eyes, no doubt wondering if she had the same power as the man who had hurt it before.

Llian hurled the lantern into the pile of timber. The light went out. Malien yelped and clutched at her head. The thranx let out a great triumphant roar and leapt down into the attic.

"What did you do that for?" she said furiously.

"I thought if the wood caught fire it wouldn't be able to get to us."

"It's not a wild animal, Llian! It's not afraid of fire. Now I've broken first, and it won't be afraid of me." She took a tiny step backward. In the semi-dark they could see the creature's shining teeth.

"What *is* a thranx afraid of?"

"Very little, I'd imagine, if it's hungry." She moved back onto the top step.

"This one can't possibly be hungry. It's eaten three of us, and who knows what else. Look at the size of its belly." The thranx's stomach was notably distended. Basitor was in there. Though he had been an enemy, Llian still took a thrill of horror from the sight, and the thought. "What does it want?"

"I don't know," said Malien. "Maybe just a place to sleep."

Suddenly the thranx dropped through the attic floor. It hit the boards of the landing hard, wings thrumming, claws scratching. Llian scrabbled backward and fell off the top step, but was caught by Galgi the weaver, for the rest of the manor's occupants were now crowded on the steps below, silently staring up.

The thranx came on, drawing a flail from a pouch at its waist. Malien stood her ground. She made a feint with her left hand. A shiny bubble appeared in the air and drifted away. The thranx showed its teeth and snapped the flail, bursting the bubble with a bright flash of purple. The gesture seemed like a sneer. Without warning it sprang.

The leap took it forward a good three spans. Its claws skidded on the splintered timber, then it snapped the flail viciously at Malien's face. The thongs cut off by Yggur had been restored. She stumbled backward just in time, but another bubble appeared, seeming to pass right through her fingers. It flashed toward the thranx, darted between the thongs of the flail and burst with a brilliant green flare against the creature's belly.

It gave a little cry, cupped its arms protectively about itself then tensed to spring again. "Quick, Malien!" Llian screeched.

Malien leapt down the steps. As she did so a third bubble slipped out of her hand to explode in the middle of the timber pile. Flames licked up the stone wall. Soon the wood was a blazing barrier across the hall.

"Get out of the way!" Malien screeched. She looked back over her shoulder. "Come on!"

The thranx sprang in the air, its wings scraped the sides of the hall and it soared above the flames. There was a mad scramble down the winding stairs. Someone dropped the lantern, which went out.

Llian heard Malien cry, "Out of the keep! Barricade the door!" The thranx came down on the lower side of the fire, reared up on its mighty wings and blocked out the light.

Llian fell the last three steps, rolled and cracked his injured shin on something. Pain flared, so excruciating that he was quite helpless. When it became bearable he crawled forward blindly, not realizing that he was going the wrong way. His head hit a wall. Llian was so dazed that his arms and legs tried to keep going.

"Bolt the door!" Malien screamed. "Wait—where's Llian?"

The thranx flew across the keep, a winged shadow, and slammed the door in their faces. In seconds it had reinforced the doorway with chests and beams. The boulder was piled on top.

Llian propped himself against the wall and waited. Blood poured down his shins. He couldn't move to save his life.

The thranx stood back with its head cocked. Evidently satisfied, it turned toward Llian, took one step and stopped. It clutched its belly while a spasm passed across it, then moved forward tentatively, never taking its eyes off him.

Llian did not move. In the past year and a half he had survived so many dangers, overcome so many insurmountable obstacles, that now that his doom was finally here he felt quite calm about it.

The thranx barricaded the front door and closed the shutters over the slit windows. Taking Llian by the shirtfront, it lifted him high in the air. The light of the burning timber was fading now. The creature drew the gray baton that it had used against Yggur on the cliff top and passed its dark light over Llian from head to foot. His bloody shins glowed luminously under the eerie flare. Again the thranx was wracked by a spasm. It dropped Llian but caught him in midair. Then, to his amazement, it simply tossed him down on the mattress.

Evidently it was no longer hungry. Obviously it did not see him as any kind of a threat. That was true enough; Llian couldn't have throttled an earthworm. But why didn't it kill him anyway?

Outside there were thuds on the back door, followed by the front, and cries that barely penetrated the thick timbers. Presumably they were trying to find out if he'd been eaten yet. He lacked the strength to answer.

The thranx folded its wings and leaned back against the wall, holding its belly. It seemed to be in pain. Llian recalled that Yggur had wounded it. It flexed its legs, squatted down but stood up straight again. One hand rubbed the small of its back. It let out a muffled groan. Instantly its head snapped toward Llian. In the void pain was weakness, and weakness death. But Llian had not moved.

He sat there for some time, watching the creature. Out of

habit he noted its every characteristic to use in his tale—the grimaces, the leg flexes, the groaning that grew ever louder. Then, after a particularly tormented cry, it squatted down and began to pant, little outrushes of air through lips formed into a trumpet.

Only now did Llian realize what was going on. The thranx must be about to give birth. All this time it had just been looking for a safe hiding place, thinking that Santhenar was as savage as the void. In that case, why had it kept him alive? The answer was obvious. Because it would need to eat again after the event, or worse, to feed him to its babies.

Llian had once seen a cat teaching its kittens how to hunt and kill. It had played with a mouse, stalking it, then letting it go while the poor creature ran back and forth in terror. By the end of the lesson the kittens, cute balls of fur, were cruel killing machines with blood-covered mouths, and the mouse a red rag on the floor. Was that what the thranx had in mind for him?

It gave a tremendous groan, cut short by a gasp, and a deluge of pink water poured from between its legs. Llian stared, fascinated yet repelled as the belly of the creature roiled. He had never witnessed a birth, not even a farm animal. The thranx let out a dreadful scream. Blood ran down one leg. Its wings beat the air. Snatching up the baton, it turned the black light on the damaged area. The spot fluoresced; the blood flow stopped. The thranx bore down again. With a grunt and a moan a head appeared in the birth canal.

And there, despite efforts that grew until the thranx was bellowing to shake the walls, it stayed. Pink foam flecked the creature's rubbery lips. Pale green drops of sweat covered its face and chest. Its nostrils expanded and contracted like beating hearts, but the baby was stuck.

The efforts went on for an hour or more. The thranx weakened visibly in that time. Llian wondered what those outside must be thinking. Surely that it had torn him apart and was devouring him gobbet by gobbet.

A faint light appeared through a crack in one shutter. It must be dawn. Llian felt light-headed from lack of sleep. Despite his peril though, and the knowledge that it surely would eat him in the end, despite knowing the fate of those up on the mountain, Llian was moved by the creature's agony.

He pulled himself to his feet but its head whipped round, baring those shiny brown teeth at him. He went still, then took another step. One arm moved sluggishly. The baton pointed directly at his heart. Llian sat down again.

Something thumped the outside of the front door. Just a testing thump, followed by silence into which came the muffled sound of many voices. It seemed that Mendark and Yggur, and the whole force that had gone down to Tolryme, were back.

The thranx gave a convulsive groan, a mighty push and suddenly the obstruction moved. The baby slid free and hit the floor with a wet slap. The mother screwed up her face in agony. Again blood gushed from her. In the growing light Llian saw it was dark purple. Once more she used the black light to cauterise the injury. Cutting the baby's cord, she took it in her arms.

The baby had a huge head, crested like the mother, though on it the crest was as soft as rubber. The arms and legs hung limp. The mother gave the child a thump in the chest, whereupon the limbs moved feebly. The child gave forth a little mewling whimper.

The mother brought her bent arms up to her chest then snapped them apart, throwing back her shoulders at the same time. The armored skin separated along seams to reveal a pair of breasts the color of pink milk. Immediately the baby squirmed in her arms and began to sniff the air. The thranx put the baby to the breast.

The crisis seemed to be over. The baby suckled noisily. The mother cradled it in her arms. Llian stared at the pair. Her eyes seemed to be closed, but if he so much as twitched he caught her smoldering glare on him.

The baby began on the second breast. Already it looked much stronger. The muscular legs kicked and one arm moved lazily. It lifted its head, sniffed the air again and looked right at Llian. The mother gave a hiss of approval.

Llian imagined her using him as a plaything, an anatomy lesson. Imagined her carefully tearing his belly open, showing the child the best bits—liver and kidneys, still-beating heart. He dwelt on the agony of being eaten alive. How long would it take to die?

Practically a cripple, the best he could manage was the most painful hobble. Probably not enough to get away from this newborn, already looking so alert and deadly. Infants have to be, to survive in the void. And there was nowhere in the keep that he could hide from the mother.

Suddenly she leapt up, tearing the child from her breast. It wailed and scratched at her. With an oscillation of her shoulders, the breasts disappeared beneath armored skin-plates. Swiftly she lashed the baby into a sling, which she threw over her shoulders. The great wings flexed, and settled back over the infant.

Llian shrank back against the wall but the thranx went past him to the door, checking the barricade. She moved painfully, as if torn by the birth, and Llian noticed that she was bleeding again.

As she reached the door something crashed against it. The lock broke, the bolt tearing right off, but the bar held. The thranx pressed her shoulder against the door. The ram struck again, splintering the timbers. She was tossed onto her side. She got up slowly, looking ill. Abandoning the door she turned toward Llian.

He reeled backward, tripped over the mattress and fell flat on his back. Rolling over, Llian found that he could not stand up. He tried to scuttle away on hands and knees. Suddenly the flail lashed out, one of the thongs coiled around his leg and the spiked ball caught in the seam of his trousers. The thranx hauled him in like a fish.

As he was dragged across the floor, the baby let out a series of little squeaks and thrust its head over its mother's shoulder. The thranx picked Llian up, holding him out in the air. Mother and child bared their teeth. Llian closed his eyes.

At that moment the ram struck again, bursting the door in. The crew of the ram were carried halfway across the keep before managing to stop. The thranx let Llian go and reared up before them like an avenging devil. Dropping the ram they scattered for their lives.

The thranx whirled, grabbed Llian, sprang in the air and the wings drove it upward. It beat its way up the stairs, laboring under the load. Llian, hanging upside down, saw Mendark and Yggur appear in the doorway.

One of Yggur's soldiers hurled a spear, which whistled between Llian's legs. Shocked, he curled himself up into a ball. Mendark or Yggur, Llian could not tell who, sent a blast of red fire up the stairs that singed the end of one leathery wingtip. The thranx was unaffected, though Llian could feel it struggling to carry him now. The birth injury must have weakened it.

It flapped harder, hung motionless for a moment then began to spiral up into the broken turret of the roof. The moon shone down through a jagged tangle of beams. Below, Llian saw Malien, Yggur and Mendark race up around the curve of the stair. Mendark set off another blast, which the thranx avoided; it made one of the rafters smolder.

Knocking Mendark's arm aside, Malien released another of those shining bubbles through her fingertips. It followed the spiraling path of the thranx, swelling as it rose. On touching Llian's foot, it enveloped his body and swelled again to become a globe a couple of spans across.

With one whispered word from Malien, frost needles expanded across the globe and it set hard. Llian felt the sphere come up against the broken roof opening and jam there.

The thranx, now out through the roof, screamed in frustration. Llian felt its mighty wings beating the air. It sent blast after blast from its baton. The baby screamed too but the bubble was impervious.

Finally the thranx simply let go, rose sluggishly into the sky, crossed before the dark moon and was gone. The shiny bubble drifted down, bursting into fragments that turned to smoke in the air. Llian lay on the floor, his legs bleeding again.

"I didn't know you could use the Secret Art," he said huskily.

"I was a master once, but Tensor cured me of it." Malien bent down over his wounds. "I don't like the look of this. Are you up to another operation, chronicler?"

"No!" he said weakly.

She lifted him to his feet and, to his surprise, embraced him. "You've had a bit of a night, Llian."

The pressure caused a sharp pain in his shoulder. Only then did he remember the intruder in the night and understand who it had been. The hand had given her away. "Faelamor!" he gasped.

"What?" Malien said sharply, letting him go. She caught him as he fell.

"There was a spy in here, not long before the thranx came." He bared his shoulder, revealing nail gouges in the pale skin that were bruised black and blue. "She wanted to know where Karan was. I think it was Faelamor."

Malien inspected the marks. "Could be! It's the size of her hand. A complication we could do without."

"She's after the construct!" said Mendark. "We've got to get it first.'

10

Pale Ghosts

It was a glorious winter's morning when Tallia and Shand set out from Gothryme. The air was still and the sun shining; as fine a day as the previous ones had been ill. Nonetheless the traveling was slow in new snow, and the cliff path very icy.

"Careful, there may be guards," said Shand.

At the top there was sign of Ghâshâd, trampled snow and burnt wood, but they saw no one. It was almost dark by the time he and Tallia arrived at the little stone pavilion beside Black Lake. The moon had not yet risen.

They reconnoitred all around, as well as they could, but found no more sign of the enemy. By the time they regained their campsite, the moon was rising past its full, the angry face already turning away. It was the fourth day after hythe. Endre, mid-winter week, was finally over. Not daring to light a fire, they dined on cold meat, bread and fruit, took a swig each from Shand's flask to warm them and turned quickly into their sleeping pouches.

Before dawn Tallia was wakened by Shand's hand on her shoulder. He handed her a hunk of dark bread and a mug of ice water. The bread was so cold that she had to gnaw at it as they walked along.

It was near midday by the time they reached the steep climb below the amphitheater. There were no tracks, for everything was covered by the night's heavy quilt. The day was still; again the sun shone brightly. Tallia eased her head over the crest. Carcharon crouched directly in front of her. In the bright sunlight she saw that part of the tower had collapsed.

Carcharon looked different, wrong, as if it had become plastic and deformed under its own weight. All the faces and angles of it were changed. "Better be careful," she said. "The whole tower could come down."

"It looks empty," said Shand. There were no guards on the walls, where previously the Ghâshâd had been everywhere. Nonetheless they crossed the arena warily. Finally, looking down on the winding track that led to the gate, they took their courage in their hands and ran.

"What a terrible, desolate place," said Tallia as they climbed the steps. "No wonder Basunez went mad."

"He must have been mad to build here in the first place!" They continued up to the top.

Tallia eyed the bronze statues outside the door with new understanding. "These are thranx! How did Basunez know how to make them so accurately?"

"I'd say his studies were more successful than anyone thought," Shand panted.

They found the gate locked, though rubble where the wall had been breached made a ramp up to the base of the gap, offering easy entrance. A breeze sighed through the broken wall. Climbing the pile, they looked into the tower at the level of the first floor. There was nothing to be seen but more rubble and drifts of snow. Tallia clambered in.

Inside, the atmosphere was even stranger. The stairs appeared different each time Tallia looked at them. Sometimes they seemed to lead down instead of up, and sometimes both down and up at the same time, impossible as that seemed. And once or twice, out of the corner of her eye, she saw a mirage Wall curving through the building.

The spiral staircase was largely intact, though a number of steps had collapsed. Here and there on the walls were abstract carvings with an ordered, crystalline geometry. They were beautifully executed but quite incomprehensible. The Ghâshâd must have done them, for they were fresh. They paused halfway up. Tallia looked out an embrasure, seeing nothing but steep rock faces and ice all the way to the bottom of the gorge, and the other side rising up as steep and bare, though not as high.

"I don't like this place," she said. "I can feel the very stones groaning."

"Well they might, the sights they have seen. But it was a strange place before Carcharon was built, and will still be when every last stone is gone. It is one of the most potent sites in all Santhenar, where the currents in the very core of the world sweep to a focus. Karan's father was fascinated by the place."

"What was he like?"

"Galliad? A strange man, in some ways. Brilliant but an outcast. He was half-Aachim, you see, and at odds with the world both here and in Shazmak. Wherever he went he was an exile."

In the topmost chamber they found a scene of devastation. A good third of the eastern wall had fallen outward, leaving the shattered roof frame sagging down to the floor. A low wall had scorch marks on it and some of the stone had melted, running down to congeal in a slaggy pile at the base. Nearby they found a huge depression in the floor as if something heavy had molded the stone like jelly. It was as smooth as glass and shaped with odd curves and corrugations reminiscent of the construct. Except for some food scraps and a broken plate, the room was empty. Carcharon had been abandoned.

The very air in the room moved sluggishly, glittering with little drifting specks of fire even when the sun was covered by cloud. Their voices changed all the time, sometimes echoing as if they spoke inside a bell, at other times sinking into the plastic walls so that they had to shout to be heard at all.

Shand sat down on the roof wreckage, drumming his heels against a rafter. He looked quite defeated.

"What's the matter, Shand? All the life seems to have gone out of you."

"I'm too old. I've nothing left to live for."

"What about finding Karan?"

"He's taken her with him. There's absolutely nothing I can do about it."

Tallia left him there. Going downstairs, she searched the whole place; every storeroom, every cupboard, the yard and all the sheds and lean-tos, mostly unroofed, that clustered against the walls. She looked in the cellars and even the water cistern. There was thick ice on the top of it. Tallia paced around the walls, peering down to see if anything had been thrown there, or anybody, but found nothing except a neat pile of waste—bones, scraps and a few broken items—in one stone bin.

Climbing up again she found Shand still staring at the molded floor. "There's nothing left," she said. "Whatever they brought with them they took away. No sign of Karan either."

He sighed. "Let's try to unravel what happened. We know that the construct worked well enough to find a way into the void, for the thranx can't have come from anywhere else."

"How do *you* know such things? Even Mendark did not know its name."

"Another time," said Shand.

"Has Rulke gone back there, do you think?"

"No one goes willingly to the void. It is a place to escape from, in desperate times to travel through, to get from one world to another. But not even the things that dwell there would drag him back—they would be too anxious to make their own escape. No, he has either gone to Aachan or he is still here."

"Here?" she wondered.

"I mean on Santh—in Shazmak with his Ghâshâd, presumably. There were many of *them* here. It would have taken more than one trip to ferry them all to Shazmak."

"And Karan too. I wonder what went wrong? The thranx must have shaken him. Look at that." She pointed to a puddle of what appeared to be frozen purple blood. "He must have wounded it, or the lorrsk that attacked Nadiril. And this hollow in the floor—I can't even imagine how that got there."

"I can," said Shand. "It's as if the construct fell on its side and the floor molded itself to its shape. Something went badly wrong."

Shand looked even older and more defeated, if that was possible. He groped blindly inside his coat for the flask, took a huge swig then offered it to her. Tallia shook her head.

"I need something hot. I'm going to make a fire."

Shand did not respond. She went down the stairs but returned looking dispirited. "No wood!" she said.

Wordlessly Shand pointed to the remains of the roof. They gathered splinters and bits of broken beams, and made a fire on the other side of the room, well away from the bloodstain and the hollow.

"Look," said Tallia, going back for more wood. "Isn't that Karan's knife?"

She pulled it out from under the rubble. They heaved the mess of timbers apart, peering underneath in case her body was trapped there, but it wasn't.

Tallia made a pot of stew. Shand sat back, occasionally sipping from his flask. Leaning against the wall, he closed his eyes. His lips moved, though whether he was talking to himself, or reciting a prayer, she did not try to find out.

"I'm so weary of the world," he said. "It's almost time to go. Almost time."

Tallia had no idea how to help him. She busied herself with a more thorough search of Carcharon, which was as fruitless as the previous one. What could be done? Shazmak was only a few days' walk from here, if the weather was kind, but it could withstand all Yggur's armies. Tallia stared up at the frozen mountains.

The day drew to a close; the wind rushed straight down the mountain at her. Time to go in. Time to eat. Shand did not appear to have moved. The fire had died down but the stew was still simmering. The stew had gummed together at the bottom of the pot. She scraped a generous helping into Shand's metal mug and waved it under his nose. He sat up.

Shand spooned down the soup as if he had not eaten in a week. "That's better!"

Tallia ate her own more delicately but with just as much appreciation. They divided what remained in the pot between them and when it was finished she broke ice off the embrasure ledge to melt for tea.

"What now?" she wondered. "Shazmak?"

"No! Much as I love Karan, Shazmak and Rulke are beyond us. They would see us coming for leagues. There's nothing we can do for her. Let's go. Carcharon isn't a place that I care to spend the night in."

"It's already dark!"

"Why so it is," Shand said in amazement. "I must have dozed."

It began to snow. The wind screamed in through the roof and the walls. They dragged wood down to a lower room that was intact and remade the fire in a proper fireplace, though even with it roaring the room never became warm.

Tallia lay awake until late, turning everything over and over in her mind. After midnight she was awakened by a reed-thin, distant cry. Her heart leapt. Could it be Karan?

Looking out, she saw something moving in the shadows of the amphitheater. Something touched with silver like moonbeams, though the moon was hidden by cloud. "Shand," she said urgently.

He woke instantly and peered out beside her. Whatever it was, it swooped and dived like a huge bird.

"What can it be? Surely not the thranx come back?"

"Surely not," he chuckled. "Let's go and see."

He strode out without a care in the world. Tallia tried to mimic his confidence but did not succeed. When they reached the lower edge of the amphitheater, he eased his head over. "Look!"

Down where the stage had once been was the ghost of a tall, rangy man in a long cloak. He was waving his arms and shouting, his movements making the cloak billow in the air, sometimes lifting him up to float across the amphitheater.

"Is it Basunez?"

"It is. I met him once, long ago. He's exhorting his masons to work harder and faster, and better, I should say. See them."

Tallia realized that there were hundreds of little pale ghosts in the arena, men and women. They were talking, playing at dice or wrestling one another, or even making ghostly love in the shadows, surely the most ethereal of all their pleasures. Occasionally Basunez's shrieks broke through, the wailing cry that Tallia had first noticed. But not a one took any notice of him.

Tallia tried to count them but it was impossible. "Hundreds must have died building this place!"

"Hundreds," he agreed. "This must be why Karan's father came up here so often, to try and learn Basunez's secrets."

"Do you think he ever did?" Tallia wondered.

"No!" Shand said quickly, with a bit of a shiver. "Ghosts don't give up their secrets, for they can never get anything in return. Come on!"

They went back to their blankets but Tallia still could not sleep. The wind howled and the ghosts of Basunez and his masons did spectral displays of their crafts until the walls crawled with them. Tallia's skin crawled too, all night. These shades were foreign to her. Back in her homeland of Crandor, the family ghosts were like invited guests. Everyone was glad to see them, for they meant good fortune.

As dawn arrived they departed, and by lunchtime were back at Black Lake. This time they made a more cheerful blaze, but neither was in a cheerful mood.

"I feel that I've let Karan down, somehow," said Tallia. It was becoming a preoccupation with her. They sat together over a cup of chard, as much to warm their fingers as their bellies.

Shand nodded. He felt the same way. "I let myself be drawn into this, bit by little bit, each time thinking that it would finish there. Now here I am, right in the middle of it. Well, no point in useless regrets."

"You're feeling better then?"

"Not really, but I'm alive, so I might as well get back to where I can be useful."

"Thurkad is the last place I want to be right now."

"I've deliberately avoided asking you before—" said Shand.

"And I appreciate it, but ask away, my friend."

"You and Mendark were once . . . close."

"We were lovers briefly, when I was a timid apprentice and he was one of the most powerful men on Santhenar. It didn't last. Mendark is too used to getting his own way. No bad thing in a Magister, I suppose, but not between us. Though he gave me the best of training, I don't think he really wanted me to become a master. He resented my successes much more than he did those of any of his other lieutenants. Since Havissard . . ."

"It was not a successful renewal," said Shand thoughtfully.

"It's changed him completely. He's become mean and calculating. He's as much obsessed with finishing Rulke as Tensor ever was. And lately he uses his power rather carelessly. He was not like that once."

Shand frowned at memories long forgotten. "He was always like that, when pressed, but until last year it had been a long time since he was pressed. The troubles have merely highlighted his true character, as yours. And mine! But that's the way of power."

"Well, perhaps I'm not up to wielding it."

"You're in good company. Though I've begun to think that avoiding it, as I have, might be just as big an evil. Mendark has done great things for the world, after all. Let's not forget that."

"I once had almost everything I wanted," she mused,

"being his trusted lieutenant and his friend. But since Havissard . . ."

"Perhaps you'll laugh to hear this, Tallia, since Mendark and I are constantly feuding, but he's basically good at heart. Mean, obsessed, conniving, but not evil. Now he sees everything he's ever worked for falling apart. His body is failing and there's no one to step into his shoes."

"They're too big for me," she said. She noticed Shand looking at her rather large feet and laughed. "But if I do go my own way, where am I to go? I want to go home to Crandor, though that would be running away. And now I have another complication."

"Jevi!"

"Yes. He's a wonderful man, and I love Lilis dearly. I care for Jevi more than for any man I've ever met. But . . ."

"What, Tallia? I never thought I'd see you at such a loss."

"He's a lovely, brave, kind, thoughtful man. But that's all he shows to me—the perfect friend."

"And that's not enough?"

"I want him, Shand. The instant he went over the cliff after Lilis, I knew it. But I'm afraid. What if he doesn't want me?"

"I'm sure he does."

"Then why doesn't he say so?" she cried in a passion.

"Do you really need me to answer that?"

"I don't know much about men, only what I learned from Mendark."

"Hardly any use in this situation!" he snorted. "I'll tell you what the problem is, shall I?"

"Please do," she murmured.

"You're rich and beautiful, powerful and well-connected. He's none of those things, Tallia. And remember his years of slavery and degradation under bel Gorst. That does terrible things to a man. How can he aspire to you?"

"I don't care about any of that."

"Easy to say, since you have it all. But he cares."

"What am I to do?" she cried, pacing back and forth.

"You'll have to work that out yourself. But take it slowly."

"I will. I think I'll stay up here for a while. I've a lot to sort out."

Shand looked up at her, startled. "Perhaps I should stay too."

"No! You don't want to, and I don't want you to stay just to keep me company, not that you wouldn't be welcome. I'll scout around here and along the path toward Shazmak. After all, when Rulke comes out again it will probably be this way, and someone must keep the watch. And for that matter the thranx could be up here, as likely as anywhere. Don't try and dissuade me. I've great need of solitude."

"I won't. That's a need I well understand. Only, be careful."

11

The Stinging Tree

After Faelamor left for Carcharon, Maigraith sat where she was for a long time, musing over what her liege had said.

Tallallame, Tallallame, your fate rests on the one which is three.

Did the "one which is three" mean the triune—Karan? Maigraith could not see how. She resumed her work with gates. Though it was easy to make portals now, she could not master using them, for there was a flaw in her that she found impossible to overcome. Most places that she thought about going to, she simply could not see, in her mind's eye, the destination.

Maigraith turned to her other work, preparing for the coming of the Faellem. She had thought herself secure in her hidden valley, but several days later, having just stepped into the river for a brief, bracing bath, she saw a bootprint in the damp soil beside the water.

Scrambling out again, she dressed without drying herself.

She was in a clearing where soft grass carpeted the ground. The trees around were giants that had known neither axe nor saw. She saw no one, but knew an army could be hiding behind such trees. Not far away, red limestone cliffs hemmed the river in on either side.

The print was very long and narrow. Moreover, the pattern of the nails in sole and heel was one she recognized as from another life. Ghâshâd! She allowed herself a moment's panic, an echo of that past life under the domination of others. Maigraith hurled the panic away, furiously stamping it into the ground, then stood still, letting calm drift over her. She was in control of her life now. What must she do?

The footmark was only hours old, and there were others nearby. Someone had walked along the water's edge heading upstream. They must have tracked Faelamor into the valley. Had the spy discovered the camp? Maigraith moved camp every week or two, and the current one was right back against the cliff.

She threw water into her stamp marks, making a concealing puddle there. Brushing out her own prints, she backtracked into the forest, obscuring her trail as she went. She saw no sign of intruders around her camp, but a thorough search must surely find it.

Swiftly she unlashed the poles and the woven sides of her shelter and took down the hammock. Climbing a little way up the cliff, she thrust them into a crack filled with fern and moss. As she hung there an alien cry echoed between the cliffs. Had they seen her? She crammed the rest of her goods in her pack and crept away from the camp, but before she had gone far there came a whistling from a little way ahead. Maigraith scrambled up a tree and waited.

There was no further sign of them. Hours went by. The hard bark made an uncomfortable perch, being heavily ridged and corrugated. It cut into her whether she sat or leaned against it. Maigraith carved some of the bark away with her knife to make a more agreeable seat, but all along the wound yellow sap began to ebb out. Moving further along the branch, her hand brushed against a leaf and the skin began to tingle, then burn. She had climbed a giant stinging tree, whose dinner-plate-sized leaves stung worse than nettles.

Maigraith was about to climb down when something flitted from tree to tree between her and the river. It was a bluebell bird, one wing dragging as if broken. After months in the forest, she was familiar with the ruse, intended to draw something away from its nest. What had disturbed it?

She eased herself along the branch to another position just as uncomfortable. It took a long, patient search, but she found it. Someone else was watching the forest from a hideout on the cliff.

There could be others as well. The Ghâshâd often worked in groups of six or more. At the battle of Casyme, the *square* had contained nine of them. Maigraith had just thought to climb down the other side of the trunk when she saw another watcher, near the river. She was neatly trapped. Faelamor's scheme would be undone.

The sun set. The watchers remained where they were. A pair of Ghâshâd appeared. Behind them in a staggered line was another pair. They were sweeping the whole valley. Impossible that they would not find her. If she fled they would follow her, and Maigraith knew how doggedly they would do that.

Besides, she had promised to remain here until the coming of the Faellem. The Ghâshâd must be gone before then. Nor could she permit them to find her storehouse caves, where she had laid up a stock of preserved food for the winter, or evidence of the gate.

A fire appeared by the river near her bathing spot.

Maigraith ate food from her pack and prepared to wait them out. It was a dark, cloudy night. The flames flickered eerily. Did they know she was here? Surely they must have sensed something, to have made camp at this spot? She stretched out a foot to climb down, but as she did a patrol passed right underneath, the guard illuminated by stray beams from the fire. The woman stopped, looked up but did not see her, then leaned against the trunk.

Cursing her, Maigraith resumed her perch. Finally the guard moved away. Feeling in her pack, Maigraith found a bobble nut and began to peel away the leathery case with her knife. She had baked the nuts in the coals only that morning, and the smell was mouth-watering.

Inside it was like four yellow globes grown together. She popped the segments apart and leaned back to enjoy them. Her hand slipped in the oozing sap. Off balance, she dropped the knife, which struck a rock on the forest floor, making a metallic clunk.

Someone shouted from the fire. Maigraith wiped her hand down her shirtfront, cursing her clumsiness, and retreated around the other side of the tree. Suddenly there were lights everywhere in the forest, Ghâshâd holding up blazing brands.

Watching the flares converging on her tree, she felt a peculiar sensation in her hand. The skin was all hot and tight. Her fingers were swelling up—already they were like wrinkled sponges. Her chest and stomach began to tingle too. The damned stinging-tree sap!

One minute her hand felt numb, the next it was so hot that it took all her self-control not to cry out. She felt faint. Maigraith wrapped her legs around the branch and tore the shirt off. Buttons went flying. She wiped her chest and stomach with the back of the shirt. She pulled out another shirt, thrust her arms through the sleeves, but before she could do up the buttons her fingers lost all feeling.

The pain was like brilliant little flashes of lightning through a nightscape of spreading numbness. In a minute, Maigraith could do nothing but cling grimly to her branch while the lights clustered around her tree and two Ghâshâd climbed up for her.

They soon pulled her down and carried her to the fire near the river. There were six of them, all much alike. They were tall and extremely lean, though one had colorless hair and skin, and as he bent over her the firelight reflected in pink eyes.

"What is the matter?" asked an old woman whose cheeks were criss-crossed all over with wrinkles. Amazingly, she looked as if she cared.

"Stinging-tree sap!" Maigraith gasped.

"Pass my bag, Rebban," said the old woman.

The albino handed it to her and she bathed the affected skin in a liquid like milk, dried it, then applied a green, mint-smelling unguent which took the worst of the pain away. She was quite gentle.

"My name is Quissan," she said.

"Why do you care?" asked Maigraith.

"Rulke ordered us to treat you with courtesy," said Quissan.

In an hour or so the swelling began to go down, though the burning sensation persisted. They fed her and questioned her into the night, particularly about Faelamor, her plans and whereabouts. Maigraith answered their questions truthfully, for the most part, for lying was not one of her skills. Besides, she knew little about what Faelamor was up to and what she did know could make no difference. One thing she did conceal,—that Faelamor had made a gate, and that she,

Maigraith, had also mastered that art. They would certainly want to know that.

Maigraith lay under a rude shelter—a piece of canvas stretched between four stakes—listening to the mutter of talk over by the fire. The Ghâshâd had been afraid of her and could not believe their good fortune to have caught her so easily.

She could not believe her stupidity. She imagined explaining this disaster to Faelamor—the humiliation, the contempt in Faelamor's eyes. I've not gone far with my new life, she thought, if just the idea of her fury can so intimidate me.

Maigraith would do anything to avoid that degrading experience. How, though? Rebban the albino was squatting just outside the shelter and his pink eyes had not once left her face. He seemed to be a rare kind of sensitive, set to watch for any trick or attempt at escape.

This was a problem as difficult as any of Calliat's Chrighms that she had solved previously. What weaknesses did they have that she could work on, in her condition? The Ghâshâd were sensitive when they linked minds in the *square*. In that state their minds were very powerful, though their bodies were correspondingly weakened. Perhaps that was the way to attack them.

First, make them so afraid that they would go into formation to defend themselves. They must! To lose her would be a humiliating defeat. Second, to strike before they were ready. Their principal weakness, as far as she knew, was a sensitivity to bright sunlight. It hurt their eyes and burned their delicate skin, for they were creatures of the far south, of cold and ice.

Maigraith felt helpless. Her wrists were bound and the pain in her hands and chest persisted, taking the edge off her thinking. How could she use their weakness to overcome them?

The fire was well stacked with wood, lighting up the whole area. Fire and light! Could she make something of that? Maigraith thought herself into the heart of the blaze, into the greedy, inanimate creature that fire was. *Consume! Consume!* That was all it wanted, to leap from stick to stick, drive out the volatile gases then devour them in blue and yellow flames above the pyre. But what it had could never be enough. It always wanted more—more fuel, more *air*.

Air was not difficult to move with the Secret Art. It was hard to control though. Maigraith stared at the stacked wood, concentrating on the air around it which was slowly being drawn into the base of the fire. She sought out the motions of the air. It had the beginnings of a pattern, curving across the ground into the fire, then up. She tried to order that structure, to amplify the little tendril currents and feed the pattern back on itself. *Whirl, wind!* Imperceptibly the air began to organize itself into currents and lazily to coil inward. It was hard work. *Stronger! Faster!* It began to form solid streams that riffled the dead grass around the fire.

Her head began to ache, and as she continued a blaze grew behind her forehead. The air kept wanting to resume its turbulent and random motions. She forced the particles back into the flow.

The fire blazed higher, drawing the air in. *Whirl, faster!* Now the current was hissing through the grass, spiraling in, being drawn up through the network of logs and, heated to burning, rushing out the top. The flames leapt high and bright. *Faster! Burn harder and hotter!*

Now it was going of its own accord. One of the Ghâshâd jumped up, shielding his eyes. *Burn! Burn everything to ashes!* The wind became a whirlwind, a mini-tornado that roared into the pyre. The flames grew so bright that they hurt Maigraith's eyes.

"What is she doing?" the man cried. He was reeling about, shielding his skin from the glare, and his eyes were watering to flood his cheeks.

"The *square*, quickly!" screamed Quissan.

"Burn them all to bones!" Maigraith shrieked, rising and throwing out her bound hands. The fire lit up like a bolt of lightning, shrivelling the high leaves of an overhanging tree.

The Ghâshâd shrieked and covered their eyes as they scrambled into position around her. Quissan passed something around, they swallowed and all linked hands. Maigraith felt the power of the *square* growing. She abandoned the fire, which was now roaring its fuel into oblivion. It needed her Art no longer, for the whirlwind was sucking leaves, bark and twigs into it from right across the clearing. She made ready a link, to strike at them before they could overpower her. To attack them in their weakness—a mental blast as bright as the fire.

The *square* was formed. They moved in on her from all directions, their bony hands reaching out. They were too strong for her. Maigraith felt a spasm of nausea and her concentration weakened. With a roar that turned into a yelp she sent her mental flare over the link. It was not strong enough. They pushed against her, six pairs of hands surrounding her skull, taking control of her and sensing what she tried to conceal.

"What are you really doing here?" cried a fanatical-looking young woman whose bony head was shaven to a day-old stubble. "What is Faelamor up to?"

Maigraith struggled. "Hold her, Culiss!" yelled Quissan, the old woman who had treated her.

The pressure was unbearable. The *square* was much too strong for her. The gate popped into her mind. Maigraith pushed it away again. The *square*, sensing victory, forced harder. Maigraith shrieked and folded up on the ground. As she did so, the aura of the gate leaked out, and the image of the cave nearby. Maigraith closed it off again but not quickly enough. The faces of the Ghâshâd were lit up in exultation. She rolled across the ground, trying to get away. Her brain hurt, but the knowledge of her blunder was worse.

She rolled onto the discarded shirt and a plan to recover from the disaster flashed into her mind. She rubbed the sap-stained cloth over her wrists and arms, then allowed the Ghâshâd to catch her.

They collected together, talking excitedly about the gate and the honor that would await them when they carried Maigraith and the secret back to Rulke. Maigraith suddenly began to scream and tear at her wrists. She wasn't pretending—the second dose of sap was agony. She came to her knees, holding her arms out.

Seeing the bloody blisters rising up on her hands and arms, someone untied her bonds while two others held her secure. Maigraith released another mental blast. It wasn't enough to harm anyone, but it shocked them enough for her to wriggle free. She ran upriver, toward her gate-stones.

They called back and forth to one another, their harsh cries ringing off the cliffs. Maigraith had to force herself to stay calm, not to fear them.

She was staggering as she turned away from the river toward the gate-stones and the cave. Let them think she was trying to flee through the gate. Her hands and arms burned unbearably. A faint path led to the cave, enough for them to follow. As she dragged herself up the hill Maigraith fumbled the four-piece stone egg out of her pocket. It was the key to the gate. She warmed it in her hands.

They approached, two by two by two. When they were

near, Maigraith slipped between the two standing spires of ironstone, swung her egg between the stones and called out for her gate. Suddenly it came alive. Not yet! she thought. Seeing the destination was her problem, but one place in the world was burned into her mind forever. She called up that basement room in Fiz Gorgo where Vartila had tormented her after Karan escaped with the Mirror.

The room flashed into her inner eye. Maigraith ducked out the other side of the spires, making sure that they saw her heading up to her cave. Then, as the Ghâshâd bunched up to pass between the stones, she fixed the image and flung open the gate. There came a roar, a tornado of dust and they vanished—one, two, three, four, five. Where was the sixth? A little way behind. Culiss, the stubble-headed young woman, was staring at the space, suspicious of the gate.

Culiss went forward tentatively, then stopped just before the two pillars. Her long neck darted this way and that. She wasn't going to go in. It would all be for nothing if she didn't. Her heart hammering, Maigraith crept around the other side of the stone. The gate was thinning. She ran up behind the woman and thrust her in the back. Culiss propped, whirled and caught Maigraith by the hair.

Maigraith struggled desperately. Behind Culiss she could see faces in the gate—Rebban and Quissan, trying to get back out. Culiss dragged Maigraith to her—she was far stronger. At the last instant, Maigraith flung her head up under the woman's jaw.

Culiss's head snapped backward and Maigraith pushed her in the chest with all her strength. The woman toppled into Rebban and Quissan. Maigraith slammed the gate closed.

She fell down between the stones, gasping. A very near thing, but she'd done it. Fiz Gorgo was two months away at this time of year. Enough, surely! But as she trudged down to the river to bathe her throbbing arms, she couldn't help but wonder why Rulke wanted her. Her heart raced at the thought of seeing him again, but it must be on her own terms.

12

THE FAELLEM

A few days later Maigraith was sitting beside the river, mending a basket, enjoying the rare winter sunshine on her back and the music of the river over the stones, when she became aware of a presence behind her. Turning slowly, because she felt in no danger, she saw three people standing beside the camp. They were two women and a man, neither young nor old.

The women were smaller than her, the man barely her own height. Their posture told of their anxiety. They were various in build, hair color and appearance, but all were Faellem. Each had the glowing, rosewood skin and the old eyes. Besides, she knew the women.

Maigraith came to her feet abruptly. It had been decades since she had seen any of them, save Faelamor, and she felt as much in awe of them as she had as a child. But she would not let them see that.

The Faellem seemed disconcerted at this confident young woman striding toward them, her glossy chestnut hair streaming out behind her, where they had expected Faelamor. They knew her, but she was not the timid, downcast child they had known.

As a rule it was not their custom to shake hands, but now the first woman put out her hand. "Greetings, Maigraith. I am Ellami. You know my sister Hallal, and cousin Gethren."

Maigraith took the offered hand, then embraced each in the proper Faellem way, her arms enclosing their shoulders, her cheek laid to each of their cheeks. She took their packs and offered fermented nectar in wooden mugs. They saluted her with the brew, and praised it, observing all the formalities. Only then did Hallal, the taller of the two women, speak the words Maigraith had been expecting.

"Where is Faelamor?" The question came out like groundup ice. "We ordered her to remain here." Hallal's tight mouth opened, then closed again. She shot a furious glance to the other two.

"She went to Carcharon to spy on Rulke," said Maigraith. Months had passed since they'd communicated with Faelamor via the link; since Faelamor had told them about her gateborne visit to Havissard, the dreadful book she'd found there, and how she had lost it to Mendark. In spite of herself, Maigraith trembled.

"Why?" choked Hallal, almost incoherent in her fury. "Why has she disobeyed the Faellem?"

"Rulke is in Carcharon. She was afraid what he was up to. And she was desperate to recover a book—"

"Enough of that!" snapped Gethren. Then, more kindly, "You may tell us the story later—the full story, in the correct order. But first we must eat."

"Are more of you coming?"

The three exchanged troubled glances. "Near half of our number—some hundreds. They are well behind. We came in haste to make a place ready. We have marched from Mirrilladell, the best part of three hundred leagues, without a day's rest."

Mirrilladell was a vast land partly embraced by the southward sweep of the Great Mountains that extended across half of the continent of Lauralin, and partly enclosed by the northward barrier of the inland seas of Milmillamel and Tallallamel. Mirrilladell was a land of endless forests, of countless lakes and bogs, of rocky hills bare of soil. It was punishingly cold in the winter, hot and sticky and riddled with every kind of crawling and biting insect on Santhenar in summer. The Faellem had dwelt there since the time of the Forbidding, and having lived there as a child Maigraith had few pleasant memories of the place. To the east Mirrilladell merged into Tarralladell, indistinguishable except that it was even bleaker.

Hallal looked exhausted. She rubbed her hand across her face (she had small hands with plump fingers, and her wrists were tiny), brushing the dark hair out of her eyes. She looked across at her sister, Ellami. Ellami shook her head.

Maigraith wondered at the lack of likeness between them. Ellami was the younger, but her hair was colorless, quite transparent, her eyes were gray instead of brown and though small she was solidly built. Her face at rest had a kind of impish quality, whereas Hallal just looked weary and worried. They both signaled with their eyes to the man. Gethren was different again, his hair a glossy brown, and he had striking dark eyebrows, long lashes and deep golden eyes, but his forehead was lined.

Gethren answered their unspoken question. His voice was melodic and very soft. "We don't know *anything*! Let us hear her story first."

Maigraith felt intimidated. Faelamor often seemed unbalanced, pursuing her objective blindly whatever the consequences. These folk were not. They were the best of an old wise race, and they would not do anything without weighing every option. They had a natural arrogance too. They were used to commanding and being obeyed. She tried to put the moment off.

"Would you care to wash, or rest, while I prepare food for you?" she said.

Hallal flicked her fingers, meaning "No!" "To be here is rest enough. Sit down. We will prepare dinner."

By this simple reversal Maigraith was stripped of authority. She sat awkwardly, feeling like a guest in her own camp, while the Faellem unpacked their goods out of remarkably capacious packs. In a short time she was eating their delicious food that she had not tasted in many years.

Their cuisine was largely vegetarian. Not that they did not eat meat or fish or fowl: they relished meats of every kind, but only in tiny portions, as flavorings. Normally they ate the freshest of vegetables, beautifully presented and subtly flavored, but more often than not raw or only seared on the outside. On the road, however, they had to eat preserved food, unlike their usual fare.

Their cookery was flavored with any of hundreds, if not thousands, of herbs, spices and essences, most unknown to any other people. They spiced their dishes with a hundred kinds of wood, as splinters thrust into a vegetable or shavings tossed into a braise, as wood dust sprinkled on the plate before serving or raspings steeped in vinegar or oil. The flavors were extraordinary. The food would have delighted Maigraith had it not brought up childhood memories that she would rather had stayed forgotten. But in the end she was glad, for what she had to offer them, gathered and preserved by her own labor, seemed very pallid stuff.

They spoke only of trivial things while they ate—the beauty of this spot that Faelamor had chosen, the hard march of the last few days over the mountain spur, the quality of the light here—and as they drank small cups of a straw-colored vintage which they flavored with chips of rosemary wood, they remarked on the color, bouquet and palate of the wine. The wine was not their own, of course. They had purchased it only last week, but it was better than any Maigraith had tasted since Thurkad.

The wine was put away, the cups and plates washed, and a bowl of yelt placed steaming before each of them. Faelamor had no taste for yelt, indeed she took little pleasure in food or drink, happy to have the same stuff month after month. Accordingly, Maigraith had long ago adapted her own tastes to monotony. She remembered yelt, though seemingly from another world, another life. She licked her lips. It was as much a dessert as a beverage: thick, rich and sweet, with a flavor like a creamy, custardy chocolate mousse but with a subtle coffee-bitterness.

She sipped her yelt. It was everything she remembered. She looked up at Gethren. His old eyes were on her—all their eyes were. She shivered. They noticed that, but did not look away.

"Now you will tell us Faelamor's story," said Gethren in that melodic voice.

Maigraith was in a bind. "I owe a d-duty to Faelamor," she stammered. "My whole life is duty—the first lesson she taught me, and the one most often beaten into me. She bade me say no more than I have done already."

"Faelamor owes a duty to the Faellem that is binding, for she fought for the honor to lead us and she swore to uphold the duty. Whereas you owe her no duty at all, and cannot! You are not one of us. Your very existence is a great sin!"

"What are you saying?" Maigraith whispered. From these people the simple statements, that would have been obvious to anyone but Maigraith, cleaved through her conditioning like a thunderbolt.

"You are not born to duty, as our species is. You owe Faelamor only what is due for your education and your upbringing, and that was paid back long ago. Neither have you sworn to us of your own will. Faelamor indoctrinated and compelled you, and that is no true duty."

Maigraith looked from one to the other, confused.

Ellami grimaced. Her face showed more than the other two. "Duty cannot be owed in isolation," she said. "You do not owe her duty merely because she says it." Her voice was harsh, after Gethren's. "It is Faelamor who fails in her duty—to the Faellem. Duty to be *one among the Faellem.* She was always arrogant. She has done a great wrong, to you not least of all. Tell us your story. Omit no part of it."

"She said that the Faellem are like a hive: she is the queen bee and you are the workers, carrying out her will with none of your own."

Ellami smote her bowl of yelt right off the table. "Faelamor is proud and must be brought low." Her eyes pierced Maigraith's like needles. "What does she think we have been doing in the hundreds of years since we expelled her for her villainy?"

"Why did you expel her?" Maigraith asked tentatively. She had often wondered. She thought that it was over the great crime her unknown parents had committed, a secret that Faelamor refused to disclose. The quest for her own background had obsessed Maigraith all her adult life, yet still she did not know who she was or where she had come from.

"We cast her out over the sin of your mother and you. Since then we have managed our lives quite well without a *queen bee*. The tale, if you please!"

Maigraith told the whole story, beginning a year and a half ago when Faelamor had sent her to steal the Mirror from Yggur, and how she, Maigraith, had forced Karan to go with her. Maigraith sipped her yelt as she told her tale, and when the bowl was empty another was put in front of her. So the afternoon passed. Late in the evening she paused, losing her voice, and Gethren prepared dinner. Ellami and Hallal went walking together down by the river. One of them, just a shadow in the firelight, pointed up at the sky. The glowing scorpion nebula was setting, the dark moon past the three-quarters. Only a few days till hythe. The scorpion reminded Maigraith of Rulke. She trembled.

The two came back and Maigraith continued. The nebula set. The dark moon passed westwards. In the early hours of the morning the wind swung around and snow began to fall. Hallal and Ellami rose as one to fetch larger logs for the fire.

Dawn came. Maigraith's voice was cracked and her eyes were red. The tale was almost done. She told them about Faelamor's gate. "An outrage!" Gethren said. And about the visit to Havissard too. She told them everything except how she felt there and what she found—the silver stylus and the piece of paper bearing the name "Aeolior."

They questioned her at length about the gold and the book, but Maigraith knew not why Faelamor had been looking for the former, nor much about the latter either.

"This gold was Aachan gold, you say?" Ellami was speaking now.

"So I believe. It had an unpleasant feel, but Faelamor was triumphant after she found it."

"It must be Yalkara's own golden jewelry," said Gethren, "that was lost after she went through the gate to Aachan. So, she didn't take it with her after all!"

"A powerful artifact," breathed Ellami.

"Perilous too!" Gethren was the cautious one. "Too perilous for us. Where is it now?"

"I don't know," said Maigraith. "Perhaps in one of our store caves. I've not seen it since the day we came back."

"Take us there at once!" cried Hallal. "It must be taken apart and scattered across the world so that it can never be used again."

They hurried up to the caves, searching everywhere and using their Faellem arts to reveal that which had been hidden. They found no trace of the gold.

"I don't like this," said Ellami. "I fear she will commit a great evil with it." They headed back to camp.

"Tomorrow," said Hallal, "we shall scan the whole valley. It must be found."

Gethren made pancakes, poured syrup over them and offered them with another brew, this time coffee so aromatic that it was intoxicating.

Maigraith concluded her tale. "Rulke is in Carcharon now, and Faelamor has gone to find out why. She is very afraid."

"As are we," said Gethren. "This year will see a transformation, one way or the other. Nothing will ever be the same again."

The tale, the confession, had left Maigraith utterly drained. She ate the food, drank the coffee and sat waiting. But their eyes dismissed her, and something akin to pity showed on Ellami's face once again. She took Maigraith's hand and led her to her shelter, even knelt down and eased her boots off, and made sure she was well covered with her blankets. Maigraith was more weary than she should have been from a night without sleep.

She lay for a while, listening to their voices: Gethren's soft, lilting tones contrasting with Ellami's harder, rougher and more excitable voice. And over them both, the quiet authority of Hallal, the one who had been rival to Faelamor eons ago, to lead them, and perhaps should have been chosen. Maigraith sensed a tinge of resentment there.

She could not make out what they were saying, except a

phrase here and there of Ellami's, and a word or two from Hallal. But of Gethren, nothing. She drifted off to sleep.

Later she woke again, or was woken by loud argument. The snow fell thickly now. The Faellem had an icing of white on their broad felt hats, an epaulet of white on each shoulder.

"I dread what she is up to," said Hallal. "She has made a gate! How can we follow someone who commits such crimes?"

"We must put her down!" cried Ellami heatedly.

"I'm afraid," said Gethren. "This will destroy us. I say we abandon her and go back to Mirrilladell."

13

A Bloody Footprint

Karan wanted to scream, to shriek and kick the snow and beat the rocks with her fists, to have a child's tantrum, get it out of her system and be better again at the end of it. She could not face being hunted by the Ghâshâd again.

But she was, and there was nothing to do but do it all over again. She bolted up the steep slope, the pack hammering her back and her heart thudding just as loudly at her sore ribs. She ran until tears of terror froze and gummed her eyelids together, until her breath burned in her side and foam accumulated on her lip and she tasted blood in her mouth.

Then, as she stumbled up the ridge, Karan saw a bloody print on the ice. She did not stop for an instant, but took it in so clearly that later on she could have drawn it perfectly from memory. Her skin broke out in goosepimples.

No human footprint this—it was the print of an unshod foot, but a foot more like a hand, with a huge square palm that could have covered her whole face, and long spread toes like clawed fingers. One side of the print was indented and the hollow, from the gouge of the claw all the way down to the heel, was filled with frozen blood so dark as to be almost black. She knew what it was—one of the lorrsk that had attacked Rulke. She scanned the snow and ice as she ran, but there was no sign of it.

Lorrsk! The hairy, human-shaped creatures that were deadly in their cunning and clever enough to work the construct on sight. Even wounded it would be match for a dozen of her. Karan wondered which one it was. Both had been injured. One had taken a gash in the thigh, while the other had fallen on its backside into that puddle of molten metal on the floor. To end up in the belly of some beast that did not even come from her world was somehow worse than any other fate she could contemplate. She had nothing to defend herself with. She ran on.

Looking back Karan saw that the Ghâshâd, slow as they were, were gaining on her. The pack was holding her back but she was dead without it. She forced herself harder, but the ridge was steeper here, and icier, and it got her nowhere. Her legs hurt; everything hurt.

She looked up. The ridge ran up, steep and broken as far as she could see. There was nowhere to hide. They would soon wear her down. Look at them, their bony shanks moving like machines! They never seemed to tire.

She thought to roll rocks at her hunters but all the rocks were embedded in snow and ice. She imagined a snowball, getting bigger and bigger as it raced down. Unfortunately the soft snow had been swept away by the wind. On she staggered, swaying from side to side in her exhaustion.

Karan looked down into the gorge. The walls were almost vertical here. It narrowed above to a vertical cleft that might have been made by a single furious hack with an axe. No, more as if the two sides of the gorge had been prised apart, for a swarm of black dykes cut across it at an angle, bridges of resistant rock but all broken in the middle.

The nearest of the Ghâshâd were almost within bowshot now, not that they carried bows. They bore no weapons. They needed none but their minds, already whispering in hers, terror and despair. Had Rulke given them that power?

The lanky figure leading them was ominously familiar. Idlis again, her perpetual hunter, her nemesis. Already she knew how his rubbery fingers would feel on her throat—like the grip of a corpse. Despair began to drain her strength away.

Above, the cleft narrowed, though it was still wider than the most desperate leap. It was a long way up to where the adjoining ridge joined hers. Not far up the gorge, the broken dykes were plastered with wind-driven snow that sometimes formed an arch of ice spanning the gap, a soaring bridge that looked as strong as steel.

Karan was not fooled for an instant. Such snow and ice bridges were commonplace here. She knew them well from walking these ridges with her father as a child. They were quite treacherous.

Karan found herself thinking that it would almost be better to throw herself into the gorge rather than be caught, or even to run across one of the bridges. Better any chance than no chance. The gorge was narrow here, only about ten paces across. It would almost be possible, she told herself, eyeing an arch of ice and snow just above her.

Never, never, never trust a snow bridge, she heard her father say. He had said that a dozen times, and he had been wise in the mountains. *They are made by the mountain sprites to trap unwary travelers. Step on one and you will fall down and be smashed to bits on the rocks, and the sprites will feed on your scraps for a month.*

It was a long time since Karan had believed in mountain

sprites, but she knew Galliad had been right. She looked over her shoulder. If she could get past the Ghâshâd there was a slim chance, for on a downhill run her agility would have the advantage over their endurance. But they were spread evenly over the ridge top, and below them she saw another line. No chance! Rulke was determined to have her.

She looked up, estimating her chances. Nil! The ridge and the ravine continued up forever. What was the point? She stopped above another ice bridge. The snow-covered ridge ran down into a lip on either side that swept out to the gentle arch of ice, a span so narrow in the middle that she could have put her arms around it. It looked strong, but she knew it was like the first ice on a pond—it would not even support a child's weight. Besides, it would be too slippery to stand on.

Karan pressed on but the brief rest had sucked all strength from her legs. Her knees wobbled and she fell down on her face. She struggled up again to see that Idlis was close.

"I can't go back again," she gasped.

"Oh yes!" he burbled. "The Master has a new plan." He smiled, a grotesque sight.

"I'll die first!" said Karan.

"We won't let you," said Idlis, spreading his arms wide and springing at her, stiff-kneed like a walking pair of scissors.

No point running now. Karan spun around then darted straight at him. Idlis laughed, but just in front of him she skidded sideways on her heel, ducked between him and the next and raced down the hill. The shock of each stride threatened to collapse her knees. The other Ghâshâd moved across to cut her off.

Karan knew with an awful certainty that she would not get through. "You'll never get me," she roared. She saw the ice arch out of the corner of her eye and a mad idea sprang into her head. I'll sled myself across. It's the only way. And if I fail, well, it can't be any worse than going back.

Body sledding was a dangerous sport that she had achieved a rare mastery of as a child, until one of her friends had fractured her skull and it had been banned by Karan's furious mother.

She ran straight for the edge of the ridge and dived over, landing hard on her chest and accelerating down the dip toward the ice arch. I'm going too fast! she thought, trying desperately to line herself up to come out the bottom of the dip along the line of the bridge. Even a slight angle and she would go straight off the edge. Karan shot down the wind-packed snow on her belly, steering with her outstretched arms, leaning to the left. She was still on the wrong angle.

I'm going to go over! The thought was a scream of terror. Then a little bump appeared in front of her, Karan smacked her hand against it with just enough force to straighten up and shot out of the dip heading along the center line of the bridge. She spread her arms apart, tracking the sides of the arch. Her chin banged on the ice, but as she hit the upcurve of the bridge she felt it crack beneath her—the crack of her doom. She rocketed across, lifting slightly in the air as she passed the crest and the bridge curved down underneath her. She settled back down light as a feather, but the ice cracked again. Karan felt herself sliding off the side, pushed back up, then just as the whole arch fell into the gorge she shot off the bridge and crashed into a mound of snow and rock on the other side.

Karan felt sure that she was going to slide back down into the chasm, but couldn't do anything about it. Opening her eyes she found that she was wedged between shattered black rocks. She worked her arms and legs. Nothing seemed to be broken though her arms, thighs, shoulders and breasts throbbed. She felt battered black and blue. There was blood on the snow—her chin was scraped raw.

She sat up. The Ghâshâd stood in a silent line at the other end of the broken arch.

"I salute you!" rasped Idlis. "But I will *still* have you."

The Ghâshâd turned like a row of machines and began to jog up the slope. Karan looked up. It would take them hours to reach the place where the two ridges joined, but that did not mean she was safe. If they were able to call to Carcharon, Rulke could reach the bottom of her ridge long before she found safety in the forest.

"You'll never have me!" Karan gasped, and staggered off. She did not stop for an hour. Then she rested for just a few minutes and continued until dusk, when she came on the familiar path that led up to Shazmak.

There she received another shock—Ghâshâd footprints in the snow, three or four of them. The marks were unmistakable, long, narrow and deeply indented, much more so than her own prints. She looked around nervously but the dark was rolling in with the snow and she could not see far enough. Squatting down, she checked the prints in the fading light. Definitely Ghâshâd, for there was the little uptick at the front from their characteristic scissor-walk. They were heading up to Shazmak, under heavy loads.

What could it signify? Had Rulke gone? Or had the construct been damaged so badly that they had to carry it back in pieces? Or did it mean nothing at all? There was no way of telling.

She groped her way down in the dark, terrified of running into more of them, and equally terrified that if she stopped to rest Idlis's band would catch her. Just as dawn was breaking, after a miserable night prey to every fear that she could possibly conjure up, she realized that the slope was growing gentler. There was only half a league of open land between her and the bridge. Across the bridge and into the forest, and down to the cliff path to Gothryme: safety. She crept down to a vantage point where she could see the bridge. Easing her head up, Karan squinted into the distance. Three stick-figures were approaching the bridge from the other side.

Had they seen her? She doubted it—their eyesight was poor. Ducking over the side of the gorge, which was less steep here, Karan climbed down toward the frozen river. She crossed it without incident, scrambled up the further side among the boulders, over the windswept crest and out of sight. She tried to follow a path where there was no telltale snow, though anyone determined enough could track her. Finally she took to her heels and ran, and did not stop until she reached the glorious shelter of her own Gothryme Forest.

The previous night a most unhappy creature had smashed apart its snow cave on the ridge above Carcharon and stood up, sniffing the air. It was the lorrsk that had fallen in the puddle of molten metal, and it was in agony. One buttock had been burned away and was now covered in huge black scabs that broke open with every movement, to leak blood and straw-colored fluid onto the ice.

The lorrsk could barely move for the pain. Every crab-wise, lurching step sent shrieks of agony from the back of its heels to the top of its head. The cold seared its bare feet. Hunger gnawed at its guts like a plague of rodents. The lorrsk raised its head higher and the scent of warm flesh came on the wind.

It crossed the ridge back and forth until it struck the trail of a creature that led back to a snow cave like its own. It knew the scent: the small red-haired female that had been in the tower when it first escaped from the void. There were only a couple of meals in it, but it would be sweet, tender flesh. The lorrsk began to track Karan up the mountainside.

Shortly it came upon another trail, many people this time, eventually following Karan and the Ghâshâd to the broken ice bridge. The lorrsk squatted at the end of the bridge for a long time, measuring the distance. Had it been whole it might have attempted the leap, but realized that it did not need to. It was not a long climb to the place where the two ridges joined. The lorrsk followed the trail of the Ghâshâd up and across onto the adjacent ridge. Here, even through the covering of recent snow it could smell the scent of many travelers. It had found the path to Shazmak and there was fresh meat not far away.

Everything will be perfect when we get back home, Karan kept thinking. In spite of her situation, she could not stop making plans for her future, for herself and Llian (if he could ever forgive her), and for Gothryme. How to rebuild it, and get free of the burden of debt and tax hanging over it.

But she was afraid. Afraid to head to the cliff path that was the only way down, therefore surely guarded; afraid to stay here; and afraid that if she somehow did get home, Rulke would come for her anyway. But hiding here availed her nothing, so after a sketchy breakfast she made her careful way through the forest toward the cliff top. As she approached she kept picking up schizophrenic flashes—*Hunt! Hunt!*—and was sure that she was sensing Ghâshâd.

Karan crept closer, using all her bushcraft and cunning, then shinnied up an evergreen tree near the edge of the forest. She did not need to go very high. From halfway up she could see that the top of the path was guarded, by at least four of them. There was no other way down.

She sat in the crook of her tree, wondering what to do. She wanted to link to Llian, to be sure he was safe, but even if she could reach him from here, she did not dare with Rulke so close.

There was really only one option—hide in the woods until they gave up or her food ran out. She headed back into the forest. It was a still, beautiful place after the snow. Karan drank up the smell of the wood, the feel of it, the calm, solitude and renewal. But it did not ease her own conflict: the rights and wrongs of what she had done in Carcharon, and what Llian must think of her for doing it.

At the most northerly extent of the Forest of Gothryme there was an old stone hut, a one-roomed dwelling sometimes used by hunters or gleaners, though seldom in the winter. It had the forest at its back and looked over the escarpment across Faidon Forest to Elludore, and east toward the Sea of Thurkad. From where she was now, near Black Lake, it was three or four leagues away; a couple of days' hard walking, in these conditions. No one would ever know she was there, if it snowed enough to cover her trail. No one would think of looking there for her.

When darkness fell Karan was still a good day from her destination, so she continued on, knowing that the moon would rise before too long. Over the past days she had grown used to walking and working in the darkness, and this was an easier, less dangerous trek than the others had been. There was a path of sorts, an old forest trail, now seldom used except by animals. But after walking in the darkness for about an hour she lost the path, or it petered out. She found herself struggling across a succession of steep gullies and ridges and could not work out where she was. Had she wandered down toward the escarpment, or up to the base of the mountain slope? There was no way of telling. It was now overcast, pitch dark.

As she floundered through the snow, the edge of a steep bank collapsed under her, precipitating her into a gully floored with rocks. A broken branch end jagged her lip. She tasted blood.

Karan stopped abruptly, feeling the gash with her fingers. It wasn't serious. She forced her way through a thicket of saplings, then without warning found herself sliding down a greasy slope. She lost her footing and crashed through ice into water. Plates of ice bumped at her knees. The water filled her boots and burned like a cold flame.

Karan was furious with herself. Now she'd have to make camp and a fire, and damn quick, else she would get frostbite. All other dangers must be ignored. Not daring to wade across in case there were deep holes, she found that where she'd fallen in was too steep to climb out. Part of the bank had collapsed, leaving a sheer overhang. Skidding along the edge for an agonizing minute, she ran into the roots of a tree hanging down into the water. They were slippery with ice but she made it up and sat down on a root to empty her boots.

The wood on the ground would be wet; she didn't even try there. Karan felt around for dead branches whose twiggy ends might be dry enough. Her labor resulted in only a handful, as the trees branched high over her head. Twice she lost her camp and once went close to going in the river again. She made a platform with wet wood to raise her pathetic pile of kindling above the snow.

Her feet were numb. Karan took off her boots and turned them upside down to drain. Ice cracked from her socks as she peeled them off. She had other socks but only the one pair of boots. She dried her feet carefully and put another pair of socks on, the best she could do.

Karan had tinder in her pack; she always carried some for such eventualities. She struck sparks into it but it would not catch. She felt around in her pack, hoping that there might be a scrap of paper. There wasn't. Her fingers encountered the round shape of a marrim, a fruit like an orange only smaller, more oval and with red flesh. Like the orange, its rind contained oil. She remembered how, as a child, she had squeezed the oil into the fire, making little flares.

Peeling the marrim with her teeth, Karan ate the mushy, half-frozen pulp. She struck sparks into her tinder, blew on it gently until she had a little patch of red, folded over the marrim skin, pointed it at the glowing patch and squeezed the skin. The tinder went out.

She tried again, holding the skin further back. This time she was rewarded by a spurt of flame that leapt up through the tinder to the nest of twigs above. A tiny, timid flame, but how welcome! It warmed her hands and her heart. But not her feet, unfortunately, and now she had to find bigger wood quickly. The light made it easier.

Soon the fire was blazing and she had enough fuel for the rest of the night. Now, hot drink and lots of it. She went in her socks down to the stream, and while the water heated, Karan put her poor feet out to the fire and at last brought some life back to them.

All she had to drink was chard, but nothing to sweeten it with. Unsweetened chard was barely palatable. She dug out the remains of the dried fruit, tore them into little pieces with her teeth and dropped them into the brew, one by one. Her lips began to tingle.

Karan toasted a hunk of bread, threw an onion into the coals, made a platform above the fire and put a large piece of eel on it. The mug of chard went down in one gulp. It burned all the way and the ginger hotness lit a fire in her belly. She finished the fish and the bread, dipped another mug of chard and sat back feeling better. Picking out a piece of the Ghâshâd fruit (as she thought of it) she sucked at it, though again the sickly aftertaste made her spit it out. One boot was beginning to smoke; she turned them hastily. They were still soaking inside. Then something very strange happened.

All of a sudden she felt dizzy and nauseous. Her head spun, her stomach churned and the forest trees seemed to be hanging upside down. Karan stood up and promptly fell over. Her whole head now glowed with warmth—a tingling, burning feeling. Instantly that disappeared, the trees and the fire too. The whole world vanished and her identity with it.

What had happened? Where was she? The ground—no, the floor—seemed to be jerking up and down beneath her. How could it be *floor*? Where was the snow? Her feet thudded nerveless on hard tiles. Her head felt awful, a dizzy, whirling sensation, like too much wine. The back of her neck prickled as if someone was standing right behind her. She tried to spin around but her body would not obey. The prickling grew—there was definitely someone there—*it felt as if someone was inside her!*

She was not alone. She—*they*—were walking along together and the other person was just as confused as she was. Karan became aware of a terrible wailing and shrieking behind her. It was a very familiar noise.

Opening her eyes, she knew where she was at once. The wailing was the sound of a gale howling through wires and around slender towers. There were engravings and thread paintings on the walls—the walls of a vast empty city. She was walking down a long hall and into a meeting room. She was in Shazmak. At least, her consciousness was.

Now she felt something rise up, as to the surface of a murky pond. Something clutched at her, trying to pull her under, trying to climb up her body to air, life and liberation. Something that was horrified and horrifying. With a shudder of realization she understood what had happened—the reverse of that night at the campsite above Narne. Her sending, her whole psyche, had leapt across space into the mind of one of the Ghâshâd, and it did not like it any more than she did. She thought of the Ghâshâd as alien, yet this mind was revealed to be a human being like herself, perhaps cruel and terrible, perhaps noble in its own way, but now uncomprehending and terrified (or perhaps comprehending too well). Certainly it was as frightened as she was.

Its mind was very strange. It seemed to think in broken sentences mixed with images, like reading a book where many of the words had been replaced with pictures that were warped, barely recognizable.

Then it began to understand that what had happened was an accident. That Karan had no idea what she'd done. That she was not trained to the control of others nor even had any knowledge of how it might be done. The other mind was no longer frightened. It calculated what to do and with ferocious intensity began to assert itself.

Other Ghâshâd appeared in front of her, giving her strange looks. She heard words forced out of her mouth—*Fliox vurnggh hwoe!*—but the language was unknown to her. Karan struggled desperately to hold on to her identity.

Suddenly the room spun, everything went blank and the next she knew she was looking up at the ceiling. A gaggle of Ghâshâd stared down at her, helping her back up. Now they were speaking at her, saying encouraging things, and slowly the Ghâshâd that was trying to get back into her mind began to force her back against a wall, giving her no way to escape. Then their voices blew away like feathers on the wind, replaced by another face; another mind. This one she could do nothing about. It was Rulke.

He roared with laughter. *My little friend, you must be very hungry if you have to eat hrux to keep alive. I thought it was you the other night, but nothing more happened. Perhaps you didn't like the taste. No matter—it grows on you.*

How much did you eat this time? Be careful, my dear Karan. Too much can kill you. One whole piece would end you, I think. You're such a little thing. Even a bit the size of a pea will give you bad dreams. Half a piece and you will not be able to keep away from it. You'll keep coming back for more, and every time you come back you'll end up here. Soon you won't want to go away again.

Don't look at me in that reproachful way. It's none of my doing. This is Ghâshâd work, and no one made you take the fruit. No one will force you to have more. That will be as you will. See, I warn you freely.

Karan's mind was boiling with terror. What had she done to herself? The one whose mind she occupied advanced on her again. She could no longer resist him. She could feel him compressing her into a tiny space up against the wall of his mind. She was losing her identity, being submerged completely, soon to become a creature under the control of the Ghâshâd.

Llian, she cried out. *Llian, help me!* There was no answer, could not be any, for she was not linking, just sending, and he was too far away. But just the thought of him helped her, and perhaps the effects of the small piece of hrux were wearing off.

Karan kicked out with all her strength and will, and the Ghâshâd whose mind and body she occupied kicked just as hard. She felt an awful pain as he broke his toes on the stone wall. Suddenly she found herself back in the forest, screaming. She had kicked the fire, scattering logs and coals across the campsite. There was a ragged gash on the end of her big toe, from which blood poured out onto the snow.

Shaking with horror, Karan hurled the contents of the pot and the mug down the bank. For good measure she washed them out with clean water, three times. Then she rebuilt the fire, gathered huge quantities of wood and built another fire nearby. She burned the remainder of the hrux and searched her pack in case there was more.

Another piece was trapped in one of the side seams, down near the bottom. Karan fished it out and put it to her lips, only realizing what she was doing at the last minute. Even then it was hard to put it down, not to eat it, and the longer she held it the harder it became, until with a great effort of will and revulsion she hurled it into the hottest part of the fire and watched it shrivel away to nothing.

Karan fixed her bleeding, throbbing toe and made another pot of chard—plain, ordinary, bitter old chard. She sat between the two fires, revelling in the unpleasant flavor until all the hrux aftertaste left her mouth, the last semblance of warmth was gone from her lips and belly, and the inside of her head no longer glowed.

I will not come! she said to herself. *You underestimate me, Rulke. I will fight you to the end.*

Suddenly he was back in her mind, as horribly near as if he whispered in her ear. He seemed amused. *You are clever, little Karan, and I respect you for it. Enjoy your triumph while you may. One day I won't need to hide in Shazmak, and then I'll call for you again. Nothing will stop me then.*

"Get out!" she shrieked aloud. "Get out of my mind. You'll never find me."

I don't need to, he chuckled. *You will come of your own accord, when the time is right.* Then he was gone.

She sank to her knees beside the fire, thanking her luck that most of the hrux had fallen out in the snow at Carcharon and been lost; and that she found the taste so unpleasant. Otherwise by now she would be in Shazmak, or on her way there, prisoner and addict. Or dead from it. And she had learned something useful too. Rulke had fled to Shazmak with his construct. Llian was safe for the moment; perhaps they both were. She could sleep easier for that. Unless he was lying. Unless he was hunting her now.

The snow began to fall heavily, enough to cover her tracks. Karan slipped into her sleeping pouch, pulled it up around her shoulders and sat sipping her chard. Finally she fell into a sleep tormented by nightmares even more strange and hallucinatory than her previous one.

14

A FEAST IN THE FOREST

In the morning Karan continued. Several more times she sensed those strange, fractured, word-and-picture sentences, and knew that the Ghâshâd were still looking for her. She finally reached the cottage in the late afternoon. It was snowing again but the wind had swung around to the east and over in that direction, toward Thurkad, the cloud was beginning to break up. The morrow promised good weather, not what she wanted at all.

She had been to the hut as a child. It had seemed much larger then. Now she saw that it was small, rustic and in need of repair. It was just a one-roomed cottage built of stone gathered nearby, roughly shaped slabs of schist laid flat like brickwork and held together with burnt limestone mortar. The roof, which overhung two tiny window holes, was clad in green slate crusted with lichen. Many of the slates were slipping. The roof overhung the windows. A scrap of veranda faced the escarpment.

To the east the forest thinned. She could see grass and

heath through the trees. In front of her the escarpment curved around to run east-west. Below and beyond was the endless expanse of Faidon Forest butting up against the mountains. Not far west the mountains rose up sheer and bare, for here the plateau was only a few hundred paces wide.

Karan took her pack inside. The earth floor was pitted where the roof had leaked. There was a rude bench and stool, and a small supply of dry wood stacked on the hearth. It must have been there for ages because as soon as she struck sparks to tinder it blazed up. There was nothing to eat of course, and her own supplies were almost gone now.

In a minute, smoke began to belch out into the room. None seemed to be going up the chimney at all. It must be blocked. Just what I need, Karan thought wearily.

She climbed onto the roof, clambered up the chimney and peered inside. It was completely clogged with old bird nests and leaves. Karan got down again, searching for a long stick to poke the mess through into the fireplace. Before she found one there came a furious roar and flames leapt out the top of the chimney. The accumulated rubbish was on fire.

Nothing she could do about it. She had experienced chimney fires before, and knew that they weren't dangerous as long as the chimney was properly built. On the other hand, the clouds of smoke made an unmistakable signal, should anyone come this way looking for her. Going inside, she stood by the warmth.

Putting water on to boil, she watched the fire gloomily, munching a lump of cheese. She'd have to go looking for food in the morning. Karan contemplated that prospect without enthusiasm. Precious little to find at this time of year, up here.

After her tea, Karan busied herself gathering wood and stacking it on the veranda until there was enough for a week of bad weather, always a risk in the mountains. Making a broom by binding dry reeds to a stick, she swept the earthen floor and removed the accumulated cobwebs. She carried water from a trickle issuing out of a gully below her, until the cauldron on the fire was full. By then it was dark. Food she could do nothing about until the morning. Tomorrow she would repair the roof, if the weather allowed.

She sat down by the fire. The room stank of burnt soot. Everything that could be done to occupy her mind had been done. She felt neither sleepy nor hungry. All she could think of was what she had done back in Carcharon, and wonder what would be the consequences of it.

She dozed, only to be woken by a sharp crack. Karan sprang up, searching for the source of the noise. Crack, crack, *crack* came from the chimney, then one whole side fell out into the snow. The chimney blaze must have weakened the mortar.

Wind howled in the gap, sending sparks, ash and smoke billowing through the room. Karan ran outside to see if she could plug the opening, but the stones proved too hot to handle. Going back inside she skimmed floating ash and charcoal off the top of her pot and made chard. It tasted like sooty mud. The hut was frigid now. Curling up in her sleeping pouch in the most sheltered corner, she closed her eyes.

She could not get to sleep. Was the Forbidding still the same now that Rulke had punctured it? What about the creatures that had escaped? One man was dead, at the least. If she'd not helped Rulke, he would still be alive. What other tragedies had resulted from her betrayal?

A little short-tailed mouse crept out of a crevice beside the fireplace, its pointed snout questing this way and that. Sitting up on its hind legs, it twitched its nose. Intelligent eyes watched her.

Karan flicked a scrap of cheese at it. The mouse scurried

back to its hole, displaying a fluffy white flag of tail. After peeping out of the crack for some time, it darted out, seized the morsel in its front paws and sat up, eating it delicately. Karan tossed it another piece and went back to her deliberations.

The revelations about her father were another puzzle. Had Basunez discovered some great secret up there? No doubt that Galliad thought he had, and had lost his life trying to find out. Karan couldn't help but feel that there was more to it, though—that somehow everything was connected, including her, the triune!

Hunger woke her at dawn. It was a fine day and she spent all morning searching for food but found absolutely nothing. After lunch, eel and onion and not much of either, she attempted to repair the chimney. More had collapsed after the fire cooled, and now she was faced with a hole larger than a door.

With no mortar to stick it together again, the best she could do was attempt a dry-stone wall, but that would take more stone than she had. It turned out to be an incredibly slow process and her fingers were raw by the time darkness put an end to the work. The job was not even half done.

The next day passed the same way. Again her search found no food. She used up all the stone, managing to block the gap sufficiently to keep the fire alight, though it gave no warmth unless she squatted right in front of it.

By the following day the need for food was becoming desperate. None of the trees nearby was of a kind that bore nuts, and she saw not a single animal track in the snow. The land here seemed to have been sterilized of anything edible, but she was afraid to go too far from the hut. Every footprint in the snow was a signpost to her enemies.

* * *

Her nights were troubled by dreams of Rulke—lingering effects of hrux, no doubt—where he appeared, always good-humored, and called her back to him. And despite her resistance she always went.

Her options were running out as rapidly as her food. She was not so pleased with the mouse these days, for it had eaten the remaining piece of her eel. Karan was constantly hungry now. Tomorrow she'd have to leave, no matter who was looking for her. There was nowhere to go but to Gothryme. She was aching for home but dreading it, too, with this burden of guilt hanging over her.

She went out the back for firewood, savagely attacking a small dead tree. It was hard work, because her hatchet was blunt and she had no sharpening stone. She gave a last hack and the tree fell, to splinter on the ground. The trunk split open. There was not much firewood in it, for inside it turned out to be full of fat white grubs nesting in digested wood.

You can eat wood grubs, if you're hungry enough. Her father's voice was in her head, from one of their camping trips in the mountains. He had always been pointing out such things—where to find water, or honey, or bird nests, what could be eaten and what must be left alone.

She eyed the grubs. Each was as big as her thumb, with a swollen body that was purple on the end, tiny brown stubs of legs and brown mouth parts at the front of its blind head. Somehow she couldn't imagine eating it. But surely grub was better than starving.

Gathering the grubs into her jacket, Karan hurried back to the hut. There she spilled her catch onto the bench and stared at the creatures.

Some of them started to wriggle, a blind questing about, as if reluctantly woken from hibernation. She picked one up, brought it to her mouth and put it down again. She arranged the grubs in rows. She changed the rows into a circle, then into lines that spelled out her name, then Llian's.

Her stomach hurt. Got to have something to eat! She closed her eyes, brought the grub to her lips again and her eyes came open involuntarily. The swollen white and purple body twitched disgustingly. Closing her eyes again she forced it into her mouth. It lay on her tongue while she tried not to vomit. Suddenly Karan felt a sharp pain. The wretched creature had bitten her. She tried to spit it out but it would not let go, even when she accidentally crushed it between her teeth.

The grub burst like a grape, flooding her mouth with what felt like thick, bitter jelly. It was disgusting! Gagging, she spat it into the fire, ripped the mouth parts off her tongue and washed her mouth out with cold chard.

She was about to fling the grubs out the door when it occurred to her that she should have cooked them. She dried her chard pot, threw the grubs in and put them on the edge of the fire to bake. It did not take very long. Picking one out, she found it withered, brown and reduced to a third of its former size. It smelled like food.

She was salivating. Karan popped the grub into her mouth, crunched it up and found that it now had a rather pleasant, sweet nutty flavor, though it felt rather scratchy as it went down. The legs, she supposed. She had just put a handful in her mouth when out of the corner of her eye she glimpsed a tall figure going past the window hole. She snatched up a half-rotten piece of wood, her only weapon. How had this intruder come so close without her talent warning her?

The door was thrust open with a creaky groan. She raised her stick.

"Karan, is it you?"

"Glmph!" she said with her mouth full. She swallowed furiously. "Tallia!"

Dropping her weapon, Karan embraced Tallia like a lost sister. "How did you find me?"

"What are you doing here?"

"Hiding! The Ghâshâd are after me." Karan moved the pot so Tallia could not see the contents.

"I think they've given up. I haven't seen any sign of them for a couple of days."

"You mean I can go home?"

"First thing in the morning!" Tallia said cheerfully.

"Well, come have some chard and tell . . . Is Llian all right?"

"Yes, though Carcharon was a disaster we haven't recovered from."

And I caused it, Karan thought, sobering up rapidly. "What happened?"

"It was a rout!" said Tallia.

"Oh!" Karan said.

"Why did you go to Carcharon, Karan?"

"Surely Llian told you?"

"He did, but I'd like to hear your version."

Karan had an inkling that things had not gone as well as she'd expected for Llian. "To bargain with Rulke for him. It was the only way to free Llian. And the strange thing was, Rulke never really wanted him at all. You were all wrong about that. It was me he was after, all along."

"What for, Karan? Why did he want you so badly?"

Karan did not want to talk about it, but Tallia's eyes burned into her, and Karan knew she could keep the secret no longer. "I'm triune!" she whispered, expecting Tallia to shrink from her in horror or disgust. "I also have a Faellem ancestor."

Tallia could not contain her astonishment. "*Triune!*" She

began to pace up and down, darting Karan sideways glances. "That explains . . . a lot. Mendark and I often wondered about you. And then what happened?"

"Once Llian was free I had to do my part of the bargain. I found the Way between the Worlds for Rulke, but everything went wrong."

"So Llian talked you into going to Carcharon?"

"Don't be stupid! It was my idea! I was sneaking out when he caught me and refused to let me go by myself. Llian was magnificent!" Karan's eyes shone. "You should have seen him! It was the bravest deed I've ever seen, the way he faced Rulke like that. Of course in the end it came to nothing. Where is Llian now? Is he safe?"

"He was when I left him in Gothryme," said Tallia carefully. She sat down at the bench.

Remembering the grubs, Karan grabbed the pot. "Tea?" she asked casually.

"What are you eating?" said Tallia. "Can I have some?"

"Haven't you got any food?" Karan held the pot well away, mortified at nearly being caught.

"Plenty!" said Tallia. "I just wondered . . ."

Karan casually emptied the grubs into the back of the fire, washed the pot out and filled it with water. They drank their chard from a pair of wooden mugs, rudely carved by some previous inhabitant. "How did you find me, Tallia?"

Tallia explained what she was doing up here. "I've been enjoying my freedom, to be perfectly honest."

"Carcharon has been abandoned, you say?"

"It was when Shand and I came up. That was on the fourth day after hythe, three days ago. Anyway, this morning, as I wandered near the edge of the escarpment about a league from here, I chanced across a small footprint in the snow. It was quite fresh; who else could it have been but you?" "It wasn't me," said Karan. "I came though the forest. And it's snowed since then."

"That's curious." Tallia sipped her tea. "I had no idea where to look so I just continued along the edge of the cliff. Even then I only discovered the hut by accident."

"A small footprint?" Karan exclaimed. "That rules out Rulke or any of the Ghâshâd. There's no one missing from Gothryme? No child or girl?"

"Not when I left. Everyone was keeping close to the manor, with the thranx about. I'm hungry. Let's see what we've got."

There was plenty: an uncut loaf, still wrapped in waxed cloth and relatively fresh; a small wheel of hard cheese, very pungent; dried meat, two kinds—one plain, the other pickled in hot spices. Tallia had the northerner's taste for spicy foods. She also had some salt fish, as well as a whole side of smoked fish.

"Smoked *fish*!" said Karan. "I stole some smoked eel from Carcharon and I can still taste the wretched stuff."

"You should have known better than snaffle the food that *they* eat, but don't dismiss mine so lightly. Bamundi is the best of all fishes, and this is the best smoked bamundi. The food of princesses."

"Smoked bamundi?" said Karan. "I don't know . . ."

Tallia pretended regret. "Suit yourself. I'm a glutton when it comes to the stuff. You know, I can't help thinking that Shand must have sneaked it out of Mendark's supplies."

"Mendark's bamundi! That's entirely different. I think I will try some."

Tallia smiled and continued pulling things out of her pack: a box of pastries filled with nutmeal and honey and flavored with blossom water. Karan was especially fond of sweet things. A bag held various spices wrapped in twists of paper. Other packets contained dried fruits and vegetables.

"In fact there seems to be everything we need for a feast, except only onions. It's quite impossible to eat smoked bamundi, especially that finest of all fish, stolen from the Magister's own larder, without onion."

Karan, who, despite her delight about the feast spread out in front of her, had been feeling more and more delinquent about her hostly duty to provide, looked up with a grin.

"I have two onions," she said cheerfully. "One each."

"Excellent! Now look what I found in Carcharon." Tallia handed Karan her knife. Karan felt quite sentimental and embraced her once more.

"Dear Malien gave that to me. I was lost without it. Do you have any more surprises?" she asked in a voice muffled by the front of Tallia's coat.

"Well, I wouldn't call it a surprise, but it will finish the feast off perfectly." Tallia reached into the bottom of her pack to retrieve a metal flask that Karan recognized.

"Yes, it's Shand's. The amount he drank while we were at Carcharon, I didn't think he'd begrudge me the rest."

Privately Karan thought that was a bit mean, but it wasn't going to stop her enjoying it when the time came.

Karan sipped her coffee, nibbled at a pastry and had a tiny sip of Shand's magical liquor. She tossed scraps to the short-tailed mouse, which had become friendly. Karan was glad to share her dinner with it now, and with the tiny heads sticking out of the crevice beside the fire. She did not know where to begin, just knew that she felt terribly guilty.

Suddenly she stretched out her arms across the table. "I know I've done wrong, Tallia. Take me—I won't resist."

Tallia pushed her hands away. "It's not my place to judge. Just tell me what you did."

"Llian matters more to me than anything. But now I'm afraid. How many people have died because of the thranx?

How many more before it's put down? How will the world be changed?"

Tallia reached across and put her finger across Karan's lips. "What happened?"

Karan took another big sip of her coffee and a small sip of the liquor and began her story. It turned into a very long tale, for though it began in Carcharon it reached back a lot further, and out in all directions—back to her childhood, to her half-Aachim father Galliad, to Tensor and the Aachim. It touched on the Nightland, and on what Tensor had revealed to her that night in the Dry Sea, and on her poor sad mad mother too. But especially on Llian and her love for him that was stronger than the earth.

Llian's every seeming act of duplicity was turned over and examined—in the Nightland, the night in Tullin, even the incident in Shazmak where he had searched her room for the Mirror. All were brought out into the light, examined, left on the table, and finally dismissed. All his splendid deeds were reviewed too: burning down the house in Narne, at the top of the tower at Katazza, his torments in Gothryme. Last and greatest of all, his magnificence in Carcharon. Her eyes were shining when she described Llian's telling.

"After all that, how could I do less for him?"

"I see you have glossed over Mendark's role in this," Tallia observed. "Please don't omit that part."

Karan sighed. "You are his deputy."

"I prefer the blunt Karan. Be honest with me."

"From the moment I met Mendark I mistrusted him, as he hated me. Now I despise him!"

"He doesn't hate you, Karan. It's just that you won't do what he wants. He has to command; to dominate and be known for his power."

Karan made fresh chard and passed Shand's flask to Tallia. They each took a generous swig.

"Had we succeeded," said Karan, "it would have been one of those deeds that are sung about in the sagas. But we didn't."

"It will be sung about nonetheless," said Tallia.

"Probably. The Aachim have a great admiration for the noble failure, more than for the all-conquering hero. Maybe that's why I still feel a trace of respect for Tensor, in spite of all his follies. Anyway, it's over now, and so is my part in the whole affair. I'm going home, and then I'm going to shut my door and have nothing more to do with the world. All I want is to look after my land and my garden, and begin to repair the damage of the war. And most of all—"

"You can't," Tallia interrupted. "You are one of the great now. The world won't let you shut it out."

Karan laughed nervously. "Nonsense. I'm just a poor farmer who can't pay her taxes. And I—"

"The great are made by their deeds! People look up to you, and I'm one of them. You have a duty to aid your country and your world. I'm sorry? What were you going to say?"

Karan was very still. "It hardly matters," she whispered. "All this turmoil and trouble, and it's not finished yet. *It's the wrong time!* What will become of Gothryme after I die? I desperately want to have a child."

Tallia spoke without thinking. "But triunes are sterile!"

Karan went as still as a statue, and the blood slowly drained from her face until she resembled a marble mask. "You have just taken away my future."

Tallia could have bitten her tongue out at the root. She sprang up but Karan stopped her with her hand. They remained in their respective positions for ages, then Karan gave a great shuddering sigh and wiped the tears away.

"Thank you for telling me," she said in a tiny voice. Now she understood Rulke's reaction when she had told him.

Tallia said no more. They were each silent, sipping their liquor and staring into the flames. Outside, the wind had come up and began to rattle the door. Karan put a block of wood against it, threw more wood on the fire, took another of the honey pastries and sat down again.

"How is Llian?" She made an effort to keep emotion out of her voice.

"Well enough, considering."

Another long pause. "And there were no . . . problems after he . . . came back without me?"

"It looked bad when he returned and you did not." Tallia did not go on.

Karan paced the room. She squatted down abruptly in front of Tallia. "There's something you're not telling me. Was he treated well? Mendark found him, you say?"

Tallia looked embarrassed and ashamed. "When the thranx burst out he was left behind. He nearly froze to death, and his legs were badly injured from the shackles."

"He was abandoned, in chains, on that terrible night?" Karan whispered. "Oh, Tallia, did no one care what happened to him?" She buried her face in her hands, living what Llian must have gone through as only a sensitive could.

"I make no excuses. It was chaos when the thranx came."

"Go on!"

"The lorrsk attacked us. Karan, it would take half the night to tell you all that happened before we got back to Gothryme. But Llian was recovering well when we left."

"You left him in Yggur's and Mendark's care? His enemies?"

"Many things have changed."

"Not enough!" said Karan coldly. "Be warned, Tallia, *anyone* who has harmed Llian is *my* enemy. I'm going at dawn, whatever the weather. You can please yourself."

15

Reality and Illusion

Karan had withdrawn into herself, brooding on Llian's sufferings. She responded to Tallia with just grunts or nods. After a while Tallia gave up and they walked along in a difficult silence for hours.

It was a miserable day. The sun had come out briefly at dawn but then the wind turned back to the west, spilling down the mountain and spitting sleet at them, hard little pellets like grains of rice. Even had they been of a mind to talk it would have been difficult, the way the wind howled in the treetops.

It had snowed heavily during the night and the forest was knee-deep in new snow, a fluffy carpet that concealed humps and hollows, fallen trees and ankle-twisting gullies. At midmorning they passed into a stand of elderly conifers, strange trees whose blade-like needles sprouted in semicircles like dancers' fans, directly from the black branches. As the pair trudged along, the day grew more gloomy. No matter how they hurried they did not seem to be getting anywhere. Every direction looked the same.

"We're lost," said Karan, coming out of her introversion. She leaned against a sapling, which dropped a clot of snow onto her shoulders. They hadn't gone much further, floundering in soft snow, before Tallia tripped over a rock, barking her shin.

"Ow!" she yelped, pulling up her trouser leg to reveal a straight cut that oozed a few drops of blood.

"Funny-shaped rock!" She brushed the snow off to reveal a hexagon of stone.

They cleared the snow away from the sides. It was a pillar like a flat-topped obelisk with writing down each side, names and dates in angry letters.

Clearing the snow out of the rudely formed characters, Karan read them aloud. "Here fell Tartim and Tartam, Hulia and Dalan, Mellusinthe and Byrn. Cursed be the name of Basunez and his workings until the seventh eternity."

"Mellusinthe!" said Tallia. "That's like your middle name, Melluselde. Was she—?"

"She was one of Basunez's seven grandchildren," said Karan, shivering. "They all were. They came up here to picnic in the forest. The oldest was only eighteen. Six of the seven died here, torn to pieces by a mountain cat, it says in our family histories."

"Then why does it curse Basunez?"

"I have no idea. That was long ago. When I studied my family histories this was just another tragedy that no one knew much about. At least I know where we are now. Let's get on."

But as they continued, Karan found herself drawn back to the children picnicking in the forest, wondering what had really happened to them. She could almost hear their cries for help, nearly sense their terror. Mountain cats had never been common here, nor did they attack with such indiscriminate violence. After seeing the statues at Carcharon, she had an unpleasant idea. *What had Basunez let out?*

After a few more hours of labor they found themselves in a part of the forest where the ground sloped down into a tangle of gullies. It began to snow even harder. Several times Karan went to turn one way around a rock or a fallen tree, only to realize that her feet had taken her in the opposite direction. It's like walking around the top of a funnel, she said to herself. The way I want to go is always the hardest, but I'm afraid of the easy option.

She stopped abruptly. "This is crazy! I know this forest, but I haven't got the faintest idea where we are."

Tallia jerked her thumb to the east. "If we go downhill, sooner or later we must reach the edge of the escarpment."

Repressing her worries, Karan followed, but the further they went in that direction the thicker the forest became, until finally in front of them it turned into a pole thicket, the slender trees growing so close together that they had to squeeze between them side on.

The ground became even steeper. "Surely this must be the edge!" exclaimed Karan irritably. "The whole wood is only half a league wide here. We could walk through it in an hour or two."

"Look!" Tallia pointed. "An open space. We must be almost there."

"I don't remember it!" Karan pushed past her, anxious to get out.

"I feel stupid," said Tallia. "I walked right by here just yesterday."

"It's a very old forest. I doubt that a tree has been cut since Basunez's time. It's always felt strange to me. My father used to talk about it." Karan pressed on quickly.

She wriggled between the last poles, having to take off

her pack to do so, and found herself in a small dell, shaped like a bowl. The snow was smooth and white, with not a mark on it. In the center the thread of water they had been following tumbled into an oval pool, about as long as Karan was tall, and ran away again. Both rivulet and pool were frozen solid. It looked just like a bowl and spoon.

"How odd," she said, so distracted that she did not take account that the thicket continued on the other side, the poles if anything even more closely spaced than where she had entered.

She turned around to Tallia, who had been just behind her. "That's odd . . ." she began, but Tallia was nowhere in sight. "Must have been further over," she said to herself, heading to the right. There was no sign here either. No, she had been right the first time. There were her tracks emerging from the forest. A shiver crept down the back of Karan's neck. Perhaps Tallia had stopped to relieve herself, though it was odd that she had not sung out.

"Tallia," she called softly.

There was no reply. Dropping her pack on the snow, Karan followed her tracks back into the forest. At least she tried to, but the trees were much closer together. Karan couldn't even get her head between the trunks now. Yet the footprints went straight through.

"Tallia!" The shiver began again, starting at the top of her head and going down her back and her arms, and up again until every hair stood on end. She ran a few paces to her right, where the thicket seemed more open, but it turned out to be as impenetrable as everywhere else. She ran back the other way. Worse yet!

"Tallia," she cried despairingly.

The trees soaked up her voice. She had called as loudly as she could, but all she heard was a frightened squeak. Black clouds squeezed out the light. The clearing became gray and threatening. High above, the slender branches interlaced, cutting the sky into drab triangles.

Karan sat down on her pack, trying to think. Things like this did not happen of their own accord. They were *made* to happen. *But made by whom?* She whirled, as if someone had whispered behind her, but there was no one there.

"This is all an illusion," she thought suddenly. "I know how to deal with illusions. They can be disbelieved out of existence."

She marched back to the place where she had come out of the forest and walked confidently up to it, retracing her footsteps. She walked straight into a pair of trees, taking the impact on hip, shoulder and forehead so hard that her head rang. The poles were as solid as the bars of a cell. She might as well have been in one.

Rulke! she thought miserably. After that night with the hrux he knew where I was. All he had to do was bring the construct back to Carcharon, when he had done his more important tasks, and attend to this minor detail. How could she have expected otherwise? He needed her.

Karan squatted by the frozen pool, slowly coming to realize that it was not Rulke at all. Illusion was not his way. He would be much more direct. The prickling began to creep up the back of her neck again. She turned, the blood congealing in her veins. An even more deadly foe, though one she had almost forgotten about over the past half year. The one who had wanted her dead in Katazza, and in Thurkad even before that. *Faelamor!*

Tallia had been just behind Karan, but approaching the clearing she felt a sharp pain in her instep, as if something had bitten her. That was odd. There weren't any insects at this time of year. Pulling off her boot she found a welt on her instep, a dull red blotch about the size of a fingernail. It began to throb. Rubbing it only made it worse.

Tallia put her boot back on and continued, but soon was confronted by the problem that Karan had encountered: though the tracks continued on, the thicket was impenetrable. She could no longer see into the glade at all. Everything had become quite gloomy.

Once she heard a cry, as if someone a long way away had called her name, but it was no more than a whisper on the wind. Another time she saw a flash of movement that might have been Karan's red hair. Then as it grew darker she could no longer tell where the clearing was. Each time she blinked it seemed to recede further.

Tallia did not lose her presence of mind. Being an adept of the Secret Art herself, she recognized that this was illusion, and how cleverly she had been separated from Karan. Remembering the small footprint, she was almost certain that it was Faelamor. Illusion was a form of the Secret Art that many practiced but few mastered, and from the seamless nature of this one it had to be worked by a great master.

Tallia could not break the illusion but she knew what to do to minimise the bewilderment. Karan could not be far away. Noting the direction of the tracks, she made her own markings. Faelamor could only conceal what she knew was there.

She had no hope of breaking Faelamor's glamour but tried anyway: all the dispelling charms that she'd learned in her apprenticeship in far-off Crandor; other cantrips she'd learned from Mendark. Nothing made the slightest difference. The illusion was unshaken.

"Faelamor!" Karan whispered, realizing that she was defenseless. Her knife was in the bottom of her pack. She looked sideways at it.

"Don't!" said Faelamor, a small woman with skin like polished rosewood and eyes as deep as the spaces between the stars.

"What do you want of me?" Karan's voice wobbled, in spite of all attempts to show no weakness.

"To talk."

"Talk! In Katazza you wanted me dead."

"Things have changed. Perhaps I'll let you go, if you tell me what I want to hear."

"I have no idea what you want to hear," Karan said.

"Don't toy with me—you're *nothing*!"

"Ah," said Karan, "but a nothing who got away from Rulke."

"Brave words, from a liar, a cheat and a murderer."

This reminded Karan of another occasion when she had been so accused. "What you accuse me of, you have done a hundredfold. *You* betrayed Shazmak! Your crimes are legion."

"The Aachim are not our species," said Faelamor indifferently. "Anyway, they are failures, scarcely human. Nothing done to another species can be a crime, else every butcher and fisher on this planet would be in the dock."

"They are as human as you or I! And I realized something as I was departing Carcharon," Karan went on.

Faelamor was drawn. "What was that?"

"I realized that Rulke had been done an injustice," Karan said. "I never found him to act other than with the honor peculiar to his kind." This was not entirely true, but true enough to say to Faelamor. "The Charon fight for their very survival."

"So do we fight for the survival of our world and our species," she replied coldly. "What did you learn about the Charon?"

Karan sorted through her memories. "I saw Rulke's overwhelming power," she said. "He could crush you and your puny illusions in an instant. He made an opening in the Forbidding. Even a thranx out of the void fled in terror from the power of his construct."

The walls of the clearing shook. It might have been someone rattling at the pole-like trees. Faelamor took control again with a gesture that sent Karan's head spinning. "What's that?" cried Faelamor. "Who else is out there?"

"Tallia," gasped Karan, her head shrieking and unable to lie.

"She is strong," Faelamor conceded. She moved her fingers and the trees around the dell hardened into an impenetrable wall.

Karan felt very frightened. "What do you want of me?" she choked. The past few minutes had been just a game, a momentary distraction to Faelamor, and now she had shown just how potent she was. In Katazza Faelamor had wanted her dead and she still didn't know why.

Faelamor moved closer. Karan flopped on her face. She would sooner have faced Rulke again; at least his motives were comprehensible. At least he laughed. But not this enemy. Nothing seemed to crack that face like waxed timber. So cold; so unyielding. Did love matter to her? Did pain? Karan understood why Maigraith was the inhibited, closed-off person that she was, having been brought up from infancy by Faelamor. Was that why Maigraith had never been able to break away from her?

"Where's Maigraith?" she asked abruptly. "What have you done with her?

Faelamor ignored her. "What really happened in Carcharon?"

"Carcharon?" Karan stalled, trying to see where Faelamor was aiming.

Faelamor was not only humorless but impatient. Waves

of sickness crashed together in Karan's head, to burst like an over-ripe boil.

"He used the construct," Karan said between spasms, "to open the Wall of the Forbidding."

"I know that! What else did he do? What did he want you for?" The soft voice was a threat. The pressure grew greater. Karan gagged into the snow. She looked up at Faelamor, her eyes running.

"He wanted me to find the Way between the Worlds for him, the path to Aachan."

"So!" said Faelamor in triumph. "He cannot find it himself, despite his wonderful construct. I didn't think he'd be able to. That's very interesting news. *And did you find it?*"

The nausea was coming again, in waves each bigger than the previous. Karan choked; her eyes flooded; her face went red and white. Despite what Rulke had done, Faelamor was far worse. She wasn't going to give her a weapon to use against him or anyone. Could she disguise a small lie? Then make it part of the character that Faelamor believed she had.

"He tried to force me," Karan repeated. "He spent days training me for it. It was so *hard*! My mind could not hold what he wanted me to do. No mind could contain all that," she said, putting a whine into her voice. "I thought I understood it, and he thought I did, and we almost achieved it too." She looked dreamy for a second. "What a mind! What a man! You cannot understand what it felt like to work with him."

Faelamor looked contemptuous. "You're just like every other woman on this wretched planet. How Rulke must have sneered as you fell under his spell—the least of all spells. All he has to do is smile and look into their eyes and they swoon. Did you share his bed as well?" She bent down over Karan. "Disgusting whey-faced creature! Surely he would not sink so low!"

"But then I saw those awful things in the void," Karan went on, enhancing the little-girl whine. "They pressed up against the Wall, slavering and rending. I was *so* frightened, the way they stared at me! One actually came through the Wall! I had to get away. Rulke should never have put me in such danger." She almost broke into a lisp. Don't overdo it, she thought. "It wasn't my fault. He should have protected me better. I begged him but he ignored me. So I broke the link when he was on the way to Aachan. How was I to know what would happen?"

Faelamor's contempt was absolute. "How did Rulke let you live after such a craven display?" She gripped Karan by the coat and dragged her forward. "What happened then?" she burst out.

"I can hardly remember. Rulke was struggling to stop the Forbidding from tearing right open." Karan tried to convey an air of childlike stupidity. "There were monsters, horrid creatures everywhere. I heard him cry out 'Thranx!' and a great winged man-beast sprang at him. They fought and he blasted it with the construct. It fled, but others came. Lorrsk! he called them, and while Rulke was struggling with them I ran away. I escaped," she corrected primly.

"I was right about you the first time," Faelamor said. "Treacherous, whining little wretch! I almost feel sorry for Rulke, thinking that he could use you. How he must regret ever seeing you. But you've taught me a great deal. He tried and failed. His confidence must be shaken. *He's weak!* Not even a thranx would have cowed him before the Nightland.

"Hold on," she continued in afterthought. Faelamor was given to soliloquy. "Don't underestimate him! When she let go it would have been a terrible blow—it would have torn his mind." Yet Faelamor allowed herself to crow a little. "Rulke is weaker than I'd dare to hope, and now he'll have to look for a new sensitive. Well, what am I to do about this one? If it hadn't been for the warning about the triune, I might have let her go. One so treacherous would do my enemies more harm than me."

Karan sat listlessly in the snow, wiping her mouth on her sleeve. Her eyes were dull. "Perhaps it *is* better to be sure," Faelamor said, flexing her fingers.

Tallia was still trying to find a way around the illusion. She knew what kind it was now, and that helped a little. Sometimes she even caught a glimpse of them as they moved. She wondered how the glamour was formed. It certainly felt solid, but it could not *be* solid. Manipulating solid matter was an entirely different branch of the Secret Art, one even the most powerful rarely mastered.

She might have cut her way into the clearing, had she an axe, but somehow she doubted it. Probably she would be unable to strike what she was trying to cut. She considered all the ways she knew to break such glamours, but none would work against the greatest illusionist of all.

Suddenly a way occurred to Tallia. How cunningly it was made must depend on what Faelamor knew about them both. An illusion that was impregnable from all possible approaches required her to visualize each such attack and make something to foil it. But one that was proof against the mind of Karan, which Faelamor had some knowledge of, might not succeed so well against the very different mind and training of Tallia, whom she did not.

How high did the illusion go? The trees here were poles about the size of her upper arm, with only an occasional twig-like branch to right or left. She moved back beyond sight of the clearing, took off her boots and socks and packed the pockets of her jacket with cones. They were the feeblest of missiles but there was nothing better.

Choosing one of the more sturdy poles, Tallia began to

climb. It was hard work, for the other trees pressed in on her, snagging her clothing so that the climb was a perpetual struggle. Sometimes, with her heavy, swaying progress, her pole would clash against another, grinding her foot between their rough bark. She almost cried out the first time it happened. When she snatched her foot out, a strip of skin was gone from either side, and blood began to drip on the snow below.

The second time it happened she was better prepared, escaping with just a mashed big toe, and as the trunks narrowed and the bark grew softer she had no more trouble.

When she was high up, seven or eight spans, she found that the illusion did weaken, up where there had seemed no need for it. Tallia could see the clearing through the branches. She crept from one trunk to another, in mortal danger if she slipped. In a few minutes she was as close to the rim of the clearing as she dared go, only a few trees from the edge. Parting the needles she peered down.

The illusion shimmered the air like a mirage but she made out Faelamor and Karan some distance away, across the other side of the dell. Faelamor's back was toward her and Karan was facing her way, though she looked dazed and fell down several times.

Tallia felt a cone out of her pocket and weighed it in her hand. It wasn't much of a weapon. Moreover, the twigs and branches were still too dense to get a good shot. It would have to be perfect, with such an inadequate missile. In Karan's present state she might not be able to help herself.

Karan fell again, and this time did not get up. Tallia hurried from trunk to trunk, gripping the thin poles with fingers and toes. She reached the edge of the clearing and drew back her arm. The pole swayed alarmingly under her. For an instant she thought it was going to snap. It did not, but to her horror the tree bent outward and kept going, for there were no trees to support it on that side. It accelerated under her weight. The snow rushed toward her.

She would land well behind Faelamor and probably injure herself. Grasping the opportunity, Tallia pushed herself off and up like a pole vaulter. The pole snapped back, she arched through the air and as Faelamor turned at the noise she struck her in the chest with her knees and all her weight behind them.

Faelamor went down as if she'd been charged by a bull and lay still with her face in the snow. The impact shook Tallia too. She wrenched Faelamor's hands behind her and bound them.

"Karan! Are you all right? Quickly, she might come round any second."

Karan sat up, looking dazed. She felt dizzy but the nausea was gone. The trees no longer appeared to be close together. The illusion had disappeared. They could walk out any way they chose.

"What are we going to do with her?"

"I know what we should do," Karan said.

Tallia silently handed her a knife.

"*Should do*, I said. Not *will do*. I can't kill a helpless person, not even *her*."

They turned her over. Faelamor was unconscious but breathing. "Leave her, then," Tallia said, "Stop her mouth and blindfold her. That will curb her powers."

They did that, quickly, and by the time they'd finished she was beginning to stir. "Come on!" Tallia screamed. They ran across the clearing, gathered Karan's pack and dived into the forest. There they stopped and looked back. Faelamor was moving her legs and arms, seemingly testing her bonds.

They collected Tallia's pack. "Oh, your poor feet," said

Karan. They were bruised blue and bloody; every step left blood on the snow.

"They hurt like blazes."

Tallia dragged her socks and boots on. The leather was stiff from the cold. They fled. Before they had gone very far there was a cry from behind. It shivered Karan's insides. Faelamor was in helpless agony, dying all alone. Karan felt all confused and twisted up inside. She stopped and would have run back.

"No!" cried Tallia, catching her wrist in an iron-hard grip.

"But she's hurt. She's in terrible pain. I can't leave her to die all alone."

"Don't be ridiculous!" Tallia spat, dragging her the other way. "She's calling you back. Her voice conjures illusions as powerful as any other. Once we're beyond hearing she can't harm you."

Karan looked distressed, feeling that she ignored a desperate entreaty, but they ran on and heard nothing more. Even after they were long out of hearing Karan felt the piteous pleas tearing at her sensitive self, then suddenly the strangeness about the landscape died away. They were safe.

They ploughed through the snow-clad heath to the edge of the cliff, a landmark nothing could disguise. They followed the winding, gully-cut edge all day, and the next. When they reached the cliff path just on dark, Karan kept going. Fretting for Llian, she went down the dangerous path at a trot.

"Wait," Tallia shouted. "This is madness. You'll kill yourself."

"Llian needs me."

"Not like this, you fool. All right, go! But I'm not going with you."

Karan stopped and waited, her breast heaving, until Tallia caught up to her. From then on they went down at a safer pace. Once at the bottom Karan was off again, running, and Tallia jogged beside her without complaint though her feet were killing her. They reached Gothryme after the middle of the night.

There was a single light on in Gothryme Manor, coming out through the shutters of the study where old Rachis kept the books. The doors were barred, so Karan rapped twice on the timbers, once, then thrice more, the knock she always used.

The shutter creaked open. "Karan!" wheezed the old man. "Is it really you?"

"It is me," she said, "whole and safe." She sprang up onto the sill and dropped lightly to the floor. "And here is Tallia back again too."

Rachis tottered and flopped back into his chair. "This is a dream surely. After hythe, and the news from Carcharon—"

"The news was wrong. It's so good to be home." She helped Tallia through the window, whereupon Tallia fell down on the floor, groaning.

"Oh, Tallia," said Karan guiltily. "I forgot all about your poor feet." She bent down and began to unfasten the laces. "Is there hot water, Rachis?"

"The cauldron is on the kitchen fire." He went out.

Tallia's socks were stuck to her lacerated feet with blood and had to be bathed off. The injuries were not serious, though rather painful. Karan chuckled to herself as she dabbed the wounds with ointment and bound up Tallia's feet.

"I don't see what there is to laugh about," Tallia said morosely.

"I was lying in the snow back there in the glade. I looked up and saw the tree falling, and you clinging there in abject terror."

"A hallucination," Tallia said sourly, "coming out of Faelamor's illusion."

"The whole top of the tree arched down," grinned Karan, "and your mouth was so wide open in your terror that I could see your tonsils."

"Nothing of the sort," said Tallia. "It was just the wind blowing my lips apart."

"Abject terror," Karan repeated, then giggled. Rachis smiled too. "The most marvelous thing I've ever seen. I could see that you were trying to distract Faelamor by flying head first into the snow, leaving me to rescue us both, but at the last minute she walked right under you. How I admired you. Had you flapped your wings I'm sure you could have flown."

"Someone has to get you out of the messes that you persist in getting yourself into," said Tallia. "So you shouldn't quibble about the means."

Karan roared with laughter. "I can't wait to tell Llian. Where is he?" She could think about nothing but falling into his arms.

"Llian was taken to Thurkad," Rachis answered.

"Taken? What do you mean?"

"For betraying you to Rulke."

PART TWO

16

AN UNUSUAL FORM OF TREATMENT

The ride to Thurkad was painful, not least because Llian knew he had failed Karan and would probably never see her again. But he never gave up hope. Every morning he woke thinking that today Tallia and Shand would appear with her, or at least with the news that she was still alive. Every night he went to his miserable blankets in despair that they had not.

The horse-drawn cart was unsprung and every bump on the road, every pothole, sent jagged pain up his legs. Lilis was driving the cart while Jevi sat beside her issuing unnecessary cautions. Malien escorted them on horseback. Yggur, Mendark, Nadiril and their entourage had left for Thurkad the previous day. The other Aachim had remained at Gothryme with Xarah, who was too ill to travel.

"Where do you stand in this business, Malien?" Llian had been wondering that for some time, for it had been months since she had taken any active part in the struggle against Rulke. She had been almost invisible since the failed attempt to seal the Nightland last summer.

She moved her horse over beside the cart. "After Tensor's folly, and our disaster down at the rift, I could not see the way. I thought it better to do nothing until it became clearer just what we were facing."

"It's pretty clear now," said Llian.

"But *I* can't combat Rulke's construct."

"Then what are you going to do?"

"Last autumn I sent messages east, by skeet, bidding my people come to a conference. After we get back to Thurkad I'm going across the sea to meet them. And what about you, chronicler? Where do you stand?"

"By Karan's side, of course!"

As she jogged along Malien reached over and turned his face to hers, peering into his eyes. After a long moment Malien let him go again. "I do believe you're telling the truth."

"Of course he is!" Lilis piped up. "Llian would not tell a lie about *her*!"

"Hush, Lilis," said Jevi. "This is not our business."

"Anything that happens to my friends is my business," she said furiously.

Malien moved her horse away from the cart and they continued in silence.

"Look out for that rock!" Jevi cried suddenly.

Pursing her lips, Lilis calmly steered around the obstacle. "I'm not five any more, Jevi," she said with just a hint of irritation.

"Are we in Mendark's domain already?" Llian called to Malien.

"I wouldn't think so, chronicler. Why do you ask?"

"No other realm spends so much on its leader and so little on the roads." He let out a tremendous groan.

"Pull over, please," Malien said to Lilis.

Lilis turned off the road, the cart wheels gouging deep tracks in the mud, and parked the cart under a leafless tree. Llian had slumped sideways in his seat.

"What's the matter?" Malien asked him.

"Every bump is like grinding broken glass into my legs."

Malien lifted his feet onto the front seat, drew up his trouser legs and began to unwrap the bandages. The left leg showed signs of healing but the right was terribly swollen and red.

"What do you think of this, Jevi? I dare say you've seen a wound or two in your time."

"Hundreds! I don't like the way the infection's got in there. Lilis, would you light a fire and get some water boiling. And be careful—"

Lilis's eyes flashed, but obediently she began to gather wood. They bathed the wound and smeared it with a paste of honey, crushed garlic and the lees from a flask of red wine.

"We're out of wine," said Malien. "Better buy some more at the next town. Do you think you could help us drink it, chronicler? Just so we can use the lees on your sores, you understand." She laughed. Llian's appetite for drink of any kind was well known.

"It's my only pleasure in life!" he said irritably.

While they were working, a throng of passers-by and fellow travelers had gathered around, staring at Llian and making jocular remarks about his probable fate.

"My cousin Marlie got the red-leg like that," said a vast, jowly woman of indefinable age. She rested her considerable bosom on the side of the cart. "A red line went up his leg to his groin, and the next we knew, it had dropped off."

"What, the leg?" asked her companion, a tiny bird-like

lady with a hideous wen on one eyelid. It looked like a third eye.

"Not his leg—*it*!" she cackled.

The small woman joined in. "What I heard, Marlie never had much use for it, even when he were a young man."

"Now Fasseli, on the other hand, he got it real bad from a wound like that," the big woman ruminated. "They cut his toes off, one by one, but do ye think that stopped it?"

"Don't know. Did it?"

"Not a bit," chuckled the big woman. "They took his foot next but the gangrene kept coming back. Treated it just like that ugly little bloke is doing here—garlic, red wine and all that. Didn't make a bit of difference. Before you knew it, the rot was up to his knee. And didn't it stink! Something putrid, it was; you couldn't even stay in the house!"

"Disgusting," said wen-eye. "You've got to chop quick and high, with the gangrene."

"Quick and high," agreed the big woman. "They took the leg off at the knee, and the next day at the hip, but it didn't make a bit of difference."

"It never does!" The small woman reached into the cart, prodding Llian's legs with her walking stick. "Take my advice, and whip them both off now, at the top. He'll be all the better for it."

Llian had been suffering their gossip in silence, but now he sat up abruptly. "Go away, you disgusting old hyenas!" he screamed.

"We were trying to help!" said the small woman. "Come on, my dear."

They continued up the road, though the big woman could not resist one last word over her shoulder. "You'll wish you'd listened to us, tomorrow."

* * *

Shortly the wagon headed off again and the torment resumed. So the day passed, and the next, with stops every few hours to bathe the wounds. The stops seemed to become more frequent, and the conferences between Malien and Jevi longer and with more head-shaking. Llian tried to read his journals but it was impossible to concentrate.

At lunchtime on the second day, Malien and Lilis were unwrapping the bandages yet again, when Lilis gave a choking cry. Malien went quite still, staring down.

"What is it?" Llian demanded, trying to sit up. Then the breeze carried a horrible smell to him, and he knew. It was rotting flesh—the women had been right. He had gangrene and Malien would have to cut his leg off, though he would probably die anyway.

Malien and Jevi went into another huddle. Lilis looked faint, but she came up and took his hand. "I'm sure you'll improve soon, Llian."

She knew better than that and so did he, but Llian went along with the pretense. "I expect you're right, Lilis. You wouldn't believe how often Malien has fixed me up, before this."

Malien came over, but not even she could joke now. "It's bad, Llian, and I don't know what to do. There are no medicines to fight gangrene. But don't give up yet. Sometimes the body does fix itself, so we'll go on for a few hours and see . . ."

"And if it's no better?" he asked desperately.

"We can't leave it any longer than that."

"You're going to chop my leg off."

"Not all of it," she said weakly.

By the next stop the small patch of bad flesh had grown perceptibly. Malien shook her head. "It's no use, Llian. I'll have to take the leg!"

"How . . . how are you going to do it?" he croaked.

"Do you really want to know?"

"Yes!"

"I'll cut through to the bone just here, below the knee, and sew up any blood vessels. Then, saw the bone through."

Llian studied his leg. In a few minutes it would be gone forever, thrown onto the fire like rubbish. He could not come to terms with it.

Malien was talking to Jevi. He nodded, mounted her horse with some difficulty, due to his arm being in a sling, and rode off. "He's gone to find someone with a saw," she said.

Again the passers-by gathered around, gawking and offering gratuitous advice. This time Malien shooed them away. They waited ages for Jevi to come back.

"There's still life, even with one leg," she said to Llian.

"How many do *you* have?" he replied bitterly.

Jevi came pounding up the road, riding the horse one-handed and yawing from side to side as if he was paddling a canoe. A long, two-handled saw was strapped to his back. Malien helped him down.

"This is all I could find," Jevi said. Its widely spaced teeth were more suited to sawing down a forest tree than cutting through bone.

"It will have to do," Malien said, frowning.

She and Jevi went into another huddle, during which they kept glancing back at Llian. He supposed they were deciding who would hold him down and who would do the cutting. They came up to the cart.

"Jevi has another idea," said Malien. "You might want to consider it, though . . . I'm not sure that I would." She shuddered delicately.

Jevi said nothing, though he glanced at Lilis, and away again.

"What is it?" screeched Llian. The travelers on the road looked around curiously.

"It's . . . you may find it disgusting," said Jevi, embarrassed, "but I saw it work once when we were shipwrecked on the Isle of Banthey. It's . . . maggots!"

"What about them?"

"They eat the dead flesh, cleaner than Malien or I can cut it away."

The idea was positively nauseating, but losing the leg was worse. "They actually eat the gangrene?"

"Love it, apparently," said Jevi, making a smacking sound with his lips.

"And it might save my leg?"

"It's a chance."

"I'd try anything in the world to keep my leg, even maggots," said Llian. "See if you can find some."

"Happens I already have," said Jevi, untying a leather bag at the saddlehorn. "There was a dead dog up the road . . ."

A dead dog! Llian wanted to vomit. "Get on with it!"

He couldn't watch as Jevi packed a handful of the white squirming things onto the wound and bound it loosely with a moist cloth. "What now?" Llian asked.

Malien, who looked decidedly ill, reached into the back of the cart and lifted out a huge flask of red. "Now we wait! Where's your mug, Llian?"

"I'll take mine out of the bottle." Raising the flask, he poured a hefty slug straight down his throat.

"What does it feel like, Llian?" Lilis asked.

"A bit ticklish around the edges!"

She went over to help Malien with the camp. Jevi sat across from Llian in the cart, evidently thinking that he needed company, though Jevi didn't actually say anything.

"How is your arm?" Llian wondered, trying to make conversation.

"Not so bad," said Jevi. He had never been heard to complain. In fact he had hardly spoken the whole trip, except to Lilis.

A long silence ensued. Llian gulped his wine, wishing Jevi would either say something or go away.

"I wonder how Tallia and Shand are getting on at Carcharon?" Llian said idly.

There was a flash of terror in Jevi's eyes, quickly hidden. How interesting, Llian thought. He's in love with her. I wonder I didn't realize it sooner.

"I hope Tallia's safe," said Llian. "She's a wonderful woman."

Jevi said something incoherent.

The wine began to work its magic. Llian, feeling a reckless thrill, pressed Jevi a bit harder. "You know," he said casually, "I think Tallia might be in love with you."

Jevi choked. "Don't be stupid! How could *she* love me? She's so—" he cried out incoherently. "Mind your own business, Llian!" He threw himself off the cart, heedless of his healing bones, and stumbled off into the scrub.

"Llian, wake up!

It was Lilis, shaking his shoulder. The sun was well up.

"What's the matter?"

"It's breakfast time."

He ate without noticing what he'd been given, and then Jevi began unwrapping the bandages. His hands were more articulate than he was, for they were careful and very gentle. Llian held his breath, expecting that putrid smell again. Jevi and Malien bent over the wound.

"How is it?" Llian demanded.

Malien shook her head. "I wouldn't have believed it."

"What?"

"The gangrene's gone, every bit."

Jevi held up one of the maggots, grinning broadly. "Fat little buggers, aren't they?"

Llian muttered something under his breath.

"What's that?" asked Malien. "Are you all right, Llian?"

Llian burst out laughing. He was dreadfully hung-over and didn't care. What a wonderful day it was. "I thought I might compose—decompose, ha!—an Ode to Maggots on the way to Thurkad. Let's go!"

17

The Apprentice Scribe

On the night of Llian's return to Thurkad a meeting was held in Nadiril's house, a splendid old villa set in its own grounds not far from the citadel. The journey had been exhausting for the old man and his chest still plagued him, while the thranx had cast a shadow over them all.

Mendark, Yggur, Malien and Lilis were also there. Yggur was clean-shaven and dressed in new blue robes, instead of his habitual black. He seemed keen to begin a new life as soon as possible. He held a mug of hot lasee, a weak yellow drink brewed from the sweet sap of the swamp sard tree. Steam curled up from the mug. He looked relaxed, and more confident than Mendark had ever seen him. The victory over the thranx had restored him to the noble Yggur he'd been before war and adversity had undermined him. The transformation was astounding, though Mendark wondered how long it would last this time.

Mendark stood beside the fireplace, sipping from a tiny bowl of gellenia, a very sweet, aromatic liquor that Shand distilled from fermented, over-ripe gellon. Stooping, he put the bowl down on the hob to warm. Its luscious peach-mango aroma filled the room.

Malien had a small glass bowl but she was not drinking. She sat back, admiring the colors in the glass, the golden liquor made red, orange and even purple by the firelight.

"How little there is between us and the void," said Nadiril, pushing himself up in bed. His pillows tumbled down. Lilis hurried to pack them in behind him.

"Thank you, child." He lifted a bloodless hand and let it fall on the covers. It made a gray blotchy lump against the snowy linen. "How easily we could be overrun."

"I want to talk about Llian," said Malien.

"Colorless Malien comes out of her shell at last," Mendark said irritably.

"Tensor taught me the failure of leadership, and you two the leadership of failures! Llian has been grossly mistreated."

"Is this guilt talking?" said Mendark.

"I do feel guilty," she replied. "Llian may be a great chronicler, but he's helpless out in the real world. I let him down at Carcharon."

"Bah!" said Mendark. "He wasn't so helpless when he led Karan up there to betray us."

"I know Llian, Mendark. I've looked into his heart, and he's innocent."

"If you'd seen him in Gothryme you might think differently," snapped Mendark. He felt that the whole room was against him.

"I'm no longer convinced either!" said Yggur. "You've been twisting the truth so long you don't know what it is any more."

"I stand on my reputation!" Mendark said furiously.

"Of course you do—you wrote it! You're a manufactured man, Mendark."

"And you're a miserable failure, Yggur!"

"The thranx would tell a different story," interjected Nadiril. "Look, Mendark, we see Llian differently now."

"I'll hear Karan's evidence before I agree," Mendark said. "Why would she give herself up to Rulke?"

"Because that's the way she is! I have to say, knowing Karan . . . well, she's not easily led." Malien sipped her drink.

"We're agreed then," said Nadiril. "This trial is over and Llian is to be freed."

"Very well," said Mendark. "Have your way, but he must be kept under house arrest until Karan returns, *or otherwise*!"

"I'll set some of my remaining Whelm to watch over him," said Yggur. "Vartila will supervise. Be assured that no harm will come to him, Malien."

Mendark forced himself to smile. The focus of power had shifted again. He felt insecure, while Yggur was resurgent. Since Havissard everything had gone wrong and he knew not how to make it right.

"Let's get to the real issue," said Yggur. "Rulke!"

"This construct freezes my blood," said Mendark, perched on his chair like a vulture on a fence. His shoulders and the fabric of the chair were covered in flakes of skin. "Rulke will annihilate us. We have no weapon to use against him. No defense!"

"Then let's get to work and find one!" said Yggur. Standing tall by the fire he looked twice the man Mendark was. His black hair swept his shoulders as he spoke. "He suffered a blow in Carcharon. Maybe he's not as great as he would have us think. It gives me new hope."

"What about Shand's plan," Malien reminded them, "to make the golden flute anew?"

"If we had a flute," said Mendark, "we could take him by surprise. Risk all to gain all—the construct!"

"The flute is not the equal of his construct," said Yggur. "All it can do is open gates from one place to another. The construct is a weapon and a defense as well. Besides, to make the flute we need Aachan red gold, and we don't have enough."

"Faelamor has plenty!" Mendark said, still bitter at the memory.

"Go play with your fantasies, Mendark!" Yggur scoffed as he strode to the door. There was no sign of his limp today. "In the *real* world I've an empire to manage and rebellions to put down, not to mention the thranx. It's been seen not far away, in Faidon Forest. I'm going after it in the morning."

Mendark, back in his room, knew he was right. The flute had to be remade. There was no other way.

But there's no gold! It positively screamed at him.

Even lying on his back, his joints burned. The last month felt to have aged him decades. The ride back to Thurkad had been torment. He limped into the bathroom to brush his teeth and caught sight of his face in the mirror. The sight was repulsive. He wanted to smash his fist through the glass. His life was running out rapidly and there was still so much to do! At the rate he was failing, he could be bedridden in months, dead within a year.

He wanted to lock the door and never come out again. The despair was not at his imminent death—he was looking forward to that, after the centuries he had lived. Death would be the ultimate experience, once his life's goals had been achieved.

But the greatest goal of all remained. Mendark loved his

city and his world with a passion, and could not die with the threat of Rulke hanging over it. Once that menace was finished forever, and Faelamor too, he would laugh in his grave.

He rang the bell and, when the servant came, called for his healers and spellbinders. While they labored, easing the knotted muscles and taut sinews, working their magic on his brittle bones and sandpaper joints, a plan began to come to life. Faelamor had the Aachan gold that should have been his. She was the key. But she was a mighty opponent. He'd need a lot of support and only one person could provide it.

Yggur had the people, the spies and the troops. He must manipulate him to find out where Faelamor's hideout was, then launch a raid on it with overwhelming strength and seize the gold. With that he would have the golden flute remade. And finally, the most daring stroke of all, he would make a gate to Shazmak and take the construct. That quest would probably fail, but if it succeeded it would establish his reputation for all time. And if by chance he *did* succeed, with the construct he could rid the world of the menace of Rulke and Faelamor forever. And Yggur, too, if he dared to stand in his way.

"Enough!" Mendark shouted, and silently everyone filed out again. They knew his needs and his moods by now. He paid enough to demand instant obedience. His body, when he slid off the table, felt better than it had in months. It wouldn't last, of course, but while it did he had plenty to do.

Encouraged that he finally had a workable plan, Mendark unlocked a small cupboard, inside which were a dozen flutes. Not magical devices—these were just musical instruments, though beautiful ones. Some were carved out of the rarest timbers the world could offer, others forged of precious metals. He selected one made of simple silver, a favorite, sat down in an armchair with a glass of brandy at his elbow and began to play.

Within minutes his swollen fingers were aching. Once he had been a master flautist, but Mendark had not played at all this last century. Two renewals ago. How the decades fleeted by!

He laid the instrument aside. His fingers had forgotten everything. The renewals must have erased the movements from his nerves. It sharpened his unhappy mood. Life and the world seemed to be slipping out of his control. All the more reason to secure his reputation while he still could. All the more reason to continue with his plan.

Mendark lay awake all night, brooding about his grievances and the lack of recognition for them. He had done great deeds for Santhenar, but his greatness, his service had not been acknowledged, and never would be. It was a festering sore. To be a part of the Histories, to have one's own strivings woven into that great tapestry, was the greatest honor anyone on Santhenar could wish for. Mendark was no more immune to that longing than any other.

Once the merest mention in a minor document had been enough to make him glow with pride. But as he grew older and more powerful, such mentions were an everyday occurrence that meant nothing. In fact they were worse than nothing, for they represented an accumulation of evidence that no doubt would be used to rewrite history one day, to show him for a fool or a scoundrel. He had to be recognized at a higher level.

Mendark had worked and schemed to have his role acknowledged in one of the great Texts of the Histories that every school student learned by heart. Eventually he achieved that goal too. But finally even that could not appease him, not even when he had his own chapter. Most important of all were the Great Tales. Then, long after Rulke was imprisoned in the Nightland, the tale of *The Taking of Rulke* was made, and at last Mendark had climbed the highest mountain of all. He was recorded in a Great Tale. His name and his deeds would be remembered whilever the Histories were kept.

But what had been, at the time, the pinnacle of his life's achievements had long since ceased to satisfy him. Like any other addiction he wanted more and more. He knew that he deserved more. The chroniclers had been ungenerous with their praise. The honor that should have been his had been spread over a dozen lesser folk, playing down his heroic deeds as they exaggerated everyone else's.

How could this be remedied? It would take no less than his own Great Tale to set out all his deeds, but the chroniclers were an unbiddable lot who allowed no interference in their affairs. Only they could agree that a tale was worthy of being called a Great Tale, and it was hundreds of years since they'd last done so. Like sainthood, to be immortalized in one's own Great Tale was something that happened only after death. Mendark did not mind that—it was posterity he was concerned with—but history tended to be rewritten. Unless he made sure of it, his tale might never be written, or written in an unfavorable light.

Well, not to be recognized is the fate of reformers. I can bear that. But when I'm dead, I can't bear to think that others will steal the credit for all I've done, and leave my name burdened with the failures and follies of the Council.

I *will* have my own Great Tale! No one deserves it more than I do. And I have the instrument right here under my thumb—Llian! He owes me for the years I supported him at the college. It won't be easy—the chroniclers are jealous of their independence—but it can be done. It must! The tale we're in now will be a Great Tale, not the *Tale of the Mirror* but *Mendark's Tale*! With these mostly comforting thoughts he slipped into sleep.

Llian was held in a ground-floor room in the citadel. It was small but clean and even had a barred window. Outside was a walled yard with a single leafless tree, an ancient thing with a warty trunk and knobbly twigs like rheumatic fingers.

At first light, Mendark appeared at Llian's door. "Your time has come, chronicler!"

"What do you mean?" asked Llian carefully.

"I want my tale told. The future must know how I've sacrificed myself for the world."

The very idea! "I'm busy with the *Tale of the Mirror* at the moment," said Llian.

"Good. You can change the name to *Mendark's Tale*, since at the heart it's the tale of my life."

Llian was thunderstruck at his arrogance. "The college would never allow it. I suggest that you employ a commercial teller."

"You ungrateful wretch! It's my tale, and you owe me fifteen years' service!" Mendark roared.

Llian felt like punching the Magister in the mouth. Instead he limped to the window, looking out as he tried to control his fury. The guards outside could not save him if Mendark really wanted him harmed. Then it occurred to him that this might be the way to find out what had really happened at the time of the Forbidding, and at Rulke's imprisonment too. Maybe he could play on Mendark's weakness to get documents that no one else had ever seen. But he would have to be careful.

"I'm well aware of my debt," said Llian. "Send down your records and I'll consider it. But, even should I agree, you know what the master chroniclers are like. Every fact must be proven— they will check the evidence themselves.

You must give me every document I ask for, and nothing will be changed save what can be proven to be wrong. Without these conditions, even if it turns out to be the greatest tale of all, it will never become a Great Tale."

Mendark looked furious, but before he could speak Yggur appeared at the door. "Of course!" said Mendark rather too quickly. He gave an insincere smile.

"This is incredible!" snapped Yggur. "The world is falling to pieces around us and all you can think of is your reputation. What will Rulke be doing while you two make your fairy tales together?" Spitting on the floor by Mendark's boot, he went out again.

The next day, Llian was sitting at his table by the window. He had made a start on sorting the first crate of Mendark's papers, but his heart was not in it. He could not concentrate for thinking about Karan. There came a tentative rap on the door.

"Come in!" he shouted, not getting up. His healing legs were extremely painful, every step pulling at the scoured and sunken flesh.

Lilis put her head in. "Can I sit here with you, Llian?"

"Of course. How is Nadiril this morning?"

"He is sleeping."

"And your father?" He already knew the answer to that question, for Jevi had been avoiding him ever since their conversation on the cart.

"Gone with Pender down the sea to Ganport."

"Leaving you all alone."

"He has to do his work," she said stoutly.

"Even with those broken bones?"

"There's plenty he can do."

"And you have nothing to do, eh?"

"No! I'm lonely. I miss Jevi, and my friend Tallia."

That was a detail Llian was curious to tease out. "Tell me, Lilis, what does Jevi think of Tallia?"

Her face was a mixture of emotions. "He thinks she is the most wonderful woman in the world."

"And what do you think?"

"I love Tallia with all my heart."

"So, what is Jevi going to do?"

"He's afraid to do anything. Oh, Llian, it's a fairy tale. He thinks that a poor sailor can never . . ."

"I don't think that would matter to Tallia," said Llian.

"Of course it would not matter to *my* Tallia," Lilis said scornfully. "But *he* doesn't know that. He doesn't understand women at all."

"Maybe he needs your help," said Llian.

"He does! Oh, Llian, this is too hard!" She changed the subject. "I wish I was back in the Great Library; it's lovely there." Her thin little face was quite animated for a moment.

"Well!" Llian sat back with a smile. "Here's a good idea. Why don't you help me with my work?"

"Oh!" said Lilis, looking as if she had just been offered the moon. "But you're so clever. How can I possibly help you?"

"Most of my work is quite ordinary, actually—checking papers, putting things in order, finding books in the archives, copying. It's only when it's all put together that it seems clever. Look at this!" He indicated the waist-high pile of documents Mendark had given him. "It's all got to be sorted and catalogued."

"Please say I can do these things for you. There's so much to learn, but since we left the library we—" she broke off, feeling disloyal. "Nadiril has been busy with important work, and now he's ill."

"Not everything you need to know can be found in books," said Llian. It was a lesson he had been slow to learn.

"Of course you can work with me. Actually, I need your help rather badly. Come, I'll show you what to do."

The next few days passed very pleasantly, with Lilis's bright presence there every day, and the documents were soon arranged in such order that he only had to think of something and it was in her hand. Sometimes too soon, for after a while he found her constant hovering to be distracting.

"Lilis," he said.

She was at his elbow in an instant. "Lilis, I'm sorry, but I just can't concentrate with you watching me all the time."

Her face dropped halfway to her ankles. "You want me to go? Of course I will," she said, trying to look dignified and totally failing.

"Of course I *don't* want you to go. But this isn't good for you, or for me. What can I get you to do?"

Lilis froze with her hand on the knob. "I will do whatever you require of me," she said, still looking hurt.

"There's one job that needs doing desperately, but it must be done perfectly. Can you copy?"

"That was the first thing Nadiril taught me," she said stiffly.

"And was he satisfied with your work?"

She hesitated. "Not completely."

"Can you make a clean copy of this?" He handed her a piece of paper covered in his own fine hand, but full of crossings-out and amendments in various inks. "But remember, there can be no mistakes. If there's anything you don't understand, you must ask."

She sharpened a fresh quill and bent her head to the task. In less time than he had expected she was at his elbow again.

"You need to check something?"

"It's done!"

"So quickly?" He took the paper. The page was beautifully scribed in a rather ornate hand in the style of Nadiril's. Though old-fashioned, it suited the text perfectly. He inspected every letter, loop, whorl and curlicue, and checked it with the original. "Close to perfect," he said beaming. "Good enough!" whereupon Lilis threw her arms around him and kissed him on the cheek.

"Is that all?" she wondered.

He laughed. "That's not even the beginning. I have the biggest job you've ever seen. Look here."

On the floor beside his desk sat three volumes bound in leather of various colors. Two were quite battered and worn, but the third was relatively new. "This is my *Tale of the Mirror*, a Great Tale surely." He crossed his fingers behind his back as he spoke, for that prerogative the master chroniclers protected jealously.

"You want *me* to copy out your tale?"

He misunderstood her. "It's a very big task, I know. Look at the mess it's in." He opened the first volume, which was far worse than the sheet she had just copied. It was a sea of colored inks, corrections, numbered emendations, inserts, loose sheets, and many of the pages were written across as well as down.

"But this is a job for a master scribe. It's too great an honor for *me*."

"An honor that great scribes charge handsomely for, and I'm penniless. Anyway, how could I work with a scribe's sour breath whining in my ear all day? I like you much better, Lilis. But if it's too hard, or you don't want—"

Lilis snatched up the volumes and held them to her youthful bosom. "Of course I want to!" she said with high scorn. "I want it more than anything, and no one will work harder to make it perfect. Where do you keep your writing paper?"

"Paper! I hadn't thought of that," said Llian. "I don't

have the money to buy even a small book. I'll see what I can scrounge or beg from Mendark. Put them back; maybe we can start after lunch. You can't use the *third* one anyway. I haven't finished writing up that tale yet. And the fourth, I don't even have a book to write it in. Now, where are my crutches?"

Llian managed to glean a small leather-bound volume of blank pages, too small for any of his tales, but it was all he could get. It was a long time before Lilis reappeared. His legs were aching. In the mid-afternoon he hobbled over to the window, staring out through the bars at the yard and the knobbly tree.

Lilis staggered in with a large bag over her shoulder.

"What's that—your lunch?" he said jovially.

Lilis opened it up and pulled out four thick packets of paper that were creamy soft to the touch.

"But . . . that's silk paper, the finest there is!" Llian exclaimed. "Where did you get it?"

"I had money saved up to search for my father, but I never used it, so I bought it myself."

For one of the few times in his life Llian was speechless. Silk paper cost an absolute fortune, at least two gold tars a ream, and she had bought four of them. He could live for a couple of years on a single tar.

"I can't let you do that," he said, feeling weak at the knees. "I can never repay you such a sum."

"I'm not poor any more, Llian," said Lilis. "After the war began, I led the Council out of the Great Hall to safety. Some of them were rich, and Tallia got the price of their lives out of each of them for me. And Mendark paid me handsomely for my help on the way to Zile last year. I put all that by to find Jevi, but didn't use much of it. Nadiril actually pays me to learn, can you believe it?"

"But such a sum!" said Llian, sinking down on the tatty rug. He'd only had one tar in his entire life.

"A Great Tale deserves the best," she said simply.

This tale would sing even if it were written on blotting paper, he thought immodestly.

"Besides," she went on, "it wasn't as much as you might think. The paper merchant knows me well now. I promised to speak to Nadiril about the contract for the Great Library, and so I will. The fellow gave me a very good price."

Llian went back in his chair. To think he had thought of her as a child. Lilis was a young woman and maturing fast. But then, after growing up on the streets and all she had been through since, how could she be anything else? In many ways she was older and wiser than he was.

He realized that she was still speaking.

"I said, have you anything else for me to copy? I want to do some practice before I start your tale."

"You can copy into this little book; I just got it."

"What do you want me to copy?" Lilis asked.

"I'll see what I can find."

18

FORTELLING AND PROPHECY

Osseion opened the door of Llian's room. "You are called to a council," he said, "and Mendark requires that you wear these bracelets. 'The first lesson!' he said to tell you." Osseion held up a long loop of chain attached to a pair of wrist manacles.

Lilis was horrified. "Osseion," she cried. "What are you doing?"

"Have no fear, Lilis child," said the soldier. "Llian is not in danger."

"Mendark wishes to remind me of my debt," said Llian, groping for his crutches. He felt quite calm now. The past months had scorched the youth out of him. What could Mendark do to him that he had not already survived? He would smile and give him what he wanted, but all the while be working quietly at his own goal. Llian held out his hands and Osseion clicked the manacles closed.

He was taken to the Magister's sumptuous apartment in the citadel. These rooms were decorated in baroque extravagance with the very best Santhenar had to offer—tapestries woven with gold and silver thread, carpets of the costliest silk, and furniture made of ebony, leopardwood and other rare timbers, inlaid with pearl and jade. At the meeting were Yggur, who had just returned from the hunt, Tensor, Mendark, Shand, recently back from Carcharon, and Malien. Nadiril was not well and had not come.

"We tracked the thranx by the ruin it left behind it," Yggur said, looking even more confident and commanding than before. His triumphs had truly ennobled him. "It was hiding in Faidon Forest, west of Muncyte, but Nadiril was right—it could not fly any distance. Eventually we cornered it there and killed it, though it did great damage first."

"And the baby?" asked Llian, remembering the birth, the blood, the fierce-eyed infant.

"It too. It was a wild little beast!"

Llian could imagine the little creature struggling for its life.

"I heard the tale at the city gates," said Shand. "They say that you struck the thranx some mighty blows, Yggur, including the one that ended it."

"I was there," said Yggur. "It took the blows of many to defeat it, and we suffered many casualties. I was lucky not to be one of them."

"Modest as always!" said Mendark caustically. He was toying nervously with a tiny chest of drawers, shaped like a whorled shell.

"Unlike you, I don't care to be praised for something that I don't deserve! What news from Carcharon, Shand?"

"Rulke's abandoned it, for the moment."

"Here's our chance," said Mendark. "Let's get to work on the flute."

"We don't have gold enough," snapped Yggur.

"Faelamor has," Mendark pointed out.

"And her plans must be well advanced, for the Faellem have been sighted coming out of the south-east," said Malien.

"I believe she is hiding in Elludore Forest," said Yggur.

"What if—" Mendark began. "No, it would never work."

"If you've an idea, spit it out!" Yggur growled.

"I was going to propose a raid on Elludore, to seize the gold. But that's no place to take an army . . ."

Yggur sprang up, pacing back and forth.

"I'm afraid what Faelamor will do with the gold," Mendark went on. "But . . . she's the match of the best soldiers I've ever seen."

"Perhaps the flute is the way, after all," said Yggur. "But it must be planned surpassingly well."

Mendark smiled to himself, though only Llian noted it.

"We had a foretelling about this business," said Malien thoughtfully.

"About Faelamor?"

"No, an answer to Rulke's foretelling. Remember what he said as we hurled him out of Katazza:

> "When the dark moon is full on mid-winter's day, I will be back. I will crack the Forbidding and open the Way between the Worlds. No one has the power to stay me. The Three Worlds will be Charon evermore."

"What was your reply, Shand?" asked Yggur.

> "Break down the golden horn,
> Wish the glass unmade,
> Fear the thrice born,
> But beware the thrice betrayed,"

said Shand.

"A load of child's nonsense!" sneered Mendark.

"It's not the first time Rulke spoke his foretelling," said Malien, deep in thought. "I heard it mentioned as a child, and a different reply, but I can't recall how that went."

"The one thing that might save us and you don't remember it!" Mendark said sarcastically. "So much for the Histories of the Aachim."

"We have a thousand foretellings," croaked Tensor. "In our slavery we baked prophets as a baker bakes buns, a dozen for every conceivable disaster, and the inconceivable too. I don't recall it either. Come, Malien; the tide won't wait."

"Where are you going?"

"Across the sea," said Malien. "To a gathering of our people. We'll be away at least a month."

"Do you know anything about such an Aachim prophecy?" Mendark asked Llian after lunch. The Magister kept shifting on his chair as though in pain.

Llian mentally ran through what he knew. "Um, there *was* something in *Tales of the Aachim*," he said after a minute.

"What?"

"It was in a book of Aachim Histories that I read in Shazmak. The *Nazhak tel Mardux*, which loosely renders as *Tales of the Aachim*. Something struck me about it even then."

"I'll strike you if you don't get to the point," said Mendark, shredding a piece of paper. "What was it?"

"I don't recall. I . . ."

"What sort of an excuse for a chronicler are you?"

Llian refused to be provoked. "The book was not in any of my languages. I had to decipher it bit by bit, and . . ."

"And you left it in Shazmak."

"It would have been a great dishonor to take it."

"You have a very selective sense of honor, you who are accused of making a pact with the greatest enemy of all."

"Falsely accused!" Llian said sharply, rising to the bait despite his vow. "To you honor is just a boast, another of the currencies you use to buy your ends. Why is it important anyway?"

"It could be the key to our dilemma," Mendark replied evasively.

Llian laughed and rattled his manacles at him. "Will things be different now that you need me?" He allowed the moment to drag out as long as he dared. Mendark looked ready to explode. "You forget that I was a master chronicler. Twice I read that book, every word; I will never forget it. That is my training. Any of us could do the same."

"But you said . . ." Mendark massaged his swollen knuckles. "Tell it, damn you!"

"In this case it's not so simple," said Llian. "I remember it in the language it's written in, which I know only haltingly. I'll have to recite it back to myself, in that tongue, and translate it as I go. It'll take all night."

"We have all night," Mendark replied, "and all tomorrow if need be. If the answer is there, we've got to have it."

Llian searched in his memories for the beginning of the book. He found it, and it took him back to that room in Shazmak more than a year ago, and the wind wailing outside.

"Remember that it's in a language I barely knew. I learned more with Tensor in Katazza, but I wouldn't say that I'm fluent."

"Begin!" said Mendark impatiently. "You chroniclers must qualify everything. You can check with Tensor, if he ever comes back."

The tale unreeled in Llian's mind. The Aachim were a people proud and strong but never secure; noble and steadfast allies but too often betrayed; the makers of great but ill-judged alliances; artists and builders of the greatest skill yet looking always to the past; finally retreating into isolation. And always, always plotting revenge on Rulke, who had brought them to Santhenar in the first place. He was the architect of all their misfortune. Back then, I hardly knew that the Aachim existed, Llian thought. But how very true the book was.

"Stop daydreaming, chronicler!" Mendark's cry broke into his thoughts. "Get on with it!"

Half the night passed before Llian found what he was looking for—a single paragraph that told of Rulke's foretelling and how it might be averted.

"*There will appear an 'instrument'*—the precise expression is *khash-zik-makattzah—and if a way can be found to use it, Santhenar can be* . . . I think the word is *redeemed. But at the end the instrument will be lost.*" Llian rubbed his forehead. "I think *khash-zik-makattzah* means *the-three-and-the-one*, but it could be *thirty and one*. I'm not sure. It's a dead language. You'll have to ask Tensor."

"I have it!" Mendark cried. "The *three* means the flute, for it was the product of three worlds: gold of Aachan for the body of the flute; precious ebony of Tallallame the other parts of it; and the genius of Shuthdar, that conceived and made it. And the *one* is the sensitive who will use it to unstitch the Forbidding and restore the balance between the Three Worlds. But at the end the instrument will be lost. Does that mean *lost*, or *destroyed*? Go through it once more, Llian."

Llian repeated the paragraph containing the foretelling.

"Perhaps there *is* a way that Rulke's prophecy can be averted. The Mirror, Shand. Quickly!"

"I'll have to get Tensor to check my translation," said Llian. "I don't know the language well enough."

"Always excuses!" Mendark said. "Do it again. The Aachim have gone across the sea."

Llian went through his translation again, explaining it all in excruciating detail.

"What can it be but *the-three-and-the-one?*" breathed Mendark when Llian had finished. "This is the sign I've been waiting for. The flute was the right way after all. Shand, you can't refuse us the Mirror now. Let's see if it shows us more than it did last time."

Shand had been dreading this moment. How he wished that he had never left Tullin. Yet he had, and once on the path there was no way to get off it.

Yet still, when he pulled the tight coil of metal from its case and it slowly unrolled and hardened into the Mirror of Aachan, he did so with the greatest reluctance. It lay open in his hand, a hard black beautiful thing inscribed with those strange silver glyphs around the border, the moon symbol in one corner and the restless quicksilver matrix reflecting his battered old face. The others were all staring at it, each with his own greed or wonderment, and Shand felt resentful. Look at them! They each think that they will get something marvelous from it. Have they forgotten that it is the Twisted Mirror, the breaker of dreams?

Look at Llian, standing there with his mouth agape. He thinks that it will tell him all the lost tales of the past. He doesn't seem like a master chronicler now. He looks more like a lecherous swineherd peeping through the bushes at the village girls at their bath, dreaming that they will offer themselves when he comes barging down to the water. But they won't—they'll run away laughing and mock him cruelly from a distance. So too this Mirror.

Look at Mendark. He imagines that it will restore him to what was once his, and give him the means to make his name ring down the generations. See how the thought has almost erased the bitter downcast of his mouth. But it will betray him. The result will be far worse than he can ever imagine.

Look at Yggur! If ever a man was made of stone it is he. Impossible to tell what's in *his* mind. But the Mirror has something, and he knows it. See how his eyes gleam, and if his face shows nothing, his posture gives him away. Sit back, Yggur! There's no more in this for you than for me. Nothing for any of us.

Shand stroked the border of the Mirror, feeling the masterwork of the engraved glyphs around the edge, unmarked by the centuries since Yalkara put them there. That had been one of the last things she'd done on Santhenar, and therefore important. He wished he knew why. What memories the Mirror aroused. How terribly sad he felt. With a swift movement he passed it to Mendark.

Mendark held it lightly on his spread fingers, his thumb resting on the engraved border. "At last!" he exulted. He touched the symbol in the corner. The scene appeared that he had produced when Karan first handed it to him in Thurkad more than a year ago. The others crowded around to see.

It was a black, desolate landscape with tall mountains in the background. Nearer was a plain dotted with steely-gray buildings shaped like ox kidneys, curve upon multiple curve. The plain was cut by an icy rift, dark and deep; a fibrous iron tower leaned from a hill to one side; a small red sun peeped fitfully through rushing storm clouds. There was no living thing in sight.

He spoke a word—*Dirgash!*—and the image disappeared. He tried another word. Other pictures appeared, views of Aachan like the first, but no more useful. Shand saw a world of huge mountains crusted with sulphur-colored snow and trickling scarlet lava. A land of plummeting canyons and furiously rushing rivers; of still, oily bogs and blue-black luminous flowers. Between the mountains were plateaux covered in gray grass, and the mounds and ruins of ancient cities. The sky was dominated by a huge orange moon hanging sullenly on the horizon and bathing all in its dreary light.

He spoke other words, and combinations of words; sentences and songs and exotic verbal symbols. New scenes appeared. Some showed people that he knew. Here was Tensor, futilely trying to direct his gate with the Twisted Mirror. Here Faelamor, staring desperately into it in Katazza, with the inside of the platinum dome reflected in the background. There the image of Karan, wild-eyed and hair matted, a big streak of mud on her face, looking down. Her head jerked up, then the Mirror went dark.

"Don't tell me the little scrag has seen more than I can!" Mendark swore, slapping the table with his open palm.

Llian was so overcome at the sight of Karan that he did not even hear the insult, but Shand did. His tanned fingers gripped Mendark's thin wrist and he squeezed so hard that the Mirror clattered to the table. Mendark lifted his other hand; his eyes met Shand's. They sat like that for half a minute, then Mendark said, "I'm sorry," and Shand released him.

"That must be just before I caught them in Fiz Gorgo," Yggur said. "Let's see if there is more."

Mendark took up the Mirror again but it now remained stubbornly blank. He could not even recover what had been there before.

"What a capricious thing it is!" he said in vexation. "I'll have to work on it overnight."

"It stays here!" said Shand vehemently.

"You're too anxious, Mendark," said Yggur. "Too angry.

Let someone else try." Plucking the Mirror out of Mendark's hand, he passed it to Llian.

"I can't," Llian said. "I've looked before." Nonetheless he tried, repeating various phrases that he had read in his books. Nothing appeared.

"If Tallia were here . . ." began Yggur.

Mendark broke in angrily, "Well she isn't! This is what you wanted all along, so stop your posturing and use it."

Yggur shot him a dark glance from those cavernous eyes. "The mistake we all made was in thinking the Mirror to be a formed, unchangeable thing. But it isn't. It's dynamic, and every use alters it, makes it more complex, more difficult. More dangerous! Perhaps it has transformed beyond anything we can do to recover . . ."

"*Get on with it!*" Mendark screamed. He felt that Yggur was taunting him.

Yggur took the Mirror from Llian, touched the symbol in a certain way and immediately images appeared, flashing quickly from one to another in much the same way as when Faelamor had used it in Katazza. Scenes of Tensor's gate; his wracked face; incoherence, mist and jumbled faces and places.

Yggur put it down again. "That's all I can find," he said, "and I know it well."

"You didn't even try," Mendark accused, furious that Yggur had found more in it than he had, and now laid it aside so casually. "You've some secret plan of your own!"

"Indeed I have not," said Yggur. "But I will not chant meaningless words at the Mirror like some village shaman, hoping that something will fit the lock. I do not have the key, and I know it. I had it for twenty years, remember. Let it go back to its guardian."

He handed it to Shand with a bow. Shand took it, feeling guiltily pleased that none of them could work it, but before he could return it to its case Llian said suddenly, "You try it, Shand!"

"No! I was just the custodian. I've never used it, and I will not!"

Yggur looked thoughtful. "Llian is right. Time for you to take off the mask, Shand. Perhaps something was left there for the custodian."

Shand looked sick. "No," he whispered. "It was not meant for me. I vowed . . ."

"Time to stop hiding behind that vow. Look on the Mirror, Shand. If it shows nothing, you are no worse off."

"You don't understand," said Shand, staring down at the cold, still surface. "You can never understand . . ."

19

THE RING

Mendark jerked upright in his chair. "Wait!" he cried. "I've just remembered something!" He hurried out, shortly to return with a package and a rolled-up piece of heavy writing paper clasped with a silver ring.

"I found these in Havissard," said Mendark, putting them on the table. Unwrapping a kid-skin wrapper he withdrew a small book bound in leather. "Also this. Faelamor dropped it on the floor of the library. I told you about it just after I returned from the east, remember?"

He handed the book to Llian. "See if you can decipher it, some time when you've got nothing to do. Try and work out why Faelamor wanted it."

Mendark looked up at Shand. "I also came across *this,*" he said, handing him the rolled-up paper and the ring. "At the time I thought that it was only of interest to a chronicler. Now I'm wondering if the custodian of the Mirror might not know something about it. What do you make of it, Shand?"

Shand took it, looking puzzled. "The workmanship is familiar," he said examining the ring. He put it down on the table, unrolled the paper and smoothed it down.

"My dearest Gyllias . . ." he read, then cried out, gazing at the leaf as if it had burned him. Cold shivers ran down Llian's back.

Shand stared at the letter without seeing it, lost somewhere in his past. Looking over his shoulder, Llian read the letter aloud:

My dearest Gyllias,

Would that I could tell you face to face, but you are still not back and I can wait no longer. Faelamor attacked me again and this time she was very strong. She dealt me a wound which may well prove mortal. My only chance is to flee back through the gate to Aachan. Beware Faelamor!

Alas, my work is not done! I fear that it will never be completed now. But I beg you, take the Mirror and guard it well, against the possibility that someone will come to restore the balance that Rulke broke with the flute. I have locked the Mirror. Its secrets are hidden to all save the One who has the key.

Take this ring, which I made with my own hands, of ore that I mined and purified here at Havissard, gold and silver and platinum all. It is the key to Havissard, and a form of protection against my enemy, and a token to give you heart in the darkness, to remind you of my undying love.

It grieves me to go this way, but go I must.

Farewell forever.

Yalkara

Shand held the Mirror in his other hand, absently stroking the engraved symbol with his fingertip, a soft, caressing touch. The Mirror suddenly exploded with light that showed every wrinkle of his craggy old face, every hair of his beard. He dropped it as if it was red hot. It fell flat on the table. They all saw the image there.

It was a woman with a striking long face, long dark hair touched with silver, and indigo eyes. She looked up, seemed to gaze at Shand, and smiled wistfully. It was the face Karan had seen on the Mirror in Yggur's library at Fiz Gorgo.

"Maigraith!" cried Yggur. "Maigraith, what has happened to you? You have aged so!" Then he looked puzzled. "Maigraith?"

"No," said Shand quietly. "It is Yalkara! Oh, Yalkara, my beloved, how I yearn for you."

The two men stared at each other.

"It *is* Yalkara," Shand said, looking down at the Mirror again. His old eyes were bright with tears. "We were lovers for an age of the world. This is how I last saw her—how she was when she left me."

"I don't think you can hide your secret any longer, Shand," said Yggur with surprising gentleness.

"I can't," he agreed. "Doing so has become worse than bringing it out into the light." He wiped away a tear. "I am—at least I was—Gyllias. I will tell you my tale."

Mendark stared at him in open-mouthed astonishment. "*You* were the great Gyllias?"

Shand gave no acknowledgment. "Over the ages Yalkara and Faelamor fought many times, but they were well matched and neither could vanquish the other. Then, not much more than three hundred years ago, Yalkara found a warp in the Forbidding, a way to escape Santhenar. It was a secret that Faelamor was desperate to have. Their last battle began in the ruins of Tar Gaarn, near Yalkara's mighty stronghold of Havissard. For her it was a most unwelcome struggle for many reasons, not least that she was with child, near her term. It was a terrible battle, hurting her more than she dared show. No one knew that she was pregnant, least of all Faelamor. That news would surely have fired *her* up. Not even I knew, for I was across the world. Half a year I had been away.

"Yalkara overcame Faelamor but was cruelly hurt inside, terribly damaged protecting her secret. She called me and I set off in haste from far away. Unfortunately the baby came early. Yalkara gave birth alone in her chamber, to a beautiful girl child. She wept for it and for us, knowing that she could neither remain on Santh nor carry it safely through the gate. It took her days to make all the preparations, always hoping that I would return in time, for I was weeks overdue.

"When I arrived she was already waiting by the gate. I ran to embrace her but she said, 'I'm sorry, Gyllias.' "

" 'What's the matter?' I cried."

" 'I am sorely wounded and no one on this world can help me. If I stay I will be dead within weeks. I love you dearly but I love my own species more. I cannot bear to die here so far from my own kind, and I cannot carry you to Aachan with me. Alas, we must part forever. But I have for you a gift. The greatest gift that any woman can give.' "

"Her whole body was wracked by spasms. She doubled over, covering her face with her hands. When she stood up again she looked tormented. From a basket she lifted a small bundle wrapped in furs, and held it out to me. I was so shocked that I just stood there, staring at her. Finally I pulled back the covers. A child lay within, a tiny baby. A beautiful little thing, with her mother's eyes—the only child I ever had.

" 'She is our daughter,' Yalkara said. 'Her name is Aeolior. Take care of her and guard her always, and when she is old enough, give her the Mirror and instruct her in its use. I have left a message for her to find there. It will comfort and guide her, for she has a destiny if a certain foretelling comes to pass. And take this gift for her, my gold. I have always worn it. Give it to her when she comes of age and bid her wear it.' "

"So saying, she took off the necklace of red gold, and her bracelet and torc, and put them in my other hand. 'I will also give you a measure of my strength and my life. I hope that you don't find it too heavy a burden in the ages that lie ahead.'

"She took my forehead between her hands (they were cool and strong, her hands; but terribly scarred). She trembled, and something passed from her to me, and then she kissed me, a delicate kiss on either cheek, and a third on my forehead. 'Do not forget. Guard Aeolior always, and when she is old enough, give her the birthright. But until then, stay here in Havissard. I have set it to protect you both. And I have a little gift for you, a ring that will permit you to come and go. Where did I put it?' She looked around for the gift—*this* ring, Mendark, and the letter—but could not recall where she'd left it. In the turmoil I thought no more about it.

"I swore that I would guard and protect Aeolior, looking down in wonderment at the tiny creature cradled in my arms.

"I never saw Yalkara cry before in all the time we had been together, but now the tears rolled down her cheeks unchecked. She took me in her arms, touched my face with her fingers, and I felt her shivery trembling. Only then did I realize how weak she was, how close to death. She kissed Aeolior, smiled at me and stepped back into the portal. How the wind howled through the gate that took her from me! She cried out a rhyme that I did not catch, and was gone from my life.

"I stared into the gate long after it had closed, until Aeolior cried and woke me. I had a new art to learn."

"That evening we went out of lonely, empty Havissard, for I wanted to show my daughter the sunset over Tar Gaarn, the Aachim city that even in its ruin was the most beautiful thing ever made on Santhenar. I gave her that, but when we tried to get back in, Havissard was closed. I had gone out without Yalkara's gift—this ring—and the protection came down and has never lifted to this day.

"That was my first failing. Aeolior and I were alone in the great world. But it did not bother me at the time. I was powerful. No one could harm *me*!

"So we lived and traveled together, Aeolior and I, and I guarded her like the precious jewel she was, and the joy I found in her was some compensation for my loss. But that was in a time when I still accounted myself important, a mover and a shaper of Santhenar. Oft-times I had to go to places where it was not safe or wise to take her. I left her in the care of friends whom I trusted utterly, with so many injunctions to guard and take care of her that it must have been quite a trial to them." His mouth curved down as he tasted the bile of self-loathing. "But one time, when I returned from my posturing and spruiking, full of pride and self-importance, I found my friends dead and Aeolior *gone*!

"I'm sorry, Llian," he said, giving him a cool stare. "I've always blamed the Zain. There was clear evidence of them at the scene, and they had strong motives. In those days I was one of their greatest enemies. Twice I exposed them to the world in their long wandering, causing them to be driven into exile yet again. Because of me, your people are persecuted to this day.

"Aeolior was still a child when I lost her. The children of the Charon grow only slowly to adulthood, and she could have passed for a girl of twelve, an old human child that is, though she was much older in years. Whatever, she was not yet a woman. She was the very image of Yalkara, even then. I came back from doing my business and she was gone. She had been well guarded, but not as well as I would have done. *Not well enough!*

"A long, long time I sought her: months; years! I could feel her, sense her sometimes, and it was as if she was in a long dreaming. Once or twice I almost reached her in *my* dreams, but always something forced me away. Decades I sought her, then one night I heard her cry out for me, her screams ringing in my nightmares. Her terror, her agony, was awful. *Awful!* Then she was gone forever.

"Guard your children with your life," he said, looking at Llian and each of them with vacant grief.

Llian looked away, busying himself with his notes for the tale. Shand continued in a bitter voice.

"I had sworn to protect Aeolior and to safeguard the Mirror for her, but a moment of carelessness undid all that. I failed her and blamed myself, so I gave away that life forever. I hid the Mirror and everything that was hers. I renounced the Secret Art, the way of the powers, and wandered in grief and abandonment."

He sank his head in his hands and his voice came back muffled. "My grief was greater than if Yalkara had left me nothing. And I was reduced to nothing, for eventually even the Mirror was sought out and taken. You ended up with it, Yggur. I don't blame you, though the foretelling about Rulke has come to pass. Aeolior is not here to use her birthright as Yalkara hoped. She is gone and I am left with nothing. Yalkara gave me part of her life and I'm now older than ever I wished to be. My strength has faded, my wits with it. I long for death but life continues to torment me."

He said no more; he looked utterly broken. No one else spoke either; there seemed nothing anyone could say.

Shand suddenly jerked upright. "Yggur, you called her Maigraith. Why? Who *is* Maigraith, this disciple of Faelamor that we hear so much of?"

"No, it's not Maigraith," said Yggur, examining the image on the Mirror. "I see that now, though the resemblance is extraordinary! Nonetheless, I believe I can tell you the rest of the tale, old man," he went on gently. "It's a sorry business. You'll get little joy from hearing it, except perhaps at the end. I came by the first fragment when I was looking for the Mirror, and found another with it, twenty years ago. After meeting Maigraith I had my spies seek out the rest. Though only now, after hearing your story, am I able to put it all together.

"You were wrong to blame the Zain, Shand. They had nothing to do with it, though the evidence was cleverly slanted that way. Faelamor took Aeolior from you."

"Faelamor?" Shand whispered. "Are you sure?" He stared at Llian in mortification. "Tell me, quickly!"

"There's no doubt whatsoever. After her last battle with Yalkara, Faelamor lay on her sick-bed for months. She was full of hatred and bitterness for the age-long defeats of the Faellem, and especially at Yalkara, whom she blamed for everything. Somehow Faelamor found out about Aeolior, and conceived a twisted plan that would revenge her on Yalkara and with luck further her own goal. As you know, Faelamor was desperate to take her people back to Tallallame, the world they were cut off from long ago. No longer would she seek some warp in the Forbidding through which the Faellem could make their escape. She would shatter the Forbidding and curse the consequences! An old Faellem foretelling had shown her the way:

"Tallallame, Tallallame,
Your fate rests on the one which is three.

"To break the Forbidding required a special kind of device empowered by the Secret Art, like the golden flute or Rulke's construct, but the Faellem were forbidden to use such things. Faelamor's way around the prohibition was to make a *human device,* a triune—*the one which is three.* But triunes were extremely rare, often mad, and almost impossible to control. The only solution was to make her own and train it from birth. How could she do that? Then she learned about Aeolior. I don't know how. She knew that Aeolior was a blending, a child of Aachan and Santhenar. From her she could make the triune and be revenged on Yalkara too.

"Faelamor took Aeolior, and, it grieves me to tell you, Shand, treated her barbarously. When Aeolior was old enough Faelamor mated her, unwilling, to a Faellem male. Such matings seldom give rise to children but Faelamor found a way to make it so, and continued the sad business until it did. Eventually a child was born. Aeolior named her Maigraith, and, my spy told me, even found joy in her. But Faelamor could not allow the child to bond with the mother or she would never be able to control it. She tore Maigraith away from her mother's breast, and in her grief and shame Aeolior killed her Faellem mate as he huddled beside her, his debasement even greater than hers, then took her own life."

"I knew something terrible had happened, when I dreamed her crying out for me," Shand wept. "Aeolior, Aeolior."

Yggur left him to his grief, speaking quietly to one of the guards. Shortly servants appeared with mugs of lasee.

Shand drank his in a single gulp, then said to Yggur, "What did Faelamor do to my grand-daughter?"

Yggur continued. "Faelamor took charge of Maigraith and schooled her for the great purpose. But the Faellem were dishonored. They drew away from Faelamor, shunning Maigraith as well. Maigraith lived a long life with Faelamor, and a lonely one, growing slowly into womanhood. She knew none of her own kind or even who she was, and though she was far cleverer than anyone around her, and stronger too, she was afraid to use her strength or her will. When she did, it was always too much, and drew attention to her. So maybe Faelamor's deeds will prove her undoing," Yggur said. "Maigraith has the talents and the strength for her purpose, but perhaps not the will.

"The first great task Faelamor set Maigraith was the taking of the Mirror, for on it, she was sure, the secret of Yalkara's flight could be found. It was in Fiz Gorgo, when I held her prisoner, that I first guessed Maigraith's origins. The eyes of the Charon give them away, for they are a most marvelous color, indigo and carmine together, though such a hue can never be described. Faelamor had given Maigraith a potion, the drug *kalash*, to conceal the color, but my Whelm took it from her and while I held her the color changed back. I then knew that she was a child of the Charon, but whose? There had been quite a few Charon blendings around at one stage, though in the early days, and again in the Clysm, they were hunted almost to extinction. She might have been hidden away, barely aging for centuries, until brought out for this task."

"She must have been," said Shand. "It is 309 years since Yalkara went through the gate."

"I didn't know Yalkara ever had a consort," Mendark said irritably.

"It was our secret. And as I said, I had a different name then," Shand replied. "Several names in fact. I was known as Gyllias in the east, but in the west, in the days of my power I was called Cheseut, which is my real name and the one Mendark knew me by."

"You must be the famous Recorder!" said Llian excitedly.

"I *was* the Recorder," Shand responded. "It took you a long time to work that out."

"The rest of Maigraith's story you know," Yggur concluded.

"Maigraith!" breathed Shand. "The daughter of our daughter, and I never knew. Karan often spoke of her. Oh, what a wonderful day! If I could just see her I would be happy to die."

Mendark did not look entirely pleased. "This makes your dereliction of duty all the greater, Shand," he said sourly.

"I don't owe *you* any duty, Mendark!"

"And Tensor recognized her heritage," Mendark continued. "Recall his words at the Conclave, when Maigraith first appeared: *Do the Charon spring up again from the earth?* Though I don't think he knew *who* she was."

"He didn't," said Llian. "Karan also saw Yalkara's face on the Mirror in Fiz Gorgo, for she mentioned it soon after I met her. But she thought it was an older Maigraith. I wonder if the Mirror recognized Maigraith even then."

Shand let out a heavy sigh. "I have done you a monumental injustice, Llian. From the very first I blamed the Zain, and I have always doubted you. I poisoned the minds of these people against you, and Karan too, as I have worked to bring your people down for centuries. No service I can do you can make up for this evil, but demand of me what you will and if it is in my power I will do it."

"I want Karan back," said Llian, "but that's beyond your power. Or anyone's . . ." He sank his head in his hands and the shackles rattled faintly.

Yggur shouted at the guards. "Bring hammer and chisel. Strike these chains off at once."

They all watched the operation. "Nonetheless," Mendark scowled, "you may not leave the citadel until we learn the truth about Karan."

Llian made a rude gesture. He felt so light that he could have floated up to the ceiling. "So that's how you knew about the thranx and the void," he said to Shand. "I always felt that there was something special about you."

"Yalkara taught me many things," Shand replied. "The answer to many of your wonderings, though not all, lies there. I have never stopped longing for her—to bring her back, or follow her to Aachan. It's been the passion of my life. A totally fruitless one!" His eyes closed. He did not speak for a long time.

"Shand!" Yggur said abruptly.

Shand shook himself out of the daydream. "Does anyone know where Maigraith is now?"

20

A Stroll in the Country

"You're looking remarkably well today, Shand," said Yggur the following day. They were taking lunch together in Yggur's rather grim workroom, though the fire was crackling cheerily.

"I feel like a young man again. No, that's not true. I feel reborn; unfortunately as an old man."

Yggur laughed. "Well, there's plenty to be done in your new life."

"Plenty to be set right! What a fool I've been!" He did not say this bitterly, but as one whose eyes had just been opened. "I've got to find Maigraith, and I know you've an idea where she might be."

"I have a number of ideas," said Yggur.

"You mentioned Elludore," said Shand. "That's a huge place."

"It is, but Faelamor has been out more than once. Did you know that she sneaked into our first meeting, after we came back from Katazza last autumn?"

"What!"

"Yes! She was very bold. I didn't realize she was inside until the Council was underway. You might have wondered at the strange course it took."

"I remember it well," said Shand. "It was full of posturing and taking positions—political nonsense! I thought you and Mendark were playing games. I was so angry that I left Thurkad straight afterwards."

Yggur leaned back in his chair, reflecting. "Well, I had to break up the meeting without alerting her. But she was too clever. Before I could seal the doors she was gone again. After that I did . . . certain things to secure our meetings. I don't know if she tried again or not.

"I knew her refuge was not far away," he went on after an interval. "Elludore was my guess, and that was confirmed a few weeks ago. Three Faellem came across the sea from the south-east. I had them followed."

"We might never find her," said Shand thoughtfully, "even if we took an army in there."

"Especially if we took an army. But that wasn't what I had in mind."

"What can two old men do that an army cannot?"

Yggur laughed. "Quite a lot, I imagine," he said. "Is the morning soon enough for you?"

Shand had never seen him so cheerful. "I think I can restrain myself."

They slipped out of Thurkad well before dawn. Yggur was heavily disguised, for he was all too recognizable. Shand was just Shand—he could look nondescript or imposing as the mood took him. Today he was like any other old man on the road. His beard, which he had started growing when he left Tullin a year ago, was now long and gray. His hair was sheared off roughly at the collar. He had his knobbly black staff in his hand. His clothes were faded, work-stained browns.

Yggur was also dressed in drab: green shirt and mud-colored trews. His jet hair was powdered to gray and he too was bearded, though his had been made during the night and glued to his face. He wrapped himself in a long cloak and pulled a baggy brown hat low over his eyes.

The guards over at the western gate looked sleepy. They checked the papers, not as thoroughly as they might have, and waved them through.

"Remind me to send them on marsh duty for a month when we return. They should never have let you through on *that* pass." Yggur's teeth flashed in the gloom.

Shand chuckled, urging his horse into a trot.

"There was a time when I would have had them whipped," said Yggur, his levity disappearing. "In the days of my misery I was as hard as stone."

"I heard what you . . . did to the Second Army," said Shand carefully.

"Most commanders would have done the same, but I'm just realizing that there can be another way."

"The thranx has changed you."

"Perhaps it has. I lived so long in terror of Rulke that it colored every aspect of my life."

"And that's gone now?"

"I think so. At Carcharon I resolved to face my fears and die, but somehow I survived. Transformed, I hope." He rubbed his cheek with his fingertips. "This beard is so damned itchy! And it stinks! What did you make it from?"

Shand chuckled. "Horsehair and fish glue."

There had been rain during the night, just enough to make slush of the dirty snow on the road. A morning breeze came off the sea. Fog drifted in patches across the fields.

The sun rose, thickening the fog, but within an hour it was gone.

"I feel that I've just put aside a great burden," said Yggur. "Is this what I really want, to spend all my days chairbound, administering an empire? Scheming, manipulating, trying to outwit Mendark and his pretenders? I was happier in those years I spent on the road, when I had nothing."

"I used to think that too," said Shand. "Tell me about it."

"I was recovering from the Proscribed Experiments. You would know all about that."

"Hearsay only. I've never heard it from Mendark."

"You won't hear the truth from Mendark!" Yggur said with a tinge of his old bitterness. "The Experiments were a different way of using the Secret Art. I won't say much about that, even to you, Shand, but you can probably guess that it was like the summoning that Rulke originally used to draw Shuthdar to Aachan, to make the golden flute for him. And a bit like the warping of place and space that goes to make up a gate."

"And the Experiments were forbidden," said Shand, sifting through ancient memories of his own, "because they often went wrong."

"No one has ever been able to codify the laws governing that branch of the Art. It's like trying to design a bird without understanding that there are laws of flight. More than once the Experiments punched a hole through into the void and let in creatures that were never intended to roam Santhenar. With terrible consequences, though of course the Council never owned up. It was just an unfortunate conjunction of the planets, people were told.

"All such experiments were proscribed a good few thousands of years ago, before the Forbidding sealed Santhenar off. Though not everyone obeyed the edict."

"Perhaps that's what Basunez was up to in Carcharon," said Shand.

"I'd say so."

"So why *did* you use the Proscribed Experiments, Yggur?"

"The Council, and particularly Mendark, was desperate to rid the world of Rulke. They saw the Experiments as the only way to trap him, and me as the only one who could control them. One Council made the prohibition; another had the power to overturn it. And of course by that time the Forbidding protected us from the worst consequences. Nothing could get through it."

Yggur's horse picked its way around a mud-filled hole in the road that could have swallowed it. Soon they were spattered with yellow mud. The sun came out momentarily.

"But the Experiments failed," said Shand, taking a swig from his water bottle.

"The Council's courage failed them at the critical time, and Mendark abandoned me when he should have supported me. He made the failure certain! Rulke possessed me, and though he was later imprisoned in the Nightland, I was left to die and blamed for the whole disaster."

"But you did not die!"

"I was driven mad though. I'd give anything to know what really happened then, but the memories are completely gone. A hundred years vanished! I rolled out of my furs one morning, looked around and *was aware*. The light of morning showed all the ugliness and squalor of my past existence—a century of beasthood. My furs reeked—ratty uncured hides, gnawed by vermin, full of fleas, lice and ticks. I stank too. The mouth of the cave was a midden of bones and shredded fur. Scavengers slunk away as I came out." Yggur scratched furiously at his beard.

"Walking hurt me. Not just a twinge but a grinding of the

bones and a spasming of the muscles along my side. The last I remembered, I had been young and strong and whole. Handsome and brilliant too, I could have had anything I ever wanted."

He went silent and they rode on until the morning was gone, Yggur lost in his memories as Shand was in his.

"This village is called Spinct."

It took some time for Shand's voice to penetrate Yggur's introspection. Yggur inspected the scattering of mud-and-thatch cottages to right and left. Most were only one or two rooms but they looked well cared for, and here and there in a front garden the first winter crocuses peeped cheerfully through the snow, as yellow as butter.

A white-haired crone smiled toothlessly at them from a front porch. A red and blue parrot squatted on her white-spattered shoulder. "Look at the ugly man! Look at the ugly man!" it squawked as they passed.

"It's talking about you!" Yggur and Shand said together, then burst out laughing.

"There are two ways we can go from here," said Shand as they approached an intersection. "The main road is more direct but it goes through several large towns. The left-hand fork is longer, but goes only by villages."

"Let's go the winding way. There's less chance I'll be recognized." Yggur lapsed back into his study, then realized that he hadn't finished his tale. "I beg your pardon, my friend."

"I'd like to hear the rest of the story, if you care to finish it."

"Why not? Doubtless there are parallels with your own life." Yggur looked away and they jogged along without speaking for a while. He was choosing his words with care, or perhaps wondering where to start. In the end he sighed and went back to where he had been before.

"What was I saying?" He paused for a long time. "I didn't even know where I was, though it was a long way from Alcifer, where the Experiments were done. I must have fled for months in my madness. Of the hundred years following that, when I was a mindless creature, just occasional flashes." Another long hesitant pause.

He mused. "Imagine how I felt that morning. I wanted to run and shout like a young man, but I was a wretched cripple. It was painful to walk, even to talk, as it still is sometimes. I'm not half the man I was.

"I came to terms with that in time. I cast off my furs, plunged into the river and rasped my skin with a piece of sandstone until the filth was gone. I cut my hair, beard and nails, got new furs. I still looked like a wild man, but at least I was a man. How was I to make a new life? I did not want employment; I was too used to solitude. I wanted to wander, to see the civilizations and ruins of Santhenar, to find out who I was *now*.

"I had to have clothes, food, coin. I might have used my powers. They remained, reduced but not lost. The hiring out of the least of them would have made me wealthy. Yet I was reluctant. The Secret Art had betrayed me."

They were now climbing toward the top of a steep hill, the horses plodding in the clinging mud. Yggur and Shand swung down simultaneously.

"So what *did* you do?"

"I became a wandering tinker. I had always been good with my hands. I fixed pots, mended chairs, windows, cartwheels—anything that was broken. I earned an honest living and traveled the four corners of Lauralin for a few hundred years more—my wizardly long life had not been taken from me either."

The road became an overgrown track. They reached the top and saw that ahead the path wound across an undulating meadow of gray turf—coarse grass that was long dead. A line of green marked the course of a rivulet, wandering back and forth to their left. The road crossed it half a league ahead. Directly in front of them, beside the road, were the ruins of a cottage. Just a chimney remained, the angle of two walls and a scatter of stone. Behind was an old fruit tree, twisted and rotten in the middle, but with one upstanding branch to which a few yellow leaves still clung. Two rotten strands of rope, forlorn remnants of a child's swing, dangled down.

"What a sad place," said Shand, this ruin making an echo in his own life.

They mounted up again but Yggur did not resume his tale. He was thinking much the same thoughts as Shand. How would it be when they found Maigraith? How would she react to him? Yggur felt insecure. Surely if she still cared she would have tried to contact him before this.

"How did you find the Mirror, Yggur?"

"I heard rumors about it."

"Long ago?"

"No, only twenty years. Just yesterday in the span of our lives, though long after I went to Fiz Gorgo and made it mine."

"So what brought you out of your tinker's life?"

"I enjoyed listening to the wandering tellers and the tavern yarns, particularly about the deeds of the great, such as Yalkara's disappearance. That was a long way from here—I spent most of my time in the east and the chilly south. But one time I had come west as far as the shore of the Sea of Thurkad, and there I heard a tale about a certain Magister of Thurkad, a great hero who single-handedly saved the world from Rulke after my follies had brought all to ruin. My memories of that time were faulty, but not so faulty that every twisted bone and warped sinew did not scream out, *Lies! Lies!*"

Shand listened in silence, but for all his liking for Yggur he could not help wondering who was doing the lying. Wondering if Yggur, after committing the great crime of the Experiments, might not have invented the story to avoid facing up to his own culpability and his own failure. The past year had demonstrated what an unstable man Yggur was. When he was up, he could be the most pleasant company. But when he was down, not even his best friend was safe.

Yggur continued. "Then I learned that Mendark was still alive. He was still Magister of Thurkad as he had been eight hundred years before, when my downfall began. He had lost nothing, yet *still* he felt compelled to aggrandize himself and destroy my reputation." Yggur twisted the reins so hard around his fist that they made red and white stripes across his skin. "That day, that minute, *that second* I resolved to revenge myself on him for that great lie.

"But I soon found that Mendark's tentacles were in every business. He was rich beyond any description of riches, while I was a wandering tinker with nothing but what I carried on my back. In eight centuries my powers had faded practically to nothing. I had forgotten most of the Secret Art, so long had it been since I'd used it. My revenge would have to be the project of lifetimes.

"I had to have a place where I could slowly build my strength, and moreover one that cost me nothing, since I had nothing. So I took over the ruin that was Fiz Gorgo. It was so far from anywhere important that for a decade no one even knew I was there. I made parts of it habitable, wrote down a book—hardly more than a pamphlet, actually—of what I remembered of the Secret Art, and began to practice it. That took the most laborious and painful effort to cram into my brain, and even more to keep there. Finally I mastered some of the simplest procedures, and that gave me something I could sell. I hired out my powers in enterprises that were dubious more often than not, gaining wealth enough to employ retainers and begin the repair of Fiz Gorgo. After that, fifty or sixty years ago, I discovered the Whelm. They had dwindled away to nothing for want of someone to serve, so I swore them to me."

"Did you know that they'd once been Ghâshâd?"

"Of course! That's why I went looking for them. I had the irony in mind, though it has bested *me* since. Anyhow, I set out to track down any device from the ancient world that could help me gain what I desired. The tavern tales were full of magical cups and rings, chalices and swords, bells and orbs, and enchanted handkerchiefs for all I knew. I made lists and set out to find them, and if necessary wrest them from their owners. I collected a great swag of them, though few lived up to their reputation."

"Including the Mirror?"

"It wasn't on my list—I came across it by accident."

"Really?" said Shand. "I have some interest in this part of your story."

"Not really accident, I suppose, since by now I had a network of spies who reported strange and unusual things to me. Some third-rate cutpurse had looted it, or stolen it from someone who had. She made a living with it at country fairs, reading futures. She must have had a minor talent, for she could make the Mirror show a different scene each time a customer looked at it, and then she told them what it meant.

"I had never heard of the Mirror of Aachan but I was interested enough to go to the future-teller myself. As soon as I saw the device I knew how valuable it was, and how old. It showed me Aachan and it showed me Rulke, though now that I think of it, never Yalkara. I took the Mirror—I paid her a fair price!—and went back to Fiz Gorgo to learn how to use it. As a spying device it was far from perfect, but it gave me an impossible advantage over my neighbors, and soon I grew powerful."

By the time they reached the stream it was mid-afternoon. They broke the journey with bread, cheese, onions and a bowl of chard or two to warm them. A south wind had come up strongly and neither was in a hurry to go back out in it. Shand put the pot back on the fire for a second brew.

Scarcely had Yggur lifted his bowl to his lips, found that it was too hot and put it down again, when they heard galloping hooves. Shortly a patrol of his own troops came up the road from the west in full flight. As they flew past they must have seen the smoke, for they wheeled and came trotting toward the camp. They were soldiers of his First Army. He knew the sergeant, a veteran called Grisk.

For once in his life Yggur did not know what to do. His disguise would fail as soon as he opened his mouth—his voice was utterly distinctive. The last thing he wanted was to be recognized, to put up with the apologies, the discussion of his plans, and probably, no matter what his orders were, being secretly watched over by them. His troops took their duty seriously.

Shand came to the rescue. "Hunch down. Look ill. If you have to speak, just whisper." He took the bowl out of Yggur's hand and held it to his lips. Yggur sipped then Shand tipped the bowl right up and a flood of hot chard poured down his windpipe. Yggur choked and spluttered. Tea dripped from his beard.

When Grisk strode up Yggur was gasping, tears flooding from his eyes. "Don't laugh," said Shand. He rose to meet the sergeant.

"Papers!" said Grisk.

Shand was already patting his pockets, looking obsequious and bobbing up and down on his toes with the expression of anxiety characteristic of the genuinely innocent when confronted by authority. Grisk frowned at the papers, which were in perfect order, but much tattered and stained. He turned toward Yggur. Shand had already anticipated him and was fumbling in the pocket of Yggur's greatcoat. He drew out the documents in their wallet, handed them to the sergeant and turned back to Yggur, whose beard was now sagging off his chin. The tea had dissolved the glue. Yggur stank of rotten fish.

"My cousin is poorly," said Shand over his shoulder, shoving the beard back in place with the heel of his hand. "I'm taking him to his daughter in Sallitt to be nursed."

Grisk inspected the papers, then peered at Yggur. He had drawn his shoulders forward and assumed a look of abject misery, punctuated by fits of coughing. Grisk examined the papers again. He looked uneasy.

Yggur hawked, coughed and hawked again, trying to clear his throat. He made a revolting gurgling, bubbling noise and finally spat a strand of mucus onto a stick in the fire, where it lay sizzling. Then he began again, hunching his shoulders and coughing until the tears started out of his eyes. He paused for a moment, managed to whisper, "Rafe at your service, sur." Hawk, hawk, gurgle, sniff. "I'll be with you in a minute, sur." Hawk. Cough.

Grisk had lost interest. He handed the papers to Shand, walked back to the patrol, who had not dismounted, and they continued up the road at a fast pace.

Shand burst out laughing.

"You can laugh!" Yggur said furiously, tearing off the beard. His cheeks were red and blistered. "You just about choked me, and I'm sure the whole roof is gone from my mouth. But . . . thank you!"

* * *

On the second night they left their horses at a village near the border of Elludore. They were heading into the deepest, oldest parts of the wood, places where there were few paths and mounts were of little use.

"Now comes the difficult bit," said Yggur, standing under the eaves of the forest.

Shand had gone back a way and was staring west, where the mountains, a wall of snow-covered peaks, rose out of forest-clad hills. He was thinking about Karan and the mistakes of his past.

"Come on!" Yggur called impatiently.

Shand shook himself out of his recurring daydream. "The wheel turns, and turns again. What will we find in Elludore?"

"Maigraith, I hope," said Yggur. "I miss her terribly, Shand. She did so much for me. After this, I'll never let her go."

Shand frowned and changed the subject. "I wonder about this gold of Faelamor's."

"So do I. Especially since Mendark is so keen on it."

"And you aren't?"

"Oh, I'm keen all right. Keen to find out what it really is and where it came from."

"You don't believe what you've heard so far?" Shand's expression was studiedly neutral.

"There's something not right about it. *I* won't be making any golden flute out of it if we ever get the stuff. But I don't like the idea of Faelamor having it either." He shrugged his pack higher.

"Then let's keep our eyes open," said Shand. He brushed past and led the way into the forest.

They walked steadily all day, south and west, hardly speaking. The going was easy in undulating country. The trees were far apart but there was a dense undergrowth, so that it was difficult to see from the path into the forest.

In the afternoon the ground began to slope upward, and here the forest became taller on rich chocolate soils scabbed with old snow. At dusk they reached the top of a ridge and found that the other side sloped steeply down into a deep ravine that cut across the path. It was too dark to work out a way around it so they made camp halfway down, where a tiny spring bubbled out from the base of a limestone scarp. Shand traced the whorls of eons-dead creatures in the stone and shivered.

"Look at this! Did you ever see such beast-forms?"

Yggur grunted.

"How old is Santhenar, that the very life in the seas has turned to rock? This must be a magical place."

"There are many such places," said Yggur, "but no one has ever worked out how to tap such old magic."

"Right," said Yggur after dinner. "We're here! Where do we start?" He unrolled a map copied onto parchment and spread it out on the ground. The forest, mapped in emerald ink, looked enormous. He measured it with his fingers.

"Twenty leagues by fifteen. That's a vast area," he said gloomily.

"What did your spies tell you?" Shand asked.

"The ones who followed the Faellem? They lost them midway into the forest; on the second day, or the third. They crossed the river and went west."

"Beyond this spur?" Shand pointed to a branch of the mountains that extended east of the main range.

"I'd say so."

They narrowed their search down to a section of forest a few leagues along a side. Shand brought out his flask of liquor and they enjoyed a tot each. They both stared at the map in the firelight. Something rustled in the forest behind.

"I once knew this forest quite well," said Shand, pouring himself another drink. "We'll find them."

"I'll have another, if you don't mind," said Yggur, pushing forward his cup. Shand poured a none too generous measure. Yggur rapped his mug against the flask. Shand glanced up, laughed and topped it up.

"I can't help it," he said with a lopsided grin. "The first cup is freely given, but the second, that I begrudge. I had another flask in my pack but it seems to have disappeared when I traveled with Tallia. If it were anyone else I would suspect robbery, but not my dear Tallia."

"Surely not!" Yggur burst out laughing. "But I'll make sure to savour it, since you've made clear it's my last. Do you have somewhere in mind?"

"I was thinking that there are places in our search area which would be ideal for her. Deep and easily defendable valleys, running back right into the mountains." Shand scratched his head. "I once panned for gold in this part of Elludore. There's still plenty here too. I wonder . . . ?"

"What are you thinking?"

"I used to practice the Secret Art, you know." Shand had a gleam in his eye as bright as flakes of gold in the bottom of a dish.

"I had guessed," Yggur chuckled. "And you have in mind a little . . . geomancy, perhaps?"

"Where better than in this ancient place?"

Shand was up at dawn, pacing back and forth as he worked out what was required. "Get up, lazybones!" he said, nudging Yggur's sleeping pouch with the toe of his boot.

"I've never been called that before," grumbled Yggur as he rolled out. "At least, not by anyone still alive!"

Shand snorted. "Climb up there, would you?" He pointed to the cliff face. "Find me a bowl-shaped stone made from that ancient rock. Then weave a little boat, from this!" Shand hacked a lock from his beard. "It will help point to Maigraith, I hope."

"I haven't had my breakfast," Yggur said sourly.

"You haven't earned any! Come on, time's a'wastin'."

Taking his dinner plate, Shand headed down to the river. "I may be some time," he said over his shoulder.

He walked along the bank for an hour or two before finding a suitable place, where gravel was trapped in rock riffles underwater. Wading into the frigid water he excavated material from the very bottom. Shand swirled gravel in his plate, rocking the dish back and forth as he spilled the coarse material over the side. He found no gold there, nor from several nearby locations, but gravel from across the river rewarded him with half a dozen flakes no bigger than grains of salt, and one larger piece of gold the size of a tealeaf. It was enough. He headed back.

At the camp, ham and onions and bread were frying in dripping. Yggur had levered out a lump of stone the size and shape of a washbasin. The strange petrified life-forms ran through it from front to back. He had also woven the hair into a tiny canoe and sealed it with tree gum.

"I found this as well." Yggur displayed some shiny yellow crystals on his palm.

"Fool's gold! Let's hope it doesn't make fools of us."

After breakfast Shand filled the basin with river water, put the true gold in one end of the canoe and the fool's gold in the other, and rested it on the edge of the basin. Holding the sides, he concentrated on the reflecting water, trying to imagine Yalkara's face on it as he had seen it in the Mirror. That was as close as he could get to Maigraith.

Shand strained with all his will, and once thought that he

did see Yalkara's shadow there. At that instant he slid the canoe into the water. It drifted halfway across, slowly revolved twice, moved slightly back the other way and stopped. The end containing the true gold was pointing west of south-west.

Shand did not consult the map. "I know where they are!"

Several days later they stood on the crest of a limestone pinnacle above a precipice, staring down into a deep and thickly wooded valley that ran right up against the sheer flank of the mountains. The rocks were saturated and moss-hung, for water poured down them most of the year. The valley was cliff-bound on either side too, and at its entrance the over-arching bluffs made a gorge with only a narrow track on one side of the river.

"This is the place," said Shand.

"I'm afraid," Yggur muttered. "I'd sooner go up against the thranx again than Faelamor. But to recover Maigraith I would . . ."

"I'm looking forward to it," Shand said with a grim smile. He rotated Yalkara's gold, silver and platinum ring on his finger.

"But even you, Shand—" Yggur said doubtfully, "great as you once were . . ."

"Yalkara taught me a lot about her. I have right on my side. And this ring, if its power has lasted. *A form of protection against my enemy,* the letter said. Not that I plan to rely on it. No, woodcraft and cunning will get us into the valley. Then we will see. But Yggur, may I say one personal thing, quite frankly? Regarding Maigraith?"

Yggur scowled. "As long as you don't plan to trade on our friendship!"

"Don't . . . have unrealistic expectations."

"I've heard enough!" Yggur snapped.

21

GYLLIAS

A snowstorm drove the Faellem into the other shelter and Maigraith heard no more. She drifted in and out of sleep for the remainder of the day, waking at dusk. The Faellem were by the fire again. Their conversation had moved on, to tales of the south that reminded Maigraith of long ago. She went out to them.

"We must find a better camp," said Gethren. "Even were we to stay, hundreds can't be accommodated here."

"There are caves further up the valley," Maigraith replied, "where the cliffs come right down to the river. They're large enough to shelter a few hundred through the winter, though in cramped circumstances."

"We like being close together. Food will be the problem. What you have put by will last our people for less than a week."

"The hunting is good in the forest," said Maigraith.

"We'd better get to work."

That day was hythe, but it passed unnoticed, for here it

was overcast and had been snowing for a week. However at moonrise Maigraith felt a foreboding and was shivery afraid all night.

She spent little time with the Faellem, who were busy hunting, fishing and smoking their catch; gathering from the nut thickets outside the valley; moving the camp upstream well past her ironstones; preparing the caves. A fortnight went by.

They began to go further afield now, on hunting and foraging trips that lasted for a week or more. They had just returned from the first of these, weary but laden with fresh meat and gatherings, when Faelamor hobbled into the camp. She moved like a crippled old woman, for her back had been damaged when Tallia crashed down on her, a fortnight ago.

Maigraith had gone down to the stream to get water. As she returned, bearing her load in wooden buckets slung from a pole over her shoulders, she saw the three Faellem standing in curious attitudes. They were arguing violently with Faelamor.

"Three hundred only!" Faelamor screamed. "What about the rest of the Faellem?"

"They swore to remain here on Santhenar," Ellami replied, leaning backward like a tree in a storm. "They will not follow you a single step. Not even if it is the only way home."

Faelamor shook from head to toe. Maigraith ducked behind a tree, thinking her liege was about to have another of her fits, but Faelamor controlled herself.

"And what do *you* say?" She gave each of them a stare that might have melted glass.

The Faellem stood up to her. "Maigraith has told us your dishonorable tale," said Gethren. "As soon as we find the book you lost, we are going *home*. To Mirrilladell!"

"Mirrilladell is not home!" Faelamor shrieked. "We are Faellem. Tallallame is our only home."

The three turned as one and walked away, their backs very straight. Faelamor roared at them but they ignored her.

"Maigraith!" she screamed.

Maigraith set down her buckets. She knew what was going to happen. Faelamor would humiliate her and remind her how useless she was. Again she would be stripped of what self-worth she had painstakingly built up.

No, not this time! The Faellem had done her a great favor. Ever since Havissard, Maigraith had known that there must be more to her life. She had been carefully preparing herself, building her strengths, exploring her weaknesses. She was nearly ready to break away.

"Yes, Faelamor?" she said calmly, emerging from behind her tree.

"You betrayed me! I ordered you to say nothing to them!"

"They are your people!" Maigraith tried to defend herself. "Why should I not answer them when they question me?"

Faelamor's rose-gold skin flushed copper. "Your duty is to *me*! Only me!"

"Why is my duty to you?"

"Because I fed you, clothed you and gave you the best education anyone on Santhenar has ever had. I gave a hundred years of my life for you!"

"You didn't do it for me! You did it to further your own wicked plans."

"It doesn't matter why I did it."

"The Faellem say that . . ."

"The Faellem are sheep!" Faelamor said contemptuously.

Maigraith found a better argument. "I am not your species at all. I cannot owe any duty to you. I repudiate you utterly." She held her breath for the attack.

Faelamor's eyes flashed and she raised one hand. Maigraith recognized the compulsion this time, though she still didn't know how to defend herself against it.

"You will—" Faelamor broke off and limped to the mouth of the cave. "There's someone out there," she whispered. Her golden eyes stared into infinity. "I know that aura, that defense. Oh, this cannot be! *She* can't have come back." She slid out the side of the cave, bent like a hunchback.

It's just the Faellem returning, thought Maigraith. Nonetheless she felt a twinge of excitement. Outside the air was still. Sugary flakes of snow drifted down to coat the rocks. She watched Faelamor creeping up the slope above the cave, only to vanish in mid-step. Maigraith shrugged, tucked her winter cloak beneath her and sat down on a log bench at the entrance. Sometimes this spot was warmed by brief shafts of sunlight.

She took out the silver stylus found in Havissard, absently playing with it, remembering how she had used it as a focus for her return trip there a few months ago. She wondered if her two shaped ironstones were still intact. The Faellem might have knocked them down. They had been very angry about Faelamor's gate—the forbidden device—but she did not know if they felt the same way about her own. It no longer mattered. Maigraith needed no such aid anymore.

She felt in her pocket for the stone egg. It slipped comfortably into her palm. Maigraith suddenly felt sure that it was as much a focus, and the mouth of the cave all the structure that she needed, to make a gate. For months she had clung on here, waiting for some spark to send her on her way. Now suddenly that possibility became an explosion of liberation. Why not? There was time for her to make a new life in a new place. Faelamor had told her a hundred times how flawed she was, how worthless. Well, let her solve her own problems!

Maigraith squeezed the egg between her folded palms, took a deep breath and focussed on using it to make a gate. Immediately the scene outside the cave began to drift, the rough brown trunks and brown fern fronds smearing together, though she had not even thought where to go. Then a stick snapped in the forest above her. Who could it be? The Faellem's woodcraft was legendary. Maigraith hesitated. There wasn't time to complete the gate and she did not want to be caught in the middle of it. She let go again.

Faelamor came sliding down the slope, her boots gouging through snow into the damp earth. She looked like a corpse wired up into a semblance of life.

"Someone's got in!" she gasped. "I felt the same warping as in Havissard. It must be Mendark, come for my gold." Rank sweat dripped from her brow.

The warping had come from Maigraith's aborted gate, but she said nothing. Faelamor's terror delighted her.

Faelamor went inside, the water bucket rattled and she reappeared, gulping from the dipper. She went quite still, then began to sway imperceptibly—a trance-like state she sometimes used to calm herself. Maigraith stood watching her, when she felt a ghostly stirring and all her skin rose up in goosepimples. Turning slowly she beheld an old man outside, barely four paces from her. His gray beard and floppy hat were coated with snow and ice. His green eyes shone. In one hand he carried a dark staff, but Maigraith felt not the least afraid.

She leaned forward, wanting to cry out: "*Who are you? What do you want here?*" but the old man did a curious thing. Shaking his head, he put a finger across his lips.

In the cave behind her, the dipper clattered to the floor. Faelamor let out a wailing cry. Maigraith did not turn around—she wanted to hold onto this strange dream for just a moment longer.

The man gave her a reassuring glance. His eyes moved past her, following Faelamor's movements. Faelamor stopped dead. It was not Mendark, but a face she had long forgotten.

The man's face changed. He became very cold, very stern. He stepped forward. Maigraith could have reached out and touched him. She wanted to.

"Gyllias!" cried Faelamor.

The man nodded. "That was my name once," he said quietly. "But I am known as Shand now. I have come for what is mine."

Shand! Maigraith tasted the name. It was a strong, kindly name. She had heard it before. Shand was Karan's friend. She looked him over—weatherbeaten old face tanned to a leathery color, a stocky frame that was still in good condition.

Faelamor spat on the floor. "You were not my match even in your prime, Gyllias, and your prime was a *very* long time ago. Even with the gift of life, as evidently you have, time has wearied you." But on the last word Faelamor's voice cracked. She thrust the fear away. "Old man. *Old fool!* Feel your old knees tremble. See the mist before your *old* eyes." She gestured in the air.

Maigraith's knees went as weak as butter. Her vision grew blurred, as if she was an old woman peering out of cataract-ridden orbs. She was so decrepit, so useless that she could scarcely remember who she was. She wanted this dear old man, so kindly when he gazed at her, so stern when he looked away, to turn aside, shaking his head as if he had been overcome by a dream, and pass out of their lives again. Faelamor had terrible powers at her command. Her illusions could drive anyone insane. Maigraith wanted no harm to come to Shand. And yet she wanted him to stay, to confront her as no one had in all her memory.

Shand laughed and the illusion fell to the ground like a discarded nightgown. "The time for games has gone, Faelamor! I am indeed old. Old as the mangrove tree that grows with its knees in the sea, year in, year out. And I am tough as the roots of the mangrove tree too. Bent I am, and brown, baked into a form that can resist any battering, as the roots of that tree make boat ribs to withstand even the hurricanes of the great ocean."

Faelamor's answer was another gesture, another simple pattern; but every muscle stood out with the effort. Maigraith fell to her knees. None of her senses seemed to work properly. Her vision shrank into a tunnel directly in front of her, outside which everything was distorted unrecognizably.

Shand waved his hand in the air and Yalkara's protecting ring shone in a fleeting beam of sunlight. The gesture was a dismissal, a refusal to believe in illusion, and instantly it was gone.

"You robbed me of my daughter," said Shand. "You took from me the most precious thing I ever had, and unmade it. Now I have come for payment."

Faelamor cast mirages in the air that would have driven anyone else mad, that had Maigraith gasping and twitching on the floor of the cave. Shand was unmoved. She tried other deceptions, the best she knew, but confidence was all and hers had evaporated before those deep green eyes, that unshakeable resolve. Her legitimacy was lost. She could not stand before the wrath of old Shand.

Maigraith saw Faelamor's courage dribble away. It was like cutting off her right hand to submit to Shand, yet Faelamor was defeated and she knew it. She put a glamour on herself and disappeared. As she went past, Shand spread his fingers at her, using the Secret Art this time, and her concealment was stripped off. She put the deception back at once, and Shand did not renew his charm, but for a fleeting second Maigraith saw her face. It was as if Faelamor screamed out in agony—a torment embarrassing to have witnessed.

Shand's eyes followed her invisible progress out into the forest. "She won't be back for a while!" he said softly.

Maigraith was utterly confused, yet at the same time felt like bursting into song. This was the greatest day of her life. She went slowly toward Shand. He took off his hat. He was a short man, only her own height. The hair was thin on the top of his head. She felt concerned for him.

"Why have you come?" she whispered. "Who are you, Shand?"

He gazed at her in wonder. "I am your grandfather." He held out his hand. She took it. "Aeolior, your mother, was my daughter, and Yalkara's. Oh Maigraith! Granddaughter!" He threw out his arms.

Such a feeling of warmth and belonging came over Maigraith that tears sprang to her eyes. They walked down the steep slope together, and downstream to a special place by the river where she sometimes came to sigh and dream—things she had only learned how to do since Havissard.

It was a little platform of gray stone, raised slightly above short grass. Behind, the tall trees of the forest ran in a sweeping curve. The platform dropped in two steps to a tiny rapid over which the transparent water chuckled merrily into a pool whose bottom of multicolored pebbles was perfectly clear. One side of the pool graded into a beach of cobbles. On the other side the sward swept around the platform in the shape of a B, and between the two rounds of the B a leaf-strewn path led into the forest. They sat together on the platform. Maigraith still held Shand's hand. She turned to him a face wet with tears.

"I've not cried since I was a child," she said. "Faelamor did not allow tears."

Maigraith was almost exploding with tension, with expectation. Shand had answers to the most important questions of her life—who she was and where she had come from. She could hardly bear to ask him.

"Tell me about Aeolior, Shand. And my father, who was he? Tell me everything."

Then, before he could begin she put a finger to his lips. "Wait—I have something to show you. These are my most important treasures and I don't even know why." She carefully unpacked her prizes, showing them to him—the silver stylus and the writing tablet with the single word, rather smeared and smudged now: *Aeolior*.

Shand stared at the relics in wonderment. "I gave that stylus to your grandmother. It was my very first gift to her. Where did you get it?"

"Faelamor and I went through a gate into Havissard. She was afraid, but I was happy there."

They clung together once more; together they wept by the river. "That stylus brings back wonderful memories, and terrible ones too," he said. "It was Yalkara's most precious possession, but she could not take it with her through the gate."

"Tell me about Aeolior."

He told her the terrible story, concluding, "And Faelamor stole her and mated her with a Faellem man to make a triune."

"Me?" she exclaimed.

"Yes, you are triune."

"Like Karan!" she whispered. "Perhaps that's why I've always been drawn to her."

Shand started, but did not question her. "Karan!" he said thoughtfully. "That explains many things. You are like her, but at the same time very different. What a coincidence! Or is it? You are, very probably, the only two triunes in existence."

"Who was my father, Shand?"

"I don't know. Perhaps only Faelamor does."

Only then did Shand remember Yggur, who had been waiting quietly all morning so as not to interfere with this time. "I have another surprise for you." He leapt to his feet and cried out, "Hoy!" in a voice that echoed in the valley.

Yggur appeared, limping, unable to hide his unease. He looked older, more worn, and his eyes were distorted behind thick glasses.

"Yggur!" she cried, leaping up and running to him, her hair flying. "Oh Yggur, how I worried about you. Faelamor told me that you were dead in Katazza."

"I was close to it," said Yggur, "but that is quite some time back now."

She embraced him too, though with more solicitude than passion. She had never before displayed her emotions in public, but now she did not care. Even Yggur shed a tear at the sight of her joy, and put out a hand to stroke her beautiful hair, though he did not. She brought them together as if they did not know one another, and sat between them, and laughed and cried and skipped and sang. Such a perfect day.

Finally Shand stood up. "We can't stay here—the longer we give Faelamor, the more time she will have to think of a way to attack us. What will you do now, Maigraith?"

Maigraith had no idea. "What do you require of me?"

"Require?" said Shand. "That life is over forever. What do *you* want from your life?"

She could not get used to the idea that they could want her and yet not want something *from* her, so inured was she to duty and to service. Freedom was not part of her existence.

"I want to know who I am, and everything about my family. I want to fit into my family Histories."

"Will you come back with us?" Yggur asked diffidently. "At least until you find yourself."

"Why do you ask so timidly? We are still friends, if we can be nothing more."

"Your life has greatly changed, and so has mine," Yggur replied softly. "I have been close to death, though," here he gave a wry smile, "evidently not as close as you were told. I have been brought very low, and though I rose up again I am greatly changed."

"Shall we go?" said Shand. "To Thurkad?"

"If that's where you want to go," said Maigraith, "I'll gladly go with you. All places are the same to me. But I *would* like to see the Mirror, if you have it."

Shand handed it to her without a word. She allowed it to unroll on the palm of her hand, then passed it back.

"It's yours," said Shand.

"Mine?" she said in amazement. "I don't see how it can be, but even if it is, I don't want to receive it here. When we reach our destination will be soon enough."

Shand put the Mirror away and they departed. They did not want to hurry, but each knew that they could not indulge themselves. The climacteric was at hand.

And on their journey to Thurkad one thing soon became quite clear. Whatever she still felt for Yggur, it was as a friend, not as a lover or a partner. That struck him hard, for it was the death of all his hopes and dreams. He did not show that face to her, but afterwards he was as hard as stone to everyone else.

22

Reunion

After leaving Gothryme, Karan and Tallia walked steadily from dawn to sunset every day, but it was hard going in the slush and took an exhausting week to reach Thurkad.

"You're very quiet lately," Karan said on the seventh day, as they climbed a stony ridge.

At the top, Tallia rested momentarily against a post-and-rail fence, which moved under her weight. "I was thinking about Lilis . . . Wondering how she is."

"And Jevi?" Karan asked, idly picking pieces of lichen off the rail.

"Him too."

In the early afternoon they trudged up to the Saboth River bridge, which was still under repair from the damage done in last summer's siege. They found the bridge to be a mess of scaffolding with just three rows of nailed-down planks across the long center span. They had to wait their turn to cross, and the wait looked like being a long one. Ahead of them a series of wagons were being maneuvered across on the planks.

Karan paced back and forth, cursing the war, the bridge, the incompetence of its builders and the stupidity of all wagon drivers, not to mention the arrogance, venality and corruption of the man who ran the city—Mendark! Tallia listened in silence.

"I'm afraid!" said Karan. "I'm sure something's happened to Llian. You know how he needs taking care of."

"It won't be long now," said Tallia. "There goes the last wagon. He's got a hell of a load on."

The wagon was so old that it was practically falling to pieces. Karan resumed her pacing. "They're so damned slow!"

"I would be too, if I were taking a horse and cart across that."

"The horse doesn't seem very happy."

The nag, a bony gray mare whose mane had been trimmed into a chevron shape, had balked in the middle. The driver was out in front, heaving at the reins, but the horse refused to budge.

"I hate this city!" Karan said. "Only in Thurkad would they do such a makeshift job. Look, there's a whole stack of timber over there that's not being used."

"Oh dear!" exclaimed Tallia.

Karan spun around. The teamster was cursing and snapping his whip at the horse's flank. She tossed her head and one back hoof skidded off the side of the plank. The mare reared up, the wagon rolled backward and the left-hand wheel went over the edge. The teamster roared, the mare screamed, the wagon tilted sideways.

"The poor horse!" shouted Karan. "Quick, Tallia!" She ran onto the middle row of planks.

Tallia followed carefully, for the planks were wet and it was a long way down to the river, which was flowing strongly after days of sleety rain. The brown flood looked perilous, and the further shore was rimmed with ice.

The driver, a podgy man of middle age, completely lacking in hair and even eyebrows, lashed furiously at the terrified horse. His cheeks were carved with lines of bitterness and frustration.

"Pull!" he screamed. "Cursed nag, pull harder!"

The mare lunged weakly against the harness, but the wagon continued to slip backward, for it was so laden that the axle was bent. Karan came racing up. "Cut it free!" she screamed, "or you'll lose the horse as well."

The teamster wailed and slashed the whip uselessly in the air. "My wife will kill me," he wept.

Karan tried to calm the frightened animal, but with the driver screaming and lashing at it the mare was beyond help. It reared up like an angry stallion, pawing the air with its front feet. Karan, who had been stroking its neck, almost went over the side.

Hanging on with one hand, she wrenched the sideboard open and let the contents spill out: wooden crates containing wine in flasks, jugs of honey and jars of preserves.

The driver lashed at Karan, catching her painfully on the shoulder. "You're ruining me!" he screamed.

Karan ran around the back, leaping across the planks. "Help, Tallia!" she shouted.

Tallia released the tailgate, the driver belaboring her with the whip all the while. The mare reared again, skidded and fell down between the middle and side planks. The wagon tipped up on its front end, and the contents rained down through the gaps. The horse hung from the harness, kicking and screaming, then the straps broke and it plummeted head first into the river.

Karan looked stricken, but the mare reappeared a long way downstream, struggled up onto the bank and limped off to the south. The wagon crashed back down again, tearing the plank out, nails and all, and fell into the scaffolding. It hung there as the last crates slid out, smashed open on the timbers and plopped into the water.

All was silent but for the wailing of the wagon driver. "You've ruined me. My wife will repudiate me." He looked up at Karan and Tallia. "I'll sue you for every grint you've got!"

Karan looked disgusted. "Sue and be damned!" she snapped, and crossed over by the further plank. The man lay down with the whip wrapped around his fist, and banged his head on the timbers over and again.

Karan had no pass. She had thrown it away long ago. That delayed them at the gate, and she was hard put to restrain herself from abusing the guards, but Tallia's face was enough to get them through. Karan was issued with temporary papers and they were waved on into the city.

They proceeded up the road to Yggur's headquarters, an old fortress high on the hill above the citadel. There they learned that Yggur had disappeared that day, without word to anyone. Shand was gone as well. "Is Llian here?" she screamed at the guard. Mud-spattered from head to foot, she looked like a refugee from the wars.

The fellow drew himself up, directing his answer to Tallia. "I believe he was held at the citadel," he said coolly.

"*Was held?*" Karan cried, and set off at a run.

"Karan, wait," yelled Tallia. "You just can't . . ." but Karan wasn't listening. Tallia limped after her.

It was not far to the citadel, and all downhill. Tallia had no hope of catching Karan. By the time she hobbled round the corner, with the massive walls towering above, the towers looking more watchful than usual, Karan was already racing up to the gates.

The iron gates stood open, a signal to Thurkad that the Magister was in control of his city. A pair of splendid guards lounged on either side in their peacock uniforms and brilliantly polished boots, though one had a yellow egg stain down the front of his coat. Karan darted in, skidded toward the guard on the right; as he raised his pike she abruptly changed direction, shot between them and hurtled across the yard for the front door.

The guard at the rear swore, "He'll have our heads for this!" and raised his spear.

Tallia shouted, "Hold it!" with all the authority she could muster. The guard turned at the familiar voice but, thinking that Tallia was also after Karan, hurled the spear.

It struck the door by Karan's shoulder. She looked back and the swinging door knocked her off her feet. She lay on the mossy flagstones, winded, watching the second guard hoist his spear. There was nothing she could do about it. As the guard's arm flashed forward Tallia swung her fist and knocked him unconscious.

Karan darted down the side of the citadel and in through a rear door. She slipped past a dozing guard, down a cross-passage, twisted the other way at the next junction and again at the one after. A stair appeared before her, leading both up and down.

She took the downward passage, trying to walk calmly down the stairs as if nothing had happened. It would not have fooled the most casual observer, for she was dripping with sweat, her face almost as red as her wild hair. Karan knew the way to the lower dungeons, having visited Llian there at the beginning of winter. She prayed that he had not been put in that desperate hole again. Further down it was darker and her appearance would have excited less attention, had there been anyone to see it. There were quite a few prisoners in the cells but she did not come to a guard until the lower level.

The fellow warned her off, though not before Karan had determined that Llian was not here. She ran up to the next level, scanned it, and the one after. Not there either. She was back on the ground floor, the one below the main entrance. Here were the offices of the citadel—bursar, bailiffs, clerks by the score. Nothing! Down the other way were kitchens and storerooms. He wouldn't be there. Karan couldn't think of anywhere else to look. She felt sure that Llian had been tried, convicted and executed.

She wandered slowly along, feeling utterly miserable. "Hoy, you!" a huge guard shouted at her from the other end of the corridor. The sound of great flat feet echoed in the hall.

Karan darted around a corner and found another hall lined with offices. Passing one whose door was open, she leapt through, slammed it behind, ran backward without looking and crashed into someone. Someone tall and incredibly strong, with cold fingers and rubbery skin that made her flesh crawl. Twisting round, she looked up at the face of Vartila the Whelm and almost passed out. Vartila looked almost as shocked. Another Whelm stood just beyond the door.

Then, astonishingly, before she had time to wonder what Whelm guards were doing in the citadel, Vartila released her. No wonder—there was nowhere to go. The shouting grew louder; she heard great bangings all the way up the corridor.

Karan pushed into the other room, needing to sit down. Her knees were weak. She looked around, and there, across the other side of the room, appearing utterly bemused as the door burst open and guards stormed in waving weapons, was Llian. He was sitting at a table with books and papers spread out in front of him. Her heart skipped a beat. Mustering all the dignity she could manage she walked quickly across and sat down beside him on the bench.

"Don't say anything," she said. Their hands clasped under the table. They both stared imperiously at the guards.

"Not a word," he replied, squeezing her hand. The two Whelm folded their arms and stood directly in the doorway, preventing access. Mendark scowled, and his scowl became deeper when he saw who it was, but the Whelm would not even allow the Magister to pass. They had their orders.

"Only this," Llian continued amiably. "And you dared call *my* rescue clumsy!"

Karan threw her arms around him and kissed him on the mouth, smearing his face with mud. Then, long before he was ready for the dream to stop, she stood up and led him across the room. As they passed by she glanced up at Vartila and raised an eyebrow. Vartila nodded. Karan continued on. She stood before Mendark. Llian's hand jerked in hers. Her green eyes met Mendark's. The whole room went still. Even Tallia, who had followed him in and was standing at the back, gave a shiver.

There would be no confrontation this time. Mendark gave an ironic little twitch of the lips. Even Vartila was smiling, a sight no one had ever seen.

"There will be no trial," Karan said. "Llian has done nothing wrong and you cannot hold him any longer."

"No trial for *Llian*!" said Mendark. "Tallia has cleared him. But you are a different matter. Don't leave Thurkad, Karan."

He stepped aside and Karan went by. Llian followed, recently off his crutches and limping badly. Vartila came after with her fellow Whelm, carrying Llian's books and papers in their arms.

Tallia strode up from behind. "You can take care of yourselves now? You don't need me?" She sounded anxious.

"Thank you, Tallia," said Llian. "I wish you well with your lover."

She went red, then rushed off.

"Where are we going?" Karan asked.

"To the master's fortress," rasped Vartila. "My orders are to guard Llian with my life."

"What about me?" Karan's voice trembled.

"I have no instructions concerning you. Nonetheless, I can anticipate my master to a certain extent." She gave a mirthless chuckle, a sound like the ratcheting of rusty gears. "Protection is extended to you as well, until Yggur returns."

Karan said nothing more, just held Llian's hand tightly as they followed Vartila to the grim stronghold up the hill. She had always known that there must be a reckoning for her work in Carcharon, but nonetheless Mendark's words had frozen her marrow. And she was dismayed by the painful hobble that was the best Llian could do. She wanted to pick him up and cradle him in her arms. She almost could have, he was so thin.

They went in through the front door. There were no lounging peacock sentries here—the guards were dressed in military drab, but they were hard-eyed and alert. Vartila led them down a broad corridor. The dark stone was undecorated and dimly lit, like a prison.

"Do you have anywhere . . . *nice*?" Karan asked in a barely audible voice. Her desire to be alone with Llian was like a living flame, but she did not want to hold their reunion in a cell. Vartila made a sound in her throat that might have been a chuckle or a sneer.

They went up several flights of stairs and along another gloomy corridor. Unlocking a creaking door, Vartila gestured them in. It was a good-sized room, though as somber as the rest of the stronghold. It could have been worse, Karan thought, tugging Llian's hand.

Vartila scissored her way across the room and drew back the curtains. Flooded with light, the room was not drab at all. The walls were half-paneled in myrtle-beech that had a peacock luster in the afternoon sunshine, and above the paneling were painted in honeyed cream. The curtains were burgundy brocade, the floor covered in a plain carpet of the same color. Through the doorway of the sitting room she saw an immense bed with six posts and a canopy, beyond which was a bathroom clad in travertine.

The bathroom had a large square tub in the middle, and next to it a five-legged stove with a cast-iron tank on top, as big as a water barrel. Vartila filled the tank, which was full of round stones, and lit the stove.

"When the water is hot," she said, "turn this tap. Be sure to keep the tank topped up or it will boil dry. I will send up your dinner." She went out.

Karan and Llian stared at one another. She felt anxious.

Llian opened his arms. "Oh, Karan," he said. "I can't believe you're here at last."

Karan leapt into his arms with such force that she knocked him over. Wrapping her arms around him, she smothered his smudged face with kisses, and they rolled across the pink travertine tiles until they fetched up against the side of the bath.

"What's that funny noise?" Llian asked a long time later.

Karan opened her eyes. The room was full of fog. "The tank is boiling!" She turned the tap and scalding water spurted into the bath, accompanied by clouds of steam. "Put the plug in. Quick! Before it all runs away."

Llian took a long time to get to his feet, she noted with dismay. By then she had done the job and the cold water was running. Soon the bath was brimming with suds. Karan sighed. "A hot bath! I can't even remember the last. Turn your back while I undress, please."

"I've never known you to be modest before," he said, wondering if her feelings had changed toward him.

"I am extremely modest, save with my chosen lover," she said archly. Llian looked crestfallen. Then she laughed and kissed him on the nose. "Llian, I haven't bathed in weeks. I'm disgustingly filthy and I don't want you to see me like that. When I am clean you can stare at my nakedness until your ears smoke. Turn your back please."

Llian grinned and went into the other room, where he found a dinner tray already waiting on the table. He locked the outside door, ate a piece of bread, arranged his papers on a desk and turned down the bed. Then Karan called, "You can come in now."

The steam was so thick that he could hardly see the bath. Karan's red hair hung down in dripping ringlets. Her face was flushed.

"Turn your head away while I undress," he said teasingly.

"Nonsense," she replied. "I intend to inspect every bit of *you*."

Llian took off his shirt. "Look how thin you are," she fretted. "I could rattle a stick down your ribs." He took off his trousers. "Oh!" said Karan, sitting up in the bath. Above each ankle was a broad red band where the ice-crusted manacles had rasped away skin and flesh. She stood up in a cascade of water, touching the sunken and scarred flesh. "Does it hurt?"

Llian did not answer. Her wet skin was the color of oiled pearls. He gazed in paralyzed distraction. "It hurts somewhat," he said after a momentous silence.

Taking his hand, she tugged him forward. "Remember the game we played at the top of the Great Tower of Katazza?"

Llian gave a crooked grin. "Which game?"

"The competition to see who had the most scars, and the best. I thrashed you soundly!"

"I remember you sneering at my injuries," said Llian, "while boasting overmuch about your own."

"You were proud and needed to be brought low. And the game—"

"Yes? Get to the point. It's cold out here."

She touched his ruined shins. "The game is over. You win!"

His smile broadened. "Since then I've been brought *very* low. You need to raise me up again."

She scanned him, up, down, middle. "I don't think so, mister chronicler!" She tugged at his hand. "Get in!"

Llian slid over the side of the tub, slipped on the wet enamel and fell into her arms.

Llian lay sleeping in an untidy sprawl across the sheets, one hand still curled about her waist. Karan could not sleep. She slid closer so that their bodies touched from shoulder to hip to ankle. He did not even twitch. This was her chosen man. She wanted no other. But their union was destined to be unfulfilled, for triunes were sterile. The line would end here. There would be no heir for beloved Gothryme, no child to pass her family Histories to, or his. What would Llian do when she told him? She had no idea. That was a future they had never discussed.

They had so much to say to each other that it could not all be said in a month. The first day they hardly talked at all, just rejoiced in being together at last, communicating by touching. For the whole day they did nothing but walk together, or just lay face to face, whispering quietly.

But after that, how much was there to tell each other!

How eagerly did he listen to Karan's tale, and though she stumbled and rambled and sometimes contradicted herself, and failed to remember quite what had happened here and there, none of that mattered. All he cared was to hear the tale in whatever manner she chose to tell it.

That took at least a day, what with late starts and occasional excursions to the roof of the fortress to look down on the citadel and the city (their Whelm guard never far away), and breaks for meals and snacks, four or five times a day, and a delicious warm clinging siesta together in the mid-afternoon, with the fire crackling on the other side of the room and the snow falling gently out the window. Discovering one another, renewing one another.

"How did you ever find the courage to do what you did in Carcharon?" asked Llian.

"I thought of you, and the courage you showed when you were battered and ill from the torments of Mendark and Rulke, when you knew that the whole world was against you, *even your lover*! Llian, I'm so sorry! But you never gave in and you never thought of yourself. You challenged Rulke to a telling to save me. I remembered how afraid you were when we parted that day, how you trembled when I embraced you. And then you just went out and did what was needed, and you did it so well.

"So how could I be less steadfast? I had to do what Rulke wanted. Anything less would have left you as you were before. I've hardly slept since, for worrying what you would think of me."

"You're the best friend any man ever had—that's what I think of you."

"But Rulke failed and so I failed too. I'm afraid, Llian. One day he'll come for me. He told me so. As soon as he's ready it will all begin, and what will the consequences be? I feel so guilty. Everything I do sets off a train of disaster."

"I have those problems too," he said.

"And what do you do about them?"

"The best I can do, and worry afterwards."

"I've learned a lot about myself over the past few months," he said some time later. "I brought all my troubles upon myself."

"What nonsense!" said Karan.

"I did! I was so set on knowing the tale that I didn't care what I did. But instead of just following the story I kept interfering to see what would happen next. I pursued the Histories recklessly, regardless of any other loyalties. I was as greedy as Mendark; as Tensor; as anyone!"

"Well—" she said. "What else have you been doing over the past few weeks, Llian? How did you fill your days, apart from pining for me?"

"That didn't leave much time." He laughed, at himself. "The same as before, Karan. Working on my tale. Or Mendark's, as he now likes to call it."

"*What?*" Karan spat her drink into the fire. "After what he did to you?"

"I owe him for my schooling and he requires the debt repaid. The obligation is real; I can't get out of it."

Karan did her best to be interested. "And how goes the tale?"

"Miserably!" he said. "It's not right. I feel that I'm demeaning my profession. Not even a great teller such as I," he gave his wonderful smile then, that lit up his whole face and warmed her too, "can make it into a tale without truth becoming the casualty."

He did not tell her his true plan. There were spies everywhere, and Mendark might even have listening devices here, like the ear Nadiril had used a few months ago.

"Then give it up. What can he do to you?"

"He can destroy me. He is very powerful still. A word

from Mendark can ensure that no one will ever hire me as a chronicler. But that's not what's stopping me . . ." his voice trailed off. He stared into the fire. She took his hand.

"What, Llian? Are you afraid of something?"

"No. The Histories behind the tale, what really happened at the time of the Proscribed Experiments—it's tantalizing. I feel as if I'm on the verge of uncovering something really interesting."

"What?"

"I don't know!" he cried, frustrated. "That's why I can't give it up."

A week had gone by since Karan's return. She was chafing to get back to Gothryme.

"They won't let you go," said Llian. "The guards on the gates will be watching for you."

"I've got to! I can't bear to be away from home any longer. Are you coming?"

"Let's go down and see."

They packed and went to an obscure western gate of Thurkad. Karan had concealed her hair and pulled her hood well down over her face. The solitary guard, a kindly-looking old woman with not a hair left on her head and ears as saggy as a bloodhound's, did not even ask for her papers.

"Go back, Karan of Bannador. It is not worth my old head to let you through."

Karan turned away, angry and embarrassed. "Let's go down to the waterfront. We'll buy passage out by ship."

"With what? I have two coppers. How much have you got?"

"A silver tar only," she said, examining the well-known contents of her pockets.

"It's no use, Karan. If we go home they'll just come and

take you back. And how can we live anywhere else with no money?"

"Why won't they let me live my life?" she wept.

That afternoon Karan decided that there was only one thing to do—beard the Magister in his office. To her surprise she was admitted instantly. He looked up at her from behind his vast ebony table.

"What do you require of me?" she asked. "Why can't I go home?"

Mendark's mouth was so thin and hard and blue and cold that Karan grew afraid. "Because you collaborated with Rulke, and there has not yet been an accounting. When Yggur and Shand return, you may be put to trial. Or . . . maybe your debt can be paid with a suitable service, *triune*!"

He smiled with his horrible lips but Karan felt cold inside. Everyone wanted to use her, just like it had been before. It was the curse of the triune. She could never escape from her heritage.

23

The Paradox of the Mirror

Llian had spent the whole week in a fruitless search for records made at the time Rulke was captured. However he could find none except those Mendark had already given him, written by the Magister himself. It was strange, since the Council kept the Histories most diligently.

Llian knew that Yggur had no memory of the incident, but surely the other members of the Council would have kept records, in this land obsessed with the Histories. He went through the lists again. The other Council members from that time had died long ago. In fact, he discovered, though young, all but Tensor had died within a year of the Experiments. Curious!

He spoke to Mendark's chief archivist but found her unhelpful, and previous interrogation of Mendark did not encourage him to do it again. Yggur had still not returned. There was only one other person who might know. Llian headed down the road to Nadiril's villa, a large square building set in its own grounds. It had a colonnaded front and a wide hall tiled in red marble.

Nadiril had not perfectly recovered from his chest complaint. The old librarian was sitting up in bed, his hands spread limply on the scarlet quilt. He looked asleep but his rheumy eyes opened at once.

"How are you, sir?" asked Llian respectfully.

"Better," he wheezed. "I may get up today. It's good of you to take the time, Llian. I'm a dull old man these days."

Llian murmured a politeness.

"But you didn't come here because you were worried about my health. You want something from me. What is it?"

Llian told him.

"Well, of course they would have written down what happened!" said Nadiril. "Every member of the Council kept the Histories, as we still do."

"There's only one record—Mendark's! No others are even listed in the catalogues."

"Hmn!" Nadiril developed a spark in his eye. "A challenge! I'm sure there's a simple explanation, but you don't want to ask Mendark, eh? Pull that cord for me and we'll breakfast together, then I'll see how I feel."

Llian had already eaten a frugal breakfast but he had the most pleasant memories of Nadiril's hospitality and was not disappointed. Afterwards they took a sedan chair up the hill to the citadel and were waved straight through the gates by the guards.

"Give me your arm," Nadiril said as they dismounted at a side door. He creaked his way down to the archives.

The archivist could refuse him nothing, since Nadiril was a member of the Council. He soon found, however, that Llian was correct—there were no other Council documents relating to the time of the Proscribed Experiments.

"You once said that dangerous documents were kept in a special place," said Llian.

Nadiril gave him a piercing glance. "So they are—the vault Yggur caught you in some time ago—but not even *those* records would describe the Experiments. Nonetheless, I'll check. You cannot come with me," he said as Llian rose. "Go through the administrative files from that time. There may be shipping records, transmittal notes or bills of lading specifying documents that were sent here. Check everything."

Llian did not see Nadiril again that day, but working into the evening he did find something of interest. He told Nadiril about it the next morning, over breakfast. The librarian was poorly, confined to bed, while Lilis hovered about looking anxious and giving Llian reproachful glares.

"Have a look at this. It had fallen down the back of an old file of shipping documents," Llian said. He passed the scrap of paper across. "It's a receipt from a woman named Uivan, for documents provided to Mendark after the death of her sister Nivan."

"Nivan was one of the seven Council members at the time," Nadiril said. He read the paper. "It lists the documents supplied. One of them is entitled *My Histories of the Experiment and the Taking of Rulke*. And the receipt is cross-signed here—the documents were received safe and complete at the citadel."

"But that's it!" said Llian, very frustrated. "There's no mention of them anywhere!"

"Nor in the secret archives," said Nadiril. "Unusual! But things can get lost in all sorts of ways in a thousand years. I'm too tired, Llian. You'd better come back tomorrow."

Nadiril closed his eyes and Lilis shooed Llian out. At the door Llian took her arm. "How are Tallia and Jevi getting on?"

"Not very well. When Tallia came back everything seemed

wonderful. Jevi was so happy to see her, then it all went wrong.

"What happened?"

"I don't know what she said to him, but he went all cold and silent. I asked him what the matter was. He wouldn't tell me. I tried to tell him that Tallia loved him but he became angry. It was terrible, Llian. Jevi has never been angry with me in my whole life. Even when I was little, and naughty, he was always patient and kind. Now he's gone away with Pender. I don't know what to do. Poor Tallia, she looks awful."

"I don't know either," said Llian. "Better leave it to them."

The next day Karan and Llian were strolling arm-in-arm past the citadel to a cheap breakfast place when they caught sight of Yggur's head above the crowd.

"I wonder where he's been?" said Llian.

"Who cares?" Karan dragged at his hand. "Come on, I'm hungry."

"Hang on, there may be news." He stood his ground and the crowd parted. "Hey, there's Shand too. Who's the woman with him?"

"It's Maigraith!" said Karan, feeling old conflicts rise to the surface. Maigraith had dragged her into this mess in the first place. But at the same time they had traveled together, shared perils together, been linked together. Karan had seen the torment in Maigraith's innermost soul. And Maigraith had led an army into Bannador, liberating Karan's country in her name. After that, Karan could forgive her anything.

"Maigraith," she shouted. "Shand!"

The three turned at her cries. "Karan!" cried Maigraith and Shand at the same time. "How did you get here?"

Karan explained. "Where have *you* been?"

Maigraith answered. "After the war in Bannador, Faelamor *compelled* me to go with her to Elludore Forest. I've been there since autumn, except for two trips to Havissard through a gate, and one or two other excursions."

"Havissard!" cried Llian. "You must tell me everything about it, for my tale."

"This is Llian, a teller," said Karan, being deliberately casual.

Maigraith inspected him minutely. "I've seen you before. It was in Narne, about a year ago. I'm glad you found Karan." She shook Llian's hand. "Karan, you cannot imagine what has happened—I have found my life. Shand is my grandfather!" She looked as happy as a child.

"Llian told me that," said Karan. "Now tell me—"

"I see you've a lot to catch up on," said Yggur, shepherding them out of the middle of the street to let an overloaded wagon go by. "Why don't you take breakfast together at my expense?"

He tossed a gold coin at Karan, who would have flung it straight back again but Llian caught it first.

"You won't join us?" Shand said to Yggur.

"This is your party. I've neglected my responsibilities too long already. We'll hold council tomorrow at nine. Don't be late!" He tipped his hat to them and strode off up the hill, with the guards who had followed him from the gate gathered round.

"I have hurt him," said Maigraith, staring after his back.

Next morning they met at Yggur's fortress, in a small room on the ground floor. As Mendark's apartment was of baroque extravagance, so Yggur's rooms were positively spartan. The chamber had an uncovered floor of wide boards, bare walls painted an ugly mud-brown and a long table with hard wooden chairs. The fireplace was set but not lit. The room was saturated with cold and damp. The meeting consisted of

Yggur, Mendark and Tallia, Nadiril in a wheeled chair, and Shand. The Aachim were still over the sea.

Karan and Llian came in late, sharing a joke. Yggur, already on his feet, scowled at them. "I have called this meeting," he began, "to review what has happened since Carcharon and to see if we can find any new ways to attack our enemies. I propose that we each tell our own tale—briefly, mind!—and then see what we can come up with."

"Seize Faelamor's gold and make the golden flute anew," said Mendark curtly.

"I like that idea even less than the last time you suggested it," Yggur replied.

"I agree with Mendark," said Shand, a wistful look in his eye.

There was a stir when Maigraith rose, last of all. Yggur was staring at her, a lost futile yearning, for Maigraith did not once look at him. She gazed at Shand, at Karan, but mostly out of the window at the roofs of the city. Yggur burns for her, Llian realized, and she won't have him.

"We've all been wrestling with the paradox of the Mirror," said Yggur. "*It can only be used by one who knows how, but that way lies within the Mirror*. Does anyone know what that means?"

No one answered.

"I've been wondering if the glyphs around the border of the Mirror have anything to do with it," said Mendark. "We know Yalkara put them there just before she went to Aachan."

Shand jumped.

"What's the matter with you?" Mendark demanded.

"Yalkara said something about that," said Shand.

"What?" cried Mendark. "What did she say?"

"The wind was howling through the gate. I couldn't hear her clearly."

"Well, see if you can work it out!" Mendark snapped. "It might be the key."

"I've been thinking about the paradox for ages," said Llian. "Actually, the answer is obvious." He gazed around the room, assuming a look of beatific simplicity.

Everyone stared at him. Mendark was the first to break. "Then what is it?" he said furiously. He had spent weeks puzzling over the paradox, without success.

Llian smiled, paused for effect, then said, "*The Mirror knows!* It was surely set to recognize Aeolior and show her how to use it."

"Aeolior is dead, you cretin!" raged Mendark.

"Ah, but I think it will open to Maigraith—"

"I'm sure it began to," Karan interrupted, "way back when she first looked at it in Fiz Gorgo. I thought it strange at the time."

"Do you have something to say, Shand?" asked Yggur.

Shand, still scratching at that memory, took a long time to answer. "The ignorant have talked for long enough. Let Maigraith speak, if she cares to."

"Yes, Maigraith, take up your birthright!" said Mendark, as imperiously as if he was giving orders to a slave. "Find what we need in it! Time is pressing."

Maigraith darted a glance at Mendark, then away quickly. "His arrogance reminds me of Faelamor," she said softly to Shand. "I'm not going back to that."

Shand squeezed her hand. "I expected to be doing this two hundred and fifty years ago," he said to the group. "But after Aeolior . . ." He eased the Mirror out of its case. A little tremor ran through him. Without looking at it, he put the tight coil of black metal in Maigraith's hand. The bright lights glinted on it, reflections shimmering down its length and back again.

"The first time I touched the Mirror, back in Fiz Gorgo,"

said Maigraith, "I felt such a fascination and a yearning, as if a whole lost world was about to open before me. Maybe it would have, if Yggur had not appeared." Her eyes met Yggur's and darted away. "I felt it calling to me then. And in Havissard I heard that call again."

Abruptly, impatiently, she opened her hand and the coil of dark metal snapped into . . . the Mirror! It reflected her face perfectly; the silky, chestnut hair that hung, quite straight, halfway down her back; the beautiful regularity of her features; the skin that was the color of honey and just as smooth; the Charon eyes, indigo crossed with carmine. Only one thing was different from the first time. Then she had been downcast, and her face had shown it. Now she looked alive.

"Llian," said Mendark peremptorily. "Copy down those glyphs. That's another matter you can work on."

They watched in silence as Llian copied the glyphs on a piece of card, checked them twice and passed the Mirror back.

"I don't know the script," he said, "though—"

"What?"

"It's strangely like . . . Yes!" he hissed. "They're the mirror image of the glyphs in Yalkara's book."

"I wonder what that can mean?" said Shand.

Maigraith stared at the Mirror without seeing it. She was thinking about Yalkara, her mother's mother. How often had Yalkara held it in her hands, using it for what purposes no one on Santhenar, probably not even Shand, ever knew? Had she wondered what her unborn daughter would be like? Had she wished that the Mirror could give her a glimpse of Aeolior's future? Surely it had not.

There was so much Maigraith wanted to know. Faelamor had taught her nothing about Yalkara, her own great enemy. And even on their journey here, Shand had scarcely spoken about her. Unraveling the past could occupy her for the rest of her life. It was part of a great mystery, one to which no one knew the answer.

"How am I meant to use the Mirror?"

"I don't know," said Shand. "My way cannot be your way, nor Aeolior's neither. The wheel has turned and you must reflect the pattern of its turning."

Maigraith moved the Mirror around in her hands, uncomfortable with these strangers feeding on her so hungrily. Had she just exchanged one tyrannous master for another? They were all staring at her, especially Yggur. All but Shand alone, who was sunk in reverie, and Karan, snuggling her cheek against Llian's shoulder. She seemed to have her hand inside his shirt. Maigraith smiled inwardly. The others all wanted something from her. But she had not gone though the past year to be mastered again so easily. She would look on the Mirror, see what it had to say, and take her own counsel. No one would tell *her* what to do, ever again.

"I can't think with everyone staring at me so," she said to Shand.

"What do you want to do?"

"Everyone wants something from me. I have to get away. Perhaps somewhere by the sea. Will you come with me, grandfather?" After a life of agonizing about who she was, the word gave her a small, tight feeling of pleasure and contentment. She was someone; she had a past and now a future. She belonged, and was loved for herself.

"I'll ask Tallia to find a place," said Shand. "She knows everything."

Shortly Tallia reappeared with an address written on a scrap of paper. Shand took it, then he and Maigraith hurried away from that abode of greedy faces to a place on the eastern side of the city, just inside the Heads.

They turned off the road to the lighthouse, down a winding, stony track. It was far enough from Thurkad that the city's stench could not be smelt, even when the wind was blowing from the west, as it was today. The path curved around a patch of wind-twisted scrub and they looked out across the outer harbor, where the blue water was flecked with foam. Waves were breaking across a bar at the entrance. Sails white, yellow and dun-colored moved up and down. They continued down the path and through a gallery forest, just a strip in the bottom of the valley.

The path wound through the rocks and scrub toward a tiny bay. Another path climbed to the top of the cliff. A gravel beach came into view. Maigraith could have tossed her hat from one end of it to the other. A cottage, barely bigger than Karan's forest hut, nestled among trees behind the beach. The windows looked across the bay. The view showed trees, water and far-off sails. They took off their packs and sat down on the porch.

"I've always wanted to live by the sea," Maigraith sighed. "I remember when I was just a little girl, playing with a battered old shell. It would have been bigger than my fist." She looked at her hand.

"Someone told me—not Faelamor, you can be sure—that the whisper I heard when I put it to my ear was the sound of the distant sea, captured there long ago. And in my childish fancy I was sure that was true, for there were times when the sound was just a whisper, the gentle waves foaming up the beach and rushing back again. Other times I heard a roaring and a crashing and a thundering that could only be the wild storm flinging gray water and green weed (and perhaps a helpless mermaid or two) against the rocks." She laughed nervously. "There was much violence, much tearing away from roots in my childhood dreaming.

"I often dreamed that I lived by that sea, with my mother and my father, and their mothers and fathers, a sister or two, even a brother. We would go for long walks across the rocks together, picking over the wrack and the drift and the strange things that lived in pools."

"You must have been lonely," said Shand, stretching his legs across the weathered boards.

"I was terribly lonely. I yearned for all the things that other children had—parents, brothers, sisters, cousins—but I was all alone. I was different. That was the first thing I knew about myself. The other children knew it too. Though I was only four or five, I was never allowed to play. I studied all day and long into the evening. At first we lived among the Faellem but when they found out what a terrible crime Faelamor had done, we were exiled."

She rested her head on Shand's shoulder, then quickly moved it again as though afraid that he would object. Shand drew her back. Maigraith gave another sigh.

"Was Faelamor your teacher?"

"Not at first. When I was little I was mostly tutored by Hana. I don't know if that was her true name. She was not

Faellem. Hana was tall with brown hair in a single plait that hung right down her back, and when she held me her skin always seemed so soft and warm. I made her into a mother, I suppose, having no other. She was kind to me. I desperately wanted a father too, but that was a forbidden topic. I've no idea who he was."

"Nor do I." Shand got up in some agitation and stared out toward the heads. The waves crashed and roared all around Shag's Rock and the Gap.

"I wish I knew. Hana understood what it was like for me because Faelamor had abducted her. She was a teacher in her own society.

"When Faelamor was away, Hana would take me for walks down to the water. I remember one place, a ridge between two lakes, the ground falling steeply to the water on both sides. I seem to recall a broken watch-tower. In winter everything was frozen, but in summer the water was so warm that we would take off our clothes and swim out to an island. It was lovely, floating there with Hana treading water beside me, watching over me.

"If it had not been for her I would have turned into a machine, which is what Faelamor wanted of me. But Hana was so kind, so loving and warm, and I knew that she, too, was a lonely prisoner. She gave me that shell and listened to my dreams about the sea. She had not seen it either, but she knew all about it. She told me stories of terrible shipwrecks, and oceans that are as warm as blood and glow with light; of towers beside the water that sent strange messages, and astounding creatures that hunted in the depths; of cruel men who sailed on tall ships, and women too, doing unspeakable things.

"But when I was eight she disappeared. One day Faelamor humiliated me for not understanding my lesson, and that night Hana came to comfort me, wiping away my tears and telling me little jokes until my misery was gone. Faelamor caught us together. I don't know what she did, but Hana went white and clutched at her head as if it would burst open. The next day she was sick and desperate. Faelamor took me away for the day's lesson. The following morning I crept into Hana's hut before dawn, but she was gone and I never saw her again.

"Faelamor was so furious that she could not speak. I suppose Hana knew too much. Faelamor went after her and I was terribly afraid for my teacher, but Faelamor did not find her. I think the Faellem must have helped Hana to escape. How else could she have gotten away from Faelamor? Not long after that the Faellem exiled us. We went far away, traveling through all the lands of the south, never staying long in one place. We never had a home after that. *Never!* How I wanted one.

"I often thought about Hana over the years, but she would be dead long ago now. The night after she disappeared I lay in bed in the darkness, weeping silently for my lost friend and for my misery. Later I woke. A full moon shone in my window and I felt stirred by something. It was cold and quiet outside: the dark shadows of the trees, the snow! I took out my shell but could not hear the sea at all. Had Faelamor cast her miserable spell over it as well?

"I traced the spirals with my fingers, outside and inside. There was something inside it, a scrap of paper folded into a pellet. It was Hana's writing. I have it still," she said, taking what appeared to be a golden bead from a chain about her neck and twisting until it separated into halves. A tiny roll of paper fell out. Unrolling it carefully she passed it to Shand. "The Whelm took it from me in Fiz Gorgo, but Yggur gave it back."

COURAGE, it said in the consciously well-formed script of a teacher. It was written in the common speech of the south-east, which Shand knew though he had not spoken it for many years. He felt his eyes grow moist for the gift of this unknown woman.

"That saved me, many times," she said. "Many times I lost heart, especially when I was becoming a woman. That was one of the most painful times for me. Faelamor tormented me so. I never knew why. I suppose it was because I reminded her of her enemy."

"Yes, you are the very image of Yalkara," said Shand. "Though a smaller version—she was a big woman."

"It must have been torment for Faelamor, seeing me growing up to so resemble her enemy. There's not much Faellem in me."

"There's enough. It just doesn't show on the outside."

"Do you know anything about my father?" she asked yet again, plaintively.

"Nothing. I'm sorry."

"Faelamor came to realize that her plan had gone wrong. She had made me, the triune that she needed, but I could not be forced into the mold she had put so much effort into constructing. I was flawed, she told me, and I think she despaired that all her work had been for nothing.

"There were times when I could think of no escape but to kill myself," said Maigraith. "I often thought of that when I was growing into womanhood. After I grew up it got better. I had achieved some mastery of the skills Faelamor had spent so long teaching me. I was able to help her, and I took satisfaction from what I was able to do, especially when it was something that she could not."

"In what way are you flawed?" asked Shand, scratching his chin.

"I had to be controllable. I could not act independently of her, or seek power for myself. She could not make someone who would break away to become a rival—that would be remaking the enemy."

"Rather ironic then, that she has brought out Yalkara in you," said Shand.

"Hardly!" Maigraith laughed. "But she must have been afraid of what I could become. She broke my spirit. That is why I failed in Fiz Gorgo, and where she first realized it. I could not impose my will on others. Since then I have developed that skill, to a degree."

"Yet you forced Karan to go to Fiz Gorgo with you."

"Poor Karan! That was not my will but Faelamor's. I would have done anything to avoid having to confess that I had failed her. Anyway, Hana's message brought me back from despair many times. But those days are so far away now." She rolled up the scrap of paper and put it back where it had come from.

Maigraith, after her initial explosion of joy in Elludore, had found it impossible to break through the reserve built up over so many years, and the demands of the company had sent her retreating back into herself. Now the sound of the sea brought all the memories and associations flooding out as if a dam had burst. "I loved that old seashell," she said with a shiver.

"What happened to it?"

"One night Faelamor found me sleeping, clutching it to me as children do with the drabbest little thing that they have made into a treasure. She threw it down and crushed it beneath her boot."

It was too long ago for Maigraith to care, though the feeling of dumb hurt was one that she was still familiar with. But Shand began to smolder. "I know the terrible isolation and loneliness the Faellem felt, when they found themselves marooned here in Santhenar. But not even Rulke would have done the things that Faelamor has done. She is utterly corrupt. Thoroughly evil!"

"Is she? I never thought that. No, it's just that the Faellem are a different human species, as the Aachim and the Charon are different. We each put our own kind first, as a dog puts its interests above those of its neighbor, the cat. She is single-minded about her own species, as you old humans are about your own race. We make so much of the rights of humankind, while denying animals any rights whatsoever."

"But animals are not human," said Shand in a tone that suggested that the issue did not warrant debating. "Well, I'm going to get this place into shape, then I'll make dinner. Can I get you anything first?"

"I want to do it with you."

And they did, enjoying the simple things like gathering wood and carrying it between them back to a heap behind the house, chopping it into lengths, collecting tinder and kindling. They made beds, cleaned away dust and cobwebs, shook out rag rugs, and when the little place was as comfortable as could be managed, and herbs and branches of aromatic shrubs had been hung up here and there in lieu of flowers, they began to prepare lunch.

Maigraith's experience of cooking extended little further than the campfire—it was not an art that Faelamor thought to be of value—and even there her productions had been austere. But Shand loved good food and took equal pleasure in preparing it. As he worked, kneading dough or beating eggs, marinating meat or creaming butter and sugar, he explained carefully what he was doing, and why, and Maigraith caught some of the pleasure from him. She was like a blind person who had just been given the gift of sight. All the world was different to her, now that she had a place in it.

They spent several days there without Maigraith even

glancing at the Mirror. Their time was taken up in clambering over the rock platforms with the sleety wind and the sea spray in their faces, or walking on the gravelly beach collecting shells. Sometimes they sat rugged up on the porch watching the sea, other times by the fire in the evenings, listening to Shand's tales and the wind in the eaves.

At first, messages came several times a day from Mendark or Yggur, but Shand tore them up and sent the messengers away. After a while they stopped coming. Then one morning Maigraith woke and knew that she was ready to use the Mirror.

She was desperate to see her grandmother's face again, and to realize the new life the Mirror had promised when first she'd taken it up in Fiz Gorgo. Perhaps it could show her Aeolior's face too. She wanted that more than anything.

Holding the Mirror in front of her, she tried to see into it. It remained no more than a metal mirror, beautiful but blank except for her reflected face. She sought out its essence as if it was a crystal that she was trying to make into a lightglass. The Mirror was indifferent. She traced the silvery glyphs around the border with a fingertip, thinking that they might be some kind of key. If they were, it was not one she could use. Maigraith shook the Mirror, cursed it, and finally, using all the power of the Secret Art at her command, attempted to force it open, to make it show Yalkara to her. The Mirror refused. It mocked her every attempt.

24

REMINISCENCES

That evening, when they were sitting on the porch again, well blanketed against the cold, taking tiny sips of yet another of Shand's liqueurs, and alternate sips of a steaming hot kind of coffee, and looking at the stars and the scorpion nebula, Maigraith asked Shand to tell her about her mother.

"I've been dreading that," he said softly. "The reopening of old wounds. Poor Aeolior! No one ever loved a child more than I loved my daughter. It would be impossible to love anyone more."

"What was she like?"

"Like other children, I suppose, though I didn't have much experience of children then. I was *much* too important for that. Aeolior was a very wilful child; clever and determined. She knew what she wanted and she would not rest until she got it, whether by wheedling me or by her own hard efforts. Yet she had a soft heart, and she was loving and mischievous too. Karan is like her in some ways.

"She would have grown up to look much like you, I

imagine. Her eyes were exactly like yours, and the curves of her face. Her hair was rather darker and wavy, like mine used to be, when I had some! She looked to be about thirteen when I lost her, though in years of Santhenar she was much older. Aeolior developed slowly, as the Charon do." His voice quavered.

"As with her, so with me," said Maigraith, and changed the subject. "Tell it some other time, if you prefer. For now, and since there are people waiting on what I do with the Mirror, even though I try my best to put them out of my mind, I would like to hear about Yalkara. And even about you, grandfather, if it does not strain your modesty too much." She said this last with a cheeky sort of a grin. It looked a little strange at first, and she gave the impression of being a little surprised at its appearance, so unused was she to joking. The grin broadened into a smile, and Shand laughed with her.

"I'll leave those tales for another day! I'll tell you what I can about Yalkara, though that may not be as much as you might suppose. We were lovers for an age, but there were great areas of her life about which she would not speak. Maybe after you've looked on the Mirror you'll know more about her than I do.

"About her previous time, before she came to Santhenar from Aachan, I know very little. About why she came here and did the things she did, and what her motives were, again almost nothing. She had an evil reputation, and was more often slandered than anyone I ever heard of. The Demon Queen they used to call her, and the Mistress of Deceits. Many other names too; worse names; foul ones! Great women attract such slander more than great men. To be great is to make decisions that affect other people, and she did not shrink from that. Yet I never knew her to do a cruel act, or even an unkind one knowingly, though she could be hard as metal to her enemies."

"How did you meet her?"

"I remember the moment I first laid eyes on her as clearly as this morning." He leaned back against the wall of the porch and closed his eyes.

The recollection stretched into minutes and the minutes into a long time. Maigraith sat watching the old man. My grandfather, she kept thinking. This man is my mother's father. There will always be a bond between us. The commonplace relationship felt so strange to her, yet so beckoning; so warming. And it spurred her to find out about the other relations she would never know—her Faellem father and his mother and father. Those grandparents could still be alive, she realized, though her father was long dead, poor abused man. Yet not as abused as her mother. Once again she was struck by the parallels between her life and Karan's. They were almost the reverse of each other. What did it signify? Or did it mean nothing at all? Was it just the kind of thing that happened to those rare few who had the misfortune to be born triune?

She realized that Shand still had not answered. He was looking quite vacant. "Shand?" she said gently.

He came out of himself like a sick fish drifting to the surface of a pond, giving her such a blank look that in spite of herself she shivered. Then he recognized her and smiled.

"I'm sorry. I find that I'm doing that more and more of late. A bad habit I got into many years ago, when I was wandering in the most abject state of misery, before I went to Tullin and found that I could be useful again. You cannot imagine what is in the mind of someone as old as I am. So many memories are tangled up together, and often it seems more pleasant, even more real, to take refuge in memory rather than remain in the present. One day I may go off into the past and never find my way back. I may forget that the now and the future exist."

Maigraith looked uncertain and afraid. "I would be desolated," she said.

Shand squeezed her hand. "That's a way off yet, never worry. Be sure that when I do go, it will be the best thing for me, because I'm utterly weary of this world. The old must make way for the young. I should not have lived this long."

"Why have you?"

"In Havissard I did not seem to age. Some enchantment of Yalkara's, no doubt. And before she left, she gave me the gift of part of her life. I often wonder what it took from her, and if she survived it." Shand came back to the present. "What were we talking about?"

"How you met Yalkara," she said.

"It was during the Clysm. Do you know about that time?"

"Of course."

He went on as if she had given the other response. "The Clysm, the wars between the Charon and the Aachim! Though when I say the Charon you must know that I do not include Yalkara. She took no direct part in that struggle. Indeed she had no army, only a small guard. The Clysm was mainly fought between the forces led by Rulke and the legions of Pitlis. Pitlis was once held to be the greatest Aachim who ever lived. He built their glorious city of Tar Gaarn, and designed Alcifer for Rulke too. But he was seduced by Rulke, and Tar Gaarn fell, and now they call Pitlis the biggest fool that ever drew breath.

"That was a desperate time for Santhenar, the worst this world has ever seen. I don't think anyone knows the true reason for the war. The Histories mostly say that Rulke began it, and that might be so. You could ask Llian the evidence for that viewpoint, if you're minded.

"Anyhow, that was when I was in the greatest flush of my manhood, full of pride and self-importance. So rash and boastful was I that I cringe to think about it. It came about that, after one terrible, bloody battle a long way away, over near Crandor, some of us held a meet on the blood-soaked field to try and find an end to it. Far better if we had gone and given comfort to the dying," he said with an edge of bitterness. "We could hear their shrieks from where we stood, but we left that to others. Important people must do *important* work!"

He paused for a sip of his coffee, which was now quite cold. "Are you cold? Shall we go in to the fire?"

"After the tale," she replied. She loved the shivery feeling of listening to his story out in the chilly air, and the stars wheeling and reflecting on the still sea.

"Our council was held under a great fig on the edge of the battlefield. It was a gigantic tree, with a trunk made of thousands of roots all twisted and woven and intergrown together. On the humped-up roots at the base we stood, one after another, and made our speeches. What rhetoric there was, and more in mine than in anyone's! And then we went down and built our alliances, and made our petty deals, and betrayed one another.

"Just as I finished my speech I noticed, on the edge of the field, a woman staring at me. That wasn't odd—everyone was watching my speech and quite a few were applauding. One or two stood to the side giving me dark looks, or turning to their own allies and their own schemes. She was a most beautiful woman, though hers was a quiet regal kind of beauty, very understated. Just like your own."

"What is beauty anyway?" said Maigraith tersely. "It is

just something to make use of if you have no useful talent. I never thought of myself as having any."

"Where did you get that notion from?"

"Faelamor often told me how repulsive I was."

"Hardly surprising, since you don't look at all Faellem, and much like her enemy. Have you never heard the tale of the ugly duckling? No? I'll tell you later on.

"As I was saying, that dark-haired woman was watching me. At the end of my speech she gave her head a little shake, as if she had not found what she was looking for, and turned away. I knew most of the important people there but I had never seen her before. What was she after? My curiosity was piqued. I had to know who she was, but no one could tell me. By the time I finished my enquiries, she was gone."

"Vanished?" asked Maigraith, who had risen right off the bench, staring at him, trying to see Yalkara reflected in his eyes.

"No, just gone, away from the slaughter fields through the forest. I ran after her, doubtless making quite a fool of myself and causing some of my allies to have second thoughts, but I was indifferent. She must have heard me, for I raced around a bend in the path and she stood there, waiting. She seemed neither frightened nor uneasy at being accosted by this madman, alone in the forest. She looked neither bothered by the intrusion nor particularly interested in it. She just waited politely, to hear what I had to say and send me on my way again.

"She wore black—a loose blouse of a lustrous material like silk, though not a wrinkle anywhere, and pantaloons of the same material. Her hair was like ebony silk and she wore red gold about her throat and forehead and wrist. Yalkara had the most flawless skin I have ever seen. She was most beautiful, perfect in every way. Then I saw that her wrists and hands were terribly scarred, as if they had been burnt.

"I ran up to her, looked into her eyes and nothing in my life was ever the same again. I, who had never wanted any woman, knew that she would be the only love of my life. If I could not have her I would have none. I would cease to exist. Every hair on my body stood on end. My stomach sweated boiling acid.

"She looked down at me, being a head taller. She inclined her head that I should speak, and a cloud passed across her face. For a moment she looked puzzled. Then she laughed, a rich mellow sound. 'I see,' she said.

" 'What is your name?' I asked politely.

"She laughed again. 'I do not give my name to strangers. You may call me Ilen, if you wish. What did you want to speak to me about?'

"I was quite bemused. I entered thereupon a rambling and almost incoherent recapitulation of my previous address. She listened to it at first politely, but with increasing impatience, looking beyond me at the forest. I grew desperate, stopped abruptly and turned away, shaking my head and feeling an utter fool. I never knew her since to suffer such a fool, and what made her do so then I cannot say. She must have seen something beneath the pomposity and the pride, for she called me back.

" 'I know what ails you, Gyllias,' she said, 'but it is beyond my power to cure. Yet if it is not a passing thing, come and see me at Lorkist' (an insignificant village in Crandor, on the other side of the mountains) 'in . . .' (she seemed to be working something out in her head) 'one year and fifteen days from today. Come to the inn on the market square and wait for me, after noon, at one of the tables outside.'

"She nodded, then turned and strode away. I watched

until she disappeared in the golden shade. I had been dismissed, though ever so politely. A year and fifteen days!

"That was the longest year of my life. Every day I thought of her; every hour. It was an obsession, and it changed everything. I had to resort to the severest mental disciplines to do my work. I, who had never needed to concentrate on anything, found that I daydreamed constantly, that sometimes I literally could not force myself to work at my task no matter how hard I tried. That quite shook me, and many of my followers fell away.

"Anyway, at length the year passed, and the fifteen days too, and you can be sure that I was there in Lorkist at the right inn and the best table well before the appointed time."

Maigraith could see the eagerness in his eyes even now; the passion that had never been quenched.

"Noon came. She did not. Well, she had said after noon, and that might mean anytime in the afternoon, or perhaps, stretching it, until midnight. I waited and waited in the cold, and just at the point when I had begun to believe that she was not going to appear, a servant approached my table. He was a man in the prime of his middle age, and about his bearing there was something that said he was honest and reliable.

" 'Are you Gyllias?' he asked me. I said that I was.

" 'Then I regret to advise you that my mistress, Ilen' (he spoke the word with a slight emphasis), 'is called away and unable to meet you, as she said she would. She bids you come again four days after endre, if you still care to.'

"My disappointment must have been writ on my face; my hopes and dreams all snatched away and replaced by this meager crumb, for he went on: 'She is very sorry to have inconvenienced you.'

"I thanked him and he turned away. I sat there for another hour or two, watching the moon drift across the sky. Endre, mid-winter week, was 370 days away, almost another entire year.

"I went about my business, and it was easier now, for some of the gloss had gone from my obsession. I worked harder at my labors than ever, and achieved great things that year, and finally endre came and I was back in Lorkist, waiting as before.

"Again the afternoon passed without sign of her. It grew cold (for Crandor at least). I was the only one sitting outside. Finally, just on dark, the servant appeared again. This time the man was most apologetic. His mistress, unable to return in time, had sent a skeet from far away, bidding me to a third rendezvous.

" 'Tell me where she is,' I said, 'and I will go to her.'

'That's not possible. Her whereabouts are guarded with the utmost secrecy. Even I do not know where to find her.'

"I began to wonder if this were not some kind of test. Perhaps the man before me was Ilen, with some illusion or change of shape on her. I implied as much, and he became distressed, so that I was fairly sure he was genuine. He then gave me another date, not so far off this time, only 150 days away.

" 'I cannot,' I said, and he looked a little surprised. 'I have business in the east, in Thurkad and Zile, and will not be in Crandor for a year or more. Indeed,' I added with perhaps justifiable annoyance, 'I have little to bring me back to Crandor again.' This will test him, I thought. If it is really Ilen in disguise, the fellow will make another appointment right now. But he did not.

" 'I have no instructions for this eventuality,' he said after a pause. 'I will have to send a message to my mistress and wait for her reply.'

"I pounced. 'How can you send her a message if you don't know where she is?' I said triumphantly.

"He gave a disdainful sniff at my lack of intelligence. 'The skeet knows,' he said coldly, referring to that huge, foultempered carrier bird. 'Please return here in seven days.'

"Seven days later he met me in the early afternoon.

" 'Ilen will also be in the east next year,' he said. 'She will find you, in Thurkad or in Zile, unless you are traveling in disguise.'

" 'I am not,' I said, 'though I use a different name there—Cheseut.'

"I sailed off to Thurkad and immersed myself in my affairs again. The war was at a critical juncture and though I was not taking part in it I was still very busy. The months passed and I thought little of her. Without further feeding, my obsession had starved itself out. Besides, I did not care to be tested so, nor for the kind of woman who would toy with me. My pride had been hurt. That's the kind of person I was then."

He smiled at Maigraith, who had not taken her eyes off him all the while. She squeezed his hand. "Tell on," she said, and her eyes shone in the starlight.

"One day I was sitting at a table at a waterfront inn in Thurkad, a place I frequented because I liked to look across the water and think, when someone stood between me and the sun. It was a cool day and I had been enjoying the warmth. I looked up, feeling just a trifle annoyed, and it was her.

"I did not smile, or welcome her, though my heart turned over. She took a seat opposite. 'I do not like to be trifled with,' I said.

" 'Nor I, but I do not play games, and my word is good. I have had much to do since we met, but now I am here.

What is it that you want? Be direct; I cannot abide waffle.' She looked just a bit anxious. My throat was dry as dust. I hardly dared to say it. It took more courage than anything I had done before.

" 'You,' I croaked. 'I want you!' Then I sweated blood, expecting a scornful rejection."

A tear ran down Maigraith's cheek. "Quick, tell me!" she cried, clutching Shand's hands.

"She smiled, just the hint of a smile. She took my hand and put it to her lips. 'That is just as well,' she said, 'since I have come to the same realization.'

"She drew me to my feet. She was very strong. We were inseparable from that day. Often apart, but inseparable. So you can understand that I still grieve for her."

Maigraith smoothed away a tear at the corner of his eye. "You must miss her very much."

"More than life itself. I would do *anything* to get her back."

"And I would do anything to help you."

"What am I to do with myself, Shand?" Maigraith asked later. "I'm so confused." Shand's story had made her appreciate how shallow had been her relationship with Yggur. She wanted so much more.

Shand looked up from the map he was drafting, a plan of the secret places of Elludore. He spent many an hour with his maps, often just staring at them as if reliving some ancient journey. "What are you confused about?"

"Once Yggur was everything to me, but now I cannot imagine why. What did I see in him? Why did I cleave to him and why do I now push him away? I hurt him badly, though I never wanted to. And there is this other thing—"

"What other thing?"

"I am afraid to tell you for fear of what you will think

of me. I saw Rulke last summer, just after he was hurled out of Katazza. He came to Thurkad in a kind of a sending. He was only half there, but when he looked at me, when he lifted me up, I felt such terrible yearnings. Yggur became a pale ghost by comparison. And I saw Rulke again, in Carcharon just before hythe. I felt the same longings, and the same terror too."

"The pull of the Charon is a powerful thing," said Shand, "as I know better than anyone. And maybe your Charon nature, that was hidden from you for so long, cries out to you."

"I don't know what to do. I'm afraid."

"I can't hope to advise you. You must do what you have to do, but make sure that you really *have* to do it. You know Rulke's reputation. Yet as I have recently learned to my cost, reputations can be wrong."

Feeling all hot and cold, Maigraith said no more.

Maigraith sat by the window with the Mirror on her lap, musing about what Shand had told her about her mother, and her mother's mother. She gazed out at the harbor, sometimes dreaming with her eyes closed, imagining her grandmother coming to her. Suddenly she felt the pressure of light on her eyelids and knew, without even opening her eyes, that Yalkara was there. The Mirror had opened.

Behind her Shand choked, but Maigraith did not notice. The symbol shimmered and burst with fire. She looked on her grandmother, the image of herself, and Yalkara looked up at her and smiled. Her lips moved. The Mirror could not give out her voice, but the words were painted in bright letters below her face.

> Aeolior, if you come to read this, I have for you a message; a warning and a task.

Aeolior—you were the most precious thing in my life and I had to abandon you. That hurt more than anything I have ever done, and doubtless it hurt you too. But if I stayed I would have died. I could take nothing with me, not even you.

Aeolior! You may wonder why I came to Santhenar, for many lies have been told about me. I begged, and the Council of the Charon allowed me to go, once we learned that the people of another world had gone between the worlds to Santhenar, and that they called themselves Faellem. I was very uneasy about them, for all that they seemed to have no powers compared to ours. You must realize that I know things that the other Charon do not. I, the youngest of the Charon, was tutored by the oldest, Djalkmah, to carry on the knowledge of our terrible first days in the void, and the time before that.

I have written that down in my last journal in Havissard, since there is no one for me to pass my knowledge to. Not even the Charon can read that script, but the Mirror will teach you when the time comes.

I was to be the watch on the Faellem. But Faelamor opposed my every work as if she had come for that very purpose, and finally she defeated me, though I made her think that mine was the victory. Beware Faelamor. She is utterly inimical to the Charon and to this world too.

Aeolior. I made the Forbidding at the death of Shuthdar—a temporary expedient. Later I found that I lacked the means to unmake it. Now it decays. Eventually it must fail, and every use of devices—I mean things powered by the Secret Art: gates, constructs, flutes, your birthright, this Mirror and even such insignificant objects as light-glasses—will hasten that failure. When it fails Santhenar will lie open to the void and cannot survive it. Your task is to dismantle the Forbidding and at the same time restore the balance between the worlds that existed before the flute.

This is what you must—

At that point Yalkara's image slowly broke up into a maze of dancing dots and the fiery writing faded. Maigraith watched, the flickering lights playing on her face, and after a while the face reappeared.

–look upon the Mirror, and it will show you what you must do.

Aeolior, fare well. We may meet some day if you succeed.

Yalkara smiled and faded away. "Oh, I hope so, more than anything," said Maigraith.

Something made her look over her shoulder. Shand was staring at the blank Mirror as if trying to see through it all the way to Aachan. He was trembling. What would I give to bring you two together again, she thought. I wonder if that is why Shand is so keen on having the flute remade?

She put the Mirror down, sorely puzzled, then took it up again. She made it open as it had before. It told her what it had just told her, and it left out what had been omitted before.

"But what does she mean? What am I supposed to do with the Mirror?"

Shand slowly roused himself from his preoccupation. "I have no idea," he said, little louder than a whisper.

"Perhaps it's damaged," she said, inspecting it carefully. "Or perhaps I am not enough like Aeolior."

"Or perhaps the Twisted Mirror is up to its tricks again," said Shand. "There's no way to tell.'

25

The Three Tasks

Faelamor was broken. Since finding the gold in Havissard there had been one setback after another. Now she had to deal with the rebellious Faellem as well. Sheep she called them, but that only showed how far she had diverged from them, over the centuries.

The three Faellem returned laden with nuts found under the snow. Faelamor was sitting at the mouth of the cave, sunk ocean-deep in despair. She looked up quickly as Gethren entered.

"I have failed," she said. "I called you out into the evil world for nothing. Maigraith is gone and all I've striven for these past three hundred years is ashes; so am I. The burden is too great to carry any longer."

If it was a plea for sympathy it did not move them. "Such a dishonorable scheme as Maigraith told us deserved to fail," said Gethren, "and I cannot but think that we're yet to hear the worst of it. My every bone aches for Tallallame, but there must be other ways. If there are not, I will remain on

Santhenar until I die, and then my bones will ache no more. If that must be the case, let the day be soon."

Faelamor did not respond. *Fail, fail, fail!* she was thinking. You begged for the task but your boast was hollow. You were trusted and you proved unworthy. Now these Faellem, and the rest, and the millions who wait for us in Tallallame, must wait in vain.

Hallal and Ellami appeared behind Gethren and stood observing for a moment. They put the supplies away carefully, washed their hands and sat down in front of Faelamor. A pair of small brown birds hopped around the rocks outside the cave, picking up seeds and crumbs.

"Remember the caution that you were given before we departed Tallallame to come to this wretched world," said Hallal. "You are *one among the Faellem*, and when there is a difficult choice, or the burden is too heavy, you must consult us. Once the choice is made we will support you whatever it is, but not if in your arrogance you do not seek our guidance. That is why we exiled you after the crime of Maigraith became known to us. We did not put our burdens on you—you took them on yourself."

"We ignored you when you first called us here!" Ellami added fiercely. "We heard you but put off answering. Do you seek our guidance at last? Is that why you called us?"

Faelamor flicked her fingers in denial.

"Or did you call because the evil scheme you hatched by yourself had at last come to fruition and you would now offer us the gift of it? If that were the case we resolved to refuse you and go back to our cold forest, even if what you offered us was the way to Tallallame at last. That is still our resolve, and if so we will call our brethren and send them back at once."

"Was that your scheme?" asked Ellami roughly.

"It was," said Faelamor.

Gethren let out a great sigh. "But it has failed!"

"Utterly," she replied, then the smooth curves of her face were wracked by wrenching spasms. Faelamor let out a wail that sent the little birds fluttering up into the treetops. Clenching her fists, she drove them into her stomach. She doubled over until she was a tiny ball of agony, then slowly went rigid on the floor of the cave.

The Faellem watched her dispassionately as she went through her ritual of grief and self-loathing. Hours passed in this state, then Gethren tapped her on the shoulder.

"Come out!" he said. "We must know what peril your folly, and worse yet, *your failure*, has put us in."

Faelamor unlocked her rigid limbs, wiped the dirt off her clothes and sat down on the ground between them. Her golden eyes were blood-red.

They listened in silence to her story.

"When I looked at Yalkara's book, with its strange but familiar writing, I was struck with terror. I could feel the glyphs writhing, trying to get off the pages to strike me down. It is an evil thing, full of lying tales about us."

"So," said Gethren, cold as the glaciers that flowed out of the Great Mountains into Mirrilladell, their adopted homeland. "Having been defeated by our greatest enemy you took her daughter and fashioned from her an even greater foe." His voice cracked like a whip. "You are a fool, Faelamor! You deserve everything you have got. We owe you nothing. Come Hallal, come Ellami," he said in disgust. "Let us call the Faellem and send them back. I can't abide the stink of this place any longer."

Hallal put her hand up. "Hold," she said. "She has fashioned a triune. What if Maigraith were to ally with Rulke? Together they could endanger Tallallame itself."

"Such folly!" said Ellami in contempt. "What are we to do?"

"I don't—" said Faelamor.

"Do you not see the threat?" Ellami cried. "Maigraith may have all the powers of the Charon, and ours too. She knows us, understands us, and after what you did to her how can she but hate us?"

"I was careful to break her spirit," said Faelamor.

"It is mending fast then, for we heard how she led an army into Bannador in defense of a friend! She could supplant us. Tallallame is vulnerable; that is why we came here in the first place. We are small and weak. Our illusions, for all their cunning, are no match for the raw power of the Charon, or their mighty machines like this construct. They could displace us from our own world."

"I can't see the way out," Gethren said.

"We have lost the option of doing nothing," said Hallal. "Give Rulke a construct that works and he will have this world and lust after ours too. As we came here to combat the Charon and their works, so we must do again. They and their devices have been our greatest threat since ever they appeared on Aachan. Nothing has changed. Somewhere in the misery of our exile we forgot what we came to Santhenar to do—bring the Charon down!"

"I accept the rebuke," Faelamor said, bowing her head. "That was our whole purpose, but we were afraid, and the Forbidding took away the urgency. We stopped trying."

"The book frightens me," Gethren said. "It must be sought out and destroyed."

"How can we do that?" said Ellami.

"Mendark surely still has it," replied Hallal. "Someone must go to Thurkad, recover the book, and we will see it burned to ashes. That is the first task."

"What about Rulke?" said Gethren.

"We must oppose him," said Ellami again. "For all his strength. For all our weakness!"

"Then we must have a device to match his," said Faelamor.

"Never!" The three voices cried out as one. "That is the greatest sin we can contemplate."

Faelamor was on her feet, a leader again, as bold as ever. "Listen to me! For more than three thousand years we opposed the Charon here. And if you recall, we tried everything that the Faellem ever knew. *Everything!* But we were powerless because we obeyed the prohibition and refused to amplify our power with magical devices. How many of us fell before we learned that? How many more fell *after*? That's why we had to shrink away and hide, and forget what we came here to do. Maigraith was my way around the prohibition—*a human device*!"

"But Maigraith is lost to you, and now she is uncontrollable," Hallal said. "We are worse off than ever."

"Then here is the second task," said Gethren. "*Maigraith must die!*"

Faelamor went rigid, her eyes almost starting out of her head. "No," she whispered. "She is everything to me, despite that I treated her so ill. It would be like cutting off my own limb."

"The limb is diseased and must go, else the whole body is threatened. *Do you put her before Tallallame?*"

"No," said Faelamor.

"We do not like it either, but it must be done."

They all looked at Faelamor. She was lost inside herself, the despair and the longing feeding on themselves until she was almost driven mad. She had failed; Maigraith was gone. She would never recover her now. In her head she knew that they were right, but her heart could never sanction it.

"I cannot do it," said Faelamor, biting her lip until the blood flowed. "Do you vote on it?"

"We do!" they said as one.

"I vote nay," said Faelamor. "I beg you, do not harm her. We are tied together, she and I."

"The vote is lost," snapped Ellami. "Do you submit to our will, or go into exile with your triune?"

Faelamor was in agony. "I cannot bear exile again," she whispered. "Ah, Maigraith! I cannot see her harmed either. You know what she means to me."

"You are overruled," Gethren said coldly.

Faelamor cast her hood over her face and scrunched herself up into a little tight ball on the ground.

The three Faellem stared at one another. "I have always liked Maigraith," said Ellami. "But I will do it if it is agreed that it must be done."

"It must be done," said Hallal, and Gethren echoed her. "But be quick; be merciful."

"It must be done," said Ellami in a voice like the stone lid sliding over a crypt. "And the other triune too—the sensitive! Karan must also die. Her death will put a spike in Rulke's plan. Are we agreed?"

"Yes," they chorused. "Karan must also die."

"Our third and most desperate task," said Ellami before they could catch their breath, "is to combat Rulke and his construct. Do you have an idea about that, Faelamor?"

Faelamor made no response. Gethren picked her up and Hallal stripped Faelamor's cloak and hood away. Her eyes were dead holes.

"Well, Faelamor?" said Ellami.

"There is only one way left," she whispered listlessly.

"What is it?"

"I have already left the path in so many ways, but this crime is of an entirely different order." She looked absolutely desperate. "We must break the prohibition and make a device of our own. We must use Yalkara's gold."

"Never!" they cried as one.

She sat up straight, terror overcoming her agony for the moment. "Listen to me," she hissed. "Where did the prohibition come from anyway? Can any of you tell me that?"

"No," said Gethren. "It is lost in the depths of time. It has always been."

"It has *not* always been. I wonder if it was not put on us to keep us down. Maybe our enemies shackled us so, in the distant past. How can we, the noblest of all the human species, endure to be so encumbered? Without such a device we have no chance against Rulke, do we?"

"We have no chance," said Gethren somberly.

"Then I say we overturn this prohibition and make ourselves a weapon that is the equal of Rulke's. It will not be easy, and we might fail, but at least we will have given our species the chance. What do you say?" Her eyes flashed fire.

"Show us the gold," said Ellami.

Faelamor brought out the jewelry she had taken from Havissard. She spilled it on the ground in front of them, a heavy chain, a bracelet, a torc, all of red gold. She touched it with her finger. It did not shock her as it had back in Havissard, but it felt most unpleasant. She passed it to Gethren, piece by piece, and he passed each piece on to the other two.

"It feels prickly," said Ellami. "Oh, I don't like the sense of it at all." She threw it back to Faelamor.

"That's because our enemy Yalkara used it. Ai!" Faelamor wailed. "How she taunted me with the Mirror, twisting our foretellings to her own purposes. How she dared me to look inside. But I did dare, and found what she had kept hidden. It is very special, this Aachan gold."

"And very dangerous," said Gethren. "Why do we need it?"

"Devices are not our way," Faelamor reminded him.

"None of us have skill with them. If we must adopt the arts of our enemies and make a sorcerous device, all the more reason to form it out of the most potent substance there is."

"Strong weapons need strong shoulders and a steady hand," said Hallal. "If we must commit this terrible crime, and I do not say that we must, then let it be with a device that is within our skill to use and to control."

"From what will we make it? Where will we find it? How will we learn to use it?" cried Faelamor. "I can make a surpassingly powerful device with this gold, for every atom resonates with its former use. But if I were to take other materials—metal or precious ebony or tusk, say—and shape them into a flute or any other device that I cared to imagine, it would remain just lifeless material. I cannot put power into it."

"Then what you cannot make and know, you should not contemplate the use of," said Gethren. "This is the greatest folly that I have ever heard. I say nay."

"Do you give up then?" Faelamor shouted in his face. "If you do, you condemn your species, here and in Tallallame too, for my very bones know how our world cries out for aid. There is no other way."

The three went into the trees and talked among themselves. Then they came back. "We will allow it," Gethren said, "so long as you make a device that is part of our tradition. No flutes! No constructs!"

"You have consulted us," Hallal continued, "as is proper, and we have laid down our rule. Now it is your duty to decide what course to take."

"Thank you," Faelamor whispered. "I would sooner make that choice here with you."

She sat for a long time with her head bowed. "Whatever I choose, the Three Worlds will be changed forever. Perhaps Tallallame is already irretrievably altered. Doubtless it has been, in the time we've been gone. But all things change, and the prohibition must be abandoned.

"I have made my choice," she said, and her voice was a knell in all their hearts. "This is our third task. We will use the gold. We will shape our own instrument with it. We will make a *nanollet*, something that every Faellem child knows how to play. With it we will smash the Forbidding asunder, and Rulke's construct too, and cast him down so low that he will never rise again. And then," she said, her eyes shining, "we will go home to Tallallame and know that our duty is done."

26

Like a Row of Dominoes

Maigraith and Shand stood in Yggur's dingy workroom, with the rest of the company gathered around them. They were all staring at the writing on the Mirror.

. . . Your task is to dismantle the Forbidding and at the same time restore the balance between the worlds that existed before the flute. This is what you must—

"The next part of the message is missing," Maigraith explained to the company. "It ends: *look upon the Mirror, and it will show you what you must do.*"

"The two sayings are linked," cried Mendark. "Recall the answer to the foretelling: *There will appear an instrument—"khash-zik-makattzah," the-three-and-the-one—and if a way can be found to use it, Santhenar can be redeemed. But at the end the instrument will be lost.*

"We know what the *three* means: gold of Aachan, precious ebony from Tallallame, and the wit and skill of the artisans of Santhenar who are to make it into the golden flute. And the *one* to use it can only mean you, Maigraith."

"How can that be right?" asked Maigraith. "Yalkara warns that the use of such devices will hasten the failure of the Forbidding. How can she have intended that the golden flute be made anew?"

"That's obvious to any fool!" snapped Mendark. "If the flute is used in the right way it will unmake the Forbidding rather than cause it to fail."

Maigraith felt panicked by Mendark's pressure. "What right way? No one knows how it was used."

"Then I suggest," Mendark said coldly, and it was clear that he found her Charon appearance unnerving, "that you spend your time trying to find the missing bits of the message rather than criticizing those who are actually trying to do something. We have precious ebony, and we have skilled goldsmiths able to work to Tensor's pattern, if we can convince him to make one. Aachan gold is all we lack to make our weapon."

He spilled the few pieces they had onto the table. They included the ring Yggur had shown them months ago, some links of fine chain and a few fragments of leaf. "It's not enough," Mendark said dismissively. "Not near."

"Yes!" said Yggur. "We've got to make a stand. Rulke exerts his strength in the west, testing us. The Ghâshâd have come out of Shazmak again. He grows stronger by the hour. We must oppose him, or fall."

Maigraith sat silent, intimidated by Mendark's aggression. She was sure that he was wrong. Then, puzzling over what she knew about Yalkara, something else occurred to her. "Is the Mirror my birthright, or something else?" she said in Shand's ear.

Shand thought for a moment. "No, not *your* birthright,

but Aeolior's. I've always thought that it was the Mirror. What else could Yalkara have meant?"

He thought for a moment, then got up. "Come outside," he said to Maigraith.

"As usual, you're off as soon as there's work to be done," Mendark said with heavy sarcasm.

Shand grinned over his shoulder, then he and Maigraith disappeared out the door.

Karan sat listening to the talk of war. She had known it was coming—her dreams of Shazmak and the void had returned a week ago. It would not be long. I've got to go home, she thought miserably. I've got to be there, this time.

"This is a waste of time," cried Yggur following hours of fruitless discussion.

"Aye," said Nadiril. "Faelamor has Yalkara's gold, that's the only certainty."

Yggur stood up abruptly. "I've got better things to do."

"We must take an army to Elludore and wrest it back from her," said Mendark.

"*You* don't have an army," Yggur said frostily, but he sat down again.

"Ah, but if I did, Yggur, I wouldn't lack the courage to lead it."

"Enough of your sly manipulation, Mendark. I've proven my courage!" Yggur riffled through the papers on his table and held up a rolled map. "But for once you're right. Maybe we should go to Elludore and seize the gold."

"She'll hide," Karan said. "You'd never find her."

"I've an idea!" cried Yggur. "Guards, clear the room!"

After everyone had gone, Mendark and Yggur kept on as if the best of friends, not bitter rivals.

"She can't hide from me," said Yggur, unrolling his map.

It was the one Shand had drawn in the seaside cabin, showing Faelamor's valley in Elludore. "I can assemble a gross of illusionists on a day's notice. We can pin her there—her perfect refuge will be a perfect trap. Look, there's only one way out, unless you're a mountaineer."

Mendark inspected the map. "Shand certainly has an eye for detail! You can truly field so many illusionists so quickly?" he asked with raised eyebrow.

"Well, perhaps not a gross, but many! As soon as I knew Faelamor had the gold I began gathering them together."

"I too," said Mendark, fascinated by the idea. "Tell me, how would you go about it?"

"See how her valley is bounded by cliffs on all sides, even where the river flows out, and that path is easily blockaded. There are one or two ways down the cliffs, but very awkward. I'd take this way in," he indicated it on the map, "though we'd need protection."

Mendark broke in. "With enough master illusionists, and the right sensitive to link and bind them together, we can sense any glamor she makes and cast our own to unbind it."

Yggur rubbed his chin. "I know that *you're* a sensitive, Mendark. But would you risk your sanity and perhaps even your life in what must be an untestable and . . . hazardous enterprise?"

"I'd prefer not to," said Mendark. "It is, as you say, a risky business, and I have other responsibilities."

"Then do you have a sensitive in mind? The wars have taken a toll of them, I know, but I could . . . provide you with a few suitable names."

"I have several in mind but I would be glad to hear of yours. Which is not to say that any sensitive would do. I must have one who can link."

"And one who has been proven under great pressure."

"Maigraith can link."

"But she is not a sensitive. Besides, Faelamor knows her too well."

"I had in mind to use someone who owes us all a debt. A triune, but a controllable one. She's such a little, incomplete thing, is Karan." Mendark smiled grimly.

"Also my choice. Bring her!" Yggur said to his guard.

Karan was led in and the matter put to her. She sat before the two stern men, afraid and intimidated. "My life has gone full circle, like it was at the beginning. Everyone wants to use me."

"Sadly, that is the fate of sensitives, blendings and most especially triunes," Yggur observed without sympathy. He might have been inspecting the horses in his stable, for she seemed to warrant no more choice than they did.

"Do I have an option? What if I should refuse?"

"We will consider *our* options," said Yggur.

But Mendark said, "This is your reckoning, Karan! You betrayed us in Carcharon and it was only blind luck that we were not overcome there. Speaking as Magister, I say that you have no choice. Either this pays for that, or you go to trial. And since you have already admitted your guilt, you will be convicted and sentenced as is appropriate for treachery. As you have such useful skills, it is probable that the sentence would be slavery as a sensitive, rather than execution."

"And the first part of my slavery would be to serve as a sensitive on this mission," said Karan.

"Precisely."

Karan bowed her head. Every one of my actions has led irresistibly to the next, she thought, since this business began. What is the point in trying to resist fate? "I will be your sensitive," she said. "When do we start?"

"At once," said Mendark. "Gather your illusionists, Yggur, and I will mine."

"So soon!" said Karan, alarmed. "How can you attack *her* with so little preparation?"

"If we delay, if Faelamor is warned, we'll never find her."

"There can't be fifty Faellem there yet," said Yggur. "I'll take a thousand of my finest soldiers. Our strength will be overwhelming."

"I'm afraid," said Karan, but they took no notice, and after that she kept silent.

"You will remain here under guard until we go, Karan," said Yggur. "Make a list of your gear and I'll send for it."

It took the best part of a day, however, before they were all assembled—an army of a thousand soldiers, hand-picked from Yggur's armies, all skilled at climbing and hiding. They were led by Vanhe, recently promoted to marshal again. With them went fifty-two illusionists, equal numbers of men and women, the men wearing black gowns with a short white cape over the shoulders, the women the converse. Also their baggage train and Mendark's guard, ten of them led by Osseion of the nine fingers, and his friend Torgsted. Llian was to be the recorder.

No one knew their destination or their purpose, save the three. Not even Llian was told until they were well out of Thurkad. They proceeded on horseback to the edge of the forest of Elludore, and thence by forced marches to their destination. A small squad guarded the entrance to the valley, to prevent any escape. The remainder climbed to the top of the dividing range, and waited.

It was the second day of spring, though it still felt like winter. The time was midnight, and the fifty-two illusionists took their places in their darkened tent, standing in a circle like so many dominoes, black-white, white-black, black-white. Llian watched silently from a corner, memorizing the scene so he could put it in his tale. He was worried, and every so often he picked up a wave of misery from Karan, who was in an agony of terror already.

Karan sat at the end of the tent outside the circle. Mendark stood across the circle from her with a short staff raised like a conductor's baton. Llian watched in some trepidation. How could it go right when Karan was in such a state? How could it anyway?

"Begin," said Mendark. "Link to the first, Karan."

Karan must have found some inner reserves of calmness, for Llian did not pick up her emotions after that. Indeed she looked almost vacant as she closed her eyes, sought out with her mind and drew a link between herself and the master illusionist. The world outside, which was all fog and shadows, blurred slightly.

"To the second, Karan." Twirling his staff, Mendark pointed it somewhat theatrically at the second illusionist.

Karan wrinkled her forehead, then sent the link to the second.

"To the third, Karan!"

On he went, around the circle and Karan following him, until each of the illusionists was linked to the next and finally, with a thump that knocked her sideways, back to Karan. Pale as a ghost, she swayed forward and had to support herself on a tent pole.

Mendark spoke to the master. "Remember, you have only two tasks. Your first and most important is to maintain a cloak over the army—to render them invisible in the fog."

"That is done," said the master in a rather foggy voice. "The conditions make it easy."

"Never underestimate this foe!" Mendark snapped. "And the second, to keep watch for any illusion that Faelamor may make to hide the way from us, *and to break that illusion whatever it takes*."

"We sense such an illusion already," said the master in sepulchral tones, "but it is weak—a nothing!"

"Beware!" said Mendark. "She's probably had a protection in place ever since Shand and Yggur were there. But if she senses you, it will grow so strong that all of you together will be troubled to overcome it. Are you ready? And you," he said to Llian, "do nothing to disturb Karan. Don't even touch her, lest it shiver the link."

The master nodded. "Now is the time!" said Mendark to Yggur's shabby little adjutant, Dolodha, who hurried out to give the word to the messengers. They ran along to the waiting army, who were to proceed in single file to the cliff track.

Mendark, walking as though his joints bothered him, followed down to where Yggur waited with Vanhe and his lieutenants.

"As soon as I give the signal, Tallia, you will lead the first squad down. Careful, it's a dangerous path. Torgsted," he said quietly, "you have always served me faithfully. Will you go down with the army and be my eyes and ears on this mission?"

"I—" Torgsted hesitated. He looked to Osseion.

"I need someone there that I can rely on utterly," said Mendark.

Torgsted's hand shook. "I feel . . . there's something not right here, Magister."

"Are you a sensitive, Torgsted?" Mendark asked with a trace of irritation.

"No, though my mother had the second sight . . . No, it's nothing! Of course I will go."

"Good. Osseion, go back up, position your troops around the tent and be ready for anything."

Osseion shook hands with Torgsted and turned away. The soldiers made no more than a rustle on the path, then silence fell again.

Llian stood in the entrance to the tent, watching Karan. She neither moved nor spoke, but once or twice she swayed on her chair. The illusionists were deathly quiet. The cold moon, an angry crescent, shone on the tent and the fog.

Then the master illusionist sang out. "She knows! Feel the strength of her illusion!"

Suddenly everything went dull. The room might have been pumped full of mist. Someone groaned.

"Ah!" cried the master. "It is hard. Oh! Oh! Hold! HOLD!" she roared. "HOLD! We're losing the way."

The silence lasted a full minute, then suddenly the mist in the room vanished. "We've done it," whispered the master. "We've broken her concealment. Look, there is the path."

For a few brief seconds, Llian saw a vision in his mind's eye, a coal-black track winding through the snow and the trees. It was the top of the path that their scouts had marked out that afternoon.

The way down to the assembly point was harder to find than they had expected, in the fog, but in the end Faelamor's illusions proved to be, somehow, not very potent. The soldiers mocked their enemy as they assembled among the trees. They had not been there long before the chief illusionist sent a messenger running to Mendark, crowing the victory.

"She was a cunning foe, but we have mastered her. We are too many and too strong. The way is cleared."

"I always thought she was overrated with large groups," said Mendark to Yggur, "though no doubt that she is peerless one to one. Tallia, are you ready?"

"I am. I have my six with me."

"You know your orders. You are to go first and get into position. When the army creates a diversion, you will find the gold and bring it back."

"Vanhe?" Yggur said softly. "Are you ready?"

The squat, bullet-headed marshal nodded.

"Remember, you're on probation, Vanhe. Fail me again and you go back to being a common soldier, for good!"

The pain showed in Vanhe's eyes, then he turned to his officers and began to issue orders.

Tallia and her group set off down the track. The fog grew thicker. She had to use all her bushcraft to keep to the path she had trod just that afternoon. And if that was not trouble enough, she found that, despite the boasts of the master illusionist, the valley was still protected with glamors that fogged her brain and made her doubt her own memory. She stopped abruptly. Which way was it here? Right or left, after these two giant trees? Right, of course, but nonetheless she stepped warily down the track, fretting that what she knew to be right was wrong.

Now the track slanted back to the left, running along a narrow ledge below the cliff top, down at the end then along the cliff ledge below that in the same direction. Tallia felt the edge of the precipice tugging at her and waited until the last of her six appeared.

"Now the path goes down the cliff and one misstep means death. We will rope together, and everyone must follow the one ahead, no matter what. If you get confused, don't step right, just STOP!"

They continued, and the glamors whirled so thick about them that even Tallia was sorely pressed to withstand them. Many times they stopped while one or other of her six was guided into the confidence that to step forward was the right thing to do.

"What would it be like without the protection of our illusionists?" said Tallia to the fellow behind her. He said nothing, but she could see the whites of his eyes.

Eventually they got down, and insofar as they could tell, in their correct position somewhere above and to the right of Faelamor's caves.

"Now we wait," said Tallia. "The army will split at the top, and half will come down a little further up the valley, the remainder on the downhill side of the caves. They will attack from both sides, creating the diversion that will let us into the caves. Not many of Faelamor's people are here yet, otherwise it would be impossible."

That would be the easy part. Tallia was less confident about her own job. She knew that Faelamor would never leave the treasure unguarded. Even if they found it they would still have to deal with her, and find the way out again.

"It won't be long now," she said, some time after the signals were due.

"It won't be long now," she said again, a long time later.

Later still, when she was growing desperately worried, she said, "I can't wait. I'm going to spy out the caves. Keep watch and if I shout, flee at once."

She knew they wouldn't flee. They were elite soldiers and here to protect her. But they obeyed orders and remained where they were.

She was scarcely out of sight when she heard, faint through the fog, the sound of a horn blowing the recall. Something had gone wrong. The army must have been spotted. They would never come to her aid now.

Tallia hesitated. She was so close to her goal. Maybe she could still use this as the diversion she needed. After Faelamor's battle with the illusionists she would be weak, perhaps already struggling with aftersickness. Tallia went on.

* * *

The soldiers were moving restlessly, wanting to go. Vanhe and his lieutenants had already walked the winding path that afternoon, making sure that there could be no possibility of confusion. Vanhe paced back and forth, anxious about the mission and his own future. He could not afford any mistake. The soldiers began to move along the path, tramping the snow down into the black soil. The track led over knife edged ridges, along cliffs that guarded the valley on all sides, between two giant trees, and turned down the cliff path. Vanhe paused between the trunks for a second. He looked around, at the shadowed ranks behind him, at the path ahead. He felt paralyzed by the responsibility.

Behind him, one of his lieutenants whispered, "We must keep to time, sir!"

Vanhe spun around. There was only one way they could go. The moon dimly illuminated the path, a winding track of black through the snow as if it was made of crushed anthracite. Yet still he hesitated.

"Sir!" called another of his lieutenants.

Vanhe gave the word. He moved out from between the two trees, turned left and disappeared into the fog. The soldiers followed close behind. They marched forward, silent and proud, the elite of four armies, confident in the leaders and their arts.

"Careful now," said the master illusionist. "Faelamor is strong and cunning—she may renew the attack at any moment. Here it comes now. Hold the path against her. *Hold the path!*"

Just then Karan began to tremble. It became an uncontrollable shake then vanished just as suddenly. "N-n-n!" she mouthed, trying to say something but unable to get the words out. "N-n-n-n!"

Llian ran to her side but was afraid to touch her, mindful of Mendark's warnings.

"N-n-n-n!" Karan's eyelids were beating like the wings of a butterfly. Her jaw clenched, she screamed out, "No!" and collapsed on the floor.

Llian tried to lift her up but she was in a stupor so deep that he could not rouse her. He looked up fearfully at the master. "How is the link?"

"It holds," she intoned. "I think we are over the worst. Most of the army is down already."

"That was quick," Llian said. "I must have lost track of time."

At that moment the master illusionist sighed and fell down on her face. The second shrieked under the pressure, bringing Osseion running in. He felt the master illusionist's throat.

"No pulse," he shouted over his shoulder to Dolodha. "Get a message to Mendark."

Now the second illusionist was writhing on the floor, seemingly trying to heave his bowels up through his mouth. His eyes rolled back into his head, he shuddered and went rigid.

"He's still alive, at least," said Osseion, as Dolodha ran back in. "Where's Mendark?"

"With Yggur. Down at the cliff top by now, I'd say."

"Did you pass the word for him?"

"Yes, but without alerting the enemy . . ." She held her hands out in a sign of helplessness. "It'll take some time."

The remaining illusionists still held the circle, black on white, white on black, all the way around, but their eyes were staring under the strain.

"I don't like this," said Osseion.

Shortly a messenger came running back, a little young

woman with a cap of yellow hair. "What's the matter?" she gasped, bursting into the tent.

"Karan is unconscious, though she still holds the link. The master is dead, and the second—" Dolodha indicated the floor. "I have the worst feeling . . ."

The messenger gasped, holding her side. "It hurts! What is the message? They've gone down already. If I have to give the alarm the whole mission must fail."

Osseion and Dolodha exchanged glances. "Should we call it off or not?"

"To sound the recall when they're halfway down might be worse," Osseion said. "We'll wait another minute."

Just then the third illusionist choked. Dark blood burst out her nose and she went rigid as a domino. Throwing her arms above her head she slowly fell backward. Then the man behind her did the same, throwing his arms up and toppling backward too, black on white, white on black, until like a row of dominoes each one knocked over the next. Soon there was not an illusionist standing.

Dolodha and Osseion watched in horror, then turned as one and raced for the flap of the tent. Dolodha got out first and did not wait for the order. "Fall back! Fall back!" she screamed and raced down the path.

Osseion pounded to the command tent, snatched a horn out of its rack and blew a blast that echoed off cliff and valley, back and forth, so low that it was like the groaning of tumbrel wheels.

There came no response. No shouts. No cries. He ran down the anthracite-black path, blowing and blowing the retreat until he had no breath left. Around a corner in the path he skidded in the mud, uncertain which way to take, then turned left. He ran down the track in the fog. A dark clad figure loomed out of the mist, its arms outstretched across the path.

"Too late," Mendark said dolefully.

The mist began to clear and Osseion said in wonderment, "But . . . this is not the way we scouted. How—"

"What proud fools we were!" said Mendark. Further down the track a shadow moved. Their feet clapped the mud down to Yggur.

"It's over," said Yggur in a dead voice, standing up on the edge of the precipice. "It's all over."

"What . . . ?" Osseion began.

"They're dead, every one," said Yggur, teetering as if to follow them. Dolodha caught his hand and eased him back. "They marched straight over the cliff in the fog and never knew it until they smashed on the rocks below. We have met a foe beyond us. Faelamor has crushed us utterly."

An updraft carried the tang of blood. "I'll go up," said Osseion, wanting to be anywhere but here, where a thousand of Yggur's finest, and Torgsted, the dearest friend he'd ever had, had just fallen to their deaths.

"Karan tried to give the warning," said Osseion, "but Faelamor was too strong. She must have known we were here from the beginning."

"She knew everything," said Yggur in a dull voice.

"Yes," said Mendark. "She was in control the whole time. She simply showed us what we wanted to see until our illusionists thought that they had beaten her. Then she worked her own *seeming* to make us see the path turn left where it went right. Simple, beautiful and deadly. Ah, Tallia, how I will miss you."

Tallia crept through the forest. Maigraith's directions were imprinted on her brain. The confusions began to ease now. She reached the entrance of the cave undetected and saw outside a clay furnace fired with charcoal. It was still glowing. Arranged about it were molds and wooden trays filled with sand. Crude work! They must have been at their forging just as the alarm went. The gold could not be far away.

She trailed her hand through the trays of sand. One was still hot but there was nothing in it. It must be in the cave. She turned and Faelamor stood directly behind her. Tallia jumped. It was surely over for her, yet Faelamor looked deathly pale in her aftersickness.

Faelamor forced a smile. "You are cleverer than I thought. Cleverer than Mendark, but not enough. Your diversion has failed and I've already hidden it." She edged to one side.

Then why are you trying to draw me away from here? Tallia thought.

"I haven't forgotten what you did to me in Gothryme Forest," said Faelamor, edging further sideways so that Tallia had to turn away from the furnace to keep her in sight.

She's sick and alone, and she knows I am not. Strike, strike now! Tallia feinted at Faelamor with her right hand and when she ducked flung a handful of casting sand from the other hand into her eyes. For an instant Faelamor was helpless and Tallia seized that moment to kick over the casting boxes. Sand flew everywhere and an odd-shaped golden object thudded into the dirt. Tallia snatched it up and ran, and as soon as she reached the trees roared for her soldiers.

"Protect my back," she gasped as they raced up the track, but though the illusions were now as thick as jelly they lacked their previous power to confuse and entice. They seemed half-hearted.

They did not encounter any Faellem in their upward rush. It was all too quiet. Maybe they were waiting further on. Halfway up they stopped for a moment's rest. Someone struck a light in their cupped hands so that Tallia could examine the golden object in the dim glow. She knew at once why the escape had been so easy. The casting was not near heavy enough for gold. It was bronze, just a trial with base metal.

She felt the failure keenly, but without support she could have done no more. She slipped it back in her pocket and they continued.

"I sent them to their deaths!" Mendark sat down, put his head in his hands and wept.

Yggur paced back and forth like a stone automaton. He could not weep; he was rigid with grief and despair. "Why did I let you manipulate me?" he raged. "This is your fault, Mendark!"

Catching sight of Karan frozen to her seat, he screamed at her. "You did this to me deliberately!" There was a froth of foam on his upper lip. He ran across and began to beat her about the head with his open hands. Karan looked up at him but made no attempt to defend herself.

"Stop it, you fool," shouted Mendark. He hobbled across and tried to pull Yggur off Karan. Osseion joined him and they carried Yggur away, still raging.

"You caused this, Karan!" screamed Yggur, pulling free and running back to attack her again. Mendark shielded her with his body. "I'll never forgive you. Never!"

Mendark struck him across the face. "Be a man, Yggur!" he said with absolute contempt. "You and I made this disaster, and Faelamor, and Karan had nothing to do with it."

Yggur collapsed on the ground. Two of the watch dragged him into a tent and stood guard over it.

"Is there any way to recover our dead?" asked Osseion. He had lost most of his friends today. "If I'd just given the alarm sooner, they could have been saved."

Mendark did not answer. A thousand lay dead at the bottom of the cliff—ten for each left alive.

"Gather your tents and your tails," said Mendark, "and put them between your legs. We're going back to Thurkad."

They made stretchers for the comatose, including Karan, struck camp and got ready to depart. Then out of the fog an exhausted band of seven appeared.

"What went wrong?" cried Tallia. "We were so close."

Mendark wept for a moment of joy in the blackest of nights. "We were sure you were dead."

"Where is the army?"

"Every one of them is lost."

"All for nothing," she said, telling her tale and showing the cast piece of bronze. "All for nothing!"

The sadly depleted caravan wended their way back down the ridge and out of Elludore Forest. Of the eleven hundred that had come in, less than a hundred departed. Yggur looked even worse than ever he had when Rulke had defeated him in Katazza.

Mendark was lower than Llian had ever seen him. His reputation had taken a blow it would never recover from. His body was blotched all over with bruises. His raw eyes leaked red tears that formed crusts on his eyelashes. He coughed constantly into a rag, and when not wiping blood off his lips, he was trying to stop it oozing out of his nose. His skin flaked off in pieces large enough to cover strawberries.

Fifteen illusionists had survived—nine women and six men—but they were badly shaken, in most cases their talents reduced to nothing. Karan was a silent, staring shadow of herself, filled with guilt. Llian walked beside her all the way to Thurkad.

"I saw it coming," she said over and over. "I saw it coming!"

The days and the nights of their journey home were the

same to her, a waking nightmare repeated again and again. One by one the flower of Yggur's armies turned left where they should have turned right and plunged to their deaths over the cliff. She kept seeing it, and she kept trying to scream out a warning, but something kept her from getting the words out.

Mendark fell in beside Llian on the second day.

"You look awful—" Llian did not finish it, expecting the Magister to snap at him as he would have of old. But Mendark did not.

"I'm dying, Llian, and it terrifies me."

"I thought—" began Llian. "You've lived so long . . . But then, I suppose the longer you live, the longer you want to."

"You misunderstand me. I'm not afraid of death, but if I die, who will defend the world against Rulke?"

Llian instinctively glanced in Yggur's direction. He was limping along, head down, arms dangling.

"I once thought so," Mendark said in a low voice. "Especially after he defeated the thranx. But Yggur will never recover from this failure."

"He's risen from adversity before," said Llian.

"And each time he falls, he goes further down. Look at his behavior in Thurkad after he failed to catch me. Look what he did in Katazza, and to the Second Army. No one can predict his behavior, and no one can rely on him."

"You've done—"

"Of course I have, terrible things. But always to advance the cause I was fighting for. I never condemned an army to death because my lover had abandoned me!" Mendark spat blood into the grass and fell silent.

27

The Burning Mountain

After Shand and Maigraith left the meeting they slowly climbed up to the top of the fortress, to look out over the city through the yellow fog of a hundred thousand chimneys.

"Yalkara had two gifts for Aeolior," said Shand, after making sure that there was no one to overhear. "The Mirror, *and* her golden jewelry. It consisted of a thick gold chain with the links irregularly shaped, an intricate bracelet and a torc. The chain was almost too heavy for the neck. She always wore her gold. It was her only vanity. At least, I thought of it as vanity, but now I'm not so sure. I never saw her without it, except on the day she left Aeolior with me."

"Would there have been enough to make a flute?" Maigraith asked, tentatively.

He considered. "I suppose so, if it was a small one. As indeed Shuthdar's was said to be. Yes, I'm sure there'd be enough. That *must* be what she intended it for!"

Maigraith digested that. "But Faelamor has Aeolior's

birthright!" The thought of it in *her* hands was enough to make Maigraith weep.

"No she hasn't! That gold isn't the birthright."

Maigraith spun around. "I don't understand. What are you saying, Shand?"

"I don't know where the gold she took from Havissard came from. But Aeolior's birthright, which Yalkara put into my hands before she went through the gate, was her own gold that she brought from Aachan."

"Are you sure?"

"Absolutely."

"Then why the secrecy?"

"It's yours now. But if Mendark and Yggur learn about it, they'll never stop pestering you. You must be free to choose what to do with it."

"Where is the gold now?"

"After Aeolior was taken from me I dug a hole in the ground and put it in, and never marked the spot, to be sure that no one else would ever find it. That was a long time ago, though not so very far away. I hid it across the Sea of Thurkad, near to the Burning Mountain, *Booreah Ngurle*, where I dwelt before Aeolior was taken."

"Can we go there?"

"Of course."

Maigraith was fuming with excitement. "Right away?"

"This very minute! Let's get our packs."

Without a word to anyone they went down to the waterfront and found that Pender was sailing that afternoon. They took ship across the Sea of Thurkad to Nilkerrand, a drab coastal town which was the gateway to the dry plains of Almadin.

Maigraith stood at the rail for most of the voyage, staring at the waves. She had crossed this sea many times, and other, greater seas too. But those voyages had been scarred by impossible burdens of duty and obligation. This trip was a holiday and she was going to enjoy it.

In Nilkerrand they boarded a fast river boat and sailed north-east up the broad River Alm, which had featured in Llian's tragic love story about Jenulka and Hengist, and their torments by the tyrant Feddil the Cruel. He had told the tale to Karan near Narne last winter.

"This is quite a roundabout way to get to our destination," said Shand, "but also the quickest, because we go most of the way by boat."

Maigraith did not care how long it took. She was enjoying every minute.

When they could go no further up the Alm, they marched overland for two days to the cliffed shores of an immense lake. "The Long Lake," said Shand, as they stood at the top of the cliff, looking over the sullen water. "Its true name is Warde Yallock, and it's the largest of many lakes that fill the rifted earth here to a depth of a thousand fathoms. It runs south-east for the best part of a hundred leagues, almost to our destination, and so by boat we can do in a few days what would take us weeks of hard marching."

A well-maintained path wound down to a prosperous town on the shore of the lake. There Shand hired a sailing skiff. They loaded their gear into it and headed south, sailing under a blustery wind and skies the color of lead. The spray stung Maigraith's cheeks and the cold wind burned them. She did not care. Everything was wonderful.

Shand broke the silence that afternoon. "Warde Yallock is positively steeped in the Histories. The first towns on Santhenar were built on its shores. More than twelve thousand years ago, the chroniclers say."

"Here?" said Maigraith, gazing at the shore, which was a tangle of erosion gullies partly clad in gray-leaved scrub. "It's hard to imagine why."

"No, right down the southern end of the lake, in a fertile land between three mighty rivers. But those towns are gone now."

"What happened to them?"

"They died out at the time of the Little Ice Age."

"A glacier ground them down?" Maigraith was intrigued at the idea.

"Nothing so exciting. The ice was a good distance away. It just became too cold and dry to grow crops."

They sailed on.

"The largest city was known as Tara-Laxus," Shand said later. "It was a powerful place in ancient times. From there Shuthdar fled to his doom. But even Tara-Laxus is gone now."

Eventually they berthed at a town surrounded by forest, and made their way unhurriedly in the direction of the Burning Mountain, whose tumbled black slopes could already be seen above the trees. Shortly they crossed into barren country where the soil was bare and stony. Smoke seemed to be issuing out of cracks in the hills all around. There was a brown haze in the air, and a reek like a coal fire.

"Funny smell for a volcano," said Maigraith, as they took lunch in the shade of a thorny tree.

"Something once ignited a seam of coal here," he replied. "Probably the volcano! The hills have been burning for five thousand years. The fires are way under the ground now, though there are places where the earth is still too hot to walk on."

Two days later, one moonless evening when the scorpion nebula gleamed from a cold clear sky, they came to the ruins of a stone cottage by a meadow. At its back was the sweep of a dark forest. It was a place of ancient memories and great sadness. They sat on the step of the cottage, looking out across the meadow. In the distance, above the trees, *Booreah Ngurle* smoked and fumed.

"The Charon had a stronghold at *Booreah Ngurle* for a thousand years," said Shand.

"Which Charon?"

"Kandor and Rulke."

"Why here?"

"It's another of those powerful places, like Carcharon. Actually, it's where the Way between the Worlds first opened. Shuthdar arrived here with the flute, and Rulke followed him. They built a massive fortress which Rulke used as a base in his hunt for the flute. A thousand Charon blendings lived there at one stage—"

"What happened?"

"A massacre. Myan and his Aachim came under a flag of truce then took the place by treachery. They slaughtered most of the blendings in their sleep and burned the rest alive. The entire line of Charon blendings was eliminated. No wonder—" Again he stopped.

"What is it, Shand?"

"I begin to understand why Rulke was so obsessed with survival. The Aachim tried to wipe out all his kind. After that he developed the Gift of Rulke, to protect himself against them."

"It seems to me," said Maigraith after a long pause, "that the Great Betrayer has been as much betrayed against."

"That may be so," said Shand. "I can see both sides. Let's get the campfire going."

They were back on the steps, washing down their dinner with bowls of yellow mil that reeked of cloves. "We dwelt together here for years, your mother and I. These lands were uninhabited then as they are now. Aeolior used to play all around this area. See that ancient hulme tree, with the spreading branches? She loved to climb in it, and swing on the swing I made her. Even then it was an old tree."

Shand got up abruptly, not bothering to wipe his eyes, and led her to a place to one side of a rocky ledge. After measuring the spaces by eye, he took a spade from his pack, cut down a sapling to make a handle and began to dig. The ground was hard but he worked steadily, and though several times he was obliged to rest he would not allow her to take a turn. "It was my task to give it," he said.

When the hole was nearly waist-deep the spade struck something hard. Shand carved the dirt and corrosion away to reveal a golden streak of metal—a brass box. It was not locked. The hinges were corroded yet it opened easily when he levered with a point of the spade. He pulled out a heavy bag whose oiled cloth was still good. When he opened the mouth of the bag, metal gleamed in the nebula's light. A thick chain, a bracelet and a torc, all of red gold. Shand presented Aeolior's birthright to her daughter—sadly, ceremoniously.

"Enough for a flute, I think. If that is how you choose."

Maigraith's hands shook as she accepted the birthright. The jewelry matched piece for piece that which Faelamor had taken from Havissard. This gold was worn silky smooth, however, while the other had been rough, as if it had never been worn. She put the gold carefully back in the pouch and returned to the step, wondering, while Shand went down to a creek for water.

Two sets of golden jewelry, almost identical. One Yalkara had brought from Aachan long, long ago. Where had the other come from? How was she to read this situation? For Yalkara to have taken such trouble, *that* gold must have held a special promise. Or a special threat!

* * *

They headed back to Thurkad the way they had come. Only once, when they were sailing back up the lake, did Shand raise the matter of the gold.

"I simply don't know what to do," she said. "To remake the flute is such a huge decision. I don't know if Yalkara would have wanted that or not. I just don't understand her design."

"Why don't you go back to the Mirror then? But when you do, know that she would not have wanted to make your decisions for you. She understood that the past cannot shackle the future."

"I'll wait for some more tangible sign," said Maigraith, and said no more about it. She trailed her hand in the water. "Tell me about this place."

They were now halfway back to the northern end of Warde Yallock, where they would return the hired boat. "As it happens, we're quite close to one of the most famous places in all the Histories," said Shand. "Huling's Tower!"

"That's where the golden flute was destroyed and the Forbidding formed."

"And where that poor crippled girl was murdered, who aroused Llian's curiosity about the whole business. I wonder where we'd be if that hadn't happened?"

She turned to face the shore. It was partly shrouded in mist, though not enough to conceal rusty cliffs rising vertically out of the water. It did not look a pleasant spot. "I'd like to go there, if it's possible." Maigraith was thinking that if it was her task to unmake the Forbidding and restore the balance between the worlds, she'd better see the place where it all began.

They continued for half an hour and more. The wind had come up and the lake was growing choppy. It was now bitterly cold on the water. Maigraith was glad when Shand, peering through the haze, grunted "There it is!" and turned the boat toward the shore.

"See it?" He pointed to the top of the rather ominous-looking cliff in front of them.

All Maigraith could see was a ragged mound the same color as the rock. However, as they sailed toward the cliff a gap opened up, a cleft-shaped inlet that ran inland for a few dozen boat lengths.

The keel scraped on rock at the end of the cove. Maigraith stepped over the bow, pulled the boat up and tied the rope to a wiry bush growing out of a crack. She looked around, wondering how they were going to get up, for the untamed cliffs surrounded them.

"There are steps cut in the rock," said Shand. "It's a bit of a scramble."

"They must have been cut a long while ago," she panted, following him up a zig-zagging path that was barely distinguishable from the rest of the cliff. The rock was like coarse sandpaper, colored pink or rusty orange, and the steps were crumbling to sand.

"More than three thousand years!" he grunted.

After a number of scares due to the treads crumbling underfoot they reached a plateau as flat as a table, covered in heath that tossed in the wind. In the distance a wall of forest curved around the place from cliff top to cliff top. Below, waves crashed sullenly at the rocks.

"That's Huling's Tower," said Shand. "All that remains of it."

Ahead a little way, on the edge of the cliff, was a mess of crumbling stone surrounded by bare land where nothing grew but lichen. Between ripples of blown sand the ground was glassy smooth.

A patch of gray-leaved bushes grew at the top of the path,

sparsely covered in black berries. Maigraith reached out to pick one. Shand caught her hand.

"Are they not edible?" she asked.

"The bush is called Assassin's Spurge," said Shand. "With good reason."

"After the death of Shuthdar the tower was taken apart, stone by stone, in the search for the golden flute. It wasn't found, of course, and afterwards the tyrant who held sway over this province (Daguar the Third, her name was) ordered that the tower be rebuilt as a perpetual monument, and a warning not to meddle with the unknown. It was put back together in exactly the state of ruin it had been in after the flute was destroyed."

They went in through an arch which was still complete, though much of the wall further on had collapsed. Ahead was a stone stair, jumbled with broken blocks of rusty sandstone. The downstairs rooms were in ruins. Maigraith scrambled up the stair. This stone was not so crumbly, the grains being fused together like sugar, while some surfaces had been melted to glass.

At the top she came out onto a flat roof with a high wall around it, though much of the wall was broken and in one place fallen stone lay in a curving heap high enough to hide behind. A wide crack ran across the roof from one side to the other, where the tower had been split open. The stone up here was also fused and glassy, except for a perfect circle on one side which was not marked at all.

Maigraith could feel worms creeping through her grave. The place was steeped in pain and horror.

Shand had clambered up on top of a piece of surviving wall. With one foot he indicated the crumbled stone in front of him. "This is the very place where Shuthdar was standing when he destroyed the flute." His foot slipped. Shand threw out his arms for balance.

"Careful!" she cried out.

"Come on up. There's a wonderful view from here."

She scrambled up beside him, as much to make sure he did not fall off as to see the view. It was magnificent, though bleak—the gray, churning lake, the dark, wet rocks below, the gloomy forest hanging back from the tower.

Shand pointed straight down. "That's where Shuthdar fell, and where he died."

Maigraith imagined herself plunging at the rocks, and turned away. "I don't like this place."

"Nor I, but I can't stop coming back to see it. What happened here has shaped the Histories for the past three thousand years."

"And is still shaping them," said Maigraith, climbing down. "Will it ever end? I'd like to finish it."

"Maybe you will. Who knows?"

Maigraith was halfway across to the stair when abruptly she screamed and leapt backward as if something had sunk fangs into her foot.

"What's the matter?" cried Shand.

Maigraith's hands were shaking so hard that she could not hold them still. She was deathly pale. "It felt as if I'd trod on something horrible; evil." The glassy stone underfoot glittered with tiny golden specks.

"Shuthdar *was* evil, no doubt of that." He helped her to a block of stone and sat her down. "Try this!" Shand held out his flask.

She gulped the fiery liquor down like water, then gave him a weak smile. "It was an awful, prickling sensation. All my nerves feel on fire."

Shand went to the place where she had been standing. "I can't feel anything, but the tower is steeped in the terrible deeds done in this place. You must be tuned into it, while I am not."

Maigraith clutched the gold around her throat and felt better. "Space and time are very thin here," she murmured. "I can feel the Wall of the Forbidding all around, as if it's radiating out in every direction. And something else. It's like a gate, waiting to be opened into the void." She felt panicky. There were forces here that she could never match. She understood nothing.

"We won't be going *that* road!" said Shand, helping her to her feet. "Have you seen enough?"

"To last me all my days."

Maigraith went back down the cliff very slowly and carefully, though her mind did not register a single crumbling step. What she'd felt up there had terrified her. The whole world was in peril if the balance was not restored. Suddenly Maigraith's purpose in life seemed much more urgent, though still she had no idea how to begin it.

They returned to Thurkad, having been away for three weeks and more, to learn about the hasty attack on Elludore and the dismal result. Karan was sunk deep into a depression that no one could raise her from. Mendark was beside himself with his own folly, he who in the past had done nothing without planning it in the minutest detail and allowing for everything that could possibly go wrong. Yggur, withdrawn and bitter against Karan and Mendark, had been brought so low that it seemed impossible he would ever rise again. The morale of his armies had been shockingly undermined. They would be easy prey for the subversion of the Ghâshâd this time.

Only one good thing had come out of the whole miserable affair. Jevi had lived in terror the whole time Tallia had been away, and the news of the disaster had broken one of the barriers inside him. Tallia and Jevi were friends again.

For all her fears, Maigraith was pleased that they had

failed to get Faelamor's gold. They would be corrupted by it just as she had been. But it did not solve her problem.

Later there was much talk, especially from Mendark, about "pooling their resources" and "pulling together", but all Maigraith could see was that she had the Mirror and he wanted it. She felt resentful. She had not freed herself from one tyrant only to accept the yoke of another. She said nothing about finding the birthright, and kept the gold well hidden.

28

The Assassin

Two nights later a shadowy figure slipped into the citadel and made her way down to the office where Llian worked. Ellami knew where it was, for she had already spied it out. The door was locked but it was no special lock and she had it open in a minute.

She closed the door behind her, conjured ghost light from her fingers and searched the room for Yalkara's book. She found it almost immediately—it was sitting on a shelf in full view. It was just as Faelamor had described it, the strange, half-familiar, hateful glyphs almost fighting themselves to get off the page at her.

Ellami closed it with a snap, tucked it into her bag and went out. One-third of her work was done—the easy third. With luck she would complete it tonight and be out of this stinking cesspool of a city before dawn. She did not want to do it. Indeed, what she had to do was a horrifying betrayal of Maigraith, but for the survival of her people there was no choice. She aimed to cut Karan's throat in her bed, then do the same for Maigraith.

Ellami got into Karan and Llian's rooms in the fortress without any trouble at all, for the Whelm guard had been withdrawn some time ago and the door was not even locked. She crept through the sitting room with her knife out, then froze. There was a light on in the bedroom. Edging her head around the door, she saw Llian sitting up in bed, reading. Where was Karan? In the bathroom? It was unlit but she checked anyway. The room was empty. After a while Llian blew out the candle and settled down on his pillow, alone.

Karan was not here. Ellami cursed. She would not be able to complete her work tonight. She crept out again and headed for Maigraith's room.

Maigraith stirred in her sleep, if what she was enduring could be called sleep, for her nights had been so restless since her return with the gold that most mornings she scarcely felt she'd slept at all. Her dilemma was impossible. She wanted to help the company with their quest. Much more than that, she wanted to open a gate to Aachan and bring Shand and Yalkara together. Every time he got that sad, yearning look in his eyes she longed to do that for him.

What else could her duty be but to remake the golden flute? Especially since that seemed the best way to achieve her own goal, to unstitch the Forbidding and restore the balance between the worlds. But if she did that, she would inevitably be opposing Rulke and her Charon heritage. She still felt troubling yearnings whenever she thought about Rulke. There seemed no solution to the puzzle.

Maigraith turned over on her side, facing the window, presenting a perfect target to Ellami as she edged in through the open door. Ellami had used no illusion of any kind—

Maigraith might have detected that. She stood absolutely still, watching her quarry for any sign that she was awake. There was none—Maigraith lay still, breathing slowly. Ellami drew her long blade and tested it with a fingertip. It was wickedly sharp.

She crept forward, holding the knife hooked so as to slip it to the tender tissues of the throat and carve them open in one movement. She had never killed anyone before, nor even thought about doing so, but this seemed the best way. Maigraith would not be able to cry out; the blood would spray away from Ellami. Four steps to go; three; two.

Maigraith rolled back onto her other side, facing the door and pillowing her head on her hand. Now she made a more difficult target in the gloom, as the left arm half-covered her throat. Ellami recalculated. A slash across the side of the neck? A stab between the ribs, or round into her back? She decided that the neck was best from here, otherwise in the dark she might hit a rib. She dared not give Maigraith any chance.

Maigraith gave a little sigh and snuggled down against her hand. That gave Ellami pause—it was a childlike sigh and it reminded her what had been done to Maigraith as a child. It made her question what she was doing. The woman on the bed was someone she knew and liked. The murder grew harder every second.

Just do it! she told herself. The future of Tallallame is at stake. Don't think about it. Get on with it and get away. She took another step, shaking in her nervousness, and kicked over a cup that Maigraith had left beside the bed.

Maigraith shot up in bed. Ellami flung herself forward, stabbing down. She was not quick enough. Maigraith rolled off the other side of the bed, hurled the covers in Ellami's face and scrabbled across the floor, desperately trying to focus on her assailant.

"No, Ellami!" she screamed.

Ellami felt shamed, but could not acknowledge Maigraith. Untangling herself from the covers she sprang, slashing wildly. She missed again; Maigraith's training had given her lightning reflexes. Now Maigraith caught her by the foot, twisted and Ellami felt her knee give—something had torn inside it. She tried to kick, overbalanced and fell on the knife.

It carved through the soft membranes of her stomach, almost coming out her back. Ellami wrenched free, scratched across the floor and ran for the door, the knife still buried in her belly.

Ellami tore the knife out and stopped the wound with her fingers. The pain was terrible. Behind her she saw Maigraith following. Ellami used a spell of concealment and vanished. Outside, the trail was washed away by rain on the dark cobbles.

Ellami barely made it to her inn. She burned the book in the fireplace of her room, stirred the ashes to dust and called frantically with her mind to Faelamor. That was a clumsy way of communicating at the best of times, but she got a message through, that the book was destroyed but both Karan and Maigraith were safe. Then she collapsed and bled to death on the hearth.

Karan had not recovered from Elludore, or Carcharon either. Every night she had nightmares where she watched the army marching to their deaths, powerless to prevent the disaster. In between those nightmares were other, older dreams, about Rulke and the construct, or the void-leech trying to drill in through her ear to suck her brains out. That ear still ached at times, and she did not hear as well as on the other side. Once she dreamed about hrux, the dried fruit that the

Ghâshâd used to link their minds together, and woke sweating, her whole body craving it.

She could not concentrate at all. Her mind was loaded with those torments, day and night, and it did no good to talk about it with Llian or anyone else. For this ailment, talking was useless. She was afraid to do anything, for her every decision resulted in a cascade of ill consequences. Not even Llian could help her. She felt quite unsupported.

The morning before the attack on Maigraith, Karan had gone out and walked the streets of Thurkad. The politicking in the citadel had no interest for her. She was chafing to get back to Gothryme. She wrote to Rachis every day, wanting to know everything that was happening there, from the state of the weather to the minutest details of agriculture and animal husbandry, but as yet there had been no reply.

The failed raid must have discharged her obligation though, for neither Mendark nor Yggur seemed interested in using her talents again. Yggur was bitterly angry with her, still blaming her for the disaster in Elludore. Mendark, however, always taking the opposite side to his enemy, was more friendly than he had ever been.

After a while she found herself at the waterfront, next to the vast old wharves. She still did not like Thurkad, but she could bear it now. Even the wharf city, that had given her horrors on her first visit as a child, she now saw to be merely squalid, rotten and overcrowded.

Karan paced along the waterfront hoping to find Pender, but though she spent hours looking she did not see *The Waif*, and the people she spoke to had not heard of him. She was in the wrong part of the port, where the larger ships unloaded cargoes from Crandor and other faraway places. Pender would go to the other side where the smaller coastal vessels docked, and the barge traffic from the river. She knew vaguely where that was—a long way from here, for the wharves stretched the best part of a league around the shoreline. Too far, in the rain.

Pulling her floppy hat down around her ears, Karan headed back. Likely that Pender would be in a tavern anyway, on a day like this. There were hundreds to choose from along the length of the waterfront. She picked one that looked less grimy than the others and went inside, but it was a dark, stinking place where people spat on the floor and everyone stared with the resentful glower of those whose sanctum has been invaded.

She had taken her hat off as she entered, and her bright hair sprang out. She stood with her hand on the latch, wondering whether or not to damn them, then decided that prudence was better and went out into the rain again. A second tavern was as bad as the first. A man who had no teeth made ugly jokes as soon as he caught sight of her. On the bar sat a wooden cage in which a sad little creature squatted with drooping shoulders, staring at the floor. It looked a cross between a monkey and a possum, with huge, watering eyes. Karan felt caged too.

The other inns looked the same. As she walked along, she came to a drab little market, a collection of half a hundred stalls, though few had customers. Stopping at a spice booth, she bought some tea spiced with citrus rind. The shopkeeper, a diminutive woman who wore dozens of filigree bracelets up one slender dark arm, weighed the tea out carefully, looked up at her with a smile, added a pinch over the weight for good measure and folded it in a little scrap of cloth.

"Good tea?" asked Karan, the way one does when unsure how much of the language the other person knows.

"Ya," she replied, giving Karan a dazzling smile that revealed few teeth but a lot of gold. "Good tea. Very, very good."

At another stall Karan bought a large slab of honeycomb. She broke off a small piece, picked the remains of a bee out of it and popped the lump in her mouth as she wandered along the wharf. The wax softened in her mouth and the beautiful strong honey dribbled out. Karan walked along, chewing the aromatic wax after all the sweetness was gone. She felt out of place in Thurkad. Llian would still be in the archives. She did not feel like going back to her room and drinking her tea alone.

Wandering off the waterfront at random through the back streets, Karan realized that the building across the road was vaguely familiar. It was the one where Shand had nursed her back to health after the Conclave. Memories of that terrible time welled up. She followed them down the alley and through a tangle of streets. Yes, here was the place where they had been interrogated by Yggur's guards. Further on she came to the steps down which they had fled into the wharf city.

At the top she looked down on the green scummy water. The steps were not as steep as she remembered, nor as long. The tide was low, exposing the platform where she had nearly drowned. The stones and beams were covered in green and pink growths. She could recall every step of that previous journey, even how she had felt—cold inside, sick, lost. She didn't feel much better now.

Karan had not intended to go any further but she suddenly found herself at the bottom, picking her way across the slippery platform, avoiding the many places where rotten timber had collapsed, or would as soon as an unwary foot stepped on it. On the other side she looked up at the huge piles and beams of the wharf city. The tarred wood was covered in weed and barnacles. She stepped into the reeking dark and stopped abruptly. Two of the lanky robed Hlune, the masters of this place, stood quite still, watching her.

Karan had been frightened of them before. But then, in the war their very existence had been threatened. The life of the city had settled back into its old grooves since then. Karan came to a sudden decision.

Holding out her hands, palms up, she said slowly and clearly, "I have come to see the Telt!" She referred to the smaller race who toiled for the Hlune. They had sheltered her a year ago, before her escape with Shand. The Telt had treated her kindly, for no reason other than that she had been their guest, and an uninvited guest at that. "My name is Karan," she added.

They looked at her blankly. She realized that there might be thousands of Telt in the wharf city. And back then she'd had dyed black hair. What was the name of the young woman who had been kind to her?

"I have come to see Cluffer the Telt. My name is Karan. I was here with Shand, one year ago."

The names did not seem to mean anything to them. They each took an arm, not roughly, and led her to the meeting place with the paneled walls where she had been questioned before. After a considerable wait, Karan was brought before the pair of elderly Hlune, who presided there on their red cedar chairs as before. The two wore only ceremonial loincloths. The man's chin-whiskers were plaited into at least a hundred braids, signifying his exalted rank. The woman's hair was similarly divided, hanging down in a fan that covered most of her chest.

"Shand is my friend," she said. "I am Karan Fyrn, of Bannador."

This time Karan was recognized, though when she repeated her request they looked bemused.

The woman felt her arm. "Karan?" she said, clicking her tongue. Then, "Shand, hah!"

"I have come to visit the Telt who sheltered me a year ago," Karan said, speaking very slowly.

The elders seemed puzzled. Perhaps the Telt never had visitors, or perhaps they never came this way.

"Telt!" Karan repeated. "I have come to see Cluffer the Telt."

"Who is Cluffer?"

Karan spelled the name out with a wet finger on the wall.

"Cluffer?" The man popped his cheeks as he followed the letters with his own finger, sounding the name out to himself. "Cluffer?"

Then suddenly he laughed. "No, no," he said, crossed out *Cluffer* with his finger and painstakingly spelled out C-L-O-G-H-E-R. "Cluffer," he repeated, with a subtle but almost imperceptible difference in pronunciation. "You see!"

"Cluffer," Karan agreed.

The woman smiled, a leathery drawing-back of the lips, and gestured to the Hlune who had brought her in. Karan was taken through the dark-timbered, wet, rotting passages of the wharf city to a room like every other room there. It was just a box of raw timber with a floor that was awash and a platform halfway up, above the tide level, on which sat half a dozen barrels and a pile of jellyfish. A dozen Telt worked there, a small, slender, pale-skinned, dark-haired, broad-nosed people. Men and women wore the same solitary garment, a scanty loincloth of drab material. They were a smiling folk, despite their miserable existence.

The Telt were busy at packing jellyfish into barrels. The vile smell of foul-jelly assaulted Karan's nostrils. The stench of the fish oil on their hair was equally overpowering. They turned and stared as one, not recognizing her.

"I am Karan," she said. She reached into her pocket and took out the tea and the honeycomb, offering it.

Someone recognized her voice and smiled. It was

Cluffer. Putting down their tools, they washed in the sea and shook hands, each clasping her two hands in their own. The man she remembered as Cluffer's lover, a slender young fellow whose hair gleamed with fish oil, went over to the urn and set the flame glowing.

They were quite reserved, much more so than before, glancing at one another but not at her. Karan realized that they did not know what to make of her. Back then she had been like them, for all she'd had in the world was a borrowed loincloth. Now she was richly dressed by their standards, far beyond them. It was too high a barrier to be overcome. Then she thought of a way.

Karan took off her coat, shirt, boots and socks, rolled her trousers up at the knee and sat down on the bare boards again, more than a little embarrassed. Goosepimples sprang up on her exposed skin. The damp went straight through her trousers. She wondered how they would react.

The Telt laughed and clapped. One by one they embraced her, then they formed a circle and hugged her in its center. Their skin was warm and very comforting.

After that they drank her spiced tea, cup after cup, until the light began to fade. One or two tiny lamps were lit, and Karan gestured to the jellyfish vats, indicating that she would be glad to take a turn at cleaning and packing them, and pressing them for their jelly. The Telt seemed to find that idea very amusing.

"Holiday!" said Cluffer with a merry grin.

They sat on the upper floor for dinner. The food was put on a single wooden platter which was worn and stained black. Before any of them took a morsel for themselves (and they all ate with their fingers) each one picked up a choice tidbit and offered it to their neighbor, or to Karan as the special guest. The one who accepted the gift first bowed, and after eating, licked the fingers of the offerer to signify appreciation. This custom was not expected of Karan, their guest, but nonetheless she copied their manners, and their way of taking food, as closely as she could. They took food only between the thumb and first two fingers of the right hand, with a fluttering movement of the free fingers, and politely licked their fingers before picking up a morsel to offer it, or to take a piece for themselves.

Dinner was not what Karan would have described as a feast, being based on jellyfish cake, the stringy material left over after all the jelly had been squeezed out. However there were other more palatable dishes. She ate spiced seaweed, mussels in a fermented bean sauce and slug-like black things that they must have gathered by diving and feeling around on the surface of the mud. The platter also held thin strands of red algae pickled in a vinegary fish sauce that stank abominably but tasted rather fine, though the algae were hard to chew and harder to swallow, being rather like eating fishing line. And at the end were served little brown pods like the bladders of a seaweed. They popped in the mouth releasing a thin, intensely sweet but slightly fish-tasting syrup.

It was good to be in the company of people who expected nothing from her. It was a delightful meal, and Karan found herself chattering away to her friends about all sorts of things, important as well as trivial, for she found their speech easier to understand than before. At the end of the meal they passed the platter to her, as guest of honor. Karan felt embarrassed, not knowing what to do with it. Then she realized that it was her privilege to lick it clean. After she had done so they clapped again and put it to one side.

A young man ran out, returning shortly with a large black bottle sealed with wax. Karan offered her knife, which they marvelled at. The wax was chiseled out and saved. The wooden tea cups appeared again. A small measure of thick, milky liquid gurgled into each.

Karan eyed hers dubiously. She had not much of a head for strong drink, and this looked very strong. Cluffer, who was directly across the table from her, raised her cup. The others did so too, then roared something that sounded like "*Caranda!*" and drained it to the last drop.

"*Caranda!*" she roared back, and hurled it down her throat. The liquor was horrible, very bitter, burning and strong, with a pungency that went up her nose like mustard, taking her breath away. Tears sprang into her eyes. Everyone laughed.

The first cup was followed by another almost at once. While recovering from that, Karan sat back against the wall, her bare shoulders touching warm shoulders on either side. Some of the Telt took out pipes and other instruments and began to play. Their songs were melancholy, for the most part. Lovely skirling melodies, but about shipwrecks or lost children, bloody battles and terrible revenges.

She wondered about the Telt. What did they want out of life? Did they dream of living free of the wharf city? But she was not sure it would be polite to ask such questions. The drink pulsed in her veins. Karan felt herself sinking into a dreamy state, and might have gone to sleep if not for the fact that her bottom was so cold and wet.

In an hour or so there was another bout of *Caranda!* followed by dancing, a slow, sinuous, complex, interwoven ballet. Karan allowed herself to be led out and they taught her a few steps, though she soon realized that it would take years to master, even if her head were not spinning. She sat down again, clapping in time to the music. When it was over, everyone resumed their seats.

"*Caranda?*" Cluffer asked.

Karan shook her head and smiled, and without any visible sign of regret Cluffer stoppered the bottle with a wooden bung and put it away.

The Telt made more tea, using up the last of her small gift. She drank another cup gratefully, for she felt cold now. It was quite late. The platter, urn, cups and instruments were packed away. Cluffer took her hand and led her to the sleeping chamber where everyone prepared for bed.

Karan felt a little stab of panic, remembering past nights there, freezing in damp seaweed all alone. That was history. They took off their loincloths, washed them in the sea and hung them up to dry. Removing her wet trousers, Karan did the same. They cleaned their teeth with seaweed. She rubbed a leathery yellow frond over her own teeth. One of the Telt gestured to the center of the big pile of woven seaweed blankets, indicating that she was to take the place of honor. She crept in, the weed tickling her skin, and they all burrowed in after. The last one blew out the light.

Now she understood what they had meant by "sharing warmth", for in the center it was beautifully warm and comforting, though the pungency of their oiled hair was, to say the least, hard to get used to. The water lapped at the slatted floor, the drink rose to her head and took her off to sleep.

Twice in the night Karan was woken by nightmares, once her familiar hideous dream of the brain-sucking leech, the second time the nightmare of the army being led to its doom over the cliff while she tried and failed to scream out a warning. Each time she was embraced by a dozen arms, and a multitude of hands stroked away the fear, the guilt and the powerlessness. Karan soon found herself drifting back into a lovely, carefree sleep.

Later she woke, lying quietly in the dark. It was a long time before she could get back to sleep. The bed was like a nest of grubs, always shifting, and every movement made the weed rustle. When the people on the outside grew cold they would wriggle into whatever inside spot presented itself; the group shifted to accommodate them and all would settle down again.

And sometimes there were other noises, whispers and giggles, though now she knew them for what they were, no longer afraid that they were secretly laughing at her. They moved all around her, breasts and knees and legs and noses, while soft hands crept across her skin. She lay there dreamily, touched by silky fire, making no protest even when they touched places that she would not normally have permitted. But she made no offers, and after a while the hands went away again.

In the morning Karan woke feeling calmer and more relaxed than she had been in months. Thanking her hosts, she donned her clothes again. But before she went they must give her a gift. They brought carvings to her, a selection of their best, and begged her to choose one. She chose a tiny, beautiful thing, a laughing child playing with a toy crab. It made her feel quite sentimental, quite sad for what she would never have.

But such a gift required an equal gift, and she had only one object the equal of theirs. Her prized knife, which Malien had given to replace the one she'd lost in Katazza. It was also a beautiful thing, made of the finest Aachim steel. She offered it, and they accepted it with laughter, hugs and tears. Then she hurried away, suddenly realizing that Llian would be worried about her.

Back in her own room, Karan understood what she had gained from them. The Telt always supported each other, and comforted each other too. She remembered how they had stood up for her last year when the Hlune had wanted to cast her onto the streets. She could not imagine them refusing to act for fear of the consequences. She must do the same. Karan felt an overwhelming relief at having made this decision after so long.

After that she was purged of her fears, if not of her failures, and those nightmares did not trouble her again.

29

A Time of Choices

The fortress was in uproar from the assassination attempt. The guards on the gate had been doubled and would not let Karan in without her pass, which she had thrown away weeks ago. She headed down to the citadel, where she encountered the same problem because of the theft from Llian's room.

Fortunately Tallia was passing at that moment and signed her in. Karan ran down to Llian's workroom to find that it was full of people. Mendark was there, furious at the breach of security, and more so at the loss of Yalkara's book. He had brought a brace of archivists, who were going through Llian's papers, to his fury. Yggur was there too. The attack on Maigraith had shaken him out of his all-pervading despair. Maigraith stood by the window looking out, apparently none the worse for her ordeal, though she seemed tired.

"This is a shocking blow," said Mendark, limping back

and forth. "A shocking blow!" The loss of the book seemed to bother him more than the attack on Maigraith.

Just like him! Karan thought.

A messenger ran in to whisper in Mendark's ear. His face fell even further. "Have all the ashes brought to me!" The fellow ran out. "The thief has been tracked to her room," Mendark announced, "but she is dead and, tragically, the book burnt. A catastrophe!"

"Her name was Ellami," said Maigraith, burying her head in her arms. "I knew her from childhood. I can hardly believe Ellami tried to kill me."

"Faelamor must have a low opinion of us. She'll try again. Be on your guard!" Mendark shook his head. "I had such hopes for the book."

"Well," said Llian, taking it all very calmly, "none of us had been able to decipher a single glyph, and I don't think I ever would have."

"Useless chronicler!" cried Mendark, stamping off. The archivists, Yggur and Tallia followed him, leaving only Karan, Llian and Maigraith in the room.

"What was this book?" asked Maigraith, who had arrived just before Karan.

Llian explained.

Maigraith let out a choking gasp. "But that was *my* book! Yalkara told me so, in the message she left on the Mirror."

"What message?" Llian asked curiously.

"I've not told anyone but Shand. The book contained the first Histories of the Charon, from the time they went into the void, and even before. It was infinitely precious." There were tears in her eyes.

"Come on," Llian said hastily. "I can't bear this place any longer."

They walked down to a park which was empty on account of the miserable weather. Llian's limp was practically gone now, though his legs would be scarred forever. He wiped the stone bench with his cloak and sat down.

Karan sat beside him, watching Maigraith pace back and forth through the mud. "What's going on, Llian? You're up to something. Maigraith, come here!"

As Maigraith sat down, Llian burst out laughing. "I still have the book," he said in a low voice. "It's here in my bag."

"What—?" Maigraith said.

"Well," he flashed his famous smile, "one time Lilis had nothing to do and wanted to practice her writing, so I set her to copying Yalkara's book. It was the copy that was stolen. I always carry the original with me, as I do my journals. They're all here."

Opening his shoulder bag, he handed her a slender volume. "No one knows there's a copy, except Lilis, and she's off with her father. I'll swear her to silence when she gets back."

Maigraith took the book as if it was the most precious object in the world. She caressed the cover and laid it against her cheek. "I can't think of any way to thank you," she said. Opening the book, she stared at the glyphs on the first page. "These are the mirror image of the ones on the Mirror of Aachan. I wonder why?"

"I have no idea," said Llian.

"Perhaps we can work on it together, if I can find the key." She stood up, slipped the book into her bag, gave a secret smile and turned away. Then she came back, giving Llian a self-conscious hug. "Thank you, Llian. After last night I have some rather urgent things to think about. I'll see you tomorrow."

Look upon the Mirror, and it will show you what you must do.

But what *must* I do, Maigraith agonized as she went back

to her room. Mendark and Yggur assumed that her destiny was to wage war against Rulke, but surely Yalkara had never intended that. Where *should* her allegiance lie? With the interests of these people, this world? The Three Worlds? With Rulke and the Charon? The conflicts were irresolvable.

Was the birthright intended to be melted down and made into a device to create gates? Yalkara may not have intended any such thing. And if they did make a new golden flute, just learning how to use it could be a perilous exercise. How was she supposed to restore the balance between the worlds anyway? Maigraith, used to being told what to do, found her choices overwhelming. In some ways Faelamor's legacy still crippled her.

The Mirror will teach you when the time comes.

She opened the Mirror, recovered Yalkara's message to Aeolior and sat quietly, reading the words over and over. Why was part of the message missing? Had it been lost over the years, or was the Mirror hiding something?

Why won't you tell me? she thought tiredly. How I need you, Yalkara. This is all too hard. Maigraith laid her head down on her arms, resting her cheek on the cold surface of the Mirror, and drifted into sleep.

Her dreams were not restful. She kept seeing Ellami creeping up on her with that hooked blade, but Maigraith was a child again and could only watch helplessly from her bed as the knife plunged at her.

The dream repeated about twenty times before Maigraith sank into a restful sleep. Suddenly she was jerked awake by a blinding glare, as if the sun shone in her eyes. She lifted her head, trying to see.

The Mirror was ablaze with light; a molten sun shone out of it. The blaze faded, revealing a green and golden land, a paradise of lake and forest, mountain and lush meadows. The viewpoint rushed toward the lake, highlighting a pavilion on its shore, carved from white marble. A woman sat by the edge, her long back resting against a five-sided column. She was tall and languid, with black hair that hid her face. Her attitude was melancholy. The fingers of one hand trailed in the water.

The lake was as still as metal, but as Maigraith watched, a breeze ruffled the surface and something appeared beneath it, like a black, reflecting teardrop.

The ripples died away and the woman rose, staring down into the water. The teardrop cleared. Inside Maigraith saw something struggling to get out. She caught her breath. A young man was trapped there, a handsome, broad-shouldered fellow with curly dark hair.

He clawed desperately at the walls of his prison, his mouth gaping wide. The woman stared, helpless to do anything. She cried out to him but the words could not be heard. She looked around frantically for something to break that prison, and Maigraith saw that the woman was Yalkara, in the flower of her youth.

She let out a wail of anguish, and Maigraith read the word from her lips. "*Gyllias!*"

The man was a younger version of Shand. Maigraith groaned aloud, for Shand was as much trapped in his teardrop world as Yalkara was in her Eden. There must be a way to bring them together.

Yalkara held out her hands to Shand, showing her helplessness. Caught up in their torment, Maigraith realized that there *was* a way to release them—the golden flute! The Mirror had shown her the path at last.

"I will give up my gold," she said aloud. "But I will not allow the flute to be used against Rulke." Then she slept.

* * *

In the morning Maigraith walked into the council of despair and dropped her jewelry on the table in front of an astonished Mendark.

"Here is Yalkara's *own* gold, Aeolior's birthright and now mine," she said. "You may use it to remake the flute."

There was a long silence.

"How did you get it back?" cried Mendark. He gave Shand a suspicious glare. Shand smiled innocently.

"This isn't the gold that Faelamor stole," said Maigraith. "This is Yalkara's *own* gold."

"Then where did the other come from?" asked Yggur.

Maigraith shrugged. "I have no idea."

"Shand?" cried Mendark in a rage.

"I don't know either," Shand replied.

"We'd better find out," said Yggur, staring down at the jewelry. "I don't like this at all. Where the hell is Llian? Maigraith?"

"Yes?"

"What condition do you put on your gold?"

Every eye turned to her. "I cannot give away my birthright. What is made of it remains mine."

Mendark looked ready to protest but must have thought better of it. "Let's see if we can make it first," he said, lowering his snake eyes. "*Then* will be time enough to decide who may use it. Indeed, who *can* use it."

"Thank you for the offer, Maigraith," Yggur said gravely. "Though I don't know that we should accept it—"

"I accept it!" roared Mendark, holding the shining gold high in the air.

Sitting down at the table, Maigraith put her head in her hands, already afraid that she had made a stupid decision. She was seized by the feeling that Yalkara would not be happy after all.

Mendark rubbed his scaling hands together, calling

loudly for an aide, and when the man came running he told him to fetch the Aachim at once.

"Are they back from overseas?" Karan asked.

"Their boat docked yesterday morning," said Tallia.

It was quite some time before they appeared, six of them. Tensor looked worse than ever. The once glorious black hair lay like a rug over the top of his head. His lips were gray as slate. Malien looked older and more resolute. Xarah was there too, fully recovered from her wound at Carcharon.

"Maigraith has brought us Yalkara's true gold," said Mendark. "Now it's your turn, Tensor. Will you show us how to make the golden flute anew?"

"Maigraith the Charon!" said Tensor bitterly. "It's Aachan gold, stolen from us!" He peered at Maigraith and shuddered, then his eyes drifted around the room to settle on Karan. They flickered at her. She went to his chair.

"Is it still your wish that I help you?" he asked in a spidery voice that only she could hear. On the trek back across the Dry Sea from Katazza he had promised her that.

"I want nothing for myself," she replied. "I would be back in Gothryme, tending my gardens."

He blessed her with a ghostly smile. "Then you've learned more than I ever did. What do you ask of me?"

She was reluctant to ask him anything. "Do you think that this is such a great crime, to remake the flute? Is it a wickedness, or a folly?"

He grimaced. His mouth was so dry that it might have been carved out of teak. He touched her cheek. "It's no crime to defend yourself, or to strike your enemy before he strikes you. It may be folly—that's what we call the bold schemes that fail."

"Does it give us a chance?"

"No one can predict the outcome to this struggle. I care

not, either way. My time is past. The decision is in your hands."

"Why is it up to me to decide? Everything I do goes wrong."

Tensor's eyes never left her face. "Because that is my price," he said at last. "Karan, as many terrible wrongs come from doing nothing as from doing the wrong thing."

She knew he was right. The doubt was there, the agony of choice, but she had made her decision.

"I ask it," she whispered.

"Then I will do it."

His grip, once so strong, felt like a loose collection of bones. He clung on to her. "Help me up! I clutch at my dignity, since I have lost everything that really matters."

They wavered their way to the front of the room. Tensor forced himself to his full height, put a hand on Karan's shoulder momentarily, then stood erect. Karan tried to sneak away.

"Stay," Tensor said out of the corner of his mouth. "It would not do for me to fall down and not be able to get up again.

"I will show you the way," he said to the group. "I and my Aachim will supervise your craftsmen in working this dangerous material. You—" (it was not clear whether he addressed Yggur, or Mendark, or all of them collectively) "—will provide us with a secure, spacious workshop, the equipment required for melting, purifying, transforming and forging the metal, and all the reagents, stills, crucibles and other tools necessary."

"It shall be done," said Yggur.

"And afterwards, everything will be destroyed by burning or melting, including the building itself and the earth beneath to a depth of half a span, and the calcine shall be dispersed across a hundred leagues of the deep sea. And you will give me your oath that the flute, if it survives, will be ground to dust, mixed with ashes to the extent of ten wagonloads and put into the deep sea as well, so that it may never be recovered." He swayed and jerked Karan closer to him.

The conditions drew a flurry of conversation and debate, but at last they agreed. Three copies of a convention were prepared, setting out each of these conditions, and everyone came forward to sign it, either as parties or witnesses.

"I have such a workroom available," Yggur said. "The old bakehouse, in the western corner of the yard, has the space you require, as well as flues and chimneys. You'll have to build your own furnace. Would you care to inspect it now?"

"I will," said Tensor.

They all trooped down. The bakehouse was a splendid old structure of polychrome brickwork and pale stone, solid and secure for it had no windows, just a back door and a front. Tensor went inside, with Yggur, Karan and the Aachim, while the others waited outside the door. After an hour or so they came out.

"It is sufficient," said Tensor. "Send down your smiths for examination. We will seal the back door. Henceforth no one may enter without my invitation. We begin in the morning."

Just after dawn the company returned to the workshop. Tensor himself opened the door, walking unaided. Maigraith stepped forward. She was dressed in a gown of black silk that showed her slender figure, and she wore Aeolior's birthright. The red-gold chain was about her throat, the bracelet on her wrist, and the torc upon her brow. From a distance she looked queenly, but close up, insecure. The tension between her and Tensor was like a live thing, for

Maigraith looked so Charon that he could scarcely bear to be in the same city with her.

"Come!" he said. "You too, Karan." They followed him inside and the door snapped shut. The Aachim were already at work.

"Maigraith, I cannot deal with *you*!" He was quivering with animosity. "My rage is too ingrained, though I know that you were not brought up Charon. Henceforth our communications must be through Karan."

"As you wish." They stood on opposite sides of the room. Maigraith was as still as a post. This is not right, she was thinking. He is my enemy, as he was Yalkara's, and will be Rulke's until the instant of his death. What would my grandmother think to see me deliver her gold into his hands?

Tensor's frame was wracked by a spasm that he could not control. Momentarily his face showed like a death's head. He was near his end, and this business would surely finish him. It was not him Maigraith had to worry about, but the ones outside the door. Make a decision, she told herself, and stick by it!

With a physical wrench she stepped forward. Taking off the torc, bracelet and chain, she held them in her hands for a moment, then with a jerky gesture put them in Tensor's hands. There were tears on her lashes.

"She may well have brought it to Santhenar for this very purpose," said Tensor, staring at her unblinking. Something showed in his eyes, an acknowledgment of her suffering.

"Why do you say that?"

"I knew her."

"Here, on Santhenar?"

"Yes, and even before. The Charon were few when they *stole* our world from us. I knew all of them, in my time."

In the background the Aachim were working quickly but carefully, though all they seemed to be doing was cleaning, removing every speck of dust from the workroom. The whole place was spotless already.

"There can be no foreign particles here," he said as if he had read her thought. "The least speck of dross will spoil it. Later today we will construct a special room for the forging, with walls that can be washed down and double doors to exclude all drafts, and a giant bellows to ensure that the air flows out and dust cannot seep in." He looked toward the other end of the room.

Maigraith saw that it was time to go. She bowed. Tensor escorted her to the door.

"It is begun," she said to the company.

30

The Golden Flute

Inside the workroom, forges were lit and bellows began to pump in preparation for the great work. Smoke issued from the chimneys. But whatever was done there was a secret well kept. No one but Karan was allowed inside, and then only after the work was finished for the day and every secret device put away again.

While the flute was being crafted, spies were dispatched to Elludore, Carcharon and other places in the east and the north, to find out what their enemies were up to. Messengers were sent to all allies, and skeets to those who were further off. One flew to Wistan, the Master of the College of the Histories in Chanthed. All favors were being called in, and all debts.

"And I trust that Wistan will treat this message with more respect than he did the last," Mendark said darkly as the skeet soared into the air. A year and a half ago he had begged Wistan to find Karan and have her brought to Thurkad. Wistan had given Llian the job, but only to get rid of him, hoping that he would fail. Mendark never forgot a favor, nor a grudge.

"I gather Tensor's having problems," Shand said to Mendark a few days later.

"Your spies must be better than mine are!"

"I picked up a bit of gossip," Shand said enigmatically. "The gold is proving difficult to work, and sometimes strange things happen in the workshop."

"Such as?"

"Well, at first they couldn't get the gold to melt, though they heated it way above the normal melt temperature. Then tools would mysteriously lose their edge without ever being used. Once the bellows pumped backward and caught fire, burning one of the smiths so badly that he had to be taken to the hospital. The artisans are terrified. Tensor is close to giving up."

"No doubt Yggur will be pleased to hear it," said Mendark.

A week went by before the Aachim first reported their progress. The company was called to the steps of the workshop and Tensor came out, looking better than any time since Katazza. He walked freely now, though not without pain. Despite the disturbing rumors, the work seemed to have been good for him. He appeared euphoric.

"It's taken more labor than we expected," he said. "There were impurities in the gold, and some most obdurate and refractory ones, but they are all gone now. And we had . . . other problems that I won't go into. It will be some time until it is finished, but we've forged the body of the flute just this morning."

He drew from its cloth wrapping a golden tube the length of his forearm and outstretched fingers. The metal was dull and rough, having not yet been cleaned from the molds. Nonetheless it was a beautiful object, and an enticing one. They all felt the pull of it. Tensor could not keep his hands off it. He kept sliding it though his fingers, fondling it. Maigraith saw Mendark gazing at it with an equal longing.

After the company had gone, Tensor called Karan and Maigraith inside. Maigraith was amazed at the summons, considering the tension between them, but it seemed Tensor had gained control over his feelings during the time of labor.

"There was a little more gold than was needed," he said. "When we weighed it at the beginning, one link of the chain was left over. Aachan gold has always been precious to me and I *hate* any Charon who has it." His hands were clenched into fists, wrapped around by those extraordinarily long fingers. "But this has been in Charon hands so long that I cannot bear to keep it. It has not been melted, just shaped into a ring. Take it, despite that you are my—No, I won't say it. *Take it and go!*" He held out to Maigraith a rather thick, plain ring, beautifully polished but unadorned. His hand shook.

Maigraith held the gold up on a fingertip. Was it a trap? She could not sense anything wrong, but she would make sure later on. She slid the ring onto her finger. "Thank you," she said.

Malien came into Karan's room while she was washing her hair in a basin.

"I must talk to you, Karan. Is Llian around?"

"He's gone to the library. What's the matter?"

"No hurry! When you're finished." She sat on the bed.

Karan rinsed her hair with several jugs of water and began to towel it dry. It took rather a while, and when she'd finished, her hair looked like a tangled fleece. Finally she mopped the floor with a towel and changed her blouse, which was saturated. She looked around for her brush.

Malien found it for her. "Would you like me to brush it for you?"

"Yes, please."

Karan sat on a chair and Malien on the bed behind her, easing the tangles out. "What did you want to talk about?" Karan wondered.

The brush stopped by her ear. "Us Aachim—and you!"

Malien's voice had the same kind of magisterial sternness that Karan remembered from Tensor, in her childhood.

"We held a great gathering of Aachim in Insoldiss," Malien went on. "The biggest held since Tar Gaarn fell. Many plans were considered there, and many discarded . . ."

"What was decided?" Karan asked.

The brush continued its work but Karan no longer found the grooming comfortable. She felt dominated, as she had never felt by Malien before.

"A number of things. I can't tell you those plans. But I can tell you that we are resolved to take our place in the great struggle. We plan to fight Rulke with whatever weapon comes to hand! And that's why I've come to you."

"Me?" Karan did not like the way this was going.

"Because of your Aachim heritage, and because you kept the Mirror from us. You owe us doubly, Karan." The brush tore painfully at a knot of hair. "Most of all because you helped the enemy in Carcharon. You know things about Rulke that we do not."

"I never expected this of you, Malien," Karan said after a long silence.

"Well, Karan, will you aid us, *or not*?"

"I have other loyalties now," Karan said fiercely. "And I haven't forgotten what the Aachim did *to me*! You demand loyalty but refuse citizenship to all who are not pure Aachim. That destroyed Emmant and it destroyed my father."

Malien's hand froze in mid-air. "You reject us when we most need your help?" she said incredulously.

"I do not. But I won't submit to emotional blackmail either! Nonetheless," she continued more calmly, "I will do what I can for the Aachim, as long as it doesn't conflict with my other responsibilities."

Malien gave her a cold stare. "Then answer me this. What's Maigraith up to with the flute?"

"I don't know what you mean."

"What does she want it for? It doesn't seem to match what I know of her."

"No it doesn't," said Karan, wondering herself. "I suppose . . . I imagine she's doing it for Shand."

"Shand!"

"Well, making the flute was his idea in the first place. And Yalkara—"

The brush froze. "Yalkara!" Malien hissed. "Of course!" She raced out, leaving the brush hanging in Karan's hair.

Maigraith checked the ring carefully, and had Shand look at it as well, but it was no different from the gold she had given Tensor the previous week. Later she sat down with the Mirror, searching for anything that might indicate how the flute was to be used. She found nothing, and began to wonder if the answer was there at all.

Who else would know anything about it? She had already asked Mendark and Yggur, but if they did know they were not saying. Tensor had been an artisan toiling for Shuthdar when the original flute had been forged in Aachan, but would he tell her? She took her courage in her hands and went back to the workshop. Tensor was busy, but would see her in half an hour as long as Karan was with her. Maigraith had no idea where Karan was. She sat down on the step.

Shortly Tensor appeared at the door, furious at the interruption. She explained what she was looking for.

"I never saw it used," he growled. "It was used only once on Aachan, by Shuthdar. He took very good care that no one was watching. Good day!"

He slammed the door. Maigraith trudged back to Yggur's stronghold. As she approached the main door Karan and Llian came out, arm-in-arm. Llian had been telling a joke, very animatedly, for he was waving his arms and Karan was laughing. They stopped when they saw her long face.

"What's the matter?" asked Karan. "You look as though you've just broken the Magister's second-best teapot." This must have been a reference to Llian's joke, for she giggled and Llian burst out laughing.

"We're going down to the city for dinner," Karan went on. Her face was flushed.

Maigraith envied her. "I don't know what to do!" she burst out.

"You know," said Llian, "I keep thinking about the glyphs inscribed on the Mirror. Why are they the mirror image of the script in Yalkara's book?"

"Hey!" said Karan. "What if it's an instruction?"

"Not much use if we can't read it," Llian replied.

"I meant, perhaps the *mirror image* is the instruction," said Karan.

They both stared at Maigraith. "Yes!" cried Llian. "Open the Mirror, Maigraith. Quick! Where's that bit of card I copied the glyphs on?" He fished it out of his bag.

No sze gwi ta sha mu no dzo ta dzo gwu cho ksi lo sze mo nu mu bu gi sze gwi gwu je ru she ksi cha vo gw'uh wi no sze ta mo va mu bu cho ksi kso fe mo nu mu gw'uh gwu ta dzo lu u lo gwi ksi lo gi mu qa kso je e i dzo ta dzo mu no she nu che mo lo cha kso pi lu ta gwu va nu vo cha ru gwi sze ya ta sze pi no sze lo je mu gwi ta sha sze e.

Maigraith handed the Mirror to him. Llian held it up, and Karan the piece of card, facing the Mirror. "What does it say?"

"Exactly the same, only reversed," said Maigraith.

"Oh well. It was a good idea though."

"Let me have a go." Maigraith reached for the Mirror. The golden ring shone on her finger.

Karan held the card up again. "That's strange," she exclaimed, staring at its reflection.

"What?"

"The glyphs aren't reflected at all, just a whole lot of letters."

"Get them down, Llian," cried Maigraith, "before they disappear."

Llian wrote down the letters below the glyphs.

"What does it mean?" he asked hopefully.

"I haven't the faintest idea," said Maigraith. "But I'll bet Shand does."

They found Shand hurrying down the main hall of the fortress. "Come in here," said Maigraith, drawing him into an empty room. "Have you any idea what this means?" She handed him the piece of card with the glyphs and the jumble of letters.

"It appears to be a message written out in the Charon syllabary," he said.

"Sorry?"

"The Charon language is written in a script where each character represents a syllable, rather than a letter as in our alphabet."

"But these glyphs aren't the secret Charon script," said Llian.

"No," said Shand, "unless it's an older version. And it may well be, because the syllabary looks much the same. Where did you get it?"

Llian explained. "What does it say?"

"I don't know. I'd have to work out how the syllables go together to form words, first. But it must be some kind of message, from Yalkara."

"Or warning!" said Karan.

"*Can* you put the syllables into words, Shand?" Maigraith asked eagerly.

"Possibly. I once knew the *spoken* Charon language fairly well, though I could not read it. It'd take a fair bit of headscratching, and the words would still need to be translated. Make me a copy, Llian. I'll start on it as soon as I get back. Sorry, but I'm in rather a hurry. I'll see you later." He hurried out without further explanation.

"Mendark's coming!" said Karan, who was guarding the door.

Llian sprang up guiltily and they ran outside, laughing.

"Come and dine with us," called Karan over her shoulder.

"I have to work," said Maigraith irritably, yearning for what they got from each other. "Besides, you look as though you'd planned a private evening."

"Nonsense!" they said together. "We can talk further while we eat," Karan added.

Llian linked his arm through Maigraith's and she could not resist any longer. She wanted to be with them; she was hungry too.

They were going to a café Llian had found on one of his jaunts into the low parts of the city and, he being Llian, they became lost three or four times and went into several undistinguished little eating houses before they finally found the place. Maigraith kept looking over her shoulder as they trekked from one establishment to another.

"What's the matter?" asked Llian.

"Oh, nothing! Ever since Ellami's attack I've felt jumpy. Once or twice I thought someone had followed us, but I must have been imagining it."

Karan shivered, though no one noticed. "Here it is," cried Llian. "It's pretty basic!"

Even so, Maigraith was not prepared for quite the austerity of the place she found herself in. It was a shack with a mud floor and a few plank benches and trestles made from raw timber. There were no other customers either, but a fire blazed in one corner. It was cozy by the fire, though a large puddle under the table left Maigraith nowhere to put her feet.

The proprietor, a stooped fellow wearing a moldy coat

and slippers, shuffled in. He bent over the table until his nose was almost touching Maigraith's. He had a tiny wrinkled mouth like a cat's bottom and it stayed closed when he spoke.

"Whoozipang?" he demanded. Black hairs sprouted out his cratered nose as luxuriantly as a walrus's moustache.

Maigraith leaned away from him, but the hairy bugle followed her until he was almost lying across the table. "Whoozipang?" he asked again.

"She is!" Karan and Llian said together, pointing at Maigraith.

"Yooispang?" The bristles quivered. Maigraith stared up his nose in fascinated horror.

"He wants to know who's paying the bill," Karan said merrily. "Obviously he doesn't trust our looks. Tell him you will, or we'll never get our dinner."

"I will pay," Maigraith said with dignity, feeling conned. Karan caught Llian's eye and they both laughed like penniless students who had just cadged a banquet. Nose Hairs shuffled out again.

"He hasn't taken our order," Maigraith grumbled.

"Doesn't need to," said Llian. "Everyone gets the same here."

The host shuffled back in with a jug of golden wine. He spilled it into three bowls, put the jug down in the center of the table with a crash that rattled the cutlery and turned away.

"Ll sen" Nuhnn," he said over his shoulder and disappeared out the back.

"What did he say?"

"I have no idea," said Karan boisterously. Just the smell of wine was enough to get her going. "Move up please. Your big backside is taking all the room."

Maigraith, whose rear was rather smaller than Karan's,

was offended. She hurriedly slid up the bench. "Ow!" she yelped.

"What's the matter now?"

"Nothing. A splinter in my . . . bottom."

"Shall I call the host to get it out for you?" Llian asked mischievously.

Maigraith was not amused by personal jokes. "I'll put up with it," she said through pursed lips.

Shortly a young woman came in, as plump and pretty as the man was grotesque. She smiled at them, especially at Llian, took their orders, all the same, naturally, and went out again.

Llian raised his bowl and they drank. The wine was better than Maigraith had expected, and after the bowl was finished and she had poured another she felt better.

"Now Maigraith," said Karan, "tell us what's bothering you. Apart from the splinter."

"I'm afraid."

"Of what?"

"Everything! Afraid that I've done the wrong thing with Aeolior's birthright. Afraid what Yalkara would think of me. Afraid what people will do with the flute."

"Then when it's made, take it and use it yourself."

"*How?*" she shouted, then ducked her head and went red in the face as the host appeared around the door, muttering imprecations. "I don't know how, Karan. I can't work out how the flute was meant to be used. No one knows, and the Mirror can't tell me."

"Or won't."

"Or won't," she agreed. "I thought you might have some ideas, Llian."

Llian drained his second bowl. He shook his head. "It's not the sort of secret that's left lying around."

The pretty waitress came back with a tray containing

many small dishes: fiery spices, pickles, mustards and thin sweet vinegar. She set it down, returning with another—equally small bowls of shredded raw meat and raw fish cut into matchsticks. Finally she eased a smoking slab of granite onto the middle of the table, and tossed the meat onto it to cook. The meal was accompanied by a mound of steamed vegetables and another of glutinous dumplings.

They ate without further talk. At the end Karan licked her fingers contentedly. "A tale would be a good way to finish this evening off," she said. "What do you have for us, Llian? None of your *Tales of Bawdry*, mind, like this afternoon." She laughed at the memory. Llian blushed, which made Karan laugh even louder. "That's not the kind of thing Maigraith wants to hear."

Being on her third bowl of wine and her natural prudishness well overcome, Maigraith would have been delighted to hear such a tale, but just then Karan very loudly said, "Hey!"

The other two sat up, wondering what was the matter. The host thrust his nose whiskers around the door, said something like "Rkle'bbos," and slammed the door again.

"What?" said Maigraith.

"Recall the tale you told in Carcharon, Llian? The part about Nassi, the young woman who worked out how Shuthdar had tricked Bandiar the sorcerer."

"Yes?"

"Was that really true?"

Llian looked pained. "We already talked about that. It was true enough."

"I'm serious. Was it true that Nassi escaped with Shuthdar and later became a great mancer and a wise woman?"

"Yes, but I don't see what you're getting at." Then suddenly he did. "She established a great house."

"A dynasty? Or do you mean a college?"

"A dynastic house, but of course many students came to learn from her, and after her death it became a college. I should have thought of that! Nassi knew more about Shuthdar's mind and work than anyone, and she saw him use the flute."

"She would be dead three thousand years," said Maigraith.

"Longer, but she may have written it in her Histories. Unfortunately, her college is at Saludith. It would take months to go there."

"I can take you there. I'll make a gate." Maigraith reached into her pocket.

"Not here!" said Llian hastily.

Giving him a stare fit for an imbecile, she brought out a handkerchief which she used to mop her brow. "It's very hot."

"The spices, and the wine," said Karan. "Are we finished?" Suddenly they needed to get outside. All thoughts of a tale were gone.

She called the waitress back. As Maigraith was paying the bill, which was only a few coppers, she looked up to see Nose Hairs watching her like a hunting skeet. His lips moved as she counted the tariff into the waitress's hand, then he turned away and they went out.

"I don't know what all the fuss was about," she said, "for such a small amount of money."

"He's always like that," said Llian. "The war drove him mad. It's a tragic tale, though a common enough one."

"Oh?" said Karan.

"He was a rich man, but he volunteered to serve in the war against Yggur and was struck down in the first hour of battle. He lay under a pile of dead for days, they say. When he came home, his wife and children were dead, and the house burned to ashes. He lost everything."

Maigraith was silent, thinking of the tragic youth who had sheltered her and Faelamor after the Conclave. The shivers running up and down her spine quite took away the levity that three bowls of wine had given her.

31

SALUDITH

"*In days of yore, old pirate Chaw,*
Was a'sailin' round the Horn—"

Llian roared out the verses, while leading them up a dark alley where the smell of human filth and rotting rubbish was more pronounced than usual.

"Hush," said Karan. "Llian, where are you taking us?"

"A shortcut! " He broke into a tuneless whistle, listing like a yacht in a high wind.

Karan looked anxiously into the darkness. "I don't like the feel of this place. It wouldn't be safe even in daylight. Let's go back." She turned toward the distant light from the street.

Llian walked into a pile of crates, sending them toppling with a crash of splintered glass. He picked himself out of the debris. "Sorry. Sorry!"

"Llian," hissed Karan. "You're drunk!" She stood in the middle of the alley with her hands on her hips. "Come on!" She set off again.

Before she had gone a dozen steps Llian made a gurgling noise, "Karan, gglmph!" and went down again.

Karan imagined it to be the kind of sound someone gave when their throat was slashed open. She snatched for her knife, but it was not there. She had given it to the Telt and forgotten to replace it. She stumbled up into the hungry dark.

All at once a white light lit the alley from one end to the other, brighter than day. It was Maigraith, holding aloft one of her globes. Four people were revealed, advancing on Karan. Llian lay on his back in the muck. Maigraith gave a cry that made Karan's hair stand up.

"Karan! Stay where you are!"

Maigraith's arm swung. The globe carved a trail through the air, landing at the feet of the nearest two attackers. Bursting in a pulse of light and sound it flung them against the wall. Neither moved after that. The second pair set off, their legs working like dressmaker's scissors. *Ghâshâd!* Karan realized. *They came for me!*

Maigraith, more calmly now, put her hand out toward the fleeing Ghâshâd. This time there was no sound, light or fury, but their legs were snatched from under them. One lay motionless. The other kept flinging out his arms and legs then drawing them back up to his chest.

Maigraith raced past, pulling a second globe out of her coat. It flared up where the attackers lay. She came running back. Karan was down on her knees beside Llian, cradling his head in her hands. Llian groaned.

"I thought they'd killed him," Karan said.

"I'm sorry, I lost my head," said Maigraith.

Karan looked around. Maigraith's globe did not show the details further down the alley. "Are they dead?"

"No," said Maigraith. "They're . . . not *dead.*" She did not elaborate.

Karan lifted Llian up. "I can walk," Llian said, holding his head in both hands. "Let's get away from here."

"They came from Shazmak," said Karan. "Thank you, Maigraith." She still felt awed by what she had seen.

"Sorry," said Maigraith. "My strength seems to come in blind rage or not at all."

"They were waiting for you," said Llian. "For *you*, Karan!"

"I know. They came to take me back. To Rulke!"

Four of Yggur's guard appeared at the other end of the alley and challenged them. Maigraith lit up her globe. They all knew her of course. She pointed to the crumpled figures. The soldiers saluted and ran that way.

"I hate Thurkad," Karan said, swearing under her breath. "How I wish I was back in Gothryme."

"You won't be safe in Gothryme," said Llian. "At least you can be protected here, as long as you don't follow idiots down dark alleys. Hold on a minute." Sitting down on the curb he put his head between his knees. "My head!" He felt it with his fingers. There was a large lump and a small amount of blood. "I don't feel very well." He got up again, walking between them with his arms over their shoulders.

The guard smirked as they wavered in through the gate. "Drunk, is he?"

"As a priest," said Maigraith soberly.

"Or a Magister," blinked Karan.

The guard guffawed, looked around uneasily in case they were overheard, and waved them on, still grinning.

In Karan's rooms they helped Llian onto the bed, took off his boots and pulled a cover over him. She blew out the lamp.

"Saludith?" said Karan, as Maigraith headed toward the door.

"I must! It's urgent now. Rulke must be ready."

"I'll come with you."

"No," Maigraith said unconvincingly.

"I need to get away from here, Maigraith. Thurkad is like a prison to me. And now, every day I'll be expecting Rulke to try again."

"All right." She looked relieved. "What about him?"

"What a duffer he is! I'd better get someone to look after him, I suppose," said Karan with studied casualness.

"Haven't you forgotten something?" said "him" coldly from the bed. "How are you going to get admittance to Saludith? How are you going to find what you're looking for there? It won't be in common speech. You won't even get in without a master chronicler."

"I suppose we'd better take him along, just in case," said Karan grudgingly, then laughed and gave Llian a hug.

They sat down on the bed to plan. They would go before dawn, and there was much to be done before then. Saludith was a long way south and would be frigid at this time of year. And they must prepare for the gate going astray.

"I'd like a few hours' sleep before we go," said Karan, when all that was done. Llian was asleep already.

"Meet me on the roof of the citadel an hour before sunrise," Maigraith said, picking up her pack.

Sometime during the night it had begun to rain, and it grew heavier with the dawning, so that when Karan and Llian reached the rooftop there were pools everywhere. A glimmer of light led them to Maigraith. Water was already dribbling down the back of Llian's neck. He wished he had never heard of Saludith. He wished he was back in his warm bed, with or without Karan. His head hurt.

Maigraith had something small and dark in her hand, like a lightglass that was not lit. She tucked its twin into a crevice on the roof. She concentrated hard, and suddenly pale-blue fire made a tracery of lines all around them, like a birdcage. The lines faded.

Maigraith swore and adjusted her hood. "There is a difficulty I hadn't thought of last night. I can't make a gate to a place I've never been to."

"I've been to Saludith," said Karan. She made a link and gave Maigraith her memories of the city.

Maigraith tried again; again she failed. "Gates can only be opened in certain places, such as here, and they can only go to certain places. But it seems Saludith is not such a place."

"Maybe Nassi chose the site for that reason," said Llian.

"This college of hers, Llian, is it actually in Saludith?"

"No, not *in*. Near, I think. I haven't been there."

"Can you remember any places near Saludith, Karan?"

Karan thought for a moment. "It was years ago. Nowhere else near there has left so clear an image in my mind that I'd risk our lives on it. Hang on! There *was* a place a day or two east of Saludith." She closed her eyes to conjure up the image. "A narrow, deep valley where all the rock was white—chalk! I remember it distinctly. I'd never seen chalk before. The roads were white, and the grass a funny yellowy-green, and on my left a track wound up to a high hill shaped like a cone. On the side facing the road, near the top, there had been a landslide, leaving white rock peering out of the side of the hill like a window. There was a cap of grass over the crown of the hill, and on that an abandoned watchtower."

It was just starting to get light. Karan renewed the link and Maigraith concentrated on the image. It was a good one—clean and strong.

"I have it," said Maigraith. "Take my hands!"

The blue tracery glowed around them, Llian's head spun and they vanished from the rooftop.

They reappeared in pitch darkness, in freezing cold and howling wind, right in the middle of a blizzard. Karan gripped Llian's hand tightly to stop herself being blown off her feet.

"Where's Maigraith?"

"I don't know," Llian shouted.

"Hang on, I'll try to find my globe."

"Don't let go!" he yelled.

Snow swirled between them and his groping fingers found only air.

"Where have you gone?" he screamed above the wind. He walked two steps and fell down an embankment. At the bottom he kept rolling, finally coming to a stop in a mound of snow.

"Karan!" he shouted, but there was no reply.

Llian stood up. The wind blew him off his feet again, so he crouched down in the snowdrift, which provided meager shelter from the howling wind. He tried to work out what had happened. They had landed on the side of a steep hill. Presumably Karan and Maigraith had also fallen down here somewhere. It had been just on dawn in Thurkad but that might be an hour later, this far south. He enveloped himself in his cloak and waited stoically for it to get light.

Eventually the sun rose to illuminate a white world. Snow whirled all about. Llian stood up, shaking it off his hood. "Karan!" he shouted.

A sheep-shaped mound not far up the hill heaved. "Oh, it's so cold."

"Why did you let go of my hand?" he said crossly.

"I didn't, you let go of mine. Have you seen her?"

"No!"

They eventually found Maigraith huddled in the snow beside a rock, with a twisted knee and a lump on her head.

"What happened?" they said together.

"I don't know. You weren't with me. The first I remember is waking with a sore head, so I crawled here and waited."

"Is this the right place?"

"We'll have to wait until it stops snowing," said Karan.

"Obviously it wasn't winter when you were last here," Llian said sourly. "Take us out of here. Anywhere!"

"I can't," Maigraith said.

"Why not?"

"I can't make another gate without resting from the first. The after-effects are bad enough as it is."

They put up their tent, with considerable difficulty, and huddled inside it all day.

That night the snow eased but in the morning Maigraith's knee was, if anything, more swollen and painful than previously. "We'll have to go back," said Karan.

Maigraith tried to visualize the rooftop. Nothing happened.

"I can't do it," she said. "I know the destination but I can't see it in my mind."

"Let me help you," said Karan. Making another link, she gave Maigraith her own image of the place.

Maigraith went rigid. "Stop!" she screamed.

"What's the matter?"

"You . . . *see* it differently from me. No, I've lost it. It's hopeless, and every try makes it worse."

Karan and Llian looked at one another. "It's going to be a long cold walk back to Thurkad," said Llian. "Two hundred leagues, the way the birds fly—I calculate we'll get there about mid-summer. Has anyone got any money?"

"Shush, Llian." Without the gate their plight was desperate. Karan had not a grint on her, of course.

"My knee isn't so bad now," said Maigraith.

The weather began to clear and shortly they saw, from

their vantage point, the town of Saludith only a league or two to the west and, about as far south, a stronghold that might have been their destination. It seemed to fit the rather vague description of the college that Llian remembered. Further along the road, a track wandered in that general direction.

By the time they reached the place it was nearly dark. Haakhaast Academy, it said in iron letters over the gate. An ancient, tottering guard asked their business. From inside his coat Llian produced a badge that proclaimed him to be a master chronicler.

"I am Llian, of Chanthed. I must consult the library on a matter of some urgency."

The guard stared at the badge, inspected Llian, then rang a bell and waved them through to the next gate. This time the inspection was more rigorous, but eventually they graduated into a courtyard and a third gate. It was open, beyond which they saw a wide hall. Once more Llian showed his badge and told his story. This time he was questioned searchingly about things that a master chronicler might be expected to know, or so Karan gathered, since she knew none of the answers.

Evidently the test was passed, for a servant ushered them into a sitting room: stone walls and floor, high timbered ceiling. The room was frigid, even near the fire. A slender woman dressed in a toga of gray silk hobbled in. She had a long pallid face and eyelids that sagged down over her eyes so she could hardly see. She wore sandals whose leather straps were as fine as string, exposing blue feet twisted with rheumatism.

"My name is Ralah. I am the Autand of this academy." She examined Llian's badge, and asked one or two other questions, which he answered, apparently to her satisfaction.

"We have to be sure," she apologized, blinking constantly. "What we have here is very precious. Precious to us anyway, though fewer and fewer come to look, or to study. Llian the Zain! I've heard of you, of course, though I've not had the privilege of hearing you tell. It's many years since I made the long journey to Chanthed, and I shall not go again. Perhaps while you are here . . ." She squinted at him and Llian saw that under the drooping lids her eyes were cloudy—she was nearly blind.

"I would be most happy to tell for you," he said. "If it's not too presumptuous, I could tell the *Tale of Nassi and Shuthdar*."

Ralah chuckled. "No, not that tale, we are steeped in it. One of the Great Tales, or even one of the lesser. Any would do! We hear so little here, and perhaps it would bring back something of the enthusiasm that we have lost. But, where are my manners?"

She pulled a bell and refreshments were brought, a sweet mild brewed drink not unlike lasee, though they called it by a different name, *mord*, and honey cakes.

"You had better tell me your business," she continued, when they were seated by the fire munching their crisp cakes. "I hear the most urgent news, by skeet, though the details take months to get here. It must be critical to have brought you all this way in winter. How is the Great North Road south of Clews Top? Usually with the snow . . ." her voice was suddenly frosty.

Llian glanced at Maigraith. "We did not come by any road, except the one outside your door," she said. "Only two days ago we were in Thurkad, in the rain. I made a portal there and brought these two with me all the way to the chalk mountain."

Ralah stared at her, not even blinking. She made a little sigh and her shoulders sagged. "It's never really lost, is it?

A thousand years it might remain hidden, but sooner or later it will out again. The miracle of gates!"

"We tried to go back when Maigraith twisted her knee, but the miracle didn't work."

"You probably weren't in quite the right place," said Ralah. "I think I can see what you've come for, but tell me the story over dinner. The whole story."

After dinner, which featured turnip in a dozen combinations, all horrible, they took a glass of vinegary port and went to their rooms. Karan and Llian's had a huge canopied bed, and the room was so cold that they were not long out of it.

In the morning they were taken to the archives, where the most precious papers were kept, including the original writings of the famous Nassi. "Here we are," said Ralah, indicating a shelf containing many rectangular boxes made of leather.

Karan reached up and was instantly rebuked. "Only the chronicler may touch these boxes. The papers are old and very fragile."

Maigraith and Karan stood in the cold aisle, watching while Ralah took Llian down the row, explaining the system to him, taking down a box now and again to show what was inside.

Llian had one of the boxes down. An odor of camphor came faintly along the aisle. "Come and look at this!" he cried. When they hurried up he said, in a voice suppressed to a whisper, "These are the very papers that Shuthdar made to trick Bandiar with." He was awed. "Imagine! Nothing else he wrote remains."

Karan was less awed. "Is it any use to us?"

"No, I don't suppose so. But imagine . . ."

Karan gave a loud sniff.

"Yes," said Llian sadly. "You're right. Another time perhaps." Closing the box, he blew a speck of dust off the spine and replaced it on the shelf with exquisite care. He took down another.

That process was repeated for the whole of the day, and several times they had to remind Llian that they were not here for his amusement, though Karan suspected that he still indulged himself as much as he dared. She was sure that he went back to the box containing Shuthdar's writings too, and spent a long time with it, but when she accused him he just smiled at her. Still, he got through many boxes, and late in the afternoon found the ones he was looking for, containing the records Nassi had made soon after fleeing with Shuthdar.

It was evident that these documents had been looked at many times, for they were in worse condition than the others, yellow and cracking to pieces. They had to be handled with such care that it took almost a minute to turn each page. The task could take weeks.

"There are copies of these papers, of course," he said, turning to Ralah.

"No copies," she said.

Llian was astounded. "But there could be a fire, or a storm might blow the roof off! Even a worm could destroy what you guard so carefully."

"It was not our founder's wish that her private papers be duplicated. We respect that wish. When they are gone, they are gone. There are, of course, copies of all our other precious documents."

Llian made a rude noise. The Histories were more important than any single person, and when he returned to Thurkad he would write out everything he had read, from his perfect chronicler's memory.

He turned back to his work. Ralah sat on a stool watching him. Karan and Maigraith paced.

* * *

The next day they started early. It was tediously slow for the watchers. The writing was crabbed, faint with age, and in an archaic dialect which was difficult even for Llian to make out. He worked through the boxes methodically, making sure that he had missed nothing, then went back to one.

"This is all I can find. May I see the catalogue?"

Ralah took him to the place. Llian went through the relevant cards, and again. "There seems to be one missing. There's a missing number."

Ralah bent over the drawer, shuffling the cards back and forth. "Oh dear!" she said, blinking furiously. "You're right."

"What was the item?" asked Maigraith.

"I don't know," said Ralah, "but it would be—"

"Something Nassi wrote about the flute," Llian said bitterly. "But it's gone, and the catalogue entry removed, and there's no copy."

Ralah said nothing.

"Do you have any idea what it said? How it was used, that is?" Llian tried to keep the frustration out of his voice.

"I am the custodian, not a chronicler. It is not *my* task to know the details of her papers, only to keep them safe for posterity."

Oh for a Nadiril here! thought Llian. Posterity is now, and you are no use at all. "How can I find out if she wrote about it some place else?"

"You can read everything in the library."

"That would take years," he said to Maigraith. Then, turning back to Ralah, "There are no masters here, or even students, who know these particular papers?"

"Alas," she said. "No more."

"Go through it all again!" Maigraith looked impatient.

Llian took the papers to a nearby table, sat down and began to read aloud. Finally he put everything back in the box. "She talks about Shuthdar playing the flute, but only in passing."

"She wrote at length about all his tricks and puzzles, but nothing at all about the most important thing of all?" said Maigraith. "Is there no mention about how he used the Secret Art to turn the music into a gate, and how he directed and controlled the gate afterwards?"

"She may have written a treatise," said Llian, "but it's not here."

"Well, what do you think? Sniff it out with your chronicler's nose."

"Such things have a way of disappearing, *especially when no copies have been made*." He directed a reproachful glare at Ralah but she was oblivious.

Ralah bent down until her nose was almost touching the page, moving her head up and down to read. Her eyes were watering. "I need my glass." She fumbled inside her toga, found nothing and put her head down to the page again. Then she turned the box over to see what was written there. Her lips moved. She looked up, her eyes focussing slowly on Llian's face.

"This is definitely the one. I went through all this some years ago, reading everything and checking the catalogue. It would astound you the number of errors I found."

Llian knew the workings of libraries all too well to be astounded at anything he found there, but he merely mumbled something that could be taken any way she pleased.

Maigraith looked along the rows of shelves. "Days are precious now. We can't waste any more time here."

Closing the box, Ralah put it back on the shelf and led them to the hall and the fire. "Lunch is ready," she said.

While they were drinking a welcome cup of tea Maigraith went through the visitors' book.

"Are you looking for anyone in particular?" asked Ralah, who had come up behind her silently.

"Faelamor, Yggur, Tensor, Mendark, Tallia, Malien for starters," Maigraith replied. "Oh, what's the use? They might have come in disguise."

"It would have to be a very good disguise," said Ralah. "Nassi made a kind of Sentinel to protect us from such intrusions, and most of them are still working. I can tell you that Faelamor has not been here, but Yggur has. Nadiril of course, and Mendark many times. He spent months here once, but that was before my time. I've not seen any of them in years."

Maigraith sighed. "Well, we need tarry here no longer."

"Someone's been here," she said once they were out of hearing, "and taken away what I came for. Someone's waiting for the flute to be made so they can take it for themselves."

"Do you have any idea who?" Karan asked.

"Faelamor, Yggur, Tensor, Mendark, for starters."

"We'll have to be more careful," said Llian. "Every villain on Santh will want the flute, once it's made."

They trudged back through the snow, walked all around the hill in a spiral upward path, and every few steps Maigraith tried to open the portal again, but without the least glimmering of success. Finally, just as the sun was setting, she slumped down in the snow.

"My head is exploding," she said.

"Then give it away," said Karan, "or we'll never get out of here."

Maigraith lay back on the snow, looking up at the white tooth of the hill, the chalk cliff towering above her, criss-crossed with narrow ledges that goats could barely have walked upon. "Where exactly did you come out of the gate?" she wondered.

"Over there, right at the base of the cliff," said Llian. "See that little shelf, then it drops away down that embankment. That's where we fell down."

"Let's try it there." Karan gave Maigraith her shoulder. She limped across in the failing light.

"This feels more like it," said Maigraith. "Yes, I think I could do it from here, if my head would just settle down. Oh, I'm all hot and cold, and my wrists and elbows ache." She rubbed snow on her inflamed cheeks.

Karan and Llian exchanged glances. "Sounds more like fever than aftersickness," Karan muttered.

Maigraith gripped hands with Karan and Llian. "Now!" she said. A feeble net of light enveloped them but went out again with a fizzing sound. Maigraith slumped down in the snow.

"I'll make camp," said Karan. "We can try again in the morning."

"No—I'm sick. I feel really sick," Maigraith groaned. Drops of sweat were running down her face but freezing before they reached her chin. "One more try—up there, as high as we can get."

She dragged herself up the cliff, across ledge after ledge, until she reached a place halfway up where the ledge petered out. She fell to her knees, holding onto the chalk face with one hand and mopping her brow with the other. She groaned and stood up, and as Llian struggled up she swayed. Her stark face was blotched with red swellings.

"This is stupid," cried Karan. "Come down!"

Maigraith gave each of them her hand. A sickly fishnet cage of light flickered around them, but as Llian pressed himself back against the cliff it faded. "Come out," Maigraith choked. "Right to the edge."

"I am right at the edge," Llian muttered. "She's mad."

Nonetheless he edged out a bit further and the light brightened.

"Further," she said, pulling him. He moved imperceptibly, it brightened a little more, though not enough. Maigraith staggered then jerked Llian to the very edge. The chalk crumbled beneath his feet and he dragged them over. Maigraith gripped their hands tightly, screamed "*Now!*" The cage of light flared into a gate and they were flung into darkness.

They crashed down onto the rooftop. It was still raining in Thurkad.

32

Breaking The Code

A sense of urgency, indeed desperation, now pervaded the company's every gathering. Time had run out and they were still hopelessly unprepared. Yggur had his armies on alert and new soldiers were being trained furiously, but their morale had sunk almost to mutiny point after the disaster in Elludore. The loss of the thousand of his finest could not be made up.

Mendark lay awake, agonizing, as he had done night after night. The world that he had protected for a thousand years was collapsing around him. There was a limit to everything and he had gone past his. He might survive for another year or two, but no longer wanted to. He tried to sit up but his muscles froze and he fell back down again, quite helpless. Oh, to have come to this!

He lay panting on his bed, wanting to die. But after his heart stopped hammering and the dizziness retreated his thoughts drifted back to Rulke. They always did, now. It was

Rulke against him. That was his life and purpose. The greatest game of all.

A new Magister was needed, a young one with fire in the blood. Tallia was strong enough, clever too, and her abilities with the Secret Art were manifest. He had trained her well. But Tallia lacked the most vital impulse of all: the iron in the soul that would drive her to do whatever was necessary to defeat the enemy. He, Mendark, would betray his best friend if that was the only way to win the war. He would even betray Tallia. It would cause him the most profound anguish, and he would regret it ever after, but if there was no other alternative he would do it.

Who am I trying to fool? he thought derisively. I'm finished! This defeat will ruin my reputation beyond hope of redemption. Not even the Great Tale can save it. That idea stirred Mendark to roll off the bed, pull a sack-like robe over his decrepitude and lurch down the hall in search of Llian. He found him in the library. Karan was there too.

"Where have you been, chronicler?" Mendark panted. "I've been looking for you for days."

Karan and Llian exchanged glances.

"Well?" cried the Magister, flexing his flaky, clawed hands.

"In Saludith!" said Llian. "Maigraith took us there, through a gate."

Mendark looked off balance. "Why?"

"Searching for clues as to how the flute might be used," said Karan.

"I've already looked there! Years ago."

"I know!" said Llian. "We didn't find anything though. The relevant document had been removed, and all record of it. Very cleverly!"

Mendark, knowing Llian was trying to force a reaction, showed no more than the wall beside him. "You're too clever, Llian, and one day it will undo you! We've all been to Saludith many times. What progress have you made on my tale?"

Llian started. "Quite a bit, though there's a long way to go. I haven't even begun to write it."

"Give me a rundown on what you *have* done so I can judge how you're going."

Llian shuffled the papers on his table. Karan was still motionless in her chair, trying to look invisible. It was perfectly obvious to Mendark that she despised him. It was also clear that Llian wasn't working on the tale and had no intention of doing so. Ungrateful wretch! His debt meant nothing to him!

"I'm not willing to tell the tale until it's done," Llian said evasively. "It's not good enough."

"I'll be the judge of that," Mendark snarled.

"The master chroniclers will be the judges," Llian pointed out coldly, "if you want it to be a Great Tale. It's not ready and I'm not saying another word until it is."

Mendark hobbled back to his room, feeling panicky. The incident highlighted how little power he had left. There wasn't ever going to be any *Mendark's Tale*. He would die a failure. He took out one of his flutes and began a rollicking jig, the very antithesis of his mood. It did not help and soon he threw it aside and went to bed. He felt the most violent, destructive urge, to wipe out the Histories and start again. One last desperate effort that would either destroy Rulke and Faelamor, or himself. That would make his name, *or ruin it!*

It would almost be worth the gamble, Mendark thought. He felt his heart begin to race at the idea of such a wager. It made him feel alive for the first time in ages. And at the end of it, succeed or fail, blessed oblivion.

His back was agonizingly painful. Mendark rolled over in bed but the new position felt worse than the old one. He'd had no peace from pain since Havissard. Why did I do it? he thought over and over again. Why couldn't I just give up and die there?

He mentally totted up the lives, the renewals. He was 1260 years old. That was not old for the Charon or Faellem species, or even some of the Aachim, but it was ancient for an old human.

The first thing he'd done after mastering the Secret Art had been to renew his body, and since then he'd done it another thirteen times, which was at least five times too many. Each time the regeneration spell forced his cells to copy themselves, more errors were introduced and more things went wrong. And the regeneration at Havissard had been under such duress that he wouldn't have been surprised if he'd ended up an insect, or an ape.

He was still a man, though a most unattractive one, and although he'd burned a fortune on the best healers and spellmasters in Thurkad, his body was not much improved. Every joint ground together as he moved. At the toilet he passed more blood than waste, and his innards roiled around inside him as if there was nothing holding them in place.

I may be the oldest old human that ever walked Santhenar, he thought. Yet my mind feels as sharp as ever, and my grasp of the Secret Art is still sound. Surely these gifts were given so I could use them for the benefit of my world. Only I can save Santhenar from that monster Rulke. But how?

That question occupied him for what remained of the night. He turned and tossed, revolved and rotated, twisted his body into every position that a ballet dancer could imagine, but none reduced the misery his bones inflicted on him. Morning came, and Mendark was in such agony that he would have cut his own throat, had there been a knife to hand.

He fell out of bed, trying to crawl to his chest of drawers, but even that was beyond him. He lay where he fell for hours more, now afraid (and how ironic that was!) that he would die there. His death would surely mean the ruin of Santhenar.

Eventually Mendark dozed and woke to find the pain diminished slightly. His corded muscles had relaxed in sleep. The answer was there, too—renewal for one last time. The spell would probably kill him—another glorious gamble!—though if it did not he must be better off. But this time he would do it properly. At Havissard he had renewed his body by himself, dying of thirst as he hung upside down in a bramble thicket. This time he would be in his own bed with the best his fortune could provide. The greatest healers and mancers, the most priceless drugs and the most powerful artifacts, to power the regeneration spell and keep it on track.

Mendark paced back and forth, organizing in his mind all that he would need: the mancers, healers, the environment, the pharmacopoeia. Sorcerous artifacts he had in plenty, though he wondered if they were strong enough. The flute would be better, but Mendark knew he lacked the strength to get it away from Tensor.

Ah, but what about the Mirror? It was practically unguarded, and Maigraith was still ill. If he could get hold of it, even a few hours would be enough. The regeneration spell did not take long. Mendark limped to the bell pull, feeling better than he had in a long time, and when Tallia herself answered the summons, he issued her with a string of orders.

The preparations were made quickly. After all, this was something that he had done many times before. By the middle of the night all was ready.

"Shall we begin?" Tallia asked. He could see her eagerness to learn. Regeneration was one of the greatest spells, and as yet he had taught her nothing about it.

"In a few minutes."

Mendark made his painful way to Maigraith's room. He had already spied her out today. She had been in a dazed sleep all afternoon. It was not implausible that he should enquire after her health, if anyone caught him. Maigraith was dozing restlessly, tossing and kicking her legs. Her face was swollen. Where would she keep the Mirror? Surely close to her. His hand slid under the pillow and there it was, a hard metal tube. He dropped it into his pocket and went out. Just as he did so Shand came by.

"She is sleeping," Mendark said, and continued down the corridor.

Back in his own chambers, he lay on the bed with the Mirror in his hand. The spellcasters and healers crowded around. Tallia hovered at the end of the bed, looking anxious. "Begin!" said Mendark.

Spring was more than a month old now but the weather had not changed. It still felt like winter—the longest in living memory. Maigraith did not know that the Mirror had been taken, for when she woke the following morning, fully recovered, it was back under her pillow where it had always been.

She was taking lunch with Karan and Llian in one of the citadel dining rooms. Yggur sat at a nearby table, reading while he ate. There came a clatter from outside. The door opened and a fresh-faced man appeared in the doorway, supported by Tallia on one side and Osseion on the other. They moved apart. The man took a tentative step forward. His knee buckled and he lurched like a newborn colt trying to find its feet. Another step, another stagger. He kept going, and his control strengthened with every movement.

"Who is it?" Maigraith heard Llian whisper. "The face is familiar."

The man, a young, slender fellow with cheeks as soft and pink as a child's, came the last few steps in a rush. He rested his hands on the table, breathing hard, then threw back his head and roared with laughter.

"It worked!" he cried. "What a wager!"

"Mendark!" gasped Maigraith.

It *was* Mendark, as he must have looked when a young man. He was a handsome fellow too, though the blooming cheeks, broad nose and full lips gave him an overly sensual air. But at the same time there was something different about him. Maigraith could not work out what it was.

"Thank you, Maigraith," said Mendark.

"What for?"

"I borrowed your Mirror in the night, for my regeneration spell."

"I should have realized," she exclaimed. Mendark's features were around the other way from his previous face.

"It won't last," Yggur said sourly, and with a trace of envy. "You'll be lucky to get a year out of it."

"I don't care!" Mendark said, bubbling with good humor. "I've lived my life and don't want another!"

"Then why did you do it?" Yggur looked bitter, frustrated.

"For the sheer gamble of it!" Mendark cried. "And for the job you're not capable of doing—finishing Rulke and Faelamor."

That afternoon the company went in procession down to the old bakehouse, as they did every day. They went away again with Tensor's curses ringing in their ears, also a daily occurrence.

"I'll tell you when it's ready!" he screamed after them.

Mendark and Yggur exchanged glances. "Well, Mendark," said Yggur, "do you still think Tensor was a good choice?"

"He was the only choice!" Mendark said cheerily.

Maigraith walked silently behind them. Since giving up her gold she felt estranged from everyone, even Shand, and it was agony.

The following day one of Yggur's spies returned from Elludore.

"What have you learned?" Llian asked at once.

"Not much, chronicler," said Yggur. "The Faellem are gathered in some hundreds in Elludore, and all approaches to the valley are sealed tight. They must have been warned, for we didn't catch any of them on the way."

"She won't get her instrument to work," said Malien. "The Faellem can never control such devices."

"After our recent experience," said Shand, "I'd suggest we don't underestimate her again."

"Then we'd better find out where the gold came from," said Malien.

"Is there any news from Shazmak?"

"None of my spies have come back from there. And there is more bad news," said Yggur. "The catastrophe in Elludore has spread like the wind. Armies are marching in Quilsin and Galardil, and in the north too. Half my empire is in rebellion. Every petty warlord in Meldorin has seen the opportunity to harass me. They know I'm weak and hardpressed." He looked it too, as if he was just going through the motions of preparing for war.

"And rumor has it that Thyllan is stirring again, across the sea," said Mendark. "I would sooner befriend you than him, Yggur."

Yggur swept off his hat and bowed from the waist. "At *your* service," he said ironically.

"I'm serious! Let's use the flute and attack Shazmak before he's ready."

"It probably won't work anyway," Yggur said apathetically.

Maigraith sat by the unlit fire for an hour, moving pieces in her mind but not finding any answers. Mendark seemed to be taking control again. She did not like the idea of him using her flute at all. She felt a presence behind her and it was Karan, standing quietly. Karan jumped at her abrupt movement.

"Hot tea," she whispered. She had a pot in her hand, and a bowl. "It's so cold in here."

"Cold doesn't bother me. I'm used to it."

"You look tired," said Karan. "Are you sure you've recovered from the fever?"

"Oh yes. It's just that I . . ." Maigraith hesitated. "I've been experimenting with gates."

"How has it gone?"

"Well enough. I don't need any kind of a gate structure any more—I can make gates with my mind now."

"Isn't that dangerous?"

"It can be, especially if the gate goes wrong. It can be . . . difficult to find the way back. But it gives me a lot of freedom, too."

"Do they often go wrong?"

"Only once, so far. The gate opened into a whirling nightmare and I had to drag myself straight home. It almost killed me; I was bedridden for a day after."

"So you weren't in a fever at all?"

"I was, but only briefly. The rest of my sickness was from the gates. I'm always exhausted now. I'm not strong enough."

"For what?"

"I panic every time I think about what lies ahead. How am I to break the Forbidding and restore the balance between the worlds, without destroying everything? I have no idea, and there is no one I can ask."

A few days later, Llian came running in to the dining room. "Quick!" he shouted to Karan and Maigraith. "There's something going on down at the bakehouse." He ran out again.

"What?" Maigraith called, pounding after him.

"I don't know. I heard Yggur ordering his troops down there on the double, then he and Mendark went after them."

By the time they reached the bakehouse there were guards everywhere. Mendark stood on the top step and Yggur beside him. Mendark thumped the hilt of his knife on the door. Karan, Maigraith and Llian pushed to the front of the crowd.

"Open up, Tensor! The building is surrounded!"

Shortly the doors did open and they were allowed inside. "Your treachery has been uncovered, Tensor!" Mendark roared. "Where is the flute?"

Tensor stood at the far end of the building, the Aachim lined up behind him. The frightened goldsmiths and woodworkers were behind them. They were all haggard, so hard had Tensor worked them.

Tensor stalked forward with little sign of the back injury that had formerly troubled him. He was furious. "I don't know what you're talking about!" he said. "We've kept our part of the bargain." He lifted an ebony and brass case off the bench, pulled on silken gloves, snapped the catches and from a bag made of black velvet silk he drew it out—the golden flute remade. Under the bright lamps it shone like liquid metal.

"It's beautiful," said Karan, reaching out to touch the wondrous thing.

"Don't touch it!" Tensor snapped, pushing her back. "You'll mar its finish."

Karan darted a glance at Maigraith, whose eyes were moist with desire for it. Mendark was staring at the flute with an equally desperate longing. "It is surely your finest work," Maigraith said.

Tensor nodded stiffly. "Its tones—"

Maigraith was stabbed by envy and rage. "What? You have played my birthright! *How dare you use it!*"

He glared at her. "We have not used it. We didn't want—"

"I doubt that anything would happen except music, without the player willing it," Mendark interrupted dryly. "That is the very foundation of the Secret Art. The power may reside in the instrument, but it takes will and talent to bring it out, otherwise any fool could pick up the flute and bring all the world to chaos."

"How do you know it will play in tune, if you have never played it?" Llian asked.

Tensor gave him a frigid stare. "In Aachan we have been making flutes for ten thousand years. Our mathematics described the instrument perfectly before it was made. When it is played every note will be perfect."

Maigraith put her hand out. "Thank you. I will take my birthright now!"

"Stand back!" he said harshly, and the Aachim put their hands on their weapons.

"But it's mine! My gold, my flute."

The Aachim guard moved to flank Tensor, five on each side. Karan could read their desires too. They thought the flute could take them home to Aachan, and all their vows meant nothing before that desperate need. Even Malien, beside her, was quivering with emotion.

We will fight Rulke with whatever weapon comes to hand, Malien had said. So this was what she'd meant.

"Not you too!" Karan whispered. "Malien, I can't believe that you would betray us for the flute."

Malien raked her fingers through thick red hair. She looked around wildly, hardly recognizing Karan.

"Malien!" Karan cried out.

Malien shook herself. "You can't possibly understand what Aachan means to us," she said softly.

Karan took her hand, wringing it frantically. "Does it mean more than friendship, than the bonds of kinship, to say nothing of all we've endured together?"

Malien shook off her hand. "Aachan, Aachan!" she whispered.

"I will not give it up to you!" Tensor screamed at Maigraith.

Karan turned back to the main conflict.

"But that was the agreement!" Maigraith was bewildered, uncomprehending. Tears poured down her face. She looked around at the company for aid, but everyone seemed captivated by the flute.

"And it dishonors me to break it, but I have watched you, *Charon*!" He spat the word out. "Every day you grow more like them. One day you will betray us to Rulke. I regret giving you that little golden ring, but I will *destroy* the flute before I let you use it to bring Yalkara back to Santhenar."

So that was what was behind the betrayal! "What about your promise to me?" Karan said furiously.

"Not even to you!" Tensor replied.

Maigraith spun around and bolted for the door. Shand cried her name but she did not appear to hear.

Mendark stood watching Tensor with narrowed eyes. "You planned this all along," he said. "If my spies had not told me of your treachery you would be gone with it by now."

"My kind must come first," said Tensor. "Surely you realize that, Mendark. I won't give it up."

"You few can't stand against my army," said Yggur.

"Should you attack, my instructions are to destroy the flute the way Shuthdar did. In which case Thurkad, and everyone in it, will cease to exist," said Tensor.

"He'd do it too," Mendark murmured in Yggur's ear.

"Then it remains here!" said Yggur. "My guards will make sure it does!"

They went out. Outside the door Karan looked for Maigraith but she had vanished.

Malien caught Karan's arm and led her down the side of the building. "Your time is now, Karan. Are you for us? If you're not, you are against us. There's no middle ground here!"

"I'm for people keeping their promises!"

"So am I. You might have thought of that when you were keeping the Mirror from us."

"And look what Tensor did with it! I did the right thing and you know it."

"Not when you worked with Rulke to show him the way back to our world, so he could keep Aachan in slavery and do the same to Santhenar!"

"You're wrong about him!" Karan said weakly.

"Four thousand years of our Histories aren't wrong! Karan, we're desperate! You've got to help us!"

"I thought the Aachim had great plans under way to deal with Rulke."

"We do. An army is forming right now but it won't get to Shazmak in time. The flute is our *only chance*!"

She looked desperate too. Karan remembered all the

good things about the Aachim, and all the kindnesses Malien had done her.

"What can I do?"

"Maigraith is the key. She can make us or unmake us. Keep watch over her. Wherever she goes, follow her, and report back to me."

The company withdrew back to the citadel, arguing furiously.

"We've got to get it back," said Mendark. "Tensor is bluffing!"

"I don't think so," said Yggur.

"Who do we have that *can* use it anyway, if Maigraith is disbarred?" asked Llian. "And if no one, what use is it?"

"A question that had been better asked before it was made!" said Yggur.

"I . . . may be able to play it," said Mendark. "I was once an accomplished flute player, as you know, and I am sensitive too. I will—"

"Ha!" said Yggur, instantly suspicious. "You've manipulated us very cleverly, Mendark. All along you wanted this, while raising false obstacles so we wouldn't realize what you were up to."

"It was proposed by Shand as long ago as the Dry Sea!" Mendark snapped. "Deciding who to use it has always been our greatest difficulty. I have studied the arts and sciences of the flute ever since. Have you not?"

"Gentlemen!" said Shand. "Suppose that Mendark can use it; let us work out a plan. A better one than the fiasco at Elludore. The flute can open the Way between the Worlds and take its user to any destination they can imagine. Perhaps it can even dissolve the Forbidding, *but it is not a weapon!* Even were we to use it to enter into the very heart of Shazmak, we would still have to defend ourselves by other means. Whereas Rulke's construct is a gate-opening device, a weapon and a shield."

"I propose that we gather our weapons, seize the flute and attack Shazmak before it's too late," said Mendark.

"How?" said Shand.

"I'm working on a plan," Mendark replied.

"It will be a bigger disaster than our last," said Yggur, "and where will we be then?"

"We won't be standing here, whining helplessly," spat Mendark, "while Rulke and Faelamor carve up our world."

Maigraith went back to the little cottage by the water and sat there, all alone. Why did I give up my birthright? she raged, over and over. Why, *why*? Everyone wants something from me but no one will help me in my need.

The thought of Tensor using her flute against Rulke was a sickening violation. She could feel the fury building up inside, overcoming her self-control as it often did. Imagining Tensor there, she stormed around the room, letting out random bursts of power that left the kitchen in a shambles. Immediately she was ashamed. She had loved her time here with Shand. She swept up the broken crockery and splintered timbers, put the furniture back in place and sat down on the porch outside, staring at the slate-colored sea.

Now she was overcome by a profound melancholy, another emotion that she was prone to. The wind turned around, blowing directly across the harbor at her and whirling the spray in her face. Maigraith sat there all day, abandoned and alone. The light faded. She allowed the dark and damp to mold itself around her, drawing all warmth and human fellow-feeling out of her. She plunged back into that state of tristesse that she had spent most of her life in, where nothing really mattered because she lacked any identity, any self. She was just a tool in the hands of others.

It must have been the middle of the night when something aroused her. She was shivering in great spasms, soaked to the skin. What would Shand say if he could see her now? The thought of her grandfather's kindly scolding made her smile in the darkness, but the humor soon disappeared. She had let Shand down. She would never reunite him and Yalkara now.

The flute is mine, whether I dare to use it or not! Whether I want it or not! How dare Tensor refuse me? After a lifetime of obeying Faelamor's orders, *no one* is going to deny me my precious inheritance!

Maigraith stripped off her wet clothes, dried herself and lit the fire. Then, as she was dressing she realized that Tensor might have done her a favor after all. By constantly insulting her Charon ancestry, he had made her think about her heritage. Everything that was Faellem she rejected, and old human was what she had been all her life. It was ordinary to her. Worse than ordinary, since they were allied to the Aachim who had just betrayed her.

Maigraith reached out for that unfulfilled Charon part of her that Havissard had awakened and Yalkara's message strengthened. If Tensor was her enemy, and Faelamor too, then maybe Charon meant friend! Perhaps it was her destiny to seek out Rulke. She began to work on a plan, to take back her flute and go to Shazmak.

It must have been the middle of the night when something awakened her. She was shivering in great spasms, soaked to the skin. What would Shaud say if he could see her now? The thought of her grandfather's kindly scolding made her smile in the darkness, but the humor soon disappeared. She had let Shaud down. She would never reclaim him and Valkara now.

But this is mine, whether I dare to use it or not. Whether I want it or not. How dare Tessor refuse me! After a lifetime of obeying Faramet's orders, no one is going to deny me my present inheritance!

Maquinar stripped off her wet clothes, dried herself and lit the fire. Then, as she was dressing she realized that Tessor might have done her a favor after all. By constantly insulting her Charon ancestry he had made her think about her heritage. Everything that was Faramet she rejected, and the Faramet was what she had been all her life. It was ordinary to her. Worse than ordinary, since they were allied to the warlord who had just betrayed her.

Instead she reached out for that unfulfilled Charon part of her that Reverand had awakened and Valkara's message strengthened. If Tessor was her enemy, and Faramet too, then maybe the Charon meant friend! Perhaps it was her destiny to seek out Kalke. She began to work on a plan, to take back her flute and go to Shazmak.

PART THREE

33

THE FIFTH WAY

It was four in the morning and Maigraith was exhausted. She knew Karan was spying on her, and getting away from her had taxed Maigraith's powers. For three nights now she had watched the workshop, and not once had Yggur's guards relaxed their vigilance. They paced, swapped over, paced again, to a complex routine. There was no time when the door was not monitored. There were Aachim guards too, inside as well as out, and they were equally vigilant.

She had already experimented with using a gate to get inside, but that had failed. The Aachim had defenses against gates. Short of using power to smash the doors wide open—not what she wanted—there was only one way left. The Aachim guards swapped over, the inside and the outside, roughly every two hours. It was the only time the door was unbarred.

Maigraith brought her mind to the pitch that would allow her to direct her power. It would have to be focused very precisely, to take out all the guards at once. Then, just before the door opened, she happened to glance at a small building across the yard and caught a faint white flicker. That was odd! She recalled seeing it before. She had thought it just a chance reflection, but now realized it was a signal. Watching the door, she caught the answering blink. Another Aachim was watching the changeover. If the signal did not come the alarm would be sounded.

Taking care of that guard was easier than she expected; the woman was not an adept. Maigraith paralyzed her and snatched the signaling globe, but by then the guards had changed and the doors were closed again. Moving closer, she covered most of the globe so that the light would seem further away, and waited for the next change.

The interval was a longer one than usual, and Maigraith worried that dawn would come first. Finally she saw a tiny blink of light. She felt that she was quite slow to respond, but the signal eventually came. The door opened. The inside guards appeared. Maigraith weighed how much power to use against them. She did not want to kill anyone. She cut back the strength of her spell.

Her conjuration whispered in the night. Every guard fell down. Racing across the paving stones she leapt through the door, bolted it, ran to the other end of the workshop and ripped open the catches on the ebony case. The flute was wrapped in fold after fold of black silky-velvet as soft as a baby's skin. She drew it out. Such a beautiful thing; it seemed almost alive when she touched it. The workmanship was exquisite.

Something thumped the door and slithered down. One of the guards recovering already? Maigraith almost panicked—she must not have used enough strength. No way to get out now without being seen, unless she killed them, an unthinkable act for her. Unless she used the flute!

No time to admire the instrument. Could she make it work? She put it to her lips, searching with her mind for the one place where she knew a gate would open—the rooftop from where they had gone to Saludith. She played a note, and another. Nothing happened.

She tried again. Still nothing! But Maigraith began to feel a faint unease, as if the world she knew had twisted slightly. She paused, unpleasantly disturbed. The unreality came and went in a series of falling and rising echoes. It was the warping associated with two forces intersecting and reinforcing one another. Someone else was using a similar power, and she knew exactly who. It had an alarming, prickling aura. Faelamor!

There came a crash on the door, then shouts outside and more bangs—axe blows. The door was shivering under the attack. She had only minutes. She tried again, playing the first half of a scale. The echoes came back, stronger than before. Maigraith reached out again, using all her strength to cut through the fog that shrouded the destination.

It was like being struck in the stomach with a stone club. The shock flung her into the side of a furnace with such force that she felt one of her ribs crack. Maigraith could not get up for a minute. Don't ever do that again! You were trying to force it. You must relax, sense it, *go with it!* Try it again. But she did not. In her hands the flute felt that it had such power, but Maigraith realized she was incapable of tapping it. Maybe the very gold had become corrupted over time. Perhaps Tensor had done something to prevent her using it. Whatever the reason, it was deadly now. The whole building had taken on a strange, distorted air.

Maigraith consigned the birthright to the floor and sat up, watching the door shake under the assault. The blade of an axe appeared through the wood, the timbers groaning as it was wrenched out again. The other resonance grew stronger.

What was Faelamor up to? Faelamor, who had sent Ellami to murder her, a betrayal so shocking that Maigraith still could not come to terms with it. She had to find out before it was too late. No choice but to go to Elludore.

There was a commotion outside and an enormous thump shook the door. The onslaught paused, only to return with greater force. The boards warped inward. The next blow would break it. Seizing a smith's hammer, Maigraith scrambled up on top of the furnace and attacked the ceiling. Black dust and plaster rained down on her. She climbed into the hole and swung the hammer at the roof. Slate went everywhere. It was already growing light.

The door was smashed open. The besiegers stormed in. Maigraith pulled herself onto the roof and ran lightly down the ridgepole, but found that the whole place was surrounded. "Up there!" someone shouted.

Would a gate work here? Maigraith sensed that she was far enough from the flute that one might. She took a mental fix on her very first gate, still the strongest, the ironstone spires in Elludore. As she conjured up the memory, the image of that place soared into her mind, clear and sharp. She reached out, silver radiance streamed about her and she tumbled wildly through space. I'm using this Art too much, she thought. Use changed the Secret Arts, sometimes in unpredictable ways. My profligacy will have a reckoning. Not this time, she prayed. *Go true!*

For an instant her control of the gate faltered, then Maigraith wrenched it back and materialized with a snap that hurt her ears. It was just short of dawn here, fifty leagues west of Thurkad, but there was light enough to see. She stood between the ironstone pillars by the river in Elludore.

Maigraith felt physically ill from the gate—the reckoning would not be long coming. Her nerves were stretched like catgut. It was some distance from here to the caves. She crept upriver. The main cave was lighted, a broad shallow opening like the mouth of a whale. Someone appeared at the entrance, looking out into the darkness, then disappeared again.

Maigraith went up the slope on her belly. There had been a frost and the trodden ground was frozen into hard ruts. She got close enough to hear talk, but not what they were talking about. Higher she crept, squirming up the track like a snake with her head forward, testing the air. She caught a word—*Shazmak!* Then someone loudly said *No!* She moved closer.

Evidently the debate had met a sticking point. Again she heard *Shazmak*, and then Faelamor's voice rang out: "Mine is the decision, is it not? Did you not pledge yourselves to follow me? Have I not done everything required of me?"

"We're afraid. This goes against everything we stand for."

"What did we come to Santhenar for, all those years ago, but to eliminate the threat of the Charon?"

"But to ally with the Great Betrayer himself . . ."

"Who said ally? I said *offer* alliance. All week we've tried to get our instrument to work, and it does, beautifully. I know it can take us home, but it can't break through the Forbidding. We know Rulke can open the Way, for he did so on mid-winter's day. He has what we lack, and I can do what he needs. When the critical moment comes, so will our opportunity."

"He will be expecting treachery. It is a risk without hope of gain. He is so much stronger than we are."

"Ah, but he does not know about our golden nanollet. He could never think that we would make such a device! And even if we gain nothing," Faelamor went on, "*so be it!* Once he is among the Three Worlds with his construct we lose everything. Tallallame cannot stand against that power. This is what we came for. *We must try!* And if, against the odds, we do succeed, we will go home in triumph and seal the Way behind us forever."

Golden nanollet? So they *had* used the gold. I've got to find out where it came from. Maigraith recalled talk of drawings stolen from Llian's college, that had told Faelamor to look in Havissard. I've seen them, Maigraith realized. They were in Faelamor's pack when first we came here. Where did I put them?

Maigraith slipped up through the trees to one of the other caves, a storehouse where Faelamor kept her gear. She emptied out the boxes and bags, rifling though Faelamor's scanty possessions. At the bottom of one bag was a flattened roll of paper.

She carried it out into the growing light, unrolled the drawings behind a tree and her hair stood on end. Maigraith stared into nowhere. No wonder Faelamor's workings had such a mad, dangerous feeling. The gold, and therefore the nanollet she'd made with it, was corrupt. The Faellem, who had little ability to control devices, had made the most perilous device of all. The only thing to do was to seize the nanollet herself. But how? She agonized too long in the growing light and suddenly there were footsteps above her. Maigraith crouched down, knowing that she was exposed. If anyone looked down she would be seen.

Faelamor appeared, hurrying across to the store cave. Ice cracked under Maigraith's foot. Faelamor spun around, crying, "Who goes?"

Maigraith bolted, slipping and skidding down the steep path.

Faelamor's cry had brought the Faellem out. Let them not recognize me, Maigraith prayed. Then she heard Faelamor's cry of rage: *"Maigraith!"*

A host of Faellem swarmed after her. She could feel herself weakening already, her mind losing focus. Her gate was half an hour downriver; she would never make it. Maigraith tried for a new gate, weeping with the strain, but something struck her hard in the shoulder, a terrible pain. "*Shand, help me!*" she screamed. Reaching out she opened a gate and, still running, fell into it.

Maigraith was buffeted about, angry lines of fire screamed all around her and she was wrenched into nowhere. Her consciousness flashed in and out, then she crashed through a plaster ceiling and landed in an untidy heap. She lay on the floor of Yggur's workroom. She looked up at him limply, then lapsed into unconsciousness. Blood ran out of her shoulder. A long arrow protruded from it.

When she came to, Yggur was attending her, with a Whelm whose name Maigraith did not know. They carried her to a chair. Yggur glared at her for a full minute, finally saying coldly, "That is a Faellem arrow!"

Her teeth chattered. Aftersickness bent her double. The arrowhead grated against her shoulder bone, right where Thyllan's knife had struck last summer.

She clung onto Yggur's hand while the Whelm worked at getting the arrow out. "There are things you were never able to tell me! I too have secrets, Yggur."

"Even leaving aside what happened at the workshop, you are abusing the Art. The Aachim are in uproar."

"I'm glad. Tensor is my enemy! I have nothing more to say."

"Very well," said Yggur, "but let me remind you of the consequences. Each gate you make must be prepared for as if it was your first. You must never go and return again in less than a day, and *never* without resting between. If you do not obey these rules, sooner or later you will lose yourself and never be able to return. Or you will come back but your wits will not."

"I know the dangers," she muttered. To be lectured by him was unbearable. "I was desperate."

"There is always a desperate need. If nothing will sway you but duty, think of all the ways you might be needed in the future. I'm afraid for you."

That was no comfort. She was silent while the Whelm finished with the wound and bound it. Maigraith laid her head down and fell into sleep.

Yggur found Shand at breakfast. "Was it Maigraith who broke into the workshop?"

"It was," said Shand. "I happened to be walking that way before dawn, just as the guards were recovering."

"What's she up to?"

"I don't know. We'd better meet today; this morning. The time is almost upon us."

"I can feel it too. I'm afraid."

"Tell me, Shand, was it an accident that you happened along?"

"Of course not. I've got into the old man's habit of rising early and walking, and I often go that way. But as soon as I woke I sensed strange forces—things I've never felt before. I ran all the way to the workshop but she was already gone."

"I felt it too."

"Do you know why Maigraith agreed to give up her gold?"

"No," said Yggur, "though I've often wondered."

"For me! She wanted the flute made so she could bring Yalkara and me together again."

Yggur almost fell off his chair. "That would be . . . controversial."

Shand laughed. "Mendark would wet himself. As for

Tensor—" He stopped abruptly. "Tensor must have found out."

"I'd say so! He'll never give up the flute now. And how about you, old friend?"

"I wish it could be." Shand shook with passion. "How I wish it! But I don't dare hope. I'll not see Yalkara again." He changed the subject. "What are we going to do about Faelamor?"

"We're so unprepared! I'll call everyone together. I'm afraid for Maigraith, Shand."

"As am I. I'll send Karan to keep watch on her. And speak to her myself when she wakes. How go your plans for war?"

"Disastrously. We had a mutiny in the Third Army last week. I put it down brutally, but that made morale even worse. You know how rumors spread." Yggur appeared anguished, and his old troubles had come back: the halting speech, the freezing of the muscles on one side of his face. "Not even my counter-rumors of our wonderful flute have made any difference."

"People are saying that it won't work; that it will do more damage to us than to him. Maybe they're right. We don't know what we're doing, do we?"

Yggur did not respond to that. "Rulke's just as good at spreading propaganda as I am. A thousand tellers have told the tale of his magical construct, and how it flew through the air, defying us. The war is lost and the battle hasn't even begun."

"There's a traitor among us," said Mendark that afternoon. He had taken the news of the attempt on the flute badly, though the anger looked out of place on his unlined face.

"How do we know it wasn't you?" said Yggur.

"You accuse *me*!" Mendark raged.

He snatched at Yggur's cloak. Yggur raised his fist. For a moment it seemed that violence would be done right there, then the door slammed open and Maigraith swayed through, looking as though all the blood had been sucked from her veins. Into the sudden silence she dropped her bombshell.

"I have been to Elludore through a gate," she said. "Faelamor is on the way to Shazmak to make alliance with Rulke. She has made her own device, *from the gold of the golden flute*." The silence was deafening.

Still no one spoke, though their faces bore identical expressions of horror.

"How do you know?" barked Mendark.

Maigraith pulled the drawings from her pocket and threw them on the table.

Llian examined them carefully. "These are the ones stolen from the college library. Look! This one shows Yalkara going into the burning tower after the golden flute was destroyed. She's not wearing her golden jewelry."

The second sketch showed Yalkara coming out of Huling's Tower again, a small figure in a large drawing. Smoke hung above the tower like an upraised fist. Her clothes were smoking, her hands blood-red, and she wore the golden chain about her throat again, the torc about her forehead, and the bracelet on her wrist.

Llian looked as if a divine truth had been revealed. "Yalkara must have used some magic to forge the molten gold into a perfect replica of the jewelry that she always wore, and worn it out of the ruins under the noses of all the watchers. How bold she was!"

"She would never say how her hands came to be so badly scarred," said Shand. "It must have happened in her haste to shape the gold."

"I felt it!" said Maigraith. "When Shand and I went to Huling's Tower. It was horrible!"

"One of them will betray the other and emerge stronger than ever," said Yggur in a defeated voice.

"We're not yet beaten," Mendark's voice rang out. "Desperate times call for desperate remedies: the forbidden, the uncontrollable! Let those of us who know such secrets meet secretly to work out a plan."

Maigraith told no one what she was going through. She had made her decision and no one was going to talk her out of it. She felt divorced from the company, her friends, even Shand.

Her wound was very painful and she felt worse as the day went on. After the meeting she went back to bed, but had a strange, fitful slumber, punctuated not by dreams but by a waking state rather like a trance, in which she got up as soon as Karan went out and packed everything that would be needed for a long journey. Knowing Karan was keeping an eye on her, she planned to slip away the first chance she got. Maigraith hid her pack, slipped back into bed and slept soundly.

After midnight she woke and the aftersickness was gone. Karan was folded up in the armchair by the fire, dozing, but woke as soon as Maigraith stirred. "How are you?" Karan asked.

"Much better, though my shoulder is very painful."

Karan checked the wound, which was inflamed, and changed the dressings. She made tea. They drank it in silence.

"I'm afraid, Karan."

"So am I."

"No, I'm *really* afraid. The whole world is turning upside down. All day I've been hearing voices, people whispering, but they seem to be on another plane. I don't understand what they're talking about, save that they want our world. I can feel them plotting—blood and violence."

"I sometimes hear voices," Karan admitted grudgingly.

"*But you're a sensitive!*" Maigraith wailed, sitting up abruptly. "I feel that I'm looking into another dimension. And now you have an aura all around you—green and black and red, and it's always shifting."

She spoke wildly, of impossible things, as if her world was different from Karan's; as if reality had shifted for her.

"It's the fever," said Karan. Feeling Maigraith's forehead, which was cool, Karan felt a twinge of alarm. "I'll get you a drink."

"The fever is gone," said Maigraith. When Karan returned with a beaker of water Maigraith was asleep.

Shortly she woke again, talking nostalgically about things they had done together in the past. "Remember how we went all the way to Fiz Gorgo together?" she said. "That was an adventure! Remember how we had to climb down into the cistern and swim through that slimy tunnel? And remember—" She laughed shrilly, in a different world.

She's gone mad! Karan thought in sudden terror. She's like a child talking about what she did on her holidays. "It wasn't an adventure, it was a horrible nightmare for us both," she said as sharply as a slap.

Maigraith shuddered and her eyes refocused visibly. She turned to Karan as if seeing her for the first time. "What am I talking about? I'm sorry for bringing you into this, Karan."

"So am I. I want to go home while I still have one!"

Later their talk drifted onto Shazmak, the journey there and what it was like inside. Only after Maigraith had gone back to sleep did Karan realize how subtly she had channelled the conversation, to learn as much as she could about the Aachim city.

Karan became alarmed, for underlying Maigraith's casual questioning was a wistful nostalgia for what might have been, and a fatalism that it was all over. And before she slept Maigraith threw her arms about Karan and kissed her, something she had never done before.

"Take care of yourself," she whispered, "and look after Shand for me."

For the moment Maigraith was sleeping soundly. It would be dawn in a few hours. Karan ran down the hall to report this vital news to Malien, who had been furious with her for not knowing about Maigraith's breaking into the workshop. Karan felt guilty about the flute too, sure that Tensor's rebellion had to do with her revelation to Malien. At the same time, the duty to Malien was also real. Both obligations added up to the same thing: if Maigraith went to Shazmak she would have to follow her.

Malien was not in her room. Karan wandered outside to the bakehouse and saw Tensor on the step, talking to one of his guards. She didn't know what to do. Was he enemy or ally now? She felt loyalties to both sides. But only Tensor could tell her what she needed to know. Taking him aside, she told him what had happened at the meeting.

"Well," he said, "I see that I don't have a mortgage on folly. What a rabble your friends are!" Presumably he referred to Mendark and Yggur. "They've had a dozen meets this winter, but what has come of them?"

"Faelamor is going to Shazmak," she reminded him.

"Shazmak!" he said wistfully. "It's as if a part of me has been amputated. If only I could see it again."

"Do you think she will ally with Rulke?"

"Ha! Which one will betray the other first?"

"But if they do put aside their differences, even for a day, think what they could do to us!"

"No one can stop her," Tensor said dismally. "Nothing can be done."

"Maigraith could."

"Don't mention her name to me!"

"You're a stupid, bigoted old fool," Karan yelled, shaking him by the shirt. "You made a promise and you went back on it."

"What?"

"You refused Maigraith her flute. Can anyone else stop Rulke and Faelamor?"

He was silent. "Can anyone?" she screeched in his face.

"No!"

"Then help me to help her."

"There's nothing I can do."

"Maigraith's going to Shazmak, and I'm going with her."

"She will betray you and return to her own!" he spat.

"I'm doing Malien's work!" Karan said furiously. "Anyway, can Maigraith make things any worse than they are now?"

"I suppose not," he said grudgingly.

"Then honor your promise!"

"Very well," Tensor said. "I have not acted honorably to you or to her, and it plagues me. What do you want?"

"Is there any way to get into Shazmak secretly?"

"There is a *fifth* way," said Tensor, his voice a bare whisper. "Known only to me now. It has not been used in two thousand years. Two thousand years—we were in our prime then. Nothing seemed beyond us."

He rambled on, talking about events she knew intimately as if they had happened in the distant past. "Then *they* finally came in disguise, and it was not until we saw them that we recognized them, for they go by a different name now. They call themselves *Whelm*!"

"Tensor!" Karan cried, calling him back abruptly. "It's urgent. Tell me the way!"

"The fifth route! Perhaps it has fallen into ruin. It's fifty years since I last checked it. We never thought to *enter* that way, only to depart. There are traps you must master on the journey. I can barely remember them now. You cannot go the fifth way by yourself." He broke off, staring sightlessly at the ceiling.

"Tell me, quickly!"

"Listen well," he said, and described the way to her, explaining all the traps and pitfalls in the path. He took a long, intricate key from a chain around his neck. "I can't think why I still have it. I'll draw you a map too." He made some cryptic scrawls on a soiled scrap of paper. "Study it well and destroy it afterwards. No, what am I thinking? Shazmak is lost forever. If you go that way, take someone you trust with you. Someone tall!"

Karan hurried back to her own rooms, where Llian was sleeping quietly. Oh, Llian! she thought, how I wish that we could go together one last time. But this is no journey for you. I would just be taking you to your death. Bending over, she kissed him on the lips. He smiled and reached out to her with his eyes closed.

She almost pulled away then, but the yearning was too strong. Putting her bag on the floor she slipped into his arms. It was so warm there; so protected; so lovely. She longed to stay, but if she did not get up now she would never be able to. Karan kissed him again, on the tip of his nose, and slid out of the bed. "Goodbye, Llian," she whispered.

Karan hurried back to Maigraith's room. She'd been longer than she had planned. She pushed the door open quietly. Maigraith's bed was empty and her clothes were gone.

Karan ran around in a panic, cursing herself for leaving Maigraith alone. She forced herself to think calmly. Her own pack still contained her traveling gear and winter garb from the trip to Saludith. It would do for the mountains too.

She raced up to her room for it, realizing as she did that she had no food. Too bad; she couldn't spare a second. How long had Maigraith been gone? It could be as much as an hour. In her weakened state it might take her some time to reach the rooftop, her favored place for making gates, and make one ready.

Karan's running footsteps echoed down the hall. She rounded the corner and crashed into Shand, who had a sheet of paper in his hand.

"Maigraith's gone!" she gasped. "The rooftop, I'd say. She's going to Shazmak!" She took the steps three at a time.

Maigraith was surrounded by a network of light, but it was not the steady pale-blue light that had seen them off to Saludith. This was a flickering red-orange and scarlet corona, intensely bright, accompanied by a sizzling sound. Karan did not even hesitate. She sprinted across the roof, shouting, "Stop!" The bright light flared, began to die and Maigraith to fade.

Shand cried out from the top of the steps, "Maigraith, wait! You must see this—" Karan dived forward into the light. There was a terrific crackle, she was flung up into the air, then the light disappeared and Karan was gone too. Shand pounded up to the spot. Nothing remained but an acrid smell that soon dispersed in the breeze. He looked down at the paper and cursed, long and violently.

34

CARCHARON

Maigraith woke soon after Karan went out. She felt much better than before, though her shoulder throbbed. She had been wondering how to get away, and now that opportunity presented itself she seized it at once. She dressed and ran to the larders. There she used a trickle of power to break the lock, stuffed her pack with food and headed for the roof.

She encountered no one during the trip to the stairs, which was just as well for she was determined to let no one, friend or otherwise, stop her. Once on the roof Maigraith prepared herself carefully. Yggur's warnings could not be ignored. This would be the third gate in a day and a half, not to mention her calamitous experience with the flute. She was taking a great risk, but she had to get to Shazmak before Faelamor did.

On the rooftop Maigraith went through the gate-making procedure methodically. There was no possibility of going direct to Shazmak because she had never been there. But she knew Carcharon. She would make a gate there and walk the rest of the way.

She conjured up memories of Carcharon. It was as clear in her mind as a picture. That was a relief. It would be an easy jump.

Maigraith worked through her preparations again, *seeing* the destination and checking in case the construct had warped the place. She could sense nothing untoward, but often dangerous places could not be sensed until you got there. Well, she had done all she could. Time to go.

As soon as she made the gate Maigraith understood how weak she was. It was a clumsy, ill sort of a portal, surrounded by a baleful cage of light. She felt how erratic it was; how poorly tuned. Still, making the gate was not the part that was so draining, or even seeing the destination. It was keeping it all together at the same time as making the jump. She tried again, but the second was worse. She was weaker and had even less control than before.

Maigraith sat down and went through her mental regimen to calm herself. "I *will* do it," she told herself, working until her head throbbed. She started again. The gate was a little better this time. Dare she risk it? She must.

Maigraith heard a cry from the top of the stair and knew that it was Karan. She panicked. She had to go. *Now!*

It was a bad jump: off balance in spite of all the time she had spent preparing. Then came the terrible realization that Karan had somehow got into the gate. Maigraith saw her flung up in the air and whirled about. There was no chance of them coming through together; Karan might materialize anywhere! Already she was disappearing, trailing off, and there was nothing to be done about it.

Maigraith reached out but she was blind. All knowledge of the destination had gone. She knew the name, but Carcharon as a place was just a distant memory.

Karan! she cried across the ether. *I'm lost, I'm lost!* She looked down into boiling clouds of nothingness. Her control of the gate had gone. Maigraith could not overcome her panic enough to find it again.

Suddenly she felt something—a questing out after her. Maigraith snatched at the link. *Where are you?* she called across it.

I don't know, Karan sent back. Her voice was calm.

I'm lost! wept Maigraith. *I've lost us both.*

Karan poured encouragement back across the link, her triune senses allowing her to duplicate what Rulke had done for her on the Way to Aachan. She was so strong, so assured that Maigraith's panic ebbed a little.

Bring me to you, Karan called. *You can do that!*

Maigraith grasped that image and tried to draw it to her. Soon she made out Karan's outline through the fog. Karan slowly drifted back to her and they clung together, spiraling down and down and down.

Keep the link. Don't let go!

I won't let go, Karan whispered in her mind. *What is the destination?*

Carcharon, of course, she whispered back. *But I can't see it any more.*

Here it is, Karan sang across the link, and the way there was like a highway, clearer than any path Maigraith had ever traveled. Carcharon loomed up before her, not as an image in her mind but the real place. She reached for it and abruptly they were snatched out of the cauldron into the ruined upper chamber of the tower, in the dark.

For a second time they clung together, crying with relief. Maigraith lay on the floor, her chest heaving. "I am utterly exhausted," she said. "I have never felt worse." She was sick over the edge of the construct-shaped hollow in the stone floor, then flopped down on her back.

"Then stop right now! You'll kill yourself."

"I don't see what we have to congratulate ourselves about," Karan said shortly, while they were taking breakfast among the ruins. The sun was rising and they were glad to see it, for Carcharon was weirder than ever now. The walls angled strangely, the stone was as soft as cheese, the light vibrated visibly. Even the air had a faint, pungent, sickly sweetness. "The gate was nothing, compared with what's ahead."

"I'll worry about that when I come to it."

"You've certainly changed since Fiz Gorgo," said Karan.

"We both have."

"I desperately need to sleep," said Karan. "Just a few hours. Can I trust you to not abandon me?"

"You can," said Maigraith. "To tell you the truth, I'm so exhausted that I couldn't even walk down the steps."

"Well, I don't trust you. What's more I don't believe you're telling the truth. Sit down here, and I'll put my head in your lap, and if you try and move I'll wake up at once."

Maigraith did as she was told, though not without a secret smile. Karan lay down and slept almost at once. Maigraith put her arms about her but did not sleep.

She knows me too well, thought Maigraith. I *will* be off if I get the chance. She sat that way for almost two hours, but finally was so cramped and cold that she had to stretch her legs. Karan's eyes snapped open. She glared at Maigraith, then smiled and patted her hand and went back to sleep.

They shared a frugal lunch, or second breakfast, and set off up the ridge to meet the Shazmak path. Maigraith felt relaxed, at ease after the turmoils of the past few days.

"Well, here we are on the road again, just the two of us. It's fitting that we should be together at the end, as we were at the beginning."

She was thinking back to their journey to Fiz Gorgo that had begun it all. How tense she'd been; how miserable. But all that was gone now. She was a different person and, even if she never returned, at least she was going with a purpose and a knowledge of her worth. And yet, how sad it was to be leaving Shand behind. She'd kept him at arm's length ever since Saludith. Had to.

And how changed *you* are, Maigraith thought. I remember how you looked that night as we crept into Fiz Gorgo: your face so pale and your eyes round with fear. But once you agreed, you did not shrink from it. Never have I seen you do so. The last year has burned the laughing child from you. Karan's face was leaner, and harder, and wiser and sadder now.

Maigraith was thinking about Yggur too. She owed him much, yet he was a part of her past. A necessary part, and a good part in some respects, but a lifetime away and ended now.

As they went up the steep ridge, Karan surreptitiously examined her friend. They *were* friends now, in spite of the way their relationship had begun. No longer did Maigraith bear that lost, unwanted look. She had found herself over the past year. But she had found this great burden too, and taken it on herself without complaint. She knew who she was and her place in the world. But she knew what the consequences were likely to be too, and so she had put the world away from her.

As they trudged along, Karan recalled Rulke's words: *You will come of your own accord when the time is right.* How right he'd been.

Karan was also thinking about Fiz Gorgo. She felt much as she had then, that she was going foolishly into something way beyond her strength. She could feel the tension building inside her, the sense of something terrible about to happen—something irrecoverable. Despite herself she began to radiate waves of anxiety, as she had that other time.

Maigraith could feel it too. Poor Karan, to be a sensitive, a prisoner of her heightened feelings. But Maigraith knew better how to deal with that now.

"When I was a child, dwelling in the vast land of Mirrilladell," she said, "there were two things (save for a mother, and a father) that I yearned for."

Karan looked up, so unexpected was this remark.

"The sea, and the mountains," Maigraith continued. "I had a taste of the sea, with my shell sighing in my ear, but I had never been to the mountains. You have not visited Mirrilladell, have you?"

"Never," Karan said softly.

"You would not like it much. It is a monotonous land—at least the child in me thought so, though going back there later I found much in it to stir my memories. It is bitter in the winter, for whether the winds blow from the uttermost pole to the south or the great mountain barrier that encloses the country in the north, preventing all commerce, they are always frigid.

"In the summer Mirrilladell is steamy and gnat-ridden, and I swear it has insects that can bite through leather. It is a place of a million lakes, and as many bogs, hills like dingy sheep, and trees that are all the same wherever you go, nothing like your beautiful forests in Meldorin.

"But from the tallest of those hummocks I could see the ramparts of the mountains, and I yearned for them. They are the greatest in all the Three Worlds, Faelamor once told me.

Six and seven thousand spans are the highest peaks, and the fang of Tirthrax at least a thousand more, reaching even beyond the upper air, they say. Imagine! You can see Tirthrax from any hill in Mirrilladell, when it is clear, and it is never the same twice."

Karan had been calculating. "Four times the height of Shazmak? Nothing could be that high."

"Tirthrax is a thing to be wondered at, but first you must see it. It is impossible to imagine."

They were now picking their way among the outcrops where Karan had made her snow cave the day after hythe. There was barely enough snow to make a cave now. The sun shone on their backs and for once there was no wind. As they climbed among knotted gray rocks, they were soon sweating.

"To the native people of Mirrilladell, Tirthrax epitomizes everything cruel, indomitable and capricious. They hate that mountain looming over their land, overshadowing everything they do. And that is one of the few beliefs the Faellem adopted from that people, for they hate it too."

"How can you hate a mountain?"

"If you can love your mountains, as you do, and the Aachim do," said Maigraith equably, "I suppose you can hate them as well. But I was captivated by it. Even more so when I realized how much *they* hated it. When I was young I used to make up stories about it."

The slope grew steeper as they walked beside the gash of the ravine, with its black dykes cutting across. Here and there a slender bridge of almost transparent ice still remained. Karan related her reckless escape across the ice bridge.

"And you lecture *me* about being careful," Maigraith said softly, looking down at the broken rocks in the bottom of the gorge. It was some time before she continued.

"Later, as my education progressed, I lost that faculty of the imagination. All that was stripped from me by the harsh regime that was my schooling and my life. It was one of the things that made it all so hard to bear—there was nowhere left for me to hide. Later I built myself another place, but it was an intellectual refuge, not nearly so comforting."

"I'd like to hear about your childhood fancies," said Karan. She identified readily with the miseries of children, her own later childhood having been so unhappy. Once again she was struck by the parallels between her life and Maigraith's.

"Most of them are gone, though Tirthrax remains. I suppose the yearnings were too strong ever to be blocked out."

Now they were on the main path to Shazmak, a steep track that wound ever upward. The wind never stopped here.

"I don't know whether there are people living in the Great Mountains. Probably they are so high that nothing could ever grow there, though at the time I thought differently. I imagined myself dwelling inside the warm heart of the mountain. Within Tirthrax there were other people, like me. Friendly people, who wanted me and cared for me. So went my dreams. You can imagine how much the mountains meant to me, especially after I lost the sea. They were the one thing that could never be taken from me, for if I climbed any hill in Mirrilladell I could see them again."

"The principal city of the Aachim is at Tirthrax," said Karan. "Set deep into the heart of the mountain."

"It must be a wonderful place."

"So I hear. I've not been there."

"Your coming is a great inconvenience," said Maigraith that evening as they ate a frugal supper. "I brought only enough food for myself. What a pest you are." But she was smiling as she said it, and passed Karan another tiny portion.

Karan stuffed the morsel in as if afraid Maigraith would snatch it back. "It's only four or five days. Even if we have nothing for the last day or two, we won't die of it."

"It won't help to be half-starved when we get there."

Karan checked the wound, squinting in the firelight. "Try this lightglass," Maigraith said, handing her one. "You can keep it."

The wound was no worse than before, but no better either. Karan bandaged Maigraith's shoulder again. "You would have had trouble doing that by yourself," she said. "And it would have disabled you worse than hunger."

They kept on, walking late into the evening, taking a brief sleep but always back on the path again by dawn. In this way they reached the top of the eastern pass into Chollaz on only the third afternoon out of Carcharon. It was good progress, but conditions had been good for walking—fine weather and the snow crusty, even at the highest altitudes.

Since Carcharon, Karan had put her fears behind her, pretending that they were on a country stroll together. They looked down toward Shazmak, though all Karan saw was a wilderness of rocky alps and precipitous canyons. She remembered the first time she'd stood here, a girl of twelve, staring into the wasteland in dismay. There had been nothing ahead but rocks and snow, and the prospect of starvation.

Karan remembered other times too—happy times mostly, going in or out of Shazmak with Rael or her other Aachim friends. Whether she'd been going or returning, there was always a thrill at this point.

All gone now. Rael had drowned in the Garr, and even that tragedy was more than a year ago. The Shazmak that she had known was gone forever. Their ancient enemies had made it their own. That, too, she had set in motion.

Maigraith must have sensed Karan's mood, for she gave

her time for herself. When it was nearly dark she put her good arm across Karan's shoulders.

"Time to make camp. You said there was a way station here?"

Rousing herself, Karan led them down a barely perceptible path to a sheltered place beneath an overhanging ledge. There they found a small, round chamber cut into the rock, with a slab of stone that could be slid across to close it against the weather.

"This is not Aachim work," said Maigraith.

"No, it's much too rude for that. It's older than their tenure here. I don't know how old."

"And were there not Sentinels too?"

"Yes, and confusions, so that unwanted visitors never found the way in. Perhaps they failed when Shazmak fell."

They had another scanty meal, rolled into their sleeping pouches and slept. At least, Karan slept. Again Maigraith felt no need of it. Her shoulder was painful but she willed it out of mind. A few stars were visible above the mountains, though by the middle of the night they were veiled in mist. She lay in the dark, thinking; watching.

In the darkest hour of the night she rose, took the remaining food from her pack and put it on the floor beside Karan. Then she bent down, touched Karan's temple with her fingertips, saying softly, "Sleep!"

Karan sighed, shrugged herself down under the covers and settled down to a sounder, deeper sleep. Maigraith threw her pack, now much lighter, over one shoulder, pulled on her boots and went outside. A three-quarter moon shone down through thick mist. She slid the stone door closed, her fingers danced on it for a moment, then she turned and headed down the path toward Shazmak, all alone.

35

MY ENEMY MY FRIEND

Maigraith felt a tense anticipation. She had finally cast off the shackles of her old life—the one Faelamor had molded for her. The future was unknown, but whatever awaited her in Shazmak the choice was her own.

And what did await her there, she wondered as she picked her way down the track in the darkness. A sliver of moonlight illuminated the path every now and then, but the mist made everything surreal. She could hardly tell the difference between cliff wall on her right and precipice to her left, and between the snow and the ice-covered stone beneath her feet.

Pressing on too quickly, thinking about what lay ahead, Maigraith trod on a slick patch and her boots skidded. She fell against the rock face, hurting her injured shoulder. As she picked herself up, Maigraith realized that her heart was going like a battering ram. The danger here was real, and more immediate than Shazmak. She could just as easily have gone over the edge.

Folding her coat under her, Maigraith sat down with her back to the cliff. Her shoulder throbbed. The river far below, tributary to the Garr, rustled in its bed. The wind sighed through frost-carved pinnacles of stone above her. Her thoughts kept coming back to Rulke, to the memory of him that hot night in Thurkad when his half-embodied sending had appeared in the storm. He had been magnificent and terrible, and when he lifted her up his fingers had been burning hot. And yet, he had seemed vulnerable too.

First Yggur, and now Rulke, she mused. Why am I drawn to powerful, ruthless men with a vulnerable side? Is it because I am so incomplete in myself? Yggur cared for me, and still does, but he doesn't care about anyone else. He's full of anger and fear, and he would do anything to get what he wants. Look what he did to Meldorin with his warring, and to the Second Army. And, she reflected, he kept from me the secret of my true heritage. He knew it all along, or guessed it, even back in Fiz Gorgo. I remember him saying, as clear as day, *Tell me where I can find Faelamor, and why she wants the Mirror, and I will tell you who your parents were, what happened to them, and why it brought such shame upon the Faellem.*

But he never did, and later when I asked him about it he pretended that he had been wrong all along. Why did he lie? Was he afraid what I would do if I knew I had Charon blood in me?

Taking out the Mirror, she stared at the silvery metal in the threads of moonlight. Ghostly images swarmed just below its surface, her past and perhaps her future too, but she did not stir a finger to bring them out. Not now. Not here!

Maigraith continued on. It was a long walk from the way station to Shazmak, but she did not dare to rest, in case Karan freed herself more quickly than expected. In the afternoon she reached the gossamer bridge beside which Karan and Llian had camped on their journey into Shazmak from Tullin. Crossing the bridge, she kept going. Several times she sensed iron Sentinels watching the track, but each time Maigraith slipped past without alarming them. It was something that she instinctively knew how to do. The night was cold and clear, not what she would have chosen. How would she get in? What would she find there? What would she do then? She had no answers.

Around the middle of the night she crossed the last bridge. Its gentle swaying under her feet made her nauseous. She was almost ill with exhaustion and hunger. Out over the middle of the Garr, the river's tumultuous passage down the gorge made a roar that even this high above was deafening. Ripples passed along the bridge. The wind was a swell that lifted it and let it fall again. At the same time it oscillated from side to side, sinuous waves passing along it like a snake crawling across sand. Maigraith felt well and truly seasick by the time she reached the other side.

Before her was a set of great gates made of wrought-iron, with towering gate posts, but they were closed. She inspected them using a glimmer from her globe. As she did so she became aware of figures beyond the gates: two of the tall Whelm. No, these ones called themselves Ghâshâd. She squeezed her lightglass and its rays streamed out between her fingers, illuminating her. She knew that she looked very strong, remote and unpredictable. She rapped on the gate.

"My name is Maigraith," she said to the first sentry. His face was scarred as if it had been rubbed with grit paper. The second was a woman, almost as tall, with a fall of raven black hair and black eyes, pretty in a gaunt sort of a way. They were Idlis and Yetchah, banished to guard duty since their vote against Rulke's tale at the great telling in Carcharon. "Take me to Rulke!" She felt a thrill run through her on saying his name.

Recognizing her, Yetchah let out a wailing cry and sprang forward, quivering with animosity. Idlis restrained her. They each took an arm, but Maigraith would not be led like a prisoner, especially not to *him*.

"Let go my arms," she said coldly, and they did so, ushering her through a roofed passageway and across the courtyard, with its amber and black flagstones, its little coiled towers, its domes of carven jade. The silver tracery on the towers made shining lines in the moonlight, but the black fountain was crusted all down one side with ice frozen like candle wax. Somehow that seemed to diminish the magnificence of Shazmak.

"Go before," she said. "Announce me!"

Perhaps these Ghâshâd knew what she had done to their fellows in Fiz Gorgo and in Bannador. Or perhaps they had orders concerning her, for they made no further attempts to secure her. At a set of double doors, three times her height, Yetchah rapped a signal. The doors opened. She spoke to the guards inside. A pair went out to do duty at the gates. Maigraith passed through; the doors slammed behind her. She had got in, but would she ever get out again?

"Come!" said Idlis in his glutinous voice.

She followed him down long corridors and up strangely twisting stairs. Yetchah trod right behind her, which made Maigraith so nervous that she was oblivious to her surroundings. She could not have told what the floors were made of, or the walls. She did not once look at the carvings and murals on every surface, or the wire sculptures hanging from the ceilings. She could have found her way out again, but that was all.

Her heart began to pound. She tried to will it to be quiet. Her mouth was dusty dry. What if she opened it to speak and only a croak came out? All sorts of fears, mostly fanciful, began to plague her. She forced them away; it took a great effort. Maigraith noted how her self-control eluded her, as it had let her down so often in the past. She had it in abundance, until she really needed it.

They entered a meeting hall, a vast space with a soaring ceiling that grew out of the walls like the curve of a shell. It made a dazzling architectural display, a demonstration of the Aachim's mastery of space and materials. The hall must have been two hundred paces long, and nearly that wide and high. Off the sides were smaller chambers with the same shell-like curves of wall blending into ceiling. Slender staircases wheeled across the walls to a series of balconies, platforms, mezzanines and subsidiary chambers, while higher stairs led to a curved ceiling which was glassy clear and showed the stars.

Right in the center of the room was a pair of staircases that looked to be made of glass and cobweb. They spun up from the floor in spirals of increasing diameter, helically coiled together then exploding apart to opposite sides of the hall near the ceiling.

And there stood Rulke, halfway between the central stairs and the wall, working at a table ten spans long. The black bulk of the construct reared up behind him. He turned away to it.

"Master," said Idlis nervously. "This woman reached the front gate undetected. She is the one you put your mark on last summer—Maigraith!"

Pushing her hood back, Maigraith stepped into the light.

"*You!*" Rulke exclaimed, setting down a mechanical device he had been working on. "When the intruder was reported I thought it was Karan. But *you*—you are more interesting yet. It is as though *she* has come back. Come forward, Maigraith."

Who did he mean? Yalkara? Maigraith walked slowly across to him, made self-conscious by the intensity of his stare. Rulke was a very big man, taller even than Yggur, and powerfully built. His hair was glossy, thick and black, as was his beard.

She walked right up to him. Their eyes met. They measured each other. Finally Rulke put out his hand. Surprised, she took it. His hand completely enclosed hers, as if he took her into himself, and his skin was hot.

Maigraith felt a tingly sensation run down her backbone, like someone breathing gently on the back of her neck. She lost track of time and self. The feeling ran up and down her spine, a delicious itchy shudder like a current flowing out of his hand into hers, charging up every nerve to red-hot wires until her whole body was afire. She squeezed her thighs together until her knees hurt. Her nerve ends throbbed, from head to toe she tensed and itched like an approaching sneeze, then with an explosive convulsion that bent her double, the swollen current discharged back through her hand into Rulke.

"Aaaahh!" he shouted, flinging out his free arm, fingers spread. Goosepimples broke out up his arms, his eyes rolled back and forth, he squeezed her hand till her fingertips went purple. She did not try to get away—Maigraith felt ecstasy for the first time in her life.

Finally Rulke opened his eyes, looked deep into hers, released her burning hand. Her slender fingers, bloodless and pale, lay across his dark palm, lingering there. He lifted her fingers to his lips, touched them momentarily, then drew back his arm.

Maigraith's hand fell to her side. She stared up into his eyes, hungering for him and aware that he knew it. They were oblivious to the Ghâshâd, assembled round them in a perfect circle, staring. Then, as though moved by a single mind, a hundred Ghâshâd roared approval, spun on their heels and left them alone in the vast chamber. Even Yetchah was gone, her jealousy replaced by revelation.

Maigraith felt weak at the knees. She shook her head, looking down, blushing scarlet in her embarrassment. The Ghâshâd had hated and feared her once, when they were Whelm. But that was before Rulke put the seal of his approval on her.

"What is the matter with me?" Rulke murmured. "I have never lost control like that before. Come to the fire. Take off your cloak and coat."

"I am comfortable," she replied, but removed the garments anyway and laid them over his arm, feeling the weight of his eyes. She was reminded of the night they met. How violently the storm had struck at the dome of the citadel, like a living creature that must smash everything to pieces. She also recalled that she had been clad in nothing but her wet shift that night.

"Don't stare so," she said, feeling that he could see right through her clothes. "It troubles me."

"I would not discomfort you in any way, but I cannot tear my eyes off you."

Nevertheless Rulke turned away. He clapped and a servant appeared, not Ghâshâd but a young man who was thin to the point of emaciation. He limped across the room and bowed low. Thick brown curls tumbled over his gaunt cheeks, then he stood before them, silently waiting. There was a dimple in his chin.

"Bring meat and drink, Jance," Rulke ordered. Jance hurried away.

Maigraith waited patiently, her head to one side. She looked quite calm, quite regal, but her insides were churning. He motioned her to a chair, waited until she sat down and drew up another before her.

"Why did you come here?" he asked.

Why had she? Rulke's strength surrounded her—in the number of the Ghâshâd; in the construct squatting in the middle of the room, black monstrous thing with a sheen as if it had been polished in oil; even more in Rulke himself. So this was what the Charon had been like. Again she felt herself drawn to him, and to that species who were so few, yet had done so much.

I suppose it's because I'm triune, she thought. Though I'm half-Faellem, I have never been able to identify with them, because of Faelamor. And Santhenar is all around me, part of me and yet less than me. But how I yearn for my Charon heritage. Can he give that to me?

"I came to prevent you from making alliance with Faelamor," she said. "I know what you have," indicating the construct with an almost imperceptible motion of her eyes, "and what you lack too. Do not ally with her, I beg you."

"Faelamor?" He raised a quizzical eyebrow. "Absurd notion!"

"Please don't."

Jance returned, bearing a low table rather awkwardly. He set it up, coming back with cutlery, dishes of food and a jug of drink. She saw the reason for his awkwardness—one hand was cut off at the wrist. Rulke poured yellow fluid into a drinking bowl and passed it to her. The cordial was hot with a peppery flavor. It went straight to the pit of her stomach and roiled there.

"Why not?" he responded.

"The Forbidding is decaying and failing. If you break it Santhenar is doomed."

"I hear you," he said. "I know the risk, but I have studied the Forbidding. I can manage it."

"There is an imbalance in it," she said. "Have you not felt

it when you used the construct? I have, every time I made a gate."

"You made a gate?" he asked, rather taken aback. He paced across to the paired stairs and back. "How so? What device did *you* use?"

"I learned from Faelamor." She described Faelamor's clumsy gate. "She lacks confidence, and competence too, but once taught I found it to be instinctive. I need no device now. As long as I can truly see the destination, all I need is in here." She tapped her forehead.

"What is it about you?" he sighed. "I've never met anyone like you."

She saw no reason not to tell him. "My father was Faellem. My other grandparents are Shand, whom you may know as Gyllias, and Yalkara. I am triune."

He sprang up. "Now I understand!"

"What?" she asked anxiously.

"Karan linked to you at Narne, and I sensed it and used it to wake my Ghâshâd. I've never understood how I could have sensed a link from the Nightland."

"How did you?"

"It was a triune-to-triune link, the rarest and most powerful of all linkings."

"We tried to link once before. At Fiz Gorgo, but it failed."

"Yggur's protection would have been too strong. So!" He let out his breath in an explosive hiss. "You make gates all by yourself! If only you can pass *that* talent on down the generations."

"Unlikely," said Maigraith with a chilly laugh, feeling her womb cramp at the thought. "Triunes are sterile." Children were not even a dream for her.

"Most are, *but not all*. And even so, there are ways to improve your chances. We Charon know *everything* there is to be known about conception."

"This is ridiculous!" she shouted, feeling very uncomfortable. Faelamor was prudish and had never talked about such things. "Irrelevant! You must listen. The Forbidding fails and your construct can only hasten it. No one understands what they are dealing with. You risk opening Santhenar to the void."

Rulke waved his hand in dismissal. "I've heard you. Tell me about this new flute. Where did it come from?"

Why shouldn't she tell him? "Tensor made it using my birthright—Yalkara's gold."

"Ahhh! So she *did* find it."

"No!" she said, speaking without thinking. "Faelamor stole *that* gold from Havissard, and I now know it's the remains of the golden flute. My birthright was Yalkara's own jewelry which she brought from Aachan."

"How can you be sure which is which?"

Maigraith went still. The question had been raised and it would not go away. How could anyone know? "By the feel of it. Yalkara's gold has a lovely old feel, like other things of hers that I have. The gold Faelamor stole feels horrible; corrupt!"

"And so it is," said Rulke. "Where is your flute?"

"I tried to use it, but it was a wild, dangerous thing. I left it behind. The next time you use the construct . . ."

"Don't lecture *me*, Maigraith!" he said fiercely. "Do you think I don't understand? Did I not lead the way out of the void to Aachan? Did I not reach across the void in ancient times, in the perilous labor of *summoning*, and pluck the accursed Shuthdar from this world to make the flute for me? That was my folly, choosing that depraved madman. Far better that I spent ten times as long and made it myself. Did I not use the construct last hythe to reach out across the void?"

"And it went wrong. Karan told me so."

"I was careless. I did not protect her as I should have. It will be different next time!"

His dark brows knitted. As he spoke she had a fleeting image of someone staggering up an endless stair of metal and stone. The tormented figure went past and she saw from the red hair and the pale face that it was Karan. Then it blinked out again.

He took her hand. "Maigraith, listen! I have done much work with the Forbidding. That's what the Nightland was made of. I will be careful."

"You have another world to return to. What do you care for Santhenar?"

"Ah, but this is a better. Aachan is fatal to us. I *do* care, more than you can ever know. More than anyone can know who has not been exiled and cast into the void to perish. I care for all the worlds!" He spoke with such vehemence that Maigraith did not know what to say.

"Look at us!" He pressed her hand between his two hands, drew her to him and looked deep into her eyes. She felt that wild thrill again.

"Once, Maigraith, when we had a world, we were many. But we were cast into the void, every one of us, *to die!* For our kind to be utterly extinguished."

Still gripping her hand, he spoke with such passion that Maigraith was captivated.

"Can you imagine what it is like in the void? It is the most violent, barbaric, barren and desperate universe. It is ever changing, and the things that dwell in it mutate just as swiftly, for that is their only chance to survive. There is no mercy there; no charity; no forgiveness. Nothing but survival matters! How they feasted on our children, our weak and our old."

She was amazed to see tears in his eyes. More amazing, she felt them in her own.

"In a month our millions were reduced to a few thousand. We learned a lot about survival in that month. We learned to defend our shelters within the barren, boiling rocks which are all that passes for worlds in the void. We learned to prey on every creature that was weaker than us, and hide from those that were stronger, or more cunning, or more intelligent."

His indigo eyes flamed. He crushed her hand painfully but she did not want him to stop.

"We could never increase, though we learned the lessons of the void and became as brutal as any. Everything there was desperate to escape, but we were more desperate, for we knew what the outside universe was like. *We once had a world, and lost it!* I love Santhenar, Maigraith, but I care for our survival more than anything."

He released her hand. Maigraith left it where it was. Rulke had disarmed her and she did not know how to deal with the situation. She began to wonder why she was here at all. Yet she was mindful of his reputation for treachery.

"Why did you come to Shazmak?" he asked.

"I told you. To prevent Faelamor from making alliance with you."

"Ridiculous notion! Yet, I will do what I must do to ensure our survival," he replied thoughtfully. "Are you a sensitive, like Karan? Can *you* find the Way between the Worlds for me?"

"I am not, and I cannot," she replied.

"Can you bring Karan here?" he asked.

Maigraith wondered what Karan was doing now. "Possibly, if I thought it was the right thing to do! Though Karan is of her own mind. What do you want her for?"

"I will not discuss my plans with you, unless . . ." He leaned forward and would have taken her hand again but she drew it back. His voice aroused her deepest yearnings.

"Come, join me! We would be a perfect partnership. Your soul is Charon, Maigraith. I know it!"

Maigraith knew it too. His words had shaken her to the core. But her intellect could not permit her emotions to take over her life in such a way.

"You know that I have another duty," she said tonelessly. "It conflicts with your plans. What's more, I am minded that you are Yggur's enemy, and treated him cruelly. He is still scarred by it."

Rulke's eyes narrowed. "I did not begin it," he said. "A great lie has been told about me. I was betrayed. Yggur attacked me, he and Mendark, the most deceitful, treacherous man who ever was born on Santhenar. I defended myself. So, you plead for Yggur now! Is he still your lover?"

"No!" she whispered. "Not since he went to Katazza." She wanted to say *Not since I set eyes on you*, but did not dare.

There was a long silence. Maigraith finally broke it. "You know what they call you?"

"Great Betrayer! There's nothing I can do to change that opinion. I know what I am—I do not deceive myself. *I* do not fawn on posterity."

She continued to pursue him, feeling a need to hear his explanation for every evil attributed to him.

"What about the Aachim? You took their world, made slaves of them and harried them mercilessly."

"Does the lion starve her cubs because she pities the lamb? Had we not gone to Aachan we would be extinct, our great species gone forever. So we took Aachan. A hundred of us mastered a world. Had they cared for their world the way we did for ours, not even a million of us could have taken it. And did we harm Aachan in any way? We did not. We preserved and protected the ancient and noble culture of the Aachim. We did not enslave them either—that's an excuse to cover up a failing that they cannot admit to themselves: they were short of courage! They were free enough.

"Even here on Santh, we did not begin the wars of the Clysm. Much that was great and fine perished in the war. I regret that."

"You make out that all the tales about you are lies. I cannot believe that."

"Of course they're not! Most *are* true. I have been cruel and relentless, and never failed to use any weapon against my enemies. I will do what is necessary for survival. Anyone who valued their own species would do the same."

"You refused to honor the bargain when Llian beat you at the telling."

"He lied and cheated, but I would expect that from an enemy. My fury was at allowing myself to be cheated in front of my servants. I was made to look a fool, and my authority with the Ghâshâd undermined. The time will come when I will suffer for it."

She kept on, bringing out every wrong she knew about. "But your tale of the conquest of Aachan showed you—"

"I acted foolishly in Aachan, as that tale told. But that was thousands of years ago, when I was young and in my heat. Who does not? Have *you* no failures that you're ashamed of? I did not try to conceal it. I am *not* without honor."

Rulke said that very simply, then walked across to the construct. He stood there looking up at it, swaying ever so slightly. He put his hand on the hard flank of the machine but seemed to take no comfort from it. Yetchah appeared but he waved her out. Maigraith watched him, wondering how much of what he told her was the truth, if anything. She could not get his reputation out of her mind, but it did not agree with what she saw, and felt.

Spinning around, he strode back to her. "What is your decision?"

"I cannot make one. I am confused." And that was the truth. "I must think."

"Then you will appreciate why I must do this," he said, moving his hands in the air. Suddenly she could not move. "If you decide to join me, your word is all I need."

She did not struggle, and that seemed to surprise him. She just looked at him, measuring him with her remarkable, sad eyes.

He clapped his hands, a noise like thunder. Yetchah and Idlis appeared at an entrance and Rulke said, "Take her to her chamber. Will you go peacefully, Maigraith, or must I restrain you? Be warned, the number of my Ghâshâd is many hundreds."

"I—I give you my parole," she said.

His relief was evident. "In that case I will take you there myself. Come with me." Dismissing the Ghâshâd, he gathered up her coat and cloak. "This way."

Maigraith walked beside him silently. She had recovered her self-possession enough to take in something of the strangeness and the magnificence of Shazmak. Rulke led her along labyrinthine passages, up ethereal silver stairs and across a gossamer bridge that linked twin towers. On the way she realized that the alien murals depicted Aachan, the world her Charon ancestors had come from. Then she could not get enough of the gloomy scapes, the towering mountains, the lava fountains and sulphur-crusted snow.

In a tower some distance away, along a corridor with many doors, Rulke stopped outside one door, opened it and waited for her to enter.

"Not a cell?"

"I understand that these rooms were Karan's, when she lived here. I thought it would be more comfortable for you."

Maigraith was touched. "Thank you."

She went in and he followed her. Inside the wind could be heard, a distant wailing. She touched the globes to light, inspected the furniture and the kitchen, wondering about Karan's life here. In the room that must have been Karan's bedchamber a crystal window had been let through the thick wall, the only window she was to see in Shazmak. It was just becoming light outside. She looked out on the towers, spires and swooping aerial walkways of Shazmak. Beyond, every craggy peak was clad in snow.

"You will want to bathe, eat and sleep," he said. "I shall send food and drink. Otherwise, this place has everything you could need. Until the morning!" Bowing, he went out.

Maigraith checked the door, expecting it to be locked, but it opened silently. She waited until an almost fawning Yetchah appeared with the promised rations, then locked the door, bathed and went to bed. There was much to think about. She could feel the Charon part of her reaching out toward the truth in what Rulke had said, feeling the loss of their world and the terror at being reduced to extinction. Yalkara had not mentioned *that*, in the message left for Aeolior. How she wished she could look upon the Mirror and see Yalkara as she was now.

She could not get to sleep. Wandering about, Maigraith found her apartment to be a large, comfortable place. She sat down on something that she interpreted to be a chair, though it was very curiously shaped. The wind shrieked outside the window.

Pulling a blanket off the bed and wrapping herself in it like a cocoon, she curled up in the chair. Maigraith woke sometime later in the thrall of desire so strong that she almost wept with it. She wanted Rulke desperately—wanted him in her bed right now. The totally foreign passion shocked her. What she'd felt for Yggur had been a pale thing beside this. Going to the window, she laid her inflamed shoulder and rosy cheek against the glass. The cold helped with both, but not with her passion, and though shortly she went back to her couch she could not sleep for the wild thoughts chasing themselves through her mind. And at the back of them all—Rulke!

36

IN THE MINES OF SHAZMAK

Karan did not rouse when Maigraith slipped away, though normally she was a light sleeper. But later in the night she began to feel cold and afraid. She dreamed that she was trying to wake but could not. The lid of her mind was held closed with an invisible web.

Morning speared chinks of sunlight in past the edges of the slab door. Karan slept on, and now the inability to wake was a suffocating thing, an admission that she was too weak and insignificant to be of any help. That hurt.

The sun rose higher. The rays fled back across the floor and disappeared. A diffuse light penetrated the gloom. The sun reached its low zenith and fell quickly toward the north and west. Finally, when it had slipped below the mountains and the last light was fading from the room, Karan wrenched the cobwebs from her brain and woke.

She felt tired and irritable, the dull feeling that comes from having slept too long. At first she thought it was morning, though it did not feel like morning, and that Maigraith must have gone out for a walk. But Maigraith's pack was gone and the small pile of food beside her own told Karan everything she needed to know. She was not surprised—it was the sort of thing Maigraith would do. Karan had been half-expecting it. That was why she had told Maigraith nothing about the secret way into Shazmak.

She must be the best part of a day ahead by now. There was no hope of catching her. Karan heaved on the door, to see the last light and breathe the open air. She heaved again. It did not budge. It was fixed somehow. She felt humiliated. Not only had she been abandoned, but locked in as well.

She examined the door. It was made from a single thick slab of the local rock, slate. With her globe she saw that the slab slid in a channel cut in the stone of the floor, and at the top was held from falling out by a metal bar bolted to the roof. It looked home-made, but quite solid. There was nothing visible restraining the door yet it would not move either way.

Whatever form of the Art Maigraith had used, it was beyond Karan's understanding, or her breaking. She felt a momentary panic—what if it stayed locked? She would die in a few days, for she had only a little water in her bottle. Surely Maigraith would have left a way out, or perhaps the closure was set to fail in a day or so.

She examined the door again, recalling how she had solved a similar problem in the sewers of Fiz Gorgo. There was no rotten stone here; the whole thing was as solid as the day it was made. She noticed, though, that over the eons the door had cut its channel deeper in the floor. What had once been a square channel was now a trench with sloping sides. At the top there was enough clearance to put her hand in the space.

Two approaches suggested themselves—to lever the door out of its channel from the bottom, or to chisel away the slate at the top and let the door fall outward. The first approach looked to be the easier but she had nothing to lever with. She took out her knife.

Even standing on her pack, Karan had to strain to reach the top of the door. The slate was soft but it would take hours, if not days, to scratch away enough for the slab to fall. The dust fell directly into her eyes all the while. Then, forcing too hard, the blade snapped off halfway down. There had been a flaw in it.

She threw the pieces on the floor and rested her forehead against the cold stone. It moved slightly. Karan put her feet against the wall, gripped the edges of the door with both hands as firmly as the limited clearance would allow and slowly straightened her legs. The bottom of the door moved a little way up the side of the channel then slid down again. Three times she tried, always with the same result. Finally she wedged it with a flake of stone. The door slipped back, crushing the flake. She lay down on her sleeping pouch and stared up at the ceiling.

What was Maigraith doing at this moment? She would be nearly to Shazmak by now. She had confided nothing to Karan about her plans. Probably she had none; could not even make any. Besides, for all Maigraith's vast abilities, Karan did not have a great deal of respect for her capacity to solve that problem. She had strength but no cunning. She lacked imagination.

She needs me, thought Karan. She'll soon be in terrible trouble and no one can help her but me. And if I don't get out of here soon, I'll be too late. Karan knew that she was being foolish. What could she hope to do against the likes of Rulke and Faelamor? But she had to support her friend. And make up for her crimes—for helping Rulke, for letting the thranx into Santhenar.

Taking up the broken hilt of her knife, Karan realized that

with its stub of blade it made a wedge of sorts. She jerked the door, jammed the wedge in and heaved again, repeating the process several times. The stone door rode up to the edge of the channel and stalled there. The space was big enough to get her head into. Edging gingerly into the space, her shoulder touched the slab and it slipped. Karan wrenched her head out, scraping her ear painfully along the side of the slab just before it slammed back against the wall. Her heart was going so hard that it hurt.

Karan could not stand up for trembling. She sat with her head in her hands, imagining what it would be like to lie here, trapped by her crushed skull, slowly dying. That must rank as one of the stupidest things you've ever done, she told herself. Don't be in such a hurry.

But the urgency had not gone away. She gave the door a truly mighty shove and the bottom rode up and over the lip. She jumped out of the way as the slab struck the floor and broke into pieces. Cold air gushed in. From the look of the stars it was nearly midnight. Taking up her pack, Karan departed.

At one or two places along the track, smaller winding paths led down to the Garr. The way Tensor had taught her about, the secret fifth way out of Shazmak, began near the bottom of the gorge, down one of these paths. She had to be on it before dawn, otherwise she would be unable to move for fear of discovery.

The night was dark, the crescent moon not yet risen, but at least the track was in good repair. She could move relatively quickly. Even so it was an anxious night. An incautious step on a patch of ice and she would be over the edge.

Karan was no more than an hour from the river path when dawn began to break. The mist thickened with the day and soon she could laugh at her earlier fear, for fog rose out of the river so dense that she could barely see her feet, and had to edge her way along by feeling the cliff with her fingertips.

Now the route became hazardous in the extreme, for this path was narrow, steep and in grave disrepair. She hurried on, afraid that she would be too late, taking risks. At a place that was too dangerous to negotiate in the fog, where the whole path had slid down into the river, she stopped for breakfast.

Once the sun was well into the sky the mist thinned rapidly, yet it was still a long way down, taking her till well after midday. The Garr swelled to a vast white torrent, pounding over endless rapids and gigantic boulders, filling all the air with spray that made pearls of moisture in her hair. The thunder of the water even drowned out her thoughts.

At the bottom a shelf had been cut into the cliff, a platform above the flood level. When she reached it, Karan saw a shaft running into the side of the mountain and at first thought that part of the cliff had fallen, revealing the entrance of the secret way. Shortly she realized that this shaft was a mine adit, for inside there were lumps of ore and a broken hand cart. The whole area was a network of tunnels, where the Aachim had mined the ore from which they had fashioned Shazmak. The secret way must be further upstream, a scramble of several hundred paces past the end of the platform, over huge blocks of wet stone.

She headed that way, recalling Tensor's directions and trying to relate them to what she saw around her. *Go upstream . . . 280 paces from the end of the platform.* But did he mean his paces or hers? Besides, it was impossible to pace out the distance over this jumble of boulders. She also remembered Tensor saying that the secret way could not be done alone. *Take someone tall*, he'd said. Too late!

Look up at the cliff. You will see that one part of it, twice the height of your head, is quite smooth, but for two small oval bosses of stone.

There was nothing like that above her, but a good distance further along, the gray rock was smooth. There she looked up. Still nothing that looked like a boss, a round lump of stone, much less two. Even higher up, three head heights, four, five, there was nothing. She sat down on a boulder, staring at the cliff. It was freezing here. The rocks were coated with frozen spray in layers that would not melt until late spring.

This had to be the spot. Karan looked down and saw a smooth round bulge of stone below her boot, and another not far off. The boulders must have fallen since Tensor was last here.

Take the key, hold it with the wards pointing vertically and to the right, and touch the flat part to the very tip of the lefthand boss, then the right, then the left again. Do this quickly. Wait for the count of ten and do the same again, but beginning with the right-hand boss and the wards of the key pointing to the left. Then stand well back.

She did exactly as she had been instructed, and waited. Nothing happened for a minute, but soon a square outline appeared in the smooth rock face and a door fell outward toward her. She leapt sideways with an involuntary yelp, slipping on the ice and bruising her knee. The door crunched against the boulder she had been sitting on. Instinctively she looked around in case someone was watching, then stepped onto the ramp.

Inside she touched the key to another, smaller boss. The door rose back into place. It became utterly dark. It was warm though—much warmer than outside. Lighting up her glass, she headed up the tunnel, ordering in her mind the various instructions to take her safely and secretly into Shazmak. This way was intended for escaping, not for entering, and there were a number of traps that had to be disarmed. The first of these was a simple pad that acted as a Sentinel. Unless she disabled it, an alert would be sent to the Sentinels in Shazmak and a block of stone would fall to seal the passage. The pad was just twenty paces in from the door. Twenty of Tensor's paces; twenty-five or more of hers. It could be disabled with a series of small taps in a bowl-shaped depression in the raw stone. That took her a while to discover, for the depression was small and high up, very inconspicuous. She went forward carefully but nothing happened. Karan judged that the Sentinels had not been alarmed.

Karan continued for a while, stopped for dinner and realized that it must be growing dark outside now. Suddenly drowsy, she lay down in her sleeping pouch and slept.

The tunnel ran, sometimes up but mostly down, in a series of looping curves that led without further interruption directly toward Shazmak. As long as she kept to Tensor's route she was safe, until she reached the foundations of Shazmak. It was quite different from that other underground way, the caverns of Bannador. Here it was quite dry. Only once or twice did she encounter water, though just a trickle along the side of the tunnel.

After a few hours the tunnel plunged steeply down. The walls were wet here and the floor slippery. Shazmak was built on a pinnacle of rock rising out of the middle of the Garr, and therefore the way must go under the river at some point. At the lower end of the decline, her lightglass showed a long stretch of water. A thrown rock indicated that it was deep. She would have to swim and hope that the tunnel was not full further on. Her small light did not reach that far.

Carrying no change of clothes, Karan undressed, put everything in her pack and drew the inner drawstring tight. With care it would stay dry. She stepped into the cold water.

In a few steps it was deeper than her toes could reach. She turned on her back, held her pack against her chest with one arm while holding the lightglass up with her other hand, and kicked along.

Almost immediately she felt uneasy, and the further she paddled the more her disquiet grew. Irrational fears began to plague her, of slimy things that dwelt in the depths below. Nonsense! It's just that I don't know how deep it is, she told herself. It's the dark and the unknown. Nothing could live in here—there's nothing to eat. It's just dead water.

Dead water! That thought was no more comforting, and now she began to think that something sat waiting for her on the other side, watching as she kicked blindly toward it. It's because I haven't any clothes on—it makes me feel vulnerable. There's nothing to worry about. This place has been sealed for centuries.

She paddled on, but could not resist the urge to look over her shoulder, expecting eyes like lamps to grow out of the darkness as she approached. Her foot kicked against a slippery, unpleasant surface. She thrashed and churned the water to foam in her desperation to get to the other side. Eventually she did, completely unscathed, to find another empty tunnel. She sat on the gritty floor to dress. As soon as she had done that Karan felt better, though so cold. She was glad of the dry clothes. But still she could not escape the feeling that there was something in the mine with her.

Karan examined the rock, which here was yellow, with veins, layers and knots of red, brown and even black. She knew nothing about mining but the dark red ore looked to be rich. Picking up a piece from the floor, she weighed it in her hand. It was very heavy. She walked along, tossing it up in the air and catching it in her hand. The light sparkled off crystals that were every bit as beautiful as rubies.

Shelling some nuts she ate them one by one, nibbling

away at their triangular sides first and then crunching into the sweet interior. They weren't bad. Karan sat down and consumed them all.

Time to get going again. As she lifted the globe the light swept across the floor, illuminating a curious and unnervingly familiar marking. The back of her neck prickled.

Holding the globe higher, she saw a dark stain on the yellow stone—the outline of a heel. The shape was suggestive. She went down on hands and knees, holding the globe close to the floor to look for other marks. She soon found one.

It was the print of a square foot like the palm of a huge hand, with just the trace of long splayed toes like fingers. She knew instantly what had made it. It was the same print, probably the same beast, as she had seen in the snow after she escaped Rulke and fled up the mountain from Carcharon. It was the massive, hairy, dwarf-shaped creature that had come out of the void and moved the levers of the construct so knowingly. She had spent that whole night in terror of it. So this was where it had got to. It must have followed the Ghâshâd back to Shazmak.

Karan cocked her head, one way and then the other. Her hearing was poor on one side—the ear that the void-leech had punctured.

Lorrsk, Rulke had called it. She sniffed the print. It had the faint odor of old blood. It was in pain, probably starving, *and in here somewhere!* It would make a meal of her and she had no weapon at all. It might have smelled her already.

Nonsense, she told herself. My adventures at Carcharon were ages ago. It must be long gone, or hunted down or starved to death, or dead from its injuries. I would have sensed it if it was near.

But the lorrsk was not gone. It had followed the Ghâshâd all the way back to Shazmak, taking one of them on the way, and later a second, slashing the man down with a single blow of its clawed hand. The meat was stringy and rank, though in the void the lorrsk had learned that any food not actually poisonous was a precious gift.

But it could not get into Shazmak, so temptingly full of live flesh. Sentinels sounded the alarm before it could get near, closing every way against it. And every movement broke open the hideous wound on its backside where it had fallen in that pool of molten metal in Carcharon. One buttock had been completely burned away and after all this time the wound had still not healed. It was now horribly infected. The pain, even for a creature inured to stoicism as the lorrsk was, was shocking.

Then one day, as its hunger grew desperate and the pain more and more unbearable, the lorrsk had chanced upon the old mine adit Karan had seen. It crept inside, grateful for protection from the winter cold, and made a living for a while on rats, bats and other small creatures. Exploring all the tunnels, it found a fresh fall of rock that had a different smell. The lorrsk broke through into the secret passage. But this, it sensed, was a dangerous place, full of traps, so it went back to the mine. When it had eaten every creature there, and still had not found a way into the larder of Shazmak, it made itself as comfortable as the injury would permit and sank into a state like hibernation, to await spring or some other opportunity.

Karan had often been afraid during the adventures of the past year and a half. Terror had been her constant companion for good parts of that time. But she had never before felt the mind-numbing dread, the absolute horror of knowing that somewhere in the dark was a desperate, starving creature at least as clever as she was, whose first aim would be to rend her limb from trunk, bite her head off and crunch her bones to powder. Her sensitive nature allowed her to imagine that far too well.

Putting the globe away, she felt her way along in the dark for a while, afraid that the light would draw attention to her. But she realized how irrational that was—the lorrsk could probably smell her like a dog and the light would make no difference. She fished it out again.

She moved, and imagined that it moved behind her, stalking her, playing with her. She stood still and knew that it waited silently for her. Every crack and groan of the rock, every drip-drip-drip of water from the roof of the cave, became a sign that the lorrsk was coming.

She wanted to scream and run in the dark, but could not. There were traps she had not yet come to, and each would take patience and dexterity to disarm, and probably a healthy dose of luck too, since she had no one to help her. If anything could be worse than being hunted by the lorrsk, it would be waiting, hanging helplessly in an Aachim trap, for it to come for her.

On she trudged, hour after hour. Surely there could not be far to go now. It was ages since she had swum beneath the river. Only two traps remained to be overcome before she could get into the lower levels of Shazmak. If she just crept along like a little mouse, surely she could get there. Karan went past a swarm of red veins that cut across the yellow rock of the tunnel. She counted them—eleven. The next trap, Tensor had told her, was just beyond this point. Once she reached Shazmak her troubles would begin again, but she wasn't going to think about that until she had to. She was exhausted but did not dare sleep.

The lorrsk grunted and rolled over in its sleep. Something had penetrated the deep slumber of its hibernation. Its grossly infected, suppurating buttock scraped against the stone, sending a shiver of agony through it.

The lorrsk rolled onto its stomach, unable to completely suppress a howl of pain, though it cut that off at once. In the void pain meant weakness, and howling about it was generally fatal. Its flabby belly reminded it of its most vital urge, but it had been hungrier than this on many an occasion. Hunger had not weakened it—the contrary! It closed its eyes and drifted back into slumber, then something snapped it wide awake and it climbed to its feet, sniffing the air.

There it was, the perfume of live meat! The lorrsk recognized the scent. It was human, female—the young woman it had seen in Carcharon and subsequently tracked up into the mountains. Compared to the stringy fare it had last eaten this was like a bouquet of roses. Saliva dripped from its mouth.

Karan was feeling with her fingers in a recess in the wall, trying to find a pad that disarmed the trap, when she heard that howl, swiftly truncated. It had found her! She started, cracking her cheek on the rough stone.

But where was it? She might be able to use this trap if the lorrsk was on the other side, but it would take nerves of steel, for she would have to wait with her light glowing to see which way it came. If it was in front of her, well and good. The trap would be between her and it, and she had better hope that it worked! If the beast was behind her she had practically no chance. All she could do was try to avoid its charge and hope that it set off the trap before it got her.

Karan brightened the lightglass and used her cloak to dust off the floor, hoping that the dimensions of the trap would be revealed. Tensor had told her that it was a big pit trap with the doors divided into two leaves that hinged down, and a long drop onto spikes. The trapdoors were designed to spring back up and lock again, in case of a second lot of intruders. But did the pit extend all the way across the tunnel, or was there room to squeeze by against the wall? He had not given her such details.

Her work was fruitless—the dust was too thick and the trapdoor so cunningly made that she could find no trace of it. What else could she do? She had a short length of rope in her pack. If she tied that around her waist and the other end to something back here, and went forward gingerly, as soon as the trap went off she could haul herself back. Hopefully! But what if it came the other way and she was tethered?

Suddenly she *sensed* the lorrsk. Karan had the globe high, scanning the passage back and forth. There it was, ahead of her: a pair of reflections that were quickly hooded. The first hurdle was passed. She watched as it approached.

Now she could see it, a shaggy outline, a man-like creature, though much bigger than her. It had a dwarfish shape, with legs the diameter of her waist but no longer than her own limbs, and a long barrel of a body. Its arms hung almost to the ground and the fingers had retractable claws the length of her fingers. The head was broad, with a domed forehead, deep-set eyes and a jaw that could have crunched through her thigh bone.

The lorrsk advanced slowly toward her wavering light. It bared its teeth then stopped, sniffing the air as if something was not quite right.

Karan was dismayed. It suspected the trap! This was a clever opponent.

The lorrsk stopped dead and the hair on its body stuck straight up. Perhaps it was also a sensitive. That would help it to survive in the void. If it was, she had an idea that might work.

Karan began to use her fear to think herself into a state of absolute terror, a state where she would broadcast that terror to every living thing around her. If she could make it strong and wild and desperate enough, perhaps it would overwhelm the lorrsk's own senses. Well, she thought wryly, thinking myself into such a state won't be hard, for I'm almost there already. And the longer it stared at her, as if working out how best to carve her up, the more terrified she became.

It's going to eat me! It was incredible, and horrible. In a minute it will be biting my head off and tearing out my arms. Or maybe it will rip my belly open and eat my liver while I'm still alive. The images were so frightening that she let out a shriek, and had to put her hands over her ears to block out the sound.

She screamed and screamed, the sounds coming out in pulses like her battering heart. Her knees collapsed. She wanted to curl up into a ball on the floor. In other crises she had been impelled to violent action, but now she was petrified with terror.

Karan realized that she was lying on her face on the floor, waiting to become a victim. Her terror was feeding back on itself, growing stronger and stronger until it was taking her over completely. Or perhaps, the thought struck her like an avalanche, *it was being fed back to her!*

Stop it! *Stop it or you really will be eaten!*

She banged her head so hard on the rough floor that she almost passed out, and that sliced through the fed-back terror. She was dripping with cold sweat and the dust had coated her like flour. Rolling over, Karan came to her knees, holding the globe up in one hand.

The lorrsk was still watching her, but now it began to move slowly forward, testing the floor beneath it with its hand-like feet. It was so big! It began to make a sound like a purring kitten and its great mouth curved open in a grin.

37

THE KEY

Llian woke not long after Karan left his bed. He was not surprised that she was gone—she often rose before dawn these days. But her fleeting appearance had disturbed his slumbers and he could not get back to sleep for worrying about an alarming possibility: that he had made a mistake in his translation from *Tales of the Aachim* weeks ago. At the time Llian had wanted Tensor to check his translation, but the Aachim had been across the sea and Mendark had demanded that it be completed at once. By the time Tensor returned, Llian was busy on other things and had put it out of his mind. Now he cursed that carelessness.

Dressing hastily, he noticed that his trousers were worn through at the knees. His boots had holes in them too. He looked even shabbier than he had in his student days, when he'd had his glorious stipend. Llian looked back on that time with considerable nostalgia now. He had worked hard and played hard too, but he'd always had a few coins in his pocket. Since arriving back in Thurkad at the beginning of this winter that had seemed to go on forever, he had not had a grint from Mendark for his service. Even the roof over his head was provided by Yggur. For months he had survived on nocturnal gleanings from the pantries and the kindness of his long-suffering friends. His ribs were like a washboard.

Sneaking down the corridors in the dark, he tried the doors of the larders. A small miracle—the lock on one was broken. Sliding in through the door like the professional pilferer he had become he stuffed his day pack with a cheese coated with poppy seeds, a round loaf, a handful of pickled onions and a wax-sealed jug of red wine. Plain fare, but Llian felt as if he had robbed the tomb of a queen of old.

He went down to the citadel. It was still dark but the guards were used to his ways and allowed him in, escorting him up to the library and rousing out an archivist to make sure nothing was lying around that he did not have permission to see. His notes were still spread across the table in wild confusion, just as he had left them the previous evening.

Eating in the Magister's library was a felony, but one Llian was so used to committing that he now did it without a thought. As soon as the archivist was gone he settled down at the table, carved a wedge of cheese, slabbed it between doorstops of bread with half a pickled onion, and opened his journal. But he could not concentrate. He gazed around at the magnificent room. The library was shaped like a stubby cross, the four arms of which were filled with cedar and rosewood bookcases of the most elegant construction, extending halfway up to the lofty ceiling. The walls were paneled in precious woods and the ceiling, which was a twelve-sided steeple, was clad in timbers equally precious but of a lighter hue.

The place had everything Llian could wish for in a library. The walls were hung with old paintings and engravings showing artists and writers at their work. The floor was covered in an exquisite carpet of knotted silk. The room was full of the scent of books and scented woods, and stuffed to the gills with volumes that he would have given his right arm for. It made all his trials worth while. He wished he could work here forever.

Llian turned the pages of his journal, found the translation, took a swig of wine from his flask and then conjured the appropriate page of *Tales of the Aachim* into his mind. He compared the two. They were the same, but one phrase still bothered him.

There will appear an instrument (khash-zik-makattzah) *and if a way can be found to use it, Santhenar can be . . . redeemed. But at the end the instrument will be lost.* Previously he had translated *khash-zik-makattzah* as *three-and-one*—the flute! But it might have meant *three plus one*, which he could make no sense of, or *thirty-one*, or with a bit of imagination, *one into three, one-third*—neither of which had any meaning that he could fathom. Mendark had dismissed all those possibilities. Llian recalled the earlier conversation to mind.

"*The* three *means the flute,*" Mendark had said, "*for it was the product of three worlds: gold of Aachan for the body of the flute; precious ebony of Tallallame the other parts of it; and the genius of Shuthdar, who was from our own world, that conceived and made it. And the* one *is the sensitive who will use it to unstitch the Forbidding and restore the balance between the Three Worlds. But at the end the instrument will be lost. Does that mean* lost, *or* destroyed?"

Perhaps that had been wishful dreaming on Mendark's part. Was it *three in* or *into one, or one made out of three?* It was impossible to tell. It must have made sense to the people who wrote it, but Llian did not know the language sufficiently well to be sure of his translation. He went looking for

Tensor but could not find him anywhere. Going back to the library past Mendark's apartment, Llian heard the sound of a flute playing, the same notes over and over again, as if Mendark was struggling to master a complex melody. He was always playing the flute these days.

Putting the journal aside, Llian returned to his other puzzle—what had really happened when Rulke had been imprisoned in the Nightland. Now he could not make sense of this story either. Disgusted with his stupidity he drank the rest of the wine, put his head on his arms and fell asleep.

Almost immediately there was a great clamor outside. Sticking his head out the door Llian saw Shand, Yggur and Tallia running up the corridor in a great flap.

"What's the matter?" Llian shouted.

Mendark jogged up from the other direction, clad in a nightgown of blue satin. "What's going on?" he demanded. He looked a lot younger than Llian felt.

"Maigraith has gone again!" cried Shand. He was very distressed.

"Go on!" said Mendark darkly.

"I had Karan watching over her, for Maigraith has been abusing her ability with gates. Unfortunately she got away in the night and made a gate from the top of the roof. Karan went after her." He gave Llian an unhappy glance. "I'm sorry, Llian. It was a strange sort of a gate—it didn't look right. Karan jumped into it at the last minute and they both disappeared. I'm dreadfully worried."

Llian hung on the door handle, staring into nowhere. It was all beginning again.

"Have you any idea where they went?" Mendark asked, and when Shand did not answer at once he shook him by the shoulder. "Have you?"

Shand pushed Mendark's hand away, though without

rancor. "I thought the gate was directed to Carcharon, though surely their true destination is—"

"What?" cried Mendark, and he suddenly looked uneasy. "Where?"

"*Shazmak!*" said Yggur explosively. "Maigraith's destination is Shazmak. She is going to Rulke."

They stared at each other, then Mendark spun around and ran for the stairs. "She's taken the flute!"

"Wait!" Yggur yelled after him. "How could she get through all those guards? Anyway, Tallia has gone down to make sure."

Mendark came back. "I need more time!" He paced the corridor. In a few minutes Tallia came running up.

"The flute's safe in the bakehouse. I saw it! Neither the guards nor the Aachim have seen Maigraith."

"So they say!" Mendark said darkly. "All along I've been right about Karan. She's gone over to Rulke too."

"Your wits have left you," said Yggur.

"Still, they don't matter. The flute is all that matters now."

"I wonder," said Yggur. "I doubt that we were ever on the right track with this flute. I should have trusted my instincts instead of allowing you to manipulate me. Better we put our faith in arms, and besiege Shazmak before he can build up his strength."

"You talk big but you never do anything!" Mendark said. "We've got to use the flute and seize his construct. Shazmak can never be taken by force."

"Only by treachery," said Llian, remembering.

"Well, you go your way and I'll go mine!" said Mendark. "But I'm not ready." He shook his head in agitation. "I'm failing at the final hurdle."

They separated, each going off on their own frantic business. Llian went back to his work but was too worried to think straight. He desperately wanted someone to talk to but everyone was too busy, even Shand.

The day dragged on. It was impossible to think for worrying about Karan. In the late morning Shand came in and slid a long piece of paper across the table.

"Here you are. It took a lot of trial and error, but I've put the syllables into what I believe are the correct words."

> No sze gwi ta sha mu no dzo ta dzo gwu cho ksi lo sze mo nu mu bu gi sze gwi gwu je ru she ksi cha vo gw'uh wi no sze ta mo va mu bu cho ksi kso fe mo nu mu gw'uh gwu ta dzo lu u lo gwi ksi lo gi mu qa kso je e i dzo ta dzo mu no she nu che mo lo cha kso pi lu ta gwu va nu vo cha ru gwi sze ya ta sze pi no sze lo je mu gwi ta sha sze e.

> Nosze gwitasha mu nodzo tadzo gwu choksi losze monu-muBugi szegwi gwuje rushe ksicha vo gw'uh wino szeta mova mu Bucho ksiksofemo numu gw'uhgwuta dzolu'u lo gwiksilo Gimuqakso je'e i'dzo Tadzo muno shenu chemo

locha ksopiluta Gwuvanu vocha rugwisze yatasze pinosze
loje mu gwita-shasze'e

"What a strange language!" Llian exclaimed. "What does it say?"

"That's rather more difficult, not least because the word order seems quite different from the syntax in our language."

"You know the Charon speech, don't you?"

"I used to," said Shand. "I had the best teacher there was, though I dare say I've forgotten most of it now. I've an inkling what this means, but let's work on it together."

Some hours later, they had come up with the following awkwardly translated lines, which observed the same word order as Shand had set out.

Held closed is reflecting plate but hides inside key
Look in interior come what you require to see there is
Take in hand firstgift be fooled nevermore
Far-seeing device truth tell
Lamented lost homeworld (repeat words) mine
Wheel stopping-point hanging from one is three-parted

"Reflecting plate means the Mirror," Llian mused. "Therefore, surely the first line is a restatement of the paradox . . ." He trailed off. Shand was staring into space, paying no attention.

"Shand?" said Llian. He shook him by the shoulder. "Shand?"

Shand floated back to reality. "Save yourself the trouble, Llian. I know what it says.

"The Mirror is locked, but within lies the key
Come, look inside, see what you want to see

Take hold of your birthright, you will see true
Then the Glass cannot lie to me or to you
Tallallame, oh my Tallallame
Your fate does rest on the one which is three

"I understand it now; it's the verse Yalkara called out as she went through the gate, that I couldn't quite catch at the time. She must have been making sure that Aeolior could use the Mirror when the time came, even if it tried to lie to her."

"So she was meant to have Yalkara's gold in hand when she used the Mirror," said Llian.

"*Then the Glass cannot lie to me or to you.* And without it, the Mirror surely has lied to her."

"And led her to Shazmak. To Rulke!"

"Yes," Shand said, crushed. He sat at the table for a very long time, head bowed, then rose to his feet and slowly went out.

Llian suddenly had an inspiration. "*Shand!*" he called out urgently.

"What is it now?"

"Remember Yalkara's book that was . . . stolen and burnt?"

Shand's head jerked up. His green eyes pierced Llian. He was quick! "You young scoundrel!" he said.

"I had Lilis make a copy, and it was the copy that was stolen."

"And you want my help to translate it."

"You said you'd do anything in your power to help me. Besides, I'm doing it for Maigraith. Are you too busy?"

"Yes," said Shand, "but I'll find the time. It's a much more difficult project, though. No doubt you know why."

"The script on the Mirror contained only thirty-three different glyphs, and there are a lot more in the Charon syllabary."

"Ninety-eight, as it happens, but the ones we know are the most common ones. And I can probably work out a few more. Shall we begin?"

They worked in Shand's rooms, more pleasant because Shand fed him at intervals, and Llian found the old man's help invaluable. Despite his protests, Shand had forgotten very little, and from the context they were able to work out the meaning of quite a few more glyphs. By the evening they had finished the first page, which seemed to be a synopsis of the book.

"Read it aloud," said Shand, and Llian did so.

Shand stood up. "This turns everything upside down."

"Everything!" Llian bent his head to the book again.

Around midnight, seeking a respite from the translating, Llian went walking outside. At the front door of the fortress he ran into Tensor, who had been checking the guards at the bakehouse. Tensor looked surprisingly friendly. But then Llian already knew how mercurial he could be.

"Chronicler! You've come about Karan!"

"Karan?" said Llian, wondering what he was talking about.

"Just before she went, she asked me if there were any secret ways into Shazmak. I told her about the fifth way. She did not mention that to you?"

Llian had a distant memory of Karan slipping into his bed, but that was all. So they *had* gone to Shazmak! "No, I came to ask you about the reading I made from *Tales of the Aachim.*"

"I wondered about your boldness in translating our work without consulting us. But it does not matter anymore. Quote me the passage."

Llian did so. "The phrase I was unsure about was *khashzik-makattzah*. I translated it as *the-three-and-the-one*, which Mendark took as a sign that the flute must be remade."

"I wish I'd known that before we began the flute," said Tensor. "That translation cannot be right."

"Then what is it?" cried Llian.

"It's not *the-three-and-the-one* but *the-three-in-one*."

"The *triune*," said Llian, feeling a chill run down his back.

"The triune!" Tensor echoed.

Llian opened his mouth but nothing came out. His stupidity had condemned Maigraith, and Karan. "Then I've made a terrible mistake. The triune *is* Aachan, Tallallame and Santhenar; *Maigraith is the instrument!* And the instrument will be lost in restoring the balance. Or . . . does it refer to Karan?"

"I don't know, chronicler."

Llian ran back up to the library. The Mirror had lured Maigraith to Shazmak. If the foretelling was correct she would die there and probably Karan with her. He spent the rest of the night going through his notes and his memories, but could shed no further light on the matter. In the early hours he put his head on his arms and dozed. Then, dreaming about *Mendark's Tale*, suddenly all the pieces clicked into place. In the chilly clarity of the pre-dawn he saw the deceit in the story, but which one was it, Mendark or Yggur?

He worked through the evidence until the dawn light came through the windows. There was little doubt, but he must confirm it. I used to be able to move people with my teller's *voice*, he thought. I'll push Mendark as far as he can be pushed, and then we'll see what happens. If that doesn't work, I'll try Yggur. *If I survive Mendark's fury!*

Llian sent a messenger boy down to find Mendark, Yggur and Shand, asking them to come to the library, for he had made a great discovery.

"What is it?" Yggur asked impatiently, the first to arrive.

"Something of great interest to you. The *greatest* interest," said Llian.

A spark ignited in Yggur's eyes, but he asked no questions.

Lilis came trotting in. She had come up to fetch something for Nadiril. "Stay for a while, Lilis," said Llian. "You may hear something of interest to Nadiril."

Eventually Mendark appeared, the last. "Well, what have you dragged me up here for?" He sounded crotchety. He looked as if he had been up all night.

Llian noted that Mendark had begun to age already. Two frown lines were etched across his brow. "I've made two discoveries," said Llian. "Here is the first. Tensor has put me on the right track at last."

"Tensor!" growled Mendark. "Already you stretch your credibility. Well, get on with it! Time is precious."

"My translation from *Tales of the Aachim* was wrong," said Llian. "The instrument was not *the-three-and-the-one*, the flute, but *the-three-in-one*, the triune. And it is the triune that will be lost."

"So the flute need never have been made," said Yggur. "I was right after all."

"Yes," said Llian.

"Nonsense!" said Mendark. "Anyway, we have it now and we will use it."

"But Maigraith has gone to Shazmak," said Llian. "If she tries to restore the balance she will be lost."

"*Restore the balance!*" Mendark's voice dripped sarcasm. "What a load of mumbo-jumbo! This confirms what I've long suspected—our master chronicler is a fraud. He is a teller, a *voice*, but there's not much wit behind it. No wonder he's incapable of making my tale."

Llian had had enough. "Do not call me fraud, you *char-*

latan!" He leapt up on the table. "Do you want to know why I cannot tell his tale?" he cried. "Because it is a lie Mendark made a thousand years ago and has cunningly reworked ever since. A deceit that has tainted the Histories since the day Rulke was imprisoned into the Nightland."

"Calm down, you two," said Yggur. "Llian, no one who was not there during the Clysm can understand what it was like. Rulke was too powerful, with his city-construct of Alcifer. If we had not stopped him we would have been enslaved just as the Aachim were. It was worth any price, even the Proscribed Experiments."

"And the failure of the Experiments?" asked Llian.

"He was too strong!" shouted Mendark. "Not even the whole Council could stop him."

"That's true as far as it goes," said Llian, using his *voice* on Mendark and taking pride in the reactions that he was forcing and, hopefully, the truths that would soon be revealed. "But that's where the great lie began. Would you like to hear the real truth, Yggur?"

Yggur was enjoying Mendark's discomfiture more than anything since the Elludore disaster. "Indeed I would!"

"I've solved the puzzle," said Llian. "The answer was in a letter written by Nivan of the Council just after the Experiments. Yggur, you were betrayed! Mendark forced Rulke into your mind."

Mendark looked shocked but recovered quickly. "Damn you!" he roared. "Cease your lies! There is no such document."

"How can you be sure?" Llian said softly, hoping Mendark would give something away.

Mendark did not. "Because I've seen them all!" he snapped. "I had to, to write the official Histories of that time. And the Council members since then have checked the documents. Yggur himself can vouch for that."

Yggur's disappointment showed. "We checked with the utmost care. Unfortunately none of us found anything out of order."

"That's because Mendark had already destroyed the evidence!" Llian said weakly. His bluff was failing and it was going to ruin him.

"The chronicler grows desperate!" Mendark sneered. "Fame is a drug he can't do without, even if he has to make up slanders to get it."

"Well, Llian?" Yggur said impatiently. "Let us see your evidence."

Yggur's trust in Llian had always been equivocal. Well, he would have to bluff harder, and his fate would rest on the bluff.

"Why is Mendark so sure about that, do you think? Because he spent a lifetime searching out and destroying every document written by that Council, but only after he had tracked down and killed its members, one by one."

"You're a liar!" grated Mendark. "This is treason and the penalty is death!"

"You deal a lot in that currency, don't you, Mendark? But you were not careful enough. This proves my argument," said Llian, producing the receipt he had found in the archives. "Nadiril confirms that it is genuine." He showed it to Shand. "It lists a document sent to Mendark by Nivan's sister, Uivan—*My Histories of the Experiment and the Taking of Rulke*."

"I remember Nivan," Yggur said thoughtfully. "She was one of the few honest people on the Council!" His eyes flashed fire at Mendark. "But I don't ever recall seeing *that* document."

"You haven't," Llian said softly. "It was never entered into the catalogue. Mendark destroyed it, and every other such document, as he murdered their authors one by one."

"You build palaces on foundations that wouldn't support a sandcastle," said Mendark, who was angry but unshaken. "Show it to me."

Llian passed the receipt to Yggur.

"The receipt is genuine," said Yggur, squinting through his glasses. "But there's still no proof of your charges. Produce the evidence or prepare to be charged with slander."

"I will produce it!" cried Llian, preparing to use his teller's gifts as he had never used them before. "Since finding this receipt I have gone through the archives. I found a copy of the document. It incriminates you, Mendark."

Mendark stood his ground, trembling with rage, but still gave nothing away. "Let's see the document!"

Llian's bluff had been called. He gasped for breath.

"You cannot! Guards," cried Mendark. "*Guards!*"

Osseion was through the door in an instant, followed by a brace of Yggur's guards. "Take him!" Mendark roared, pointing at Llian.

Osseion slowly stepped forward, but Yggur said softly, "Leave him be, Osseion. We will hear Llian. Chronicler, prove your case *if you can.* You have one minute."

"I don't even need a minute," Llian said arrogantly. "Look at this, Yggur! Mendark used you as bait in his trap. I have the proof right here." He leapt up on the table and with a theatrical flourish pulled a much-folded piece of yellowed parchment out of his shirt. Llian held it high, then thrust it in Yggur's face.

"Here, read Nivan's record aloud," Llian raged. "I'll tell you what it says. This is what Mendark did to you—"

Yggur took the paper and let the folds fall open. It stretched down to his waist. He moved the document up past his eyes. He stared at Mendark and slowly his face grew colder and colder.

"Be silent!" Mendark screamed. "I will silence you!" He

threw out his arm and a flame leapt forth, setting fire to Llian's coat. Yggur raised his own hand. Mendark sprang out of the way. Shand tossed Llian onto the floor, rolling him over and over to put out the flames. Lilis, standing quietly in the background, ducked to safety under the table.

Mendark, running backward, swung his arm in a circle. Flames burst out among the books and papers on the table, leapt to the bookshelf beside the table, to a rack of scrolls nearby.

"No!" Llian shrieked. He elbowed Shand out of the way but it was too late. The papers on the table blazed higher than his head. He snatched his bag of precious journals, on the floor beside the table, from the fire. The cover of one was burning but he stamped it out.

Mendark sent fire leaping into the bookshelves. Flames licked across the carpet between him and the company.

"A burning," he said calmly, standing back to stare at the pyre of blazing books. "A cleansing! The past is gone now. I have cleansed the Histories. My life no longer exists."

He watched until the conflagration reached the top of the shelves and roared up into the beautiful paneled ceiling, then walked though the swirling fire across the room and out the far door, which he gently closed behind him.

Row after row of shelves gushed flames; burning papers spilled out of boxes that had preserved them for centuries. The whole room was on fire. Llian wept for the priceless records that would be lost forever. He stood there, oblivious to the heat, the smoke and the cinders settling onto his hair. His clothes were still smoldering, his beard singed to stubble.

A bookshelf toppled behind him, sending a whoomph of fire licking at his trouser leg. The room was full of smoke. Flames leapt up between him and the door. He ran back and forth but could not find the way out. Everyone else had fled and he was trapped.

He was going to burn to death with the library. The teller in him appreciated the irony.

Llian sprang up on the table among the papers now burnt to ash, trying to see a way out. The smoke and heat were worse up here. Another bookshelf crashed down, the flare singeing most of his hair off. He smacked it out and sat down on the table, cradling his precious journals to his chest.

"Llian!" It was Shand's voice. Another voice called his name, Lilis. Llian could not see either of them.

"Here!" he screamed hoarsely. His throat hurt.

"Llian, where are you?"

He shouted and kept shouting, and eventually Shand, crawling along the floor, found him. "You fool, get down!"

Llian found that the air was better at floor level, though he could see nothing. "How do we get back out?"

"Lilis is by the door," Shand shouted above the roar of the flames. "Lilis?"

"Here," came her voice.

"Hold my hand, Llian." Crawling along, they eventually found the door, and Lilis, and safety.

"So," Shand said, supporting Llian on his shoulder, for he was choking. A silent Lilis gave him her shoulder too. "The villain is unmasked at last. We will find more evil afoot before the day is out. Come on!"

At the door Llian looked back. The heat hurt his eyes, but the burning library hurt much more. "This is all my fault!" he said, and would have wept but that the fire dried up his tears as they formed. "I pushed him to see what would happen. This is the result. Why did I not keep to my books and leave the intrigue to others?"

"Why indeed?" said Shand. "But at least we know."

Gripping his journals tightly, Llian closed the door behind him for the last time.

Already the halls were clotted with servants and retainers, running this way and that, hugging things too precious to leave, or treasures they might as well have if everything else was to be destroyed. A few servants dashed toward the library carrying buckets, but when they saw the size of the fire they dropped their pails and ran back again. By the time Shand and Llian pushed down the choked stairs to the main level, the ceilings were scorching.

They reached the great hall. Yggur was there, standing tall, calming the panic, dispatching guards up to the higher floors to rouse the sleepers and down to the dungeons to get the prisoners out. He did not try to take from the avaricious the treasures they had pilfered.

"What does it matter now? Better that anyone have them than they be destroyed, and no doubt they will be stolen again before the night is out."

The citadel was doomed, though most of the people from the upper floors were led to safety. Those that remained could not be saved, unless they chose to leap, for now the fire was licking even into the Great Hall. They raced outside, getting well clear, and shortly the great dome sagged, copper running in rivers, and crashed down into the ruin. They turned up the hill to Yggur's stronghold and the workshop where the flute was held.

"By the way, Shand," Yggur said, smiling fiercely, "don't ever play at cards with Llian." He took the folded piece of parchment out of his shirt.

Shand scanned it and burst out laughing. "An inventory of a carpet warehouse! You devil, Llian! It's lucky you were right, or not all of us together could have saved you."

Before they reached the fortress two of the Aachim guard came running down, shouting incoherently. One, a muscle-bound man, had a curtain of blood down his face from a gash on the temple.

"The golden flute is gone!" they cried together. "Mendark came upon us like a storm, blasted down your guards and ours, and got away with the flute."

"I didn't think, somehow, that he was going to commit suicide," Yggur said. "Where has he gone, Stentex?" he asked the Aachim with the bloody face.

"No one knows!"

Tensor appeared behind them. He looked shattered. "Well, Tensor!" said Shand. "Whose side are you on now?"

"Not ours!" Yggur said. "We don't want you!"

"Will you join with us in this chase?" asked Shand, ignoring Yggur. "Or do we fight each other all the way?"

Tensor took a long time to answer. "We will not oppose you, until we catch him. After that, the flute goes to the strongest, and I fervently hope that is us."

"Your word on it, Tensor?"

Tensor offered his hand. "My word." His voice was barely audible.

Like a whirlwind they made themselves ready for pursuit. Llian was clothed in new gear from the stores, for his shabby clothes were ruined. Still, a couple of hours had gone by before they uncovered Mendark's tracks and were ready to go after him. A message came from the west gate that he had ridden through like the wind and disappeared down the Tuldis road in the direction of Bannador, leading a string of horses.

"He has a lead of two hours and the best horses in Thurkad," said Yggur. "Unless he breaks a leg we won't catch him. Where has he gone? Why didn't he use the flute to make a gate?"

Shand had the answer. "Because Maigraith's departure

has so warped reality here that it's no longer possible to make a gate; not even with the flute."

"How do you know that?"

"*I know!* Now, at what place might a gate still be made when all others have failed? Karan's mad ancestor Basunez located it precisely. *Carcharon!*"

They rode like fury all day and through the night, stopping before dawn for a few hours' rest and to get fresh horses. At sunrise they continued. The company comprised Yggur, his timid little adjutant Dolodha, Vartila and another Whelm. Shand was there too, with Llian, a shocked and silent Tallia, Lilis, Jevi and Osseion, equally moody. Tensor rode awkwardly beside Malien, with four Aachim. Tensor forced himself, though every jolting stride was a torment. Malien's eyes were sick with fear and failure. The other Aachim were to follow. Nadiril had been informed but was not well enough to go on this hunt.

They rode through the day, changing horses again at midday. In the afternoon they came on a tall black horse, dead in the slush on the road; ridden to death. Tallia looked down at the great beast, and then away up the road.

"I might have done the same if the need was dire enough," she said, but Llian could tell by the set of her mouth how she felt about it.

Shand swung down to feel the beast's muzzle. "It's still warm; can't have been dead an hour. We're gaining." He hobbled back, grimacing. The hard riding had chafed the skin off his thighs.

They rode on and on.

The following night they arrived at Gothryme, stopping only long enough to give Rachis the news. Mendark had been through less than an hour ago, they learned, riding past at great speed without a hallo.

They reached the bottom of the cliff. Another beautiful black horse stood in the moonlight, its flanks covered in foam. It was quietly cropping the gray grass. They left their own with him and started up.

They made no ground on the way up the cliff, Mendark proving to be remarkably fit. "The people who helped renew his body have a lot to answer for," said Yggur, with a cold stare at Tallia.

She did not reply.

"I've got to stop for a rest, no matter what," gasped Shand when they were halfway up. The sun was rising. "We're too slow. Send someone ahead. Someone quick, and powerful enough to match him."

"I'll go," Tallia whispered. Mendark had betrayed everything she stood for.

"And I with you," said Jevi. They had ridden stirrup to stirrup for the past day and a half.

"And I," said Malien.

"I'll come too," said Osseion. "I have repudiated my oath."

At the top of the cliff the four hurried on, walking quickly at first, then breaking into a jog, then walking some more, jogging some more. Even so, they came out of Gothryme Forest in the afternoon to see that Mendark, in the distance, was halfway up the ridge to Carcharon.

Now they ran. Mendark began to jog but even his youthful body could not keep it up. It grew dark. The moon came out, a horned crescent. It was slow work here, the slope being icy. By the end of the long race they were but ten minutes behind and closing the gap. Tallia and Jevi were well ahead of the other two when they reached the steps. Mendark was silhouetted at the crest of the knotted buttress of rock, pointing down, then he disappeared over the top.

They had to climb the last pitch cautiously, for Mendark's blast had melted the snow and the steps were now icy. The last hundred paces were agonizingly slow. At the top they sprinted across the amphitheater but the race was already lost. Mendark was just going through the open door of Carcharon.

On they ran, down the dip and up the steep stairs to the front door of Carcharon. Past leering gargoyles, in through the doors, up the broken staircase, leaping over rubble and mounds of ice, up and up. Tallia and Jevi emerged together, gasping the inadequate air, at the very top of the tower.

Mendark stood in the construct-shaped depression in the floor. He had aged more, looking middle-aged now. He had the flute to his lips. The first strange, haunting notes emerged. Tallia put out her hand.

"No, Mendark . . ." she pleaded.

Mendark blew the tune in a higher key. They heard a frightful din as though the stones of the wall gnashed themselves together. Half a hundred tormented ghosts wisped out of the rock, Basunez among them. On even his angry face there was a look of horror. Then they vanished into smoke as the walls of Carcharon wobbled like custard. Jevi hurled himself at Mendark but was too late. When the distorting glass that was the space between them cleared again, the Magister was gone.

38

Ecstasy and Agony

Maigraith remained in her prison chamber in Shazmak, on parole. She was well fed and comfortable, but afraid. Afraid of Rulke, who came frequently, pressing her to ally with him, but overpoweringly drawn to him too. She wanted to help him, to be his mate, to share his bed. The unfamiliar urges frightened her. And she was afraid for Karan, who would certainly follow her here. Whatever choice she made the consequences would be ill.

Maigraith could have broken out, even with the Ghâshâd guarding her, but she had no idea what to do after that. If Rulke was telling the truth, what she knew about him must be a lie. Even so, his plans endangered the whole world, and Faelamor was a greater danger. But if she, Maigraith, did nothing, or if she tried and failed, that might be worse yet. So she festered, and fretted about Karan, and burned for Rulke as the hours passed.

That afternoon he came yet again. This time he looked

uncertain. Then, to her astonishment, he went down on his knees before her.

"Maigraith," he sighed, taking her hand. "I am struck dumb by you. We would make a perfect partnership. But I can't find the words to say what I want to say to you." He rested his bearded cheek on her knee.

The transformation made Maigraith hideously uncomfortable, for all that she was troubled by similar yearnings. This was not Rulke. It could not be!

"You must have had a thousand lovers," she said.

"I have coupled some," he admitted, "but I have only loved once since I came to your world. Even that was an uneven match, and a tragic loss."

"Tell me!"

"When Alcifer was complete, I wanted to populate it with children of my own species. Who was I to mate with? Yalkara was the only Charon woman on Santhenar, but that match was impossible. Not even to ensure the survival of our species would she pair with *me*. My only option was one of the halfCharon, blendings of Charon and Aachim that we brought here with us. That would be better than nothing, but I wanted my children to be full Charon. How could that be done? I wrestled with various sordid schemes. Once in my desperation I even thought to strip the eggs out of Yalkara, fertilize them with my own seed, and put them in one of the blending women. Shameful thought. I could not do it!

"I mated the blendings as a farmer might breed goats to bring out a particular strain. The result of those unions looked like true Charon but I knew they were not. I tried to punch a hole through the Forbidding and bring a mate from Aachan, but that failed too. Then I became captivated by one of my blendings.

"It was an unequal match, for I was age-old while she was barely nubile. Nonetheless, we were betrothed and she was ready to march into Alcifer and take her place on the throne beside mine. But it was never to be. The corrupt Council used her as the bait in a trap for me—their so-called Proscribed Experiments. Though I did everything I was capable of, I could not save her, nor in the end myself. She went to a cruel and pointless death, and I into the Nightland."

He spoke truth, her very soul knew it. Rulke had been greatly wronged. She looked into his eyes.

"So, what are *your* plans, Maigraith?"

"I have none. But I must know what you plan, if I am to consider allying with you."

"Have you heard the tale I told Llian in Carcharon? How we were treacherously cast into the void, and came out of it on the very brink of extinction? How a mere hundred of us took Aachan, to give us the chance to regenerate our species?"

"I heard the tale and was moved by it," she said.

He jumped up, to pace restlessly backward and forwards. Then he sat down again and took her hand. "Maigraith, I am going to trust you with the very fate of our species. This is the terrible truth: do you know how many Charon there are?"

"I imagine that you are legion by now, in Aachan."

"But we could not flourish in Aachan!" he raged. "We have never been fecund, like humans and Faellem, or even the Aachim species. Aachan was somehow hostile to us. We are less than a hundred now, and most are age-old.

"*We are so few!* Our hope became our nightmare—our sanctuary our prison. That's why we had to come to Santhenar. We had to get off Aachan to a world where we could increase. That's why I had the flute made in the first place. A perilous labor, but worth the risk if it could open the Way between the Worlds and free us from Aachan."

"But Shuthdar stole the flute," she said.

"And began the agony that still wracks us to this day. The Forbidding trapped us here—Yalkara, Kandor and I. Not enough to begin our species anew, even were Yalkara and I not mortal enemies."

"Why so?"

"An ancient feud between our families, which I will not go into. Anyway, as we were trapped here, the rest of the Charon were trapped on Aachan, slowly losing their potency, growing ever more desperate. Everything I've done since I came to Santhenar—*every single thing!*—had but one objective: to break through the Forbidding and bring the rest of my species here. To multiply before it was too late. To save my kind from extinction."

"That is not how the Histories tell it."

"Of course not! Every dictator, every tyrant needs an enemy to distract attention from his own shortcomings, and I made the perfect enemy. But enough of that. If you have no plans, at least tell me what your objective is."

"My destiny is to restore the balance between the worlds that Shuthdar broke, though I don't know how."

He leapt to his feet. "Then we are utterly opposed!" His fists were clenched into knuckled balls the size of grapefruit.

"Can we not work together?"

"To restore the balance necessarily means the end of the Forbidding. I might never find the Way then."

"But to breach the Forbidding is a terrible risk," said Maigraith.

"I have done it. I know how."

"And it was a disaster."

"A tiny flaw in the construct, remedied now. I've worked on my own weaknesses too. Maigraith, with the Forbidding gone I might never find Aachan again. Everything is so changed now, you see. I cannot take the risk. We Charon stand on a precipice, and only I can save us. Once I have brought them here it will be a different matter. I will gladly help you then."

"I don't dare to take *that* risk," said Maigraith. "The Mirror tells me that the whole void could swarm into Santhenar. That will be the end of old human kind."

"The Mirror lies!" he said furiously. "It is an Aachim thing, always trying to frustrate our ends."

"Not to me!" she replied, unshaken.

"Even to you!"

"Well, I am resolute." She stood up, her chin lifted, her back very straight. She looked him in the eye. "Neither can I yield."

The moment was drawn out. Then Rulke said, "I cannot allow you to thwart me. The future of my species is at stake."

"And my world! I am only one-quarter Charon, remember!"

"But it is quite dominant. You are more Charon than anything else."

"I am triune. The Three Worlds are my mother and my father, the four human species my children. How can I buy your future at the expense of another's?"

"This is torment!" cried Rulke "But if you will force me to the choice, I must put my own species first—no matter what my feelings toward you."

"What can you possibly feel toward me? You've only known me two days."

"I've been waiting for you for twice a thousand years. You have shown me an opportunity that none of us has ever had before."

"I'm sorry," she said, and she was. So terribly, terribly sorry.

"Then we must do battle." Rulke whirled and went out.

"And you will certainly defeat me," she said to herself, "for in my heart I don't want to fight you, and for all my words I can't impose my will on you."

A few minutes later he rushed back in. "Show it to me!"

Very tentatively Maigraith brought out the Mirror. "Sit beside me," he said. "Show me what it showed you."

She did so.

"And the message from Yalkara?"

That was harder, because it was a private treasure that she did not want to share with anyone. But then, Rulke was Charon too. She found Yalkara's message. Again there was that disconcerting gap in the middle. "See," she said. "It must be because I have not enough Charon blood in me."

"The Mirror lies, I told you, and when it is prevented from lying it cheats and conceals. Give it here."

He gripped the Mirror in his strong hands, staring deep into it, matching his will with its own. The image of Yalkara faded to nothing. The Mirror's surface changed from silver to gold and back again, then a torrent of light poured out of it, so bright that he flinched. "No, you don't!" he cried. "Not to me!" He held the Mirror high, forcing until his hands shook, then suddenly the face of Yalkara reappeared, and the writing ran across the bottom as it had before. But now the missing passage was complete.

> This is what you must do. Aeolior, the Mirror will try to deceive you, but your birthright is proof against it. Wear the gold and the Mirror will be forced to show true. The gold will protect you too, if you wear it. Never let it out of your hands. Never, never allow it to be used in any other way, for if you do the protection will be lost and the gold will become as dangerous as the gold that came from the golden flute. Do not be hasty. Spend a lifetime preparing yourself, and when you are ready, remember, take hold of your

birthright and look upon the Mirror, and it will show you what you must do.

Aeolior, fare well. We may meet some day if you succeed.

The bright letters faded away. Maigraith sat staring at the Mirror, devastated by her blunder. After all her careful thought, all her agonizing, she could hardly have made a worse decision if she had set out to.

"So!" said Rulke. "You could not have known, but now you do! You handed your birthright to our enemies, the protection is lost, and now Tensor has made the most deadly device that could ever be made from it."

Maigraith found herself shaking uncontrollably. "I didn't know!" she wept. "It lied to me. I can never trust the Mirror to show me what to do. Can you recover the secret from it, Rulke?"

"Not without the gold. Maybe not with it either, after Tensor's work."

"What am I to do?"

"You'll have to find another way. I may be able to help you when the time comes, if you will agree not to oppose me now."

"I—I will think about it."

He sprang to his feet and without saying another word disappeared out the door.

Maigraith drifted out of sleep, thinking about Rulke, yearning for him. That snapped her wide awake. I do yearn for him, she realized. I want him body and soul. I know it absolutely, no room for doubt.

She played back the scene of their first meeting here, revelling in the ecstasy of his remembered touch. Surges of heat coursed their way down her body at the remembrance. Even her toes felt hot. Every nerve was a heated filament inside her. Her skin was so sensitive that she flung off the covers and bathed in the freezing air.

There came a single tap on the door. Rulke! She flung on a gown hanging on the wall. It must have been one Karan had worn as a girl, for it was far too small. No matter. Maigraith went to the door, holding the robe together with one hand. The soles of her feet felt so exquisite that she could hardly bear to put them on the floor. She opened the door.

Rulke stood there, carrying a basket in one hand. She ached for him; she felt that she was melting inside. "Come in," Maigraith said, in such turmoil that she could no longer think to hold closed her gown. Rulke's eye touched on the swell of one breast. He dropped the basket just inside the door with a crash of crockery.

Giving him her hand, she led him to the bedchamber. She shook her shoulders so that the robe sighed into a heap on the floor.

"What happened to your shoulder?" he asked, touching the red wound with his fingertips.

"A Faellem arrow. It's nothing."

"I'll call my healer. Idlis will soon have you better."

"In the morning!" Sitting on the side of the pallet she attended to his trouser buckle and shirt buttons. His skin was smooth and dark, not hairy as Yggur had been. She found the difference marvelously sensual.

Maigraith drew him down to her. His fingers carved a fiery path down her throat.

"There is more than one way to do battle," she said, hooking her arm around his neck and pulling him closer to her.

* * *

That was how Faelamor found them. To break into Shazmak undetected had taken every atom of skill and experience in her long life as the greatest illusionist of all, for she was the first enemy Rulke had protected himself against. But Faelamor knew Shazmak, knew the Sentinels and the secret ways too. Even so, had not Rulke been so distracted she would never have achieved it.

She had entered not long after Maigraith, and in her nocturnal prowlings had been shocked witless to learn from the chatter of the Ghâshâd that Maigraith was here.

It had taken another day and night to find her, and Faelamor was worn out. Maintaining her disguise against the collective will of the ever-vigilant Ghâshâd was harder than ever. But she did it. She found the chamber that had once been Karan's, turned the handle without a sound and slid within. There was no noise, no movement. The apartment was dimly lit by the dawn light. Faelamor crept to the open bedroom door, easing her head inside. The first thing she saw was a dark foot dangling over the side of the pallet. Two feet; dark long legs, massive thighs half-covering slender legs that were pale by comparison—more the color of honey.

They lay asleep in each other's arms, still in the tangle of their lovemaking. Maigraith's hair was fanned across the gray silk of the pillow. Faelamor shuddered. Her hand shook. She almost cried out in her grief and loss. Had she a dagger she would have plunged it through them both.

Too late! Rulke stirred. She must not be seen. Faelamor pulled the tattered shrouds of her illusion around her and withdrew silently, creeping away to a distant part of Shazmak, there to lick her wounds and plot her next moves.

What game do they play? She risks much, to dally like that with Rulke, and so does he. Could he be smitten by

Maigraith, his judgment perhaps failing? I see an opportunity.

Why is she here? Surely to seize the construct for herself. But she's not strong enough. I broke her will myself, lest she come to overpower me. Rulke will sway her to his side, as he has already seduced her. They will try to open the Way, and might succeed too. I must prevent that, whatever it costs. I will make him a better offer.

Once the gate is made I will batter it wide open and shatter the Forbidding. I will break his toy to bits. Whatever is at the heart of it I will take with me so that it can never be remade. While they struggle to hold back the void we will be away to Tallallame at last. But I cannot do it at a distance. I must be close to him. *I must see the gate!*

In the afternoon Faelamor was discovered just outside the gates of Shazmak. She wore a submissive, hangdog air, as if trying to break into Shazmak had been a last desperate gamble that had failed. Rulke's eyes narrowed as she was led in, a small woman in white robe and sandals, with a satchel slung over her shoulder. He signed her to speak first.

"I have come to make you an offer," she said, her manner that of one who was despairing, failing. "Your sensitive has abandoned you, as my creature did me. I know you can open the Way, but you cannot trace out the shifting paths to Aachan or to Tallallame."

"You don't know what I can or can't do."

"I forced the truth out of Karan, how you used her, and how she failed you out of the cowardice that is her way of life."

For an instant Rulke looked perplexed, then he burst out laughing. "She did not fail me," he roared. "I failed her! There is no braver person on Santhenar than Karan Elienor Fyrn. Oh, this is rich! She has fooled you utterly."

"Whatever," Faelamor said, as cold as a glacier in her mortification. "Here is an offer. I can find the paths between the worlds but I need Maigraith to crack open the Forbidding. Or you! Together we can achieve all our aims. You know what we Faellem want—Tallallame, nothing more. We will leave this world and never return. You can have Santhenar and Aachan too, if you wish it. But we will guard Tallallame with all our strength!"

Rulke considered. Faelamor could never be trusted. Nonetheless the proposition interested him. His long searching had uncovered no other sensitive with Karan's particular talent. And Faelamor was right: to find the Way was probably beyond him. But Faelamor was wily and more treacherous than anyone. What she said was as much a web of illusion as what she did. The advantage of her own species was of paramount importance to her too, and anything she did to any other people to gain that advantage would bother her no more than a butcher frets about cutting the throats of a flock.

"There may be some small way you can assist me," he said, feigning indifference. "I will think on it. Meanwhile you must remain in Shazmak and submit to confinement. Take her away!"

Ghâshâd guards marched Faelamor to an apartment with only one exit, and guarded her turn and turn about. She submitted willingly, well pleased with her bargain. Not even Rulke would be able to hold her when her hour of most desperate need came—after he opened the Way through the Forbidding for her.

That morning Idlis had appeared, inspected Maigraith's wound, bathed it, dusted it with powder and bandaged it up again. Not long after, the Sentinels sounded all over Shazmak. Maigraith wondered what had caused the alarm but there was no one around to ask.

In the night Rulke came to her chamber once more. She was waiting for him. She had thought of nothing all day but what they had done in the night, and what they would do again tonight, if she had pleased him as much as he had her.

"Faelamor is here," he said, easing his way through the door with a heavily laden tray. "What does she really want?"

Maigraith felt a shooting pain in her chest. She lost her breath. How Faelamor could oppress her, even after all this time. "What did she say she wanted?"

He told her.

"I'm sure that is the truth. But know she hates and fears you, so—"

"She will betray me at the critical moment!"

"And do her best to erase you from the world. *Don't do it!*" she cried in anguish, feeling what his fate must be, feeling her loss.

"Why not?" Rulke asked. "On whose behalf do you speak?"

She couldn't say it. "I—I speak on behalf of the Three Worlds, if I speak for anything, and I have a better right to that than anyone." But she yearned for the Charon too—her people!

"Perhaps you do." Then suddenly: "Do you know who your father was?"

The question caught her completely off-guard, as he no doubt intended. That was something Faelamor had refused to speak about. "He was Faellem. That's all I know. He is long dead."

Rulke regarded her impassively.

She felt like screaming out, "Do you know? *Tell me!*" But she would not show that weakness. She fixed him with the same cool gaze as she had before. For all their passion in the night, this was a game and she had small skill at it. Far better that she be direct.

"Rulke," she said, wanting him desperately, and wanting to please him too, but not at hazard of the only world she knew. "I cannot aid you. The risk is too great."

Rulke tossed his head. The black curls quivered. His shirt was cut low at the front. The sight of his chest stirred her. I've got to have you, she thought. Taking his hand, she pressed her lips to it.

He groaned. "This is torment!"

"For me too," she murmured. "But this is the only world I know, and I care for it as much as you do for your own kind. I can't."

"Then we will talk no more about it." He stood up, but Maigraith held his hand and rose with him.

"Do you dally with me?" he asked roughly.

Maigraith was sweating. What did he really feel about her? She must know: at the price of her dignity, even her humiliation.

"I know nothing of coquetry or feminine wiles," she replied. "Let me be honest. I want you, now and forever. My body aches for you. Say that you feel the same, or not, and end it."

They stared into each other's eyes. What was he thinking? What was he going to do? Great Betrayer! Never trust him. The silence stretched out to infinity, until Maigraith wanted to crawl into a hole and die. Rulke looked stern, implacable, utterly dominating. Then she saw that his face was a mask, behind which he was just as afraid and uncertain as she was. She put out her hands.

Without taking his eyes off her for a moment, Rulke took from his finger a golden ring. She could have put two of her fingers in it. He closed his fist about it, squeezing and compressing until beads of sweat appeared on his brow. He spoke a word, baring his teeth in a grimace as a wisp of smoke trailed out the end of his fist. She wanted to cry, "No! Don't hurt yourself!" but was as much captured by his eyes as he was by hers.

Suddenly Rulke plunged his fist into a pitcher of wine, quenching the ring with a hiss. He pulled out his hand; opened it. The ring lay on his steaming palm, much smaller now. Spreading her fingers he slipped it on. It was still quite hot. It fitted her slender finger perfectly.

Maigraith held her hand out, gazing at the ring in wonderment. What could she give him in return? Then she realized that she had the perfect gift. Feeling in her scrip she found the red-gold ring—the single link of Yalkara's chain left over from the making of the flute. She stroked her ring finger around the circle, faster and faster, until the gold began to glow and resonate and sing like a wine glass.

"Hold out your hand," she said. She rolled the ring, which was now as soft as putty, onto Rulke's broad finger. The tone sank lower and lower, the glow died down and the gold hardened to fit him as perfectly as hers did her.

"I want you too, now and forever," he echoed.

"It is done," she agreed. "Forever!"

They reached for each other but just then something strange happened outside, a subtle working that was familiar, for it had the print Maigraith had learned when she and Faelamor had made the gate to Havissard together.

"Faelamor!" Rulke cried, and ran for the door. "Stay here!"

The door crashed shut. Maigraith ran after him but this time found the lock immoveable. She sat down on the edge of the bed, aching with unfulfilled passion. What was Faelamor up to?

Rulke did not come back and shortly Maigraith sensed a strange, throbbing warping, very powerful. He was using the construct. Surely he had not allied with Faelamor in spite of her warnings? Cold fear almost overwhelmed her. She had found her mate and now she was going to lose him again.

Already she could feel the mismatch in the reverberations between the two: the lack of phase that became a noisy chaos. Sometimes it abruptly died down to nothing, one canceling the other, while at other times it rose up in a shriek as one strangeness added itself to the other. Could they not feel it? Or did they not care? How could Rulke not care, unless all he had told her so earnestly, and all she had believed, was just a fabric of lies by the Great Betrayer?

I will not believe that, she thought. He must not fully realize. All that about the Way and the void—that is delusion. He knows how it used to be, but *that is not how it is any longer*. It's different now, and the Forbidding is decaying. We are in deadly peril and only I can stop it.

Maigraith focussed the entire power of her mind on the lock. Someone else might have used a little strength and a lot of cunning and worked the lock, but Maigraith had too much of the one and not enough of the other. The lock flew to pieces and the door into splinters. She kicked the kindling out of the way. Yetchah tried to stop her but Maigraith raised her fist. The look on her face was so terrible that Yetchah froze.

"Hinder me and there will be nothing left of you but a print on that wall," Maigraith said.

Yetchah was wise enough to obey. The Ghâshâd were superlative guards but Maigraith had grown beyond their power. She ran past, heading down to the vast hall where the construct was.

On the way she passed a band of Ghâshâd arguing furiously. She caught only a snatch of their conversation but it was enough to make her deathly afraid.

"Llian's telling was true," said Idlis, "and we must learn from it."

"We are sworn," replied a squat fellow who looked different from the others. He was short and stout, his legs were bowed and his skin was as gray as steel. His name was Jark-un, the leader of the band that had hunted Karan from Fiz Gorgo a year and a half ago.

"How can we serve a master who is such a fool?" whispered an elderly woman. Her eyes were a glassy yellow and one arm shook constantly.

"We are sworn, Tyone," Jark-un repeated, as if that was the answer to everything.

"Not to Faelamor!" Idlis said with a shudder.

So it *was* true, and now his most faithful servants preached sedition. Rulke was surely doomed. Maigraith hurtled through the marble halls and across the cobwebby walkways of Shazmak, terrified that she would be too late. She skidded into the Great Hall, searching for Rulke.

Despite her emotions, she could not but marvel at the genius of the Aachim who had created the vast space, with its walls soaring up to that curving, shell-like, transparent ceiling, the delicate stairs like wire and glass, the balconies and platforms that seemed to hang in the air. Then her eye was drawn down and down, to that black, strangely curved and impossibly dense object that was the very antithesis of Shazmak—the construct!

The construct was operating, warping the spaces all around. Even the light curved toward it as it went past. It had the opposite effect on the floor, which sagged beneath it like a sheet of rubber pulled down by a steel ball. Rulke stood tall on the top of the construct with his hands on the levers. Faelamor sat on a mat on the floor, her eyes closed, apparently linked with him. Maigraith knew what they were attempting to do: Karan had explained it to her. Rulke was trying to make a perforation through the Forbidding with his construct, and Faelamor to reach through it and find the forever changing Way between the Worlds, the Way to Aachan.

As Maigraith hesitated in the doorway, a curving, shimmering surface sprang into view, like an enormous soap bubble cutting through walls, floor and distant ceiling. It spanned the whole vast room—the Wall of the Forbidding made visible. Rulke twisted a knob. A lens of light sprang into being before the construct. He brought the lens to bear on the Wall, focussing it to a small circle.

Maigraith crept forward, but before she was close Faelamor roused, staring at her with those cold eyes that seemed to have no bottom to them. The Wall faded from view again.

Rulke cried out, "Leave her be!" but he was in the middle of his working and dared not stop.

Faelamor did something with her eyes and Maigraith was unable to stand. She had never encountered such an enchantment before and could not defend herself against it.

All her senses were cut off, except sight. She could hear nothing, feel nothing, not even her feet on the floor. The whole room looped the loop. Her inner ears prickled, then Maigraith felt the most nauseating dizziness she had ever experienced. Nothing was *up*, nothing *down*. Her nerveless legs collapsed under her.

Maigraith's head spun, far worse than being drunk. She tried to speak but could not remember any words. Her tongue snaked back down her throat. She clawed it out, gagging and choking until she could only lie down with her cheek on the stone, shuddering. Still her brain whirled.

It was a long time before she could get up but as soon as she did she was hurled down again. Maigraith pretended to rise, fell back with a groan, made another show, this time even weaker, and lay prone. She did not have the strength to face Faelamor. But Faelamor was using such prodigious forces that surely she must suffer for it.

Maigraith lay motionless on the floor, watching as the Wall of the Forbidding appeared once more. Faelamor paid her no more attention and Maigraith began to feel better, though now she was careful not to show it.

She had to husband her strength. Rulke was in deadly danger. He was dependent on Faelamor, for he needed her to find *his* Way. His plan was weak. He must have been desperate to try it. Once the Forbidding was opened, Faelamor could attack him and he would not be able to defend himself, for fear of the void emptying itself into Santhenar.

Maigraith gathered her strength, fueling her hatred of Faelamor for the chance that must come. All around her things were changing, warping and twisting in a way that was difficult for her to slide her mind around. It was a great risk she was taking. If she left it too long . . .

Then Maigraith felt the first faint stirring of another force, again familiar. Someone was using the flute. She recognized the dangerous aura first felt in Havissard. Mendark! The company must be near. She felt an overwhelming sense of relief—someone to share the load with. Then she realized what it really meant. The perilous flute might dissolve the decaying Forbidding completely. If that happened, nothing could save Santhenar.

39

THE SOUNDING OF THE SENTINELS

Tallia stood staring at the hollow. "Everything I've worked for these past eleven years is undone," she whispered. The Magister she had served so faithfully had betrayed her. Jevi was nursing a badly wrenched wrist. Osseion propped himself up against the wall, panting. The rest of the company straggled slowly in.

"Mendark, I did not like the tone of that flute at all," said Malien. "Beware!"

"Who will do the duties of the Magister now?" Tallia asked mournfully.

"You must!" gasped a red-faced Shand. "You've been his deputy long enough."

"He kept his secrets to himself," she said.

"Why don't you look to Jevi's injury," said Shand, clapping her on the shoulder.

"Jevi hurt?" Tallia shook herself out of her malaise. She fell on her knees before him. "Jevi, I'm sorry. What must you think of me?"

"I think you've suffered a worse blow than a sprained wrist," he said. "But nonetheless I would be glad to have it attended. And then . . ." he looked up at her and smiled, "I would help you with your own hurt."

Tallia threw her arms around him and wept. He held her, saying nothing at all, but when she'd finished he mopped the tears away, as gentle as ever.

"Don't let me go, Jevi. Don't ever let me go."

"I won't let you go, Tallia!" And then he surprised her, and everyone else, and himself too, by kissing her full on the lips.

"We've got to get to Shazmak," said Yggur, shaking his head.

"By the time we do it will be long over," said Malien, as Tensor dragged himself up the stairs, more dead than alive, supported by two Aachim. "Tensor, can you make us a gate?" The irony was not lost on her, nor on Tensor either.

"Hah!" Tensor fell to his knees, arching his back, trying to find the position that caused him the least pain. Finding none, he lay down on the floor. The breakneck pursuit had treated him cruelly.

"I swore that I would not," he said, "and I will not, unless it is the last hope."

"If we can't get there today," said Yggur, "it will be no hope."

"It would be quicker for you to walk there," said Tensor. "I'm no triune, as Maigraith is, combining the talents of all the worlds. Nor have I the flute to aid me. My first gate took me weeks. Even now, with help, it would take many days. You must look elsewhere."

"I have not the talent," said Yggur.

"Nor I. I've failed and Aachan is doomed." Malien cast herself on the floor in despair.

"Not yet!" said Shand. "I swore that I would never use

my powers again. But time cancels all oaths, if you have the misfortune to live long enough. Nor have I made a gate before, but I know how, and this is probably the only place that a weak vessel such as I could make one. Even so, I will need your strong shoulders and your broad backs.

"Tallia, I remember how you labored in Katazza to give Karan and Llian the chance to come back. You can use those skills here. You, too, Yggur. Tensor, advise me!"

"How will you find the destination?" asked Llian, fascinated.

"The destination is Shazmak," said Shand. "Look at the floor, molded in the form of the construct. *Like calls to like*—it will be a lodestone to our needle. Get out of the way, Llian."

Llian stepped back. Shand moved back and forth around the depression, eventually settling on the spot near the embrasure where Karan had sat when she found the Way for Rulke.

"This is a good place," he said. "Let me think about it for a while. I suggest we all eat and sleep first. Making gates requires a full belly and a clear head."

It was after midnight before they were ready to begin. People were sleeping everywhere. Shand roused them with a roar.

"Give me your hands, Tallia," he said. "Put your back to my back, Yggur."

Tallia stood facing him, gripping his hands, and Yggur at his back. Shand concentrated.

"What will you use for a focus?" Llian broke into his thoughts.

"Be quiet, pest!" Shand thundered, looking very unlike his shabby old self. Then, relenting, "Watch carefully now, if you would put this in your tale."

On one hand Shand wore the ring Yalkara had forged for

him as a parting gift. In the other he had his black staff. He closed his hands around Tallia's and drew them up till the knuckles touched his forehead. The ring began to shimmer. The shimmer spread to his hand, then his arm, enveloped his whole body and expanded until it came to the depression in the floor. It curved away around that to form a doughnut with a bite out of it.

"This is a special kind of gate," came Shand's voice, slightly muffled. "It will remain here, once I anchor it . . ." his voice was strained, "*Thus!* When you step inside and I reach out to the destination, it will stretch toward Shazmak, compressing the distance between here and there into just a few steps. But you will always be inside the gate as long as you stay within the light. Make sure that you do. Other gates send you and receive you, but in between the gates you are *between*, not *within*. Between is a particularly dangerous place to be, just now."

As they stepped into the gate, the shimmer became a golden-colored veil. A dozen questions trembled on Llian's lips but he was afraid to ask them.

Now they were all in but one. Tensor stood by the broken wall, looking out listlessly. Shand called but he did not hear. The outside world was thinning; he was barely visible now. Abruptly Shand tugged the ring off his finger, put it in Llian's hand saying, "Hold this tight. Don't drop it. Think of nothing!" and stepped out of the mist.

The veil abruptly changed color and began to pulse. Llian closed his eyes, clinging to the ring, feeling that any minute it might turn into smoke and disappear. The colors began to oscillate around the surface of the doughnut.

Shand put his hand on Tensor's shoulders. "Come, Tensor. We need you."

"This is the end of the world!" he replied.

"Do you want to end it in Carcharon?"

"It doesn't matter!" However, Tensor allowed himself to be led through the veil of light and Llian surrendered the ring thankfully.

"Why did you tell me not to think?" he asked, fearing that they might have been whipped to some inconceivable destination by the pure power of his thought.

Shand laughed. "Because it would change the colors."

"How would that alter things?"

"It would frighten you," he chuckled. "You have no power to direct a gate, Llian."

"Oh," said Llian. "But in the Nightland . . ."

"That was a set gate. Whoever stepped within it would go to the same place. Except Rulke, of course, who might direct it anywhere that it was possible for a gate to go. *Now cease your chatter!*"

Llian shut up. Shand put the ring to his forehead once more, the doughnut formed into a golden cocoon that began to elongate, first slowly then faster and faster, though strangely the other end did not seem to be much further away. In less than a minute it stopped extending.

"Wait!" snapped Shand, stepping to the leading edge of the cocoon, and through it into nothing. A minute later he reappeared.

Looking at the faces in the gate, Llian found no comfort anywhere. Everyone else was as afraid as he was.

"Come forward, to the edge of the light," Shand said. "But on your life, *no further*."

"What are we going to find there?" Yggur muttered.

"Calamity!" cried Tensor.

They went slowly forward, walking on the spongy base of the cocoon. Llian did not dare imagine what held him up in case it dissolved and dropped him into blackness. The distance between Carcharon and Shazmak was reduced to nothing, as if they stood at two ends of a great ovoid hall.

Mist was all around except directly in front of them. There, distant but brought to a clear focus, they saw a clot of darkness shot with red flame: *the construct!*

Karan moaned deep down in her chest—she could not help it. There was no strength in her arms and legs. She worked her muscles, praying harder than she had ever prayed in her life that the trap would go off. This was a desperately ferocious opponent.

The creature crept forward, another step and another. The trap must have failed. Karan flexed her legs. Now it was only half a dozen paces away, just a bound from those massive thighs. She looked into its eyes and fell into pools as wild as the River Garr outside.

The thigh muscles corded, the lorrsk inched forward and without warning sprang at her. Karan had lightning-fast reflexes but she could not even move, it was so quick. Or had it used some mesmerizing power against her?

The trap snapped down beneath it. Instead of leaping high and landing on top of her, the lorrsk's feet slipped on the down-swinging trapdoor and its leap went flat. It landed a body length away and her side of the trap dropped as well. The floor tilted right under Karan's feet—she must have been standing on the edge, but been too light to set it off.

The lorrsk flung its immensely long arm at her. Karan tried to throw herself backward but her feet slipped and she fell flat on her back with her legs dangling over the edge of the trap. The lorrsk's clawed fingers slashed between her spread legs, tore through the fabric of her trousers and caught the edge of the trapdoor.

Karan let out a terrified squeak—the claws were hooked through her pants just below the crotch. If it fell it would take her with it. She dropped the lightglass to scratch at the floor for any kind of handhold. Her fingers found a crack as the trapdoor dropped right open. The lorrsk fell hard, which forced a grunt out. Its joints cracked and the weight ripped the claws out of their hold. Karan was jerked so hard that the back of her head banged on the floor. She felt herself being pulled over the edge, then her trouser-leg tore from crotch to ankle.

The lorrsk slammed the fingers of its left hand into the crack between trapdoor and floor. This hold held. One claw was pulled right out, but somehow the creature managed to hang on. It swung there, its weight suspended on three fingers. She expected the doors to spring closed again but the weight of the lorrsk held them open. Karan was balanced on a knife-edge. She dared not move lest her legs pull her over.

The lorrsk groaned and thrashed about with its right arm, but couldn't quite catch hold of Karan. One slash tore through her other trouser leg, shredding it as well and rasping down the inside of her thigh like sandpaper. Karan flung her legs up in the air, certain that she was going to fall, but somehow her legs passed the point of balance and she rolled backward out of the way.

She scrambled to her feet, gasping. Would the lorrsk fall or get out? With a wild lunge it caught the top of the trap with one claw of its right hand, making an unpleasant scraping sound on the metal trap. It was going to succeed.

She jumped up, retrieved her glass and felt around in the recess for the trapdoor release. Then the lorrsk spoke.

"Hwix thrung? Hwix tjart?"

It was not just a ravening beast. It was a thinking creature, like her. It must have sensed her hesitation for suddenly her mind was flooded with images. She saw a cave lit by a tiny fire, around which was a family of lorrsk. One, just like the creature here, held a haunch of something over a fire, while its mate played with two furry balls, baby lorrsk. Another, between them in size, was inscribing what could only be characters on the wall of the cave. Outside, a pair of red suns glowed in a purple sky. Its longing for its family and its nest, for a place that was not the terrible void, flooded her with emotions. Was it trying to show that it was human too, or just to weaken her?

She forced the images out of her mind. "That may be so," she said, "but if you catch me you'll eat me!"

Her fingers caught a knob in the recess. The trapdoors sprang up again. The lorrsk wrenched one hand out but the other fingers were trapped between the edge of the trapdoor and the floor. It screamed, then stood up, stamping on the trap with one foot, trying to set it off again. The trap shivered but did not open.

Karan did not wait to see what happened. There was a tiny gap between the edge of the trap and the wall, the width of a narrow board. She ran for it, one, two, three, four steps on dangerously wobbly knees. To her amazement she made it across. Karan raced up the tunnel without looking back.

Behind her the lorrsk kept screaming. Had it got free or had it fallen? She wasn't waiting to find out, just pounded on with her shredded trousers flapping, until her knees would no longer hold her up. She lurched around a corner and ran head-on into a wall of rock.

Almost there! she thought, rubbing a bruised forehead. Back twenty paces was a side tunnel, if she could find the key to open it. She went back, searching for a hidden plate that would open the way up into Shazmak.

Here she encountered an unexpected difficulty. A vein of quartz pointed to the plate that must be pressed to open the door, but it was at the highest reach of an Aachim, much too high for her. She held up the lightglass, looking fearfully down the tunnel.

Her dismal foreboding was realized. Two pinpoints of

light appeared in the distance. She sprang high but could not reach the plate. She sprang again—not even as high as the first time.

Now Karan heard a curious wet plopping noise, like longdead fish being repeatedly slapped down on a slab. It turned the blood in her veins to ice. It was the lorrsk, and though just a dark shape a long way down the tunnel, she could sense it in her mind's eye as clearly as if a light shone on it.

She watched it come. Blood poured down its legs from the freshly opened buttock wound. Its huge hand-feet, wet with blood, slap-plopped the floor as it lurched stiff-legged toward her. Its long arms hung down, one hand dripping dark blood where it had torn the fingers off in its desperation to get out of the trap. The mouth was a toothed hole, the eyes bayonets fixed on her. Only death would stop it this time.

Karan backed across the passage, ran and sprang as high as she could. It was an awkward jump, since she had to hold the lightglass in her other hand. Her outstretched fingers slapped the side of the plate. The door did not open. Heel first, then fingers! She backed up, ran and leapt again.

Her elbow struck the wall, jarring the lightglass out of her hand. It struck the floor, cracked and went out. Karan dived for it and managed to coax a dim light out of the larger piece.

Flap-slap! Flap-slap! The lorrsk was close. It must have been as exhausted as she was, but it had survived the void. It kept on doggedly. Well, it wasn't going to have her! Her knees were wobbling as she prepared for another attempt, her last. She leapt, stretching up as high as she could go. The heel of her hand struck the plate, then her fingers, one after another. Something groaned behind the wall and part of it slid away to reveal a dark tunnel that led up into blackness.

Karan landed like a cat, twisted, and as the lorrsk swung its claws at her she ducked under its arm, reeling from the stench of its gangrenous wound, and up the passage. Somewhere to her left was the mechanism that would seal it behind her. One of the stones of the wall—for this was cut stone, not native rock, and therefore part of Shazmak—worked a counterweighted block. But which one? She couldn't tell in this light, and there wasn't time to experiment. The lorrsk rushed after her. It seemed to have found a new reservoir of strength.

She ran up the passage, slapping at the stones with her left hand, desperately hoping that one of them was the lever. She only hurt her hand. Ahead was a flight of stairs that led straight up—high steps meant for the long Aachim stride. Karan took them two at a time, sobbing and gasping, all the way to a landing where she had to rest no matter what. Her side was on fire and her breath came in huge, shuddering gasps.

The lorrsk had fallen behind in the ascent but it was still coming, one step at a time, with a deadly implacability. She knew it could keep this up all day, whereas another half hour would finish her. She moved on, step by step now, and every tread hurt more than the previous one.

How far was there to go? Karan had no idea—there was endless darkness above her. What was at the top? Tensor had not told her. She must keep going, just this step, just the next.

And somehow she did, up and up those endless stairs, a thousand steps and more. She climbed until the stitch in her side disappeared, and kept climbing until it came back again and would not go away. She climbed until the flesh of her legs felt to be melting, until every muscle was on fire and every sinew as tight as wire, until her throat burned and her stomach heaved bile up into the back of her nose, until her head was a serrated rasping pain that drove all thoughts away but terror. Finally Karan saw that she was approaching the top of the stairs.

She looked down. The lorrsk was only twenty steps below her, its feet still flapping the stone in that dead-fish zombie gait. The fur on its chest was matted with sweat and dried saliva that formed white crusts all the way down to its groin.

She looked up. Let there be a door, Karan prayed, and let it be open. She went up the last steps on hands and knees. Ahead she saw an iron Sentinel beside a studded metal door that was closed. If only it was not locked. She staggered to it and tried the handle. Locked! It did not even quiver under her shoulder. She was trapped! There was absolutely nowhere to go. Tensor hadn't told her how to open this one.

Sobbing and choking, Karan screamed out, "Help me, help me!" She called over and over again at the shrillest pitch of her voice, a shriek of despair and terror. She pounded on the door with her fists and kicked it with her feet. Finding a piece of broken stone on the floor, she crashed it against the door, making the metal ring like a drum. Behind her the lorrsk lurched up the last steps.

"What's that?" Rulke said, staring at Faelamor as if she had betrayed him. She looked as puzzled as he was.

"It is a device," he said. "Though not operated with much skill." He paused, sniffing the air. "At least, not with any skill that I am familiar with."

"But a danger to us both," said Faelamor.

Maigraith lay motionless on the floor, waiting for an opportunity.

Faelamor shouted, "I remember that aura. *It's Mendark!"*

"Quickly!" said Rulke. "Before he gets here."

Once more Rulke focussed the light-lens on the wall of the Forbidding. A larger lens formed there and soap-bubble colors raced back and forth across the surface. Abruptly the colors vanished and the lens began to wobble back and forth like a bag of jelly. The floor shook. The vibration became audible, a subliminal rumble.

"Now!" roared Rulke. As he spoke the whole shimmering Wall of the Forbidding rang like a vast gong and Mendark appeared on a balcony high above them, wrapped in a radiating sphere of light. The golden flute was in his hand.

Rulke swore, the construct swung round at his command and through the light-lens a doughnut-shaped pulse fanned up at the balcony. Mendark put the flute to his lips and vanished. The whole room tried to turn itself inside out. Maigraith choked up a clot of bile, that being all she had left in her. The Wall of the Forbidding whipped back and forth across the room, and though it was completely intangible, each time it passed through her Maigraith was wracked by another spasm of disorientation and nausea. Yet even in that desperate state she was capable of wondering how it could pass through her, but be the same on the other side.

The construct spun crazily, upside down, while Rulke struggled to control it. Eventually it answered his command again. He brought the machine down to the floor and sat for a moment clutching his stomach. With a supreme effort he stopped his guts from heaving back out of his mouth. Sweat drops on his brow were the size of peas.

Scarcely had he begun again when another interruption occurred. This time the gate meshed so smoothly that no one realized it was coming until the golden cocoon appeared in the distance. It stopped on the far side of the room and Shand stepped forth. Rulke recognized him this time. "Gyllias!" he swore.

Llian looked everywhere for Karan. He could not see her.

The construct drifted toward the company, giving off a ground-shaking rumble that made Llian's bones and teeth ache. The floor rose and fell beneath him like the swell out in the Great Ocean.

It was close now, and huge. The potency of it depressed the floor all around, like a saucer, and that deepened until the machine hung above the bottom of a bowl into which loose objects began to drift. The floor curved steeply down right in front of them. A low table with a wine flask on it slid past Llian into the bowl, the wine spilling and forming a trail of red droplets behind it. Before reaching the construct, table, flask and wine vanished in a puff of mist.

Even inside Shand's gate Llian felt the pull of the device—its gravity was dragging everything to it. His feet slipped on the suddenly slick surface.

Llian stared at the construct in terror and amazement. What wonders would Rulke do with it? He felt an urge to take up the offer Rulke had made long ago, to be part of the great adventure. Rulke was magnificent, no question of it. Who was to say that he was not the fittest, the one who would, in the end, do the greatest good for Santhenar? The temptation was overwhelming.

Someone put a hand on Llian's shoulder. Malien's voice was soft in his ear. "Be strong, chronicler." The pressure eased lightly.

"Gyllias!" Rulke said in a low voice. "Be careful what you do. I have Maigraith here."

"If you harm her . . ."

"We have sworn to one another! But this project is critical to my kind. I won't let anyone stop me."

"It is a perilous experiment," Shand replied.

The Forbidding began to flicker and fade, and just as suddenly flared bright again.

"It's decaying," screamed Faelamor. "Get it back, *quickly*!"

"One matter is more urgent," said Rulke. "I would have speech with Llian. Send him forth."

Ignoring Shand's warnings, Llian sprang right out of the gate. "Where's Karan?" he shouted.

"You tell me, chronicler," Rulke replied.

"She went with Maigraith," said Shand.

"Where is she, Maigraith?"

"I put her to sleep and locked her in the way station at the eastern pass," Maigraith said tonelessly. She looked quite drawn. "But she would be free long ago."

"Find her!" Rulke roared at the Ghâshâd.

"Help!" Karan screamed, over and over again. The lorrsk's head appeared above the top of the stairs. Step by step it lurched into view: chest, belly, thighs, blood-wet flapping feet. It stood on the top step, its mouth opened in a horrible rictus, then staggered toward her.

The hairy arms reached out. The claws extended. One mutilated hand was drenched with blood. Forcing herself back against the door, Karan hurled her rock. It bounced uselessly off one mighty shoulder. She frantically tried to think of some way to attack it, but there was no way.

One way! Snatching up another rock, she crashed it against the conical witch's hat of the Sentinel. Light burst out of it and it boomed, a hollow echo that made the door vibrate. Then it began to sound the alarm, an awful clanging that set her teeth on edge. It had not recognized her as an enemy, else it would have given her a disabling shock. She ducked in behind it. The lorrsk slapped up to the Sentinel, reached over and was given a blast that raised every hair on its body and sent it reeling off the edge of the landing. Karan prayed that it would fall all the way to the bottom, but it reappeared. This time it advanced slowly, deliberately. Karan knew it was over.

Springing, the lorrsk kicked the Sentinel with both feet, so hard that it was ripped off its mountings. Her leg was crunched against the wall. The device toppled, clanging more loudly than ever. The lorrsk took another discharge but had achieved its goal. Karan's cover was gone. She limped to the door and pounded on it with her rock.

Back it crept, flap-slap! flap-slap! Karan could smell the sweat, the gangrene, the blood. "Open up!" she screamed. The door opened and the curious face of a Ghâshâd guard was framed in the gap. She darted through, evaded the grasp of the first guard and the second behind him, and careered across the room into the uncertain safety of Shazmak.

The first guard cursed and slammed the door. It was smashed open so hard that one of the hinges tore off. The guard went flying across the room. The second, backpedalling furiously, reached for a rack of spears.

Karan fled. Let them fight it out! Ahead, another corridor crossed hers. Not knowing this part of Shazmak, one way seemed as good as another. She hobbled along the corridor, turned down another and up a third, one that was dimly lighted—probably not much used. A good distance along she flopped onto the floor and lay there until the hammering in her chest had died down.

That was a mistake, for when she tried to get up her leg muscles had seized. She tried to massage them back to usefulness. Against all odds she had survived. She was inside

Shazmak. She did not know where yet, but soon she must come into familiar ways. All she had to do was hide from the Ghâshâd, evade the lorrsk if it had survived and find Maigraith without getting caught by Rulke, or her enemy Faelamor.

Child's play, Karan thought, after what I've just been through. At that moment there came a hollow *Boom!* followed by a *clang, clang, clang!*. All the Sentinels in Shazmak were sounding at once.

40

THE NANOLLET

Karan played hide and seek with the Ghâshâd, and for all she knew with the lorrsk too, for what must have been a full day. She lost track of time after a while. Once she had been completely at home in Shazmak, and, inquisitive and mischievous child that she had been, had explored practically every part of that vast city. She knew the secret tunnels, the service corridors and ducts, the stairways that were practically never used. And she knew how to evade the Sentinels too, as long as they were not specifically set to recognize her. A few hundred, even a few thousand Ghâshâd, were nothing compared to the vast emptiness of Shazmak.

Once or twice she felt comfortable enough to hide in an empty chamber, lock the doors (she always picked one with two doors) and sleep for a while, though her restless sleep was filled with nightmares of running, hiding and always being discovered. Endless, cycling dreams, like this pursuit—like her life! Every time, after a few hours, the nightmares forced her on. The fear of being caught by the lorrsk overcame every other emotion.

And Karan grew increasingly afraid for Maigraith; that she had helped her into a situation which was beyond Maigraith's ability to manage. So Karan had to keep on, trekking her circuitous way across Shazmak, following her senses to Maigraith, *and to Rulke!*

After some time Idlis came running back. "The Sentinels don't show her," he said. "But I have a report on that incident yesterday, when they sounded in the abandoned part of Shazmak, where the door goes into the old mines."

"Go on," said Rulke ominously. "Where the guards failed in their duty and ran away!"

"No, something broke in from the mines. We found the leg of one guard halfway down the stairs, still with its boot on, and the brass buckle of the second. That's all that was left of them . . ."

"What else? Come on!"

"Bloody prints," said Idlis. "It was one of the beasts that came out of the void in Carcharon. A lorrsk, and it's somewhere in Shazmak."

"A tougher opponent than I thought," said Rulke. "Turn up the Sentinels so that not even a rat can get past them. Go after it, in pairs."

"Karan!" croaked Tensor from Shand's gate chamber, now swollen to cover half the room.

"What is it?" cried Rulke.

"I taught her the secret way into Shazmak, through the mines."

Rulke cursed. "Then no doubt it's had her as well."

Llian reeled drunkenly. Rulke held him up with one hand.

"She must have disarmed all the traps along the way,"

said Tensor, "else the creature would never have found the entrance."

"There were one or two prints in the dust," said Idlis, "but we can't tell if she came through."

"She's here!" Rulke roared his delight. "What a woman. Find her!"

Faelamor stood up on tiptoes, looking haggard. The construct swung around to face her.

"Sweat!" he said. "I may not need you after all."

The Wall boomed again. Tensor, tottering on his toes, waved a fist from which a feeble radiance spluttered. "You'll not have Karan," he shouted.

For an instant Rulke looked rattled. "Get out of my hair!" he roared, "or I'll finish the lot of you." He moved his levers, spun his wheels and a barrier slammed down between the cocoon and the construct, dividing the room from floor to ceiling like a seamless sheet of glass.

Llian hammered on it. It was immoveable. "Do something," he shouted, kicking the glass, but it proved impervious to everything, even Shand's gate.

Rulke had buffeted Mendark away to somewhere *between*—a place not unlike the Nightland. Mendark was not sure how to get out of it. He tumbled through space lit with fireworks, then put the flute to his lips again.

For all his study of the instrument—and he had spent half a lifetime learning about it, secretly hoping that he could make it again some day—he was not ready. The flute did not answer his playing as it should have. Mendark began to fear that he had lost the ability.

Hundreds of years ago he had gone to Saludith and stolen the one paper Nassi had written, that told how Shuthdar had used the flute. He'd had a dozen instruments made since then, as perfect replicas of the original as could be made, the only difference being that they were ordinary flutes from ordinary gold.

He had spent lifetimes playing them, mastering the intricacies of the instrument, until he was, in truth, one of the greatest flute players on Santhenar. But eventually, despairing that the golden flute would ever be remade, he had laid the instrument aside. Only after Katazza had he taken it up again, but his fingers had forgotten the paths of the notes. He was still very good, but he was no longer master of his instrument or of himself.

Well, in the next few hours he would either be victorious or dead. Probably dead, he told himself. He was not Rulke's match; nowhere near. But at least he would have tried.

Mendark put the flute to his lips and blew. A single pure low tone came forth—soft and gentle. It meshed with a curious weft of unreality, some constantly changing point beyond all known dimensions. A green and golden luminance grew around him. Even the air began to glow, so that the tendrils of mist undulating before him gleamed darker than the enveloping sky, and his breath hung like liquid gold in the brittle air. Mendark maintained the tone, the color, while he sought for the perfect contact. He screwed his courage tighter and blew the note up a fraction.

But in the middle of his playing he felt a terrible pang, a feeling that his world was in awful danger. The path that he had been seeking coiled away like a swimming snake. With an audible snap everything faded to rainbow shadows, though still his breath hung golden there. Then all became as insubstantial as the mist.

What had gone wrong? He blew another note and it was as if the flute had exploded in his face. He tumbled in the air. His teeth felt to be rattling around his mouth, though when he felt with his tongue they were all still in place.

Maybe the Mirror had lied. He had always been aware of

that risk. The flute would kill him. Maybe he would starve in this dismal place. He strained to the utmost, to recover the genius his fingers had once had. Putting the flute to his bruised lips again, he recalled to mind a high balcony in the Great Hall of Shazmak, a place where he could wait unobserved, and blew the gentlest note he was capable of. The scene shifted but it still showed only fog.

Mendark clenched his eyes into focus, whispered another note and became aware of a dark clot of power somewhere in front of him. It was the construct. He had opened a gate back into Shazmak, and before him was the enemy. It was going to be all right after all.

The scene resolved. Rulke was arrayed in black with a scarlet cape. He was standing astride his construct, the device potent beyond all potency, a coruscation of ebony and adamant, exuding power, terrible in its strength. Fear almost overwhelmed Mendark, but this time he would not give way to it. He settled like thistledown on his balcony, made himself as comfortable as his throbbing mouth would allow, and prepared to wait it out.

Karan had taken refuge in a larder in a part of the city abandoned since Shazmak had fallen a year ago. She found edible food there: the pickled and highly spiced meats that the Aachim so loved, as well as dried fruits and vegetables, and cheeses protected in wax. After eating until she could cram nothing more in, she tapped water from a glass tank, curled up on the floor and slept for a few hours more.

This time she was woken not by nightmares but by surreal sensations, as if something had shivered Shazmak to its foundations. It had to be the construct. Rulke must be attacking the Forbidding again.

Karan gulped another drink, ducked her head out the door to check that the way was clear and set off like a limping, hobbled wraith on the last leg of a marathon. Her shredded trousers hung from her waist like a grass skirt. Her senses had gone into overload, and occasionally she caught a glimpse, just fleetingly out of the corner of her eye, though it was never there when she looked directly at it, of the shimmering Wall of the Forbidding made visible.

The pit of her stomach alternated with fire and nausea. Faelamor was here already, Karan was sure. She could sense an unpleasant shifting of reality that might have been Faelamor, using her own mad instrument. Maigraith was in terrible danger. They all were. She had to stop it before it was too late.

Running around a corner Karan saw a group of Ghâshâd deep in discussion, at the other end of a long hall.

"The master is a fool," said one, "How dare he ally with Faelamor, his enemy for all time?"

"He is still our sworn master," said another fiercely.

"Well, I—"

She turned to run back the other way.

"Halt, Karan of Bannador!" someone shouted.

She raced back through the doorway, turned left and ducked up a narrow stair onto a mezzanine level. Peering through the rail, she saw them flood after her. Go the other way, she prayed, but of course a pair turned up her stairs.

She ran silently back, but before reaching the other side they topped the stairs and spotted her.

"Stop!" came their harsh cries.

Karan flung the door open and slammed it behind her. It was only a matter of time. And yet the overheard debate had given her a glimmer of hope. The Ghâshâd were having second thoughts about their master. If it were to come to a critical pass, and he did not have their help, there might be a chance after all.

She continued up the stairs, quite mechanically now. The

construct and the Forbidding had fogged her mind with multiple dimensions. How changed Shazmak is, she kept thinking. How familiar, for all the passages and stairs and towers remained. Yet inside, how different it felt. The uniquely Aachim feeling that had been here for a thousand years was quite gone.

She reached the top of the stairs, knowing that she was near her destination. As she brushed past a squat Sentinel, it sounded, jolting her with a shock that numbed her arm to the elbow. That had not happened before. She yelped and jumped halfway across the corridor. The next one she passed went off too, though she managed to avoid its charge. She began to despair of ever finding Maigraith. There was no way to hide from the Ghâshâd now.

The lens in the Wall pulsed like a beating heart, developing clear pinholes that slowly began to coalesce. Alarming bodyparts pressed against the transparencies—knowing eyes, serrated claws, leathery wings tipped with spines. Soon the whole center part of the lens was transparent, and a wild thing clawed at it, trying to get out of the void into Santhenar. Maigraith felt a black mist of foreboding settle over her. She glanced at Faelamor, who was resting on her haunches like a panther about to spring.

"Don't do it, Rulke! Faelamor will betray you," she said to herself. Maigraith realized that she was sweating all the terrors of the world for him. Her way became clear at last.

The construct drifted, passing between her and Faelamor, and Maigraith sprang up on the side.

"I will help you!" she shouted, holding up her hand.

Rulke reached down and heaved her up beside him. With a great roar of triumph he spun the machine around.

Faelamor attacked with a sickening hallucination that had Rulke clinging to the side of the construct. He did not lose control for an instant. "Do your worst," he shouted at her. "I designed it to buffer your Art."

He swung the lens of light directly at her. Faelamor screamed, the vision was cut off and she writhed as if pinned to the floor with a spike. She clutched her belly and groaned. She rolled from side to side and shrieked. She flung herself about in marvels of dexterity that would have astounded a gymnast. She did everything possible to get away, but could not.

Faelamor went absolutely still, then flung phantasms back at Rulke that had the company on their backs. The images hurt Rulke but she could not break him, nor escape the impaling light.

Finally she was spent. She stood still, her chest heaving, her clothes and hair plastered to her skin with sweat. She was just a small woman, showing her age in sunken eye and flabby skin, no match for the big man and the implacable device that he rode.

Her shoulders dropped. She was defeated. She looked terrified, but Maigraith felt no pity for her.

Then Faelamor looked up at Rulke, her face twisted and she screamed out a word, a screech of desperation. "*Mariem!*"

Maigraith felt a chill of horror, though she had no idea why. Rulke froze into a pillar of ice. The blood drained away, leaving his dark face a muddy color. He swayed on the construct, having to embrace his levers to stop himself from falling down. The construct lurched and its nose screeched across the floor.

"Where—did you get—that name?" he choked. His words came out in bubbles, as if he spoke through a mouthful of blood. "That is our secret name, the single memory of our life before the void. It is all we have left from our lost world." His voice became a scream of rage and pain. "*Where did you get that name?*"

For a moment he was paralyzed, and a moment was all Faelamor needed. She had screamed the name in desperation. Nothing else could possibly have diverted him. From the satchel over her shoulder she whipped an object made of red gold and precious ebony wood. It was a Faellem nanollet, a small instrument with a complexity of sounding boards and resonating chambers, and strung with layers of golden strings. She tapped one of the chambers and a low drone came forth.

Rulke stared, unable to comprehend. Then suddenly he did. "*Tallallame!*" he cried. "Tallallame, Tal-lal-la-me. Faellem. Fay-el-lem. Mariem. *Mari-em!*" Tasting the words. The names. Feeling the pain. The loss. The crime. The greatest betrayal of all—*genocide*!

He struck a knob with one knee and before Faelamor could use her nanollet she was flung backward against the barrier that kept the company at bay. She lay limp as a rag, still clutching the instrument, spitting blood.

"It was you that cast us into the void to die! *You!*"

"Not I," she said. Blood ran down her chin to soil her white gown. "That was generations before my birth."

"The taint has passed down the generations. The stink of it is on all the Faellem. You reek of it—you taunt me with it! I will torment you until the end of time. I will *never* let you go."

He spun a little wheel and the lens of light shrank to a pinpoint that drifted in an oval around her heart. Her gown began to smoke.

"Tallallame was your home too," she said. "Now it cries out for aid. Would you ruin your world for something done so long ago?"

"We were remade in the void. We have no world save what we take for ourselves."

"You are cruel," she wept. An oval of cloth fell from the front of her gown, but the golden skin beneath was unmarked.

"Cruelty we learned at the hands of masters." Rulke was quite implacable.

"Everything I did was for my people and my world."

"And what I do, I do for my own species. Now you die, Faelamor. And then you die again, and again, *and again*!"

He drew back his levers. "Rulke," Maigraith said urgently. "Remember that the nanollet was made from the gold of the golden flute."

Again Rulke hesitated, but Faelamor's helplessness was another trick and she was too quick for him. She struck a desperate chord, a mournful wail that ended in a whip-crack, the sound of the Forbidding trying to tear itself apart.

The transparency starred in the middle and, with a screech like air escaping from the stretched mouth of a balloon, a tear appeared in the middle of the lens.

"No!" he screamed. "That gold is corrupt; you must never—"

Faelamor struck another chord. "You give me no choice," she whispered.

"It will destroy us all. It will be your nemesis," said Rulke.

The world turned inside out. The internal spaces of the construct became its outside. A vent opened in the Forbidding: gaping, uncontrollable, madly swelling and contracting. A multitude of creatures clawed at the opening, then it snapped shut again. Rulke appeared, disappeared, reappeared, inside the construct and then out of it. He wheeled through the air, crashed down on his back and did not move.

Maigraith scrabbled across the floor, touching his brow with moist fingers.

The vent tore open again and the boldest of the creatures thrust its head into the gap. It was the size of a small barrel, with a red horny crest on top, tipped with spikes.

Rulke groaned a word. The construct radiated a soft light on the vent. The creature screeched, jerked its head back and the puncture sealed itself over. Something clattered on the floor: an amputated horn, a bloody claw. The Forbidding tried to shake itself to pieces. Rulke staggered toward the construct like a drunken man, and with Maigraith's help gained it. Faelamor struck another chord on the nanollet. Another vent opened in the Forbidding, and another. Rulke swung his lens of light and Faelamor was hurled between the double staircases that spiraled around each other all the way up to the translucent ceiling of that vast hall. She crawled into shelter, her nose dribbling blood.

Llian, Shand and the rest of the company beat their fists on the glass barrier. All they could do was watch. A horde of creatures now scratched at the vents. If they broke through, everyone in Shazmak would die.

"Do something!" Llian screeched at Yggur.

"We've got to get in there," said Tallia. "Lend me your strength again, Yggur."

"There's nothing I can do," said Yggur. He had already fired one of his colored blasts at Faelamor, but it had refracted unpredictably through the barrier, destroying several treads of the glass staircase. Molten glass made a fringe of threads that hung down from one step. "If I try again I might kill Maigraith. *Maybe I should*, since she's gone over to my enemy."

Shand seized him by the collar and shook the big man.

"I'm sorry, Shand," Yggur said meekly, his fury evaporating again. "Take no notice. My rage is all that's left of me."

"Look!" called Lilis. "It's Karan." She pointed to a doorway, where Karan was just staggering in. Karan looked over her shoulder then stumbled away as a dozen Ghâshâd came after her. Her hair was wild, her face scarlet.

The sight of Karan set Llian mad with longing. Swinging a heavy metal chair back over his head, he smashed it against the barrier with all his strength. It bounced back just as hard, nearly knocking his head off. He skidded across the floor on his knees while the chair went the other way. He looked up at Shand and Malien.

"You'll not break it," they said at the same time.

They tried everything they could think of, but the barrier was impervious. They could not get round it either, for all the exits on their side of the room were blocked by the same material. They were neatly trapped.

41

Extinction with Dignity

Karan lurched into the Great Hall and saw Rulke across the room. He looked nearly as bad as she felt. Maigraith was next to him. She was safe! But Karan's relief was changed to incredulity when Maigraith gave Rulke her shoulder and they scrambled up onto the construct. What on earth had happened?

"What are we going to do?" she heard Maigraith shout.

Karan followed Maigraith's pointing arm. The clawing and scratching at the Wall was deafening. She dashed around the side of the central stairs and was brought up short by the glassy barrier, and by the sight of Llian banging on it. He was in a frightful state. Practically all his hair was gone, what was left was frizzed up in a clot on one side of his head, and his beard was singed to stubble.

In her state it was all too difficult to take in. Llian was shouting at her and pointing over her shoulder, but she could not make out what he was saying. Going to the barrier, she pressed her hands against the outline of his. Malien came up beside him, screaming through the glass. Karan knew what *she* was saying. "Stop Rulke, whatever it takes!"

"I'll try to hold it!" Rulke shouted to Maigraith.

"Maigraith," Karan screamed. "What are you doing?"

"It's Karan!" Maigraith cried.

Rulke sent the construct soaring her way. Karan watched the black object hurtle toward her. She couldn't run any more.

"Karan," Maigraith yelled. "You've got to help us!"

Karan backed away, thinking that Rulke had taken control of her. The company hammered frantically on the barrier. What were they trying to tell her?

"Karan!" Maigraith roared. "Faelamor will destroy the world."

Karan looked from Llian to Malien, to Maigraith, to Rulke. How could she decide?

"She's lying!" shrieked Faelamor from up the stairs. "She's in league with Rulke."

If there is one person I'll never trust it's her, Karan thought. Even Rulke is a better choice.

She held up her hands, and knew as she did that Malien could never forgive this betrayal. Maigraith hauled her up the side, sobbing and throwing her arms around her.

"No time for that!" cried Rulke. "Karan, show us the way to Aachan, before it's too late."

Faelamor began to crawl up the pearly stair like a decrepit old washerwoman. "What about her?" said Maigraith.

"I haven't the strength."

Karan was remembering the horrible finale to her previous attempt to find the Way. "I can't do it!" she gasped.

"What will *they* do to Gothryme when they get in?" Rulke said, pointing to the Wall. "And never doubt that Faelamor will let them in. If you truly can't do it, we are all finished. But if there is an ounce of hope in you, I beg you, try! I will support you."

"You said that before," Karan murmured. Her eyes slid past his gimlet eyes and fixed on Llian, who had his hands flat out on the glass barrier in an attitude of desperation. His eyes were as wide as soup bowls.

"I'll try," she said, "but I have had . . . something of a day already. I'm a little tired."

Gripping her hands, Rulke gave her a fiery kiss on the mouth that set her lips ablaze. "And so am I," he said with a fierce grin, "but we'll do our damnedest. Are you ready?"

Her throat was dry. Karan reached for a flask sitting in an open compartment, gulping the sweet cordial down. "I'm ready!" she gasped, though she felt as wobbly as a custard. She linked to Maigraith and to Rulke, and the link with Maigraith was like being encased in diamond. Karan felt utterly protected, sheltered and cared for—nothing could harm her this time.

Rulke cried out through the punctured Forbidding for Aachan, for the Charon. His longing reverberated across the void, leaping from Way to Way with Karan, secure in the knowledge that Maigraith guarded them back in Santhenar. And bolstered by Maigraith's unique triune talents, developed from the decades of training with Faelamor and her own urgent need to meet her Charon ancestors, they found it.

Who's there? The voice spoke in their heads, so clearly that she might have been beside them on the construct. It was a deep woman's voice with a rasp to it as if she had lived her life in smoky rooms. *Rulke, can it be you?*

"*Yalkara!*" Maigraith whispered across the link. She knew this voice.

"Yalkara!" Rulke cried harshly. "I can't see you. Show yourself. I'm desperate!"

He conjured a bubble out of the wall of the Forbidding. It floated in the air before them like a shiny metal ball, and the whole universe seemed to be reflected in it, curving away in all directions to infinity. The reflections in front of them misted, cleared and a face appeared that Maigraith knew almost as well as her own. It was Yalkara, but she was much older than she had appeared on the Mirror. The long hair was completely silver now. Yalkara's lips moved but her voice spoke in their heads.

"Yalkara!" Rulke screamed. "Call the Hundred together. Our time is now, but the precipice yawns."

Who is this with you? Yalkara whispered. *Can it be her?*

"I am Maigraith," she said. "Aeolior's daughter. Faelamor mated her to a Faellem to make a triune—me! Aeolior is dead. Rulke and I have sworn to each other forever."

Maigraith—Aeolior! said Yalkara. She looked stunned.

"And here is my friend Karan, triune too." She pointed at Karan.

So like Elienor, said Yalkara.

"Quickly," Rulke said. "The Forbidding is decaying and must fail. Faelamor has made a nanollet device, and Mendark a new flute from your gold."

"But I warned—"

"The Twisted Mirror!" snapped Rulke. "It would take too long to explain. Besides, I have a device that surpasses them all—my construct!" His voice rang with pride. "I can bring you here at last, and ensure the survival of our species. But I don't dare open the Way from here, not with Faelamor rampant. Can you open it from Aachan and bring yourselves to my gate?"

You have come at the last possible moment, she replied.

We despaired and were near to finishing ourselves. It won't be easy, but I think I can do it.

Together they made rudimentary gates at her end and his, but Rulke kept his gate firmly closed.

I will seek out the Way to Santhenar from this end. These are very unstable gates, Rulke. Can't you hold the Forbidding any better than this?

"I'll be lucky to hold it at all," he said grimly. "Faelamor's nanollet is made from the golden flute."

She's insane!

"Or desperate! Come quickly! It's going to be a harsh passage. Send the most important first, because it'll get worse."

Only ten of us are still fertile. Four men and six women. Guard them well. Without them we are extinct.

Rulke changed his mind. "No! Send the strongest. Protect the fertile ones till the last." As he spoke, a burst of static misted over the mirror globe and Yalkara faded.

Rulke used the construct to fashion a chamber in the Wall, as far away from the lens as possible. It had the form of a silver egg, with a round door at the front like a porthole.

I have traced back the Way to Santhenar, said Yalkara. Something rang against his chamber like a hammer on an anvil.

"I can barely hold it." Sweat dripped off his chin. "I've lost them! No, it's all right, *it's all right!*"

He banged the porthole open and a woman appeared in the chamber. She was naked, as was everyone who passed between the worlds, limp and defenseless. The chamber clouded over as something tried to force the door closed again. Rulke worked feverishly at his controls. "Run, get them out while I hold it!" he said to Maigraith and Karan. "Ah, this is hard."

Maigraith and Karan dragged the woman out, and seven more Charon after her. It was a struggle to haul them over the lip through the small porthole, for they were big people. Maigraith's shoulder was bloody before they had finished. The arrow wound had broken open again.

Each Charon was as bewildered and helpless as a baby. The passage had shaken them. But Rulke was exultant, as were the faces of the other Charon in the reflecting sphere.

"It's getting harder to hold!" Rulke shouted to Yalkara. "Better come quickly, if you're coming. Maigraith, hold this." She climbed back up while he sprang down from the construct and lifted the last two out, both men, as gently as if they were his own children.

The Charon lay scattered over the floor, stunned from the brutal journey. "We've got to get them into the protection of the construct. Come through!" he shouted to Yalkara, whose face had just reappeared on the reflecting sphere.

We're almost ready, she sighed. *Oh, this is the greatest day of our lives!*

"And mine," said Rulke. His smile stretched from one side of his face to the other. His eyes shone like indigo suns. "We've waited four thousand years for this," he said to Maigraith.

Rulke picked up the first of the Charon under his arms, a woman as tall as he was, big in the breast and the hips. She groaned and tossed her long black hair. Her bare feet slithered across the tiles.

At that moment Faelamor stood up high on the central stair. Supporting herself on the glass rail like a crazed witch she played a veritable symphony of sounds on the nanollet—an achingly haunting tune that brought tears to Karan's eyes, a lamentation for the death of a world.

What? screamed Yalkara. *What's that? No, Rulke, quickly—*

Rulke spun around. High in the air another lens was forming in the Forbidding, all by itself.

The lens solidified into an oval gate that shone like metal. "No!" Rulke moaned, dropping the woman. "Maigraith, get them into the construct. I've got to stop her."

He ran in leaping bounds toward the construct but Faelamor brought down her final deception, the greatest of her long life. Suddenly the floor moved under Rulke as if he was running on a treadmill. He ran harder but still made no progress.

"The construct may be proof against my enchantments," sneered Faelamor, "*but you are not!*"

Rulke pounded away, running faster than any human had ever run. For a few seconds he seemed to be gaining, then the floor swept him backward again.

The oval gate opened and a creature sprang through. It was almost as tall as the construct, with huge intelligent eyes and clawed wingtips. The wings soared over it, casting it into an impenetrable shadow.

"What is *that*?" cried Maigraith.

"It looks like a thranx," Karan muttered.

Rulke abandoned the fruitless chase. "It's a kind of a thranx," he said, his chest heaving. "*The worst kind!*" His clothes dripped sweat which puddled on the floor. "One of the most fearsome creatures in the void. It is violent, but clever too. And I don't even have a weapon."

The thranx, a female, braked its fall with a snap of leathery wings and landed skidding on the floor.

"Kill them," screamed Faelamor, now on a balcony high above. "Kill them all and you can have your own world."

The thranx cracked its wings again and headed with soaring bounds toward the ten helpless Charon. The head of another thranx emerged through the gate. It flapped down in the same direction.

Karan disappeared out a side door. "I can't blame you," Rulke sighed, but a moment later she came racing back with a horde of Ghâshâd behind her. One of them, the squat one called Jark-un, cried, "Master!" and flung a long sword to him.

Plucking it out of the air, Rulke leapt at the first thranx. It towered over him. The thranx was blindingly fast. It flicked a wing at him and the spiked leading edge tore open his shoulder.

Rulke sprang back and to one side, stabbing at the thranx's plated knee, aiming for the joins. His sword tip skated across armor as hard as metal. The thranx kicked him in the hip, knocking him off his feet. Rulke skidded across the floor, desperately trying to hold on to his sword.

Over near the door a band of Ghâshâd had begun to attack the second thranx but they were hopelessly outmatched. One lay dead already. A dozen others pressed the attack, then the thranx spun around, ripped a length of rail off a side stair and swung it like a scythe. Half a dozen Ghâshâd were bowled over, and not one of them got up again. The thranx sent the twisted rail flying across the room at Rulke's back, then leapt among the helpless Charon.

Karan caught sight of Faelamor's impassive face. It showed nothing—neither joy nor triumph, just a deadly implacability.

She doesn't care about any of us, Karan thought. Another band of Ghâshâd surrounded the second thranx. They fought with more cunning than the first group, for they managed to put a spear in the back of the creature. The injury did not hinder it noticeably.

Maigraith and Rulke fought side-by-side but were surely being defeated. Rulke bore half a dozen gashes and was tiring rapidly. Maigraith's thigh was torn open to the knee, her injured shoulder useless. The thranx seemed to be unharmed. High up Karan saw a third thranx at Faelamor's gate, but it was having trouble getting through.

Karan knew it was futile for her to attack such a creature, but by circling round she had come right up to the construct. Suddenly inspired, she scrambled up its curving flank and flopped into the seat. In front of her was a bank of six levers, a console with glowing yellow plates, several small wheels and a shrubbery of colored knobs. On the floor five crescent-shaped pedals protruded in a row. She remembered which levers Rulke had used to control it. What she did not know was how he used his mind to direct it.

Here goes! Stretching her left foot forward, she stamped on the left-hand pedal, having to come right out of the seat to do so. The machine was not designed for someone as small as she. The construct shuddered. She eased back the central pair of levers. It bucked, whined but did not move. *Forward!* she sent frantically. Colored lines appeared on the glowing plates. Lights flashed from one end of the spectrum to the other. *Why won't you go, stupid machine?*

The construct tilted back and took off at a steep angle. Karan hung on desperately, in danger of being flung over the rear. Now it began to climb vertically, rocketing toward the distant ceiling. A siren went off in her ear. *Use the levers!* She pushed one forward.

The construct turned on its side, veered crabwise across the room and caromed off the glassy barrier behind which the company watched helplessly. Karan hung on by a finger. Her knee hit a blue knob, evidently a kind of throttle, for the machine slowed down, giving her a chance to experiment with the second lever. The construct resumed an even keel, drifting slowly in the air. High above, the third thranx was coming through the gate.

Her airborne chariot curved around the room, heading up toward the balcony from which Faelamor had wrought so much damage. Faelamor's hands were moving frantically, casting a deception that Karan knew would render her helpless. From this high, the fall would kill her.

She wrenched the blue knob right out. The construct took off as if inertia had never been discovered and shot toward the pair of helically coiled staircases. The siren blasted again. Karan was paralyzed, afraid to touch the levers. At the last moment her hand moved by instinct, nudged one lever sideways, the construct altered course fractionally and shot between the twin spirals, almost taking her head off. Out the other side it roared up toward Faelamor's balcony.

Before either of them could react, it smashed into the balcony from underneath, knocking most of it away. Karan's head hit the flaring hood, she blanked out momentarily, but recovered to find the construct spinning crazily across the room. She lost sight of Faelamor. The battle down below came into view.

Rulke was down. Maigraith stood over him, a frail forlorn figure overwhelmed by the might of the thranx. Karan tried to point the construct at them but the controls no longer seemed to work. Maybe the blow had robbed her of the capacity to control it. The siren emitted high-pitched screams, the lights were a firework display, the glowing plates went mad. The machine flopped across the room like a beached fish. She approached the melee, watching with horrified eyes as the thranx drew itself up for the death blow. Karan pushed her levers back and forth uselessly, feeling her own despair and fury building, then the construct gave a lurch, crossed overhead and all the lights went out.

It dropped out of the air, crushing the thranx down flat. Karan fell off, landed like a cat and scrabbled across on hands and knees, terrified that she had killed Maigraith and Rulke.

"Are you all right?" she choked, dragging her friend out from underneath.

Maigraith helped Rulke up. "Just!" She was staring at the upcurving base of the construct above her. "You missed us by a finger," she said in an awed voice. "How did you manage it?"

Karan did not answer. She watched the death throes of the thranx, its wing spikes rattling across the corrugated underside of the construct. The ruined wing flexed and retracted, over and again.

Rulke could hardly stand. He gripped Karan's shoulder like a vice, wordless thanks, then staggered off to find the other Charon.

The second thranx lay still with a dozen spears in it, front and back. Many of the Ghâshâd were dead. "Another few seconds and it would have been too late," said Rulke. "Thank—"

They turned around the body of the thranx, its bulk and upturned wings shielding them from what was beyond. The Charon were tattered and torn like a tiger's playthings. All ten were dead.

Rulke crushed his fists together, the Charon way of grief. For a full minute he did not move. Then his face grew as cold as the continent of ice at the uttermost pole. "I will avenge you," he ground out, "no matter what it takes! Even if I have to come back from the dead to do so. You will rue this deed for a hundred centuries, Faelamor! I curse you and your descendants *until the end of time itself!"*

Reaching into Maigraith's coat, he plucked out the Mirror and wrested it to his will. "Let her try to use that ever again."

They looked up. Faelamor had disappeared from the smashed balcony. Her gate was gone too, but on the floor directly beneath lay the body of the third thranx, still twitching among the shreds of its vast wings. At least, all of it from the hips up.

"The gate must have closed when it was halfway through," said Karan, shuddering.

The thranx writhed, one wing flapped like a banner in the wind, and died.

With a flick of his wrist Rulke woke the globe once more. "You saw?" he whispered to Yalkara. She did not need to answer—it was written in the ravines of her face.

"One last try," he said. "Come all of you, at once."

It is over, Rulke, Yalkara sent.

"No, I have control back now."

You're too late. They were the last! The rest of us are as barren as the tombs that you will lay them in.

Rulke was trembling. "What about you, Yalkara? You're the youngest. You've proven your fertility."

Look at me, Rulke! I gave away half my life, and alas my fertility went with it. I am an old woman now. Our extinction is inevitable.

"*No!*" Rulke screamed. "No! It cannot be. I will not allow it. Come to Santhenar. There are ways. We can harvest their eggs and seed, and plant them—"

A host of Charon appeared, reflected in the brilliant curve behind her. They were called the Hundred, though barely seventy remained. They were all old now. *No!* they said as one. *Some things are not meant to be. Let us at least face extinction with dignity.*

"I will do it anyway," he said in an aside to Maigraith, "if I can just get them here." He looked into Yalkara's eyes. "Please come."

No, Rulke, said Yalkara. *What time we have left will be bitter enough without spending it on a foreign world. Come back to Aachan. We will go to our extinction together.*

42

The Thrice Betrayed

Faelamor crouched high on the other side of the hall, out of sight. Karan's onslaught on the balcony had almost sent her to her death, but her will kept her hanging on. At least the Charon were dead, one threat eliminated. I am almost there, she told herself, and began her own working.

The mist that enveloped her extruded another lobe, which extended outward. At the other end it stopped before a crowd of Faellem, gathered together in Elludore, forty leagues and more away. They could have been a colony of minds, so regular was the linking. They made a perfect, translucent sphere, flecked regularly on the outside with each will, slowly revolving one way and then another, and in the center a greater spot, a darker will than any, directing the whole. Faelamor had gone on to the next stage of her plan, the linking of all the wills of the Faellem.

"Not even Rulke can stand against this force," she said to her people.

The Faellem stepped between the trees and into the pale

green light, that misty gate-lobe, and out of that into Shazmak. They gathered on the platform, waiting for Faelamor.

"We should never have doubted you!" they cried. "Show us the Way, Faelamor. Lead us home to Tallallame!" There was not a dry eye among them.

"And Maigraith lives. She did not harm us after all," said Faelamor. "I am glad about that."

"She could have, but she has not," Gethren agreed.

"Two things remain to be done," Faelamor caressed the golden strings of her nanollet. The music raised tiny ripples up Gethren's bare arms. "First we must rid ourselves of Rulke and his construct," she said, "else he will go back to Aachan and do it all again, and we will forever be looking over our shoulders. When the deed is done we will force Maigraith to burst apart the Forbidding. Then we can return to Tallallame with honor."

"Faelamor," cried Hallal. "Put down your instrument. It is no longer needed. We have committed crimes enough."

"I cannot," cried Faelamor. "If I let Rulke live, sooner or later he will come for us. While I distract him, fetch Maigraith back." She began to play her nanollet again, more wildly than before.

Llian, watching the struggle between Rulke and Faelamor, was in an agony of frustration. Tallia had been working with Shand and Malien for what seemed hours, but nothing had made any impression on the barrier.

Yggur had given up. He just stood with his great hands pressed against the glass. "Maigraith!" he wailed. "How could you do this to me?"

Shand took him by the arm. "It's over, Yggur. What was between you and Maigraith ended long ago."

Yggur turned a blotched face to him. "She doesn't know what she's doing. He's bewitched her."

"Look how they work together, Yggur!" Shand shook him hard. "They were born for each other."

"She's mine. I've got to have her!"

"You must accept it, Yggur."

"I can't!" he screamed. "*I just can't!*"

Malien drew Shand away. "I need to talk to you," she whispered. "Seeing Rulke here, and Faelamor, and thinking about all that's happened, I wonder if he's the real enemy now. And there's Mendark . . ."

"I wonder too—" said Shand. He broke off as Yalkara's face appeared on the reflecting sphere. "Yalkara!" he roared, but reflections on the barrier concealed him from her. Shand just stood there, staring at her, and no one could rouse him.

The drum-tight Wall of the Forbidding began to lash back and forth. Smoke gushed from underneath the construct. The stairs and balconies shook; the whole of Shazmak felt ready to implode. While Rulke struggled to hold it all together, a squad of Faellem crept out of a doorway, pelted across the room and seized Maigraith. Faelamor was among them, sheltering them with her illusions.

The webs protecting the Faellem were like sticky threads that caught Maigraith's arms and legs. She cried out for help but Faelamor hit her with a confusion at point-blank range. Maigraith could not move. Faelamor rifled through her pouch and plucked out the Mirror.

"This is the last step," she said to her people. "Time to find the hidden Way to Aachan. Bring her!"

They formed a circle around Faelamor, shielding her with their bodies and their minds while she sought within the Mirror. "I have it!" she exulted. They marched off, still surrounding her.

At Karan's cry, Rulke sent the construct after the little band of Faellem. He came up as close as he could, nudging it forward in little jerks, but dared not use power while Maigraith was in the middle.

"Keep back!" said Faelamor, making sure that Maigraith was between her and him. "She is my hostage."

Rulke's eyes could have burned right through her.

"Take us home," the Faellem begged. "Leave her."

"Not while Rulke lives," said Faelamor. Flickering images from the Mirror still reflected on her cheeks.

"What are you doing?" asked Hallal.

"I'm following Yalkara's trace back to Aachan," she said, taunting Rulke. "She will relish this irony, her own device used to unmake her kind." Faelamor stood up, looked deep into the Mirror and, one-handed, played three chords.

The Forbidding rumbled and the assemblage of creatures clustered outside disappeared as if they had been sucked down a plughole.

"What have you done?" the Faellem cried.

"I've opened the void into Aachan. Soon the Charon will be no more." As she spoke, the reflecting metallic sphere that showed the mourning Charon vanished.

Faelamor turned to Rulke. "Our enemies are finished now, all save one. Now to end the last."

Rulke was strangely calm. "Out of your instrument I have forged a better—one that will outlast your kind."

"Then use it! Go to Aachan, if you have the courage. Defend your people. It will save me the trouble of dealing with you."

Rulke hesitated, torn between the Charon and Maigraith, the past and the future. In his mind's eye, as clearly as if it were shown on the sphere, he saw the remaining Charon torn to pieces by the creatures from the void. Only he could save them. But if he went to Aachan, Faelamor would finish Maigraith and his future would be gone.

"What am I to do?" he said to Karan, or perhaps to himself. "How can I abandon the Hundred, my life? Or Maigraith, my love and my future?" Smiting the cowl with his fist, he flung the levers over hard. The construct whirled around the little group in a tight circle, so fast that it was no more than a blur. The blood rushed to Karan's feet; she grew faint. She knew the agony he was going through but there was nothing she could do to help him. Finally he slowed the machine to a crawl. "What do you say, Karan?"

"I would choose the future, if I was forced to choose. But of course," she said with a trace of bitterness that she could not overcome, "being triune, *I have no future*."

Rulke squeezed her little hand in his. "Nothing is certain in life," he said, grounding the construct directly in front of Faelamor. "I choose the future."

"Your choice is irrelevant," said Faelamor. "I cannot allow even one of you to live." She stroked her fingers across the strings of the nanollet for the last time.

The Wall faded, churned and the outside layer split into a thousand panes that drifted in the air, casting distorted reflections everywhere. Red smoke wafted out from underneath the construct. A vent the size of Gothryme Manor opened in the Wall but nothing came through it.

"You did your work too well!" Rulke snapped. He spun a wheel. The construct groaned but did not move. Smoke belched out of it from a dozen places. The light-lens faded. Cursing, he jumped off, sword in hand. Karan slipped down the other side, out of sight of the Faellem.

Faelamor back-pedaled away from his long sword, moving her hand feebly in the air.

"Your glamors are useless, this close to it," he said.

She backed slowly around the front. Karan held her breath. One more step, she thought. Just take one more step! Faelamor stepped back another step.

Lashing out with her foot, Karan kicked the nanollet

from under Faelamor's arm. It skidded under the construct. There was an explosion and the sound of rending metal. The construct leapt in the air. When the clouds of magenta smoke cleared Karan saw that one side was torn open, leaving jagged wings of black metal protruding out, and dark complex innards revealed. The machine drifted in slow circles, listing so far sideways that one of the wings screeched on the floor. An oval plate the size of a cartwheel fell off the underside, clanging on the tiles. Inside that cavity something burned like a white-hot furnace.

Maigraith lay on the floor, concussed by the blast. The construct was still drifting in a circle, heading directly for her.

"Maigraith!" Karan shouted. "Get out of the way!"

Maigraith moved feebly. Karan ran and tried to pull her out of the way. She felt so weak. As she heaved, the furnace blast from the inside of the construct passed right over Maigraith's outflung arm. Her skin blistered like a roasted chicken. Maigraith screamed. Rulke came running up and helped Karan pull her free.

Maigraith hardly recognized him. Rulke held her face between his huge hands and tried to remove Faelamor's confusion, but as soon as he let her go she fell down again.

The construct, circling slowly, passed directly over the fallen nanollet. There was a hiss like steam escaping. The instrument glowed red, blue and violet-black. Then, in an explosion that sent all three flying through the air, it disappeared.

Karan was hurled backward against the spiraling stairs. There was a sickening crack. She gave a little cry and slid down onto the floor like a boneless carcass. Her legs were at a strange angle. She couldn't move. The pain was agonizing.

Rulke, who was unharmed, ran to Karan. "I can never

thank you for what you've done today," he said, then froze. "Karan? Are you all right?"

She was rambling to herself, in a delirium of pain. "All my fault. Llian! Father? *Father!*"

Rulke picked her up, her arms and legs dangling like a sick swan. She screamed. He set her down by the construct, which had settled lower, its dimensions seemingly more squat, more menacing. After making her as comfortable as he could, he began ripping the metal skin off the machine, desperately trying to get it going again.

Llian could see that Karan was terribly injured. He felt an almost irresistible urge to run at the glass and burst it with his head.

Karan arched her back, her mouth opening in a silent scream. Llian could feel her agony. She was radiating it in a sending that shivered its way up the spines and nerves of everyone in the room. She was dying! She needed him desperately. Tears washed channels down his grimy face.

He saw Maigraith lurch over to Rulke, who had his construct working again. Rulke stopped the huge hole in the wall down to the size of a hoop. Nothing had come out of it for ages.

Llian turned an agonized face to Malien and Tallia.

"I'm sorry, chronicler," said Malien. "We've done everything we can, and it hasn't worked. "I've nothing left in me," said Yggur listlessly. "Please do something."

"Mendark said you'd never amount to anything!" Llian said as cruelly as he could. "Shand?"

Shand had not noticed. He was still gazing at the place where Yalkara's image had appeared, oblivious to everything else.

Llian turned away from the barrier. Wiping the tears off,

he smudged the dust into the trail of a comet on his brow. There is always a way, he said to himself. "Tensor!"

Tensor, sitting on the floor with his head sunk in his lap, did not answer.

"Tensor!" He shouted in the Aachim's ear and struck him on the shoulder.

Tensor raised his head, looking Llian in the eye. "She's finished, chronicler!" There were tears in his eyes too. "We all are. We won't see out the day."

"Be damned! You owe me a debt and I call on you to pay it."

"I owe *you* a debt, chronicler? I can't think why."

"You kidnapped me, dragged me all the way to Katazza and used me there. You wronged me, yet still I aided you with your gate."

Tensor appeared to struggle to recall that time. "I cannot see where the debt is, but after today, what will it matter? Ask your boon, chronicler."

"Smash down this barrier. Karan is dying all alone. I've got to go to her."

Tensor peered through the glass wall and focussed on Karan. "What can I do when everyone else has failed?"

"Use the potency that you made for the destroying of Rulke."

"The destroying of Rulke," said Tensor wonderingly. "That was my life's work, once. I don't think I can get the potency back, chronicler. I am wasted, empty."

"Try!" said Llian imperiously. "Remember how you hated Rulke once. Remember all that the Charon have done to your people since they came out of the void."

"I was hot with hate once," Tensor said, shaking his head.

"Bring that hate out again," Llian cried recklessly, urging Tensor on with tales of Rulke that he knew were no longer true, lies made up to ensure that the Charon remained the

Great Enemy. He put every iota of his teller's *voice* into it. Nothing mattered any more, except Karan. "Remember the Clysm, remember—"

"Llian!" Malien called. "This is unwise."

"Remember how the Hundred took your world," Llian shouted. "Remember how Rulke crippled you in Katazza!"

"I do remember!" Tensor lurched to his feet.

"And do you remember your potency?" Llian was jumping up and down, shouting and waving his arms. His spittle spattered Tensor's coat front.

"I remember that too," said Tensor, holding up his fist. Wisps of radiance began to rise from it like vapor. He stared at the tenuous strands.

"And is your potency the equal of this barrier Rulke has put between you and Karan?" Llian said wildly, caught up in the ecstasy of this creature that he was creating. "Look at her, lying there in her agony, bleeding inside."

"Enough, Llian," said Malien, advancing on him. "Shand, help me!" She shook him hard.

Shand roused from his dreams of Yalkara. "Llian, stop it!"

"It is the equal of Rulke itself," said Tensor, standing tall and brandishing his radiant fist.

"Then smash the barrier down—"

Tallia whipped her hand across Llian's mouth. Shand pinioned his hands. They dragged him away. "You bloody fool," Shand hissed in his face. "I warned you about this after the citadel burned. Do you realize what you could have—"

He broke off, staring at Tensor, whose upraised fist now glowed as bright as a furnace. "Look at him there," husked Tensor, "embracing Maigraith while Karan lies dying at his feet. They are my enemies both. My time has come at last."

Tensor drew himself up by will alone. He reached for the

sky, tottering on his emaciated legs, and his face was alive with hate. Thrusting out his fist, he roared forth his rage. The crystalline barrier shattered to fragments that sparkled in the air then struck the floor with a roar like a waterfall.

"*Beware the thrice betrayed!*" Tensor bellowed. He thrust his hand toward Rulke and Maigraith, exactly as he had that night at the Conclave a year ago, when he had destroyed Nelissa and taken back the Mirror.

Shand and Malien were powerless to stop him. They watched in horror, helpless to prevent the tragedy.

43

LIEBESTOD

Rulke's head jerked up and he saw his nemesis. He could have escaped, had he cared to leave Maigraith behind, had he fought back. But Maigraith was clinging to him, barely able to stand. He knew Tensor would strike her down as well.

Rulke swept Maigraith behind him, shielding her with his body. A jet of ruby came from Tensor's hand and struck Rulke full in the chest. For a moment his great frame seemed to glow. His feet slipped on the floor as he was pushed backward by an irresistible force. Once this potency would have been no more than a flea bite but the day had taken a dreadful toll of him.

"Help me!" he cried to his Ghâshâd, but where once they would have obeyed instantly, now they hesitated momentarily. It was just enough. By the time the nearest of them raised their spears Tensor was ready for them. He swung his arm and they were tossed in all directions.

"Tensor, stop!" screamed Shand. "What are you doing?

Oh, you bloody fool!" He sprang forward, but Tensor held out his other hand and Shand could not get near him.

The jet of light struck Rulke once more. He windmilled the air with his arms. Maigraith was blown sideways, to disappear behind the stairs. Rulke's feet struggled for a purchase, but he was tossed into the air. Soaring like a paper cut-out on the wind, he slammed into the side of the construct. Rulke flung his arms and legs out, roaring so loudly that the spiral staircases oscillated.

He raised a mighty fist and it seemed that he would fling Tensor's potency in his face. Llian ducked for cover. Then Rulke suddenly collapsed as if all the air had been let out of him.

Llian picked himself up. Everyone near, except himself, had been affected by the potency. Malien was on hands and knees, retching. Shand looked dazed and had a cut above one eye. Yggur lay twitching on the floor. The rest of the company were strewn about the room.

Llian raced forward, crunching over broken glass, and saw that Rulke had been impaled on one of the horns of metal torn away from the side of the construct. The jagged black thorn protruded out through his side. Yet still Tensor screamed at his enemy, still the ruby jet roared out of him like water out of a fire hose. Tensor began to shrink down and wither, as if projecting his entire essence into that rod of fire.

"Master!" cried Vartila the Whelm. Sprinting right across the room she struck Tensor down savagely. The beam arced across the ceiling and went out.

"You stupid, stupid fools!" said Shand, lurching to his feet. "Tensor, all your names are folly. Look what you've done, Llian."

Malien hobbled over to Tensor, her lover once and long ago. "I have done well, Malien," he said.

Her face showed nothing but contempt. "You are not Tensor!" she said. "You are Pitlis the Second, the most contemptible fool that ever lived." She did not tear her blouse in grief for him this time. She ripped his shirt off his back, dropped the tatters on the floor and put her head in her hands. "The Aachim are cursed!"

Vartila hurled herself through the heaped-up fragments of glass to Rulke. "Master," she cried, falling to her knees and taking his hand. "I was blind to you, master, but I know you now. Forgive me, master."

Rulke took Vartila's hand and smiled. "Thank you, most faithful servant. But it's over now. You're free."

Tears poured down Vartila's face. "What am I to do with *freedom*?" She spat the word out like blasphemy. "All I ever wanted was to serve my master." She vainly tried to stem Rulke's wound with her fists.

Rulke writhed on the metal thorn. No one could think him their enemy any more, so great was his agony; so great his nobility. "Does Maigraith live?" he groaned.

"Yes," said Vartila. "She lies yonder."

"Attend her injuries, faithful servant, then bring her to me."

Llian took Karan's hand. She did not recognize him. He tried to straighten her broken body but she screamed and screamed. He could do nothing to stop it. Shand and Malien ran to her. Llian was hopping around in such distress that Shand pushed him off.

"Go away, you bloody fool! See to Rulke."

Llian crept up to the Charon. He touched the black metal spear.

"I did this!" Llian said bitterly. "I am the stupidest man that ever drew breath."

Rulke smiled a smile of sorts. "You are," he agreed. "But are you not a chronicler? This was my fate all along, Llian. Help me off this barb."

Rulke put out his hand. Llian gave his, braced himself and strained hard. The thorn crept into the wound. Rulke's lips curled apart to show bloody gums. "Harder!" he gasped. He appeared to lose consciousness, then Llian gave a mighty heave and Rulke subsided to the floor. Blood gushed out of the chasm in his side. All around, Llian saw the horrified faces of the Ghâshâd, conscious that they might have saved their master, but had not.

Rulke choked. Llian wiped blood from his mouth. The Charon stared at his shaking hand as though unable to believe that he could ever have come to this.

"Where's Karan?" he asked in a kind of a daze.

"Right here," said Llian.

Turning his head, Rulke saw her lying there, still but for an occasional shudder. "Thank you, Karan." He took her limp hand in his, and her pain eased, though his grew worse. "I've a gift for you."

"The Gift of Rulke!" murmured Llian. "I hope it's not a poisoned chalice like the last one."

Rulke awkwardly felt inside his coat and brought out a black bead the size of a pill, in a clear case.

"What is it?" Karan whispered.

"The least I can do for you. Use it if you get better. If not, it won't matter." He pressed the case into Karan's hand and closed her fluttering fingers around it. "And I've something for you too, Llian."

"I don't deserve a reward," Llian said bitterly.

"I want you to have it anyway."

Fumbling at his throat, Rulke lifted over his head a tiny key made of silver, on a silver chain.

"My spies told me that you lost a tale, chronicler. Here is a better! But you'll have to earn it." He dropped the chain over Llian's head. With the movement his scarlet blood flooded onto the white floor. Rulke appeared to admire the patterns it made on the tiles. "The pain is even worse than the last time," he whispered.

"I don't know where to begin," said Llian stupidly.

"Begin in Alcifer." Rulke closed his eyes, went still, then seemed to find another reserve of strength. "We are extinct, chronicler. The Charon will live on only in your tales. Will you take them on for me?"

Llian wiped his mouth again. Rulke's side still ebbed blood. His dark complexion had faded to pale gray.

"Yes, I swear it," cried Llian, riddled with guilt and desperate to atone.

"But make sure you tell the truth about us. All of it!"

"The Histories *are* truth!" said Llian. "The best we can recover from the past."

Rulke looked at him pityingly. "Dear boy! You have failed the final test. You believe what you were taught. Everyone else may believe, but the masters must know the truth. *History is as it is written*, that is the only truth. Enough of that. I would speak to my enemy Tensor, before I die. Bring him here!"

Tensor was carried across and laid next to Rulke and Karan.

"Karan," Tensor said in the husk that remained of his voice. Her eyes fluttered open. She was in great pain. "Forgive me for shaping you, for trying to destroy your triune talents. I did it for the best of reasons."

Karan took his huge dark hand in her small pale one. His hand was even colder than hers, and so withered now. She turned her head painfully, looking into his eyes. "I hated you for it, but what does it matter now?" she whispered, and closed her eyes again.

"So, my enemy!" said Rulke. "You Aachim will have your freedom, and your world, after all."

"It's too late for us," said Tensor. "We are a species rich in folly but short on courage. We used you as an excuse for so long that we no longer know how to face the world by ourselves."

"But the Aachim will live on in Aachan. And here."

"Diminished!" Tensor said scornfully. "But tell me, how do my people fare?"

"On Aachan?" asked Rulke. "They are legion, I believe, and not much reduced by their servitude."

"I would have loved to see Aachan again."

"But you never will."

"No, I never will. But at least I go knowing that I have finished you at last," said Tensor.

"I wish you joy of your victory," said Rulke, and held out his hand.

Tensor's face wrenched. "You have defeated me, *and* outmannered me," he said. Then he toppled sideways, dead.

Maigraith, supported by Vartila, labored across. She stood beside Rulke like a marble statue, staring down at the hideous gash in her lover's side. She was utterly still. "You gave your life for me," she said.

"We made vows together," he replied simply. It encapsulated everything there was to be said.

"I will never forget you," she said.

"I will be part of you forever."

"What will happen to your people now, my love?"

Rulke looked up at Maigraith. "*We* will not dwindle away to nothing. The void is the only place left. It may remake us, but most likely it will erase us utterly, like the ten billion species that have come and gone since the ancestral mite. If we are to be extinct, we will face it bravely. We will embrace it."

Maigraith went to her knees and laid her head on his breast. "What am I to do, Rulke?"

He held her with one arm. "It hurts, Maigraith! I'm so sorry. Mourn me as you see fit, then follow your destiny."

"I don't know how," she said plaintively. "How *can* I restore the balance between the worlds?"

Rulke coughed shiny blood onto the floor. "Only Yalkara knows what she intended. Take the construct to Aachan." He choked. "If she has survived, tell Yalkara of my death and beg her assistance." His eyelids fluttered.

"How we would have loved, you and I," he went on. "But it was not to be."

She gripped his hand. "*I once loved, and was loved.*" She dropped a feather kiss on his eyelids.

"And the fruit of our love will shake the Three Worlds to their underpinnings. But this is the end of the Charon." Rulke closed his eyes for the last time.

His death turned Maigraith inside out, the marble-statue calmness wrenched into a feral rage over the futility of it all. "*I will not allow it!*" she screamed at the construct and the Wall and the place where Faelamor had disappeared. "I will reach even beyond the grave to bring him back."

Mendark had been quietly biding his time, watching from his balcony for an opportunity. And though he had never really expected it, that chance had now come. The construct was unattended. He had coveted it since the instant he'd heard of it. With it he would seal the Forbidding and rid himself of his enemies forever.

But when that was done, what opportunities the construct presented him! He would order Santhenar the way he had always wanted to; perhaps the other worlds too. Mendark felt a surge of excitement such as he had not felt in a hundred years.

He crept down the stairs. Faelamor was nowhere to be seen. No one was watching; they were all busy with the dead and the dying. The construct was between them and him. He climbed the hidden side, fell into the seat and sat in silence for a few moments, savoring this time of triumph. Putting his hands to the controls, Mendark began to think himself into the way of controlling the machine.

He pressed buttons, eased back levers and prepared to deal with the first of his enemies—Yggur! Nothing happened. He tried again. The construct was absolutely dead.

There came a piping cry from below. "It's Mendark!" Lilis's thin arm was pointing directly at him.

Mendark would have struck her down if he could have. What was one child before the security of the world, before his great destiny? He did not get the chance. In a few seconds the construct was surrounded.

"Come down!" Yggur said coldly.

"Stand back," Mendark cried, holding the flute up so they could all see it. "I have the flute and the construct too."

"It will be the death of you," said Shand.

"Shut up, you old fool! I'll be glad to see the end of *you*."

Raising the flute, Mendark drew the notes out of his memory and began to play a melody so wild that his mind could scarcely encompass it.

"Not on the construct!" screamed Shand.

Too late! Abruptly the whole room twisted and turned back on itself, writhing with impossible colors and music. Mendark's eyes burned with splinters, as of colored ice. Then the whole fabric of the Forbidding began to peel apart layer by layer, like a burning book. Bits of shredded Wall floated in the air, charred flakes as from the death of a library. The flute had betrayed him. The Forbidding was coming apart!

Once more he played, exerting all his mind and will to tune himself to the Forbidding and seal it tight. Too late he realized that he did not know how. Everything was different now. The whole Wall became transparent, allowing him to see what waited on the other side. The shapes and spaces of *beyond* shivered. A shadow appeared in the mazy void, then another. The flute had called a hundred creatures, a thousand. A veritable army was gathering on the other side of the Wall.

An approaching army of thranx and lorrsk, and a hundred other creatures that looked just as bloody. In the infinite history of the void there had never been such an alliance, but the ripe plum of Santhenar was worth putting aside old feuds for. Mendark slowly rose to his feet, staring at the nightmare. The hand holding the flute fell to his side. There were hundreds upon uncounted hundreds of them. Then, as his focus moved progressively out from the Wall, the hundreds became thousands and the thousands millions, marching in ranks, in planes and layers, in three-dimensional arrays from every direction. Marching to war against Santhenar. The world that he loved more than life was doomed. And he had doomed it.

Mendark lifted the flute then lowered it again. He dared not tamper with the Forbidding now. Was there another way?

As he pondered, something stirred among the dead on the floor. It was the second thranx, still stuck with spears. From the shadows it hurled a broken spear at Mendark, smashing the golden flute out of his hand. The instrument rang out on the floor, a single pure note that sent a shimmering along the transparent layers of the Forbidding. The thranx crawled toward the flute.

Mendark cursed and shook his throbbing hand. Then, suddenly understanding what the problem had been, he laughed for joy. The two devices had been interfering with each other. He banged the levers over and the construct moved. "Keep it!" he roared. "This is what I came for."

He swung the construct around smoothly. The remnant of the company were all in its path. The Wall first, or his enemies? Yggur's fingers were working, preparing to blast him. Several of the Aachim raised their bows. And, he saw with dismay, even faithful Tallia was speaking urgently to Shand, surely plotting his ruin. They all wanted the construct for themselves. But none of them could save the world. Only he could do that. He directed the construct toward his enemies.

"No, Mendark!" wept Tallia. "Is this how you would have posterity remember you?" She held out her hands to him.

Not even Tallia could be allowed to stand in his way. He prepared to blast her down. But as they faced each other, something stung his eyes. Dear Tallia, they'd shared such times together. It was harder than he'd imagined. But I *will* do it! Mendark thought. Before he could wrench the control rod the thranx forced itself to its feet. The spears quivered like the quills of a spiny anteater. It put the flute to its lips and blew. The construct bucked, turned over and Mendark was flung off. He landed on his feet, running forward to stop himself from falling, but he ran one step too far.

The thranx swung its powerful arm and claws like daggers ripped through Mendark's middle, sending him tumbling through the air. He began to drag himself back to the construct, leaving a trail of blood. The thranx began a different melody.

In the background, the vanguard reached the Wall and pressed against it. The Wall molded itself to their shapes like a rubber sheet.

"What's it doing?" Lilis whispered.

"It's calling its own," said Malien.

"Mendark!" screamed Tallia. "Stop them!"

Mendark tried to climb the construct but slipped in his blood and fell down again. He looked up at the wondrous machine and wept.

"Mendark!" Tallia shrieked. "Stop it, quickly!"

She tried to run to him but Jevi and Lilis held her back. Mendark forced himself to his knees, moved his hands in a spell and the flute glowed red-hot. The thranx screeched and dropped it. Mendark stood upright but his entrails began to spill out of his belly. He looked down at the fatal wound, pressed the innards back in and duck-walked to the flute. As he raised it, white smoke came from his fingers and his mouth. He blew a plangent series of notes.

A cyst grew around Mendark. It swelled with every note and rushed outward to envelop everyone in the room. The thranx was tumbled backward until it came between the cyst and a side wall, where it was squashed to a smear.

"Is it all over now?" Lilis asked, staring at the ranks of creatures that stretched to infinity across the void.

The cyst continued to grow until it touched the Wall. It bonded to it, plugging the tiny vent and clouding over the Wall. But they all knew that what waited on the other side was only a blink away.

Jevi brushed Lilis's shining hair off her face. "No, Lilis, it's not over yet. Not near!"

The strain began to tell on Mendark. Would he fail before the work was complete? The cyst stopped growing. He weakened, fell to his knees, clutched at his belly, played on. Then all at once the air rushed out of his lungs. A bloody bubble grew out the end of the flute to burst in a discord. The note failed, the flute fell and Mendark lay dead.

Tallia ran to the man she had served so faithfully for so

long, to perform her last service. Stooping over the body, she smoothed his hair, closed his eyes and arranged his robes so that they covered the horrible wound. Then she carried him slowly across to the others. He looked quite small in her arms. There she sat, looking down at him, her beautiful face cold.

"I will see that this deed is recorded for the future," she said, "though I doubt that it will balance the others. My oath is undone, my service ended."

44

Going Home

Maigraith, pacing back and forth in a daze of grief, saw Faelamor appear near the bottom of the central stair. Shand, Yggur and Malien came the other way, preparing for the greatest battle of their lives.

Maigraith held up one hand. "Stay back! This is between her and me."

Faelamor positioned herself at the point where the cyst curved away from the Wall. "This is the weak point," she said to Hallal. "We will open it here."

"You'll destroy the world!" said Shand.

"*I* can control it," she replied coldly.

Faelamor reached out. The Wall was now so thin that it parted in front of her. Through a crack she peered beyond, searching for the path to Tallallame. She needed no one to find that track for her. "I have it," she said, and opened *her* Way.

"You see," whispered Karan, "I never did harm you. How could I have? I never understood why you feared me so."

Faelamor looked across at Karan, lying between the bodies of Tensor and Rulke. "It was not the triune endangered us after all! It was the forbidden device, *the-three-and-the-one*. Why couldn't I see it?"

The Way became a shining funnel. All around it the alien armies swarmed. When the Wall finally fell apart only Faelamor would be able to stem their flood, but Faelamor was going home.

Maigraith paced up to Faelamor, whose face showed anguish; guilt too. "Now is the moment I trained you for, Maigraith. Why did you abandon me?"

"You sent Ellami to kill me!" Maigraith whispered, still finding it impossible to comprehend.

"Not I," said Faelamor. "I could never harm you. The Faellem voted that you die."

"Voted?" shrieked Maigraith. "So my life is no more than an election that you couldn't be bothered to rig!"

"I tried. They won the vote! It was the worst day of my existence. I could not stop them."

Catching sight of Rulke's sword lying on the floor, Maigraith snatched it up. "I'll show you how!" she screamed.

Faelamor put her hand out. "You can't!" she said. "I made you so you could never turn on me."

All Maigraith could see were those golden flecks in her eyes. She felt torn apart between her hatred of Faelamor and the chains of the compulsion. "I will not . . ." she began, but Faelamor screwed her control tighter.

Maigraith was helpless, as she had always been. Then, thinking about all she had done the past year, she knew that only fear of Faelamor held her back. She had grown beyond her.

Could she overcome that fear and strike Faelamor down? Maigraith thought of her dead lover and that fear was gone forever. With a shrill laugh she raised the sword. "I've broken your compulsion *and* your conditioning. Are you ready to die, Faelamor?"

The answer was in Faelamor's eyes—the sudden terror, the realization that, after all, Maigraith had beaten her. "Go on then," said Faelamor. "Have your revenge. Let it be all the sweeter for the knowledge that I die having gone so close to my duty, and *failed*." There were tears in her eyes.

Maigraith held the sword high, taking pleasure from her opponent's pain. Remembering Rulke's last bloody moments she wanted, more than anything, to see Faelamor suffer the same way.

"Do it quickly!" said Faelamor in a cracked voice.

The Faellem stared at the frozen tableau. None stirred to Faelamor's aid. Did they not dare, or did they not care? The minutes passed.

Abruptly Maigraith lowered the sword, slapping Faelamor on one cheek with the side of the blade. "Go home!" she said harshly.

A shiver passed over Faelamor's face. She looked frail now. "Happy are the Faellem," she murmured, "to put all their burdens on their leader. Have I the strength for the last act?"

The Wall rippled. Something hideous and unbearably potent reached in beside the funnel and gripped her by the calf. It pulled, trying to draw her in. She dashed it away like a fly. Blood ran down her leg from three claw marks.

"You won't stop me?" she said to Maigraith.

"No," said Maigraith, numb in her agony. Suddenly Faelamor seemed lost. "Was it worth it, for this? Does this justify the ruin I heaped upon the world, and on the child who would have been greater than me?"

Bowing her head, Faelamor took Maigraith's slender hand in her own small one, and a single golden tear fell on

Maigraith's wrist. Maigraith wrenched away. "It was not worth it," Faelamor whispered. "I must atone. I take this duty on myself, in penance for my crimes."

Faelamor stood up straight and the years dropped from her. She looked as she must have done all those countless centuries ago, when she first led the Faellem to Santhenar.

"*I am the Faellem!*" Faelamor cried in her glory and her grandeur, holding open the Way between the Worlds by will alone. "Come, my people! Now is the time. We are going home!"

The first approached and pressed his lips to Faelamor's hand. He hesitated. Putting her hand on his shoulder, she gave a gentle push. He leapt, the Way snatched him and he disappeared. The second came forward, a little old woman with silver hair like Faelamor's, and did the same. Then another man, similar in size and features to the woman. Faelamor counted them past.

Without warning the glowing funnel shuddered as it was struck a massive blow. A crack gaped between the Way and the Wall. A man-shaped creature squeezed in through the space and like a balloon pumping up it expanded to its full size, as big as Rulke. It was a lorrsk-like thing with massive arms and legs, an enormous chest and a head that came out of its shoulders without recourse to a neck. Claws scraped on the floor as it leapt and struck at Faelamor. The sleeve of her shirt was torn off. Two bloody gouges opened up from shoulder to elbow.

Faelamor shuddered. "Sixty-one, sixty-two—" Her voice, counting her people past, cracked. She moved her free hand in the air and the lumpen creature doubled up. But the diversion had allowed another in, and a third. They attacked her all at once, clawing at her back and her legs, trying to hamstring her. Despite the power of her glamors, fading but still strong, they landed a blow here and there.

She writhed under their strokes but her will held her firm. Nothing could stay Faelamor's iron command, at this moment she had waited for so long.

The Faellem were passing her quickly now, just a tap on the shoulder for each, then through the gate and gone. Suddenly Faelamor went down under the weight of her attackers. They were all about her: snapping, rending. The gate quivered, the Way shook again. "Two hundred and fifty-six, two hundred and fifty-seven—" She pulled herself to her feet and swept her bloody arm in a circle, scattering her assailants. The creatures hurled themselves away from her as if they had been stung. The last of the Faellem passed through. The funnel of the Way narrowed. Faelamor staggered and fell to her knees.

"My duty is done at last!" she gasped. "I can scarcely believe it." Sitting down on the floor, she wept for the centuries of trial and torment that were finally over. Wiping her face clean, she stood up. "I had one last task for you, Maigraith, if ever I got this far. To hold open the Way for me so I could be the last to go."

"Go!" spat Maigraith, "I *will* hold it! It will be worth it to see you gone forever."

Faelamor did not move. "Now that my duty is done I must tie up all the ends. It doesn't matter whether I get home or not." She bent down over Karan. Karan trembled.

"You once did me service at great cost to yourself," Faelamor said. "You carried the Mirror faithfully all the way from Fiz Gorgo to Thurkad, in fulfilment of Maigraith's obligation to me. You have never been paid for that service."

"It doesn't matter," whispered Karan. "I'm dying."

"Perhaps you are," said Faelamor, touching Karan's forehead. The pain suddenly lifted from her. "I cannot see the future. But I must pay my debts, every last one. What goods that I and the Faellem have, I leave to you and your estate, to do with as you will. These things may be found in the cave in Elludore where Gyllias . . . found Maigraith." She slipped an ebony bracelet off her wrist onto Karan's. "They are protected by a perpetual illusion, but this will dispel it."

"Go!" Maigraith shrieked. "It's too late to atone now, and too little. If you spent a thousand years on your knees you could not make up for what you have done."

"You're right," Faelamor said. Her face was frozen solid. "To think that I so abused my own child. I can't imagine why, anymore. I was obsessed."

Maigraith's legs collapsed beneath her. "*No, No!*" she screamed. "You are not my mother. Aeolior was my mother."

Squatting down, Faelamor took Maigraith by the shoulders, desperate to embrace her but unable to. "Maigraith, here is the truth you have been searching for all your life. I am your other grandmother. It was my own son Galgilliel, poor frail emotional boy, whom I forced to mate with Aeolior until the evil business was done. I destroyed him too."

Maigraith's went hysterical, beating Faelamor about the face with her hands. "*No!* I refuse to believe your wicked lies! How could you do this to me? You are a monster!"

Faelamor did not defend herself. "I am, but will you give me your hand anyway? Will you forgive me before I go, granddaughter?"

Maigraith swung her fists like wheels. "Never! I spit in your face."

Faelamor made no attempt to defend herself. "I deserve no better. I acted that my own species may survive, ignoring all other considerations. Move clear, granddaughter. I will go through the Way by myself. My people have gone home. My duty is done. My fate doesn't matter.

"I am the Faellem," she whispered, saluting Karan, saluting Maigraith, saluting them all. "*I am Tallallame!*" That cry echoed in the room.

The Way narrowed again. "Fare well, my granddaughter. Forgive me."

Faelamor leapt through the gate. It held for a moment then snapped tight like a steel stocking. They saw her face wracked by an excruciation. An explosive flare of blue and white light obliterated the gate, the funnel of the Way and all the creatures lurking nearby. The hole in the Wall fused over. The Faellem had gone home.

Maigraith looked in the Mirror, watching them all the way to Tallallame. They emerged triumphant on their own world, even Faelamor. Maigraith flung down the Mirror and the image froze in place.

"There is no justice anywhere in the Three Worlds!" she said to Karan.

Karan coughed and groaned. The pain had come back. "What did you expect from the Twisted Mirror?"

The great oval chamber of Shand's gate stretched out into two teardrops separated by a thread, one in Carcharon, the other in Shazmak. The thread snapped the two back together. Shazmak vanished, and the gate with it. The company were left alone to stare at the ice-covered walls of Carcharon. The gate had failed and Karan lay dreadfully injured in Shazmak, at least four days march away.

Shand turned to Llian. "She was Tallallame, and Tallallame was her. I wonder what they will find there. Santhenar was not the only world affected by the Forbidding."

"Make the gate again," Llian wept. "Karan is dying!"

"I don't think I can," said Shand. "Everything is changed now."

If Carcharon had been strange before, now it was positively bizarre. The walls were sometimes as soft as cheese, sometimes hard as metal, and they were never in the same place twice. There were wormholes through them too, like tunnels connecting different places in the void. The broken stone staircase appeared to spiral in a dozen directions at once, and ghastly, terrifying specters trudged up and down it, working devices that sprayed doughnuts of unreality in all directions. The air changed color constantly. Shards of every noise in the sound spectrum stabbed through their eardrums.

Shand, Tallia and Malien went into a huddle, trying to block out Carcharon and recover the gate. Yggur joined them, desperate to get back to Maigraith.

"This is going to take a while," Shand grunted as they strained against the warped fabric of space and time.

"I don't understand what happened between Faelamor and Rulke," said Malien. "For a moment he was helpless."

"Llian can tell you," grunted Shand.

Llian, rubbing red-raw eyes, shook his head. He was quite as tormented as Faelamor had been.

"We need to know!" snapped Yggur as he worked at some obscure process with Tallia.

Llian made a visible effort. "Part of the tale comes from Yalkara's book. That's where I found out the very beginning of the business."

"I thought the book was destroyed unread," said Yggur suspiciously.

"Another tale, for another time." Llian managed a weak smile. "This is what it said—a summary of it, anyway.

"Long ago in Tallallame there were two human races—Mariem and Faellem. The Faellem's talents were of the mind, and they were numerous. The Mariem were clever with devices and machines, but not fecund. Over time the two races grew apart as they each developed their particular talents and cultures. They did not interbreed, and became quite distinct peoples.

"The Mariem accumulated wealth and power, for they had built a civilization with machines that did their work for them. Feeling no kinship with nature, they set out to tame it. They cleared the beautiful forests that had once covered whole continents. They moved rivers, carved roads through the wilderness and built vast cities. The Faellem were forced back into the most rugged lands and the poorest, as the Mariem used more and more of the world's wealth for their civilization.

"The Faellem had a totally different outlook. Their kinship with the land was total, for they knew themselves to be just one species in a vast web of life. They felt no need for the trappings of civilization, save the arts. Their life was of the mind. They never cut down a tree, or slew an animal, without a prayer of thanks for the gift. They built no cities, used no machines. Their arts and their culture were simple, but very beautiful."

Yggur cursed and sprang out of the way as the process he had been working on failed in an explosion of purple cinders. The broken walls curved over them, oscillating like rubber. "I can't do it!" he said hoarsely. "Carcharon is too strange."

"I've an idea," Malien suggested. She spoke in his ear.

Yggur nodded. "It's worth a try."

Malien conjured up one of her bubbles and grew it around them all. Inside, the weirdness of Carcharon was blocked out, though it could still be heard and felt. It was completely dark, so Shand created light with his knobbly staff and they went back to their work on the gate.

"Continue, Llian," said Malien.

"The Faellem realized that the Mariem were going to wipe them out. Once the forests were gone they would have no place to live, nor any reason to. The Mariem would destroy them, not from malice but from simple greedy indifference, and the beautiful world they were the custodians of would be no more.

"The Faellem had to find a way to curb the Mariem and reclaim Tallallame. In their desperation they bred their most talented and sensitive people together like farmyard animals, to develop their powers of mind and illusion so highly that the Mariem would not be able to resist them.

"The Mariem had been experimenting with gates, so they could travel instantly from one part of Tallallame to another. Their first were crude, clumsy devices that seldom worked properly, but the Faellem knew their enemies would soon perfect them, and when they did, no place on Tallallame would be safe. The Faellem learned how these gates worked, and how the Mariem used their minds to direct them from one place to another. Experimenting with their own vastly superior mind-powers, they forced a gate to go wrong. They directed it to the worst nightmare of beasts and barrenness they could imagine. To their astonishment the gate opened a way off Tallallame into an unknown place teeming with desperate life—the void!"

Llian slumped down on the low wall. His voice had gone hoarse. He looked ghastly. "Has anyone got a drink?" he croaked.

Shand tossed a flask to him. Llian took a huge swig, thinking that it was water. The liquor roared down his throat and lit a fire in his belly. "Thank you," he choked.

"So the Faellem began it all!" said Malien.

"Yes!" He went on with the tale. "Here was an opportunity to save Tallallame. The collective wills of the most sensitive Faellem made a mass illusion, a pied piper for adults, and one by one the whole population of the Mariem were led through the gate, thinking that they went to their own wonderful world. As soon as they ended up in the void they knew differently, but it was too late. The Faellem had sealed the gate and it could not be reopened.

"The Faellem busied themselves with regenerating beautiful Tallallame. They broke the dams, tore down the cities and planted the forests anew. That other race was eliminated from the Histories of Tallallame, and all use of the machines and magical devices that had almost ruined their world was forbidden. Eventually the genocide was reduced to just a rumor, a frightening myth. Within a millennium, nature had covered all trace of the Mariem.

"And in the void, that desperate place where nothing matters but survival, most were dead within days. In a month the millions were reduced to a few thousand. Of those, over thousands of years a small number adapted. Things evolve rapidly in the void if they do survive, so that those who came out and took Aachan, not many more than a hundred, were quite different from those that went in. They were a new human species and they took a new name, Charon, after a frigid moonlet at the furthest extremity of the void. All they could remember of their former life was their name, and their betrayal.

"The survival of the species now meant everything to the Charon. To Rulke that purpose was unquenchable. But they did not thrive on Aachan. For some reason the Charon were infertile there. So Rulke commissioned the golden flute, to open the way to Santhenar and offer them another chance. But Shuthdar stole the flute, and that crime led to war after war, misery after misery, calamity after calamity, all the way down the ages to today."

"How is it going?" Osseion asked while Llian slaked his thirst, with icy water this time.

"A little progress," Shand replied. "It's tiring work though."

"I feel quite sleepy," said Malien.

"Open the sphere for a minute," said Shand. "Let some fresh air in. And Mendark, Llian? I suppose you've worked that out too?"

"Yes," said Yggur. "I very much want to hear that."

Llian wiped his mouth and continued. "The Aachim and the Charon fought many battles on Santh, though at first neither was numerous and the world scarcely noticed them. That changed in the Clysm, when Mendark convinced the Council to side with the Aachim. His propaganda gave the Charon an evil reputation. Mendark's strength was dependent on having a common enemy, and this was a lie that was in the interests of most. So much of the past had been lost in the Clysm that it was difficult to check afterwards. As Rulke said *History is as it is written.* Terrible deeds were done against the Charon and they retaliated in kind.

"Had Mendark not been so concerned about his reputation I might never have discovered the truth. He had only been able to capture Rulke by betraying you, Yggur."

"How?" cried Yggur. "How did he do it?"

"In the last battle he knew that the Council would be defeated. There was only one chance to save the world and Mendark seized it. He *forced* the Proscribed Experiments to fail and when Rulke attacked your mind, Yggur, Mendark forced Rulke's consciousness inside it. You went mad and Rulke could not find his way out. Tensor captured his now helpless body and they expelled him into the Nightland. Mendark had saved the world, but only by betraying you, his closest friend. You were supposed to die, but instead you escaped and no one could find you. Little wonder Mendark was terrified when you reappeared."

Yggur clenched his fists in fury. The memories were too awful. "Air!" he gasped.

Malien let the frigid, hallucinatory air into the sphere again. Llian went on with his story.

"Within a year of Rulke being put away, most of the Council were dead. Mendark slew them one by one, in case they realized what he had done. Had you not disappeared he would have finished you too. Tensor alone was spared.

"But ever after, Mendark lived in fear that one of the Council had written down the truth that would destroy his reputation forever. So he amassed a vast store of ancient documents to disguise his true intent, which was to seek out and destroy every record that could possibly link his name to the crime. It was the greatest library from that time ever put together. But it's all gone now, except what I have copies of, and what I remember.

"Mendark could not bear to have once been great, and then to fail and lose his reputation. History treats its heroes randomly. He felt that he had never had his due and was desperate to renew his name with one last heroic deed. So when the opportunity of the flute came, he could not resist it."

"How did he know how to use it?" asked Malien. "No one else did."

"He had been looking for it, and preparing for it, all his life. He spent months at Saludith. Perhaps he found the answer there, and took it away so no one else ever could."

"But why did the flute go so wrong?"

"The gold was corrupted by time, as all things carried between the worlds eventually are. He knew that risk but was convinced he could overcome it. He wasn't strong enough."

"Why did the Faellem come to Santhenar in the first place?" asked Tallia.

"They had thought that they were alone in the universe, after the Mariem were sent into the void. Then Shuthdar used the flute and they knew that they were far from alone. Theirs was just one of the Three Worlds, and the Way between the Worlds was open. It let things out of the void into Tallallame. The Faellem were not troubled by them, for they were used to dealing with wild creatures, but they knew that the most dangerous creatures of all dwelt on the other worlds—*other human species!*

"The Faellem went the perilous way to Santhenar to find out what had happened, and to restore the Three Worlds to the closed-off places that they had always been. Once they arrived here they found three more human species, and all were makers and users of the forbidden machines that so terrified them. They were too numerous for the Faellem to do anything about, except for one species.

"The Charon were so familiar and so threatening, for all that there were but three of them on Santhenar. The Faellem knew that they were vulnerable, but not how vulnerable. Because the other species were so powerful, they had to work from the shadows. Then the Forbidding trapped them—"

"I think I have it," cried Shand. "If only we're not too late! Into the gate, quick as you can!"

45

THE FATE OF THE FAELLEM

One by one the Faellem emerged from the gate into Tallallame, as naked as was everyone who passed between the worlds. They came out at a sacred meeting place, a grassy hillside shaped like a curving pyramid, standing above tall forest. It was dark but dawn could not be far off, for there was a light in the east.

Faelamor emerged last of all, so covered in welts and claw marks that she was barely recognizable. She lay on the grass and could not get up. The Faellem lifted her high to show her her world. She embraced them one by one, and everyone was weeping. Millennia had passed since they left for Santhenar.

"We have done it," Faelamor whispered. "Our world is safe; our enemy is no more. We are free at last."

"But look at the cost," said Hallal. "Look what you did to Galgilliel and Aeolior, and Maigraith too. We are all culpable. We warped, we twisted and we extinguished the

Charon, as we did our best to eliminate the Mariem before them."

"I did it for Tallallame," said Faelamor.

"You emptied the void into Aachan," said Hallal. "That was not necessary. You changed Aachan forever."

"I had no choice," said Faelamor. "We are the noblest of all the human kinds. Look how we cared for our world, as no other species ever has."

The wind shifted and they caught the smell of burning wood and leaves. A faint cry came on the breeze.

"What's that?" hissed Hallal, straining her eyes against the gloom.

The burning smell grew stronger until they knew that it could only be a forest fire, and a big one too. Overlaid with that they caught the reek of burning flesh.

The sun wrenched itself over the horizon and through the thunderheads of brown smoke they saw glimpses of the horrible scene. Vast tracts of forest were burning, as far as could be seen, and even in the furthest distance smoke made columns in the air as big as mountains.

"What's happened?" Faelamor whispered. The sun shone on her face, and her golden skin had withered. Her eyes were dull raisins in two deep craters. "What's gone wrong? I don't understand."

The Faellem had gone down the hill, seeking news. Faelamor remained on the pyramidal hillside, staring into the drifting smoke. High above, winged creatures soared and wheeled on thermals created by the fires. They seemed at home in the chaos. Terrifyingly so.

As she watched, one folded back its wings and went into a steep glide, right into the billowing smoke. A long while later it flapped out again, holding something vaguely human in its claws. It was closer now, and Faelamor saw clearly how the leathery wings clubbed the air out of the way. No such beast had inhabited Tallallame when she'd lived here. Now she could see dozens.

Faelamor felt a terrific pain inside her, as if that creature was tearing at her vitals. Suddenly she did understand. Time passes differently in the Three Worlds, and Tallallame was only a pale shadow of the paradise she remembered. In the peaceful beauty of its forests, violent, desperate creatures now stalked.

The vent she had directed with the Mirror had emptied the void not into Aachan, as she intended, but into Tallallame. The Twisted Mirror had betrayed her yet again.

All morning she sat on the grass, alone, as she had been alone for so many years. What was to be done? This was a greater trial than any she'd faced on Santhenar. How could she save her world? She felt so old, so tired. I must rally the Faellem, she thought. We are millions, and no doubt there are gatherings nearby, directing the fighting of the fires and the defense against the void-creatures. She made a broadcast link, to find out where they were and what they were up to, but where once she would have picked up a whole world of minds, now she sensed nothing but mindless terror. What had gone wrong? That terror echoed in her own head.

She limped down the hill to find the gathering. In the valley below was a Faellem town—a beautiful place they had inhabited for ten thousand years. That's where they would be.

But in the valley she found nothing but ruins, so old that the stone was overgrown and crumbling. It looked as if no one had dwelt here for ten centuries. She sat on a column, staring up into the trees. Hours she remained there, not knowing what to do. Finally, in her exhaustion, Faelamor leaned back against the stone wall and dozed.

* * *

A banshee shriek woke her. Faelamor leapt up as a winged shape plummeted through the treetops, snapping and snarling. It was one of the winged creatures she'd seen earlier. It settled on a high limb, darting a beaked head forward on its long neck, trying to get at something hiding in the uppermost branches. Something that looked very human as it weaved and ducked among the foliage.

Suddenly the creature's head flashed forward, incredibly fast for such a large beast, and caught the human by the arm. It let out such a scream of terror that Faelamor wanted to run away. There was a melee in the treetops; then they fell together, bounced off the end of a branch and kept falling, wheeling in the air.

The great wings flashed just above the ground. The creature landed awkwardly and its prey—a young Faellem woman—tore free. Scrabbling across the leaf litter, she came face to face with Faelamor.

They stared at each other. The young woman could have been a daughter, for she had the same colorless hair, translucent skin and golden eyes. She was a beautiful creature. Or would have been, had she not been dressed like a beast, in tatters of moldy fur. She was dirty, and she stank. Faelamor was profoundly disgusted.

The woman threw out her arms to Faelamor, making a series of grunts that could only be interpreted as a cry for help.

The winged creature arched its wings, staring at them. It's afraid of me, Faelamor thought. It recognizes my power.

The woman again made that grunted plea. Faelamor wanted to help her but was paralyzed by the realization that her people here on Tallallame, who had been the noblest of all the human species, had been reduced to this. She had destroyed a whole species, and corrupted herself, for this animal?

The young woman gave up, ducked past Faelamor and

tried to hide in the ruins. The winged creature sprang, the beaked head darted forward and caught her by one slender ankle. The woman struggled desperately. Faelamor did nothing.

The ankle was transferred from beak to claw. The creature gave Faelamor a knowing look, leapt into the air, flapped up through the treetops and disappeared. Faelamor had to sit down. The woman's cries kept echoing through her mind.

She understood it all now. The Faellem who had remained on Tallallame, who had once been so plentiful, now dwelt in caves and the tops of trees, little more than beasts, and were dreadfully afraid. Over the millennia they had stagnated. After expelling the Mariem into the void, their mind-powers had given them so much control over their lives that they no longer had to strive, and the genocide of their rivals meant that they were unchallenged masters of their own world. They had forgotten that, outside Tallallame, the struggle for existence continued as relentlessly as ever.

The forest was already reclaiming their great arts, and the fires would take the rest. The Faellem had lost their humanity and were now sinking down the one-way slide to beasthood. They would survive, but only to paw and grunt at the priceless treasures of their civilization, until time turned the last of them to dust.

There's nothing left of us, thought Faelamor as she crawled back up the hill to her followers. The Faellem are finished.

"Our whole life and purpose has been a lie," she said to Gethren. "If only I had listened. But I was too proud. I refused to believe that any device could get the better of me. What a fool I am! I said it a long time ago and never realized: *I looked on the Mirror in Katazza and saw what I wanted to see.*"

"We deserve this fate," said Gethren. "We lost our nobility when we betrayed the Mariem. We chose the wrong way and we have followed it ever since."

"I *led* you the wrong way. I am the Faellem, and I am Tallallame!" said Faelamor, weeping as she looked upon the ruin of her world. "This evil has come from my own. It must be immolated."

She went down into the forest to a place where three grand trees had fallen together and were blazing fiercely. The Faellem cried out to her. "We can defeat this enemy too," said Hallal. "We can reclaim our world."

Faelamor would not hear them. "Our enemy is ourselves," she said. She marched forward, never flinching as her colorless hair seared off to expose the death's head of her skull. She reached out to embrace the pyre, to burn all the evil away.

And just as they had followed her every decision for so long, one by one the Faellem followed her into the flames.

46

A Genuine Hero

In Shazmak there remained only Maigraith, Karan and the staring Ghâshâd. When Faelamor disappeared, that fiery explosion had sealed the tattered remnant of the Forbidding over again.

Maigraith took Karan's hand. There were tears in her eyes as she looked down at the broken body of her friend. Karan opened her green eyes, liquid with pain, and smiled a wan smile.

"We have done it, you and I," she whispered. "Who would have thought it?" Her eyes drifted closed and she seemed to shrink in on herself. Her pale face went as smooth and still as wax.

Maigraith was in an agony of shock and grief so deep that she felt no pain from her own wounds, and they were many. The arm that had gone beneath the construct was covered in weeping blisters. Her thigh was torn open to the knee. She was scratched, battered and bruised all over. But her work was not over yet. She steeled herself to complete the job—

to restore the balance between the worlds. If only she had not given away her birthright. But how was she to find the way to Aachan? Her least gates on Santhenar were apt to go wrong because she could not *see* the destination clearly enough.

"Don't go!" said Maigraith, stroking Karan's red curls. She laid her hand across Karan's brow, wiping the beads of dampness away. "Stay with me—we have one final task."

Karan's eyes fluttered open, though it took a supreme effort. They were cloudy, but Maigraith took Karan's limp hand; it tightened and her malachite eyes grew clear again.

"What is it?" Karan whispered.

"The Forbidding is only hanging together by a thread, but the balance has not been restored. At every seam of the globe the creatures that dwell in the void gain entrance. I must make things the way they were before the flute. That is my destiny."

"How can *I* help you?" Karan's voice was barely audible.

"I cannot do it alone. The balance was broken, in Aachan. It can only be restored there."

"Once before you pressured me so very hard. Look what you got me into that time. Now Rulke is dead," whispered Karan, "and Tensor too, and Mendark, and every one of the Charon, and half the Ghâshâd. Shazmak is a sea of blood, and all because of you and me."

"Rulke is dead!" Maigraith echoed, staring into eternity.

"Where's Llian? I must speak to him before I die."

"I don't know where Llian is. Karan, listen! I must reach across to Aachan and work with the Charon, if any survive. But I do not know the Way. Only you can find it now. Will you help me?"

"The pain is killing me." Karan writhed, slipping into delirium. "I want Llian. This is my dying wish, which you must honor."

"Then the fate of the Three Worlds is sealed, and we will fail under the weight of the void. We cannot survive."

"I can't help you," said Karan. "How can I sense the Way? The pain takes away everything from my mind." She looked up suddenly and her eyes were fever-bright. *"Llian, where are you, Llian?"*

Taking Karan in her arms, Maigraith carried her to a couch. There she arranged her broken limbs with cushions so that they troubled her as little as possible, but still the pain was terrible.

Maigraith sat beside her, holding her hand. Of course she must honor Karan's dying wish, if she possibly could. The Forbidding would surely hold for a bit yet.

Where could the company have got to? Most likely Shand's strange gate had carried them back to Carcharon. She tried to sense the Way there, but since Faelamor's departure everything had changed. She could not visualize Carcharon at all.

Karan stirred. "Llian!" she moaned.

"I can't find him."

Karan began to pant in little short breaths. Maigraith gave her some water, after which she seemed a little stronger. Karan closed her eyes.

After some time Maigraith realized that the remaining Ghâshâd were gathered round, staring at them both. All they had striven for was undone, and they had failed their master in his time of greatest need. Rulke's death had freed them but diminished them. They no longer had a purpose in life.

Vartila the Whelm was the lowest of them all. Vartila, who had not recognized her master until it was too late, who had only become Ghâshâd at the moment of their greatest failure—Vartila was completely undone.

"What was my life for?" she wept. "Nothing at all!"

"People," said Maigraith. "Rulke is dead and the

Ghâshâd are no more. There is nothing for you here. Go back to what you were before Rulke first made you his, if you would live. Swear that you will take no master any more."

Vartila and the other Ghâshâd took that vow, then turned away, cowed, fearful and alone in the world, and went back to hide in their southern forests. All except one. "Are you coming, Idlis?" asked Yetchah, looking back longingly at him. They had been together constantly these last few days.

"I'll follow, wherever you go," he said. "But first, I have unfinished business here."

Idlis looked down at Karan, and on his face there was an expression as close to tenderness as his blocky features would allow.

"If only Rulke had listened," he said to himself. "I warned him—Llian's telling was not a fable but a prediction. Rulke would not hear me. Llian made the tale better than he knew. *From nothing we came—to nothing do we return.*"

He turned to Maigraith. "I am a healer," he reminded her. His thick voice was gentle now. "For more than a year I have owed Karan the debt of my life." Crouching down, he took Karan's hand with his skeletal fingers. "Once before you refused my aid," he said, referring to the dreadful injuries she had taken when she choked his dog to death. "Will you let me help you this time?"

"I would be most grateful," Karan whispered. She did not fear him any longer.

"She is cold," he said to Maigraith. "Bring two braziers, some blankets and a hot drink."

While Maigraith did that, Idlis cut off Karan's garments and laid her out on the couch. He exclaimed at her many scars, and particularly at her hand and wrist. "Poor Whelp!" he said wistfully, thinking of his dog.

After covering her with blankets, he went away, shortly to return with a purple phial. He put a few drops of the secret fluid on Karan's tongue.

"Is that better?"

"A little," she whispered, "but now my head spins so."

He probed her flesh, but his touch was infinitely gentle. Taking her hips in his hands, he eased them this way and that, trying to tease the broken bones back together. Karan screamed.

Idlis looked grave. "She should feel nothing at all," he said to Maigraith. "I don't dare give a stronger dose. I have only one remedy left, but I am afraid to use it on her."

"Anything," gasped Karan, squirming, which only made the pain of her shattered bones worse.

"It is the drug hrux," he said to Karan. "You have tasted it before, have you not?"

"Twice," said Karan with a shudder, remembering the dried Ghâshâd fruit that she had accidentally taken from Carcharon. It had given her such schizophrenic dreams. Just the mention of it sent her body arching in yearning.

Idlis frowned. "It could kill you, in your state, or possess you ever after." He explained to Maigraith. "Hrux is a deadly drug. We used it when we all wanted to work together with one mind, to *sense* and to *control*. It was employed by the *square* against you when you fought the Second Army in Bannador last summer."

Maigraith remembered that day very well, the feeling that she was opposed by a community of minds and wills.

"But to her, and to you too, Maigraith, it is the most addictive drug there is. She has tasted it twice already. A third time and she may never be free of the yearning for it. And it has other effects too, as varied as the people who take it. Who knows what it might do to a triune?"

Maigraith wept. "If it doesn't kill her, you say?"

Idlis nodded. "It may. But nothing else can lift the pain from her."

"Karan," Maigraith said, spotting Karan's hand with her tears. "I am a cold, unfeeling woman, as you know. How can I demand from you what I cannot do myself? But—"

"Say what you want," snapped Karan.

"Will you take this hrux and offer me the chance to restore the balance? I swear—"

"I—" said Karan.

"Don't be hasty," Maigraith interrupted. "It may kill you."

"Or if you become addicted and cannot get it, you will wish it had," said Idlis.

"What's the difference?" Karan screamed. "I'm dying! If I can put that off and do this thing as well, then give me the hrux."

"Very well," said Idlis. "I will begin with a small dose. It's just possible that you may get away without ill effects." He cut off a piece of hrux about the size of a pea and put it in her mouth.

It was chewy in a leathery sort of a way, like an overly dried apricot. "My mouth burns," she said.

After an interval Idlis took her hips in his hands again and tried once more to ease the bones back in place. Karan screamed.

Idlis looked up at Maigraith. "It's done nothing! I'll have to give a bigger dose."

It took a second piece and then a third before the pain diminished enough for Idlis to put her fractured pelvis back together. When that was done, and it was not done quickly, he straightened her legs, smoothing the flesh with his hands, and all of a sudden the stress went from her face. He fixed her bones, cleaned the many cuts and abrasions, and bound them with clean cloth. Finally he drew the blankets over her again. Even his iron-hard features showed weariness.

"I thought her back was broken," he said to Maigraith, who was standing at the head of the couch. "But it is not—only the pelvis, though that in three places, and both legs high up. One hip is dislocated, and sundry other bones broken too. Only time can fuse them together, but I have put them back as they should be. Bones are my special skill. Now we must encase her hips in plaster, and her legs, else she may never walk again. Perhaps she may not anyway. And as for childbirth . . ." he shook his head. "Best that pregnancy be avoided altogether."

"She is triune," said Maigraith coolly.

"Nonetheless!" said Idlis. "Tonight I will build a metal frame for her lower body, to force the bones to heal true."

He set to work with plaster, and when that was finished said to Maigraith, "You may begin your own work. But take it slowly. She is weak and has lost blood inside, and the hrux, as I said, is dangerous. For your sake as well as for hers, don't push her too hard. But first let me attend your injuries, or I will be laying you beside her."

Karan felt quite strange, as if she was floating above her broken body. There was no pain; she felt no sensations whatever. But there was work to do. She drew a link between herself and Maigraith. The hrux made that easy, for she was halfway into the world of dreams and hallucinations anyway, but the link was a tenuous, wavery thing.

Maigraith hammered the fatal metal thorn down flat, climbed the construct and sat in the high seat. She worked the controls and instantly a section of the Wall thinned to gauze. The armies clawed against the other side. She let out a gasp.

"Maigraith, are you all right?"

"I can hardly breathe," said Maigraith. "My throat feels closed up. I know I'm not strong enough."

"I can't help you," said Karan.

"I know!" Forcing calm on herself, Maigraith spoke over the link. *I'm ready. Now do your part, if you can.*

Karan sought out through the Wall for that wandering, ethereal path that was the Way between the Worlds, the path from Santhenar to Aachan. In spite of the chaos of the Forbidding the Way was easier to find than before. Perhaps the pain and the drug stripped away all distractions and allowed her mind to focus on just one thing.

I have it, she said across the link. *See, here it is!*

Maigraith used the construct as she had seen Rulke do, wrenched with her mind and opened the Way. At once the armies of the void renewed their assault, and the Wall began to flutter as it had done before.

"Show me the Council chamber of the Charon," cried Maigraith in a great voice. "The place where Rulke spoke with Yalkara." Using the construct, she created a golden globe in the center of the wall, to give vision to Karan's inner seeings. It was surrounded by an iridescent doughnut shape that shone with distorted reflections.

Karan brought forth the image onto the globe, though with difficulty. The pain was growing again in spite of the hrux. The image wavered.

"Hold it!" Maigraith yelled.

Karan firmed the image, which showed the Charon discussing the upheavals in the void and the imminent breakdown of the Forbidding. Yalkara looked up suddenly.

"You live!" called Maigraith to her grandmother.

Rulke?

"It is I, Maigraith. Noble Rulke is dead."

How did he die?

"Tensor struck him down with a potency. Rulke saved me at the expense of his own life."

He sacrificed everything for you? That is—she broke off. *Forgive me!*

"I don't know," said Maigraith dumbly.

Then the experiment in Santhenar has truly failed, said another, *and our species is finished.*

He tore off his shirt and cast himself on the floor in grief and loss, an Aachim custom that the Charon had adopted. Then the one next to him tore off hers, and the rest did likewise, and Yalkara rent her blouse last of all. Finally she stirred.

If it is the end, let us go to it bravely, as he would have done. Thank you for bringing us the news.

"Wait, the Forbidding is failing! Will you show me how to restore the balance between the worlds?"

You must bring the construct here. It can't be done anywhere else.

While they spoke the Wall of the Forbidding had begun to reverberate back and forth across the room, and each time it snapped the other way it made a boom that shook the building like an earthquake. Cracks appeared in a side wall. One of the staircases fell down with a shocking clatter.

"Don't go," said Karan aloud. "I can't hold the link. You'll be trapped there."

"I must," said Maigraith. "This is what I was born for. Don't lose sight of the Way, whatever you do."

Despite Karan's pleas, Maigraith bound Rulke's body to the side of the construct, in a desperate hope that they could bring him back. She looked down at Karan, shuddering on her couch, and tickled the levers. The globe became transparent. An aurora of pastel colors flickered around it. A landscape rushed across the globe, distorted as if reflected onto its curving inner surface. Karan saw a gloomy plain dotted with buildings growing out of the ground like clusters of metallic bubbles. Several were circled by platforms that resembled planetary rings. Volcanoes were erupting everywhere, flooding red lava down to overwhelm the bubble clusters.

Maigraith roared in pain, then she and the construct vanished. The landscape faded from the globe, to be replaced by the Charon again. With a thunderous roar, the construct with Maigraith atop it, materialized in the center of the council chamber. The great table around which the Charon sat was shattered to kindling, though they seemed unfazed.

"Thank you," said Yalkara, brushing splinters off her face and arms. "This construct will be Rulke's monument, temple and tomb. We cannot cower here, dwindling to nothing, dying out one by one. There can be no greater agony than to know that you are the last of your species. We shall leap hand in hand into the eternal night. We will take the construct into the void."

"First show me how to restore the balance," said Maigraith.

"You cannot alter the balance with the construct," the Charon cried. "*You* are the instrument. *You* must do it."

In restoring the balance the instrument will be lost, said Karan across the link.

"Lost to Santhenar!" said Yalkara.

The Charon explained what had to be done. "It will be hard," said Yalkara. "None of us could do it."

"I know what to do," said Maigraith. "My whole life's purpose was for this task."

Suddenly, incomprehensible visions flashed through Karan's mind and across the brilliant sphere. Everything flickered and wavered. Her pain was growing again.

"*Hold the link!*" Maigraith screamed.

As she spoke the door was smashed open and a horde of

Aachim pushed through. They were heavily armed, their faces resolute. They had rebelled against their masters at last.

"Stand firm!" Yalkara shouted. She leapt right over the construct and caught Maigraith about the waist, supporting her while the Charon made a wall before their enemies.

As Yalkara and Maigraith strove together, weird visions spun through Karan's mind. The images on the globe whirled sickeningly, then it blanked out. Karan tried to get it back but the sphere remained dark.

Behind her there were running footsteps and incoherent cries of joy. The company had returned through their hastily constructed gate from Carcharon—Shand, Yggur, Llian, all of them. Llian ran to Karan, weeping for joy, but she put her hand up.

"Not now!" she gasped, and turned back to the globe, forcing through her pain to recover the link and the Way. Everything was changed again. She found something and brought it out on the surface—an array of dancing dots that had a vaguely human shape. "That's Maigraith," she said, and all at once the dots resolved into Maigraith and the room was back again, though now everything was tinged with dark auras like an indigo and black rainbow.

Shand stood as rigid as a post, staring at Yalkara. His arms hung straight down. His fists were clenched. Malien, beside him, was shaking with her own conflict. She wanted the Aachim to seize the construct and free their world, but not at the expense of the Forbidding that protected this one.

The Charon's council chamber was in uproar, Aachim and Charon in wild melee. Then, as Karan watched, helpless, a muscular Aachim man crept out from behind the construct and struck Maigraith down without warning. Leaping over her, he climbed onto the construct. A dozen more Aachim followed him. Maigraith groaned and rolled over.

"Maigraith, flee!" cried Karan.

"*How can I?*" her cry returned.

The first Aachim took the wheel. A rumble shook the room. The watchers in Shazmak saw the globe vibrate. A yellow light came out of an aperture at the front of the construct, so bright that it carved smoking channels in the air. It splashed on the wall of the chamber, searing it away. Outside, an orange moon hung in the black sky, so big and bright that it might have been suspended in a tree. Volcanoes were erupting everywhere, flooding red lava toward them.

"Flee!" screamed Yggur, and his cry was transmitted through Karan all the way to Aachan.

"*Not without the construct,*" Maigraith shouted, shaking her head. Hurling away an Aachim woman who resembled Karan, she advanced, shielding her eyes. The beam shot from the aperture again, vaporized the remains of the table and moved jerkily toward her. The room began to fill with smoke.

"Can no one help her?" Karan screeched.

"What about my people?" said Malien, staring hungrily at Aachan. "What about *my* world?"

The Charon seemed paralyzed. An eternity passed in a few seconds. Yggur's face contorted. He shot out his hand. His back arched. His eyes bulged. Calling up aspects of the Secret Art that he had lost in his decades of madness, he did something that had never been done before. A bolt of blue fire seared through the Wall, across the Way between the Worlds, into the chamber, and turned the construct into a glowing cinder. The Aachim went in all directions.

Maigraith's face looked out from the globe. She reached out her arms to Karan as if she could pull her through, but it was too late. The Way slowly collapsed in on itself. The sphere vanished. The luminous layers of the Forbidding flared bright and disappeared forever.

It was over. The balance had been restored. Yggur crashed down on his face and could not even move a finger. Karan fell back with a little cry.

Llian laid his head upon her breast, thinking her dead. But she moved under him, and her warm breath came past his face in a little sigh. "What on earth happened to your hair?" she said, opening her eyes and smiling fondly at him.

"A fire. But this time *I* didn't light it," he said hastily. He was referring to his clumsy rescue in Narne, when he had burned the house down while they were still trapped inside, and had to break through the floor to get out.

That reminded her of one of his earliest absurdities. "*My name's Llian. I've come to save you,*" she quoted dreamily, and smiled up at him in that teasing way she had.

"I thought you were dead!" he said accusingly.

She snorted, opened her eyes and put her free arm across his shoulders. "I was near enough to it a while ago, but I am better now. So very much better, Llian."

The hrux had begun to wear off. Karan hurt all over. Not as badly as before, but badly enough to take away every worry about the carnage here, and the loss of Maigraith, and all the other dead.

Yggur lay not far away, tossing and turning in a hideous version of aftersickness. The superhuman blast had torn him inside. He looked like a dried-out cadaver, though Idlis had said that he would recover.

Llian sat with Karan for an hour, then was called away to corpse duty. There were many dead, and each must be honored according to their own customs. The creatures that had come out of the void had to be destroyed to prevent disease.

So it was that Karan was alone when the lorrsk that had hunted her throughout the tunnels eventually tracked her down. It had spent most of the day in hiding, for fear of the

Sentinels, but it was much bolder now. For the past few hours, when the Sentinels sounded, no one had come to investigate.

The lorrsk was a dreadful, ruined, slavering thing, for it had been terribly hurt before it overcame the two Ghâshâd at the mine gate, and their sinewy flesh had not slaked its desperate hunger. It had tracked Karan all this way, cunningly evading the few Ghâshâd patrols, stung and blasted by a hundred Sentinels. One arm hung half-severed and useless, and three fingers were gone from its other hand. It was gouged and rent and half its fur had been burnt off. The ghastly buttock was a pulpy, gangrenous mess.

But it had found what it was looking for—the juicy red-haired woman, and this time she *looked* completely helpless. It hobbled across the room, so intent on her that it did not even notice Yggur until it trod on his face.

Yggur shrieked and the lorrsk jumped sideways a couple of spans. Karan snapped awake. At first she thought it was a hallucination brought on by the hrux, but no hallucination could be that horrible. The great room was empty. There was no one to help her.

"Oh, Llian," she thought aloud. "Just when I believed it was all over. Where are you now?"

She stared at the lorrsk. "What can I do? I can't do anything at all." The lorrsk, remembering her previous tricks, stood motionless, gauging her. Then, rather gingerly, it reached out for her unprotected belly.

Out of the corner of her eye Karan saw the object of her hopes and fears. Llian, coming back for the next body, must have heard Yggur's cry.

"*Karan!*" he screamed. Snatching up Rulke's sword, he ran straight at the lorrsk, brandishing the huge weapon like a butcher his cleaver.

"Oh, Llian," she said calmly, "this is not a good idea at all. You won't even get one blow in."

The lorrsk turned away with terrifying speed, despite its injuries, and hurled itself at Llian. He flailed the sword furiously, the creature ducked and Llian, completely off balance, fell to one knee right in its path. It swung its arm, its huge hand connecting with Llian's side with a thump like a butcher dismembering a carcass. Llian was hurled through the air to land on his shoulder, somehow still clutching the sword. His shirt had been ripped off. There were bloody gashes across his side.

No one could survive such a blow from a lorrsk's claws. This was the end of the line. Karan felt the most unutterable agony.

Then, miraculously, Llian moved his legs. He groaned and tried to sit up. The lorrsk flapped after him. There was only one thing that could possibly be done, and this was the only time Karan could have done it, while the hrux still pulsed through her brain. She hurled her fury at the lorrsk in a violent sending, the twin of her accidental sending into the mind of the Ghâshâd, that night in Gothryme Forest after her second dose of hrux.

She found herself in an alien, desperate mind, more in pain than she was. She saw though its eyes, felt it raise its good arm to tear Llian apart, and with an effort that was like lifting a boulder she tried to seize control. Fighting muscles that were ten times as strong as hers, fighting a will the equal of her own, all Karan could do was force the swing to go high. The blow passed just over Llian's head. The lorrsk bellowed and flung her back out again.

Then, with her own eyes she saw the most incredible sight. Llian came to his knees and hurled the sword underarm up at the creature as if he was pitching manure with a shovel. It was a hopeless, agricultural throw. Karan was just steeling herself for another sending when the razor edge carved along the side of the lorrsk's neck, bursting an artery. The creature danced around in a circle and fell flat on the floor in front of her, dead.

She looked down at the ruined hand. The two remaining claws were broken to stumps. That was all that had saved Llian from being disemboweled.

Llian wobbled across. There were two great gouges across his ribs. "Don't say it," he said as he put his arms around her.

"*I've come to save you?*" She gave a muffled giggle. "I wasn't going to."

"I never wanted to be a hero anyway, just a teller."

"Well, you are now. A genuine hero. But then, you always were to me.'

47

FOREVER EXILES

In the morning Idlis reappeared with a metal and leather frame made to fit over the plaster casts. It ran from Karan's waist to her feet. They put her in it and he adjusted the straps and the tension of various springs which pulled on her feet and kept the bones straight.

"This will keep everything in place until the bones have grown back together," he said to Llian. "She must stay in it for at least six weeks, and may not be moved for two."

Llian eyed the contraption. "It looks hideously uncomfortable. And how will you . . . ?"

Karan laughed. "Attend to my bodily functions, you mean? I will have a nurse, of course. If you truly love me you will do that for me, and when I finally get out I will reward you. And myself, naturally."

Idlis took Karan's small hand and kissed it. Her skin no longer shrank from the rubbery feel of his skin. He felt like a friend to her now.

He said, "I will come to Gothryme on this day once a

year, in case you need hrux. There is no other way of getting it, for no one else knows how it is made. If you should need me, send a message to Pymir, a place on the southern shore of the Karama Malama—the Sea of Mists. I must go after Yetchah." His eyes were moist. "Fare well!"

"Fare well," said Karan. "There is a future for you now. Come to Gothryme if ever you need *me*."

Malien came over, to stand by Karan's stretcher. "Do you hate and despise me?" Karan asked in a small voice.

Bending over, Malien pushed the hair from her brow. "You are kin, Karan, and I will always love you."

"But I betrayed my kin and helped Rulke."

"And once again you were right to do so. It's done with, Karan."

Karan heaved a vast sigh.

"But can you forgive us, Karan, for all the Aachim did to you and your family?" It was Malien's turn to look anxious.

"Malien . . ."

"Yes, Karan?"

"You didn't finish brushing my hair," Karan said, referring to their fight in Thurkad weeks ago.

"I'll do it right away." She laughed. "And to show my contrition, I'll even use my own brush, since no doubt you've lost yours."

"Now that *is* a favor!" Karan said cheekily. "First your boots, then your hairbrush. When I next go east, maybe you will give up your bed for me too."

"Don't push it!" Malien laughed.

The Aachim closeted themselves with Tensor, prepared the body and kept vigil over it for a day and a night, playing their plangent instruments and speaking their threnodies. The following dawn they buried him in the tomb reserved long ago, in the catacombs of old Shazmak, sealing him in with a simple, dignified ceremony.

"He will not leave his beloved Shazmak again," said Malien. "And none of us will ever go home to Aachan. We are forever exiles."

"Does that matter after all this time?" Llian asked. "Your ancestors were born here, surely?"

"They were, but the longing is burned deep into our souls. Aachan is a place we all dream of making our pilgrimage to." She sighed heavily. "I'm worried now. Did you see the volcanoes erupting? What's happening to my world?"

"Is there anything you can do?"

"No!" said Malien. "Whatever fate is in store for my people on Aachan, good or bad, they're on their own."

"What will you do with yourselves now?" Llian wondered.

"We'll go off to our eastern cities, I expect, and make our way in the world somehow. We were never as great as we thought we were, but we're survivors. Our long march of folly is finished. And it gives us heart to know that our slavery on Aachan is over. We could have ended it ourselves four thousand years ago, had we the courage to challenge the Charon. Had we known how vulnerable they really were. But we didn't."

Mendark they entombed in Shazmak too, and the other dead. All that remained of the nanollet was a film of gold and soot on the floor. The Aachim smashed the tiles to powder and threw it bit by bit into the Garr, along with the ashes of the dead creatures that had come out of the void. In its last flight the construct had passed over the flute and melted it into a puddle that had seeped into the cracked floor. They chiseled that out and cast it into the Garr as well. It was not what they had pledged to do before the flute was made, but it was the best they could manage now.

When all that work was done, Karan, still in her plaster and her frame, was bound to a stretcher. Only ten days had gone by but they could delay no longer. There was much to be done in the real world, the only one they'd ever know.

They made their way out of Shazmak for the last time, on foot, for Shand's gate had failed when the Forbidding dissolved. All those who knew how to make gates were dead now, or lost, except Shand alone. He was a downcast automaton. Having lost Yalkara and now Maigraith, there seemed no reason to go on living.

"Why don't you try to make another gate, just to get us safely to Gothryme?" Llian asked as they stood at the end of the glorious cobweb bridge. Karan was already suffering.

"I don't want to know if gates still work," Shand snapped. "The secret will die with me! There are some things we are better off without."

"What about you, Yggur?"

"If I had a hundred gates at my disposal I wouldn't make one to help *her*," he said coldly. He blamed the loss of Maigraith on Karan too.

The road was steep and long, and the nights hard, especially on the windswept track beside the Garr. Karan was hideously uncomfortable, for every careful step by her bearers sent such a jolt of pain through her that she wept, and at night it was still cold enough for the tears to freeze on her cheeks. She lay awake, remembering how hrux had taken the pain away, and wanting it now. It wasn't a desperate longing, no more than an itch, but always there.

On the way Llian took Shand aside. "Some time back, you said you would make up for what you did to me."

"I did," said Shand indifferently. "What do you ask of me?"

"Karan had an old silver chain that we found in Katazza. You pawned it for her when I was in Yggur's cells in Thurkad. The chain is very precious to her. If you can get it back . . ."

Shand jerked like a pair of frog's legs on an alchemist's battery. "It might be . . . difficult to recover. Because of the war, I mean."

"Will you try?"

"I will," Shand spoke to the other side of the road, and strode on ahead.

At their pace it took five days to travel out of the high mountains and onto the ridge path that led down past Carcharon to Gothryme Forest. Late on the sixth day they passed the bleak ruin, standing on its ridge like a broken bottle. Karan's eyes misted over, thinking about her father. Her yearning for the solace of hrux grew stronger.

They kept going that night, unwilling to camp on the path, and at the bottom crossed over the stone bridge. The gullies she had walked across after hythe were running now and soon would be impassable torrents. Spring was on the way at last.

They broke their fast in the pavilion by Black Lake, rested for an hour and then headed on. The stretcher-bearers trod carefully down the cliff path. The steps were wet with melt. Llian, taking his turn at the back of Karan's stretcher, was lost in memories.

"What's the matter?" Karan asked.

"Oh, I was just thinking. Last time I came down *I* was on the stretcher. And then, just here the thranx appeared."

"Well, you don't have to worry about that—it's long dead."

"But how many more are at large now?"

The last part of the journey seemed interminable, but finally they were down, splashing through mud among the granite tors where the first green shoots of spring had begun to appear, and along the well-worn track to Gothryme Manor. Karan had a momentary fear that some disaster had befallen her home, but its stone chimneys and green slate roofs appeared over the top of the hill. Gothryme stood before them just as it always had looked, a little, old place, rather shabby, with the weathered scaffolding extending down one wing and the gardens drab and bare.

"It looks deserted," said Karan, fretting.

They turned around between the two wings and saw half a dozen children chasing one another across the garden beds, and in and out through the half-built walls. One of the cherry trees in the orchard was just coming into bloom. The children shouted and ran to stare at the strangers. People appeared at the back door, and among them Karan saw the white hair and tall stooped figure of old Rachis, the mainstay of Gothryme and of her life since her father's death. She let out a great sigh. Everything was going to be all right after all.

They wanted to carry her up to her bedroom and put her in the great square bed, but, although in considerable pain, Karan was having none of that. "Put me down just there," she said, indicating the space between the fire and the window in the old keep. "I'm sleeping there until my plaster comes off. I want to see everything."

That night they had a banquet, feasting on surplus Aachim food carried down from Shazmak (though more than one of the Gothryme folk complained about the weird foreign stuff), and wine from Karan's cellar. A whole stack of wood was burned, so that everyone could bathe away the mud of the past week. Karan itched unbearably under her plaster but had to be content with a wet cloth.

At Gothryme they heard news for the first time in weeks, and it was not good news. Strange creatures had appeared from nowhere, all over Meldorin. Creatures out of mythology: intelligent ones like lorrsk and thranx, but wild beasts too, large and small, in every form imaginable. Elludore Forest was especially thick with them.

The following afternoon Karan was back on her stretcher, checking on the condition of the gardens and the rebuilding work, when a stranger rode up to the front door with an escort of two soldiers. "Who can that be?" she wondered idly, making pencil marks on her garden plan.

"One of Yggur's lieutenants with dispatches, I suppose," said Llian.

"I'd better go and make him welcome. Carry me in, please."

Entering the hall she saw a rather thickset man with black eyes and a crooked nose, talking to Yggur. His legs were long and spindly, making him look top-heavy. "He doesn't look like a soldier," she said. "He looks like a clerk."

"Or a tax collector!"

She stared at Llian. Karan had forgotten about that problem.

Yggur gestured in her direction, whereupon spindleshanks headed across to her. "Karan Elienor Melluselde Fyrn?"

"That is my name."

"I am Garlish Tunk, tax collector for the district called the Hills of Bannador. Here is my warrant." Opening a leather case he displayed a document inscribed on parchment with black ink. It bore Yggur's seal at the bottom.

Karan did not even glance at it. It was hardly likely that he was an impostor. "I know who you are."

"Your remit," said Tunk, "is assessed at 540 tars. Here is the audit." He handed her a paper scroll tied with a black ribbon.

"An appropriate decoration," she said, not looking at it either.

"Please check the audit," said the tax man. "The rule of law applies in Yggur's realm, and he requires everything to be done regular."

Karan read the paper. So many tars for her house; so many for the land, the road and the bridges; a head tax on her tenants and workers; the tax on her fishing rights to part of the River Ryme; another tax on the forest of Gothryme.

"What's this? A tax on the forest?"

"It contains much valuable timber."

"It's worthless. There's no way to get it down."

"Do you relinquish the title then?"

Karan said nothing. Give up the title to land! It was unthinkable.

"I cannot pay your 540 tars," she said.

He frowned. "How much are you unable to pay?"

"Any of it! I have no money at all."

"Cannot pay!" He wrote that down. "Then what steps are you prepared to take to discharge your obligation?"

"I have no obligation!" she said furiously. "Bannador is a sovereign realm. Why should I pay to repair the damage of the war your master brought against my country, destroying the land and ruining me? Damn you! I refuse!"

"I will take that as being an appeal to Lord Yggur," he said, and called him across.

Karan glared at Yggur, scarcely able to believe that he required such a sum of her after all that had happened. "A quarter of that sum would bankrupt me."

"The realm is in ruins and has to be rebuilt," he replied with icy calm. His rage against her was as strong as ever.

"It was you who ruined it!" she snapped.

"That's history! Everyone must contribute."

"You had no trouble raising money for your stupid wars!"

"You have more than most, Karan. Surely you have ways of paying the debt."

"I have none," she said. "All my resources are used up. There is only one possibility."

"And what is that?"

"Faelamor owed me a debt of some hundreds of tars."

"Really?" said Yggur. "How so?" His eyes glinted dangerously.

She hesitated. "Payment for my trip to Fiz Gorgo to steal your Mirror."

Yggur almost had a fit. "You're not improving your case!" he snapped.

"What she left in Elludore is mine, if I can get it." Karan fingered the ebony bracelet that would dissolve the illusions there.

"What good is that to me? The roads and bridges must be repaired *now*. Elludore is rife with beasts. It may never be safe to go there."

Shand came up behind Yggur and put a hand on his shoulder. If anyone had influence over the man it was he. "In this particular case there are mitigating circumstances," Shand said. "I think that an argument can be made for an extension."

One side of Yggur's face twitched, then he nodded coldly. "Very well! In view of your situation, Karan, and what you have done for us, which I acknowledge, I will give you grace until the end of autumn. But if it is not paid then, your lands and possessions to the value of your taxes are forfeit."

The problem was only postponed. The sum would hardly be more affordable in the autumn even after the best of seasons.

* * *

The next morning the company continued on to Thurkad, for there was Santhenar to be ordered, and all sorts of creatures to be hunted down. The world had to be remade.

"And someone must make it," said Yggur as he dragged himself onto his horse. "Though what is the point I cannot imagine."

Karan waved them off through the doorway. Llian came back inside.

"Well, it's all over. At last!" He wandered aimlessly around the hall and went out in the direction of the kitchen.

It's not all over, Karan thought. Nothing ever is. She lay back on her bed, staring up at the blackened beams. The manor was completely quiet.

Her healing bones ached, and again she felt that desire for hrux. She pushed it away, as she was used to doing, but this time it came back stronger than ever. Karan turned her head so she could see the fire, but that also reminded her of the drug, and how she had burned it that night up in Gothryme Forest. Right now she would have scratched through the burning coals to get it, to feel that rush of power and invincibility. To escape the pain and despair.

"Are you going to leave me too?" Karan said that afternoon. "I suppose you'll be off to the college any day now. I dare say you're getting bored with me."

"I wasn't planning to," Llian said, and tickled her feet just to annoy her, and to see her helpless laughter.

"I am reckoning up every one of your unkind deeds," Karan said, rather more irritably than usual, for the discomfort was unbearable and she had not had a good night's sleep since Shazmak. "Don't think that I won't exact a price when I'm better."

Llian was not intimidated. He pulled the blankets up, tucked her in, then sat beside her on a cushion. "What are you doing?" she asked, suspicious, but when he held out his hand she slipped hers in it.

"What's the matter, Karan?"

She burst into tears.

"I've been looking forward to this day for nearly two years," she wept. "But it's all gone wrong. Look at me! I'm a useless cripple and Yggur's going to take Gothryme away. And . . . and . . ."

"And what, Karan?"

She turned her head away. "It's too awful. I'm no good. I want you to go away. Go back to the college and find someone else."

Llian was taken aback, but decided to put her to the test. "Actually," he said thoughtfully, "I do have a friend at the college. She's not at all like you though. She's tall and elegant, with beautiful dark hair and she has big—"

Karan gasped, punched him in the belly, then tried to scrunch her upper half into a ball.

"I was teasing you," he said softly. He untangled her arms from around her head. "So, you don't want me to go away after all."

"No!" she whispered.

"Let's see if I can work out what the problem is," said Llian. "Do you think, because you can't have children, that I don't want you?"

She sat up painfully. "How did you know I can't have children?"

"You're triune!" He hugged her tightly. "I've known for ages."

"And . . . you still want me?" she said as if she couldn't believe him. "Don't you like children?" She sounded suspicious.

"I'd love to have children. But I want you more."

They lay together for some time. It was awkward because of her casts. Karan was still as tense as wire.

"There's something else, isn't there?" he said.

"Isn't that enough?" she cried.

"Tell me, Karan!"

"It's hrux! I want it all the time now. I thought the longing would go away but it's stronger every day. I can hardly think of anything else."

Llian sat silently. Hrux addiction was something that only she could overcome. All he could do was support her as best he could. But how? Then he saw the way. In fact it had been on his mind all the way home from Shazmak.

"I wonder, would you like to hear a little tale?" he said.

"A tale?" she said irritably.

"A bedtime story." He put on his best teller's voice.

"It's not bedtime!"

"Nonetheless! It begins like this: Once upon a time—"

"Is it romantic? I like romantic tales best."

"It could be," Llian said.

"But not sad, like the one about Jenulka and Hengist. I couldn't bear a sad tale today."

"Not particularly sad."

Karan sighed and snuggled her head against his shoulder. "Well, at least it begins in the right way," she said grudgingly. "The traditional way."

"Once upon a time there was a small girl with red curly hair and eyes as green as bottles. She was a cheerful child, even when it was hard to be cheerful, and that was most of the time. Her father was dead, and her mother too, and she lived with her mother's elderly cousins who treated her very badly. The only hope in the poor girl's life was a dream she kept having. Then, after she grew up, her life was so miserable that she completely lost the dream."

"What dream?" Karan asked suspiciously.

"Well," said Llian with a sly grin, "she knew that, of all men, tellers were the handsomest, the boldest and the best lovers."

Karan gave a derisive snort. "Poor fool!"

It's working! Llian thought. "And since she was little, she had dreamed about wedding a teller."

"Oh really?"

"And not just any teller. She had her eye on a master chronicler of the College of the Histories, and he the handsomest and boldest of them all."

"I look forward to you introducing me to him," Karan said with mock sarcasm.

"Ah, what a man he was, for his was an inner beauty that made her sing inside."

"That's what all the ugly ones say!"

"Hush!" said Llian. "When the teller smiled at her it was like the sun coming out after a week of rain. And when she heard him tell his tales it made her dissolve inside.

"Now comes the bad bit," said Karan.

"Unfortunately, this teller had one or two character defects, though of the *teensiest* kind—"

"I think I know this story," murmured Karan, squeezing his hand. "He was vain beyond all vanity and proud of his art to the point of arrogance! He knew nothing but thought he knew everything. He was so curious that he pried into everyone's business—he just couldn't stop himself. What's more, at every single other thing he was so useless that it's a wonder he managed to feed himself. He could never walk down a step without falling on his face. The wonder is—"

"You've heard it already," Llian said sorrowfully. "And the wonder is—?"

She practiced fluttering her eyelashes a couple of times. "The wonder is that she, who was so beautiful that the moon hid its face when she went outside, who was clever and resourceful and brave and kind—"

"Yes?" said Llian impatiently. "What is this wonder?"

She smiled enigmatically, looking up from under lowered eyelashes. "The wonder is that she loved him so," she said softly. "Go on with the tale, Llian. What did this paragon of a teller do?"

"It happens that, not long after fate threw them together, he fell upon hard times. No fault of his own, you understand—"

"Of course not."

"They were hunted across the world and had many adventures together. Horrible, gruesome adventures, which is good. That kind make the best telling—"

"Don't bother with all the tedious details," said Karan. "What happens at the end? That's all I want to know."

"It's bad manners to interrupt the teller. I'm sure I've told you that before." He sighed loudly. "Very well. Though they had traveled the world together, sharing everything, there was one thing he had never been able to say to her—"

"What?" cried Karan, shaking him. "What couldn't he tell her?"

Llian smiled. She had forgotten all about the pain, and her longing for hrux had vanished.

"Stop grinning like a loon and finish the story!" she shouted. Rachis put his white head around the door briefly, smiled and went away again.

"He loved her more than the moon and the stars—"

"What about his college and his books?" she interrupted, but now there was a shining light in her eyes.

Llian pressed her hand to his lips. "He loved her more than his college, his books, his pens and paper, his writing desk, his ink bottle—"

"Get on with it!" Karan cried in a frenzy. "She knew all

that long ago." She tried to sit up. Llian helped her, very gently.

"But . . ." he paused deliberately.

"Quick, quick!"

"This great teller, this master of all the words in the dictionary, could not find the courage to say those four little words that had been in his heart for more than a year. Poor man, he was terrified."

"Poor stupid girl!" said Karan. "She should have said them for him."

"If only she had," said Llian. "What a silly, miserable duffer he was. Because—and now I find that the story does end sadly after all—he never did."

"And that's the end?" she exclaimed. "What about 'and they lived happily ever after'?"

"That's a different tale. Karan?"

"Yes, Llian?"

He opened his mouth but no words came out.

"Will you marry me?" they both said at the same instant, and fell down on the bed, laughing and crying and hugging one another.

"What's the matter with you," asked Karan a few nights later, when it was late and the house was quiet. Llian had been unusually subdued all afternoon. "I thought I'd made you the happiest man in the world."

"You have, yet I'm stricken by my crimes. I am shaken to my bootstraps."

"What crimes?"

"Collaborating with Tensor in Katazza; taunting Mendark so that he burnt down the archives and stole the flute; driving Tensor into a fury that led to him destroying Rulke. What pride I took in using my teller's *voice*, and in my ability to manipulate him! What reckless joy it gave me! And look how tragic the consequences!"

"Well, you may rue them, while knowing that if you had not acted, things might have been very much worse. I would be dead, for one."

"I feel so guilty. My curiosity was fatal. I will give up being a chronicler and a teller too. It is the only way. I shall labor in your fields from dawn to dusk to atone for my crimes."

"You would be the most useless and miserable laborer in the whole of Bannador," she said with a heartless laugh. "I would probably sack you before lunchtime. Anyway, that's all past and done, and we have to look to the future. Think of all the good you've done with your tales and your Histories."

Llian sat listlessly. "How are you going to support yourself?" she continued. "Not to mention contributing to this place, which burns money like firewood and never makes any. Did you not promise Rulke that you'd write the Histories of the Charon? And what about the people of Bannador, who have suffered so in the past two years? Are they not entitled to hear the *Tale of the Mirror?*"

"You're right, I suppose," he said, not quite so unhappily.

"You also have to tell the full tale to the college. You can't get around that. It's your duty as a master chronicler."

Llian perked up at that thought.

"Besides, how could I possibly bond to a farmhand? That would make me very unhappy. Ever since I was a little girl I dreamed about wedding a teller. There's even a tale about it."

That was a busy, indeed a desperate time. Meldorin was harried by thranx and bands of lesser creatures, and they did almost as much damage as the previous year's war had done.

Even Thurkad was attacked on one terrible day at the end of spring.

Llian had many calls to go to Thurkad and other places to tell his tale. He had handsome offers too, but refused them all.

"It's not finished," he said in each case, "and when it is, first I must tell it in Chanthed."

He stayed at Karan's side, comforting her and attending to her needs, and putting up with her mischief and her temper. And that was very great, when finally she got out of her chair and tried to walk with sticks. But surprisingly, even in her worst moments she felt no desire for hrux. That longing had completely gone.

"Today is the day!" said Karan early one morning about a month after their return. It was the seventh day of Bolland, the first month of summer.

"What day?" Llian wondered.

"*It's six weeks!* The day I get my plaster off! You can't possibly imagine how much I've longed for this day."

The metal frame was taken apart, the plaster casts carefully sawn through and cracked away from her hips and each leg. Karan was helped into a chair.

"Oh, it feels funny to sit on my bottom, after so long on my back. I can feel my bones creaking." She looked down at her withered legs. They were like straight, blanched sticks, her knees were mere knobs in the middle and her ankles stuck out. "Oh, yuk. I'm so ugly! Help me with my trousers, quick."

When that was done, Karan put her hands on the arms of her chair and tried to push herself to her feet. She got halfway up and fell down again. "Don't just stand there like a fool!" she shouted. "Help me up!"

Llian gave her his arms and heaved her onto her feet but

her legs would not hold her up. She sagged sideways, almost pulling him over. Karan burst into tears.

"Put me back," she said. "It's no use, my legs don't work any more. I'm a useless cripple."

Rachis came by. "Karan child," he said, "you're taking it too quickly. After all this time, you have to build up your muscles before you can expect to walk."

"I can't even stand up!" she wailed.

"But if you exercise first, tomorrow or the next day you will. And a few days after that you'll take your first step. Soon you'll be walking everywhere. I've seen it many times." He went out, whistling.

"That's so," said Llian. "I've often heard about it."

Karan dried her angry tears. "I'll believe you then, though it doesn't seem possible. Now, run me a bath and put me in it please, so that I can get rid of this awful itching. And you'd better stay to make sure that I don't drown, and to lift me out again. And then you can carry me up the stairs to my bed, where I will claim my reward for the last six weeks, and offer you your own."

After a few days Karan was able to get around by herself, though she was on crutches for another month. Llian had recovered from his malaise by now. Freed from constantly needing to attend her, he threw himself back into his work. There had been a message from the College of the Histories. He was to tell the tale at the Graduation Telling, only two months away. Old Wistan had nominated it as a Great Tale, and all the master chroniclers would be there to vote. There was an incredible amount to do if the *Tale of the Mirror* was to be ready in time.

Llian allowed himself to dream about that. The first new Great Tale in hundreds of years. His tale! Surely they would vote for it. And old Wistan was well past his time. Last year he had talked about passing on—and the need for the college to have a new, young master. And, with the tale to his name, perhaps he, Llian, would be the one . . .

Llian suddenly burst out laughing, at himself, and where his daydreams had led him. I am truly incorrigible, he told himself. But, can I not dream?

There finally came a day when Karan was able to cast aside her sticks. Soon she was walking and running everywhere, and taking such pleasure that she was able to, though she knew she would never get back the fleetness and agility of before. To the end of her days she walked with a slight limp, and in winter especially her bones troubled her.

One evening Shand appeared at the front door of the keep. "Shand, it's good to see you," Llian said merrily, for the old man had not been back since their return from Shazmak. "Come in!"

"I can't stay." Shand looked uncomfortable. "I've too much to do." Thrusting a small package into Llian's hands, he immediately headed back down the path.

Puzzled, Llian went back inside, unwrapping the package. Within a box of white wood, nestled on a crumpled piece of midnight-blue velvet, was the silver chain Shand had once pawned for Karan. It had been cleaned and looked as beautiful as the day the master craftsman had made it.

Llian examined it carefully. Inside was the engraved "shu" character, Shuthdar's mark, and it was quite worn. A thrill went through Llian at the sight of it—to think he held in his hands something made by a legend, four thousand years ago. And there on the clasp, the letters widely spaced, in a wavery hand that was not worn at all, were the letters F I A C H R A—the name of the crippled girl whose mysterious death had started it all. Surely that proved it was Shuthdar's gift to her.

"Karan!" he yelled. "Look what Shand has brought back!"

Karan came running. "Oh, Shand, thank you!" she cried. She held the silver chain to her cheek. She looked around. "Where is he?"

"He didn't stay."

"*Why not?* Why has he gone? At this time of night?" She ran out the door.

"I don't think he wanted to be asked questions," Llian said.

Shortly she returned arm-in-arm with a notably incommunicative Shand. Karan was practically floating in the air. Shand, however, would not even relate how he had recovered the chain. He said little at dinner and retired straight after.

Karan bathed and scooted up the stairs to her room, wrapped in a threadbare towel. Llian was in bed already, apparently asleep. She brushed her hair, hung the towel over a chair and slipped Fiachra's chain over her head. Karan slid into the sheets and burrowed her way into Llian's warm spot. Rousing, he took her in his arms. Soon they both slept.

Karan dreamed the Histories. She dreamed herself into Llian's *Tale of the Forbidding*, the way he had told it right at the beginning. She could see him, just as he had looked on stage that night of the Graduation Telling, two years ago. Karan saw herself too, living the Great Tale and her heart going out to the teller.

But with that strange self-awareness that comes in dreams, Karan realized that she had dreamed right into Huling's Tower on the Long Lake. She could see herself there, a ghostly image at the top of the stairs, looking over the walls to the water on one side and the semicircle of burning forest on the others. Shuthdar's enemies were coming and nothing would be allowed to stand in their way.

Karan turned, dream-slow. Shuthdar, as gruesome a wreck as could ever be imagined, was staring right through her. Poisoned by the metals he had spent so long crafting, his very bones had been deformed. His legs and arms were knots of wasted muscle that clothed bones as gnarled as tree roots. His skin was eroded like a half-peeled potato, while his fingers were twisted, arthritic claws.

But it was his face that was the ultimate horror. It was equally eroded, equally deformed, while his shrunken lips gaped open to display the most hideous travesty of his craftsmanship. His false teeth were iron that did not fit the weeping cave of his mouth—rusty, misshapen things that stained lips, beard and shirt blood-red.

Karan cried out in her sleep. Or was it Karan the ghost, for Shuthdar's gaze fixed on her before slipping to one side? His eyes softened, his ghastly mouth curved into a smile. Turning as well, Karan saw the crippled girl sitting on the flat roof nearby. Her twisted legs were tucked up under a long skirt. Fiachra was lovely, a small heart-shaped face framed by thick black hair. There were pearls of perspiration on her brow from the magical dance Shuthdar had given her.

The girl looked up at the monster with such adoration that Karan caught her breath. Shuthdar spoke and Fiachra's face lit up, though his words were inaudible. He pointed to the burning forest. She shook her head, and the look that passed between them made Karan sing inside. Shuthdar took a chain from around his neck—the chain that had carried Karan into the dream—and scratched Fiachra's name on it. It was a protection against what was to come. He slipped it over her head, touched her cheek with the back of his hand, then scuttled up onto the wall, flute in hand.

Outlined against the ghastly moon, the dark side full and

reflecting across the lake, he brandished the flute at his enemies and blew a single blast.

Everything vanished in rainbow-colored shockwaves that thundered out in all directions. The tower fractured. Waves burst over the ruins. Time slipped sideways, and when it resumed Shuthdar had disappeared and the top of the tower was rubble. Hidden behind a wall of debris, a shimmering cylinder enclosed the sleeping girl.

As Karan's ghost reached out, the cylinder burst and Fiachra roused. She scratched at the wall, crying out for Shuthdar, but he was dead. All that remained was a slowly congealing puddle of gold, the remains of the flute. The girl sank weeping behind the rubble.

Time shifted again. A tall specter appeared on the stair. It fell on the gold with a cry of exultation, using a great spell to mold it into three pieces of jewelry. Karan saw smoke rise from the specter's hands, proof that it was flesh and blood. Finally the job was done, the jewelry quenched in a puddle. The specter looked up suddenly, realizing that it was being watched. It sprang up onto the wall. The crippled girl made a futile attempt to get away but the specter plunged a long pin into her back. Fiachra cried out, stiffened and did not move again.

Karan groaned aloud. Though she knew she was dreaming, and knew that the murder was more than three thousand years old, it was as shocking as if it had been done in her own bedroom.

The specter turned abruptly and for the first time Karan saw its face. It was a woman, tall and broad of shoulder, with black hair, a long, beautiful face and searing indigo eyes. Yalkara! It all fell into place!

The specter lunged at Karan's ghost with bloodstained, blistered hands. Karan screamed and woke in Llian's arms.

* * *

"So Yalkara killed her," Llian said in the morning, as Karan and he were taking breakfast with Shand. Karan had just finished telling them the chain-inspired dream.

"I thought as much, as soon as I saw the drawings Faelamor stole from the library," Shand said sadly. He picked at his food. "But the chain confirmed it. Once I held it in my hand again I knew what had happened. The metal was imprinted with the deeds done in the tower—the destruction of the flute, the protection, the murder, the Forbidding! Oh, Yalkara! What an ignoble deed, to kill a helpless girl."

"I suppose she felt that she had no choice," said Llian. "The gold was too warped and deadly ever to be used again. No one could be trusted with it, so no one must know that she had it. The crippled girl had to die."

"And did she kill Kandor, too, when he found out about it long after?" asked Karan.

"To kill one of her own, one of the Hundred, would have been a far, far different thing," said Shand.

"I don't understand why Yalkara didn't get rid of the gold," said Karan. "Why didn't she grind it to dust and scatter it across the waters so that it could never be recovered? Why leave it around to be found and used, if it was so perilous?"

"I suppose she kept it in case her need was desperate," said Shand. "Remember that Havissard was the safest place on Santhenar; it was impregnable. Remember, too, that Aachan gold was incredibly precious. Then, when she had to flee unexpectedly, she was too badly hurt to do anything with it, and she could not take it with her." He sighed. "Ah, Yalkara, even knowing about this crime, even after all this time I still ache for you."

"So how did Kandor end up with the chain?" asked Karan.

"He was one of the thousands outside when the flute was

destroyed," Llian replied. "And later, knowing that the girl had been murdered, he took the chain from her neck, thinking that the evidence might be read from it. Whoever had the gold would hold the greatest power on Santhenar. He coveted that power, for Kandor was always insecure. That's why he put everything into making his empire. He had to display his strength and have other people envy him for it. And fear him!"

Shand took up the story. "But all the while he knew that he was second-rate. He could not read the murderer's name from the chain. Worse, someone much greater than him had the gold yet did nothing with it. And when the Sea of Perion began to dry up Kandor realized that only one power could save him.

"Descending into paranoid madness he built the Great Tower of Katazza, following the same pattern as the chain. The congruence between the two was a form of sympathetic magic. But also a boast—'I know what you're up to, but my Art is greater'."

"The boast was empty. The sea went dry and Kandor's empire failed with it. Now believing that Rulke had the gold, Kandor wrote those letters to bring him and Yalkara together, hoping to expose Rulke and cause his downfall.

"But Yalkara refused to come, and Rulke, in a letter of his own, accused Kandor of treachery. So Kandor betrayed Rulke to the Council, through the woman he was betrothed to. And Mendark, knowing that Kandor could destroy his reputation, had him killed.'

48

THE GREAT TALE

In the last month of summer, Karan, Llian and Shand made the journey across the mountains to Chanthed for the Graduation Telling. It was a painful trip for Karan. Her bones hurt most of the time.

On arriving in Chanthed they found many friends there—Tallia, Jevi, now first mate on *The Waif*, Lilis and Nadiril, Malien and Asper, and even Pender. The other Aachim were fighting a colony of thranx on the other side of Lauralin. Malien looked older, and her red hair was threaded with silver. She did not say much. The fate of Aachan, and her inability to do anything about it, was a constant preoccupation.

"Pender!" Karan exclaimed, "Just look at you! You are magnificent!"

Magnificent was perhaps overstating it, but all things are relative and Pender had done his best. The stubble that habitually graced his jowls had been carefully removed. He was dressed in clothes that were, if not the height of fashion in the waterfront inns of Thurkad, at least clean and new. They had even been pressed, though not very well, and the belly straining at his coat buttons showed that he'd had a prosperous year. He was as round as a bottle.

Pender grinned and opened his arms. He'd never had much time for Llian, but Karan was a great favorite. "It's been a good year for trade, eh! I am thinking that I might buy a new boat."

"Oh, you're not going to sell *The Waif*, are you?" said Lilis. "I would be very sorry to see her go." Lilis had also grown over the past months. She was still small but not quite so skinny. She was rounder in the hips, fuller in the chest—definitely a woman now.

"Well, Lilis, I can't sail two boats at once, can I? And I have to pay Tallia back her share, eh!" He went on in a stage whisper. "Now don't tell anyone, but I might sell her to your father."

Lilis's face blossomed like a flower opening in the sunshine. "Jevi," she shrieked so that every head in the room turned. "Jevi, Jevi! Pender is going to sell *The Waif* to you!"

Jevi, who was just behind her, smiled and said, "Yes, we've talked about it already. Can you imagine me owning my own boat? I never dreamed of such a thing. I am a new man, Lilis."

Tallia came up and put her arms around him. "I liked the old one well enough, but I am happy for you."

"So, what are your plans?" Pender wondered, turning back to Lilis.

"There's plenty to do. I have to finish copying Llian's tale for the Great Library. And I'm not even halfway through my apprenticeship. Come over here, Pender, say hello to Nadiril. You'll like him very much."

* * *

Llian still had to resolve one final detail before he could tell his *Tale of the Mirror*. "Why did Yalkara engrave those glyphs around the Mirror?" he asked the company, who were gathered by the fire in their inn. "And why the moon symbol? Do you know, Shand?"

"I believe so. We worked part of it out just before Mendark's fire, if you recall. In their final battle, Faelamor had forced Yalkara to reveal that the key to making gates lay within the Mirror. Yalkara was so afraid that she changed the Mirror at once. She then engraved the script there, to be certain Aeolior would still be able to use it. Apparently she taunted Faelamor with the verses too, though she left out the third and fourth lines, which were meant only for Aeolior. This is how it goes, and the emphases are important:

"The Mirror is locked, but within lies the key
Come, look inside; see what *you* want to see
Take hold of your birthright; you will see true
Then the Glass cannot lie to me or to you
Tallallame, oh my Tallallame
Your fate *does* rest on the one which is three

"The message had several layers," Shand explained. "Once Yalkara let slip the secret of gates, Faelamor saw the way home to Tallallame at last. At that point she began her three-hundred-year-long plan.

"Yalkara's message was an enticement to Faelamor to look into the Mirror and, combined with that ancient Faellem prophecy, one impossible for her to resist. It was also a sneer—*See what* you *want to see*!—that Faelamor was not strong enough to make the Twisted Mirror show true. And a prediction about the fate of Tallallame that emphasized Faelamor's misunderstanding about the triune."

"And the moon symbol?" asked Lilis, fascinated. "Was that to Faelamor too?"

"Not at all!" Shand replied. "It was for Aeolior alone, an illustration of Yalkara's only hope, that the Charon blend with the other species. Look at it!" Shand sketched it on a scrap of paper.

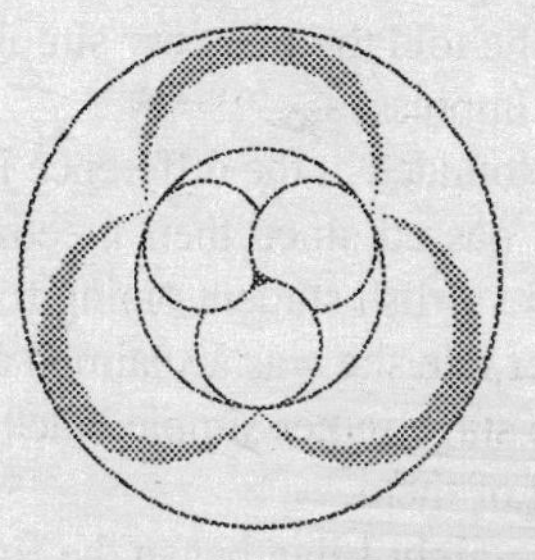

"The outer circle symbolizes us old humans, the ancestral human species, complete but insufficient (to her mind anyway); too primitive. The three scarlet crescents depict the Faellem, Charon and Aachim—powerful but all, in some ways, incomplete."

"And the inner circle?" asked Karan.

"The three golden balls must represent the triune," said Llian, "set in a completed circle which, I imagine, is meant to depict a new kind of human."

Malien, who had sat quietly through the discourse, now finished it. "That part might also represent the cells of the human embryo. But the symbol was also a threat to deter us from ever using the Mirror again, for it's a reworking of an old Aachim doom symbol. We were all terrified when we saw it. Even Tensor, though his lust for the Mirror's secrets outweighed his fear of it."

* * *

This year the honor of the final night of the Graduation Telling had been awarded to Llian's friend Thandiwe, though of course she could not tell the *Tale of the Mirror*. Instead she retold the very first Great Tale, *Nulki's Saga*, a tragic story from *before*. It, alone of all the Great Tales, dated from the time prior to Shuthdar's stealing of the golden flute. Though Thandiwe was a chronicler rather than a master teller, she told the tale very simply and touchingly. Even Llian was impressed.

Karan was astounded at the difference in Thandiwe. Less than a year had passed since their meeting, but Thandiwe was no longer the girlish student pining for her lover. At the conclusion of her tale she was acclaimed as a master chronicler, and on the stage in her simple black gown she looked the equal of any of them.

The following night Llian began the first part of the *Tale of the Mirror*. The tale was in four parts, to be told on four successive nights. Two years had gone by since his retelling of the *Tale of the Forbidding* that had begun the tale.

"The first part of the *Tale of the Mirror* is called *A Shadow on the Glass*," began Llian, "and it was that fleeting appearance of Yalkara's face on the Mirror in Fiz Gorgo . . ."

The *Tale of the Mirror* was finally told. Llian bowed his head. There was absolute silence. Then, up the back someone let out a great roar. A young woman echoed it from across the hall, and suddenly the whole room was on its feet, roaring, yelling and screaming their acclamation. Ovation followed ovation until it was put to rest by the students swarming onto the stage and carrying Llian across and back, and up and down the hall through the audience a dozen times.

At last, exhausted by cheering, they set him down again

and trooped back to their places. Old Wistan shuffled up to the stage. He was quite frail now, and a thickset master had to help him up the steps.

Wistan nodded to Llian, rather curtly, and moved forward to the front of the stage. "A fine tale!" he said. "A wonderful tale, I'm sure we all agree. And now comes the time that I have been waiting for all my life, as no doubt many of you have too. Every master chronicler is here tonight." He read out sixty-four names, one by one, very slowly and deliberately.

Karan, sitting in the front row in the place of the guest of honor, thirty-one masters to her left, an equal number to her right, was absolutely burning with impatience.

Wistan reached the end of the list. The last three names were Thandiwe, Llian and himself. "My fellow masters, distinguished visitors, students, I will be brief. I hereby nominate the *Tale of the Mirror* to be a Great Tale. The master chroniclers have all read the documents, spoken to the witnesses and checked the facts. Now you have heard the tale told by a master. What say you? Is it a Great Tale? Yea or nay? Answer one by one, if you please, and the Recorder will register your vote."

He paused for effect. Karan felt a momentary twinge of unease, though it passed swiftly.

"Master Quendryth, what say you?"

A small, white-haired woman stood up at the very end of the row. She nodded to Llian, to Wistan and to her fellow masters. "Yea!" she said in a husky voice. "It is a Great Tale." Without further word she sat down again.

"Master Laarni?" called Wistan.

The dark-faced man next to Karan sprang to his feet. "Yea!" he roared, making sure there was no doubt of his opinion. "A Great Tale! A very Great Tale! Note down my vote carefully, Recorder!" He sat down with a thump that rocked the whole row of seats.

"Master Cherith?" cried Wistan. A fleshy, black-clad woman of barely middle age rose from the other side of the room.

"Yea!" she said softly. Then she smiled, infecting the whole room with her good humor. "A Great Tale it is, Master Wistan."

"Master Thandiwe?" said Wistan.

The youngest of all the masters, Thandiwe stood up. Karan noticed Llian staring at her and again felt a little stab of jealousy. Thandiwe looked truly breathtaking tonight, in a sheath of red satin that hugged her voluptuous form. She gave her vote, for the Great Tale, and sat down quickly.

So it went on, back and forth across the front row. Finally all had voted but one, the Master of the College of the Histories. Llian could not vote, of course. Again Karan felt that twinge of unease. This honor meant everything to Llian. Wistan had hated Llian once. What if, despite all, he still did?

Wistan said not a word. The room was silent. Karan's unease grew. Then Quendryth's seat creaked and Karan realized that the master of the college was waiting to be asked.

"Master Wistan," said Quendryth. "You have checked the documents, questioned the witnesses and heard the *Tale of the Mirror*. What do you say? Is the tale worthy of the highest honor?"

"The tale is worthy of my vote," said Wistan, then paused. He looked ancient, exhausted, grim of face.

The pause stretched out to minutes. Karan could hear the heavy breath of Laarni beside her. She couldn't breathe at all. Her chest hurt.

"And what is your vote?"

Wistan took a deep breath. He swayed on his feet. "It . . .

it is a Great Tale," he whispered, and had to sit down. "The *Tale of the Mirror* is a Great Tale, the twenty-third."

The roar shook the tiles in the distant roof. The whole room stood. Slowly Karan rose too, moved to tears. Oh, Llian, she thought, you have what you wanted at last.

Llian now stood alone in the middle of the great stage and the tears ran down his face unchecked.

When the clamor finally died down, Wistan took the stage again. "There are two final matters to be attended to," he said. "I have been master here for more than fifty years. I have seen the college safely through the war and into the new age. I have heard the Great Tale. My health is failing rapidly and I no longer have any reason to keep going. It is time to pass the burden on. Tonight, before we leave, we will elect a new master."

A stir went through the audience, like a wind blowing dry bracken across the yard. Wistan held up a shaky hand. "The old world is gone forever. A new master is required, and a fresh start for the new age. Propose none of the superannuated old guard. Go for youth, talent and integrity, and trust that wisdom will develop. I call for nominations!"

"Master Llian," sang out a voice in the crowd.

Llian stepped forward, nodding his acceptance. Even after all the acclaim he positively shone with eagerness for this final honor. It would signal that the outcast Zain was accepted at last.

Karan was torn between conflicting desires. Did Llian want to be master more than he wanted her? If he got it, he would have to live in Chanthed. But how could she cling to him if he wanted to go?

The Recorder carefully inscribed his name in an ancient red book. "Other nominations," called Wistan from his chair.

"Master Laarni," shouted a master across the aisle from Karan.

"Do you accept the nomination, Laarni?" asked Wistan.

The dark man beside Karan stood. He bowed to the stage and to the man who had nominated him. "I do not! I am of the old age." He sat down again.

Wistan scanned the room. No one moved. "Come on!" he said irritably. "There are half a dozen here tonight worthy of the honor."

After a long pause, two others were nominated. Both declined. The election seemed a *fait accompli.*

Wistan's face spasmed. He stood up, creaking forward painfully to the very edge of the stage, and his cloudy eyes sought one face among the row of masters. "There must be a vote," Wistan whispered. "I nominate Master Thandiwe Moorn."

Thandiwe almost fell off her chair. A mutter of astonishment went through the hall. Llian looked incredulous. Then Thandiwe stood up and Karan's heart went out to her, for the young master's face was as red as her gown and she was trembling almost to fall down.

"Do you accept the nomination, Thandiwe?" asked Wistan.

"I am unworthy of it, much less the position," she said softly.

"I think otherwise. The new master of the college must be young, as you are. Must be brilliant—no one could disagree that you are. Must love the Histories as much as they love life itself. But most of all, the new master must have impartiality and integrity. I say you have all of these attributes. Again I propose you."

Thandiwe looked him in the eye. "You are wise and I am not. Surely you see what I cannot. I accept the nomination."

"Then take your place on the stage and wait our judgment. Are there any further nominations?" There were not. "Come, Masters, we must discuss the merit of the candidates."

Burly Laarni supported Wistan into the adjacent debating chamber. The masters followed and the door thudded closed. The audience began to chatter among themselves. Llian and Thandiwe sat on their separate chairs. Llian leaned back, and it took all of his teller's self-control to maintain a blank face. Thandiwe looked as if she wanted the floor to open and take her away from the torment.

Nothing happened for a very long time. From the other side of the door Karan heard raised voices, a long and spirited debate. Finally the door opened and the masters emerged. They spread across the back of the stage, muttering to one another. The two candidates were urged forward. The masters all put slips of paper into a box, which the Recorder counted out and, with painful slowness, entered into the red book.

Finally the Recorder looked up. "It is done, Master."

"Have you a majority for one candidate."

"I have, Master Wistan."

"What is the majority?"

"Forty to twenty-two."

Wistan smiled. "A clear win! A good start for the new master. And the name of the winner?"

The Recorder handed Wistan a long slip of paper. Wistan walked along the line, showing the votes and the count to each of the masters except the two candidates. Each nodded their acceptance of the vote. Wistan came to the front of the stage, between Thandiwe and Llian.

"Will the candidates rise?"

Llian and Thandiwe stood up.

"The winner," said Wistan, displaying the biggest smile

anyone in the college had ever seen, "by the margin of forty votes to twenty-two, is Master Thandiwe Moorn."

The audience was stunned to silence. The momentary look of consternation, followed by dismay and humiliation, on Llian's face must have delighted his enemies. He hid it quickly. Forcing a smile that fooled no one, Llian put out his hand to Thandiwe. He would have been delighted for her had she beaten anyone else, but this was more than he was capable of.

"You will make a fine master," he said. "I wish you well."

Thandiwe could not smile back. There were tears of disbelief in her eyes. She kept shaking her head. Llian bowed to her, to Wistan and the assembled masters, and turned to leave the stage.

Wistan motioned him to stay. "Thandiwe Moorn, you have been elected the seventy-fifth Master of the College of the Histories. Do you accept the election?"

Thandiwe firmed her shoulders. "I do, Master Wistan," she said softly.

"You will take up your position upon my death, which is," he gave a wry smile, "expected imminently. I congratulate you." He shook her hand.

Again Llian turned to go. "Stay a moment, Llian," cried Wistan in a voice suddenly loud and firm. "There is one last matter to attend to."

Llian sprang back to center stage as if he expected a consolation prize. Wistan gestured the masters forward.

"Master Llian," said Wistan, "you have made a new Great Tale, and been acclaimed for it. You are a great chronicler, and a great teller too, no doubt of it. Perhaps the greatest of the age that has just ended."

Llian bowed to Wistan and to the audience. Again Karan felt that prickle of unease.

"But Llian, as I said to you more than once when you were a student here, *Genius without ethics is a deadly commodity*. Just how deadly I never realized. A great chronicler you may be, Llian, but you are not a worthy master. Your tale proves your dishonor. You betrayed your calling in Katazza by collaborating with Tensor, and betrayed it again in the Nightland."

Wistan held up his hand as Llian began to defend himself. "You've had your say—four long nights of it—and now I will have mine. Those crimes might have been forgiven, done under duress as they no doubt were. But not what you did next. You meddled in the Histories, Llian. You manipulated Mendark in Thurkad just to find the answer to a historical curiosity. The result—a hundred prisoners burned to death in the citadel cells, and a priceless library of the Histories destroyed."

He paused. Llian looked as if he had been punched in the face.

"And then in Shazmak you did it again. Perhaps worse! You manipulated Tensor using your teller's gifts . . ." Wistan almost choked on his fury, "causing the death of noble Rulke and all the consequences that flowed from that to this day. Have you anything to say now, Llian?"

You stinking hypocrite! Karan thought. The whole world hated and feared Rulke until his death, and did all they could to destroy him.

"No!" whispered Llian. "Nothing at all. Everything you say is true. I accept your rebuke and vow to mend my character."

"This is not a rebuke!" snapped Wistan. "You are corrupt, Llian. You are unworthy to be a master chronicler. You must be taught a lesson."

Llian bowed his head. "I've learned that lesson!"

"You haven't! How could you, a Zain, think to be master of this college?" Wistan's voice positively dripped malice.

Karan wondered whether the friendliness of the previous year had been hypocrisy, too, or if Llian's behavior had merely reinforced old prejudices. Wistan had desperately wanted the honor of the Great Tale, but now that he had it would make no concession to the detested Zain.

"I raised the least of us to the position of the greatest," Wistan continued, "to demonstrate that you could *never* be acceptable to us!"

Llian went white. The whites of Thandiwe's eyes could be seen. She was quivering with fury.

"Accordingly, by my right as master of the college you are hereby stripped of the honor. You are master chronicler no longer. Give me your badge."

Llian was so shocked that he staggered and would have fallen off the stage had not Thandiwe caught his arm. He fumbled in his pocket, brought out the master's badge that was more precious than his life, and handed it to Wistan.

Wistan looked around at the assembled masters. "Does anyone disagree with this judgment?"

Several masters scowled and scuffled their feet. "No point, is there?" shouted Laarni. "Not all of us together have the power to reverse your decision!"

Wistan drew a small ceremonial mallet from his robes, smashed the badge on the floor and swept the fragments off the stage with the side of his foot. "Leave us, Llian! You have no place here among the masters." Then Wistan put on a nauseating smile that revealed black gums and stained teeth. "But you are still a great teller. Go on with your telling with our blessing and goodwill."

"But . . ." said Llian.

The smile became a rictus. "I could have taken away

your honor *before* you told your tale," snapped Wistan. "No Great Tale beside your name then, Llian!"

"Nor yours neither, you bloody hypocrite!" Laarni roared.

One of the masters whispered in Thandiwe's ear. "Wait a minute!" she said. "You haven't consulted me!"

Wistan was taken aback by her sudden boldness. He conferred with the other masters, then turned back to her. "The master-elect may vote on this decision. How do you vote, Thandiwe? Vote for integrity!"

"Integrity?" She choked on it. "The word has been on your tongue so long that it stinks like your breath, Wistan. Thankfully your time is over."

"Vote!" he snarled.

"I vote against you, Wistan. There are a dozen masters here today whose crimes are greater than Llian's."

"The master-elect's vote is null," said Wistan, "because of her well-known conflict of interest. My decision stands, my last as master!"

"And here is my first!" snapped Thandiwe. "Llian will be reinstated immediately once I take office."

"You can't!" said Wistan. "A master who has been dismissed can't be considered for readmission in less than seven years. And that requires a two-thirds majority of all the master chroniclers."

Thandiwe clenched her fists, then turned away, controlling herself with an effort. "Llian, you have indeed been a great master chronicler. You have done much for the reputation of the college, and for the Histories too, in spite of your . . . failings. But who among us does not have faults? I know I do. Perhaps you will do great things again. It is my decision that we review your conduct, and consider your case again, in seven years."

"How dare you!" Wistan's boiled-egg eyes almost bulged

out of his head with his fury, but there was nothing he could do about it.

"I haven't finished!" Thandiwe said. "At the same time, when our heads have cooled, we will vote on the record of Master Wistan. Perhaps the masters will strike *him* from the record. Posterity must know the truth about all of us, especially those who have the honor of being master of the college!" She turned to Llian. "I'm sorry, Llian, I can do no more. Fare you well!"

Karan watched as, completely numb, Llian went down the steps, down the aisle and outside. The show was over.

49

The End of the Tale

Lian was very quiet on the long journey home. The loss of his honor seemed to have stripped away all the self-confidence that gaining it had previously brought him. To Karan's mind he was not the chronicler she knew and loved at all. He was more the shy, awkward young man he must have been as a student, no longer sure of his place in the world. Karan did not like the transformation, but she could not see what to do to help him.

The night of their return to Gothryme, Karan was rearranging the clothes in her drawers when she came upon the small black bead that Rulke had given her.

Taking it out of its clear case, she weighed it in her hand. It was light and as black as licorice. "The least I can do for you," Rulke had said. That could have a thousand meanings. Was it an ornament, a good-luck charm, a magical talisman or even a tablet?

She sniffed but it had no odor at all. She licked it. The bead had a faint, ethereal taste, as elusive as week-old musk.

Karan popped the bead in her mouth. It lay on her tongue, slowly dissolving, and a little tickling sensation ran through her.

"Llian!" she called.

"Yes?"

"Come upstairs."

They went on with their lives. Llian worked away quietly, completing the copies of his Great Tale, even going so far as to decorate some of the capitals with gold and silver leaf, and ink made from powdered chips off the piece of lapis lazuli he had carried all the way from the Great Tower of Katazza. Illumination was an art he had some skill at, since his mother and sisters followed that trade. He would spend the winter on the copies, making sure that the three to be sent to Chanthed in the spring were perfect. He had planned to take them personally, but felt like an exile now. Lilis's copy would remain in the Great Library.

And after that? Llian no longer knew what to do with himself. The Histories were his life but he was forbidden to work on them, except in the way that any unschooled amateur might. All libraries were closed to him, and all archives.

He had spent a lot of time thinking about his future, in particular about the key Rulke had given him. Llian hid that in a secret place. One day, if he was ever reinstated as a master chronicler, he would follow that tale and write the Histories of the Charon as he had promised Rulke. He must be reinstated! That obligation could never be put aside.

Llian had decided to put his notes relating to *Mendark's Tale*, which were in one of the journals saved from the fire, into the archives of the library at Chanthed. One day another student would come along to tell it for posterity, and maybe even make it into the Great Tale that Mendark had so coveted. Llian never would.

So the weeks went by, unhappily for Llian. Once he had loved scribe's work, but now even copying out his Great Tale was a chore, though not one he neglected. Nothing but his best was good enough for the *Tale of the Mirror.*

When his eyes could no longer focus, or he could no longer hold his hand steady, Llian wandered listlessly about the manor. He tried many jobs and succeeded at none of them, for he could do nothing well except writing and telling, and there was little need for either at Gothryme. He was miserable, and so was whoever he worked with, for they had to do the job again after he was finished.

"This isn't working, Llian," Karan said one day, as kindly as she could.

"I'm not earning my keep, am I?"

"Of course you are! But you've got to do what you're good at, not disrupt the whole place for the sake of keeping busy."

The next day Llian took his pack and set off down the road, telling his tales for money wherever he could find an audience. He was away for weeks, going as far as Thurkad. He returned with a small bag of coin, for which Karan was grateful, though Llian did not enjoy the experience nearly as much as he once had. He was terribly lonely on the road, and being a teller only reminded him how much he wanted to be a master chronicler again.

"There's nothing I can do here!" he said a few days after his return. "I feel quite useless."

Karan thought about asking him to search out her own Family Histories, to find out what her father had been up to in Carcharon. That was something she never stopped thinking about. But, afraid that Llian might uncover something unpleasant, she desisted.

* * *

At the end of autumn everyone gathered before Karan's blazing hearth again, telling each other what had gone on over the past months. There were heroic tales of struggles with beasts and monsters; tragic tales too. Karan's own story took not much time at all, for they could see her season in her garden, orchard and fields. In Gothryme, the drought had ended and the harvest was good. The building work was still a long way from completion though, for want of coin. The year had not been *that* good, and now it was tax time again.

Karan was dreading that, for there was no possibility of going to Elludore to recover Faelamor's debt. That place was so full of lorrsk that it would probably never be reclaimed. She felt sure Gothryme would be taken from her this time.

The tiny dose of the Histories had done nothing to cure Llian who was still miserable. The telling and copying only made him long for what he could no longer have. Outside a sleety rain began to fall. It was getting dark already. Shand pulled his chair closer to the fire and unsealed a flask of gellon liqueur, the first of a crate he'd shipped down from Tullin. He poured a generous cup for each of them, hardly begrudging it at all.

"You know that verse about the *thrice betrayed*?" said Yggur. "All the time I thought it meant you."

"Me?" laughed Shand. "No, the Aachim were the thrice-betrayed. Betrayed by Rulke when Tar Gaarn fell; then betrayed by Faelamor when Shazmak was overcome; but most of all betrayed by their own inescapable folly."

Tallia sipped her liqueur, sitting silently by the fire. Surely she was missing Jevi, who was away with Pender down the coast.

"Do you think Mendark was corrupt all the time?" she

said to nobody in particular. She still felt deceived by what he had done.

Shand replied. "No, he always cared for Santhenar and Thurkad. His faults were too great a love for power and its trappings, and too great a concern for his own reputation. Anything was justifiable if it kept him in power, for he believed that he was the only one capable of standing against the enemy."

"Yet he was greater than he seemed," Yggur said. "Though he was my enemy, right to the end he was guiding the affairs of Santhenar. We owe a lot to him. No one could have been more protective of our world. Nonetheless, his crimes were terrible ones, not easily forgiven."

"Know too that he was past his time, as I am," said Shand. "Life had become a burden to Mendark. He would not have been sorry to go. But he loved to gamble, and the chance of seizing the construct was too great a gamble to resist. Even so, he did the right thing in the end. He may get his Great Tale after all, one day."

Yggur grimaced and changed the subject. He wasn't feeling *that* generous. "A thranx was sighted only a few leagues from here the other day. How many of them got through, do you think?"

"Dozens, if not hundreds," said Malien. "And thousands of lesser creatures. Enough for them to breed, in the wild places. We will never be rid of them."

"What troubled times we live in!" exclaimed Yggur. "Sometimes I wonder how ordinary people can bear to go on with their lives, working their holdings and bringing children into the world when it can all be snatched away so brutally."

"It's an uncertain world," agreed Shand. "An uncertain future. Who would plan for it?"

"I would!" snorted Karan. "While the great spout philosophy, the humble must go to work for their daily bread. If we don't get started on the future we will wither as the Aachim did. Did you see my new gardens? I am going to make Gothryme bloom like a little bit of paradise. And maybe even make enough to pay my *taxes*," she added, glaring at Yggur, for she expected his tax collector any day now.

Yggur still ached for Maigraith, his pain seeming to grow greater with time. "If only there were a way to bring her back," he said into his wine cup after dinner. "She brought hope into my life and I abandoned her."

"I grieve for her too," said old Shand. "But at least she is with Yalkara."

"I thought the longing would grow less with time," said Yggur, "but every day it hurts more. I wish I could bring her back."

"You can't, and even if you could she may not want to . . . renew the relationship."

"I know that!" Yggur snarled. "But I trapped her in Aachan. I just can't cope with that. If only I knew she was all right."

There was a long silence. Karan used her arms to push herself up in her seat. "She is!" she said softly.

Yggur almost fell off his chair. He stared at her, but she just sat there, smiling. Llian, who knew all too well her mischievous ways, said, "You're unkind, Karan. Tell him, if you know something."

"Maigraith has never been able to break my link unless I allowed it," she said. "It's still there, a little warm knot in my mind. I can't use it across the abyss but I know she is still alive."

"Why didn't you tell me this before?" Yggur said furiously.

"I've been too preoccupied with other things," she said, smiling sweetly. "Like my taxes."

"Oh, damn your taxes!" he roared.

"I wish you would."

"Very well! Get me pen and paper quick, before I change my mind."

Llian ran across with fresh leaves and a pen. Yggur scribbled something on the sheets, signed each, sealed them and Shand and Llian witnessed them.

Yggur read it out. "The bearer, Karan Elienor Melluselde Fyrn, is hereby absolved of all taxes, duties, levies, rates, tributes and other imposts for a period of ten years from this date, in acknowledgment of her service to the state. Will that do?" He handed the documents to Karan.

"Very handsomely," she replied, keeping one and handing the other back. "Let's drink to it."

But when they were well into their drinks Yggur raised the issue again. "If only the flute hadn't been destroyed, we might have opened the Way and tracked her down with your link. I don't suppose . . ."

"No, Yggur," Shand said gently. Having given up that hope for himself he could not bear to see it reopened. "No chance whatsoever." They lapsed back into silence.

Later that night, Karan and Llian were sitting by the fire after everyone else had gone to bed. Karan took a deep breath. "Llian—" she began.

"You know," said Llian, returning to the topic that so often troubled him, "I thought I knew everything once—everything was so certain when I was young."

"You're still young, only thirty!"

"I feel twenty years older than I did when I met you. But I meant, after I became a chronicler. You can never know how that changed me. Almost overnight I went from being a penniless, persecuted kid to being someone that people looked up to. It transformed my life! I had respect and an important place in the world. I belonged! But now, if I went back to the college I'd feel like a trespasser. It's all gone. I threw it away."

Karan felt her fury at Wistan stirring. "You were foolish, but you didn't deserve what Wistan did to you. You were the victim of a malicious, Zain-hating old man."

"I caused Mendark to burn down the archives, and lots of prisoners died."

"No you didn't! You pushed him but he chose to do it."

"I was responsible for Rulke's death. I'll never forgive myself for that."

"No you weren't! You were trying to save my life. Tensor killed Rulke, not you."

"Ah, but how I enjoyed that power to manipulate. I deserved to have my mastership stripped from me."

"If everyone who enjoyed using power were to be punished, few people in Santhenar would escape. There used to be jokes about the unscrupulous masters."

"So there were," Llian remembered. "I used to tell them myself. There was Gissini the Pervert, Relch the Plagiarist, Mara the Fraud—what a liar she was! None of them was ever punished."

"Including Wistan, who forced you into the affair of the Mirror in the first place to get rid of you. Disgusting old hypocrite! He made sure the college accepted the Great Tale before he cast you out."

Llian was pleased to be defended so stoutly, though not completely mollified. "I was stupid though. I want my master's honor back, more than anything!"

She took his hand. "I'm sure you'll get it back, Llian. Now—"

"I'm not!" he snapped.

Karan moved in her chair. She had something important to say to him, but couldn't find the words among all his prattle. "Llian—"

"What a terrible world it is," he interrupted again. "Look at the last two years. Look at the Histories! Life is a lottery. It's not the fittest who survive at all, otherwise we would all be slaving for the Charon until the end of time. It is the least unlucky, and there is just a grain in the balance."

"Am I supposed to be comforted by that?" Karan retorted. "What of our future together? What of our children's future?"

"Children?" he said dreamily. "Triunes can't have children." Then something in the tone of her voice made him look up. Karan's beautiful, malachite-green eyes were liquid bright, gazing at him in wonder. Her cheeks were glazed with tears. She put out her hand, and he took it and drew her to him.

"Well, maybe my injuries, or the hrux, or more likely Rulke's Gift, unblocked something. *I'm pregnant!*"

EPILOGUE

"Too well I see and rue the dire event,
That with sad overthrow and foul defeat
Hath lost us Heav'n . . ."
MILTON, *PARADISE LOST*

Maigraith had lost the will to live. For weeks she lay in a coma of depression, unable to speak. Then one morning her senses woke of their own accord and she opened her eyes. Her grandmother sat by her bed, watching Aachan's small red sun set over peaks as jagged and uninviting as broken black glass. A huge orange moon hung in the sky, so low that Maigraith could feel its weight making tides in her belly. She had been devastated by the loss of Rulke; then finally her lethargy had given way to fury and irrational urges to avenge his death. But she was helpless to do anything about it. Gates would no longer work.

"Maigraith!" Yalkara was at her side instantly. "I thought you would never wake."

Maigraith opened her mouth but only a croak came out. She had practically forgotten how to speak. "I long for Rulke so badly," she whispered.

"I'm so very sorry!" Yalkara brushed Maigraith's hair

back with her fingers. "If only I could do something for you, but I cannot."

"If there were a way to bring him back, I would reach beyond the grave to do it. I would do *anything*!"

"He can never be recovered, Maigraith."

"Then I will devote my life to the revenge he swore, whatever it takes."

"That's just as pointless. Tensor is dead."

"But the Faellem have everything they ever wanted."

"Have they?" said Yalkara.

Plucking the Mirror out of Maigraith's coat she conjured a vision of the bloody hell that was Tallallame. It looked as if the whole world was on fire. The once beautiful forests were just black spikes in a sea of ash. Yalkara cried out in anguish and several of the Charon came running. They all stared at the ruins of what had been their world, before the Mariem had been cast into the void.

"They might as well be dead," said Yalkara in a whisper. "See, Rulke *is* avenged, and they did it to themselves."

"The Twisted Mirror," Maigraith said bitterly, but still she had to turn her head away. "It lies!"

"Not to me!"

"I'm sure Faelamor survived it."

"Look!" said Yalkara, thrusting the Mirror into her face. "Look, and know that revenge is pointless."

The scene shifted, shifted again, then settled on one place. It was a clearing snowy with ash, in the middle of which lay a small pile of unrecognizable bones. Maigraith knew, without knowing how, that they were Faelamor's. Only then did she weep for the grandmother she had spent most of her life with and never known.

The Charon mourned for Tallallame, an ancestral memory but a very powerful one. No world could come up to it.

Its loss was the final blow. "I have but one wish left," said Yalkara, "and that is to lead my people back into the void."

Maigraith slumped into a heap. "I never asked who my Faellem grandfather was, and now I will never know. I have nothing to live for any more. I will come with you, Grandmother."

"Nonsense! We choose the void willingly, knowing what it is like. You have no conception. Think about Rulke's sacrifice. Think about his parting words."

"*The fruit of our love will shake the Three Worlds to their underpinnings*," she quoted. "I don't know what he meant."

"I wonder," said Yalkara thoughtfully. Drawing up Maigraith's shirt she put those terribly scarred hands on her belly. Maigraith felt soothed, at peace. She was drifting off to sleep when Yalkara's cry broke into her thoughts.

"*A miracle!*" Yalkara was shaking with emotion. "A miracle has occurred."

"What?" Maigraith asked sleepily.

"His parting gift. Rulke has quickened you."

"Impossible!" said Maigraith. "I am sterile. Faelamor told me so."

"And you believed her? Of course *she* would say that. She was terrified of the triune and everything you represented! No, there's no doubt about it. We know *everything* about conception."

"Rulke said that too," Maigraith said, and smiled for the first time since his death.

Yalkara looked up, her eyes brimming, and called her people to her. "This is our greatest day in a thousand years."

The Hundred, what was left of them, all gathered round Maigraith, touching her as if she was a saint, a miraculous vessel, their way forward into the future.

"This gives me hope," cried a sage, a graybeard sodden with tears. "I see that it will be the first of a new human species. Our extinction is a rebirth—a species that has a better hope of survival than we ever did."

"My plan has taken on a life of its own," Yalkara said to herself, "and in a way I never expected. Alas, I'll never see how it turns out."

"What do you mean?" cried Maigraith, whose hearing was keen. "Did you plan this all along?"

"Not in the way you're thinking, Granddaughter," Yalkara replied calmly. "But I knew—as Rulke did not—that we Charon were no longer a viable species. One hundred was not enough—we lost too much of our heritage in the void. Our only chance was to breed with the other human species and find a way to make the offspring viable."

"Then you will stay?" Maigraith asked, holding her grandmother's scarred hands.

"No, child. Our time is past. I was the youngest of the Charon, but I gave half my life away, and now Aachan has withered my ovaries as it shriveled the gonads of each of us. We have already made the decision to go."

"But . . ." said Maigraith.

"Maigraith, the extinction of a species makes all other human tragedies insignificant. It has always been my destiny to lead my people. How can I abandon them now? But to know that you carry our seed into the future, that from you may spring a new species, is all that we need."

Maigraith faced the thought of life on Aachan without them. "Even the void would be better than remaining here after you have gone."

"But you are triune! You are at home on any of the Three Worlds, in any of the human cultures."

"Or none!" she said bitterly. "So did Faelamor warp me."

"We would not leave you to suffer our fate," said Yalkara. "Besides, this world is surely doomed. We will try to send you back to Santhenar, before we go. Do you have friends to support you? The coming months will be difficult."

Maigraith thought about those left behind. "There is Karan, if she is still alive—the best friend anyone ever had."

"Good! Are there others?"

"Malien, Tallia, Yggur, Llian! Yes," she said, realizing for the first time in her life that she had friends. "And of course, dear Shand, who is everything to me."

"Shand?" frowned Yalkara.

"My grandfather, Gyllias!"

Yalkara might have been struck by lightning. "Gyllias lives? And he found you?"

"He lives, and he still longs for you. Will you not come back to Santhenar now?"

Yalkara fell to her knees. "Gyllias!" she screamed. "Gyllias," she repeated in a whisper. "How I love you. Gyllias! I want you still—"

A cry disturbed her. The Charon had all gathered round and were staring desperately at her, afraid she would abandon them. They were old people now; much older than her.

"Don't leave us, Yalkara," wept the bearded old sage. "Not in our most desperate need!"

Yalkara looked from them to Maigraith, and back again. She put her arm around Maigraith's shoulders and led her to a bench.

"Look at my people," she said softly. "We have been together, sharing everything, since the Hundred came out of the void. We seventy are the last Charon left in the universe and we are dying one by one. We can't bear that any longer. We have vowed to leap into the void together. All for all. They depend on me, and I need them."

"But, Gyllias—"

"I want to see him desperately. I want to go with you, too. But I can't, Maigraith. It's too late now. Far too late!"

Yalkara rocked back onto her knees and stood up. Her forehead was smudged with a crescent moon of dust. "The past cannot be recovered. I *cannot* linger on in Santhenar knowing that the rest of my kind are gone. Not even for Gyllias would I be *the last*. I will go with them into the void."

Maigraith shivered. "You're right, Grandmother. I'm used to looking after myself. But poor Shand! How will I tell him?"

"Tell him the truth. He will understand. Our lives have run their course. But first we must find a way to send you back."

The Charon took heart from this new project. They set to work to extract what they could from the ruins of the construct and build a device to open the Way again. That was a thankless task and a very long one. More than half a year had gone by before they completed a device to do the job. It was quite simple—just a flared tube of metal like a hunting horn, but of exquisite make.

They stood Maigraith on a burnished plate of brass set in the floor and the remaining Hundred embraced her, one by one. Last of all, Yalkara watered Maigraith's slender shoulders and hugely swollen belly with her tears.

"Please come with me," Maigraith begged, clinging to her grandmother's scarred hands. "I'm afraid. I want you there for my time."

"I can't. Things are different now. The Way between the Worlds will be much harder to find and to cross than before. This horn is good for two blasts only—one to send you to Santhenar; one to take us home to the void. We are not sorry to go, not now. Are you prepared?"

"Yes!" she squeaked.

"Be ready for anything. You may not end up quite where you hope. The passage may hurt. And you will arrive there naked, for I can send nothing but you."

"I came here with all my goods," said Maigraith. "I must at least have the ring Rulke gave me."

"The construct *carried* you here," said Yalkara, "and all your goods too. This horn just *sends* you." She consulted the others. "I'll try to send the ring with you as well, but don't be surprised if you lose it. Now, link with me."

They linked and Maigraith showed Yalkara her destination, Gothryme Manor. Yalkara traced out the Way between the Worlds for the last time, the way to Santhenar, and that *was* much harder than it had been before.

"You're ready?"

Maigraith looked into her grandmother's eyes, took a deep breath and nodded.

"Wait," said Yalkara. "You won't be needing this." She took the Mirror from Maigraith's pocket. "I'll take it with me into the void where it can't do any more harm." Then she thought of something. "Oh, Maigraith!"

"Yes?"

"There are still some Faellem left on Santh, I believe. In the wilds of Mirrilladell."

"That is so," said Maigraith, wondering what she was getting at. "Many did refuse to join Faelamor in Elludore."

"If you were to go there, you might find someone who knew Faelamor's consort in ancient times. Your other grandfather."

"Thank you," said Maigraith. "I will, one day."

"And Maigraith?"

"Yes, Yalkara?"

Yalkara clutched her hand, squeezing so hard that it hurt. "Tell Gyllias . . . tell Shand . . . I have never stopped loving him. I never will!" She abruptly let go. "Go now."

"Fare well."

"Fare well, fare well!" chorused the Charon.

The horn blatted. Maigraith felt turned inside out. The baby kicked frantically. Aachan vanished. She whirled through nothingness, keeping a desperate grip on that image of Gothryme. Her finger burned as if the ring had turned to molten gold. She closed her fist, and closed the other fist over it as tightly as she possibly could, willing it to come with her. Everything went blank, she lost her way, found it again and with a crack that hurt her eardrums and sent the baby into a fury, she landed on her bottom on the threadbare rug before the fire in Karan's living room.

The room was empty. It was just on dark. Maigraith got up, unsteady on her pins. She leaned on the edge of a table, knocking it down and collapsing onto her knees. Her belly felt much heavier than it had on Aachan. She was as naked as the child within her. Her hand and ring-finger burned unbearably.

She opened her fist. The ring was still there, but it was melted into strands like four wires twisted together, with a button of gold at front and back. It was still scorching hot. She wrenched it off and the skin came with it. Her finger was burned around the circle so deeply that the scar would never leave her. The other burn scars ran up her arm past the elbow. Like my grandmother, she thought. Maigraith slipped the ring onto a finger of her right hand and never took it off again.

A thin old man with white hair appeared in the doorway. His manners were far too good to show his astonishment. Helping Maigraith to her feet, he swept a tablecloth around her and settled her back into a chair before the fire.

"And who . . . ? Ah, I remember you," Rachis said. He shouted through the doorway. "Karan! Come quickly!"

Karan limped in. Her hair stood on end. Then she leapt right across the room to embrace Maigraith.

"Maigraith!" she shrieked. "How did you get here? And look how fat you are. *Why, you're pregnant!"*

"So I am," said Maigraith, smiling. "To Rulke. It's so good to be home."

"How did you get here?"

"Yalkara found a way to send me back. Oh Karan, I have no idea what I am going to do with my life, but I feel that I belong for the first time."

"Well, there is one complication—"

Just then Yggur came in to see what the fuss was about. When he saw Maigraith he went pale, and one side of his face froze the way it had done when he was still possessed by Rulke. He staggered, his knee gave way, then he came on, limping badly. Shand stood behind him in the doorway, his eyes shining.

"Maigraith," Yggur whispered, holding out his arms. "I tried to find a way to bring you back."

She took his hand but did not embrace him. "I see," Yggur said, abruptly turning away.

"Is Yalkara . . . ?" began Shand.

"She lives," said Maigraith.

"Did you tell her about me?" The yearning in Shand's eyes was awful.

"Yes," said Maigraith, wanting to run away from his hopeless longing. She took him in her arms instead. "She said she will never stop loving you."

Shand stiffened. "She's not coming, is she?"

"No. She wanted to, so very badly but she could not abandon her people. They are going back to the void."

Shand hung his head in his hands. His voice reflected off the floor. "I should have given her up when she went through the gate. But hope would not die."

He walked over to the window and stood there looking out.

"Maigraith," said Yggur. "I cannot get you out of my mind. I want you more than ever. Will you come back to me?"

"No," she said as gently as she was able. "I can't, Yggur, though I wish you all the best. Besides, how would it be when I gave birth to the son of your lifelong enemy?"

"A—bitter—day," he said haltingly, though it was not clear whether he referred to that day or this.

Maigraith held her breath. Yggur was going through a terrible struggle. His strength of character was also his weakness. Would he rise above it, or would it overwhelm him?

"There was a time when I would not have been able to accept such a blow," he said. "Before Carcharon I would have had to break something; *or someone*!" He forced himself to smile and gave her his hand. "I wish you well."

He turned and limped away. "I will go back to Fiz Gorgo for a time," he said to Shand.

"Nobly done," said Shand. "But who will look after your empire? Who will rule unruly Thurkad?"

"It's yours, if you want it."

Shand laughed. "Of course I don't want it. Give it to your ablest general, until a new Council can be elected. Or, better still, to Tallia."

"I'm not up to it," said Tallia, shaking her long black hair. "I don't want to be Magister."

"You've passed the most important test then," said Shand. "And here is a challenge. Look at the mess Thurkad and Meldorin are in. Who else has the strength and the wisdom, and the *compassion*, to right all the wrongs that have been done?"

"I—"

"Would you not do good things that no other Magister would? What if Thyllan were to come back? What if there were no Magister at all, and one of Yggur's generals were to rule, say?"

"They are hard men," said Tallia, reflecting. "And Thyllan is a fool and a monster. Very well, if you ask it and the Council supports it, I will take it on for a year. But no longer. I have other plans now. We're going to sail back to Crandor once Lilis finishes her apprenticeship."

"Maybe we'll come with you," said Llian. "Take our baby to see its grandparents."

"What do you say, Yggur?" said Shand.

"I can think of no better choice," he said, and gave her his hand. "Fare well."

"What could I do?" said Maigraith after the door closed behind him. "It was over long ago."

At that moment Malien came in from outside. On seeing Maigraith she went pale, then, most uncharacteristically, ran and took her hand. "How fare my people, Maigraith?" she whispered.

"I did not see them after the construct was destroyed," said Maigraith. "They went back to their own cities. But Aachan is in its death agony. Ten thousand volcanoes were erupting when I left. I don't see how the Aachim can survive."

Malien let her hand fall. "And there is nothing I can do about it." She slumped into a chair, staring at the fire.

No one said anything for a full minute. But to Maigraith's surprise, Malien got up again, and she was smiling.

"Adversity only strengthens our resolve," Malien said. "If there is a way to survive, my people will find it, as they have always done. And I must be just as strong. I have much to do. Fare well!" She embraced them all and hurried out.

"So what will *you* do, Shand?" Karan asked.

Shand smiled. "Suddenly I have everything to live for." He embraced Maigraith. "I was sure I'd lost you too. I'll stay for a while, at least until my great-grandchild is born, and your child too, Karan. You've no idea how much I'm looking forward to being a great-grandfather. And then? Back to Tullin I suppose. That's not so far away that I won't see you often. In Tullin I'll tend my gellon trees and lay down liqueurs for the children, until my time is up."

Llian crawled into bed, looking as gloomy as he had every night since returning from the college.

"What's the matter?" Karan asked irritably. The baby was already hard work and his everlasting depression was wearing her out.

"The usual problem," he said, staring at the wall.

Karan couldn't take it any more. "Well, find something to do with your life!" she said furiously. "Our baby needs a contented father, not a miserable one." Blowing out the lamp, she presented him with her rigid back.

Llian lay awake, staring into the darkness as he went through his situation over and again. It was obvious that there were only two things in the world he was suited for—being a master chronicler and a teller. But to Llian the two professions were hand in glove; he had to have both.

I will find something to do! he thought. Damn the college and the master chroniclers. Damn the old master and the new one too! No one will tell me that I can't practice my art. I'll make my living by being a teller, and be a chronicler in secret. I'll begin on Rulke's Tale. The defiance gave him a powerful thrill, like the time in the Nightland when Rulke had offered him the forbidden knowledge. *I will have it!* I can't do otherwise. Maybe I am corrupt, but *I'll have what I want and pay the price*, whatever that may be.

* * *

In the middle of the night Karan gave a sharp cry and thrust herself up in bed.

Llian sleepily stroked her brow. "What's the matter?"

"My bones hurt."

"You've been lying in the same position too long."

"You don't understand! When I move it feels like my hips are made of broken glass."

He turned her over, settled her with pillows and began to rub her back. It did not make things any better.

"I think . . ." Karan stopped, sweating and shivering at the same time. Giving birth was another of her nightmares. She imagined her pelvic bones splintering under the strain. But far worse, that terrifying craving had come back stronger than before. She wanted hrux. How she wanted the drug, but she was afraid of it too. Afraid she would never be free of it—afraid that if she did succumb it would damage her baby.

"What?" he cried.

"I think you'd better send for Idlis."

"Right now?" Llian exclaimed, and had she not grabbed his wrist he would have fallen out of bed. "The baby's not coming already?"

Karan found herself smiling. How ignorant he was. "Not for another six months, silly! Send for him in the morning! And ask . . . ask him to bring some hrux with him.

Llian took her hand. "Hrux!" he shivered. "Are you sure?"

She did not respond for a long time. "I'd forgotten it for months, but when I woke the craving was back again. I need it desperately, Llian."

He held her. "Are you sure?"

She gave a great shudder. "*No!*" she raged. "No hrux!

"Karan?"

"I think I can manage it," she said. He could feel her desire for it. Her whole body was trembling. "Hold me tightly, Llian. I need you more than I ever have."

"I'll always be here, Karan," he said. "I'll help you. Together we can overcome it."

Karan lay back and closed her eyes. "Yes, Llian. Together we can do anything. And we will."

The next day Karan, Maigraith, Llian and Shand were sitting together on the veranda enjoying the wintry sun. Llian turned to Maigraith, who was staring dreamily into space.

"Maigraith," he said.

"Mmm?"

"I do so wonder about the Charon. When you were in Aachan . . . did you ever talk to Yalkara about her life? Or the other Charon?"

"Constantly."

"What about the void. Did they mention that place?"

Karan looked up through half-closed eyelids. Llian was sitting forward as if about to spring from his chair in eagerness. His eyes were shining, a look she had not seen since Chanthed. She smiled to herself and closed her eyes again. It felt good in the sun today. She did not want hrux at all. And for once she had absolutely nothing to do. No one required anything of her.

"Enough to fill volumes," said Maigraith. She rolled over, cow-like in her contentment.

"Do you think . . . you could tell me some of those tales?"

By the time the sun went down the floor around Llian was littered in papers covered in his fine script, and he was still writing furiously. He looked deliriously happy.

Maigraith held up her right hand, inspecting the strange ring, just four twisted wires and two blobs of gold.

"Maigraith, you look so fulfilled," Karan observed.

"That's funny, isn't it," Maigraith replied. "I never knew how to be happy before. I lacked the capacity for it."

"But you've lost so much!"

"All I ever wanted was to know who I was."

"What about Rulke?"

Maigraith smiled but said nothing at all.

"You loved him very deeply."

"I *do*; and in my memories I will always have him. That is enough." She paused. "There is one thing, though."

"What?" asked Karan.

"If your daughter and my son were to mate," said Maigraith, "triunes both—"

"Begone, serpent!" said Karan. "We have yet to deliver them, and we don't know what we'll deliver."

"I know what I know," said Maigraith complacently. "Who else can a triune's son mate with but a triune's daughter. From our loins spring a new people, a new species, perhaps with more of the strengths and fewer of the weaknesses than those that engendered us. Let us agree to pair them, now."

Karan felt a stab of alarm. Had fate manipulated her all along to bring about this end? Or had her father, with his experiments up at Carcharon? She hastily swerved away from *that* thought.

This had to be stopped at once. She moved uncomfortably on her chair. Though her own pregnancy was not far advanced, her damaged bones ached all the time. Remembering Idlis's warning, she did not even want to think about childbirth.

"We are the complement of each other," Karan said. "Both orphaned, both *shaped*, both triune, but completely different. If you won't learn from your own life, then at least listen to what I've learned from mine. There's been more than enough manipulating of children in this tale. Give them the freedom of their own future. In any case, a new species will still be human—just as frail and just as foolish as the ones it sprang from. Just as good and just as evil. How can it differ in its humanity? That's what makes us what we are."

Maigraith was no longer listening. She closed her eyes, drawn far, far away. Distantly she heard the blatt of a hunting horn. *Fare well!* echoed in her mind. Then the whispery link between her and Yalkara was gone forever.

She looked up. Shand's eyes were on her. His eyes were wet too. "Just you and me now," he said.

"Just the three of us," she replied, enfolding her glorious belly with her arms.

THE END

Author's Note

The View from the Mirror, though published in four books, was conceived and written as a single novel. When I began it a dozen years ago, I intended to write a long epic fantasy with no objective other than to entertain as best as I could.

I did, however, want to create something distinct from the Eurocentric tradition of popular fantasy that has developed over the past few decades. Accordingly, the work is not medieval or feudal by any description of the terms. It is not set in a version of the Middle Ages, real or imaginary. There is no struggle of good versus evil. My women are not oppressed victims or marginalized figures, but real characters who get into as many difficulties as the men do, and get out of them by their own cleverness.

I also wanted to develop a world where the geography was realistic, and different, where culture and history were important, where people make mistakes and things don't always work and everything, particularly magic, comes at a cost.

The story was written, and rewritten, continuously between September 1987 and March 1999, though its origins go back another decade. In the late 1970s, faced with the forbidding task of completing my doctoral thesis, I seized on any distraction to delay it. One of these was the creation of an alternative world, complete with maps large enough to cover walls, and all the details—human, geographical and biological—that go to make up such a world. This project continued for several years after the wretched thesis was finally submitted, and accepted, until in the early eighties the demands of family, house renovation and work extinguished my interest in world building.

A Shadow on the Glass, when I finally began it five years later, went through twenty very tough drafts, many written in hotel rooms across the eastern hemisphere. The other books took nearly as much work—an extended writing apprenticeship! No doubt the keen-eyed reader will pick up errors, for which I alone am responsible. With hindsight I find some aspects of the work dissatisfy me, and were I beginning the novel again would do it rather differently. But *History is as it is written*. It can't be taken back.

Ian Irvine, 1999

Glossary

of Characters, Names and Places

Aachan: One of the Three Worlds, the world of the Aachim and, after its conquest, the Charon.

Aachim: The human species native to Aachan, who were conquered by the Charon. The Aachim are a clever people, great artisans and engineers, but melancholy and prone to hubris. After they were brought to Santhenar the Aachim flourished, but were betrayed and ruined in the Clysm, and withdrew from the world to their vast mountain fortress cities.

Aftersickness: Sickness that people suffer after using the Secret Art, or being close when someone else uses such power, or even after using a native talent. Sensitives are very prone to it.

Alcifer: The last and greatest of Rulke's cities, designed by Pitlis the Aachim.

Asper: An Aachim healer, one of Tensor's company.

Bannador: A long, narrow and hilly land on the western side of Iagador. Karan's homeland. Bannador is the closest land to Shazmak and was ruined in the war between Yggur's forces and the Ghâshâd's.

Basitor: A bitter Aachim who survived the sacking of Shazmak and accompanied Tensor to Katazza.

Basunez: A distant ancestor of Karan's. He built Carcharon, carrying out forbidden experiments there, and later went mad.

Benie: Cook's boy at Gothryme Manor.

Blending: A child of the union between two of the four different human species. Blendings are rare, and often deranged, but can have remarkable talents.

Booreah Ngurle: The burning mountain, or fiery mountain, a volcanic peak in the forests east of Almadin. The Charon once had a stronghold there.

Calendar: Santhenar's year is roughly 395.7 days and contains twelve months, each of thirty-three days.

Calliat: A philosopher and mystic of ancient times. See **Forty-Nine Chrighms.**

Carcharon: A walled tower built on a rugged ridge high above Gothryme Forest. It was constructed by Karan's mad ancestor Basunez at a node where the Secret Art was especially powerful.

Chacalot: A large water-dwelling reptile, somewhat resembling a crocodile.

Chanthed: A town in northern Meldorin, in the foothills of the mountains. The College of the Histories is situated there.

Chard: A kind of tea.

Charon: One of the four human species, the master people of the world of Aachan. They fled out of the void to take Aachan from the Aachim, and took their name from a frigid moonlet at the furthest extremity of the void. They have strange eyes, indigo or carmine, or sometimes both together, depending on the light.

Chronicler: A historian. A graduate in the art and science of recording and maintaining the Histories.

Citadel: The Magister's palace in Thurkad, an enormous fortified building of baroque extravagance.

Clysm: A series of wars between the Charon and the Aachim beginning around 1500 years ago, resulting in the almost total devastation of Santhenar.

College of the Histories: The oldest of the colleges for the instruction of those who would be chroniclers or tellers of the Histories, or even lowly bards or king's singers. It was set up at Chanthed soon after the time of the Forbidding.

Compulsion: A form of the Secret Art; a way of forcing someone to do something against their will.

Construct: A machine at least partly powered by the Secret Art.

Council; also **Council of Iagador**, **Council of Santhenar**, **Great Council**, **High Council**: An alliance of the powerful. With the Aachim it made the Nightland and cast Rulke into it. After that it had two purposes—to continue the great project and to maintain the watch upon Rulke.

Crandor: A rich, tropical land on the north-eastern side of Lauralin. Tallia's homeland.

Dolodha: A timid messenger girl to Yggur, now promoted to adjutant.

Dunnet: A secluded land within Elludore Forest, now Faelamor's hideout.

Elienor: A great heroine of the Aachim from the time when the Charon invaded Aachan.

Ellami: A Faellem woman, Hallal's sister.

Elludore: A large forested land, north and west of Thurkad.

Emmant: A half-Aachim, librarian at Shazmak, who conceived a violent lust for Karan and attacked her. She killed him in Thurkad.

Faelamor: Leader of the Faellem species who came to Santhenar soon after Rulke, to keep watch on the Charon and maintain the balance between the worlds. Maigraith's liege.

Faellem: The human species who inhabit the world of Tallallame. They are a small, dour people who are forbidden to use machines and particularly magical devices, but are masters of disguise and illusion. Faelamor's band were trapped on Santh by the Forbidding, and constantly search for a way home.

Festival of Chanthed: An annual festival held in Chanthed in the autumn, at which the Histories are told by the masters and students of the College.

Fiz Gorgo: A fortress city in Orist, flooded in ancient times, now restored; the stronghold of Yggur.

Flute; also **golden flute**: A device made in Aachan at the behest of Rulke, by the genius smith Shuthdar. It was subsequently stolen by him and taken back to Santhenar. When played by one who is sensitive, it could be used to open the Way between the Worlds. It was destroyed by Shuthdar at the time of the Forbidding.

Forbidding: See ***Tale of the Forbidding***.

Fortress: Yggur's headquarters in Thurkad, a plain old building which looks down on the Magister's citadel.

Forty-Nine Chrighms of Calliat: A series of linked enigmas and paradoxes so complex that, thirteen hundred years after Calliat's death, only one had been solved. Maigraith has recently solved many of them.

Fyrn: The family name of Karan of Bannador, from her mother's side.

Galliad: Karan's father, who was half-Aachim. He was killed when Karan was a child.

Gannel: A river beginning near Chanthed and flowing through the mountains to the sea at Ganport.

Garr, Garrflood: The largest river in Meldorin. It arises to the west of Shazmak and runs to the Sea of Thurkad east of Sith.

Gate: A structure controlled by the Secret Art, which permits people to move instantly from one place to another. Also called a portal.

Gellon: A fruit tasting something between a mango and a peach.

Gethren: A Faellem man.

Ghâshâd: The ancient, mortal enemies of the Aachim. They were corrupted and swore allegiance to Rulke after the Zain rebelled two thousand years ago, but when Rulke was put in the Nightland a thousand years later they forgot their destiny and took a new name, Whelm. Roused by Rulke through Karan's link to Maigraith, they became Ghâshâd again and sacked Shazmak just before the Conclave.

Gift of Rulke; also **Curse of Rulke**: Knowledge given by Rulke to the Zain, enhancing their resistance to the mind-breaking potencies of the Aachim. It left stigmata that identified them as Zain.

Glass: Colloquial term for the Mirror of Aachan.

Gothryme: Karan's impoverished manor near Tolryme in Bannador.

Great Betrayer: Rulke.

Great Library: Founded at Zile by the Zain in the time of the Empire of Zur. The library was sacked when the Zain were exiled, but was subsequently re-established. Its current librarian is Nadiril the Sage.

Great Mountains: The largest and highest belt of mountains on Santhenar, enclosing the south-eastern part of the continent of Lauralin.

Great Project: A way sought by the Council to banish the Charon from Santh forever.

Great Tales: The greatest stories from the Histories of Santhenar; traditionally told at the Festival of Chanthed and on important ceremonial occasions throughout Santhenar. A tale can become a Great Tale only by the unanimous decision of the master chroniclers. In four thousand years only twenty-two Great Tales have ever been made.

Grint: A copper coin of small value.

Gyllias: The Recorder.

Hakasha-ka-najisska: A forbidden potency (mind-blasting spell) developed by the Aachim against the Charon. Zain carrying the Gift of Rulke are immune to it.

Hallal: A Faellem woman, longtime rival to Faelamor.

Hana: Maigraith's teacher when she was a child.

Havissard: Yalkara's abandoned stronghold near Tar Gaarn. Faelamor found the Aachim gold hidden there; also a book which she recognized as deadly to the Faellem.

Histories, The: The vast collection of records which tell more than four thousand years of recorded history on Santhenar. The Histories consist of historical documents written or held by the chroniclers, as well as the tales, songs, legends and lore of the peoples of Santhenar and the invading peoples from the other worlds, told by the tellers. The culture of Santhenar is interwoven with and inseparable from the Histories and the most vital longing anyone can have is to be mentioned in them.

Hlune: The lanky people who rule the wharf city of Thurkad and control all ship-borne commerce there.

Huling's Tower: The place where Shuthdar destroyed the golden flute and the crippled girl was murdered.

Human species: There are four distinct human species: the Aachim of Aachan, the Faellem of Tallallame, the old humans of Santhenar and the Charon who came out of the void. All but old humans can be very long-lived. Matings between the different species rarely produce children (see **blending**).

Hundred, the: The Charon who survived the taking of Aachan. Rulke is the greatest of them all.

Hythe: Mid-winter's day, the fourth day of endre, mid-winter week. Hythe is a day of particular ill-omen.

Iagador: The land that lies between the mountains and the Sea of Thurkad.

Idlis: Formerly the least of the Whelm, also a healer and long-time hunter of Karan and the Mirror. Karan spared his life three times, a debt that must be repaid. He became Ghâshâd and served Rulke, though voting against him in the telling competititon.

Jark-un: The leader of a band of the Whelm, once rival to Vartila, but now a Ghâshâd. Unlike others of his kind, he is short and stout.

Jepperand: A province on the western side of the mountains of Crandor. Home to the Zain; Llian's birthplace.

Jevi (Jevander): Lilis's father, taken by a press-gang seven years ago.

Kandor: One of the three Charon who came to Santhenar. He was killed after the end of the Clysm, the only Charon to die on Santh.

Karama Malama: The Sea of Mists, south of the Sea of Thurkad.

Karan: A woman of the house of Fyrn, but with blood of the Aachim from her father, Galliad, and old human and Faellem blood from her mother. This makes her triune. She is also a sensitive and lives at Gothryme.

Lar: An honorific used in Thurkad.

Lasee: A pale-yellow brewed drink, mildly intoxicating, and ubiquitous in Orist; fermented from the sweet sap of the sard tree.

Lauralin: The continent east of the Sea of Thurkad.

League: About 5000 paces, three miles or five kilometers.

Librarian: Nadiril the Sage.

Lightglass: A device made of crystal and metal that emits light after being touched.

Lilis: A street urchin in Thurkad, rescued by Tallia and now apprenticed to Nadiril.

Link, linking; also **talent of linking**: A joining of minds, by which thoughts and feelings can be shared, and support given. Sometimes used for domination.

Llian: A Zain from Jepperand. He is a master chronicler and a teller. Banished from his college, he fell in with Karan. He has an insatiable curiosity for the Histories.

Lorrsk: An intelligent creature living in the void, it is humanoid in shape though massively built. Some are sensitives.

Magister: A mancer and chief of the Council. Mendark has been Magister for a thousand years, save for a brief period when illegally overthrown by Thyllan. After the disaster at Katazza he went to Havissard, where he nearly died and had to renew his body.

Maigraith: An orphan brought up and trained by Faelamor for some unknown purpose. She is a master of the Secret Art. After the Conclave she led Yggur's army to war in Bannador. Subsequently Faelamor took control of her again.

Malien: An Aachim; Rael's mother; once consort of Tensor. After Tensor's rebellion in Katazza she took over leadership of the Aachim.

Mancer: A wizard or sorcerer; someone who is a master of the Secret Art. Also necromanter.

Master chronicler: One who has mastered the study of the Histories and graduated with highest honor from the College.

Master of Chanthed: Currently Wistan; the Master of the College of the Histories is also nominal leader of Chanthed.

Meldorin: The large island that lies to the immediate west of the Sea of Thurkad and the continent of Lauralin.

Mendark: See **Magister.**

Mirror of Aachan: A device made by the Aachim in Aachan for seeing things at a distance. In Santhenar it changed and twisted reality and so the Aachim hid it away. It also developed a memory, retaining the imprints of things it had seen. Stolen by Yalkara, the Mirror was used by her to find a warp in the Forbidding and escape back to Aachan. After the Conclave, Tensor found in it the secret of making gates. Shand now has it.

Moon: The moon revolves around Santhenar about every thirty days. However one side (the dark face) is blotched red and black by volcanic activity, and because the moon rotates on its axis much more slowly, the dark face is fully turned toward Santh only every couple of months. This rarely coincides with a full moon, but when it does it is a time of ill-omen.

Nadiril: The head of the Great Library and a member of the Council.

Nanollet: A small musical instrument that every Faellem child learns how to play. Made of wood and metal, it has a complexity of sounding boards and resonating chambers.

Narne: A town and port at the navigable extremity of the Garr.

Nazhak tel Mardux: A book of Aachim tales that Llian committed to memory in Shazmak. Also called Tales of the Aachim.

Nightland: A place, distant from the world of reality, wherein Rulke was kept prisoner. In Katazza, Tensor made a gate into the Nightland to drag Rulke forth and revenge himself upon him, but only succeeded in letting Rulke out.

Nilkerrand: A fortified city across the sea from Thurkad.

Old human: The original human species on Santhenar and by far the most numerous.

Osseion: The captain of Mendark's guard, a huge dark man.

Pender: A masterly sailor who carried Karan and Llian from Narne to Sith, and later to Thurkad. After the Conclave he helped Karan and Shand to escape from Thurkad, and was subsequently hired by Mendark.

Perion, Empire of: Kandor's empire, which collapsed after the Sea of Perion dried up.

Pitlis: A great Aachim of the distant past, whose folly betrayed the great city of Tar Gaarn to Rulke and broke the power of the Aachim. The architect who designed Tar Gaarn and Alcifer, he was slain by Rulke.

Portal: See **gate**.

Potency: An all-powerful, mind-breaking spell developed by the Aachim as a weapon against the Charon, but effective against all but those Zain who bear the Gift of Rulke.

Proscribed Experiments: Sorcerous procedures designed to find a flaw in the Forbidding which could be used to banish Rulke forever. Hazardous because of the risk of Rulke taking control of the experimenter.

Rachis: Karan's steward at Gothryme Manor.

Rael: An Aachim, half-cousin to Karan, son of Malien and Tensor. He was drowned helping Karan to escape from Shazmak.

Recorder: The person who set down the tales of the four great battles of Faelamor and Yalkara, among many other tales. He is thought to have taken the Mirror (after Yalkara finally defeated Faelamor and fled Santh) and hidden it against some future need. His name was Gyllias.

Renderer's Tablet: A semi-mythical key to the secret script of the Charon.

Rula: The Magister before Mendark. She was regarded as the greatest of all.

Rulke: A Charon of Aachan. He enticed Shuthdar to Aachan to make the golden flute, and so began all the troubles. After the Clysm he was imprisoned in the Nightland until a way could be found to banish him back to Aachan. When Tensor opened a gate into the Nightland Rulke escaped, later occupying Shazmak and Carcharon.

Santhenar, Santh: The least of the Three Worlds, home of the old human peoples.

Sea of Thurkad: The long sea that divides Meldorin from the continent of Lauralin.

Secret Art: The use of magical or sorcerous powers (mancing). An art that very few can use and then only after extensive training. Notable mancers include Mendark, Yggur, Maigraith, Rulke, Tensor and Faelamor, though each has quite different strengths and weaknesses. Tallia has considerable skill but as yet insufficient training.

Sending: A message, thoughts or feelings sent from one mind to another.

Sentinels: Devices that keep watch and sound an alarm.

Shalah: A young Aachim woman, twin to Xarah.

Shand: An old man who works at the inn at Tullin and is more than he seems. A friend of Karan's late father, Shand rescued Karan from the Conclave, smuggled her out of Thurkad and accompanied her on a trek all the way to Katazza in the middle of the Dry Sea.

Shazmak: The forgotten city of the Aachim, in the mountains west of Bannador. It was captured by the Ghâshâd, after they were woken from their long years as Whelm.

Shuthdar: An old human of Santhenar, the maker of the golden flute. After he destroyed the flute and himself, the Forbidding came down, closing the Way between the Worlds.

Sith: A free city and trading nation built on an island in the River Garr, in southern Iagador.

Span: The distance spanned by the stretched arms of a tall man. About six feet, or slightly less than two meters.

Stassor: A city of the Aachim, in eastern Lauralin.

Tale of the Forbidding: Greatest of the Great Tales, it tells of the final destruction of the flute by Shuthdar more than three thousand years ago, and how the Forbidding sealed Santhenar off from the other two worlds.

Talent: A native skill or gift, usually honed by extensive training.

Tales of the Aachim: An ancient summary history of the Aachim, the Nazhak tel Mardux, prepared soon after the founding of Shazmak. Llian read and memorized it in Shazmak so he could translate it later.

Tallallame: One of the Three Worlds, the home of the Faellem. A beautiful, mountainous world covered in forest.

Tallia bel Soon: Mendark's chief lieutenant. She is a mancer and a master of combat with and without weapons. Tallia comes from Crandor.

Tar: A silver coin widely used in Meldorin. Enough to keep a family for several weeks.

Tar Gaarn: Principal city of the Aachim in the time of the Clysm; it was sacked by Rulke.

Tell: A gold coin to the value of twenty silver tars.

Teller: One who has mastered the ritual telling of the tales that form part of the Histories of Santhenar.

Telling Competition: In Carcharon, Llian challenged Rulke to a telling. Llian won but was accused of cheating and thrown out of Carcharon.

Tensor: The leader of the Aachim. He saw it as his destiny to restore the Aachim and finally take their revenge on Rulke, who betrayed and ruined them. He is proud to the point of folly.

Thandiwe: A student at the College in Chanthed and friend of Llian.

Thranx: A massive winged humanoid creature out of the void. Highly intelligent and able to use the Secret Art.

Three Worlds: Santhenar, Aachan and Tallallame.

Thurkad: An ancient, populous city on the River Saboth and the Sea of Thurkad, known for its wealth and corruption. Seat of the Council and the Magister. Yggur's First Army is now based there.

Thyllan: Warlord of Iagador and member of the Council. He intrigued against Mendark but was subsequently humiliated by Maigraith in single combat.

Tirthrax: The principal city of the Aachim, in the Great Mountains.

Tolryme: A town in northern Bannador, close to Karan's family seat, Gothryme.

Torgsted: One of Mendark's guard. A cheerful, reliable fellow now returned from spying on Thyllan.

Triune: A double blending—one with the blood of all Three Worlds, three different human species. They are extremely rare and almost always infertile. They may have remarkable abilities. Karan is one.

Tullin: A tiny village in the mountains south of Chanthed. Shand lives there.

Twisted Mirror: The Mirror of Aachan, made in Aachan and given to Tensor, who smuggled it with him to Santhenar. Like all objects taken between the worlds, it changed and became treacherous. So called because it does not always show true.

Vanhe: Formerly one of Yggur's mid-ranking officers, he was forced to take command after all of Yggur's generals were killed. Later, after returning from Katazza to find Maigraith gone, Yggur broke Vahne to private.

Vartila: The leader of a band of the Whelm. She remained Whelm and served Yggur after most of her people reverted to Ghâshâd.

Voice: The ability of great tellers to move their audience to any emotion they choose by the sheer power of their words.

Void, the: The spaces between the Three Worlds. A Darwinian place where life is more brutal and fleeting than anywhere. The void teems with the most exotic life imaginable, for nothing survives there without remaking itself constantly.

Void-leech: An amorphous creature.

Vuula Fyrn: Karan's mother, a lyrist. She committed suicide soon after Karan's father, Galliad, was killed.

Wahn Barre: The Crow Mountains. Yalkara, the Mistress of Deceits, had a stronghold there, Havissard.

Waif*, *The: Pender's third boat, formerly a blacklisted smuggler's vessel, *Black Opal.*

Way between the Worlds: The secret, forever-changing and ethereal paths that permit the difficult passage between the Three Worlds. They were closed off by the Forbidding.

Whelm: Servants of Yggur, his terror-guard. See also **Ghâshâd.**

Wistan: The seventy-fourth Master of the College of the Histories and of Chanthed.

Xarah: A young Aachim woman, twin to Shalah who was killed in Katazza.

Yalkara: The last of the three Charon who came to Santhenar to find the flute and return it to Aachan. She took the Mirror and used it to find a warp in the Forbidding, then fled Santh, leaving the Mirror behind.

Yetchah: A young Whelm woman who hunted Llian from Chanthed to Tullin. She became Ghâshâd and harbors a hopeless passion for Rulke.

Yggur: A great and powerful mancer and sworn enemy of Mendark. Formerly a member of the Council, his stronghold is at Fiz Gorgo. After Karan stole the Mirror his armies overran most of southern Meldorin, capturing Thurkad where he now dwells. He and Maigraith became lovers. Yggur hates and fears Rulke from the time Rulke possessed him before he was imprisoned in the Nightland.

Zain: A scholarly race who once dwelt in Zile and founded the Great Library. They made a pact with Rulke and after his fall most were slaughtered and the remnant exiled.

Zile: A city in the north-west of the island of Meldorin. Once capital of the Empire of Zur, now chiefly famous for the Great Library.

Guide to Pronunciation

There are many languages and dialects used on Santhenar by the four human species. While it is impossible to be definitive in such a brief note, the following generalizations normally apply.

There are no silent letters, and double consonants are generally pronounced as two separate letters; for example, *Yggur* is pronounced *Ig-ger*, and *Faellem* as *Fael-lem*. The letter *c* is usually pronounced as *k*, except in *mancer* and *Alcifer*, where it is pronounced as *s*. The combination *ch* is generally pronounced as in *church*, except in *Aachim* and *Charon*, where it is pronounced as *k*.

Aachim Ar'-kim
Charon Kar'-on
Fyrn Firn
Iagador Eye-aga'-dor
Lasee Lar'-say
Maigraith May'-gray-ith
Rael Ray'-il
Whelm H'-welm
Xarah Zha'-rah
Chanthed Chan-thed'
Faelamor Fay-el'-amor
Ghâshâd G-harsh'-ard
Karan Ka-ran'
Llian Lee'-an
Neid Nee'-id
Shuthdar Shoo'-th-dar'
Yggur Ig'-ger